MY OLD HOME

MY
OLD
HOME

A Novel of Exile

Orville Schell

PANTHEON BOOKS

NEW YORK

All rights reserved. Published in the United States by Pantheon Books, a division of Penguin Random House LLC, New York, and distributed in Canada by Penguin Random House Canada Limited, Toronto.

Pantheon Books and colophon are registered trademarks of Penguin Random House LLC.

Grateful acknowledgment is made to Rowman & Littlefield Publishing Group for permission to reprint an excerpt from *Shanghai Faithful: Betrayal and Forgiveness in a Chinese Christian Family* by Jennifer Lin. Copyright © 2017 by Jennifer Lin. Reprinted by permission of Rowman & Littlefield Publishing Group. All rights reserved.

Library of Congress Cataloging-in-Publication Data
Name: Schell, Orville, author.
Title: My old home: a novel of exile / Orville Schell.
Description: New York: Pantheon Books, 2021.
Identifiers: LCCN 2020021047 (print). LCCN 2020021048 (ebook).
    ISBN 9780593315811 (hardcover). ISBN 9780593315828 (ebook).
Classification: LCC PS3619.C34755 M9 2021 (print) | LCC PS3619.C34755
    (ebook) | DDC 813/.6—dc23
LC record available at lccn.loc.gov/2020021047
LC ebook record available at lccn.loc.gov/2020021048

www.pantheonbooks.com

Jacket images: (people) Ryan Ten/Alamy; (Qinghai sky) Yiming Li/E+ and
    (background) Abigail 210986/iStock, rumblefis/iStock, all Getty Images
Jacket design by Emily Mahon

Printed in the United States of America
First Edition

9 8 7 6 5 4 3 2 1

For my dear wife, Baifang,
without whom I would never have
fully become myself

He is despised and rejected of men; a man of great sorrows and
acquainted with grief: and we hid as it were our faces from him;
He was despised and we esteemed him not. Surely he hath borne
our griefs and carried our sorrows. . . .
He was oppressed and he was afflicted, yet he opened not his mouth:
He is brought as a lamb to the slaughter and as a sheep before
her shearers is dumb, so he openeth not his mouth.
He was taken from prison and from judgment: And who shall
declare his generation? For, he was cut off out of the land of the
living.

—*Isaiah 53: 3–8*

Music will save the world.

—*Pablo Casals*

Music is joy that man cannot help but feel. And since . . . man must
have his joy and joy must have its expression, if that expression is
not guided by the principle of the "way," (道), then it will inevitably
become disordered. The former kings hated disorder and therefore
created musical forms in the form of odes and hymns as guides.
In this way they made certain that the voice could fully express
feelings of joy without becoming wild and filled with abandon;
that the forms would be well-ordered but not unduly restrictive;
that the directness, complexity, intensity and tempo of the musical
performances would be proper and arouse the best in man's nature
so that evil and improper sentiments would find no opening by
which to enter.

—*Xunzi* 荀子

PART
ONE

1

WITHOUT DESTRUCTION

THERE CAN BE NO CONSTRUCTION!

LONG AFTER the sky had drained of daylight, Li Tongshu (李同书) had still not arrived back home. As Chairman Mao's Great Proletarian Cultural Revolution (伟大的无产阶级文化大革命) had gathered a frightening momentum in the summer of 1966, he rarely returned home before dark and his fourteen-year-old son, Li Wende (李文德), often found himself sitting alone in their sparsely furnished room inside the once-elegant complex of gardens and halls that was known as Willow Courtyard (柳园). Besides two beds, a small round wooden table, a wardrobe, and a tall wooden case with glass doors to protect the books and music inside from the dry dustiness of Beijing, their only piece of furniture of any distinction was a Steinway upright piano.

Li Wende, known as Little Li in the neighborhood, was an unusually handsome boy, tall for his age but with a look of tentativeness that played about his eyes. As he sat on his father's piano bench and waited, the fall wind whistling under the eaves of the sloping tiled roof made the single lightbulb hanging from the rafters swing and cast ominous, undulating shadows across the silent room. When, at last, footsteps sounded outside, Little Li ran to the door. Seeing the familiar silhouette of his father walking from the gate with his head lowered and shoulders hunched against the brisk fall night, he felt relieved. But as soon as he stepped through the door, his somber expression made the boy's heart sink.

"Where were you?" he anxiously asked his father.

"I had to get some things at the Conservatory," he answered, and then wordlessly set about preparing some cold steamed buns and pickled vegetables for dinner.

When they finally sat down to eat and he took one of his son's hands in his own, and very softly intoned: "Almighty God, we thank you for this food. Bless us and keep us, make your light to shine upon us and be gracious unto us."

Because religious expression of any kind was forbidden, Little Li usually felt uneasy during these moments of whispered prayer. However, tonight he felt reassured by his father's hand.

"Are you . . . ?" he began.

"This afternoon Red Guards dragged Ma Sicong to the Conservatory for a struggle session [批斗会]," interjected his father. "They attacked him as a 'bourgeois intellectual' [资产阶级知识分子] and a 'Christian' [基督徒], capped him with a dunce hat, taunted him as an 'ox ghost and a snake spirit' [牛鬼 蛇神], and then paraded him around the courtyard."

"How do you know?" asked Little Li with alarm.

"I saw them."

"Did anyone help Professor Ma?"

"No." Li Tongshu cast his eyes downward, afraid to let his gaze meet that of his son. "Now, I've been told I am on the Red Guards' list." Little Li froze with fear.

With Beijing streets besieged by Red Guard actions, Little Li and his friend Little Wang had found all the drama exciting. But now as he studied his father's somber face, he felt only guilt and regret.

"For what crimes are you on their list?" he asked. Other people might be secret "capitalist agents" or "counterrevolutionaries," but his own father?

"For my U.S. training, your American mother, and my love of Western music."

"Will they demand a confession?"

"If one has committed no wrong, how can one confess?" riposted Li Tongshu defiantly. Then, in a softer tone, "In case anything happens to me, you must promise you'll always . . ."

"But what can happen to you, Father?"

"We are in uncertain times, son."

"But . . ."

"If anything does happen," he continued, "promise me you'll do everything Granny Sun tells you and always honor our family name." His voice cracked with emotion.

Granny Sun was the elderly widow who lived across the yard. She'd been married to a professor of literature from Yanjing University who'd once owned their entire courtyard complex of halls, gardens, verandas, and ponds, where his extended family and all its servants had lived for generations. However, when Willow Courtyard was nationalized by Mao's new revolutionary government in 1949 and partitioned up among a host of new tenants; Granny Sun, her husband, and their young daughter were forced to move all their Ming Dynasty furniture, artwork, books, and papers into a single hall. After arriving from San Francisco, Li Tongshu and his American-born wife, Vivian Knight, were assigned the room across the yard from theirs. A short while later, Professor Sun passed away from heart failure; Granny Sun was sure he'd died from dispossession of his beloved family home. However, she bore no grudges against the others who'd moved into their former home. In fact, after her daughter was assigned a job in Tianjin, she'd taken a special liking to Little Li.

Li Tongshu was quietly cleaning up after dinner when, just as a wild animal freezes upon hearing the snap of a twig in the forest, he suddenly froze. Holding a bowl in one hand and the kitchen cleaver in the other, he walked to the front door and cracked it open to listen. From the other side of the gray brick wall that surrounded their courtyard came the muffled din of agitated voices and the thudding of a drum. A moment later, a strident pounding sounded on their gate.

"What is it?" a panicked Little Li asked.

"You must put on your coat," ordered his father.

"But what is it?" His father did not answer. Instead, as if he were acting out a script long since committed to memory, he walked to his piano, sat down on the bench, lifted the fallboard, positioned his slender hands over the keyboard, and began to play J. S. Bach's chorale "Jesu, Joy of Man's Desiring." As the music suffused the room like a sweet fragrance, it reminded Little Li of how his father had played such chorales at night when he was younger, as he fell asleep. Whenever his father played this particular transcription, he always began with the simple hymnlike melody, before slowly building the piece from the bottom up, part by part, as he imagined Bach had composed it. As he played, he sang along softly:

Glad am I who have my Saviour
From him will I never part.

He restoreth my sagging spirits,
Be I sad or sick at heart.
While cares may vex and troubles grieve me,
Yet will Jesus never leave me.

Little Li had always waited with anticipation for the moment when the descant line finally entered before allowing himself to float off to sleep on the wings of the chorale's lullaby-like purity. But, whereas Li Tongshu usually played chorales with extraordinary gentleness, now his eyes were closed and his face upturned, as if he were straining to hear some faraway call. As the din in the alley swelled, he pounded out the chorale melody with ever fiercer resolution. Then, just as he introduced the familiar obbligato, the front gate flew open with a splintering crash, and the cacophony of hostile, hoarse voices, pounding drums, and clashing gongs grew suddenly louder. From watching other "counterrevolutionary elements" (反革命分子) paraded and attacked in public, Little Li knew his father's hour of judgment had arrived.

"Down with the American spy Li Tongshu!" shrieked an angry voice from the shadows. "Down with all bourgeois music and foreign spies!" another voice responded. Li Tongshu continued to stubbornly hammer out the chorale.

"Father!" cried Little Li, running to the piano. "You must stop!" But, as if music might somehow tame the strident voices outside, he kept playing. "They're in the courtyard! Stop!"

Only when he tugged at his sleeve did his father open his eyes. But instead of stopping, he continued playing. Just then a tall Red Guard in a khaki-colored greatcoat appeared on the veranda and, surprised to see a boy standing beside a grown man at a piano, cast a hesitant glance back toward his comrades, who'd fallen silent. As the music floated through the open door out into the darkness, the intruders seemed unsure how to proceed against such unexpected enemies of the people, and, like a film projector frozen on a single frame, for a moment the scene remained in a state of suspended animation.

"Long Live Chairman Mao!" a voice finally cried out. "Down with all running dogs of American imperialism!" shouted another, as the tall Red Guard began waving others up onto the veranda.

"Down with all counterrevolutionary elements!" an adolescent voice bleated to the rhythmic beat of a drum.

Little Li knew that once accusations of "counterrevolution" were uttered they left stains that no power on earth was capable of cleansing. They were demonic spells that removed a person from the ranks of the "people" (人民) and banished him to the ranks of "class enemies" (阶级敌人), a category of political damnation from which there was no reprieve. But if his father did not oppose the revolution, why didn't he stop playing and defend himself? Why was he so bullheaded? Hadn't Chairman Mao himself deputized Red Guards as his own personal emissaries to help save China's revolution from all the "bad elements" (坏分子) out to sabotage it? Little Li himself had been spellbound by the panache of the Red Guards and yearned to participate in their audacious movement. However, because of his bad "family background" (家庭背景), he'd only been able to stand on the sidelines as the Great Proletarian Cultural Revolution marched forward.

"Father, stop!" he pleaded again as a burly Red Guard, whom he recognized as a woodwind student from the Conservatory, rushed into their room. "Tell them you support Chairman Mao and that there's been a mistake!"

Another Red Guard pushed over their rickety wooden table, ripped off one of its legs, and lunged toward the piano.

"No!" Little Li cried out, trying to block his advance. "My father's only a musician!"

"Your father believes 'the moon's rounder in America than China' [美国的月亮比中国的圆]!" screamed the Red Guard, pushing Little Li aside. "If you know what's good for you, you'll break with his rotten lineage now!" Filled with vituperation so that the tendons on his neck stood out, as taut as piano strings, he yanked the piano bench out from beneath Li Tongshu and hurled it across the room. But Li Tongshu kept on playing, crouching before his piano, pounding out the chorale so it sounded more like a military march than a hymn.

"Insult the broad masses with your decadent music and you'll feel their righteous wrath!" shrieked the Red Guard as drops of spit shot from his mouth like fat from a hot wok.

With Li Tongshu still refusing to stop, the Red Guard swung

the table leg against his shoulders with such force that it knocked him to the floor; the music ceased with an eerie suddenness. Little Li started to his father's side, but had hardly taken a step before he was grabbed and shoved against the wall by another Red Guard.

"Your old man opposes Chairman Mao's revolutionary line!" he screamed. "Be done with him!"

As his father was being dragged outside, several Red Guards struggled to overturn their heavy hardwood wardrobe. Only after rocking it back and forth did they succeed in toppling it with a triumphant cheer. Next they tipped over the bookcase, sending shelves of musical scores and books skating across the floor. An anthology of Tang Dynasty poems, its spine snapped like the backbone of a delicate creature, landed at Little Li's feet and fluttered open. A startled spider with a shiny black body scuttled from its pages, and Little Li was about to kneel and whisk it to safety when, as if being blown by a gust of wind, it streaked toward his bed. However, before it could reach safety, a Red Guard spotted it and crushed it under his shoe, leaving only a splotch of yellow goo with two rows of delicate legs extending from each side like eyelashes.

"Class enemies do not deserve such a merciful fate!" he sneered at Little Li.

As younger Red Guards began hauling armfuls of music and books to the garden and dumping them under the willow tree, their panting breath made jets of steam in the cold night air. One pimply youth picked up an illustrated book entitled *Great Churches of Europe* and thumbed quizzically through its color plates of cathedrals before slamming it shut, toting it outside, and hurling it onto the growing pile beneath the tree.

"Religion is the opium of the masses!" he proclaimed contemptuously.

Little Li knew each of its illustrations, and where every one of these books sat on their shelves. Even as colleagues had purged their homes of anything that might be used as evidence of bourgeois Western leaning, Li Tongshu had refused to hide or destroy his own books or scores. He'd long since decided that seeking to conceal them would be as foolish as trying to hide himself.

When the tall Red Guard contemptuously kicked a book of Bach chorales toward him, it was so close Little Li could see the inscription on its cover written in his father's hand: "'In Bach, all the seeds of music are found, as the world is contained in God.' Gustav Mahler." Hoping to tuck it inconspicuously into his coat, he leaned over.

"What are you up to now?" a girl wearing a brace of Mao buttons challenged him.

"Nothing. I just . . ."

"Give it up!" she demanded with an outstretched hand. Little Li penitently withdrew the music from his coat. "You'll never hide such Western pollution from the dictatorship of the proletariat!" she jeered as she tried to rip the collection in half. However, it was so thick that she had to settle for tearing loose several pages at a time and ripping them up individually.

"Let's see you hide those inside your coat!" she taunted, pointing to the heap of shredded paper on the floor.

"What's your name?" demanded the tall Red Guard disdainfully as he walked over.

"It's Li . . ." he began, halting in mid-sentence.

"Have you swallowed your tongue?" laughed the Red Guard. Little Li had always felt humiliated when kids mocked him for having a "feudalistic" (封建) name—Li Wende (李文德), Li the Literate and Virtuous. During the political campaign against "the Four Olds" (四旧)—old traditional customs, habits, culture, and thinking—that had recently swept the country, he'd begged his father to change his name to something like Serve the People Li (李为民), but his father had refused.

"State your full name!" insisted the Red Guard.

"My name is . . . Li Wende [李文德]," he finally admitted, almost inaudibly.

"So—here we have a lover of bourgeois literature and virtue," jeered his tormentor, planting both hands authoritatively on his hips and turning to address the other Red Guards in the room.

"But I'm a good student of Chairman Mao," protested Little Li.

"The people have no interest in your alibis," rejoined the tall Red Guard. "You can no more hide your class background than a tiger can hide his stripes. If you insist on changing your name, Son of a Dog Li [李狗崽] would be more appropriate." He laughed. Then he leaned down, picked up a stack of books and scores, and thrust them into Little Li's arms. "So—show us on whose side you really stand." He pointed to the door. With the words "Son of a Dog Li" burning in his ears, Little Li submissively carried the books outside.

"We must all dare to criticize the ideological crimes of our reactionary parents, little friend," said an older girl who intercepted him on the veranda. She spoke with conviction, but not without sympathy. "If you're loyal to Chairman Mao, you'll help rid our socialist Motherland of such decadent things." She pointed to the books. Then she added, "Remember, you're not alone. Most of us have had to criticize our own rightist parents. It's our revolutionary duty. As our Chairman teaches us, 'Where the broom does not reach, the dust will not vanish by itself.'" Little Li felt a rush of gratitude toward her, and a flash of resentment toward his father. Why had he married an American? Why did he so stubbornly insist on playing his treasonous Bach all the time, even when Red Guards had come to promote Mao's revolution? "So show us your true colors!" the girl coaxed, pointing to the growing pile of their family effects.

Little Li marched as resolutely as he could toward the pile of books, scrolls, and music heaped under the willow tree. It seemed as if the entire neighborhood had gathered in Willow Courtyard, and all eyes were now focused on him. At the very back of the crowd, he spotted Fu Qiangmin, Strengthen the People Fu, a short, wiry man from the Conservatory who, while studying piano in Warsaw, had taken the eponymous Russian name, Fyodor. Both he and Li Tongshu taught keyboard, and at first Fyodor Fu had worshipped his colleague's musical abilities. However, as the party's increasingly anti-American posture became clear, his admiration turned to condescension, and by the time Fu gave up the piano to become the Conservatory's Communist Party secretary, Li Tongshu had become an easy target. Little Li was sure Fu was behind this attack. But, desperate to appear strong, grown-up, and loyal to Chairman Mao, as he approached the pile he cried out, "Chairman Mao is the red, red sun in our hearts!" and hurled his armload of books onto the pile. No sooner had he done so than the tall Red Guard appeared with a kerosene-soaked torch, which he lit with his cigarette lighter and thrust into Little Li's hands.

"Now we'll see whether the son of Li Tongshu intends to sweep away the black poison of counterrevolution or stubbornly defend his renegade father."

Transfixed by the sudden silence in the courtyard and the gaudy flames dancing at the end of the torch, Little Li could not move. But, knowing he was being watched, he finally drew himself up and cried out, "Long live Chairman Mao!"

However, at the last moment, his fourteen-year-old voice cracked. Burning with embarrassment, he flung the torch onto the pile. But instead of the roar of approval he'd expected, he was rewarded only with more silence. Paralyzed, he watched as a single, delicate tongue of blue flame licked up at the yellow cover of a G. Schirmer edition of Mozart's Piano Concerto No. 2. Slowly, the cover darkened and curled, before finally bursting into full flame and incinerating into a few weightless flakes of black ash fringed with orange that floated drunkenly up through the leafless branches of the willow tree. As the flames spread to *The Anna Magdalena Bach Book* and then *The Goldberg Variations,* their pages of antlike black notes on bone-white paper puffed, one after another, into flame. Soon the entire library of scores that his father had brought back from America to help "build a new China" (建设新中国) had vanished. "Is this what death is like?" wondered Little Li. At one moment a flesh-and-blood person like his mother was here; the next, gone, just like these scores?

Little Li's trance was broken when a package of the royal-blue-and-crimson-edged aerograms sent by his mother after leaving Beijing sailed overhead and landed in the fire. In an instant, their sheerness was incinerated in serial bursts of flame.

Then something landed that sent a cloud of sparks into the air like a swarm of angry incandescent insects. It was the photograph of his mother and father that had hung above their piano since he was born. Taken of them standing in front of the Golden Gate Bridge in San Francisco just before they were married, this photo had provided him with his only visual connection to his departed mother and her American homeland. How many hours had he spent kneeling on his father's piano bench, staring up at the photo, into his mother's unblinking eyes? Sometimes he'd even dare imagine that if he stared long enough she might step out of the frame, descend from her shrine on the wall, throw her arms around him, and beg his forgiveness for leaving. So he instinctively lunged now to retrieve the photo. But just as he did, a Red Guard grabbed his collar and yanked him back; in that moment, with a snap, the glass in the picture frame shattered, and the milky image of his parents burst into flame.

The drum began beating again, and the Red Guards began raucously singing: "We are Chairman Mao's Red Guards, tempering ourselves in great waves and wind; Armed with Mao Zedong Thought, we'll wipe out all pests and vermin!" Their voices were so out of tune; Little Li knew his father would scorn their singing. But where had they dragged him? In the dancing shadows, Little Li searched the crowd. He spotted his closest friend, Little Wang, who lived at the other end of Big Sheep Wool Alley, and Granny Sun, who was standing in her doorway looking small and worried, but nowhere did he see his father. Whereas only moments before his stubbornness had angered Little Li, now he felt only longing.

"To rebel is justified!" a voice brayed. "We must love Chairman Mao and with our heart and soul carry his revolution through to the end!"

"There can be no construction without destruction [不破不立]!" bleated another voice, echoing Mao's famous line.

Tears welled up in Little Li's eyes until everything appeared as if he were looking through a rain-streaked window. Ashamed, he wiped his eyes with his cuffs. Only then did he see that Granny Sun was on her veranda, frantically beckoning to him. Taking advantage of the distracting chants, he edged back into the shadowy throng. When he finally reached her doorway, she ushered him brusquely inside, threw the lock, and turned out the light.

"Here, drink this," she whispered, pouring a cup of hot water from her thermos, making him realize how parched he was. "It's dangerous," she reproached. "You mustn't go out."

"But where's my father?"

"Shhhh!" was all she replied.

When the crowd outside gave up a collective murmur, Little Li rushed to the window. The burly Red Guard was back on their veranda, triumphantly holding the leather case in which his father kept his 78 rpm phonograph records of Beethoven's five piano concertos, nine symphonies and one opera, *Fidelio*. Wrenching it open, he began sailing the ebony discs into the air with all the delight of a child launching toy flying saucers. Each time, the drum beat and he let another record sail into the darkness. The first hit the trunk of the willow tree and shattered. The next two sailed erratically out among the onlookers, who scattered as if being attacked by rabid bats. But the next few glided with graceful precision right into the fire, where they slowly drooped into unearthly shapes before melting into puddles of tarlike goo and combusting into jets of flame and black smoke.

There was an unexpected splintering crash. Four Red Guards were using their piano as a battering ram to break through the doorway. Each time the instrument hit the doorframe, a cheer went up. Then, as with an explosive report the piano knocked the door off its hinges. A scrum of Red Guards dragged it down the veranda and pushed it up over the railing to the edge of the bonfire.

"Down with the instruments of American imperialism!" exulted one Red Guard, who triumphantly mounted the instrument as if it were a barricade, wrenched loose its hardwood top, and hurled it onto the flames. Then, waving their cleaver like a conductor gone mad, he began hacking at the keyboard and filling the courtyard with one jarring, dissonant chord after another.

Several Red Guards gathered around the overturned instrument and strained against its weight until they finally managed to tip it up on end, where it teetered hesitantly for a moment before falling in slow motion into the fire, where it gave up a noise like a wounded beast crying out its last. As flames hungrily licked at its lacquer finish, its sides began blistering and bubbling like roasting skin.

When Granny Sun let out a gasp, Little Li lifted his gaze from the smoldering instrument. There was his father standing on their veranda; a cardboard dunce cap inscribed with the characters "American Spy!" (美国间谍) was clapped on his head, a rope was tied around his neck, and he was being pulled by the tall Red Guard toward a table set with their meat cleaver and a copy of *The Quotations from Chairman Mao*. Li Tongshu stood motionless, jaws clenched, eyes squeezed shut, and face drained of color. His slender hands, clasped before him as if in prayer, glowed in the firelight with the eerie whiteness of marble.

"American spy Li is on trial as a member of the black reactionary gang who has ceaselessly sought to champion decadent Western music over our own proletarian Chinese music," intoned the tall Red Guard. Then, opening the Little Red Book from the tabletop, he began reading with scriptural authority: "Everything reactionary is the same. If you don't hit it, it will not fall." Then he turned to face Li Tongshu. "By claiming the superiority of capitalist culture over socialist culture, you've sown inferiority in the hearts of our young people. Now, American spy Li, you must make a self-criticism! You must confess!"

"No leniency for those who do not confess!" shouted the crowd.

Li Tongshu tilted his head upward, but said nothing.

"So—you're too good to respond to the call of the masses?" challenged the tall Red Guard, a cruel smile bending the corners of his mouth. "You may play the piano, but that does not make you fit to be called Chinese!" Li Tongshu opened his eyes, slowly raised an accusatory forefinger toward the burning piano, and, in a voice loud enough for everyone in the courtyard to hear, proclaimed, "May it be the will of heaven that our Motherland survives this disgrace!" He pulled the dunce cap from his head and threw it into the fire.

For a moment, the tall Red Guard seemed uncertain how to respond. But, realizing he'd been challenged, he finally called out in stentorian tones, "Bow your head before the people, American spy Li!"

"To rebel is justified!" someone cried out.

"You must confess your crimes!" shrieked a young woman, who leapt onto the veranda and spat into the face of Li Tongshu. He neither flinched nor opened his eyes. Little Li would have rushed into the courtyard to his side, but just then there was a flash of silver in the firelight. In horror he watched as the cleaver rose and fell. Even from inside Granny Sun's room he could hear the dull thwacking sound like a butcher chopping meat on a block as the cleaver came down again and again on his father's hands.

"Father!" he screamed.

"Hush, child! Hush!" hissed Granny Sun, clapping a palm over his mouth.

Stunned by what he'd just done, the tall Red Guard backed away, an expression of shock softening his hard, young face. Li Tongshu's mouth was agape in agony, his face a death mask as he raised his hands over his head like a conductor who's just finished leading a monumental work and is waiting for the last reverberations from in the orchestra to die away before allowing the audience to applaud. As blood cascaded down his forearms onto the tabletop, an unearthly silence descended over the courtyard, so that onlookers could hear the sizzling sound as flames feasted on the piano's lacquered sides.

2

HEADS ARE NOT LIKE LEEKS

WHEN LITTLE LI awoke, it took him several moments to remember where he was and what had happened the night before. Leaping from bed, he ran to Granny Sun's window. Wisps of smoke still curled up from the heaps of half-burned books and music. With its charred sides and tangle of snapped strings erupting from inside, their piano looked like a disabled implement of war. Ash had fallen over the courtyard like snow, clothing and papers were strewn everywhere, and their front door lay on the veranda in a shower of shattered glass that glittered in the morning sun like ice crystals. He pulled on his clothing and was just opening the door when Granny Sun awakened.

"What are you up to now, stupid boy?" she challenged.

"Going out to save some of our things."

"No, you're not!" she commanded, sitting bolt upright in bed.

"But I see our radio!" he protested. On the ground under the willow tree lay their Flying Deer–brand radio, its brown plastic cowling seemingly intact.

"Don't you go out there!" she snapped, laboring out of bed. "Young people aren't smart enough to know when to be afraid! 'Newborn calves haven't the wits to be fearful of tigers' [初生牛犊不怕虎]."

"But maybe our radio still works. I could just get it, come right back, and . . ."

"How can you be such a 'dumb melon' [傻瓜]? Who knows when the Red Guards might return?" she reproved. "And your father would . . ."

"But where is he?"

"Hush!" she rejoined, squeezing her eyes shut so her whole face became even more wrinkled.

"But what about his hands?"

"Don't be thinking about such things," she said, checking the lock on the door. "There's no way. You must wait!"

"For what?"

"You've no patience!" Her voice was full of exasperation.

As he stared out the grimy window, he thought, "If I could just cross the garden and step onto our veranda, perhaps everything would magically return to normal."

"Oh, that lovely willow tree you and your father brought back to life!" said Granny Sun, noticing him staring toward it. "Do you know what the willow signifies in Chinese poetry?"

"No," he responded without interest.

"The poet Tao Qian [陶潜] used it as the symbol of constancy and loyalty in times of hardship."

"Do you think Father will be all right?"

"Heaven only knows what 'fate' [命] decrees for any of us. It's best not to think of it."

Until that night, the months of Little Li's life at Willow Courtyard had ticked by with a repetitive predictability. In spite of his mother's departure, his father's exile during the Anti-Rightist Campaign in 1957, and his return home in 1959, life on Big Sheep Wool Alley had seemed almost immutable. Each day he got up, ate breakfast, and bicycled to the Conservatory where his father taught, and he attended the lower school attached to it. Upon returning in the afternoon, he played with his friends in the surrounding network of alleys, or *hutongs* (胡同), that honeycombed old Beijing, practiced his flute, ate his dinner, and then did his homework. Once he was in bed, his father always read him a story, often from one of the illustrated English-language books his mother sent from San Francisco.

"Your mother would never want you to forget her mother tongue," he insisted.

Because he also held that his son could never become a truly "civilized person" (有教养的人) without also having a knowledge of Chinese history, by the time he was eight Little Li had memorized the names and dates of all the major dynasties. And in his child's mind this succession of imperial reigns was like a string of sausages, a clever ploy for dividing up a very long stretch of confusing history into discrete lengths to give each period an understandable shape. He also imagined the repeating days, weeks, months, and years that made up his own life as similar, an endless and reassuring succession. But, seeing Willow Courtyard in ruins, he had the sensation now that, just as dynasties of yore had risen and fallen, a period of his life had now irretrievably ended. The comforting cycles of time and concentric circles of protection that he had once imagined as radiating protectively out around him from Willow Courtyard and Big Sheep Wool Alley had been breached in a way that might now irreversibly change things.

His thoughts were interrupted when two Red Guards from the night before unexpectedly sauntered into the courtyard through the smashed front gate and walked toward their veranda. Little Li watched as they pasted a sheet of white paper emblazoned with bold black characters on the brick wall beside the shattered door frame into their room. Whereas the night before they'd been filled with revolutionary zeal, now they went about their task with all the matter-of-factness of municipal workers. When Granny Sun went out to the public latrine later, he darted over to see what they'd posted.

Chairman Mao Tells Us:
MAKE THE PAST SERVE THE PRESENT AND MAKE WHAT IS
FOREIGN SERVE CHINA.
Remember this, American spy Li Tongshu!

He suddenly regretted his impatience with his father and his yearning to run away with a Red Guard troop to free himself from contamination of his family legacy; recalling this now, he was overcome with remorse. Why hadn't he left the safety of Granny Sun's room to help his father?

Later that morning, as he was finishing a bowl of porridge, Dr. Song Shaoming, his father's oldest friend, came unexpectedly through the gate. As he stopped to survey the destruction, Little Li opened Granny Sun's door.

"Uncle Song! Over here!" he called out.

"Good heavens!" exclaimed the doctor as he embraced the boy. "What happened?" His intelligent eyes were streaked with red. Dr. Song was a tall, lanky man with a fringe of hair tumbling out from beneath his faded cap. He wore a khaki-colored greatcoat with a synthetic fur collar over a faded gray Mao suit from whose trouser cuffs protruded two pairs of different-colored long underwear. He carried the same black leather medical bag emblazoned with a red cross that he'd brought back from San Francisco after receiving his medical degree at UCSF. Tucked under the other arm was a bundle wrapped in newspaper. "As soon as I heard, I came over. Are you all right?"

"They burned our books, our records, our piano, hurt Father's hand and took him away!" Little Li had to bite his lower lip to keep it from trembling.

"I understand," said Dr. Song, putting a reassuring arm around the boy's shoulders.

"Do you know where he is?"

"I have a lead," replied Dr. Song wearily. "Do you know where Building Two is at the Conservatory?"

"It's where his studio is."

"Can you show me how to get there?"

"But what good will it do?"

"Your father may be there, and he'll need a doctor."

"Will he be all right?" asked Little Li.

"We'll see," replied Dr. Song unconvincingly. "We must go right away and you must dress warmly."

Little Li put on his coat as Dr. Song asked Granny Sun for a thermos of hot water, which he handed Little Li to carry.

They rode down the Avenue of Eternal Peace past Tiananmen Gate and did not slow down until they were nearing the familiar walls of the old Qiye Palace (七爷府), the birthplace of China's second-to-last imperial ruler, the Guangxu Emperor (光绪皇帝), which had been reassigned to the Central Conservatory of Music in 1949. Every inch of the high brick wall surrounding the sprawling compound was now plastered with "wall posters" (大字报) denouncing faculty members of the shuttered school so that it hardly looked like a school of music. Just as they were nearing the back gate, Dr. Song veered so abruptly down a side alley that Little Li almost fell off the bike and dropped the fragile thermos.

"There are Red Guards in the courtyard!" whispered Dr. Song. "We mustn't be seen!"

A blast of static crackled from loudspeakers in the compound, followed by a high-pitched electronic squeal and a strident voice:

"All comrades take notice: the struggle session against the bour-geois violinist Ma Sicong and the reactionary pianist Liu Shikun will soon commence! Down with all reactionary musicians!"

Ma Sicong and Liu Shikun were two of China's most renowned classical musicians. Ma had studied in France and returned to become the first president of the new Conservatory, and it was he who had personally invited Li Tongshu to return from San Francisco to teach. Liu Shikun was the recipient of the Special Prize at the 1956 Liszt International Piano Competition in Budapest (for which he was given a strand of Franz Liszt's hair), and shared second place in the 1958 Tchaikovsky Competition in Moscow, behind the U.S. pianist Van Cliburn. As a burst of martial music followed, Dr. Song and Little Li pressed themselves against the alley wall, unsure whether to advance or to retreat.

"There are too many people in the courtyard right now!" whispered Dr. Song.

"But I know how we can get in through a back entrance!"

"Where?"

"It's not far. Shall we go?"

"Yes."

Little Li, who knew each and every one of the winding *hutong*s that veined the neighborhood around the Conservatory, led Dr. Song to a battered wooden gate that breached the high brick wall on the rear side of the compound. "This leads to the canteen," he said breathlessly. "And with school closed, there shouldn't be anyone there."

"How can we get in?" asked Dr. Song, tugging at the padlock affixed to the wooden door.

"Boost me up," said Little Li, pointing to a ledge above the gate.

Dr. Song lifted Little Li onto his shoulders and strained to hold him steady as he stood upright and began feeling along the dusty ledge overhead for the smooth, cold surface of the key he hoped was still there. But all he dislodged was a shower of leaves and twigs down onto Dr. Song's head. He was about to give up when there was a chimelike clinking sound as the key hit the ground.

"How did you know it was there?" Dr. Song asked with a broad smile.

"The cooks used to allow their friends to sneak in through this door after hours to steal food from the canteen," replied Little Li, jumping down to pick up the tarnished key. As he unlocked the padlock and swung the door open, its parched hinges groaned. Dr. Song froze in fear of being detected.

"Where's Building Two?" he finally asked.

"Follow me," whispered Little Li, and they stole around the back of the canteen and down a passageway where heaps of broken desks and overturned pianos were piled. "Wait here—I'll see if the coast is clear."

Little Li hurried out into the main courtyard, to the fishpond under several ancient cypress trees. With the closure of schools that summer, the fountain had been shut off, the goldfish stolen, and the remaining water had turned into a vile brew of filth and algae. But this once-sylvan fishpond was to suffer one further indignity: it became the dumping ground for thousands of musical scores looted from the Conservatory library by Red Guards and had been turned into a bog of filthy papier-mâché. Stealing behind the pool and down another passageway, Little Li was relieved to find that the back entrance to Building 2 was open.

As Dr. Song nervously waited for Little Li's return, he noticed that he was standing right under a wall poster emblazoned with a quotation from the tsarina of China's new socialist arts and culture, Mao's third wife, Jiang Qing.

> *It is inconceivable that in our socialist country led by the Communist Party the dominant position on the stage is not occupied by the workers, peasants, and soldiers who are the real creators of history and the true masters of our country.*

He knew that Jiang Qing sat at the apex of the Cultural Revolution leadership, and that she'd just lectured an assembly of high-school students, saying: "We do not fear chaos. Chaos and order are inseparable." Then she'd added for good measure, "We don't advocate beating people, but beating people is no big deal." How Chinese culture had come to this left his head swimming.

"There's a group of Red Guards at the end of the courtyard, but I know a way around them," said a panting Little Li, who was suddenly back at his side.

"Your father would be proud of you, my boy."

"Follow me," he commanded. Burning with pride, he led Dr. Song to Building 2.

"And where's Room 317?"

"Upstairs."

On the third floor, they were just about to start down the corridor when Dr. Song yanked Little Li's collar.

"There are two Red Guards playing cards at the end of the hallway," he reported, pointing through a small pane of glass in the hallway door.

When one of the Red Guards stood up and started toward them, Dr. Song pulled Little Li sideways into the latrine, which emitted an overpowering reek of stale urine. No sooner had they ducked into a toilet stall than the door opened and one of the Red Guards entered a neighboring stall. As Dr. Song and Little Li stood absolutely still, they heard the door slam, a belt buckle jingle, and then a bassoonlike crepitation. They did not move until the door opened again and the sound of footsteps had faded down the stairwell. Upon regaining the hallway, they were relieved to find only one Red Guard now on watch outside Room 317.

"Leave the talking to me," ordered Dr. Song as they approached the lone guard. "Good afternoon," he began, authoritatively proffering his hand to the short, ruddy-faced boy of no more than sixteen years. "I've been sent by Beijing Capital Hospital to treat the American spy Li Tongshu, who I believe is being held in Room 317." Hearing his father referred to as a spy made Little Li's heart skip. He was about to protest when Dr. Song squeezed his hand.

"Well, I can't . . ." began the Red Guard, looking at the closed studio door. His thick provincial accent marked him as one of the thousands of young revolutionary pilgrims now pouring into Beijing from the provinces to "link up" (串联) with other Red Guards in the capital.

"I understand," soothed Dr. Song. "However, I must carry out my revolutionary duties as a people's doctor." He extracted a document bearing the official red seal of his hospital.

"But I've been ordered not to let anyone into this room."

"You're correct to carry out your own responsibilities with diligence," rejoined Dr. Song, with faintly disguised impatience. "And

I'll report to the relevant authorities that you've been doing your job faithfully. However, I, too, must do mine, to treat those in need."

"Just a minute," said the Red Guard. He ran down the hallway and called into the lavatory, "Xiao Peng, are you still in here?" There was no answer. "Strict orders from the revolutionary command have ordered us not to let anyone into this room," he insisted upon returning. "Li Tongshu is an enemy of Chairman Mao's mass line and . . ." He was clearly uncomfortable about refusing this older man bearing an official document.

"Chairman Mao also tells us, 'Even the most poisonous weeds can be reformed through criticism and self-criticism,'" countered Dr. Song.

"Well . . . I'm not sure . . . ," stuttered the Red Guard.

"As a doctor, I have the revolutionary duty to treat even traitors, so that they, too, may learn to better serve socialism," continued Dr. Song. Then he reached into his overcoat and extracted the package wrapped in newspaper and, with the same precision with which he performed surgery, unwrapped it, took out two steamed buns (包子), and offered them to the agitated Red Guard.

"Go ahead," soothed Dr. Song. "To make revolution, one must also eat." He put a reassuring hand on the young man's shoulder. The boy cautiously accepted a bun and, after a hesitant first bite, began eating ravenously.

Suddenly something stirred inside the studio. Little Li looked up just as a gaunt face appeared in the small pane of glass in the studio door. It was his father.

"I must do my duty," said Dr. Song, opening the door and walking in defiantly just as Li Tongshu slumped back against the wall. Little Li ran in as well and squatted down beside his father, who tried to raise his arms to embrace him. But, because he could not use his crippled hands, he had to clutch his son's head to his chest between his elbows. As he did, Dr. Song shut the door and set a chair behind the doorknob.

"So—you found me," Li Tongshu croaked in the half-light.

"My dear friend" was all Dr. Song could utter through the waves of emotion overcoming him. Then, turning to Little Li, he said, "We must work rapidly and quietly."

"Can we help him?" asked Little Li, horrified by the sight of his father sprawled on the floor holding his mangled hands out in front of him like a sleepwalker.

"Just do as I say," whispered Dr. Song. He took off his coat, draped it over the shoulders of his shivering friend, knelt beside him, and opened his medical bag. Only when Dr. Song took Li Tongshu's hands in his own to examine them did Little Li comprehend the magnitude of what had befallen his father. His grossly swollen knuckles were caked with dried blood and dirt, and his fingers looked more like talons than human appendages; he knew that these battered fingers would never fly over a keyboard again. As Dr. Song studied the wounds, his friend averted his pain-drowsed eyes, perhaps still unwilling to accept the full measure of the disaster that had befallen him.

"Please pour some boiled water into the thermos top," Dr. Song ordered Little Li. Then he spread a white cloth across his friend's knees, snipped lengths of gauze from a roll, dipped them into the boiling-hot water, and began to scrub the scabrous wounds. Dr. Song's own fingers were as white, delicate, and smooth as those of a woman and went about their grisly task with all the skill and dexterity of Li Tongshu's own fingers when they had still been able to ripple over the keys of a piano. But now his hands trembled so violently that Dr. Song had to hold them between his knees as if in a vise to steady them. When Li Tongshu let out a moan of agony, Dr. Song grimaced, extracted a silver hypodermic from his bag, loaded it with morphine from a small rubber-tipped bottle, pulled his friend's trousers down over one hip, and plunged the needle into his thigh. Li Tongshu uttered a noise that sounded more like the growl of a wild animal than a human cry. After scrubbing the dried blood off and pruning away the necrotic flesh, Dr. Song covered the gaping wounds with antiseptic, wound them in gauze, splinted the broken knuckles with wooden tongue depressors, and bandaged both hands with gauze and adhesive.

By the time Dr. Song finished, Li Tongshu's eyes were closed in a morphine-induced stupor, and his face was as gray as the cold concrete floor beneath him. Dr. Song was fixing his own greatcoat around his friend's shoulders when the chair blockading the door flew across the room.

"If you don't hurry, I'm going to report you!" barked the Red Guard.

"Of course! Of course!" replied Dr. Song without looking up.

"I'm not fooling," insisted the Red Guard. "If you don't want trouble, you'll go!"

"We're just leaving," replied Dr. Song as he buttoned his coat around the motionless form of his friend. When he'd snapped his medical bag shut, he placed the remaining steamed buns and the thermos beside the inert form of Li Tongshu.

"Goodbye, my old friend," he whispered. "May the Lord bless you and keep you!"

"Forgive them," murmured Li Tongshu.

"You must say farewell now," Dr. Song urged Little Li. Teeth chattering from cold and fear, he knelt beside his father. It was then he saw that he'd scrawled, "Save the children [救救孩子]" with his own blood on the wall behind his head, a plea the renowned writer Lu Xun had made famous in his short story "The Diary of a Madman" (狂人记) decades before.

"Goodbye, Papa," he mumbled. Li Tongshu's eyes, dull and drowsy with shock and morphine, flickered open. "My son!" was all he could manage to rasp out before the Red Guard called out, "The others are coming!"

"Hurry!" urged Dr. Song.

Just as they reached the stairwell, the other Red Guards entered the hallway at the far end.

3

THE STINKING NINTH CATEGORY

AFTER THE Red Guard attack, Granny Sun would not permit Little Li to go outside, even to salvage their effects.

"It's still too dangerous, and there's no telling what might happen," she reprimanded. Only after several days did she finally relent and let him go to the public latrine rather than the chamber pot. But as soon as he was outside, two rival neighborhood boys spotted him.

"Li Wende is the blackest of the black!" they mercilessly taunted as he ran into the latrine. "I bet your shit is darker than coal!" They were yelling so loudly that people living on the alley began coming out to see what the commotion was. Little Li was so afraid his tormentors would march right into the latrine and catch him in a compromised posture that he didn't dare even to unbuckle his trousers.

"Why don't you come back out, Li the Literate and Virtuous?" they jeered as he cowered inside. "Are you afraid of the wrath of the people?"

Finally, he had to brave their gauntlet of derision, but with a new respect for Granny Sun's curfew.

"I hope you've learned your lesson!" she said reprovingly after he returned.

Sitting in her dark, claustrophobic room as she knitted and prattled on about life in "old Beijing" left him so bored that he began perusing the piles of her husband's old books at the back of her room. He found a string-bound edition of *The Dream of the Red Chamber* (红楼梦) by Cao Xueqin (曹雪芹), which his father loved. As he read, he came upon one of the book's most famous lines:

*"We have arrived at the realm of illusion," a Daoist
monk said to Shi Ying as they walked in a dream together
through a memorial archway leading into the Phantom
Realm of the Great Void, on which a couplet was written:
"When the unreal is taken for the real, then the real
becomes unreal. When nonexistence is taken for existence,
then existence becomes nonexistence."* (假作真时真亦假 无
为有处有还无)

*Shi Ying was trying to follow through the archway when
he heard a crash, as if the mountains had collapsed and
the earth parted. He awoke with a start to see nothing but
bright sun shining down on the courtyard outside, and the
broad leaves of a plantain tree casting a cool shadow.*

Little Li wished the courtyard scene outside Granny Sun's window was only another "phantom realm" born of his own imagination from which he, too, might awaken. But it was no fantasy. There were his father's overturned piano, burned books, and charred scores. The only way this bleak tableau seemed to bear out the lines he'd just read was in suggesting that even the greatest households are mutable, and in the end all men are only pawns in an enigmatic game of endless change in which it is often impossible to distinguish reality from illusion, because reality frequently ends up being every bit as strange as fantasy.

Little Li could not stop thinking about his father. Where was he? How were his hands? What would become of him? He felt remorse not only for sometimes having been so impatient and disloyal, but for failing to help him. Equally painful was the recognition that a flesh-and-blood human being who'd been so present in his life at one moment could disappear so completely the next and yet still live on so vividly in memory. As he lay in Granny Sun's room, waiting for sleep to arrest his turbulent thoughts, both his father and his mother now seemed no more permanent than blocks of ice left out in the hot sun. Was his father now destined to fade into milky blankness, as his mother had? Just as he'd once tried to conjure up images of her to fix her face in his mind's eye, he now sought to do the same with his father, hoping that such mental calisthenics would help fortify his powers of memory. However, no matter how hard he tried to freeze-frame calming images of his father playing the piano, writing letters, or cultivating his garden, they kept being overridden by harrowing images of him gaping up at his bleeding hands in stupefied horror.

Hoping that music might help him maintain another kind of connection, Little Li started practicing the flute again. But since the only permissible works were now "model" pieces approved by Jiang Qing—proletarian anthems such as "Socialism Is Good," "The Screws of the Revolution Will Never Rust," and "We Are All Socialist Sunflowers"—his repertoire was limited. But knowing his father loved variations, he began improvising on these revolutionary songs, trying to imagine how Bach might have spun his spare opening *Goldberg* aria into thirty different variations, or how Beethoven had taken a banal oom-pah-pah waltz and transformed it into his thirty-three *Diabelli Variations*. His own efforts created a bizarre fusion designed to deceive anyone walking into the courtyard unannounced, because he could slide from his improvisation back to the approved revolutionary anthem in an instant. He called these improvisations his *Sibuxiang Symphony* (四不像交响曲), literally *The Four Unlike Any Others Symphony*, an allusion to a mythic Chinese creature said to have the antlers of a deer, the tail of a donkey, the hooves of a cow, and the neck of a camel.

Granny Sun's only offspring was a thirty-year-old unmarried daughter who worked in Tianjin and had the default facial expression of someone who's just bitten into an unripe persimmon. She unexpectedly reappeared in Willow Courtyard one day, wearing a khaki-colored army jacket pinned with so many Mao buttons that she looked armor-plated. Seeing that an interloper had supplanted her, she refused to speak directly to Little Li. Instead, she addressed only her mother, saying such things as:

"Why don't you get the boy to fetch some more hot water?"

"Let's send the boy to the market to make him useful."

Her homecoming gift was a white ceramic bust of Chairman Mao, which she instructed her mother to display on a Ming Dynasty side table like a protective tutelary god, a prophylaxis against Little Li's fallen state of political grace. Her homecoming turned out not to be dedicated to visiting her mother, but to purging their household of incriminating evidence, lest she become sullied by the reliquary of "feudal" things left behind by her father. Forgoing any discussion about what should be saved, she set about burning her father's voluminous collection of art, books, and papers in Granny Sun's small metal stove.

"Didn't Chairman Mao warn us, 'If you read too many books, in the end they will petrify your mind'?" she scolded her protesting mother. "We must not waste time sticking our noses in useless books from the feudal past!" For two days, smoke poured from their stovepipe as Granny Sun wept. She tried to save a set of ancient books, a box of letters, then a photo of her husband in a scholar's robe, but her daughter refused. "Remnants of the Four Olds have no place in new China," she militantly proclaimed.

"But maybe we could just . . ." Granny Sun began in protest; her daughter hushed her to silence.

When all evidence of her father's once-cosmopolitan life was purged from the room, the daughter unceremoniously decamped for her Tianjin factory, leaving her mother bereft of almost everything that had given her life continuity with the past. And so she turned even more to Little Li for consolation. Since he'd already lived with her in 1958 after the Anti-Rightist Campaign, when his father had been "sent down" (下放) to the countryside, she'd come to accept, even love, him. And he'd become so devoted to her that, even after his father's return in 1959, he continued to fetch her hot water from the nearby boiler, shop for her, clean the ashes from her stove, bring her vegetables from their garden, and sometimes just sit with her as she puttered around her dark, cluttered room. But, as fond as she was of him, she, too, sometimes became anxious about the consequences of sheltering the son of a "rightist."

"How's that 'half-breed' [混血] you've taken in?" a neighbor pointedly asked one day.

"Don't talk that way to a grown woman, Comrade Weng!" she shot back. Such talk angered her, and it wounded Little Li.

After returning from the market one evening, as Little Li put down the things he'd just bought, he accidentally knocked over her new ceramic bust of Chairman Mao. When Granny Sun saw what he'd done, her face became as pale as the shards of white porcelain on the floor.

"Look what you've done, you reckless child!" she erupted.

"I'm sorry, Granny Sun!" he pleaded. "I'm so sorry!"

"There's no good in you!" she scolded. "Sometimes I don't know why I took you in."

"I didn't mean it! Really! I didn't!" he sputtered.

Mortified, he would have bolted out the door if they hadn't heard unexpected voices in the courtyard. Granny Sun, terrified that his dastardly act would be discovered and reported, stopped scolding, threw both locks on the door, and began frantically cleaning up the incriminating evidence. In panic, she grabbed one of her precious cotton pillowcases, went down on her knees, and began sweeping the razor-sharp fragments of porcelain into it with her bare hands. Little Li just stood against the wall in shamefaced silence. Only when the voices outside finally departed did she order him to pulverize the shards in the pillowcase by pounding them with a brick. As he hammered away, he felt as if he were flagellating himself, not just for his sin of carelessness, but for having been born into such an infected family. He did not stop until his fingers were raw and the shattered bust was no more than a handful of white grit inside the tattered pillowcase. After dark, Granny Sun ordered him to take the incriminating remains out to Big Sheep Wool Alley and sprinkle them like seasoning on the ground in the dark.

One day, Little Li heard that all the youths in the neighborhood were going to be registered for a special Red Rebel Brigade. He barely slept that night. When he looked in the mirror the next morning and saw the ineffaceable hints of his half-Caucasian mother in his otherwise Chinese features, he dreaded the prospect of still more rejection and humiliation. His foreign features would forever preclude him from full acceptance in the prejudiced world to which fate had consigned him, and as he walked to the school where the registration was being held the next morning, he felt like a prisoner on his way to a place of execution. Had there been some way to erase the disfigurement he'd received from his mother, even though it meant the excision of some physical part of himself, he would not have hesitated. His spirits were hardly lifted by the slogan written on an easel blackboard at the school's front gate: *IF THE FATHER IS A HERO, HIS SON IS A GOOD PATRIOT. IF THE FATHER IS A REACTIONARY, HIS SON IS A BASTARD.* (老子英雄儿好汉 老子反动儿混蛋.)

Inside, middle-school students were already queued up for registration. Once in line, Little Li watched intently, so that by the time his turn came he would, at least, understand the procedure. After a quick grilling, a tall Red Guard was directing each candidate to one of three tables, the first draped in crimson, the second in gray, the third in black. Each represented a level of "class status" (阶级成分), in descending order of odiousness. For a student to be registered at the red table, his parents had to be from the ranks of the "five red categories" (红五类)—namely, the workers, poor peasants, revolutionary soldiers, and revolutionary cadres. Students with ambiguous class status were sent to the gray table, where they were called upon to prove their revolutionary credentials. Those from the dreaded "five black categories" (黑五类)—landlords, rich peasants, counterrevolutionaries, rightists, and other "bad elements"—were consigned to the ignominious black table.

For a revolution that made so much of egalitarianism, the Chinese communist revolution had produced a system riven with just as many social and political hierarchies as the "old society" (旧社会) it opposed. Behind its smoke screen of equality lay a towering pyramid of differentiated party positions and attendant privileges that were hauntingly similar to the very hierarchies that had formed the traditional core of Confucian/scholar-gentry rule (封建礼教) that Mao's revolution had sought to overturn. And no child was unaffected when a parent was "labeled" (打成) a "counterrevolutionary," publicly pilloried, and sent into exile. For not only were such children left abandoned; they were unable even to look up to their vanished parents. Ever since his own father was "labeled a rightist" and "sent down" in 1958, Little Li had registered each fluctuation in his political fortunes like a delicately calibrated seismic device. And now he was sure his "bad family background" would deny him even the gray table.

"Next!" the presiding Red Guard called out. A short boy at the head of the line marched forward and stood rigidly at attention.

"Name, grade, and family class background?" challenged the tall Red Guard.

"Liu Jun [刘军]. Middle school, first year. Both parents in the People's Liberation Army," the boy proudly proclaimed.

"Red table. Next!" commanded the tall Red Guard with swaggering authority.

"Wei Yihua [魏一华]. Middle school, second year. My father was a revolutionary martyr and my mother's a doctor."

"Red table!" the tall Red Guard responded without hesitation, as a flood of relief swept across the girl's face. "Next!"

"Han Wei [韩伟]. Beginning middle school. My mother works in an office, and my father . . ." Here the boy's voice trailed off and his gaze fell to the floor.

"Speak up!"

"My father's . . . a professor," the boy said in a barely audible voice.

"Black table!" commanded the tall Red Guard, so peremptorily that a titter went up. The crestfallen boy marched to the black table, where a Red Guard with a poster-perfect expression of proletarian righteousness registered him for political damnation.

Little Li dreaded the moment when he, too, would have to announce not only that his father was a professor of classical music but that his mother had been an American. Couldn't she at least have been Russian, Hungarian, or Albanian? And couldn't his father have foreseen what was now happening and changed his profession? Little Li's heart was beating like an engine gone haywire, and sweat was beading on his brow.

"Next!" demanded the tall Red Guard. "State your name."

"Li Wende!"

"Ah, so we have one of those charming bourgeois names," retorted his inquisitor, not even allowing Little Li to announce his grade in school.

"And just what do your parents do?" His top lip curled in derision.

"My mother's gone, and my father's a teacher."

"A teacher! And, pray tell, what does he teach?"

"He teaches . . ." Little Li did not want to let the next words escape.

"And what does he teach?" taunted the tall Red Guard, enjoying tormenting his prey. Because he felt so deeply disgraced, Little Li became tongue-tied. "If you think you'll escape the judgment of the masses by refusing to answer, you're deceiving yourself with wishful thinking," jeered the Red Guard.

"He teaches . . ." Little Li stammered, but still could not bring himself to say the loathsome words "classical music" (古典音乐).

"Speak up!"

"But I support Chairman Mao and his revolutionary mass line!" Little Li protested awkwardly, though even as he tried to defend himself, he felt overpowered by guilt and dishonor.

"What does this father of yours teach?" persisted the Red Guard. "Let the masses know!"

"Classical music," said Little Li in a whisper.

"Louder, so everyone can hear!"

"Classical music!"

"And classical music from where?"

"From the West."

"So that's why you look like an American imperialist?" said the tall Red Guard with a cruel laugh.

"No! I'm really not—"

"Save the empty talk for the black table!" the Red Guard interrupted. Every eye in the room was now fixed on Little Li, and their sniggering censure pierced his flesh like knives. "Welcome to the table for sons and daughters of 'the old stinking ninth category' [臭老九]," derided the Red Guard as he started toward the black table. "This label will serve as a warning to those who pretend not to know who the enemy really is."

As he picked up the pen to sign this list of infamy. Little Li felt so shamed and demeaned that, had there been some way to expiate himself by disowning his father and mother, he would have done so on the spot. But since even this pathway was foreclosed, he numbly signed the black register and walked back to Willow Courtyard despising himself, his mother, and his father, even as he missed them. However, at the same time that he hoped nobody else would learn of his humiliation, he paradoxically yearned to have everyone know: at least that would give him occasion to plead his innocence. Although a part of his immature self knew he'd done nothing wrong, the cloud of damning accusation left by the black table enveloped him in such a cloud of guilt that it seemed to him his punishment was actually justified. There was something about having been publicly shamed that made it impossible to feel he'd not, in fact, done something very wrong. For the ability of a person to maintain a belief in his own innocence is far too weak to stand against such gale-force winds of external indictment, especially when sanctioned by society, the state, and the "Great Leader" himself. If those in authority could level such charges without any objection from anybody, must not some grievous wrong have actually been committed?

Perhaps, if his father had not been gone, he could have helped Little Li make sense out of the waves of self-condemnation that now swept over him. During his own Shanxi exile ten years before, after the Anti-Rightist Campaign, Li Tongshu, too, had come to know how accusation and punishment demand the fabrication of concrete crimes as the process by which a crime begs a punishment becomes so perverted that a punishment ends up begging a crime. He had also begun blaming himself for his separation from his son. After all, if punishment presupposes a crime, who better than an alleged offender to invent a crime to fit his punishment? While pondering such vagaries in the solitude of the Taihang Mountains, one day, he'd undergone a moment of epiphany of his own and found himself crying out, while mulching apple trees high on a terraced field: "Hats off to the Chinese Communist Party for confecting such a masterful strategy! In its war against class oppression, the party masterfully transforms us, 'the people,' into accomplices in our own oppression. And then, because it helps make our miserable fates seem more explicable, we trick ourselves into cultivating our own sense of culpability. Whoever imagined that the party possessed such a profound understanding of human psychology?"

Like a madman, he raged away, addressing the fruit trees around him as if they were a human audience. "How proud Chairman Mao must be to end up the designer of an auto-culpability machine of such exquisite design that his victims line up to participate in their own subjugation, to become their own indicters and jailers, while the party, the real criminals, are relieved not only of any burden of wrongdoing, but also of the expense and bother of hiring more secret police and building more penal colonies. In this masterfully engineered system, we the innocent miraculously surrender our innocence, accept your accusation, torment our souls with guilt, and then inflict punishment on ourselves! Your brilliance is unbounded! You, Chairman Mao, are truly a Great Helmsman, teacher, and conjurer!" As he ranted on, Li Tongshu began laughing quite hysterically.

When he finally trudged down the mountainside that evening, another element in the party's virtuosic formula of auto-oppression occurred to him: For the party, even abject surrender was not enough. Victims were expected both to accept their guilt and to participate in their own punishment, and then to continue "demonstrating loyalty" (表态) to the eternal infallibility of the very party that was victimizing them by declaring its unfailing "correctness" (正确). As if they were ancient "sons of heaven" (天子), whatever these latter-day communist emperors did was right because they possessed their own latter-day "mandate of heaven" (天命), and "heaven" could never be wrong. What's more, the party liked its victims to be silent, passive, and contrite, so even if it later deigned to "rehabilitate" (平反) someone it had cashiered, for the victim to protest innocence before the party was ready to grant such ritual absolution was considered unpardonable effrontery! It was the party's exclusive prerogative to make and unmake its victims, and it alone was entitled to issue pardons, something it did only when this served its own purposes, and then usually only after one "correct political line" had been replaced by a new and even more "correct" political line and a new leader had ascended the party throne. (Never mind if said "new line" was completely at odds with its precursor.) And when the whole travesty was finally said and done, the aggrieved were still expected to agree that, under the "historical circumstances," their persecutions, incarcerations, exiles, et al., were "correct". . . at least until that moment when the perfidious party decided to "reverse a verdict" (翻案). Even then, victims were supposed both to continue pretending no wrongdoing had ever been perpetrated and to express gratitude for the party's magnanimity in changing their minds.

Whenever Little Li asked Granny Sun what had happened to his father, she reproved him. "Don't always be asking about such things," she chided with a mixture of fear and irritation. "When your father's verdict is decided, the responsible authorities will notify us."

Although she'd forbidden him to go to the Conservatory, the only way he could think of to find out anything about what had happened to his father was to comb the wall posters there, where mention was often made of professors under criticism. So, one afternoon, he told Granny Sun he was going out to play chess with Little Wang—"Virtuous Nation Wang," Wang Dehua (王德华)—who lived at the far end of Big Sheep Wool Alley. With one ear that stuck out like a tree fungus, buckteeth, pockmarked cheeks, and hair that stuck up so he perennially looked as if he'd just woken up, he was not a comely boy. Although his father and Granny Sun viewed him as brash and uncouth, Little Li considered Little Wang his best friend, and they were jokingly referred to in their neighborhood as the "Two Virtuous Ones" (二德)," from the character meaning "virtue" (德), which their names shared.

Instead of playing chess, the "Two Virtuous Ones" rode Little Li's bike to the Conservatory, where, after months of "red terror" (红色恐怖) and fighting between Red Guard factions, the campus was a wasteland. At the front gate hung a banner: "Without Violence There Can Be No Change" (没有暴力就没有改变). Windows were broken, smashed desks and chairs were piled in heaps, and several pianos lay overturned outside the recital hall. Pages from musical scores blew hither and thither across the courtyard, where almost every vertical surface was shaggy with wall posters. The boys skimmed as many as they could, looking for the surname Li (李), but nowhere did they see any mention of Li Tongshu. They were about to leave when it occurred to Little Li to look in his father's old studio. Stealing around to the back of Building 2, they maneuvered themselves through a smashed window, and bounded up the familiar staircase to Room 317. It was empty, with its door sagging on a single hinge, the light switch smashed and the blackboard shattered. The only sign that his father had been there was the dark-brown stain on the dirty concrete floor and the four crude characters written in blood on the scarred wall: "Save the children!"

As they were departing, Little Li spotted the Red Guard who'd pushed their piano into the bonfire, coming through the back gate on his bicycle. Little Li wanted to run over and ask him if he knew where his father had been sent, but he resisted the temptation. Instead, once he'd parked and walked insouciantly away, Little Li pulled his scarf up over his mouth, stole over to the boy's bike, and stabbed its tires with his pocketknife. The hissing sound of escaping air was sublime.

The next morning, Little Li arose before dawn, hoping to catch Dr. Song before he left for the hospital. Since all the lightbulbs in the concrete stairwell of his apartment building had long since burned out or been stolen, he had to grope his way past the jungle of locked bikes in the entryway. He hurried up the stairs to the fifth floor and knocked.

"What is it, my boy?" asked Dr. Song with concern when he discovered who was outside.

"Do you know where my father is?"

"I don't. All I know is that he was sent away for 'ideological remolding' [思想改造]."

"Will they care for his hands there?"

"I think so."

"What will they make him do?"

"Go to political study classes and do manual labor."

"Can you help him?"

"I cannot," sighed Dr. Song, putting an arm around his shoulders. "I'm powerless."

"Is he really a bad person?"

"I want you to listen carefully to me, Little Li," began Dr. Song after another long sigh. "Your father is being punished precisely because he is a good, not a bad, person." Little Li was trying to concentrate on what Dr. Song was saying, but he kept seeing his father's bloodied hands. "Your father's an upright soul living in a time of madness. But he has great inner strength, and as you grow up, I hope you, too, will find such strength. For now, you're only a boy, and you must be careful." He gave Little Li's shoulder a reassuring squeeze. "You must be very careful."

"I'll try."

"Try for your father's sake, as well as your own." He looked intently at Little Li, then said, "I'm already late for surgery. I must go."

When he was with Dr. Song, Little Li felt sheltered, and as they walked down the dark stairwell, he wished they did not have to part. Not knowing what else to do, he boarded the first bus that came by and did not get off until it reached the end of its route, at Iron Lion Tomb. As a pale sun was rising in a slate-gray sky, he was aimlessly walking when he spotted a crowd gathered on the sidewalk in front of a brick building. At any time of day or night, Beijingers thronged around traffic accidents, arguments with street vendors, fistfights, or marital feuds, engaging in what was colloquially known as "watching the heat and noise" (看热闹). But it was still early in the morning, and this crowd showed none of the hall-marks of normal gawkers. Instead of milling around and chattering, people were standing in a subdued semicircle, staring silently down at something on the sidewalk. Only one man was looking up. Following his gaze, Little Li saw that it was fixed on an open window on the top floor of the building where two lace curtains billowed out in the chilly wind. As Little Li squeezed through the throng of onlookers, he spotted a blue cap lying on the dusty pavement. Standing on tiptoes to peer over people's shoulders, he also saw the pale sun reflecting off something on the sidewalk. When he drew closer, he realized it was a pool of blood, as red as the crimson color drenching the armbands and political posters extolling Chairman Mao and his revolution. As the pool's circumference slowly expanded, the tightly packed crowd edged backward, as if out of respect for its advance. Only when Little Li succeeded in making his way to the very front of the throng did he see that a man in a blue Mao suit and traditional-style cotton-soled shoes was sprawled on the concrete.

"Did he jump?" he asked one of the bystanders.

"Nobody saw what happened."

In the window above, framed by the two fluttering curtains, there suddenly appeared the pale, distraught face of an older woman. However, as soon as others in the crowd looked up at her, she pulled back inside, like a frightened animal recoiling into its burrow.

Slowly, Little Li made his way around the edge of the crowd until he was standing just behind the fallen man, but all he could see was the nape of his neck, as pale as steamed fish, and a few wisps of hair, as gray as the sky, fluttering in the breeze. One of his arms looked as if it had been attached backward to this body. Only when the man in front of him stepped aside did Little Li catch sight of a book splayed open on the sidewalk. It was the same edition of the Confucian *Analects* owned by his father. Involuntarily Little Li fell to his knees behind the lifeless figure.

"Oh no!" he cried out. Aware only of a feeling of overpowering dread, he began shaking the shoulders of the inert figure. "I'm so sorry, Father!" he choked, as the crowd murmured in confusion.

Only when an old man in a long greatcoat and earmuffs knelt

beside Little Li and whispered something in his ear did he snap to, as if from a trance. Leaping up, he stepped in front of the fallen figure, gazed into his face, blinked, put his hands to his temples, and let out an animal-like howl. "Dear heaven! It's not him!"

Spinning around, he began to run.

4

"MY OLD MAN hasn't come home for two nights, and my mother's out of her mind," exclaimed Little Wang, unexpectedly appearing outside Granny Sun's door. "She made me go out to the Tsinghua University campus last night to look for him!"

"Did you find him?" asked Little Li.

"No, but I found a wall poster calling him 'an indelible reactionary unfit to teach the Chinese proletariat,' and then I ran into one of his students, who said he'd heard that several professors from his department had been brought before a mass struggle session. But he didn't know anything more. When I told my mother, she started wailing, 'It's just his fate!'"

"So—what are you going to do?"

"Don't know," replied Little Wang with an uncharacteristic lack of certainty.

"We should go back together?" proposed Little Li.

"But it's bedlam there. Red Guards are everywhere, and if they figure out who we are, they'll beat the crap out of us."

"We'll go anyway," insisted Little Li resolutely.

"All right." Little Wang said this deferentially.

The university's arched main gate—erected when the school was founded, with funds that had been returned to China's last dynasty by the United States, from the Boxer Rebellion Indemnity Fund, was now a heap of rubble strung with a banner: "World in Great Disorder: Excellent Situation! [天下大乱形势大好]" The thousands of Red Guards who'd taken up residence on the campus had won their struggle against the "work teams" (工作队) that had been sent to the university by President Liu Shaoqi that summer in an attempt to "lower the temperature" of what was becoming an increasingly turbulent situation. Emboldened by Mao's challenge to "bombard the headquarters" (炮打司令部), the hotheaded young Red Guard leaders who'd taken over the campus viewed Liu as a "revisionist Chinese Khrushchev and Deng Xiaoping as his co-conspirator." There were now so many wall posters that extra temporary rattan walls had been erected, and for hours the boys scanned these makeshift galleries for information on Little Wang's father. They found nothing.

"At least there's no bad news," offered Little Li gamely.

"That's not going to calm my mother down," said a discouraged Little Wang.

As darkness fell, they were about to leave when Little Li noticed that the Grand Auditorium was ablaze with lights. When they reached its pillared portico, they found throngs of students pushing into the theater where a pretty young woman costumed in a form-fitting military-style jacket and trousers with a broad leather belt cinched around her slender waist was onstage defiantly singing:

Open fire at the black gang, open fire at the black gang!
Resolutely strike down the handful of anti-party,
*   counterrevolutionary elements!*
Take the black lid off, the better to see black hearts!
*   Mao Zedong Thought is a demon-exposing mirror.*
Demons and ghosts, don't imagine you can get away. . . .
The fortress of reaction must resolutely be attacked and
*   smashed!*

As the crowd cheered, a young man wearing a crimson armband strode onstage with martial authority.

"Comrades," he began grandiloquently, "I am Kuai Dafu, leader of the Jinggangshan Red Guard Regiment." Kuai, a chemical engineering student, headed a militant Red Guard faction that gained notoriety by publicly humiliating the wife of President Liu Shaoqi when she'd appeared on campus with a "work team." "We are in a life-and-death struggle with the forces of bourgeois reaction who are seeking to subvert the mass line of Chairman Mao," Kuai continued; the crowd roared. Just then, an elderly man with his hands bound behind his back was pushed out onstage. A placard around his neck read "Yu Shicheng: member of the black gang from the Department of the History of Sciences who has taken the capitalist road."

"Professor Yu was a ringleader supporting the counterrevolutionary activities of the 'work-teams' sent on campus to suppress our revolutionary movement," thundered Kuai, gesturing contemptuously toward the old man. "Having stubbornly clung to his reactionary line, he will now show his repentance by singing for the people!"

As if on cue, a stocky Red Guard stepped out in front of the hapless professor, pulled a pencil out of his pocket, and began waving it like a baton, as if he were an orchestra conductor. "Sing! Sing!" Sing!" chanted the crowd, stomping their feet. The old man stared vacantly out at the packed auditorium.

"Are the people going to hear 'The Black Gang Song'?" challenged the Red Guard.

Finally, the dazed professor croaked out a few lines in a voice that sounded like a record player set on the wrong speed.

I am an ox ghost and a snake spirit.
I am a member of the anti-party black gang.
I stand guilty before the people.
If I am ever dishonest again,
May I be crushed and smashed to pieces!

"Louder!" shrieked a youth in the front row, provoking hoots of derision. Sensing that his struggle session was turning into a circus, Kuai snatched the pencil from the stocky Red Guard, waved him offstage and cried.

"Confess your bourgeois crimes!" he demanded, glowering at the unfortunate professor.

"Confess! Confess! Confess!" roared the audience.

When the old man did not respond, two other Red Guards emerged from the wings, threw one end of a rope over the trusses in the stage loft, and fastened the other to the professor's bound wrists.

"Sing! Sing! Sing!" the crowd kept chanting.

Still the old professor refused, so they yanked him off his feet and into the excruciatingly painful "jet-plane position" (坐飞机),

so known because a victim's arms were swept behind him like the wings of a jet fighter. As the old man twisted in lazy circles in the air, a young man in a jacket festooned with Mao buttons vaulted onstage and thrust an accusing finger in the dangling victim's face.

"Traitor of the people," he screamed, "what have you to say?"

"That those who enslave others can never be free," the old man finally rasped out.

"How dare you?" shrieked the youth, striking him with his fists as if he were a punching bag. "This is just a warning!" he screamed, as the old man's body went limp.

"Lower the prisoner," ordered Kuai Dafu.

"Next time, there will be no such leniency, and the house of Yu will not tolerate being tainted by your bourgeois reactionary line!" cried the youth as the old man landed on the stage floor crumpled in a motionless heap. "Long Live Chairman Mao! Long Live the Cultural Revolution!" screamed the youth, and spat on the man's inert form.

"If no one stops him, that Yu Bin will be his father's death," murmured a voice behind Little Li. "There's no end to what that boy will do to prove he's redder than anyone else."

Little Li turned to see who was speaking; it was a young woman, conversing with a friend. Realizing they'd been overheard, she froze, then turned and hurriedly left the hall. Back onstage, the overwrought youth had turned to the audience. With a theatrical gesture, he grabbed his largest Mao badge and ripped open his tunic with such force that several buttons flew out into the audience. Then, raising the badge above his head as the stage lights shimmered off the halo of golden sunbursts radiating from Mao's head, Yu Bin cried out, "Long live our Great Helmsman! Down with all capitalist roaders!" and stabbed its long pin through the nipple of his left breast. With blood trickling down his pale chest, he triumphantly closed the clasp and swooned to the floor beside his motionless father. Little Li bolted from the auditorium. When Little Wang found him, he was leaning against a tree, sobbing.

"You shouldn't go to such places," chided Granny Sun the next morning. "And your father would agree with me." Seeing that Little Li became more reflective at the mention of his father, she added, "When I think of your father, I always think of the aphorism 'To allow the spittle to dry on one's face without wiping it off'

[唾面自干]." Seeing the perplexed look on Little Li's face, she asked, "Do you know what it means?"

"No."

"It refers to Lou Shide [娄师德], an upright Confucian 'gentleman' [君子] from the Tang Dynasty who, when asked by his elder brother what he'd do if someone spat on him in contempt, declared he wouldn't acknowledge such a base act even by wiping the spittle from his face. You know, child, forbearance is sometimes the most honorable way to rebuke baseness."

"You mean just refuse to react?"

"Yes. Refuse to dignify an insult with any response at all. Exercise forbearance [涵养], like your dear father."

When another month had passed and still Li Tongshu had neither returned nor written, without telling Granny Sun, Little Li went back to the Conservatory.

"Can you tell me where my father, Li Tongshu, has been sent?" he asked one of the few administrative staffers still on duty.

"It's not clear," she replied blankly.

"How can I find out?" he pressed.

"The relevant department will inform you when you need to know."

As more and more urban parents came under investigation and disappeared, a growing number of young people found themselves on their own, making it a time of enormous anxiety and loneliness, but paradoxically, also a time of liberation and freedom. With their parents gone, the Two Virtuous Ones felt closer kinship than ever. Since school was closed, they hung out together almost every day, free to go where they wanted, do what they wished, eat as they pleased, and return home when they chose. It did not take long for them, like many others, to replace their vanished families with new fraternities of young people who were also living by their wits. Many also began to get into trouble, and it wasn't long before Little Wang himself was detained for stealing an onion cake from a vendor next to the train station and sent off for a month of "ideological re-education" with two other neighborhood boys, who'd been caught necking with girls in Ritan Park (日坛公园). Their new "school" was officially known as "the Academy for Mao Zedong Thought" (毛泽东思想学习班), but they proudly referred to it as "the Academy for Crookery and Hoodlumism" (小偷流氓学习班).

"At least I finally got a degree!" boasted Little Wang facetiously when he came home, released early because there was not enough food to feed the "students."

In November 1966, Chairman Mao had given a speech urging young Chinese to initiate "a great link up" (大串联) by traveling the country and sharing their revolutionary experiences. As a result, public transport was made free, and hotels, restaurants, schools, and universities were instructed to welcome these political pilgrims as "Chairman Mao's own guests" (毛主席的客人). In no time, China became a massive traveling youth festival. The Two Virtuous Ones were not quite old enough to "link up" outside of Beijing themselves, but they could interact with the tens of thousands of provincial Red Guards who began flooding into the capital with no idea where to find shelter, food, which revolutionary shrines to visit, and were more than willing to consign themselves into the custody of these two savvy young Beijingers. And the boys thrilled at the chance to escape the odium of their class backgrounds and be able to participate in the excitement. However, even though Little Li found the demonstrations, rallies, and struggle sessions rousing, each time a victim was actually paraded down the street or abused, he could not help seeing the face of his father. Whipsawed between a yearning to be included and revulsion, he was riven by an insoluble contradiction.

One day, as he and Little Wang roamed the Peking University's campus, they came upon a wall poster that stunned them. In a confession, none other than Deng Xiaoping shamefacedly had expressed his "deep remorse" for having "increased the arrogance of the bourgeoisie" and "deflated the morale of the proletariat."

> I have not stood on the side of the masses, have opposed the mass movement and pursued a line which is in absolute opposition to the policies of Comrade Mao Zedong. . . . Worse still, I have rarely reported to and asked advice of the Chairman. . . . In the final analysis, my way of thinking and style of work are completely incompatible with Mao Zedong Thought. . . . I have shown myself not to be a good student of Chairman Mao and am absolutely unsuited to my present position of responsibility. . . .

Though I have gone astray on the road of politics, with the radiance of Mao Zedong Thought lighting my path I should have the fortitude to pick myself up and go on. . . .

In conclusion, Deng unctuously proclaimed:

Long live the Great Proletarian Revolution!
Long live invincible Mao Zedong Thought!
Long live the great teacher!
Long live the Great Helmsman and great leader Chairman
   Mao!

With moderate leaders like Deng deposed, Red Guard factions were now waging open warfare throughout the city. Sometimes they even attacked foreign diplomatic missions. When during the summer of 1967 the Two Virtuous Ones heard that a demonstration was planned at the British Legation, they decided to go and have a look. They arrived in Sanlitun (三里屯) diplomatic area to find thousands of young protesters outside the gates of the mission, with a loudspeaker blaring speeches condemning the arrests of journalists from the New China News Agency in the British crown colony of Hong Kong.

"We resolutely protest the arrest of patriotic Chinese journalists by the British imperialists!" bellowed a Red Guard standing on a jury-rigged dais. "Who here dares say that the Red Guards, under the great leadership of Chairman Mao, cannot handle foreign policy? We must seize power from the weak-kneed document readers in the Foreign Ministry who are too civilized and cowardly to confront the British imperialists. This is a revolution! Our revolution!" The crowd chanted back: "Seize the hour! Seize the day! Down with British imperialism! Down with British colonialism in Hong Kong!"

British diplomats had been watching a Peter Sellers film inside when demonstrators outside began assaulting the metal fence surrounding their mission with crowbars and mattocks. When a section finally fell and they poured into the leafy compound, Little Li saw one youth climb onto the legation roof and cut the power and phone lines while another smashed a large window in the brick building, set a handful of dry hay on fire, and shoved it inside. As the panicked diplomatic staff streamed out—like bees escaping a hive when a keeper approaches with a smoker—their only avenue of egress was through the jeering mob. Covering their heads with their bare arms, they ran the gauntlet as screaming protesters beat them with bamboo canes and shouted, "Kill, kill, kill the English devils [杀杀杀英国鬼子]!" One man, in a sleeveless white shirt, with a security badge around his neck identifying him as Chargé d'Affaires Donald Hopson, became trapped right in front of Little Li, as four Red Guards holding a large portrait of Chairman Mao thrashed him with their canes and chanted: "Bow! Bow to Chairman Mao! Bow to the red, red sun in our hearts!" Hopson steadfastly refused.

"I know the British have been our oppressors," a subdued Little Wang offered as the two boys walked home afterward, "but, still, aren't they people?"

"Sometimes I don't know what side I'm on," answered Little Li.

"Things are getting pretty crazy!" added Little Wang, evincing none of his usual bravado.

Red Guard factions were now regularly attacking against each other, even using rifles, grenades, and mortars. So, it was with relief that the Two Virtuous Ones learned that everyone from their school over the age of thirteen would be mustered into a "youth work brigade" and sent to the countryside to "participate in labor" (参加劳动).

In preparation, Granny Sun stuffed an extra change of clothing and a raincoat into a rice sack with Little Li's quilt and sewed on two straps so he could wear it like a pack. Then she filled his canteen with boiling water and wrapped four steamed buns in a sheet of newspaper, and he marched off for the countryside. No one was more excited to find himself positioned behind the portrait of Chairman Mao and the brace of red banners whipping in the breeze that led their march. Since there was no place along their route able to accommodate the brigade for the night, Monitor Wu, an eighteen-year-old who claimed to be joining the PLA (The People's Liberation Army), kept them marching. By midnight, Little Li had blisters on both feet and was so tired he could hardly keep his eyes open. When it began to rain and the column halted so everyone could don rain gear, he'd gotten only one arm into the sleeve of his plastic raincoat when, in the flickering beams of flashlights, he noticed that the paint on the placard of Chairman Mao leaning against a poplar tree was beginning to run. Feeling suddenly wide awake, he stripped off his raincoat and gallantly fastened it around the poster. Then he defiantly cried out, "Long Live Chairman Mao!" He was thrilled when others in the brigade responded, "For ten thousand years!" Even though Little Li was soon soaked to the bone, never had discomfort felt so satisfying.

For the next two months, they lived on the Beijing-Pyongyang People's Friendship Commune, where, from dawn to dusk, they sickled wheat, tied it into sheaves, and fed them into a pedal-pumped threshing machine. Although laboring under the hot sun was exhausting, Little Li did not mind, for, as long as he met his daily quota, the local peasants couldn't have cared less about his "class background." At last, he was having a chance to prove himself through his own deeds. Nor did he care that their lodgings were nothing more than a crudely built lean-to with no doors, running water, or electricity. What mattered was the camaraderie and the fact that every night they all gathered on the threshing floor to "report to Chairman Mao" (晚汇报), perform skits, sing revolutionary songs, do loyalty dances, and enjoy themselves. Sitting under the stars on a summer evening, by the flickering light of oil lamps, as crickets gave voice around them, offered Little Li an unfamiliar sense of belonging and well-being.

He slept beside Little Wang, and they soon gathered enough sidekicks to become known as the "Wang Gang" (王帮). After curfew, they gossiped about girls, told dirty jokes, traded insults, and held farting contests that were almost always won by a pudgy older boy surnamed Qi (齐), a homonym for the character meaning "gas" (气). It was this lad's amazingly musical ability to emit sustained crepitations in different tones that earned him the nickname "Gasman Qí," or Qiqi (齐气).

"We know why the Gasman can cut such amazing farts," joked Little Wang. "His father is an electrical engineer and when he was little, hooked his butt up to a power plant to generate electricity for the masses." Everyone roared with laughter as the Gasman chimed in with a perfectly timed cadenza. "He should get an award for 'serving the people.'"

By stealing over to the girls' bunkhouse at night, crouching behind the back wall, and listening through the cracks in the lathing to the chatter inside, the Wang Gang liked to imagine themselves as guerrilla fighters. One night, while out on a maneuver, they heard a strange groaning coming from inside the girls' bunkhouse. The next morning, Little Wang made a dramatic report back to the other boys.

"All right, listen up!" he began with all the flair of an intelligence operative making critical report. "Last night, while on a recon patrol to the girls' bunkhouse, the Wang Gang documented two girls together under the same quilt, moaning." When his announcement elicited mostly bewilderment, Little Wang dismissively asked, "Hey! Don't you idiots know girls like to do it together, too?"

He was met with more silence and blank stares. The truth was that even though these boys had matured, no one had ever had anything very helpful to tell them about navigating the confusing shoals of puberty, infatuation, and courtship, much less love, sex, and marriage. There was such a vacuum of knowledge among them that when they began to be besieged by uncontrollable urges, many thought they were going mad. And when girls started having their periods, not a few were so uninformed about biology they feared they were hemorrhaging.

One of Little Li's favorite collective nighttime activities was the telling of lurid, and probably mostly apocryphal, stories of voyeurism, in which the older boys competed to impress the younger, more gullible boys with tales of derring-do. The most self-promotional of these older boys was Hou Da, who, because of the triangular shape of his skull, was known as Hatchet Head Hou (斧头侯). He was the progenitor of an event that became camp legend. After collecting a purse of two yuan, Hatchet Head promised to award the entire sum to the boy who could win a round pound. Many of the younger boys had little idea what he was talking about, but were still eager to contribute to the kitty. However, the game was fixed. Everyone except a very unpopular boy, Lin Yang, was alerted ahead of time that this competition was a setup and they were not to do anything more than make spurious slapping noises in the dark after the flashlights went out and the so-called contest began. This was to be the night when Lin—who was almost universally disliked for his ass-kissing to Monitor Wu—would get his comeuppance.

"All right! Ready for the big event?" announced Hatchet Head once all the boys were sitting along the sleeping ledge. "Tonight one lucky winner will get this valuable cash prize!" He shone his flashlight on the purse he'd collected and then back on each expectant face.

"Can't wait to get going," offered Little Wang helpfully.

"All right, then! On your mark!" Hatchet Head cried out. "When I turn off my flashlight, that's the signal! And remember, whoever shoots first gets the money!" He waved the prize money above his head. The shadowy darkness was punctuated by a few titters. As soon as Hatchet Head extinguished his flashlight, a furious pounding commenced, followed by some overly theatrical moaning and a few bursts of uncontrollable laughter. Then, just after someone gave a deeply synthetic sigh of ecstasy, Lin Yang emitted a climactic yelp and, in a tremulous but triumphant voice, proclaimed, "I'm almost at the finish line!"

"Go for the gold, Comrade Lin!" someone urged, causing an eruption of snickering.

"Victory!" a panting Lin Yang finally proclaimed exuberantly. "Triumph is mine!"

"Looks like we have a winner!" announced Hatchet Head, shining his flashlight right at the hapless champion, who was crumpled over his victorious climax. "We hereby crown you 'the King of Shooting Down Airplanes' [打飞机大王]!"

A wave of nervous tittering swept among the other boys, all of whom were now watching with a horrified fascination as it slowly dawned on the hapless champ that he'd been duped. Holding up his glistening hand in the merciless beam of Hatchet Head's flashlight, the newly crowned king let out an agonized howl. The last anyone saw of King Lin was as he was bolting from the lean-to out into the darkness. It was later rumored he'd walked all the way back to his grandmother's house in Beijing in the dead of night.

Little Li knew no more about the mesmerizing topic of sex than what he was able to glean from touts like Little Wang and Hatchet Head Hou. Despite Mao's own personal debauchery, search as one might through his vast *Collected Works*, there was no wisdom to be had on boy-girl relations. Nor did any volume at the Xinhua Bookstore on Wangfujing Street (王府井) have anything helpful to say on this inscrutable subject.

There was nothing at the Beijing-Pyongyang People's Friendship Commune that inflamed the prurience of these randy boys more than Hatchet Head's most prized possession: a pubic hair he claimed came from his seventeen-year-old sister. He kept it sealed in a dog-eared envelope inside his jacket and exhibited it only on special occasions . . . or for any boy willing to pony up five cents. Little Li had seen it once, when, in a moment of uncharacteristic charity to celebrate King Lin's exodus, Hatchet Head decided to exhibit his treasure free of charge. He was disappointed to find that it consisted of nothing more than a short, curly black hair. However, when Hatchet Head began regaling his gullible assemblage with tales of a girl on his *hutong* who would "shoot the cannon" with any boy who dared ask, every boy became bug-eyed with fascination. Sensing that there was far too much unrestrained carnal energy rampaging through his young charges, Monitor Wu gathered them all together one day after lunch for a lecture on tempering themselves against unrestrained infatuations with members of the opposite sex.

"We are here to advance Chairman Mao's Great Proletarian Revolution by toiling in solidarity with the peasantry to increase our nation's grain yield," he admonished. "To become distracted from this great calling is not just to engage in unhealthy individualism, but to separate ourselves from the broad masses of the people and our hosts!"

The boys were soon treated to another extra-moral lesson in biology. Coming back from the fields one evening, Little Wang spotted what looked like a pair of albino eels napping in a nearby canal. Only after snagging them with a long stick did he discover they were actually two used condoms. He brought them back to camp and displayed them on a rock in front of the boys' barracks with all the pride of a hunter who'd just bagged a rare trophy. Then he laughingly announced he was going to undertake a scientific experiment. Pulling the condoms over the necks of two empty beer bottles, he stole out after dark and set up his "experiment" on top of the wall around the threshing floor, right in front of the girls' barracks.

When everyone returned from the fields the next day for lunch, they all beheld a startling sight. As the noonday sun heated the air inside the bottles and it expanded, the two condoms slowly became tumescent. And just as the girls returned for the midday meal and temperatures hit their zenith, they became completely upright, their little reservoir tips as erect as aroused nipples. Watching them bob cheerfully in the breeze, the excited boys were unable to suppress squeals of laughter. As word spread among the girls, they, too, began tittering and giggling, so that soon the whole brigade was snickering. The "experiment" ended when Monitor Wu stood up, marched angrily to the wall, threw the offending bottles into the tall grass, and then ordered all the boys to line up on the threshing floor.

"No one will leave here until the perpetrator of this vile deed makes a full confession," he proclaimed sternly. At first his threats were met by silence. Then someone in the back row laughed. "Silence!" Monitor Wu ordered. But then there was another snicker, and soon irrepressible gales of giggling were erupting like a string of firecrackers. "Enough of this! We will take other measures!" he threatened. Leaving the boys standing, he disappeared into the commune office. When he re-emerged, he was accompanied by an elderly peasant with a wizened, shamanistic face.

"Comrade Zhao is from the local production brigade and will show us how 'poisonous weeds' [毒草] who refuse to confess their crimes are unmasked here in the countryside."

He beckoned the old man forward as if summoning a scent-sniffing hound. Old Zhao walked over to the first boy in line and let his eyes flutter closed as he held an open palm over the top his head, as if divining the vibrational emanations of his psychic aura. Mumbling incomprehensibly, he moved methodically from one suspect to the next, causing all the other boys to fall apprehensively silent. Did this old-timer possess special folk powers of divination capable of sensing telltale signs of guilt? No one dared move. Then, just as Old Zhao reached Little Wang, the silence was rent by a crepitation from Gasman Qi. It was followed by a strange yelp from the other side that sounded as if someone was trying to suppress an epic sneeze. The outbursts caused the whole brigade to erupt in laughter. Undeterred, the old peasant pointed a crooked finger right at Little Wang.

"Him!" he said, like a wizard. And perhaps he was a wizard. How the old guy knew who had masterminded the prank, nobody ever figured out, but Little Wang was promptly sent home.

Everyone was stunned, and not a little titillated, when, several weeks later, news swept the brigade that two girls investigating noises they thought came from a wounded animal stumbled on none other than Monitor Wu, facedown in a rick of wheat straw, on top of the nurse from the local commune health clinic, "making clouds and rain" (云雨). Thereafter, it was widely believed that the condoms Little Wang had employed in his "science experiment" were from Monitor Wu's politically incorrect trysts with said nurse. In any event, the next day, both Monitor Wu and the nurse disappeared.

When the work brigade was finally ordered back to Beijing, as soon as Little Li reached Willow Courtyard, Granny Sun handed him a letter. It bore a Henan Province postmark and was addressed in a scrawl that looked like that of a very small child. His father's calligraphy, once so refined, was now so twisted and graceless that Little Li could hardly make sense of it.

> *My dear son:*
> *Be assured that things are all right with me. My life here in the Henan countryside is quite simple. Every day I arise at dawn to join in labor with the peasantry, who have been most gracious. Also, the clinic here has cared for my hands.*
> *I hope that you are heeding Granny Sun. No amount of gratitude from our family will ever be able to fully recompense her for what she's been doing. Please give her my heartfelt greetings and thanks.*
> *And write to me at this address when you can.*
> *I want to know what you are doing, how you are. Above all, I want you to know that not a single hour passes when I do not think of you.*
> *Your father*

Little Li read this all-too-brief missive again and again, as if a more careful textual examination might reveal new hidden meanings. But no amount of effort allowed him to pierce its impenetrable matter-of-factness. Little Li was relieved to receive, at last, evidence that his father was still alive and well. But as he replied, the idea of ever being drawn back into his father's gravitational field filled him with apprehension.

5

ONE COLD December morning in 1968, just after the "East Is Red" reveille ended, a stentorian voice reverberated out over Big Sheep Wool Alley: "Young intellectuals must go to the countryside to be re-educated by the poor and lower-middle peasants. We must persuade children of cadres and all those who have completed middle school, high school, or college to go to the countryside. We must mobilize the country to bring this movement to fruition, and all comrades in the countryside should welcome these young intellectuals."

Mao Zedong had launched his latest mass movement. The millions of self-styled Red Guards who'd been spreading havoc in China's cities were now to be dispatched as "educated youths" (知识青年) to China's "countryside, border regions and wherever the country needs you most" (到农村去, 到边疆去,到祖国最需要的地方去). With fond memories of his summer at the Beijing-Pyongyang People's Friendship Commune, Little Li was initially excited by Mao's call.

Several weeks later, a notice arrived from his school summoning his class to a meeting. There he was handed a summons from the "Office for Sending Educated Youths to the Countryside" headlined: "Answering Chairman Mao's Call to Go Down to the Countryside and Up into the Mountains [上山下乡] to Participate in National Reconstruction in One of Our Country's Vast Border Regions." Attached was a document affixed with a vermilion seal.

December 2, 1968
Name: Li Wende
Age: 16
Family Class Background: Intellectual

Address: 14 Big Sheep Wool Alley, East City, Beijing
Departure Date: January 16, 1969, 5:00 a.m., Beijing
    Railroad Station
Destination: Xining, Qinghai Province
Local Unit: To be determined by local authorities

In his call describing participation in his new mass move-ment, Mao had used the word "persuade" (说服). But in reality his order left no choice. When "the Chairman" spoke, obedience was expected. As his "chosen successor" (接班人), Marshal Lin Biao, had put it: "If we understand Chairman Mao's words, we put them into practice. But even if we don't understand them, we must put them into practice anyway."

But why, when most other students from his school were being "assigned" (分配) to Inner Mongolia and Manchuria, was he being sent to Qinghai in the far west, a remote, inhospitable, and unpopulated wilderness where ethnic Han populations gave way to Tibetan, Muslim, Mongolian? While his teachers droned on in geography class, Little Li had often stared up at the map of China on their classroom wall and wondered what was out there in the empty, trackless void of Qinghai, Tibet, and Xinjiang. The characters 青 and 海 that composed the province's name meant "green" and "sea," and on his classroom map the area was left largely empty and marked simply as "grasslands" and "desert." During imperial times, officials who fell out of favor were often exiled there. In more recent times, Chairman Mao had himself passed through Qinghai on his marathon Long March from 1934 to 1935, as his Red Army fled encirclement by Chiang Kai-shek's Nationalist forces. But since 1949, Qinghai had acquired a more sinister renown: the site of many of the camps for "reform through education" (劳教) and "reform through labor" (劳改), which were the backbone of China's immense archipelago of penal colonies.

As Little Li looked out Granny Sun's window at the willow tree he and his father had nursed back to life, the remains of the garden his father had once so lovingly cultivated, and their room, it was hard to comprehend that he was about to be spun out of these familiar surroundings into the unknown. Would those things now disappear just as his mother and father had, leaving him marooned with nothing more than fading memories? The recognition that, besides his father, Granny Sun, and Little Wang, there was no one on earth who cared where he ended up, and that in a few days even they would have no idea where he was, made him feel suddenly invisible. Realizing he hadn't had a chance to tell Little Wang he was leaving, he ran to his friend's house and banged on the door. But there was no answer, and he returned to Granny Sun's in a state of near panic, to find her wrapping his flute case in newspaper and laying out those few articles of clothing that constituted his wardrobe so she could sew them up with his quilt inside the same rice sack he'd taken to the Beijing-Pyongyang People's Friendship Commune. But his bundle of possessions seemed hardly sufficient for such a long trip with so many uncertainties. Noticing how sober he'd become, she tried to cheer him by insisting that she and Willow Courtyard would always be awaiting his return.

The next morning, Little Li rallied outside the Conservatory with other students being "sent down," and they marched together to Tiananmen Square for a ceremonial farewell. There, in front of the white marble Bridge Over Golden Waters, they stood under a banner inscribed with a quotation from Mao: "The Countryside Is Another Kind of University [农村也是大学]" like the tens of thousands of other youths before them who were also steeling themselves before departure with this ritual. Trying to maintain a stalwart front as his troupe looked up at Mao's famous portrait, Little Li thrust his fist into the air and incanted the Oath of Educated Youth:

> *The reddest of red suns in our hearts and the greatest of*
>   *leaders,*
>
> *O Chairman Mao! We, your most loyal Red Guards,*
> *swear this oath:*
> *Your great thoughts are the brightest of beacons that*
> *guide the steps of the peoples of the world toward*
> *revolution! We shall be eternally loyal, eternally and*
> *without limits boundlessly faithful to your thought, and*
> *boundlessly loyal to your revolutionary line. The road*
> *ahead is tortuous, but your radiant thought will light the*
> *way. . . . We shall follow your revolutionary path until the*
> *end and never look back!*

When the ceremony ended, six older boys unexpectedly broke ranks and, with tears in their eyes, knelt to offer "blood letters" (血书), testimonials written in blood drawn from their own fingers, swearing that they would go "wherever Chairman Mao and the Motherland most needs me."

After a sleepless night, Little Li arose before dawn, dressed, slung his possessions over his shoulder, and, with Granny Sun hobbling along beside him, and a metallic taste of fear in his parched mouth, made his way to the train station.

"You must drink and eat," Granny Sun kept insisting as they walked, even stopping to buy him two fried oil sticks (油条) and a bottle of soy milk.

The train terminal was draped with a giant banner: "Better a Socialist Train That's Late Than a Capitalist Train That Is On Time!" Although it was only 5:00 a.m., the esplanade in front was already crowded with young people and their families, carrying bundles of bedding and winter clothing hung with shoes, pots, and canteens; it looked as if it had been occupied by a horde of wartime refugees rather than a corps of "educated youths" on their way to "make revolution." As the bell tower struck the hour by chiming out an electronic rendition of "The East Is Red," Little Li experienced none of the excitement he'd imagined. Instead, he felt only dread. What is more, standing among thousands of other milling "educated youths" who were with their parents, he felt awkward beside this elderly woman.

"Maybe I better go now!" he suddenly blurted out.

"Will you be careful?" asked Granny Sun anxiously.

"Yes," he stammered numbly. She stared at him with perplexed eyes as strands of her gray hair blew back and forth across her furrowed brow in the chill breeze. Was she expecting him to shake her hand, put an arm around her shoulders, perhaps even hug her goodbye? He had no idea how to enact a ritual of parting with this woman who was not even from his own family, but to whom he owed so much.

"You won't speak out too much, will you?" she pleaded.

"No, no!"

"And . . . you'll write your father?"

"Yes! Yes!" he said with exasperation.

The mention of his father was like a bee sting. For an instant, he visualized him at his piano, but his father seemed more like a character from a book he'd once read than a real parent. He felt dizzy, unable to cope with what was happening. He wanted this agony to end, yet at the same time he wanted it to go on forever. Sensing how uncomfortable he was, Granny Sun took one of his hands and pressed it to her cheek. Then, as tears pearled in the corners of her eyes, she squeezed some money into his palm, lowered her head, turned, and hobbled off. If there had not been so many people watching, he would have run after her, perhaps even told her how much he loved her. Instead, he let the moment slip away. But then everywhere mothers and fathers were standing awkwardly beside their children, no one knowing what the proper deportment was for such a moment. Nearby stood two parents and a boy with a bundle of effects twice as large as his own.

"Make sure you wear your padded jacket," the father was saying. "It'll be very cold in Mongolia."

"Yes, yes!" insisted the embarrassed boy.

"And don't forget to write," insisted the boy's mother, chin quivering. She reached out to straighten the collar of his tunic, as if this small sartorial rectification might help her son through the hardships ahead. The boy glanced over at Little Li and, seeing he was being watched, became even more flustered.

"No! I mean . . . yes! Of course," he rejoined impatiently. "Ma, you just don't need to—"

"All right! All right! Just don't say it like that!" she interrupted in frustration.

Dazed as Little Li was, he could not tear his eyes from this family clumsily trying to express the deep but suppressed sentiments welling up inside each of them. He hoped that this one family would somehow manage to overcome their paralysis: for if just one of them could succeed in expressing what they were feeling, he felt he, too, might somehow be redeemed. So when the father unexpectedly reached out to put a consoling hand on his son's shoulder, Little Li's heart jumped. But just then a distant train whistle hooted and the loudspeakers came alive: "Departing for Hohehot, Inner Mongolia Autonomous Region, Train Number Fifty-five on Track Eight." As if he'd touched an exposed wire, the father jerked his hand back. The boy mumbled something and, trying to keep his composure, shouldered his things, nodded a goodbye, and marched toward the terminal. Only when he reached the steps did he stop and for a moment look helplessly back at his weeping mother and father.

How had the expression of sentiment become so forbidden that these most irresistible of human emotions became so stifled? Maybe this was why his own father had so loved *The Dream of the Red Chamber,* where the novel's hero, Bao Yu, never gets around to expressing his deep love for Dai Yu before he's ordered by the family matriarch into an arranged marriage with someone else. Only then does he cry out to his beloved: "I always thought you could read my heart!" But, it was too late.

Little Li liked to imagine that, as an American, his mother would have acted differently. But he was sure that if his father were sending him off, he would conduct himself just like these other parents. He seemed to find emotional release only at his piano, in a solitary rapture that came not from being with others, but from being alone with Bach and his God, who for him were one and the same. Once there had been a Confucian prescription for every category of human behavior and interaction: how a son should relate to his father, a wife to her husband, a subject to his ruler, and even an emperor to "heaven" (天). There were ritual forms and ceremonies for every occasion, showing love, hatred, gratitude, respect, commitment, disagreement, and displeasure, which gave people guidelines for how to deport themselves. But the myriad revolutions of the twentieth century had so mercilessly attacked these traditions as the source of China's national weakness that human relations had been set adrift in a compass-less void. How should a son show respect to a father who'd been labeled a class enemy? What was the proper way of venerating a grandparent who'd disappeared into the gulag? How should one mourn a mother who was politically contaminated by her place of birth? And if one's father had been executed as a landlord or imprisoned as a counterrevolutionary, should one still express filial devotion? With no one knowing what kind of behavior was appropriate, sentiment was left to bottle up unexpressed until people just exploded, or a frightened boy about to be flung out into the unknown was left standing beside his parents, who were unable to take him in their arms.

By the time the tomato-red sun began silhouetting the two pagoda-like towers of the train station against the smoky winter sky, Little Li still did not know when or how he was departing. Not until 9:00 a.m. did four green Shanghai sedans with curtained rear windows drive up to the front of the terminal. Four officials, each accompanied by a factotum carrying a sheaf of documents, disembarked, and were immediately mobbed. Competing with hooting train whistles, the clamor of voices, and the din of martial music, the assistants began giving commands. It took hours for them to bring any semblance of order to the unruly free-for-all of anxious supplicants that surged around them. Little Li did not reach the front of a line until afternoon.

"Where can I find out what train I'm on?" he asked.

"Name and school?" snapped one of the harried assistants without looking up.

"Li Wende, Conservatory Middle School," he replied, trying to sound grown-up. The assistant combed through a dog-eared list on his clipboard.

"Oh!" he exclaimed, as if he hadn't really expected to find Little Li's name. "Take the ten p.m. to Zhengzhou, and change for Xian and Xining!"

"And where am I being assigned?"

"Local authorities will instruct you upon arrival," growled the assistant, reaching into a black vinyl bag and handing Little Li a ticket, before turning to the next supplicant. On the back of the ticket, underneath a Mao quotation, were some instructions:

> *Educated youths who have come to board trains must*
> *hold high the great banner of Mao Zedong Thought, must*
> *always put proletarian politics in command, and must*
> *stop holding hands with their parents five minutes before*
> *departure. Moreover, as your train pulls out of the station,*
> *you must wave your booklets of Mao quotations and shout*
> *revolutionary slogans.*

Gathering up his things, Little Li walked into the crowded terminal, found a place to sit against a wall, and, after drinking his soy milk, fell asleep. He awakened only fifteen minutes before his train was due to leave, and because there were no more empty seats, he was forced to sit in the aisle of the last car. Before they'd even left the terminal, his car had filled with a choking cloud of smoke as boys no older than he lit up to act cool (玩儿帅). For several hours, he resisted drinking from his canteen, because he feared that if he went to the lavatory he'd lose his place on the aisle floor. Normally, he hardly thought about his body, but now it was making all sorts of demands. It was suffocated, exhausted, hungry, and thirsty, and needed to relieve itself, all at once. He was suddenly aware that, just as it produced saliva, mucus, earwax, blood, dandruff, hair, piss, gas, and shit, it also demanded food, water, medicine, air, and rest. By the time they neared Shijiazhuang, he so urgently needed to piss that he nudged the boy sleeping beside him and asked if he'd hold his space while he was gone. Then he waded down the trash-strewn aisle, over a battlefield of sprawled bodies, to the lavatory, where he was stunned to find that it, too, was filled with passengers. One of them desultorily gestured him toward the platform at the very end of the car. As he opened the door and stepped out into the cold, deafening darkness, he was on the verge of losing control. To his great relief and disgust, he saw that the corrugated steel plates of the platform already boasted a miniature mountain range of frozen human waste. This was an inglorious way to start his revolutionary odyssey.

On his next leg, from Xian, he got a seat only by sprinting down the platform when the gate opened, his pack bouncing on his back like the hump of a camel. Most of the passengers in his car were "educated youths" from Shanghai, being sent to China's westernmost province, Xinjiang, and they were in high spirits, joking, laughing, singing, eating dried watermelon seeds and spitting shells unceremoniously onto the floor. Little Li envied the way the boys and girls cavalierly flirted, and was particularly captivated by a tall girl with luscious pink lips and silky hair who sat beside a handsome young man who had a shock of hair flopping down over his forehead and a cigarette drooping rakishly from one corner of his mouth. The way she gazed up at him hinted at mysteries of the male-female interaction that were still as unfathomable to him as quantum physics. The young man's charm and bravado seemed to have neutralized her resistance like the sting of a spider that stuns its prey as a prelude to being slowly wrapped in gossamer thread and devoured. This unabashedly flirtatious couple seemed to belong to a rare species that, even in the vortex of revolution, managed to let desire spring forth. Of all the counterrevolutionary forces, surely sexual attraction was the most subversive. So how was it that he, Little Li, could be so powerfully attracted to and so terrified by girls at the same time? In the company of girls for whom he felt no physical attraction, he was completely relaxed, whereas around an object of desire he became immobilized. There was something about the wanting that threw him so off course he could hardly imagine actually touching a flesh-and-blood girl that he desired.

As he had walked around Beijing, he'd sometimes played a game in which he pretended that by the end of a given block he'd have to choose one of the young women he'd just passed as a partner. But since he had only the vaguest sense of how a disrobed woman actually looked, much less how lovers communicated in the alien tongue of physical intimacy, it was impossible for him to imagine completely what would happen next. He'd seen dancers in leotards performing Jiang Qing's eight "model works" (八个样板戏), and watched female gymnasts compete in body-hugging tights, but the little he knew about the opposite sex came secondhand from the likes of Little Wang and Hatchet Head Hou. He was like a person blind from birth trying to imagine the shape of something from other people's descriptions.

It was only when the young man sitting across the aisle and his girlfriend nodded off that he dared really study her. With her head bobbing to the swaying of the train car, he would have liked to reach over and stroke her silky hair, caress the jadelike smoothness of her cheeks, and cup her breasts in his hands. But even though she was only a few meters away, she was as inaccessible as an actress on a movie screen. To distract himself, he picked up a dog-eared copy of the *People's Daily* that had been discarded in the aisle. It featured a front-page story about a "model youth," Jin Xunhua, whose energies were focused not on fevered imaginings of female breasts, but on heroic efforts to "serve the people." In a letter home from the countryside to his parents, he wrote:

> *My hands bleed, while those of poor and middle-lower peasants do not. Why? It proves that my hands and thoughts have long since been distanced from the peasants and workers, distanced from manual labor, contaminated*

by revisionist poison, and that I need to spend a long time toughening them up among the workers and peasants.

Compared with such lofty, unselfish sentiments, Little Li's yearnings seemed petty and base. If the revolutionary spirit was as powerful as sex for others, what was wrong with him? Maybe he did deserve to be in the "stinking ninth category" after all.

When, late the next night, the train finally pulled into Xining, Qinghai Province's far-flung capital, there were hardly any passengers left on board. In spite of feeling drugged by smoke and fatigue, as soon as Little Li stepped out onto the platform into the bracingly cold, clear air he was jolted awake.

"Where are you from?" he asked two boys who were also standing by their packs on the platform.

"Shanghai," one replied, appearing every bit as lost.

"Are you 'educated youths'?"

"Yes."

"Do you know where you're assigned?"

"No."

Little Li shook his head and forced a smile. Not knowing where to go or what else to do, the three exhausted boys piled their packs around them to help break the chill wind, sat down back to back to keep warm, and fell asleep on the station platform.

6

THE EDGE OF THE WORLD

IT WAS still dark when three Liberation trucks pulled up alongside the train platform and six PLA soldiers disembarked.

"You the 'educated youths'?" one of the soldiers challenged, looking with no small distaste at the encampment of half-awake boys.

"So it seems," replied Little Li, struggling to remember where he was.

"Load your things onto the second truck," the soldier ordered without further ceremony.

"Where are we going?" asked one of the other boys.

"Wherever the truck in front of us goes," snidely replied another of the soldiers.

As the convoy set off, the sun was just rising over the drab city. Even along Yangtze River Avenue, one of the capital's main streets, there was no activity or color except for one old man harnessed like a donkey to a cart heaped with cabbage heads that glowed jade green in the gray morning light. Leaving Xining through a gate in what remained of its ancient city wall, their convoy set out across Qinghai's boundless desert grasslands, leaving a wake of dust clouds billowing up behind it. It was freezing cold, and despite his cocoonlike greatcoat and fur-lined hat with earflaps, Little Li was soon so chilled he could hardly move; he kept hoping they'd stop so he could warm himself and get something to eat and drink. Instead, like sailing ships set on one tack for a long ocean voyage, the convoy kept forging down the perfectly straight gravel road toward the horizon. Finally, he fell asleep.

It was not until they forded a river that he woke. Everything in the truck was coated with a thick film of dust, and he had a sore throat, a raging thirst, and a pounding headache made worse by the pitching and heaving of the truck as they crossed the rocky riverbed. As the convoy growled up the far bank and picked up speed again, Little Li's attention was caught by something silhouetted against the distant horizon. From far away it looked like a fortress, but as they drew closer he saw guard towers and brick walls trimmed with swirls of concertina wire. At a checkpoint, guards waved them through as soon as they saw that their drivers were PLA soldiers. A battered signpost read: "NEW PHILOSOPHY FARM REFORM THROUGH LABOR CAMP [新哲学劳改农场], GONGHE COUNTY [共和县], QINGHAI PROVINCE [青海省]." Every province in China was known for certain "specialties" (特点): Guangdong for its food, merchants, and proximity to Hong Kong; Shanxi for its vinegar, ancient banks, and coal mines; Jiangsu for its silk and beautiful women; Shandong for Confucius and peonies; and Qinghai for its prison camps.

Through the clouds of dust, Little Li saw an unexpected blur of blue. Only when their convoy had finally stopped and the dust had settled was he able to discern that it was a column of men with shaven heads wearing tattered blue uniforms, carrying picks and shovels. When he jumped down from the truck bed, he was so cold, stiff, and sore he could hardly move. He was just wondering what to do next when a man in blue appeared by his side with a bucket of water, a ladle, and a basket of corn cakes (窝头).

"You must be very thirsty and hungry, little brother [小伙子]," he said, offering a sad but beatific smile. "People passing through are usually so parched. Drink as much as you like."

The kindness in this man's eyes, the sweet, clear coldness of the water, and the promise of something to eat boosted Little Li's spirits. Only after he'd slaked his thirst and devoured a corn cake did he look up. Before him stood a small man of his father's generation with a scar slashed across one side of his face, which glowed with a strange goodness. As Little Li returned the ladle to his bucket, the man smiled in a way that seemed to say, "I understand everything in your heart. There is no need to speak." Giving Little Li's shoulder a reassuring squeeze, all he said was, "Take care of yourself, little brother."

"Thank you," replied Little Li. He'd hardly spoken since his departure from Beijing, and his voice surprised him, as if he hadn't really expected it to keep up with him as he made his way across

China. After they'd refueled and departed again, just as the vibrations of a bell continue to reverberate long after it is tolled, thise old man's face lingered in Little Li's mind's eye.

It was long after dark when their convoy pulled into a compound, and a gatekeeper with a flashlight unceremoniously herded the three boys into a warehouse.

"You can sleep here," he said without inflection. Little Li spread out his bedding on the filthy floor and fell into an exhausted slumber.

He was awakened the next morning by a beam of sunlight lancing through a crack in the boarded window. He was in a storage shed filled with old school desks and chairs. His tongue felt as dry as a piece of felt, and he was famished. Since the other boys were still sleeping, he got up quietly and went outside, where the white light radiating down from the gray sky was so blinding he had to shield his eyes. As they adjusted, he saw he was inside a school compound.

"Excuse me, Comrade?" he tremulously asked a man reading a tattered newspaper at the gatehouse. "Where are we?"

"What kind of a question is that?" he responded, taking off his glasses to see what manner of imbecile was addressing him.

"I mean, what's the name of this town?"

"What's your unit?" he challenged.

"Well, we just arrived and I'm . . ."

"Oh, you're one of those so-called 'educated youths' they hauled in here last night. Well, you're at the Number Two Elementary School in Gonghe [共和], but we're closed for reorganization."

"And, where is Gonghe?" Little Li continued hesitantly.

"Where is Gonghe?" asked the gatekeeper, as if he were being asked by an alien what planet they were on. "You've never heard of Gonghe?"

"I . . . Well . . ." stammered Little Li.

"Gonghe is the county seat of the Hainan Tibetan Autonomous Prefecture in Qinghai, China's largest province. Did you learn nothing in school?"

"We came in last night after dark, and . . ."

"Where do you come from?" said the gatekeeper, glowering.

"Beijing."

"Oh, Beijing, is it?" he repeated, as if that explained everything. "Well, nothing you've learned there is going to help you out here."

"Is there any place I can get something to eat?"

"Go out through the gate and turn left on Victory Boulevard," he replied, then turned back to his paper.

The grungy Red Star Restaurant was presided over by an unsmiling woman with a red-cheeked two-year-old wearing a pair of crotchless pants from which his pecker protruded like the rubber air valve on an inner tube. Little Li sat down at a rickety wooden table facing the dusty main street. As he gulped down a large bowl of rice porridge, the boy, who had rivulets of snot oozing from his nostrils and congealing like ice on his upper lip, stared at him with unblinking wonder.

"Where do you come from?" Little Li finally asked the woman, who was also staring.

"Me?" She pointed at her nose, surprised at being questioned.

"Are you Tibetan?"

"Half Tibetan and half Han," she announced in an almost unintelligible accent. "My mother was a herder [牧民] and my father was Chinese, but I never met him. I grew up with them."

"Them?"

"The Goloks."

"The Goloks?" he asked.

"You don't know the Goloks?" she asked in surprise. "We're the Tibetan nomads who've always lived around here." She shrugged. "Some people think *golok* means 'to lose your head,' because sometimes we chop the heads off our enemies!" She gave a pleased shriek of laughter. "Or maybe it means 'rebel.' Who knows? But you can recognize our menfolk, because they have long hair, wear sheepskin robes, and have daggers on their belts. We're very fierce."

"Fierce?"

"We have a reputation for liking to kill people!" She let out another burst of self-satisfied laughter. "You must be from far away."

"Yes. From the capital."

"You mean, Xining?"

"No, Beijing."

"Aiyaaa! Besides prisoners, we don't see many outsiders here!"

He paid with the money Granny Sun had given him and set off down the street. Gonghe was a squalid, run-down backwater whose most distinguishing features were the piles of cinders, rubble, and refuse unceremoniously heaped along its sidewalks. Victory Boulevard's only adornments were its wrought-iron streetlights with glass globes shaped like flames (most of which had been broken) and a few leafless saplings protruding from the sidewalk like dirty toothpicks. The only prominent edifice was the Communist Party headquarters, a four-story building of recent vintage that rose above the other low-lying, ramshackle structures with commanding pretension. But even this signature monument lost the little grandeur conferred by distance as one approached. The national crest—five gold stars and the outline of the Gate of Heavenly Peace on a field of crimson—over its entryway was fading and tipping to one side. And its front plate-glass window was marred by a huge crack that someone had sought to mend with black electrical tape. The only daubs of color in this bleak tableau were two banners—*"To Rebel Is Justified"* and *"Down with American Imperialism and Its Running Dogs"*—that drooped from the surrounding brick wall. The Cultural Revolution had evidently reached Gonghe, although it was difficult to imagine the woman running the Red Star Restaurant becoming incensed over American imperialism.

The most colorful part of this forlorn outpost was definitely the Goloks. Their men's long hair, broad-brimmed felt hats, embroidered yak-skin boots, and robelike sheepskin outer garments fastened at the waist with sashes hung with daggers lent them a dashing, even menacing, air. The women's even more colorful dress featured brightly embroidered aprons hung with silver amulets; their hair was plaited in long braids adorned with coral-and-turquoise-encrusted silver jewelry. Though such getups would have gotten any Han Chinese branded as a "bourgeois element," Tibetans were permitted to continue wearing their traditional costumes even now, a prerogative afforded to all China's fifty-five official minority groups. It had never really occurred to Little Li that humans might wear stylish, even flamboyant, garments and accessories just for the pure pleasure of it. Even before the Cultural Revolution, such displays had been frowned on as manifestations of excessive individualism. As taboos against such self-expression gained momentum under Mao, fashion became buried ever deeper under an avalanche of baggy Mao suits. But reveling in their dashing outfits, these Goloks looked as if they'd been specially costumed for a lavish theatrical production. Making it obvious why Chinese films, ballets, and operas so often included roles for ethnic minorities. It was not simply that the party's culture overlords wanted to propagandize for the PRC as a multiethnic state, they also needed to inject some color, flash, and drama into their otherwise dreary cultural fare.

Farther down Victory Boulevard, Little Li came upon a crowd of Golok idlers gathered around a sheet of plywood hanging from a tree branch that had a dolphin-shaped MiG fighter jet painted on it with a hole cut out just above the shoulders of a cartoon pilot whose body protruded from the plane's fuselage. For fifty cents, a customer could poke his head through the hole and have a snapshot taken as if he were piloting the plane. One after another, Goloks were poking their grinning faces through the hole to mug for friends, but as far as Little Li could discern, none ever paid to have a photo taken, leaving the Han Chinese proprietor scowling. It was easy to be impressed by the handsome, weathered faces and the playful manner of these tribal people, who broke into toothy smiles at the slightest excuse. When Little Li made a funny face at a small boy, his Tibetan mother began giggling so mirthfully that Little Li himself smiled for the first time in days. But at the same time, he felt plagued by a familiar frustration: he was again the eternal observer. As others acted, he was always an accessory watching from the sidelines—the opposite of Little Wang, who not only knew what was going on, but made things happen, so that when they were together he felt attached to an alternate propulsion mechanism. But why was he dwelling on such absurd things now? Here he was exhausted, hungry, alone, and exiled in one of the most godforsaken parts of the planet, and he was gawking at a pack of nomads!

Little Li was on the verge of heading back to the schoolyard when two white-uniformed policemen swept down Victory Boulevard on motorcycles, causing a frightened street cleaner to scamper to the curb, a horseman to clop hurriedly down a side street, and pedestrians to scatter. However, people soon began regathering in silent groups, as if anticipating that something special was about to happen. And it was not long before a phalanx of primary-school children, each carrying a small wooden stool, came parading down the broad boulevard. They were followed by a motorcycle with a sidecar and flashing lights leading an open jeep filled with a group of stern young men wearing red armbands. Next came a shiny new truck bearing a massive portrait of Chairman Mao. Then a second, older truck appeared with two expressionless youths in regimental greatcoats and fur-lined hats standing like charioteers behind the cab, flanking two prisoners with shaven heads and hands bound behind their backs. The first had a face as pale as the sunless winter sky and a white placard around his neck reading "GUO LIANGSHU: HISTORICAL COUNTERREVOLUTIONARY GUOMINDANG SPY." The second wore a blood-streaked shirt and a placard reading "WANG SONGTAO: COUNTERREVOLUTIONARY" slashed through with a crimson "X." The very last truck carried a young Tibetan with a shaven pate, his skin bleached gray, lips as pale as dust, and eyes so filled with terror they looked as if they might explode from his head; he wore a placard reading "SPREADER OF COUNTERREVOLUTIONARY TIBETAN INDEPENDENCE PROPAGANDA."

As soon as this procession had passed, onlookers streamed back onto the boulevard to follow it, as if they were holiday promenaders. Tagging along, Little Li soon found himself on a dusty sports field adjacent to the very school where he'd slept. Here the parading children were already seated on their stools in front of a makeshift stage draped with a banner reading "LENIENCY TO THOSE WHO CONFESS: SEVERITY TO THOSE WHO RESIST (坦白从宽 抗拒从严)." The prisoners waited in their trucks behind a soccer goal as martial music blared. When some speeches began, the sound system was so poor that Little Li could make out only snatches of what was being said: "We must resolutely crush all . . ." "Those who have taken the capitalist road cannot . . ." "Tibetan independence will never succeed in . . ." A moment of silence was followed by the amplified sound of someone voiding his rheum. Then a voice that mixed militancy, righteousness, and hysteria read out the charges against each prisoner. Then the trucks started their engines again and as they snaked across the sports field, the crowd followed. At what looked like a dry riverbed, the prisoners were pushed off the trucks and the crowd became so silent that Little Li could hear the breeze rattling the dry poplar leaves. A young guard grabbed the blindfolded Tibetan and twisted his arm until he fell to his knees.

"The world is so dark!" he cried out.

"Shut up!" yelled the guard, cramming a rag into his mouth. The motionless onlookers hardly seemed to breathe.

"Mama, let's go!" a child cried.

An order was barked, a pistol raised, and a popping noise sounded. The prisoner's head kicked back, and his body slumped forward. A murmur rippled through the crowd. Lowering his pistol, the executioner disgustedly flicked away something that had splattered onto his cuff. The next prisoner was pushed forward. People were walking backward now. Then, after another popping sound, they began running, as if something were chasing them. Suddenly Little Li, too, was clamoring up the rocky bank. He didn't stop running until he reached the storage shed where they'd spent the night. Finding no sign of the other two "educated youths," he threw himself onto his quilt and fell into a tormented sleep. He was in the middle of a nightmare in which he was being commanded by the conductor of his school orchestra to choose several of his fellow musicians for execution when he smelled smoke and awakened. A short man with hooded eyelids and a cigarette drooping from his mouth was standing over him.

"You are Li Wende?" he said, as both a statement and a question.

"Yes."

"You were absent when your group departed," he replied curtly.

"Can I rejoin them?" Little Li asked, wanting nothing more than to get out of Gonghe.

"You must wait to be reassigned."

"Where?"

"Unclear. Our director must arrange it. Come with me."

As he followed the man out, Little Li tried to calm himself: since he'd never known where he was being sent, reassignment hardly meant a worse place.

Inside a dark reception room, under a set of faded portraits of Mao, Marx, Engels, Lenin, and Stalin, sat a portly man with several long hairs growing from a mole on his chin.

"I am Director Shen of the Number Two Elementary School, charged with handling 'educated youths' in the region." He consulted a file on his desk. "So—you're from Beijing and play the flute."

"Yes," replied Little Li.

"Well, I'm not sure there will be much call for the flute out here," he said with a sneer. "Now, it says here that you were originally assigned to the Gonghe County Song and Dance Troupe."

"Really?" interjected Little Li, brightening at the idea.

"But it is now inconvenient to keep to that assignment."

"Why?"

"Because the unit has been disbanded." He laughed mockingly.

"So where will I be sent?"

"You would have gone back to Xining with the others, but since that's no longer an option, we'll have to find an alternative." He consulted what appeared to be a list while lovingly stroking the hairs growing out of his mole. "Well, I'm afraid we'll be obliged to assign you to Yak Springs," he finally said.

"Where's that?"

"Yak Springs is" . . . —Comrade Shen stopped to remove the top from a cup on his desk, and made a loud slurping noise as he sucked up a mouthful of tea—"a remote outpost that will give you the opportunity to steel yourself with a new spirit of hard struggle and self-reliance. As our party teaches, 'We must fear no adversity in our willingness to promote revolution.'" Director Shen spat his mouthful of tea leaves out onto the dusty floor. "As Chairman Mao teaches, 'Work is struggle.' At Yak Springs you'll have plenty of opportunity for both."

"Is there a cultural troupe in Yak Springs?" Little Li asked hopefully.

"A cultural troupe?" Director Shen gave a loud guffaw. "Besides the odd nomad, there are hardly any people out there on the grasslands around Yak Springs. But, as Comrade Lei Feng tells us, we must all be willing to become never-rusting screws in the machine of revolution and bravely go wherever the party has a need. Isn't that true?" Little Li nodded unenthusiastically.

When Little Li awakened before dawn the next morning, two trucks loaded with fifty-gallon drums of gasoline were waiting at the front gate. A driver wearing so many layers of clothing under his greatcoat that he looked as if he'd been pneumatically inflated gestured for Little Li to climb into the back of the second vehicle.

"Where's Yak Springs?" he asked.

"On the old northwestern route to Lhasa," the driver answered. "And unless you wanna get your pecker frozen off hanging it off the back of the truck, you'd better take a good long piss now."

After returning from the latrine, Little Li climbed into the bed of the second truck. They soon found themselves out in grasslands where the only signs of human habitation were occasional black yak-hair tents that from a distance looked like giant insects stretching their wings. These were the dwellings of the Golok nomads who eked out an existence from their herds of yak and sheep in this unforgiving land. But as bleak as it was, after the chaotic confinement of Beijing and its predatory politics, Little Li found something unexpectedly soothing about such boundless openness and solitude.

With the lead truck whipping up choking clouds of dust, despite the infinitude of crystal-clear air, it was impossible for Little Li to inhale deeply. He tried hunkering down in one corner of his truck bed, fastening the flaps of his fur-lined hat under his chin, and pulling his head inside his greatcoat as if he were a tortoise. But his nostrils were soon caked with dust, his body stiff from the cold, and his head aching from the relentless jolting. Then he discovered that if he squeezed his eyes closed tightly, he could coax forth streaks of cheerful orange and red from somewhere deep inside his skull that made him feel a little less despairing.

At dusk, the road began rising into a low range of mountains, and as the trucks growled up the serpentine grade toward a pass, the plumes of dust subsided and Little Li stood up to look around. As they crested the ridge, the vista that opened up before them was like a hallucination: the setting sun was bathing distant snow-covered peaks in myriad hues of gold and turning the clouds a salmon pink. Then, as darkness fell and a full moon rose, it crowned these same towering summits with halos of silver that silhouetted them against the black sky, reminding him of the steeples of the great cathedrals of Europe he'd loved in his mother's book. And with moonlight illuminating the roadway, the drivers turned off their headlights so that the stars overhead twinkled with such a dazzling brightness that the firmament seemed ready to rain down diamonds. With engines complaining in low gear, brakes squealing, and the crystalline air rife with the acrid smell of burning metal, the trucks began their descent to the valley floor below in the moonlight, Little Li was able to discern the outline of a square compound set to one side of the road like a floating raft tied to a long dock.

The trucks finally slowed as they reached a battered wooden placard fixed to an unprepossessing Tibetan-style sod wall:

YAK SPRINGS WAY STATION
NO. 6 QINGHAI-SICHUAN HIGHWAY MAINTENANCE BUREAU
GOLOK TIBETAN AUTONOMOUS PREFECTURE
QINGHAI PROVINCE

After they turned in through a breach in the wall and the drivers turned off their truck engines, the only sound was the soft soughing of the wind blowing unobstructed across the broad valley. Looking around, he saw that the compound consisted of a collection of shabby structures with adobe walls and tile roofs sprouting grass. The one building of any distinction boasted a tin roof, a concrete stoop, and a flagpole constructed of plumber's pipe painted yellow flying a tattered Chinese flag. Stiff-legged, Little Li jumped down from his truck and followed the drivers into the building where they were greeted by a lobby portrait of Chairman Mao encrusted with dust and grime.

"Where can I find someone in charge?" Little Li asked a driver, who gestured toward a closed door marked "Office." Little Li knocked, a gesture that seemed absurdly formal in this setting.

"Enter," a muffled voice answered.

Upon opening the door, Little Li found himself in a room enveloped by a penumbra of cigarette smoke. Barely visible was a wiry man in a stylish Mao suit seated behind a desk that, because the legs on one side were slightly shorter than on the other, threw the whole room out of perspective. Ostentatiously displayed on his tilting desktop was a telephone, covered in a thick layer of dust (hinting that it was vestigial); a large official stone seal; and a brass nameplate announcing in black characters "WU YANG: STATION CHIEF" (吴阳站长). Behind this display of power symbols sat a man whose eyes were deep-set in a skull-like face that was topped by a comb-over confected from what appeared to be no more than several strands of hair trained to make several laps back and forth across their host's bald pate. What is more, when Station Chief Wu deigned to look up, Little Li noticed that one of his eyes wandered, creating the unnerving impression of being scrutinized by two people at once.

"Old Liu!" Station Chief Wu urgently called out, as if summoning an offstage actor who had missed an entrance cue. A moment later, a short bald man materialized in the doorway.

"Station Chief Wu, I am present," he announced, holding his own lamp up to Little Li's face to have a better look at the visitor.

"We seem to have an outsider here!" announced Station Chief Wu.

"I was told in Gonghe that I'd been assigned here," offered Little Li tentatively.

"Here?" Station Chief Wu asked in surprise.

"I'm the 'educated youth' from Beijing."

"Oh!" exclaimed Old Liu, as if he'd suddenly recalled something. "Yes, yes. Station Chief Wu, you'll recall we had some discussions about another—"

"All right! All right! Just take care of him," commanded Station Chief Wu.

"Of course!" replied his factotum with a servile smile.

"I appreciate your help," said Little Li, hoping to curry some favor with his new overlord.

"No matter," said Station Chief Wu, and returned his attention to a document on his desk.

"You must be hungry," said Old Liu in a way that was almost feminine.

"I am," said Little Li gratefully as they left the office.

"Then we'll see if Master Chef Wang [王大厨] can make you some noodles. Afterward, I'll take you out back so you can rest." Little Li had not eaten since Gonghe, and the smell of food caused waves of suppressed hunger pangs to seize his body. "Oh, Master Chef Wang!" Old Liu sang out in a strangely operatic voice as they entered the almost empty canteen. "Will you feed this boy? After his long trip, he needs to eat."

Master Chef Wang was a scurvy-looking man whose potbelly was upholstered by a filthy apron. His other most distinguishing feature was an enormous gold front tooth, which gleamed from his mouth like a headlight. Having just been recalled to prepare dinner for the drivers, he was not pleased by yet another request, and only after a bout of scowling did he consent to throw another handful of noodles into his enormous carbon-encrusted wok and fan his fading fire back to flame with his bellows.

When Little Li finished eating, it was all he could do to shoulder his pack and follow Old Liu outside into the cold. They were passing a strange structure built on stilts that was silhouetted against the moonlit sky when Old Liu stopped.

"Here we have the latrine," he announced. "Just go up that ladder, but don't be surprised by the pigs." Little Li had no idea what he was talking about, but was too tired to ask.

In front of a long, low building with stamped-earth walls, Old Liu stopped again. "As a matter of historical information, PLA soldiers were billeted here in the 1950s and '60s, when the Red Army was suppressing Golok rebels who opposed the reunification of our Motherland," said Old Liu, gesturing with a sweep of his arm like a tour guide toward the vast emptiness lost in darkness beyond the compound walls.

"Am I to sleep here?" asked Little Li, weary and in no mood for a local-history lesson.

"You can sleep anywhere here you like," replied Old Liu as he opened the door. "Just have a look around. Breakfast is at five-thirty." Then, handing Little Li a candle, he departed. In the flickering light, Little Li saw he was in a windowless shed filled with piles of junk covered in dust and draped with cobwebs. Even if it had not been dark and he hadn't been cold, dirty, and tired, it would have been a daunting task to fix up even a small corner of this ruin. Though only a few days had elapsed since his departure, Beijing already felt light-years away. He stood in the flickering light, feeling as if he'd slipped through the space-time continuum into a parallel universe from which he might never find his way back out.

7

LITTLE LI was unrolling his bedding on the littered floor when he noticed a sliver of light shining through a crack in the wall. Then he felt a draft of cold air and turned to see a silhouette standing in the doorway.

"Are you the new 'educated youth'?" a gravelly voice asked.

"Yes," replied Little Li, unable to see the face of the speaker.

"I'm your welcome committee!" the voice said, with a rueful laugh. When he raised his candle, Little Li was surprised to see before him a tall, handsome boy with a head of tousled hair and a face burned brown by the sun who looked to be a year or two older than him. But beneath his unkempt exterior, Little Li could also discern a certain fineness of features.

"I'm Liang Shan (梁善) from Shanghai," said the boy, proffering his hand. "You can call me Little Liang."

"I'm from Beijing," replied Little Li in astonishment.

"Ah, Beijing! Unfortunately, out here it doesn't matter where we're from, because everyone except the Goloks is from elsewhere."

"Yeah. I just met Station Chief Wu, Master Chef Wang, and Old Liu," replied Little Li with a wry laugh. "Is that the local leadership?"

"You might say." Little Liang's voice dripped with sarcasm. "Wu thinks of himself as our Great Leader [伟大领袖]. He controls the politics, and that bandit Master Chef Wang controls the food. These are the two currencies here. Then there's 'Legs of the Dogs Liu' [狗腿子刘], who'll do whatever his master tells him. Everyone calls him Eunuch Liu [刘太监] behind his back."

"Why?"

"Well, just take a look at the guy!"

"You don't sound very content."

"Content?" erupted Little Liang, wrinkling his nose and spitting at the wall. "Yak Springs is lonely, the food is crap, the leaders are despots, and there is nothing to do except slave in the quarry or on the road. Welcome to nowhere!" Shivering, Little Li gave a yawn. "Until you've had a chance to fix up a space for yourself, why don't you bunk in with me," offered Little Liang. "Except for one small end of the building that I've made livable, this place is a dump!" He gestured disgustedly at the mess around them.

"That would be nice," managed Little Li through his fatigue.

He was even more grateful when he saw the so-called room Little Liang had fixed up with old bricks, scraps of wood, cardboard cartons, plastic fertilizer-sacks, shipping pallets, even an old oil drum he'd fashioned into a washstand. And, to keep drafts from whistling in around the window, he'd pasted layers of newspaper over the cracks.

"You can put your quilt next to mine," said Little Liang, gesturing toward the sleeping platform. Deeply appreciative, Little Li started arranging his bedding. However, his teeth were now audibly chattering from the cold, fatigue, and the trauma of the last few days.

"Are you sick?" asked Little Liang with a sudden softness.

"No, I'm just cold and messed up." Little Li forced a smile.

"I've got an idea!" Little Liang suddenly interjected. "Put your coat and shoes back on and follow me!"

Little Li reluctantly obliged and followed him back out into the darkness. As the freezing air hit his face, he regretted his decision. Nonetheless, touched by Little Liang's solicitude, he followed him through a side door out of the compound and down a rocky path into a shallow gully. There Little Liang paused, reached down, picked up a copper ladle hanging on a post, and scooped up some water from a pool bubbling out from under a rock beside the path.

"You must be thirsty!" Only as Little Li drank did he realize how parched he was. Never had water tasted so sweet, cold, and pure. As they came around a bend in the path, he was surprised by a white phantasm billowing up into the moonlight.

"What is it?" asked Little Li suspiciously.

"Yak Springs! We're going to warm you up!" As they drew nearer, Little Li saw that it was steam swirling out of a crude wooden shack. When Little Liang wrenched open its door hinged with two wide straps of leather and shone his flashlight inside, through the roiling clouds of steam Little Li made out three rock-lined pools, fed with bubbling water so hot it warmed the whole interior. "Go in!" urged Little Liang with custodial pride. "The first pool is the coolest, so we'll start there. When you get used to that, we can move up."

As they undressed, Little Li had never seen a boy Little Liang's age with such broad shoulders and such a muscular body. Whatever he'd been doing here at Yak Springs, he'd gained an impressive physique.

When Little Li put a foot tentatively into the first pool, he let out a gasp, and involuntarily pulled back. However, not wanting to seem unmanly while Little Liang was plunging right in, he held his breath, stepped into the pool and forced himself to slowly sit down. He felt his blood was going to boil. But then the searing sensation began to turn to warmth, and he became so relaxed he was unsure he would be able to stand up again.

"Do you dare try the second pool?" asked Little Liang after a few minutes.

"Sure," replied Little Li. But he was not so sure.

"Okay, but you have to be careful!" Little Liang warned. "It's easy to faint when you come out. So—do like this." He stood up, bent over, and put his head between his legs. Then, as he dunked himself in the second pool, he let out a yelp. Not to be outdone, Little Li followed suit. The sensation was like being plunged into a wok of boiling oil. However, as his body adjusted and he became infused with a pleasing sense of warmth, all his fatigue vanished. He felt reborn.

In an almost yogic trance, the boys lumbered out of the water, threw on their clothes, and stumbled back to the compound under a star-struck sky. Lying beneath his quilt beside his unexpected new comrade, Little Li felt so miraculously delivered that, despite his fatigue, when Little Liang asked about his trip, he recounted the events of the past few days, even the execution.

"Where was this?" asked Little Liang.

"Gonghe. There was something about the way that old man's head jerked back when . . ." He was not able to go on. "How long have you been here?" he suddenly asked, wanting to change the subject.

"Almost six months."

"What do your parents do?"

"Before they got 'sent down,' they worked at the Shanghai Museum of Art and History."

"Where did you live?"

"Oh, in a pretty nice government apartment. But, with my folks gone, I worry that the government will let new people move in so, when I get homesick, I have to remind myself that maybe I'm missing a home that isn't there anymore. And what about your parents?"

"My father also got 'sent down'."

"And your mother?"

"Well . . ." sighed Little Li. He was not sure how to proceed.

"Is she still alive?"

"Actually, she died, but . . . in the United States."

"In America?" exclaimed Little Liang, sitting bolt upright.

"Yes."

"Was she American?"

"Half American. She had to leave Beijing when I was small."

"Aiyaaa! I thought I saw something in your face. So—you've got a little bit of foreign-devil [洋鬼子] blood in you, eh?"

"Yeah," replied Little Li. "But keep it a secret. As soon as people learn about my mother, everything gets crazy."

"Of course, of course! But did you ever really live with her?"

"Not since I was about five."

"Where did she go?"

"She had to go back to San Francisco, to see her father, who was ill." He pointed over his head, as if America was just over the compound wall. "But she died there before she could come back."

"Aiya! Didn't you miss her?"

"I missed the idea of her, especially after my father got 'sent down' the first time, during the Anti-Rightist Campaign. Now I'm not sure what I miss." There was a long pause.

"You'll go crazy out here if you start missing people, thinking about home, and wondering what might happen to you. Remember, 'Distant waters cannot quench immediate thirst' [远水不解近渴]. It's all out of our hands, so I just try to go on one day at a time."

"And what do they have you doing here?"

"Cracking rocks to make gravel and filling in potholes on the highway. So it's my good fortune they sent you. I don't know how much longer I would have lasted alone!"

"I never expect much good fortune," offered Little Li. "Sometimes I think I just scare good fortune away!" He began to shudder.

"There's no need to talk about such things now," said Little Liang reassuringly, reaching over to pull his quilt up around Little Li's shoulders. "Are you cold?"

"I don't know what I am."

As Little Liang put an arm around Little Li's shoulders, he felt cold and hot, lonely and succored, anxious and relieved, sleepy and awake, and tired and energized all at once. He was not sure exactly what was happening, but he no longer cared. As Little Liang's hands strayed, tripping mysterious forces within him, he felt only too glad to be able to turn control over to someone else. Then, suddenly, someone was trying to shake him awake.

"Get up!" a voice was saying. Grudgingly, Little Li opened his eyes to find Little Liang standing over him with a candle. Because it was still dark, he wanted nothing more than to roll over and go back to sleep in the cocoon of his quilt. "If you don't get up, you won't get anything to eat until supper!" persisted Little Liang.

Little Li dragged himself out of bed, dressed, and followed his new friend across the still, dark compound to the Administration Building. After the crystal-clear Qinghai night and starry sky, coming into the smoky, grimy confines of the Yak Springs canteen was like entering another universe. Its pale-green walls were covered with the same mossy patina of grit and grime that adorned Mao's entryway portrait; the concrete floor was strewn with a permanent litter of cigarette butts, ashes, burned matches, toothpicks, and other detritus; the tops of its wobbly tables were sticky to the touch from years of spilled food and dirt; and the air was dense with a greasy smog of cigarette smoke, scorched cooking oil, and fumes from the poorly ventilated yak-dung fire under Master Chef Wang's Stygian wok. To associate the appellation "Master Chef" with this sour-faced noodle-slinger was to mock the hallowed Confucian notion of the "rectification of names" (正名), aimed at keeping the meaning of words aligned with the reality they purported to describe through a process of constant rectification. As the Sage warned: "When names for things lose their integrity, language then ceases to accord with the truth of things. (名不正则言不顺)." The only part of Master Chef Wang's craft in which he truly excelled was pyrotechnics, when he induced his greasy wok periodically to burst into flame. It was a feat in which he perversely delighted, although sometimes his conflagrations were so large he needed to douse them with water, lest they incinerate not only someone's dinner but the whole canteen.

"Where's your bowl?" he snarled as Little Li approached. "Do you think this is a rest home for retired Politburo members?"

"Don't worry," Little Liang offered cheerfully, passing his own tin bowl to Little Li. "I'll eat afterward."

As dawn broke after breakfast, Little Li could see where he was for the first time. The Yak Springs compound sat in a treeless valley that stretched away to a panorama of foothills, that rose to a range of distant snowcapped peaks just then being struck by sunlight. Never had Little Li seen such undisturbed emptiness.

Because the leaders of Yak Springs hardly seemed to notice their newest member, for the next few days, after Little Liang left to work on the road each morning, he busied himself in the former barracks clearing away piles of debris, spiderwebs, and sheep manure to slowly carve out a small, serviceable corner for himself. It was not until several days later, when he was on the roof under a cobalt-blue sky filled with enormous fluffy clouds, fixing the cracked tiles over his new sleeping platform, that Eunuch Liu reappeared. With all the solemnity of a subaltern informing a visiting legate of an audience with the emperor, he announced, "Our station chief will now discuss your work assignment with you."

"Now?" asked Little Li.

"He's managed to fit you in this morning."

Little Li climbed down and followed Eunuch Liu into the Administration Building.

"Enter," responded Station Chief Wu when his assistant knocked on his closed office door. Once inside, Eunuch Liu took up a position standing unobtrusively at attention against the back wall. The smoke was so thick that Little Li was able to take only the shallowest of breaths. "And you are?" Station Chief Wu began imperiously.

"Li Wende."

"From . . . ?"

"Beijing."

"We usually draw from Shanghai. If you come from Beijing, you must have an interesting family background."

"My father was a musician," began Little Li, immediately thinking better of saying more.

"A musician?" said Station Chief Wu, flashing a smile that exposed a horrific set of yellowing teeth and diseased gums. "And it says here you play the . . . the flute, is it?"

"Yes."

"Well, you're not going to have much of an audience out here, except maybe an occasional yak or drunken nomad! Am I right, Comrade Liu?" He turned to his factotum, who quickly acknowledged the correctness of his superior's dictum with a bout of unctuous head bobbing. "And weren't you supposed to be sent elsewhere?"

"It is difficult to explain," stammered Little Li, not wanting to go into the details of how he'd missed his ride in Gonghe.

"And"—Station Chief Wu slapped a folder on his desk—"it says here you're of 'mixed blood'." He extracted a new smoke from a crumpled pack of Victory cigarettes, lit it with the still-smoldering butt of the last, and inhaled a satisfying lungful of smoke.

"Yes." Little Li nodded, deeply unhappy to hear that news of his mixed parentage had followed him all the way up here, onto the Tibetan Plateau.

"Well, I don't suppose anyone's going to get corrupted by a little American blood at the Drogyu Quarry, doing gravel production and road maintenance." He went into a phlegmy spasm that mixed laughing and coughing. Still apparently curious about that foreign part of Little Li, Station Chief Wu studied his face for a few uncomfortable moments. "We have no foreigners up here, unless you count the Goloks!" He winked knowingly at Eunuch Liu, took another languorous drag on his fresh smoke, made an O-shape with his lips, and let a coil of smoke rings curl out past his yellowed teeth. As they drifted lazily up to his nostrils, he resourcefully reinhaled them. So engrossed did Little Li become in this ingenious recycling system, which enabled Station Chief Wu to sit in his airtight office and keep reinhaling the same smoke, that he momentarily tuned out the monologue. "So—that's that!" Station Chief Wu suddenly concluded. "Old Liu, will you make sure our 'educated youth' here is at the equipment shed at six tomorrow morning, so Superintendent Peng can issue him the relevant tools?" This order sent his obsequious beadle into another bout of head bobbing. By the time Little Li reached the outside, he was gasping like a floundering man who's managed to paddle back to the surface just in the nick of time to save himself from drowning. But he also felt something else. When he'd entered Station Chief Wu's office, he'd felt intimidated by the notion of the highest authority at Yak Springs. However, his audience had transformed Station Chief Wu into an absurd presence. The idea that a person of such vanity and pretension had taken root out here on the outer edge of civilization seemed ludicrous and laughable.

After breakfast the next morning, Superintendent Peng, a short, dyspeptic man of few words who oversaw roadwork, issued him a shovel, a short-handled maul, a beefy steel chisel, a small battered wooden stool, two woven rattan baskets, and a carrying pole. As he and Little Liang set off down the road to the quarry, it was a beautiful clear day, and the distant snow-clad mountains stood out like the jagged teeth of a saw silhouetted against the azure sky.

"That's Anymachen, the highest peak in the range," said Little Liang, pointing to a distant pinnacle that shimmered in the morning sun. "Tibetan Buddhists believe it's a 'divine mountain' [神山], the abode of powerful deities. Most Goloks who live here aspire, sometime in their lives, to do a *kora,* or circumambulation, around it, by prostrating themselves over and over, to earn 'merit,' or good karma, for their next reincarnation!"

"Are there many Goloks around?" asked Little Li.

"Oh yeah! They're out there, but you can't always see 'em," he said with a laugh. "But when they come into Yak Springs to ship their hides, they camp out across the road, at the old caravanserai. And when they get drinking, they can carry on all night!"

"Are there any monasteries nearby?"

"Chairman Mao closed them all. But when it comes to the Lord Buddha, Goloks don't give up easily!"

The Drogyu Quarry had been blasted out of a hillside by PLA demolition crews, who returned once a year with a truckload of dynamite to detonate new slabs of rock off the quarry face. Without a mechanical grinding machine, it was the boys' job to reduce the resulting pile of scree into pieces of gravel the size of almonds, using nothing more than steel chisels and mauls. As soon as they arrived, Little Liang sat down on his stool in front of a boulder and began matter-of-factly chipping away. With delicate taps of his maul on his chisel, as deftly as a master gem cutter flaking a diamond, he effortlessly made pieces of gravel fly off, one after another. Little Li chose a small boulder, positioned his stool, and set to work himself. But each time he struck his chisel, it bounced off the stone face with an arm-numbing clang. Turning to watch his friend, he discerned how Little Liang combed the rock's surface for hairline fractures before he began chipping, with all the tenacity of a wood-boring termite undeterred by the prospect of turning a giant log into a pile of sawdust.

With their steel chisels making a gamelan-like symphony of metallic sounds, Little Li couldn't help thinking about a mythic story so admired by Chairman Mao that every child had to study it in school, "The Old Man Who Moved the Mountain" (愚公移山). It told of an old-timer who lived in the Taihang Mountains (where his own father had been sent during the Anti-Rightist Campaign) and who became so exasperated by a mountain blocking his village's access to the outside world that he began to chip slowly away at it. When others laughed at his foolishness, he insisted that, if everyone would only keep at the task, in a few generations the mountain would be gone. Impressed by his determination, the God of the Mountains rewarded him by removing it. Mao was said to love the story because it showed the diligence and tenacity of ordinary people.

Only when the sun began to dip did the boys head back to the compound. As they went, Little Liang proved a fountainhead of information about Yak Springs.

"What's the story on Master Chef Wang?" asked Little Li.

"They say he was a health official in Wuxi who got pissed off at his boss during the Anti-Rightist Campaign and got 'sent down.' It's the old story: if you refuse to 'kiss the horse's ass' [拍马屁], it's all over!"

With his unprepossessing moon-shaped face, little pig eyes, and paunch liveried in an eternally greasy apron, Master Chef Wang presided over his canteen from the commanding heights of a platform on which his wok was installed, like the first mate on the poop deck of a great sailing ship. What gave him his authority was neither his commanding perch nor his gastronomical skill, but the fact that he got to determine what and how much "inmates" (牢友), as they called themselves, got to eat. And eating was the most important part of the diminished lives of those unfortunate enough to be marooned at Yak Springs. "Since the canteen is the only place where there's any food for miles around, that old turtle egg [王八蛋] is able to exploit his position to favor those he likes and punish those he doesn't," explained Little Liang. "And, like 'the son of heaven' [天子], he's convinced he's always right."

Master Chef Wang had secured a kind of divine right of chefs, which enabled him to turn cooking into a form of revenge rather than art. And he was not above making his cuisine tasteless just to deny inmates one of the few sensory pleasures still left them. In his kitchen, there were only two ways meat appeared on the menu: (1) when an aging sheep or yak dropped dead as a nomad family passed by; (2) when the compound's two pigs were finally slaughtered for the Spring Festival during the Chinese New Year. The only other fare inmates could really look forward to on a regular basis was rice. However, the rice allotted Yak Springs was the lowest grade, and often wormy as well. Inmates joked that mealy worms at least helped boost their meager protein intake! And, compared with their usual diet of half-rotten sweet potatoes, ancient turnips, limp cabbage, dried bean curd, and corn cakes, infested rice was still viewed as a luxury.

Master Chef Wang announced meals by striking a steel truck axle that hung outside the canteen's back door. When it was hit with a maul, it emitted a dull metallic sound that was no more sonorous than the meals it announced were tasty. But, despite the low regard in which Master Chef Wang's cuisine was held, as soon as his tocsin was sounded, inmates and drivers overnighting at the caravanserai across the road nonetheless came running.

"No matter how bad the slop, no one objects, because complaints only lead to retaliation," explained Little Liang. "There's a famous Yak Springs story about a teacher from Shanghai who'd somehow managed to get rehabilitated, but just before he was scheduled to go home, he found three boiled worms floating in his cabbage soup. Emboldened because he was about to leave, he blew up at Master Chef Wang right in front of all the other inmates. 'You old turtle egg!' he screamed. 'How dare you steal the good rice for yourself and your boss and feed us this wormy crap?'"

"And how did Master Chef Wang take it?" asked Little Li, excited by the idea of such an overt challenge to authority. (There was not a single inmate who did not entertain such fantasies of revolt.)

"Well, the old bugger didn't immediately respond," continued Little Liang. "But the next night, as inmates lined up to receive their dole, the teacher was surprised when Master Chef Wang served him an especially generous helping, even garnishing it with an added dollop from another pot that he often saved for the favored few. It was not until the teacher sat down and had slurped up his first few mouthfuls that he discovered something odd at the bottom of his bowl. Fishing it out, he found a long, finely tapered tail still attached to a tiny asshole and a pair of hind feet swinging from his chopsticks. Fricasseed rat! He dropped it on the tabletop, bolted from the canteen, and ate nothing more until his truck convoy left Yak Springs two days later. No one has openly criticized Master Chef's culinary skills since. However, the incident gave rise to a new name for our chef: 'Old Turtle Egg Wang' [老王八蛋]. Of course, no one ever dared utter this nickname in his presence. However, one morning just after I arrived, someone loaded a bucket with shit from the caravanserai outhouse and scrawled *'Fuck Wangbadan's Ancestors for Eight Generations!'* on the front wall of the Administration Building. Station Master Wu had to hire some Goloks to scrape the insult off, and Master Chef Wang punished everyone by not serving rice for two months."

If an inmate missed a meal, the only possible reprieve lay in the small, dusty, glass-topped case parked just outside the canteen, under Chairman Mao's portrait. Here candy, crackers, soap, cigarettes, and a small inventory of jars, cans, and bottles of cheap liquor (白干) were for sale. The fact that the liquor was 150-proof and smelled like industrial solvent did not deter truckers and herdsmen from imbibing it while sucking on chunks of rock salt as they played drinking games, cursed, and fought until they collapsed in a drunken stupor. Master Chef Wang controlled the key to the case, and opened it only after actual cash was shown. But, with the exception of cigarettes and liquor, few things in his "store" were ever actually sold—not because inmates did not covet them, but because they had so little money. So the pyramid of canned Liberation pears, Double Happiness lychees, Red Star donkey meat, and Flying Fish mackerel remained largely undisturbed, their labels slowly fading.

For Little Li, this display came to seem more like an untouchable offering at a religious shrine than actual edibles. Nonetheless, the mere existence of such goods incited powerful yearnings. As he lay under his quilt at night, he often dreamed of spiriting a can or jar out from under Master Chef Wang's nose and secretly gorging himself on it in blissful solitude. But the master chef watched over his cache like a hawk, and everyone knew that if anything was ever missing, reprisal would be swift and draconian. So Little Li was left to satisfy his cravings by revisiting memories of the delicacies sent by his mother long ago.

Every Chinese New Year there was a moment of gastronomical relief at Yak Springs, as the two piglets that arrived from Xining each year—and were by compound tradition named Nikita and Nina, after the much-reviled revisionist Soviet leader Nikita Khrushchev and his wife—were finally slaughtered. So grateful were inmates for this annual bounty of pork that when it was at last served they ate with all the wary concentration of wild animals, fearful that at any moment a competitor might sneak up and snatch a fresh kill from their mouths. No one gave a second thought to how these pigs were fattened—not only on the compound's meager output of garbage, but also on the far more reliable supply chain, the Yak Springs latrine, that wooden platform under a tin roof perched on stilts over one end of Nikita and Nina's sty that Eunich Liu had pointed out to Little Li that first night. New arrivals were forced to acclimatize quickly to the mayhem that accompanied the evacuation of one's bowels. As soon as a person approached the ladder leading to the catbird seats, the ravenous hogs stampeded over to do battle with each other for the most advantageous position underneath. As trousers were lowered and a patron squatted over one of the slits in the latrine floor, the crescendo of frenzied oinking and squealing that swelled from below sounded almost as if the two porkers were already under the butcher's knife. Simultaneously trying to nip each other and stand up on their hind hooves like pirouetting circus animals, this husband-and-wife team vied with each other to snatch each turd right out of the air. The idea of dangling one's private parts over such bestial competition took more than a little getting used to.

When Little Li mounted the platform for the first time, the commotion below so unnerved him that his already impacted bowels seized up and he was unable to extrude more than a single, pellet-like offering that nonetheless sent the always expectant Khrush-chevs into a state of high dudgeon. Only as he became a veteran did he come to enjoy the comedic distraction of this couple's theatrical quarrelings. The voracious appetites of the Khrushchevs and the inexhaustible quantities of fresh wind that knifed across the Qing-hai grasslands kept this outhouse a model of socialist hygiene.

There was one other unexpected hazard attached to the act of elimination at Yak Springs. The copies of the *People's Daily* that arrived episodically on passing convoys for the political edification of inmates also provided their only available source of toilet paper. After being read, the newspapers were ripped into strips and given a second life in the privy. But before the official propaganda organ of the Chinese Communist Party could undergo this transubstantiation, an editorial challenge had to be met: someone had to make sure that no piece of any newspaper bearing the name of, a quotation from, or photograph depicting Chairman Mao ended up on latrine duty. This responsibility fell to Station Chief Wu, who took a strange comfort from the fact that he could not imagine being sent to a place of exile more undesirable than where he already was. Nonetheless, to afford himself maximum deniability, he deputized Eunuch Liu to undertake the sensitive and time-consuming task of reading every page of every newspaper as carefully as a censor reading copy to make sure that nothing escaped scrutiny. The ubiquity of Chairman Mao's utterances and photos made the task particularly onerous. After cutting and snipping around each photo and quotation with exacting care to ensure that all sensitive material was properly excised, Eunuch Liu ended up having to withhold most of each issue from "service to the people," creating a chronic shortage of politically corrected toilet paper.

8

STATION CHIEF WU

IN HIS tireless efforts to enhance his standing at Yak Springs, Station Chief Wu felt his exalted position demanded a proper uniform. He may not have been able to wear elaborate ceremonial robes or feathered hats like imperial officials of old, but as Station Chief he alone felt entitled to wear the kind of four-pocketed Mao jacket favored by high party officials. Despite Mao's ideology of egalitarianism, men like Station Chief Wu continued to yearn for such trappings. Especially critical to his self-esteem was a meeting room adjoining his office, its three stuffed chairs accessorized with the kind of lace antimacassars favored by ranking officials throughout China. However, to his great chagrin, one chair was missing an antimacassar, leaving one arm infuriatingly bare. But his reception room suffered another, even more galling affliction: there was no one at Yak Springs of sufficiently high station to sit in these chairs with Station Chief Wu. What's more, because such ranking personages rarely passed through Yak Springs Way, he was denied the opportunity to use his cherished throne room at all.

Station Chief Wu's most precious symbol of suzerainty by far was his "secretary" (秘书), Eunuch Liu. No self-important official in China could consider himself complete without an inferior-in-waiting to do his bidding. How Station Chief Wu acquired Eunuch Liu, nobody knew, but his entire purpose in life seemed to be to serve his master. The origins of his moniker were equally unclear, but were rumored to have grown out of insinuations that because, like imperial eunuchs of yore, he had a high-pitched voice and a bullet-shaped bald head and was short and heavyset, he must have only one testicle, or possibly none. How he managed to maintain his ample girth on Master Chef Wang's unappetizing fare was no mystery: closeness to the throne gave him special access.

According to Little Liang, Station Chief Wu had once served as a mid-level administrator at an engineering institute in Lanzhou from which he'd been expelled during the Anti-Rightist Campaign, although no one knew exactly what offense he'd committed. However, he had such a distaste for the outdoors that even when the weather was fair he almost never left the Administration Building. The closest anyone had ever seen him come to actual manual labor was once when a ranking highway official from Gonghe unexpectedly appeared and he'd dug up a single ceremonial shovelful of earth to preside over the dedication of a new bridge that was within the way station's jurisdiction. His evident aversion to physical labor earned him the nickname "Comrade Inaction" (无为同志), a play on the notion of "nonaction" (无为) that the classical sage Laozi (老子) had enshrined millennia ago as an essential principle of Daoism. This theory propounded the notion that all things happen most felicitously without overt human striving, so the best approach to life and government is a stance of inaction and noninterference. As Laozi famously declared, "Through nonaction, everything comes into being" (無為而治). Station Chief Wu's version of "inaction" was to get others to do things for him while he sat in his office behind his listing desk drinking tea, smoking cigarettes, and nibbling snacks delivered by Eunuch Liu. Like a riparian marine creature that knows it's dangerous to swim both too far upstream, into fresher water, and too far downstream, into saltier water, Station Chief Wu's excursions beyond the confines of his office were limited to evacuating his bowels and those unavoidable times when he was forced to go to the parking area to greet visitors. As a result, his pale skin bore none of the hallmarks of the other, swarthy Yak Springs inmates, who'd become so scorched by the high-altitude sun that their faces were as brown as raisins, their arms and hands bronzed and covered with scars and calluses. The only parts of Station Chief Wu's doughy body that were tanned were his delicate nicotine-stained fingers. In effect, he was living a double sentence: First, his state-imposed sentence of exile to Yak Springs. Second, his self-imposed confinement to his office.

Like so many others of his generation whose opportunities for sensual pleasure had been narrowed by the revolution's puritanism, Station Chief Wu had only cigarettes, snacks, and the power of his office as his indulgences. Indeed, his soul had been so defoliated by the exigencies of life, it was difficult to imagine him engaging in any real enjoyments. Since sexual relations require a member of the opposite sex (of which there were none at Yak Springs) as well as a capacity for some measure of reciprocity (a trait not in Station Chief Wu's playbook), this world was foreclosed to him. Moreover, everything about his being, from his mossy yellow teeth and ludicrous comb-over to his unprepossessing body, repelled one from even imagining sexual congress. Nonetheless, the question of sex was one of the great imponderables hovering over not only Station Chief Wu and Yak Springs, but Mao's whole revolution. Because there is no more self-indulgent human activity, sex was the revolution's nemesis. Although Mao got special dispensation for the serial wives and concubines he kept in the old imperial tradition, his minions were expected to subdue their urges for self-gratification and focus on "serving the people" (为人民服务), "raising high the banner of class struggle" (高举阶级斗争的旗帜), and "making revolution" (干革命).

As far as Little Li could discern, the only enjoyments his boss truly looked forward to were smoking and pleasing superiors. But because there were so few superiors to toady before, he was left to pleasure himself only with cigarettes. Indeed, he was married to tobacco, having to awaken at least once each night to light up or risk going into nicotine withdrawal while slumbering, and the odor of burning tobacco exuded by his clothing, hair, and pores was overpowering. He was like a piece of yak jerky so well cured in a smokehouse that the meat finally turns into a mummified, if pungent relic of its original organic self.

Station Chief Wu was a secretive man, especially about his past life. The only place such facts about a person were recorded was one's official "dossier" (档案) kept on each person. Such files were considered "internal" (内部) documents, so subjects themselves were never allowed to see them, and at Yak Springs only Station Chief Wu had access to these materials, a privilege that constituted no small portion of his power. The dossiers, which were kept in a file cabinet behind his desk, were lodestones that drew into their malevolent field of gravity a wide array of information, including school transcripts, evaluations from former work-unit leaders; reports from informants; random critiques of political views; press articles; self-criticisms and confessions; notes on time in exile; rumors about relations with friends, family, spouses, and mistresses; police records; surveillance reports; and hearsay about any personal peccadilloes, especially sexual indiscretions. Since reporting on others was considered a demonstration of loyalty to the party, not even friendships or marriages were sacrosanct barriers to snitching. And once a piece of information landed in a person's dossiers, it followed them forever, determining thereafter into which schools they were admitted, what jobs they were given, how rapidly they got promoted or demoted, when they could give birth, if they got "sent down," whether they got dispatched to a reform-through-labor camp or locked up in a prison, and even where they could be buried.

Having been victimized for more than a century by the imperialist Great Powers, the Chinese Communist Party had defiantly taken over the role of China's victimizer-in-chief. Its message to foreigners seemed to be: "Give us a chance to oppress ourselves! It's only fair!" And the party was triumphant in harnessing Leninist organization and discipline to bring the dark art of self-oppression to "a higher stage of development," as Marx might have put it. With suspicion, disloyalty, character assassination, and betrayal the rule rather than the exception, the very notion of friendship became so corrupted that trust vanished, lives were broken, families destroyed, and people killed, as the very DNA of China's social genome mutated into a new pathology, with these traits destined to continue re-expressing themselves for generations to come.

So painful was the past that no one wanted to dwell on it. And even in his immaturity, Little Li could not bring himself to blame Station Chief Wu, Eunuch Liu, Master Chef Wang, or anyone else, for that matter, for wanting to forget. In fact, he wished he wasn't so obsessed with trying to remember his own past. What was to be gained by reliving dead events? More wrongs had been done, and more collective pain inflicted, than could ever be set right. Instead of remonstrating, people had learned to remain silent and dedicate themselves to whatever task was set before them by whatever master was installed above them. If one was assigned to make gravel, one made gravel without complaining. One did what one was told because things just worked out better that way. Not perfectly, but better. Mainly, one survived. Only the most foolhardy imagined they could ever struggle successfully against such a system.

One morning, while visiting the latrine, Station Chief Wu came upon a strip from the *People's Daily* that, despite Eunuch Liu's best lustration efforts, contained a fragment showing one of Chairman Mao's ears. That evening, he strode into the canteen at dinnertime with Eunuch Liu in tow.

"Your attention, please, for a message from our leadership, Station Chief Wu," a grim-faced Eunuch Liu began, his head hanging like that of a small child who's just been caught doing something naughty.

"A grave offense has taken place within our own unit, and the offender now wishes to make a clean breast of it with a public 'self-criticism' [自我批评]," intoned Station Chief Wu severely. Then he turned to Eunuch Liu.

"Well, I . . . I . . ." began Eunuch Liu. "I want to thank our station chief for giving me a chance to criticize my low level of political vigilance in carrying out those responsibilities entrusted to me by our unit. I have failed to apply myself resolutely to serving the people and must now dedicate myself to rectifying my errors." Here he began sobbing so piteously that he could not continue. By now his fellow inmates had all stopped eating and were staring blankly at the floor, having no idea what was happening. When, after several minutes, Eunuch Liu had still not regained his composure, an agitated Station Chief Wu was forced to step forward again.

"All right, that's quite enough," he chided. "You're here to make a self-criticism, not blubber like a child!" By now his roving eye was spastically gyrating around the canteen, like a radar antenna gone berserk. "You will show your contrition by placing yourself on duty in the latrine from sunup to sundown for three days, so such errors are not repeated!"

Alas, after a single day without having Eunuch Liu at his beck and call, Station Chief Wu was so undone that he quietly summoned him back from the latrine.

Several months later, another copy of the *People's Daily* intruded into the normally uneventful lives of Yak Springs inmates, in a very different way. While he was taking his daily constitutional, a strip of newspaper that had been consigned to latrine duty caught Station Chief Wu's eye. On this particular fragment he chanced upon several paragraphs from a story recounting how an official who'd been dubbed a "rightist" and sent to do manual labor on a state-run hog farm in Hunan Province had redeemed himself, and even gotten "rehabilitated," by building a "loyalty wall" (忠字墙) emblazoned with a giant portrait of Chairman Mao. The column told how this "hero of the people" not only continued slopping hogs, but also set about teaching other "rightists" at the farm how to perform "loyalty dances" (忠字舞) in front of his new shrine, as paeans to Chairman Mao's leadership. So impressed with these expressions of devotion was the farm's Revolutionary Committee that they not only rehabilitated its architect, but turned him into a national hero celebrated in the *People's Daily*. Filled with zeal to imitate this inspiring example, Station Chief Wu appeared in the canteen once again.

"Our leader, Station Chief Wu, has a few important words on a bold new project that everyone will surely welcome," began Eunuch Liu. Inmates and visiting truck drivers looked up from their bowls with annoyance at having their dinners interrupted.

"Good evening, Comrades," began Station Chief Wu, grinning broadly. "Despite our remoteness here at Yak Springs, I know we all feel deep solidarity with the great revolutionary upsurge taking place throughout our Motherland. Because it is only natural to want to play an active role in this great struggle, our unit has decided to undertake a special project, the first of its kind in these parts—a loyalty wall." Station Chief Wu paused here as if expecting an ovation. However, when, instead of clapping, his audience just sat in silent stupefaction, even though thrown off by their lack of enthusiasm, he was finally forced to continue. "So . . . We'll have further announcements about this important initiative in the future." As soon as he finished, the nonplussed inmates and drivers returned thankfully to the solemn task of mastication.

"What's he up to now?" asked Little Li, rolling his eyes.

"He wants to kiss some superior's ass to get himself out of here," replied Little Liang. "But first he has to figure out a way to lure a big ass out here to kiss!"

Despite his unenthusiastic reception in the canteen, Station Chief Wu remained filled with fevered visions of rehabilitation and pressed on. First he conscripted a group of Goloks to erect a twenty-foot-high wall of air-dried earthen bricks facing the parking area just inside the main gate. Then he ordered Little Li and Little Liang to plaster it with mud and whitewash it with lime. Finally, he inveigled the Provincial Propaganda Department to dispatch a poster artist to paint the wall with a gargantuan mural of Chairman Mao standing heroically before a scarlet sunrise. Then, below Mao's beaming visage Station Chief Wu wrote in his own hand, "The Reddest of Red Suns in Our Hearts."

"This wall shows the leadership abilities of our very own Station Chief Wu," proclaimed Eunuch Liu proudly when Little Li and Little Liang found him admiring the wall one morning as they were leaving for the quarry.

"Aiyaaa!" exclaimed Little Liang, shaking his head, as soon as they were out of earshot. "It's like putting makeup on a yak! At least the wall adds a touch of color to things!"

The biggest fans of the loyalty wall turned out to be the Goloks, who spent hours admiring Chairman Mao's smiling face, as if he were a Buddhist deity.

A week later, Station Chief Wu again sent Eunuch Liu to the canteen, this time to call a pre-breakfast rally in front of the new wall. Once in the parking area, the assembled inmates, truck drivers, and Golok hangers-on were surprised to find that, even though Mao's beaming likeness had already been on view for several days, it was now draped with a canvas tarp. When everyone had finally assembled, Eunuch Liu again stepped forward.

"Good morning, Comrades. This is a historic day for Yak Springs. And, now . . ." He gave a rope affixed to a grommet in the tarp a yank. When the tarp refused to slide off the wall, he began pulling it with both hands, as if trimming a sail in a stiff breeze, so that when the tarp finally fell, so did he. After getting up and dusting himself off, he announced: "Now we present Station Chief Wu."

"The leadership is immensely proud of our new wall and wants to thank all comrades who've helped erect it," began Station Chief Wu, his wild eye spinning manically. Then, turning to face his wall, he raised one hand in a clenched salute. Most of those assembled in the parking lot cared nothing about Station Chief Wu's wall. All they cared about was their interrupted breakfast. But Station Chief Wu persevered. "So let the ceremony begin!" he continued, despite the hopelessness of ever winning his command audience's enthusiasm. When nothing happened, he commanded again, only louder, "Let the ceremony begin!" Only then did Eunuch Liu trot back out from behind the wall with an ancient accordion strapped to his chest. Even though only two or three onlookers clapped, he patted his chest emotionally, as if he were giving a concert-hall debut. Then his instrument wheezed to life and he began singing in a voice that was not half bad:

> *Socialism is good! Socialism is good!*
> *People of socialist countries have high social status.*
> *Reactionaries are overthrown and the imperialists tuck*
>   *their tails between their legs and flee!*
>   *The entire country is united by a tide in socialist*
> *construction!*

Clearly imagining himself following the script of the celebrated hog-farm hero heralded in the *People's Daily,* Station Chief Wu began his own version of a loyalty dance that involved flailing his arms around in the air to suggest dazzling beams of socialist radiance emanating forth from the persona of Chairman Mao.

"Everybody together now!" cried out Eunuch Liu. "Ah-one, two, three, four!"

Road Superintendent Peng began halfheartedly waving his arms in solidarity for a few moments, but no one else moved. They were all too flabbergasted by the sight of Station Chief Wu outdoors, without a cigarette in his mouth, singing and dancing as Eunuch Liu accompanied him on the accordion and singing.

> *The Communist Party's good! The Communist Party's*
>   *good!*
> *The Communist Party guides China on the way to power*
>   *and wealth.*
> *The power of people is invincible,*
> *The resistance of reactionary cliques is destined to fail.*
> *The cause of socialism will definitely be victorious,*
> *A communist society will definitely come true, will*
>   *definitely come true!*

It was a gross miscalculation for Station Chief Wu ever to have imagined that these onlookers would become inspired enough by his project to act as a volunteer corps de ballet. Not only did they have no idea how to dance, they had no interest in learning. What is more, many of the truck drivers were so hung over from the night before, it was all they could do to stand up. But the verses kept coming and the whole affair did not finally end until the accordion music suddenly stopped with a sound of rushing air and Eunuch Liu futilely pumping his ancient instrument.

"Aiyaaa! My equipment's broken," he wailed. It was an odd turn of phrase, because he made it sound as if he were a technician announcing the malfunction of an irrigation pump or an electrical transformer.

"What the fuck?" yelped Station Chief Wu.

"It sprang a leak," lamented Eunuch Liu, pointing to his hapless accordion.

A week later, Station Chief Wu was treated to an even greater indignity. Just before an important official was due to visit Yak Springs for an inspection tour, the compound was hit by a torrential thunderstorm. Since the artist who'd done the Mao rendering on his loyalty wall had failed to use oil-based paints, Mao's visage began to weep and blur, and by the storm's end the heroic fresco had melted into a mud-streaked rainbow and Station Chief Wu's paean to The Chairman had turned from a hopeful asset into a grave liability. Since no one at the compound had the artistic skills to restore the portrait before the inspection, Station Chief Wu became paralyzed with panic. The next morning, he ordered all inmates to again rally in the parking area before breakfast. Hearing the commotion, yak herders who'd been camping at the caravanserai and the drivers from a Lhasa-bound convoy promptly also drifted over to see what was up. As everyone milled around in front of the ill-fated loyalty wall, Station Chief Wu ordered Superintendent Peng to fasten a stout rope around its base. Next he commandeered a truck from the passing convoy and ordered its unhappy driver to tie the other end of the rope to his rear bumper, start his engine, rev it to high rpms, and then pop the clutch. But when the truck lurched forward, there was a sound like a rifle shot: the rope snapped and whipsawed into the onlookers, knocking over three Goloks.

"Find a thicker rope and pull this turtle egg of a wall down!" screamed Station Chief Wu, ignoring the fallen nomads.

When Superintendent Peng reappeared with a steel cable, Station Chief Wu marshaled the now even less enthusiastic truck driver for another attempt on the stubborn wall. This time when he revved his truck engine and released the clutch, the air was rent by a noise like two railway locomotives colliding head-on. As the dust and exhaust slowly cleared, the disbelieving crowd found that while the loyalty wall was still standing, the rear end of the truck— the back bumper, a piece of the chassis, the differential, the rear axle, and two back wheels—had been parted from the rest of the vehicle as if by means of the imperial form of punishment (五马分尸) by which a living victim's body was pulled apart by five horses. The agitated driver leapt out of his listing truck cab, gaped for a moment at his drawn-and-quartered vehicle, and began cursing. Everyone in the now silent crowd was staring at Station Chief Wu, who was in turn gaping helplessly at the dismembered truck and then at his wall, his errant eye bulging as if at any moment it might explode from its socket like a musket ball. Removing his Mao cap, he clutched his comb-over as though that might help him think his way out of this mess.

"All right, everyone line up again!" he finally ordered, gesturing almost hysterically toward the slack cable. "When I give the order, grab onto this cunt of a cable and pull this stinking wall down!" When no one moved, he screamed hysterically to his factotum, "Old Liu, get these Golok slackers moving!"

In desperation, Eunuch Liu began trying to rally the gawking nomads. But since few spoke Chinese, they just stared at him. However, Little Li thought he saw a hint of merriment in the eyes of several—not just because they were part of some real excitement, but also because they were getting to watch disaster befall a Han Chinese overlord. When everyone had been cajoled back in line along the cable, Station Chief Wu desperately began counting again.

"Ah-one, two, three! Pull! Pull!" he urged his motley chain gang. But they only halfheartedly tugged on the cable. "Yank this fucking wall down!" he shrieked, gesticulating wildly at two Goloks who were only pretending to pull. The tug-of-war team gave one more yank, but the wall didn't even tremble, causing Station Chief Wu to keep casting furtive glances toward the gate, as if he feared the inspection team might pull in at any moment, catch him in a compromised position, and send him off to an even more godforsaken place of exile . . . if such a place existed.

"Pull this stinking wall down—now!" he screamed.

When still nothing happened, Eunuch Liu stepped forward and, standing on tiptoes, whispered something into his master's ear. As Station Chief Wu registered his retainer's advice, a look of relief flooded his face and he gestured to Little Li and Little Liang.

"You two, come here!" he cried out. Hesitantly, the boys left their positions on the cable. "All right, I want you to climb up and fasten a rope to the top of the wall."

Standing on his friend's shoulders, Little Li managed to levitate a noose around the top of the wall, where it would have maximum torque when pulled. Then Superintendent Peng fastened the other end to the cable.

"All right, one, two, three . . . pull!" barked Station Chief Wu once the tug-of-war team was repositioned along the cable. This time, the wall trembled. "Are you fucking dead people?" he bellowed. "Pull harder!" The wall teetered. "Pour on the oil and pull!" he screamed again. Finally his beloved loyalty wall came crashing down.

When the dust cleared and Station Chief Wu came into view once more, he was hunched over the rubble, his body heaving as if he were being racked by seizures. Nobody moved to soothe him until, finally, Eunuch Liu ran over, put an arm tenderly around his waist, and, as if he were guiding a wounded comrade from the battlefield, walked him slowly back to the Administration Building.

The end of Station Chief Wu's ill-fated loyalty wall only made the atmosphere around the Administrative Building more poisonous. Little Li could, of course, walk out the front gate and escape the compound's petty concerns, which he did each day. As severe as it was out on the grasslands, he'd grown to love being alone in the wind and sun with the frieze of snow-clad peaks rimming the distant horizon. Sometimes, when he went out without Little Liang, he brought along his flute. However, when he first opened its case, under the vast blueness of the Tibetan sky, his flute's slender silver barrel and delicate keys nestling in their purple velvet bed seemed so irrevocably from another world that he hardly dared take the joints out and put them together. And when he finally did hold the instrument in his tanned, callused hands and began playing, its thin, tremulous sound was so quickly taken up by the emptiness around him, his flute seemed far too refined a thing for such a rough, remote wilderness. Sometimes as he played he felt he himself might evanesce into nothingness, just like his music. But he slowly became accustomed to the lack of resonance when playing outdoors, and was soon enjoying his musical soliloquies. They helped him remain connected not only to music but to all that he'd left behind.

With each passing day spent on these otherworldly grasslands, Little Li felt a little more as if he were being slowly forged into a different being, almost as if he was being reincarnated, Tibetan Buddhist–fashion. Only when he was lying wrapped in his quilt—one of the few remaining concrete things that still linked him to his Beijing past—did these two disconnected worlds regain any physical connection. One night, as he lay waiting to fall asleep, he recalled how a grade-school history teacher had once shown his class a photograph of the Shroud of Turin in Italy and mocked the Catholic faithful who believed it was imprinted with an image of Christ's face as victims of "feudal superstitions" foisted by members of the "aristocratic Italian ruling classes" on gullible "peasants and workers" to make them forget their grinding class oppression. He'd nonetheless been fascinated by the idea that millennia ago such an ancient shroud might have actually touched the face of Jesus. Just as the recognition that his father, Granny Sun, and even his mother had once lovingly washed and folded his quilt helped link his own past to the present, the idea of such an ancient shroud helped make history seem alive. But just as often he wondered if it was not better just to let the past go. What good did it do anyone to hold on to it? His father's books, music, piano, and garden no longer existed, and even their home might now be gone. Perhaps it was better not to cling to the memory of such things that no longer existed. As he lay beneath his quilt, he felt caught in a riptide that was slowly carrying him farther away from the shores of his own past, out into the uncharted waters of an unknowable future.

9

ROAD TO NOWHERE

"HAVE YOU ever thought about trying to escape from Yak Springs?" Little Li asked Little Liang one night, while they were soaking in the hot springs.

"Escape?" his friend gasped, shocked by the audacity of the question. "It's senseless even to think about such things!" Then, lowering his voice as if he feared that even here someone might be eavesdropping, he added, "Even if we got away from the compound, you know we'd never be able to return home. So where would we go?"

"Maybe we could get across the border to—"

"Are you crazy?" interrupted Little Liang. "We'd never get near a border, much less across it! As soon as Station Chief Wu saw we were missing, he'd file a report, and they'd be after us! And, then when they caught us, let's not even think what they'd do! Yak Springs would seem like paradise compared with where we'd be sent!" They both fell silent.

A neophyte might well imagine that a country as vast, varied, and populous as China would present endless opportunities for fugitives to lose themselves in its overcrowded enormity. But the system of controls set up by the party was so all-embracing that there was virtually no possibility of living outside its confines: to buy food one needed "ration coupons" (粮票); to purchase train tickets or stay in hotels one needed "work unit" (工作单位) "letters of introduction" (介紹信); and everyone was anchored to their pre-scribed places of residence by their "household registration card" (户口本). Chinese society was so well regimented that exiting it was virtually impossible.

"Do you think we'll be here forever?" wondered Little Li.

"Heaven knows!" responded Little Liang. "Maybe you can

arrange for us both to go to America! How about that?" he added facetiously. "You're half American. We'll find your people, go to Hollywood, buy flashy cars, marry beautiful girls with blond hair and big tits!"

"Glad your picture of America is so clear and positive," replied Little Li. He was amused by his friend's jest, but it was also a reminder that part of him was American, even out here in Yak Springs. As he lay in bed that night, he remained so riled up by their talk of escape that he couldn't sleep. Not knowing what else to do, he dressed, stole through the compound, and slipped out the front gate. It was, he thought, ironic that this was one of the few unguarded gates in China. But, then, it was an exit to nowhere. Yak Springs was a bizarre contradiction: absolute freedom and complete confinement.

Able to see no more than the dimmest outline of the gray road stretching away before him in the starlight, he began walking. In Beijing he'd been able to imagine life as having a direction: if he practiced his flute and studied hard, he could expect to become a respectable musician, be assigned a job, get married, and have a child. But life at Yak Springs was lacking both goals and a destination. It was true that his past life had been punctuated by interruptions, unexplained cancellations, and dashed hopes; nonetheless, it had retained a general sense of forward motion and purpose. Now it had been stripped of both and he feared he'd never see Beijing, his father, Granny Sun, or Little Wang again.

It was a moonless night, and in the inky darkness his father appeared in a series of visions that unspooled spontaneously like dreams. He was playing the piano, sitting in stony silence at their kitchen table, and staring in horror at his bloody hands after the Red Guard attack. Oh, those horrible mangled hands that had clasped together for so many prayers and played so much beautiful music! How could such an image ever be forgotten? And did his father still think of him? Did he curse his foolishness for leaving San Francisco? Was he regretful now about having been so different and willful? Did anyone back in Beijing still remember him? Did he, Li Wende, matter to anyone? He felt utterly insignificant.

China had been victim of so much tumult, tragedy, and hurt. Suddenly there'd be an empty chair at a dinner table, a missing place in a bed, clothes left hanging unworn in a wardrobe, or a bicycle gathering dust in an entryway. People disappeared, jobs were canceled, friendships were destroyed, and marriages ended, all without explanation, often without even a farewell. Then, just as suddenly and unexpectedly as they'd vanished, years later people reappeared, but so aged and eroded that sometimes even family members didn't at first recognize them. As he grew older, Little Li had come to realize that he was living in a world of permanent disorder. Chairman Mao had famously proclaimed, "World in great disorder: excellent situation! [天下大乱, 形势大好]." Disorder for him seemed to be an organizing principle. He lived to overturn things. Under his guidance, one moment's infallible "correct line" (正确路线) became the next moment's completely "incorrect line," so that a friend became an enemy and a loving child became an adversary. Those who protested were the first to disappear, while those who accommodated survived. However, even abject collaborators found no permanent refuge, for the party had nothing but contempt for those who faithfully obeyed it. The more obedient a person was, the more reviled he or she became, because the party so despised China's historical powerlessness and subservience that it was repelled by the spectacle of its own people being bullied into submission, even by itself. Those who tried to maintain moral clarity in such a maelstrom of perfidy and opportunism were viewed as quaint, unreliable throwbacks to a "feudal" world that traded in the obsolete currency of personal honor. And because the party no longer gave its minions the option of leaving to study abroad, as Li Tongshu had been able to do under Chiang Kai-shek, there was no exit. The outside world had once served as a last haven for those wishing to opt out of the Chinese whirlwind. Under Mao this exit, too, had been closed.

When he was a child, he had loved to pretend he was blind and then make his way by touch, sound, and smell to the latrine on Big Sheep Wool Alley. Now it was so dark he did not need to close his eyes to have to feel his way along the road with his feet. In Beijing, of course, he'd actually been going someplace, if only to the latrine. Now, forgotten, forsaken, and forlorn, he was going nowhere. Perhaps, he thought, he should just jump off the top of the quarry and be done with his meaningless life. What was he saving himself for, to make more gravel? But to commit suicide here where no one would notice or care seemed more absurd than to go on living! The old man lying on the sidewalk in a pool of blood near Iron Lion Tomb had at least had someone peering in horror from a window upstairs to mourn his loss. But out here, who'd notice a death? With no danger of being overheard, he began crying out to the road as if it were a person, which in a cryptic way it was for him. After all, he'd spent as much time working on it as in any other place in his life.

"I walk on you every day, Road, but you take me nowhere!" he cried out in anguish as if it were a living being. "Will you ever take me someplace? Do I still have a purpose?" He was beginning to wail now. "I curse you, Road, and I curse the revolution that made you! Down with the Chinese Communist Party! Down with the dictatorship of the proletariat, and down with the Cultural Revolution!"

Even in the middle of this dark night, in the desolation of Qinghai, he half expected some higher authority to rain retribution down on him. But when he stopped to listen, all that came back was the sighing of the wind. Emboldened, he allowed even more forbidden sentiments to gush forth. "The party's the enemy of the people! Long live Li Tongshu and American imperialism! Down with the counterrevolutionary revisionists Station Chief Wu Wei and Master Chef Wangbadan!" He bawled these insults out into the void until he'd disgorged every heresy he could summon up. But all of it was just swallowed up by the infinitude of indifference around him, and in the end, he felt so ridiculous that he was overcome by a fit of crazed laughter. Then everything began spinning. Kneeling on the road to stop his dizziness, he clasped his hands above his head and, with the gravel he himself had chipped and transported cutting into his knees, he cried out, "Father! Father! Where are you?"

All he wanted at this moment was to know that someone, somewhere, still cared for him, so that he could entertain some small hope of reunion at some distant time. He felt like running away, but there was no place to run. As Little Liang had reminded him, China was one huge penitentiary, made up of concentric circles of ever smaller and more self-contained prisons, one inside the other ad infinitum, like those nesting matryoshka dolls he'd seen as a child in the Moscow Restaurant at the Beijing Exhibition Center. Lying on a tuft of grass along the roadway, he gazed up into the vault of stars above and felt woefully earthbound. He was not sure how long he lay there. When he did finally get up, a hint of pink was suffusing the sky over the Anymachen Range and he started trudging back to the compound. There, he wrapped himself in his old quilt, fell asleep, and dreamed of Willow Courtyard.

So remote was Yak Springs that no broadband radio signals reached it, and the few newspapers that arrived via truck were the only connection inmates had with the world beyond. Unfortunately, Little Li did not always get a chance to read these papers before they were exfoliated by Eunuch Liu and sent on to their final socialist mission. And keeping up with the news in latrine format was as frustrating as piecing together scattered fragments of classical texts written thousands of years ago on "bamboo scripts" (竹简) left buried in tombs. Just as one began a revelatory paragraph, it would infuriatingly end. But he was stunned, one day in 1972, to read a fragment of a privy article noting that U.S. President Richard Nixon had been to Beijing. Still, he had no idea what this meant. For, from what he could learn from subsequent newspapers, the Cultural Revolution still raged, Mao was still in charge, and the party was still "putting politics in command" (政治挂帅).

One evening, Station Chief Wu made another mealtime appearance, this time to announce that henceforth inmates would be required to remain in the canteen Monday nights after dinner for "political study sessions" (政治学习会). The first topic would be Mao's 1945 warning on the need to engage in constant ideological housecleaning. "As we say, dust will accumulate if a room is not cleaned regularly, and our faces will get dirty if they are not washed regularly," he'd written. "Our comrades' minds and our party's work may also collect dust and also need sweeping and washing."

"All right, who would like to kick off the first of these very important discussions with a comment on our chosen text?" Station Chief Wu began the first session, after Eunuch Liu had done his usual introduction. He was met by dead silence, with everyone trying to avoid making eye contact—which was difficult, given his roaming eyeball. "How should we here in Yak Springs view the idea that 'our faces will get dirty if they are not washed regularly'?" he persevered. Except for Superintendent Peng, who cleared his throat, there were still no responses. "All right," he finally proclaimed with irritation, "it's clear that political consciousness in our unit is extremely low, so, for our next session, we'll assign a text for all comrades to read in advance and write an analysis." Someone groaned.

But there was a problem with this plan, too: there were no written texts available in Yak Springs. Station Chief Wu's remedy was to deputize Eunuch Liu to choose an editorial from an old *People's Daily* and read it out loud to the class. His first choice was entitled "Never Forget Class Struggle."

"All right, now that we've had a chance to absorb this important theoretical analysis, who'd like to summarize it for us?" asked Station Chief Wu, gazing hopefully out over his parish of bored tutees, several of whom had nodded off during the liturgical reading. As far as Little Li could detect, there was no one dreaming about waging class warfare at Yak Springs. When there were no volunteers, he called, in desperation, on Eunuch Liu.

"Well . . ." he began, quickly realizing that despite having the editorial read out loud, he hadn't a thought in his head. "Well . . . I'd like to ask the leadership if I might study the text more closely tonight and give a more complete report tomorrow." There were several snickers.

"Clearly, we need more 'thought work' [思想工作] in our unit," rebuked Station Chief Wu angrily, and summarily concluded the study session.

Several days later, a chalkboard appeared next to the entrance to the canteen, and Station Chief Wu charged Little Liang with providing a short summation of each week's study topic in multicolored chalk. Little Liang was furious at being drawn into such a futile exercise, until he learned that the new assignment would afford him a whole day off from roadwork each week. For the next study session, Station Chief Wu chose a turgid editorial on the dangers of "taking the capitalist road" and ordered all inmates to write a paragraph of analysis.

"What the fuck am I supposed to write?" cursed Little Liang. "There is no one here in the compound actually 'taking the capitalist road,' because there's no capital and no such road to be taken! Then there's the inconvenient fact that, with the exception of the Goloks and truck drivers, virtually every inmate here was involuntarily born into a bad 'class category' and is still paying for it!"

"Maybe that's what you should write: 'The broad masses at Yak Springs will never forget class struggle, because class struggle is what got us all exiled here,' " replied Little Li, laughing.

It was not long before no one paid any mind to the chalkboard or their study sessions. Indeed, soon even Station Chief Wu lost interest and sent Little Liang back to the quarry. However, he underwent an alchemical change upon receiving word that a provincial military official would soon pass through Yak Springs. At this, he summoned Little Liang to his office and ordered him to revive the lapsed chalkboard and inscribe it with Mao's famous appraisal of American military might: "All reactionaries are paper tigers." So anxious did he become over the pending visit that he made Little Liang rewrite the slogan three times.

Then, one morning, inmates arrived in the canteen for breakfast to find that someone had etched the chalkboard with the bright-red outline of a giant erection and dangling scrotum emblazoned with the English letters "USA," so it looked as if an American guided missile were about to score a direct hit on Mao's slogan. Every time a person entered the canteen and saw the chalkboard, a new burst of snickering rippled through the room. However, when Master Chef Wang spotted the outrage, he made a beeline for Station Chief Wu's office. Moments later, his door flew open, and he stormed into the canteen. After studying the offending drawing for a moment, Station Chief Wu glowered at the breakfasting inmates as if they were all collectively responsible, ripped the chalkboard from the wall, stomped its gray slate into shards on the floor and then commanded all inmates to muster in the parking area. One by one he called on each to step forward, thrust his right fist into the air, and deny any complicity in this dastardly act. Little Li feared his American parentage would automatically turn suspicion on him, and was greatly relieved when, before his turn came around, Eunuch Liu appeared and announced that a truck driver who'd just departed was under suspicion. But as inmates walked back to the canteen, Little Liang winked.

"No truck driver could ever draw a dick that beautiful," he whispered to his friend.

When the military official's trip was canceled, the chalkboard and what came to be referred to as "the Big Incident" (大事件) were soon forgotten.

Although chipping gravel was hardly his ideal of "service to the people," by now Little Li had become so deft at this primitive craft that he could almost work with his eyes closed. Gravel was the life's blood of the highway, and after every piece was laboriously hand-produced by the boys, it had to be carried by basket and carrying pole to wherever it was needed to grade the roadbed or fill potholes. But Little Li had come to experience the admittedly tedious, repetitive nature of their work as strangely satisfying. With gravel, you knew exactly where you stood: how long you'd worked and how much you'd produced. To handle gravel was to know the tyranny of weight, but at least your achievements were measurable and incontrovertible. There was no arguing with a ton of gravel. Nor could any political challenge refute the fact that the stretch of road assigned to the care of the two boys was without potholes.

When Liang Shan was precipitously taken off road duty by Superintendent Peng and assigned to the truckers' camp across the highway to manage passing convoys, he welcomed the lighter assignment. It was only when, several weeks later, he was also ordered to vacate the living space he'd fashioned in the old barracks and move into a dilapidated sod hut next to the truck parking area that the full logic of his reassignment became apparent.

"That turtle egg is stealing my place!" he ranted. "So much for serving the people! But before I walk out the door the last time, I'm going to—"

"Be careful!" interrupted Little Li, worried by such unrestrained wrath. The next morning, when the compound witnessed an unprecedented act of defiance, his concern proved justified. As Superintendent Peng was just gulping down a mouthful of noodles, Little Liang marched to his table.

"You may be a superintendent, but you're also a useless piece of counterrevolutionary yak shit who steals the people's property!" he announced in a voice loud enough for everyone in the canteen to hear. With dripping noodles still hanging out of his mouth, Superintendent Peng looked up at his accuser and blinked. Then, after seeming to swallow, he stood up and began wagging a threatening forefinger in Little Liang's face.

"With this kind of hoodlum attitude [流氓态度], you're headed for big trouble!" he managed before beginning to snort and gasp like a drowning man. Then, as his face turned radish red, he keeled over onto the floor. Springing from his wok, Master Chef Wang flipped the fallen superintendent onto his back and was pounding on his chest with his big greasy hands when a tangle of half-chewed noodles exploded from his mouth and landed at the feet of Little Liang, who kicked it back onto his tormentor.

"What the fuck's going on here?" yelled Station Chief Wu, running into the canteen from his office to see what all the commotion was about, only to find his road superintendent on the floor coughing violently with noodles emerging from one nostril.

Then, Superintendent Peng suddenly sat up and frantically began trying to extract the offending noodles from his nose. But each time he pulled, he succeeded only in breaking off a short section. Little Liang, who'd been glowering at the indisposed superintendent, now turned his wrath on Station Chief Wu.

"You call yourself a leader?" he snarled, looking directly at the dumbstruck station chief, whose errant eye had begun swiveling madly out of control. "You allow this gangster to steal a young person's things and you do nothing? You're just as much an embarrassment to Chairman Mao's revolution as this dog dick, Peng! It's no small wonder they shipped you both out here to Shitville!" With that, he turned and stormed out of the canteen, leaving Superintendent Peng still trying to extract noodles from his nose and Station Chief Wu smoldering with rage.

As Little Li worked on the road alone that day, he replayed the unlikely scene he'd just witnessed over and over again in his head, each time enjoying it more. There were so many petty tyrants ruling over so many intimidated people that almost everyone entertained fantasies of such rebellion. But whenever authority was challenged and face was lost, even here at the edge of the world, retaliation brooked neither delay nor appeal. Liang Shan had snapped, a not uncommon end in China, where so many indignities were heaped on people's heads that they were finally reduced to such a state of subsurvience they no longer cared what happened. He was sure that such unbridled anger would be his friend's undoing, just as it had been for all those other righteous rebels he'd read about in school—the Boxers, Taipings, White Lotus, Red Turbans—who'd revolted and been crushed, their leaders beheaded. Rebellion was the Chinese people's only remedy for injustice. Indeed, it was out of this very tradition that Mao's own communist revolution had been born.

As soon as Little Li got back to the compound that evening, he went in search of Little Liang, but he was nowhere to be found. Hurrying back across the road to Station Chief Wu's office, he rapped on the door.

"Enter," came the familiar voice from within.

"What happened to Liang Shan?" he asked, his voice trembling.

"Gone!"

"Gone?"

"Reassigned."

"Reassigned where?"

"Not your business."

"When did he go?"

"This morning."

Being nearly the same age and having worked and lived together for so long, he and Little Liang had become inseparable. But now he'd vanished, just like everyone else of importance in his life and he was devastated. From here on, Little Li's only companion would be solitude. On his way to the quarry the next morning, he lay down in the grass beside the road and gazed up at the hawks, eagles, and lammergeiers soaring in lazy, effortless circles overhead. They were able to fly wherever they wished, yet chose to stay here, hovering almost motionless in the sky.

In the weeks that followed, Little Li often left his roadwork to wander alone in the foothills. Here, where there was no one to "seal mouths and knot tongues (缄口结舌)," all fear of being watched, criticized, and censured lifted like a fever breaking. The thought that this landscape had for millennia remained as unchanged as the constellations of stars and planets that blinked down on Yak Springs at night was comforting. As he trekked up the foothills toward celestial peaks beyond, he felt as if he was ascending a heavenly staircase where the feckless world from which he'd been expelled was in abeyance. Enthralled, he watched as squalls gathered in the mountains, then swept down over the hills to weep great curtains of gray rain onto the grasslands. As suddenly as they came, they moved on, leaving a great blue sky filled with puffy white clouds washed clean as new-fallen snow. Maybe, he thought, this is what his mother's inscription on the back of the photo of her with his father in front of the Golden Gate Bridge had meant. He'd never been able to figure out how hills could deliver help or where the words *"I will lift up mine eyes unto the hills, from whence cometh my help"* had come from. Now he thought he understood something of their import, for these foothills and mountains did radiate a sublime sense of beauty and peace. So, henceforth, just as Tibetans incanted *"Om mani padme om,"* "The jewel in the lotus," over and over as their mantra, he recited this as his.

Out of loneliness, he often talked to himself as he roamed. Sometimes he spoke to his father, even to God, although he was not sure who God was. But, while stalking blue bharal sheep and Mongolian gazelles just to watch how they moved, he felt the presence of something ineffable. One day, he chanced upon a snow leopard soaking up the warmth of the afternoon sun on a rocky outcrop as it groomed its milky, spotted fur with its pink tongue. Crouching behind a boulder, he watched until it arched its tawny back and effortlessly padded away. He was about to move on himself when, out of the corner of one eye, he saw something else move as a snow-leopard cub bounded ebulliently after its mother. Only when the spell the animals had cast was broken did he finally leave.

When the snows came, the landscape vanished into such a blur of white that even one's own hands held out at arm's length sometimes became invisible. The day his first really big blizzard hit, Little Li had been alone at the quarry, and snow began falling so fast he hadn't gotten halfway back to the compound before the road vanished beneath his feet. Sometimes storms were so intense that no one was able to go outside for days. He found such snow days unbearable. With nothing to do, inmates gathered in the canteen, around the stove, to play Go and cards, smoke, and vie for the few books available, each ripped into numbered segments so that several people could simultaneously read one book. Trapped in the canteen's sublime ugliness, Little Li felt all the more as if his life was an old boxcar that had been run off onto a siding and forgotten. By the time a big storm abated, he was always pining to get out again. But often the sun was so dazzlingly intense on the fresh, white, fluffy snow, like sifted flour on the valley floor, that anyone venturing outside had to don goggles to avoid blindness.

The only reliable way to mark the passage of years at Yak Springs was by the seasons. Little Li always felt immense relief when spring finally approached, the snows melted, and the monsoon rains began reawakening the drab, duff-colored grasslands. He was astounded by how something so seemingly lifeless so quickly became reborn. The land around Beijing had been so exhausted by so many millennia of abuse that nature seemed to have all but lost its will to keep up its normal seasonal cycles. Here, however, was nature untrammeled, marching proudly and confidently through its paces. And spring was an ecstasy of renewal. First the grasslands turned an iridescent green. Then they erupted into rainbows of brilliantly colored wildflowers with successive waves of blossoms springing from the once frozen earth as if fed by subterranean springs of color. A carpet of yellow poppylike blossoms was followed by a blanket of deep purple in luxuriant grapelike bunches, then a sea of delicate pink. To gaze at the promiscuous palette of yellows, reds, purples, whites, and pinks that carpeted the valley floor was like seeing a beam of intense light refracted through a prism. He couldn't help thinking how much his father would have loved these upwellings of spontaneous blooming, which required no human ministration because they had not yet suffered any human disruption.

Walking to the quarry as the valley was being reborn, it was reassuring to know that here, at least, there were still cycles of nature undisturbed by human intrusion. The grasslands were a reminder of the stubborn will to life that exists in all living things, and its beauty made Little Li glad to be alive. It also left him pining to share it all with someone else. This was the same feeling he'd experienced when hearing a beautiful piece of music: he immediately wanted to tell someone and share it.

As he roamed these foothills, he often fantasized that a beautiful young woman would magically appear and be so overcome by the lonely beauty around them that she would just fall into his arms. Alas, such fantasies were as manifestly preposterous as hopes of escaping to America. Nonetheless, he could not resist them. Lacking any contact with members of the opposite sex, would he be denied the chance to know, perhaps even love, a woman? For him, women were still only exotic figments of his fevered imagination, barely imaginable as flesh-and-blood creatures, much less as partners in the kinds of intimate acts in which couples were alleged to engage.

Thinking about all the ragged lacunae being created in his life by exile left Little Li filled with a consternation so deep it often bordered on panic whose only antidote was to extract whatever pleasure he could from the austere beauty of the terrain around him. And sometimes these strangely beautiful hills and majestic mountains did seem almost alive. Did not the Goloks believe such peaks, passes, lakes, and caves were the abodes of powerful living spirits?

One afternoon, as he reached the top of a pass at almost three thousand meters, he sat down beside a mani wall, built from thousands of pieces of slate laboriously inscribed with Buddhist prayers stacked one on top of another. Gazing out at the snowcapped grandeur of Anymachen, he recalled the Tang Dynasty poem his father had made him memorize when he was a boy, "Lu Mountain" by Li Bai (李白).

Let me reach those Sublime Hills
Where peace comes to the quiet heart.
No more need to find the magic cup.
I'll wash the dust, there, from my face,
And live in those regions that I love,
Separated from the Human World.

In the canteen at breakfast one morning, Eunuch Liu unexpectedly trotted over to announce, "You are wanted in Station Chief Wu's office."

Little Li's knock was answered by a grunt. As he stepped into the penumbra of smoke inside, Station Chief Wu did not at first even acknowledge his presence. Only after several minutes had passed did he rise from his chair and, with a look of distaste, push a brown envelope inscribed with red characters across his desktop.

"A letter," he said with disapprobation, as if receiving mail were a counterrevolutionary offense.

"Thank you," replied Little Li as he took the letter. It was addressed in a spidery, childlike scrawl and came from the Pingyuan May 7 Cadre School in Henan Province. Hurrying out of the

Administration Building, he sat down on the stoop and with trembling hands opened the envelope.

> *My dear son:*
>   *Our good doctor friend managed to learn your whereabouts and sent me this address. I sincerely hope this letter reaches you. I am sure you've had much anxiety about my whereabouts and well-being. Just know that I am all right, as I hope you are. Know also that each day I think of you and of that moment when we may see each other again.*
>   *Until then, I remain,*
>   *Your father*

As if someone had suddenly thrown an electrical switch, Little Li felt his father's presence again. Learning, at last, that he was "all right," whatever that meant, not only came as a relief, but allowed the future to come to life again. The thought that there was still someone out there, after all, who was waiting for him triggered waves of feeling. Little Li still missed home, but so much scar tissue had formed over the wounds left by all the forced separations that they had begun to throb with less intensity. And although he had not wished it, as he'd drifted ever farther away from the shores of Beijing, his father, too, had become more of an abstraction than an actual human parent. But this letter ripped the scab off his old wound, and as he sat down to write a reply, the torrent of memories and feelings that rushed in left him so dizzy he hardly knew what he was writing:

> *Dear Father:*
>   *I was so glad to receive your letter, to at last learn where you are, and that you are all right.*
>   *Please know that I, too, am fine, out here in Qinghai. I will write soon again and tell you more after I've had a chance to collect my thoughts. For now I simply wanted to let you know that your letter reached me and that there is no reason to worry on my account.*
>   *Your son*

When Little Li's letter arrived at his *School* in the mountains of western Henan Province, Li Tongshu, too, experienced an initial sense of relief that was profound. But as he held the letter in one trembling hand he was assaulted by waves of emotion that left him feeling both indissolubly linked to and irrevocably severed from both his son, and the complexity of his own past and his Californian wife.

PART TWO

10

TO BUILD "A NEW CHINA"

WHEN HE'D walked out onstage for his graduation recital at the San Francisco Conservatory of Music in 1949, Li Tongshu had been one of the first Chinese to study there. He'd also been the very first to concentrate on the keyboard music of J. S. Bach, a composer far less popular in China than others like Mozart, Beethoven, and Chopin. Moreover, Li had chosen to play sections of the *Goldberg Variations*, a work of great abstraction and complexity that Bach had described as "written for music lovers." When he'd first heard Wanda Landowska's 1945 recording of the work on the harpsichord, he'd fallen in love with it. The opening aria and thirty subsequent variations—one variation a delicate filigree of cheerfulness, the next replete with wistfulness, the third brimming with brash forcefulness—gave him entrance to a whole musical universe. He loved how the *Variations* were at once grand and serene, humorous and serious, how the hands crossed and chased each other up and down the keyboard like animals at play.

As he sat down at the Steinway grand onstage, he was comforted to see his friend Dr. Song Shaoming (宋劭明) smiling in the front row. He'd been studying medicine at the University of California, San Francisco (UCSF) Medical Center, and they'd met through the Chinese Overseas Students' Association to become such good friends they decided to rent an apartment together. But as soon as Li Tongshu began playing that evening, he lost all awareness of both his friend and the rest of the audience; when the last notes of the restated aria finally faded away and applause began, he felt as if he were awakening from an intense dream.

Several weeks later, he was standing on the balcony of their Willard Street apartment, watching an evening fog roll in under the Golden Gate Bridge, when there was a knock on their door.

It was a Western Union messenger with a telegram from China. Upon opening it, Li Tongshu was stunned to find an invitation "to return home and help build a new China" by joining the faculty at the new Central Conservatory of Music just then being organized in Beijing under the patronage of China's Premier Zhou Enlai. Li had come to love San Francisco while living there, but understood how difficult it would be for an immigrant, especially an Asian, to find his way as a professional musician in America. And now that Chiang Kai-shek's Nationalist forces had been vanquished by Mao Zedong's Red Army, maybe after more than a century of foreign occupation, disunity, revolution, world war, and civil strife, the "sick man of East Asia" (东亚病夫) was, at last, on the threshold of recovery. And so, as he read the telegram, he felt an unexpected rush of homesickness and patriotism. National regeneration was a beguiling hope, especially for a people who'd been stripped of the ability to dream of greatness for more than a century.

Li Tongshu was then twenty-six years old and already engaged to Vivian Knight, a twenty-two-year-old violin student whose father, Rev. Josiah Knight, had been an Episcopalian missionary to Shanghai. Eager to dedicate his life to Christian service in Asia, he'd been inspired by an article in the English-language *Chinese Recorder and Missionary Journal* proclaiming China a nation that had "contributed to world civilization her quota of truth which her ancient sages and heroes discovered." But, continued the president of Trinity College in Fujian, Lin Pu-chi, of China: "In no era of her prolonged history did she need, nay hunger for, more truth than she does at present." China, he wrote, "craves for new, practical truths in relation to every phase of her national existence. In the arts, in science, in government, and in all civic problems, she craves for the right principles." Reverend Knight answered this call.

The 1920s and '30s were a time when Chinese had turned hopefully to the West for models of how to reform their country into a modern, prosperous, and democratic nation, and Josiah Knight believed that, just as the Chinese craved "the right principles" and the love of God, they also yearned for the truth of the "shining city on a hill," as John Winthrop had proclaimed the Massachusetts Bay Colony and its experiment in democracy. So, with a single suitcase and his Bible, he set out in 1923 for Shanghai, dedicated to leading more Chinese to Christ and liberty. It was while singing in the Saint Peter's Church choir in the port city's International Settlement that he met his future wife. Bai Wei, a young Chinese who'd studied at the missionary-run McTyeire High School for Girls—attended by the famous sisters Song Meiling and Song Qingling, who'd ended up as wives to Chiang Kai-shek and Sun Yat-sen—went on to study at Saint John's University, which was then attracting some of the brightest, most ambitious students in China. A year later, Josiah Knight surprised the Shanghai Anglican community, in which interracial marriages were still few, by betrothing Bai Wei. In 1928 she gave birth to Vivian Knight.

When she turned nine, in 1937, the year Japan began its long occupation of China, the Knight family left for San Francisco, where because of her interest in music and talent as a violinist, she was admitted to the San Francisco Conservatory of Music.

Li Tongshu, whom she met in a harmony class, was tall and handsome. He wore his hair parted down the center, in the manner favored by Westernized Chinese intellectuals and artists of the day, and had just arrived from Beijing to study keyboard and Vivian fell in love with him at first sight. She admired his air of quiet sovereignty, especially when he sat down at the piano. Even when performing, he seemed to play only for himself. And when, in conversation, he often did little more than nod his head, she concluded that this distrust of words was what enabled him to express himself so eloquently through music.

When they got married, their best man was Dr. Song Shaoming, who was just finishing his internship in surgical oncology at UCSF and had accepted an invitation from Peking Union Medical College Hospital to serve his residency in Beijing. So, when Li Tongshu received his invitation, the two friends felt destiny was uniting them. However, Li Tongshu was less certain about returning home, and devoured every bit of news coming out of their homeland as he tried to make up his mind. He was wary of Mao's disrespect for religion, but didn't want to challenge his friend, because he knew that, while attending Shandong University in Jinan, Song had joined a communist youth group out of sympathy for the plight of the common man.

"I understand your desire to be optimistic, but who can say what Mao will come to?" Li Tongshu cautioned. "I'm a Christian and a classical musician, and communism makes me very. . . Well, I've never liked the idea of one party running everything. Look at Stalin, Tojo, Hitler, and Mussolini. I prefer Bach: with him all voices are free to contend equally." He laughed.

"You treat your bloody music as if it was a living creature," replied his friend. "I'm trying to save physical bodies, not souls." This time they both laughed.

"So—you've really decided. You'll go back?" asked Li Tongshu.

"Yes, and I hope we'll go together."

"I've grown pretty fond of life here," mused Li Tongshu. "I mean, look out the window! Here everything's so open, we can think and breathe freely."

"But this isn't our home, Tongshu." A hint of stridency entered his friend's voice. "After all, we're Chinese, not Americans."

"True, but at heart, Shaoming, I'm sometimes unsure what I am. As Lu Xun wrote, maybe I'm just 'something stuck in-between' [中间物]."

"You're a cultural mongrel, all right," said Dr. Song, chuckling. "But wouldn't you like to know more about what's going on back home now that China's on the edge of such a big change? Several friends have written saying that, with Chiang Kai-shek's corrupt government finally gone, they're filled with optimism. And just yesterday I came across an article quoting an essay by Mao Zedong himself in which he claims that 'all of China is seething with enthusiasm'! Maybe it's propaganda, but for a change it's nice to read something positive about our hapless land."

"Perhaps so, but I'm not sure Mao's bunch will ever appreciate the likes of me," Li Tongshu said, trying to be tactful, because he knew his friend's hopes grew out of a long-thwarted desire to see their battered country whole, healthy, and self-reliant again, a sentiment shared by almost every patriotic Chinese.

"Well, have a look and tell me what you think, anyway." Song handed Li the essay.

"Honestly, what impresses me," responded Li Tongshu after scanning it, "is where Mao insists that some Chinese intellectuals still harbor 'illusions about the United States', and are easily seduced by the 'honeyed words' of Western leaders, and 'still want to wait and see' before choosing sides. He even writes that there's a 'wide gap between these people and ourselves.' I mean, he's talking about us, Shaoming!" He pointed to his chest with both index fingers.

"I understand, Tongshu. Maybe our different views come from being in different fields. Yours centers on self-expression, mine on caring for others. I might be able to make a real contribution in medical care."

"God knows our poor old misbegotten country does need some kind of a revolution, but I'm not sure a person like me will ever fit into Mao's version of it. Still, I'll admit to feeling honored to be invited back. A big piece of me would like to be a part of whatever is coming together there."

When he raised the question of returning with Vivian, her reaction surprised him.

"Don't forget, Tongshu," she replied, "I, too, was both born there and am half Chinese. So there's more than a little of China imprinted on my genes; there must be something about one's country of birth that's inescapable. But . . ." She hesitated. "If we did go back, we should keep our eyes wide open. After all, China is having a revolution, and as Mao himself put it, 'A revolution is not a dinner party—"

"Yes, yes!" he interrupted. "I know the quote, too: and he says a revolution is not 'writing an essay, or painting a picture, or doing embroidery—"

"So, let's not be naïve, especially about religion," she interrupted.

"That's what I keep telling Shaoming. But there's something about the idea of a Chinese rejuvenation that excites him . . . and me, too."

"Perhaps it's my missionary family background speaking, but without hope any landscape becomes bleak!"

Still, despite Song Shaoming's endless urging, the couple held off deciding. What finally helped them make up their minds was the growing number of well-known Chinese writers, diplomats, musicians, scientists, and artists living and studying abroad who were deciding to return to help "build a new China."

"Did you see that both Mao Dun [茅盾] and Lao She [老舍] are going back?" Song Shaoming excitedly announced one morning at breakfast. Mao Dun was a world-renowned novelist who'd been living in Hong Kong, while Lao She was a prize-winning writer of stories about old Beijing who'd been residing in New York.

"And I heard that Huang Feili [黄飞立] and Zhou Xiaoyan [周小燕] have announced that they're returning to Shanghai, too," added Li Tongshu. Huang was a young conductor studying with Paul Hindemith at Yale University while Zhou was China's best-known young Western opera singer, who had been studying in Paris. "How can so many accomplished, well-known people be wrong?" he wondered.

It was not until the French-educated violinist Ma Sicong (马思聪), the founding president of the new Central Conservatory of Music, and himself a returnee, sent a follow-up telegram urging him not to miss "this chance to join the new faculty" that Li Tongshu and Vivian finally made their decision. And so in March 1950 they boarded the SS *President Hayes* with Song Shaoming in San Francisco, bound for Hong Kong. However, because the British government there viewed them as "probable communists," they were not allowed to disembark in the colony. Instead, they were offloaded onto a small Chinese steamer in Hong Kong Harbor and taken directly up the Pearl River to Canton. As they headed north by rail through the war-ravaged landscape, Li Tongshu saw signs of Mao and his new government everywhere. Portraits of him hung in every train station, quotations from his work were scrawled on walls and chimneys, and revolutionary anthems about his leadership blared in every train car; Li Tongshu couldn't help wondering if they'd made the right decision. Nonetheless, upon finally reaching Beijing, he felt a rush of sentimental affection for this city in which he'd grown up, especially when they were welcomed as "patriotic intellectuals" (爱国知识分子) by the new government and assigned to live in one of the many traditional courtyard houses that were honeycombed by Beijing's network of alleyways (胡同). Number 14 Big Sheep Wool Alley (大羊毛胡同) in the East City District had been the residence of Granny Sun's husband's family for generations. Because of the weeping willows that shaded its gardens and cascaded over its brick walls, it had come to be known as Willow Courtyard. But, when Mao's new government swept into power and nationalized all private property, it was confiscated and divided up, with each room being assigned to a separate tenant. When Li Tongshu's upright piano finally arrived from San Francisco, and their new home became filled with music; it helped create an aura of cosmopolitanism around the young couple that drew many of the most promising young musicians at the Conservatory into their circle.

"Are you glad you're back?" Vivian asked as they sat on the veranda one evening, watching swallows loop through the air.

"Yes," he replied, but with a hesitation that worried her. "Everything is familiar, but also changed. I'm just glad you're here with me."

In fact, Li Tongshu found Beijing so changed by Mao's new "people's government" that the city often felt quite alien. What's more, he had to be away from home several days a week, because the Conservatory was temporarily located in Tianjin while its new campus was being finished in Beijing. He found his students talented and eager, but their grasp of the interior meaning of Western musical works was primitive. Easily touched by Schubert, Beethoven, and Romantic composers, most of them were nonplussed when it came to Bach. Of course, given the years of privation most had endured while moving from city to city during World War II and the Civil War, Li Tongshu found it hardly surprising.

Even as almost everyone talked nonstop about "national reconstruction," the immediate physical world around them was falling apart. Because all property was now owned collectively, or by "the people," upkeep was at once everyone's and no one's responsibility. The Municipal Housing Administration supposedly managed Willow Courtyard and collected small rents from each tenant, but they were nominal, and afforded no reserve for upkeep. And since the tenants themselves were rarely able to agree on acceptable divisions of labor, much less cost sharing, when collectively used things wore out or broke down they usually went unrepaired. It was not long before Willow Courtyard's once-elegant gardens had withered, its willow trees ran wild, and the rock pond that was once covered with lily pads and alive with brightly colored goldfish became a fetid sump fed only by the rusting outdoor tap from which residents drew their household water.

"Perhaps we should fix up our own place a little," Vivian proposed. Li Tongshu did not reply, because he knew that, if they improved their room while everything else fell further into disrepair, they would be viewed as harboring a "bourgeois mentality." So, as Willow Courtyard's previously imposing vermilion posts and lintels flaked and peeled, as its clay roof tiles cracked, and its

brick walls sprouted weeds, with no one to whom one could complain, they were left to look on helplessly. Vivian could not prevent
herself from comparing Beijing to San Francisco, a city in a process
of constant expansion and renewal. Aware of his wife's growing
sense of disappointment, Li Tongshu urged her to take heart from
the fact that beggars were gone from the streets and houses of ill-
repute closed.

"At least they're trying to build a new China," he said.

"Indeed, they are," she replied sardonically, "all undertaken
with the assistance of our new 'Soviet big brother' [苏联老大哥],
Joseph Stalin."

As Mao Zedong had himself bluntly put it: "We belong to the
side of the anti-imperialist front headed by the Soviet Union, and
so we can turn only to this side for genuine and friendly assistance,
not the side of the imperialist front." And when, that fall, the Chinese People's Liberation Army unexpectedly crossed the Yalu River
to clash with U.S. and UN forces in Korea and no slogan was more
popular than "North Korea's Friends Are Our Friends; North
Korea's Enemies Are Our Enemies," Li Tongshu could not sleep
for nights. As far as Mao was now concerned, "Sitting on the fence
will not do." Instead, he insisted, China had "to choose between
the alternatives of either killing the tiger or being eaten by it."
Recalling with regret Mao's essay about intellectuals and artists
stubbornly maintaining "illusions about the United States," which
he'd read in San Francisco, Li Tongshu felt increasingly regretful of
his decision to come home. Then, one morning, he was summoned
by the Conservatory party secretary (党委书记) for a "chat" (谈话).

"Comrade Li, we are so honored that a musician of your stature felt the patriotic call to come home and help rebuild our new
socialist people's republic," he began, after lowering himself into
one of the thronelike upholstered chairs adorned with lace antimacassars that he had arrayed in that unique regimental U-shape
favored as office décor by ranking party cadres.

"My wife and I are pleased to make whatever contribution we
can," responded Li Tongshu.

"Indeed! Indeed!" muttered the secretary dismissively. "And we
welcome all patriotic fellow countrymen home to join our struggle.
However . . ." Here he paused for a moment, and pursed his lips
together. "To rectify any incorrect tendencies in ideological view-

point that might have been picked up while living overseas, our party has set up a program of special study that will—"

"Does that include me?" interrupted Li Tongshu, offended by the insinuation that he might harbor "incorrect tendencies in ideological viewpoint."

"Oh, let's not misunderstand anything here," the secretary hastened to add with synthetic good cheer. "These special study sessions are really a gift to you from the party, designed for your own good! All 'returned intellectuals' are being given this opportunity to improve their ideological understanding, so they can make even greater contributions to the Chinese revolution." His face fixed itself in a self-satisfied grin.

"Have returnees been adjudged to be spreading incorrect ideological thinking?"

"Oh, no, no!" interjected the secretary, waving away the idea as if it were an unpleasant smell. "I assure you these study sessions are not punishment. No, no! Not at all! They are completely for your own benefit!"

"And what will they entail?" pressed Li Tongshu anxiously.

"Well, yes, they will take a few months of your time, but they will also give you a chance to better understand our party's new political line and develop a keener awareness of your own class stance. And, of course, they will present you with an incomparable opportunity to examine past mistakes and shortcomings in your own work and prepare a 'self-criticism' [自我批评], even to write a short 'autobiography' using Marxist-Leninist theory to analyze your bourgeois class background. This will assist you in reforming your thinking so it will be more in line with the broad masses of the people, and—"

"What is wrong with my thinking as it is?" challenged Li Tongshu, though he immediately realized his tone was too belligerent.

"Oh, I think you understand quite well," answered the secretary with a sudden coolness. "It's sometimes necessary to make a clear break with the past."

"And what does all this have to do with music?"

"Of course, music's important," he responded, regaining only some of his earlier insincere good cheer. "And, yes, everyone can appreciate music, enjoy your Bachs, Mozarts, Beethovens, and . . ."

Here he stopped, as if he'd suddenly come to the end of the list of Western composers he was immediately willing to recall. "But, having been educated in America, perhaps you have not yet fully had a chance to analyze how all art and culture have class origins. And Chairman Mao teaches us that, before we can remake a new China, we must first remake ourselves. Is that not true?" He opened his palms up, as if the point was too obvious to be disputed. "And because comrades with spouses from other lands may have developed different ways of looking at things, well . . . it's quite natural to guard vigilantly against incorrect tendencies, especially now that the U.S. imperialists are fighting Chinese volunteers in Korea."

When he arrived back at Willow Courtyard, Vivian instantly sensed that something was wrong. "What is it?" she asked.

"Sit with me, Vivian," he said softly, walking to the piano.

"Of course," she replied, fearful of pushing him to express himself before he'd worked out his real feelings at the piano. As they sat down, he began one of his favorite harmonizations of the chorale *Jesu meine Freude, Jesus My Joy,* playing slowly and deliberately, emphasizing each voice moving against the others as the base line propelled the whole piece forward like a beating heart. And when he came to the final resolving chord, he was so reluctant to let it go, he held the pedal down until its last reverberations died away on their own. What he loved about these short, seemingly simple, but actually profound musical meditations was their order and brevity, the way Bach kept them obedient to his laws of harmony even as he allowed them to be so inventive. Each of the four individual voices had its own integrity, yet they still formed a perfect unity. Playing these chorales gave him momentary admission into a world that still had coherence. If only human beings could be so perfect.

"Vivian, do you know what Haydn said about Bach?" he asked, turning to her even as his fingers still hovered over the keyboard.

"No, I don't."

"He said, 'Johann Sebastian Bach is at the center of the sun and hence the man from whom all true music has proceeded.'" A flicker of a smile lit up his face. "The more I play any piece of his, the more I love it. They never wear out." As he began playing again, she put her head on his shoulder. As a violinist, she, too, loved Bach, especially the suites and sonatas for violin and piano. But she stood in awe of her husband's mystical connection to this music; in a way she couldn't explain, she believed his love of Bach was what also enabled him to love her. But his troubled expression now filled her with disquiet.

"You're worried, aren't you?" she said after he finished the last bar.

"I am. The party secretary summoned me today for a lecture on ideology."

"What did he say?"

"It wasn't what he said, but what he implied—namely, that because I studied abroad, you are American, and we are Christians, we are thrice tainted."

"I'm not sure what else we can do except hope and pray," she replied somberly. "My father loved the Serenity Prayer and I find myself depending on it now, too."

"How does it go?"

" 'God, grant me the serenity to accept the things I cannot change; the courage to change the things I can; and the wisdom to know the difference.' " He sighed. "You know, most of the foreign churches now have had to close or join the so-called Triple Independence Patriotic Movement," she continued. "They're being pressured to adopt all kinds of lingo about becoming 'self-governing, self-supporting, and self-propagating,' and to cut off all ties with overseas church organizations. Clergy are being ordered to give 'patriotic' sermons, and even hymns are being rewritten." She began singing:

Chinese Christians, love your country:
Increase production;
Do your best to support the Korean front,
For country, for the Lord's church;
Quickly donate weapons of war to defeat the American
*   wolves.*

"Before we get too worried, Vivian, let's wait and see what happens. Maybe, once the government gets more established, they'll relax." She nodded, but he could tell she was unconvinced.

In the months that followed, Mao's efforts to politically remake China accelerated. First came a call to "resolutely destroy the old society" (坚决打倒旧社会) and a growing number of urban intellectuals were labeled "counterrevolutionary elements" (反革命分子).

At the same time from the countryside came whisperings of extensive land expropriations and "people's tribunals" carrying out executions of rural "big landlords" (大地主). So, when they were summoned to an official convocation, Li Tongshu and Vivian were surprised. The fact that the meeting was being held in the Hall of Remembered Benevolence (怀仁堂) inside the elite South and Central Lakes Compound (中南海)—the cloistered preserve from which imperial families had ruled China since the Ming Dynasty moved to Beijing in 1421, and into which Mao had chosen to move his new "people's government"—would include hundreds of the most prominent members of Beijing's intelligentsia, and would be hosted by Premier Zhou Enlai (who'd spent several years in France and was considered the most sophisticated of China's new peasant leaders) suggested the importance the party imputed to it.

"For a communist, he certainly is debonair," whispered Vivian when finally Zhou swept onstage to a round of applause.

"He looks to the podium born," Li Tongshu whispered back.

Indeed, with his elegantly tailored gray Mao suit and perfectly groomed hair, Zhou was suave and impressive. But Li Tongshu also found him a bit too polished. And it did not take long for him to get to his real point: Western-trained intellectuals and artists needed to purge themselves of "mistaken thinking of the bourgeois class" and adopt what he called "the correct stand, viewpoint, and methods of the working class" and create a culture that "is nationalist in form but socialist in content" and always "proletarian in nature." As they left the hall, Li Tongshu felt foolish for having clapped so ardently at the outset.

"We were summoned for a warning to ready ourselves for a brotherhood of socialist culture controlled by the state," she said somberly as they walked home.

"We have no choice but to wait and see," he said, not knowing how else to reply.

"Wait for what?" she countered glumly. "He's telling people like us to dissolve our old selves or be counted as the enemy! You heard what he said: artists should give up all 'the old stuff they've learned in England and America twenty or thirty years ago,' cease being 'slaves to the West' [洋奴] and become foot soldiers in the party's new 'cultural army' [文化大军]."

During the following months, the few Western musicians still in Chinese orchestras were replaced by counterparts from Soviet Bloc countries. Concert programs became increasingly foliated with works by Russian composers, such as Borodin, Tchaikovsky, Kalinnikov, Glinka, and Rimsky-Korsakov. Chopin was tolerated, but only because he was Polish, and Poland was now part of the Soviet Bloc. Like an inclement weather system that quietly moves in, the atmosphere of openness and diversity that had prevailed at the outset of this new people's republic was clouding over with political campaigns now coming one after another. First came a Campaign to Suppress Counterrevolutionaries (镇压反革命分子运动), aimed at supporters of Chiang Kai-shek's former Nationalist government. Then came the "Three-Antis" and the "Five-Antis" (三反五反) campaigns, the former attacking corruption, waste, and bureaucracy, the latter bribery, theft of state property, tax evasion, cheating on government contracts, and stealing state economic information. Next came rumors that Mao had ordered all party branches to assign each "work unit" (单位) a target requiring local leaders to arrest a designated number of "counterrevolutionaries." One October morning in 1951, a worried Dr. Song arrived at Willow Courtyard with a "confidential document" (内部文件) that a patient had slipped him.

"This is not the revolution I thought I was joining," he whispered, handing his old friend the document:

"The subjection of counterrevolutionaries to forced labor is an indispensable means for the liquidation of the counterrevolutionary class," Chairman Mao was proclaiming. "We must execute about ten thousand to several tens of thousands of embezzlers nationwide before we can solve this problem."

Li Tongshu was horrified. It was almost as if Mao were giving a directive to a steel mill to smelt a designated tonnage of ore, or to a collective farm to produce so many kilos of grain. In his people's republic, even political movements and purges required targets and that they be met by galvanizing tens of thousands of local cadres to dispatch the requisite number of "counterrevolutionaries." In Guangxi Province alone, Mao's acolyte, Tao Zhu (陶铸), was proudly boasting: "450,000 bandits pacified; 40,000 killed, one third of which may or may not have deserved death." The thought that accountants with abacuses were sitting somewhere ensuring that party-decreed "quotas" (指标) for "counterrevolutionary" victims were being faithfully fulfilled was chilling. Tongshu felt so racked with guilt for having dragged his wife into this maelstrom that he did not share everything he learned with her. However, she could see how the changing situation weighed on him.

As the fires of extremist revolution drew closer to institutions like the Central Conservatory, which used to be relatively sequestered, and as more people were accused of political crimes and forced to make public confessions, a wave of suicides swept the city. Vivian was particularly unnerved by the case of the renowned physicist Zhou Peiyuan (周培源), because before coming to Tsinghua University he'd studied at the University of Chicago and Caltech, even worked with Albert Einstein. Now he was writing humiliating self-denunciations:

> *During the four years of my first sojourn in the U.S., I saw only the skyscrapers, automobiles, and the licentious and shamelessly free spending life of the exploiting classes, but I did not see the tragic exploitation of the toiling masses. . . . I erroneously thought democracy was good and that the people had free speech. . . . But what I did not realize was that the American president and so-called government officials were the slaves of monopoly capitalists. . . . I became an instrument of American imperialism and yet I felt it was my honor.*

"How have so many sophisticated people with such good intentions ended up groveling so abjectly?" Vivian asked sorrowfully.

"Intellectuals and artists returning from abroad are so unfamiliar with Leninist practices, they easily get intimidated and confused," he responded. "Remember what Confucius admonished: 'When the archer misses the center of the target, he turns around and seeks for the cause of failure in himself' [射有似乎君子失諸正鵠反求諸其身]. The party exploits our tendency to blame ourselves."

"It's a discovery that comes late for us," she answered taciturnly.

There were, however, moments of brightness. One winter night in 1952, just as Li Tongshu was drifting off to sleep, Vivian took one of his hands and drew it to her belly.

"I have a secret, Tongshu," she whispered.

"A secret?" he asked with concern.

"A nice secret."

"And what's your nice . . . ?"

"I'm pregnant," she whispered. He was so moved he could neither speak nor move. "Aren't you happy?" she asked.

"Yes. Yes!" he gasped, taking her in his arms.

"I didn't want to tell you until I was sure."

That fall, they were treated to a "big happiness" (大喜), the birth of a son, and they named him Li Wende (李文德), Li the Literate and Virtuous. His birth allowed them to turn from the outer world of political turmoil back into themselves, and they fell in love again, this time through their child.

"Small children are one of the last bulwarks against the revolution's occupation of private life," Li Tongshu wryly observed one evening, while holding his new son as Vivian prepared dinner.

"And they have one other singular virtue," she added. "They cannot be pressured, hectored, or bullied into saying anything on command, much less be harangued into silence."

"I love the thought that not even the highest official in the land cannot prevent an unhappy child from protesting," he said, laughing. "No matter how mighty the leader, how grand the political system, or how powerful his army, not even autocrats can make a hungry baby stop howling without succoring it. Babies are the original dissidents. They have real power!"

"Does that mean our son has the makings of a 'bad element'?" joked Vivian.

"Chinese never much liked individualism," he added. "Do you know what that little Chen boy down the alley told me the other day? He said that, because he's left-handed, his mother whacks him on the knuckles with chopsticks if he doesn't eat with his right hand. She even puts hot pepper on his left thumb to prevent him from sucking it."

"We Chinese do love our systems of control!" She laughed ruefully.

As he grew, Little Li enjoyed his child's world of sitting in his mother's lap on Big Sheep Wool Alley on hot summer evenings as little girls skipped rope, boys played "attack the city" (攻城), old men hunched over chessboards, and ancient grannies with bound feet and chicken-feather fans gossiped through toothless gums. He loved holding his father's hand as they walked to the old Ming

Dynasty Observatory on the City Wall for a summer popsicle (冰棍) or a wintertime stick of candied hawthorn berries (糖葫芦). That was where the great beyond began, which loomed in Little Li's impressionable young mind as a terrifying, unexplored wasteland into which a child might stray, never to be found. While following a cat one afternoon, he'd wandered so far from Big Sheep Wool Alley that he was unable to find his way home. Weeping his eyes out, he was convinced he was lost for all eternity, when his distressed mother suddenly appeared, wiped his tears, consoled him, and brought him back to the safety of Willow Courtyard.

Each spring, Little Li eagerly awaited the return of the swallows that nested under the eaves of their veranda. He loved to watch as they wheeled and dived around the courtyard, catching insects. He waited eagerly for the time each spring when his father would boost him onto his shoulders so he could peek into their mud nests to see if there were any eggs. The reassuring, childlike scale of things in the *hutong*s, the repetition of daily events, and the familiar faces in their neighborhood made Big Sheep Wool Alley seem as immutable as the great City Wall surrounding old Beijing. Punctuated by eight majestic gates, and boasting a promenade along its top as wide as any avenue in the city, this monumental brick rampart rose off the North China Plain like a fantastic dream to give Beijing a fairy-tale aura.

By age four, he was memorizing two new lines each morning of the "Three Character Classic" (三字經), a text children had been learning since time immemorial to inculcate them with the basic precepts of Confucianism:

> *When people are born, They are by nature good.*
> *Though their characters are similar, They develop*
>   *differently.*
> *If they are not taught, Their natures will change.*
> *In teaching what is most precious is focusing*
>   [人之初 性本善 性相近 習相遠 苟不教 性乃遷 教之道
>   貴以專].

After he'd memorized the entire text, his father started him on calligraphy with a brush and ink. And when an old flute turned up at the Conservatory, he began teaching him music as well. It was a strict daily regimen that Little Li found tiresome, but his father brooked no protest. The fact that they spoke English at home, owned a piano, had shelves of Western as well as Chinese books, and lived in a house filled with music was the natural order of things. His very first intimation of his otherness—that he was the offspring of a Eurasian mother with an American passport and a Chinese father trained abroad—came one day when a neighborhood boy was playing with him in Willow Courtyard.

"Aiyaaa!" his friend suddenly blurted out. "Your house is so strange. I don't understand a word your mother and father say."

"They're speaking English," Little Li innocently explained.

"English?" his perplexed friend asked. Little Li was not sure how to reply.

Then, one evening, while they were playing on Big Sheep Wool Alley, an older boy cried out, "Hey, now we know why Li Wende is so weird: his parents talk gibberish!" The other kids howled with laughter, and Little Li burned with mortification.

"Why can't we be like normal people and speak Chinese?" he protested.

"You must never lose touch with the language of either parent," his father insisted in English. But what Little Li yearned for was not fluency in English, skill in calligraphy, being able to recite the classics, or talent playing the flute; he wanted the admiration of his friends and someday to be able to wear the crimson bandanna of the China Youth Pioneers (中国少年先锋队) at school.

One morning, as Li Tongshu was sitting in the very back row of a "political study" session that all Conservatory faculty were required to attend, to purge themselves of "unreformed Western ideology," a trumpet player known for his leftist views stood up, pointed an accusing finger right at him, and indignantly charged, "Is it not true, Li Tongshu, that the real reason you returned to China with your American wife was to spy on the Motherland for the U.S. imperialists?"

Heads that had been drooping in boredom snapped to attention. When no one in the room—and there were many who knew Li Tongshu well—rose to his defense, he felt compelled to speak up himself. "You are misinformed," he countered, in as even-tempered a voice as he could muster. "You—"

"Misinformed?" interrupted the trumpeter. "Don't think we are so blind we don't see who you are."

"I am only a musician," responded Li Tongshu, frightened and incensed at the same time. "I have done nothing more than study abroad, like many others." He did not dare say "in America," because he knew he would only incur more guilt by association.

"There is no such thing as someone who's only a musician," his accuser rejoined. "Everyone has a class stand, and you will never hide your own indelible class blackness with lies. It's plain for all to see that you and your family are the kind that love to run under the skirts of foreigners."

"These charges have no basis in fact. I—"

"You must come clean, Li Tongshu!" interrupted his accuser. "Confess your errors and draw a clear line between yourself and America!"

"I returned home to help build the new Conservatory and a new China. That's all!" he futilely protested.

"You have not only a bad class background and a pessimistic worldview, but an unrepentant attitude," continued the trumpeter. "If you refuse to acknowledge your errors, you'll come to no good!"

An unnerving silence fell over the room. Fearing that further rebuttal would only provoke a more damning indictment, Li Tongshu said nothing more, but he knew a milestone had passed. He'd been "capped" (被扣帽子), an expression used for when someone was publicly accused. For once the figurative cap of accusation was clapped onto someone's head, the political stain was impossible to expunge. Friends would soon find it inconvenient to interact with the accused, neighbors would look the other way as he or she passed, colleagues would shun that person in the corridors and even family members might quarantine "capped" victims, as if they'd become infected by a highly contagious disease.

It was only a matter of days before a student left his tutelage to take up the accordion instead, so he could perform with mobile propaganda troupes and "better serve the people [为人民服务]." Then another young man announced he wished to transfer to the Composition Department, only to turn up later studying with another keyboard professor, who'd been trained in Moscow. Li Tongshu said nothing to anyone. He was left to seek solace in his wife, music, and religion, the very things that were his undoing.

"Did you think me blind to what was happening?" Vivian

asked almost indignantly when her husband finally confided his concerns. "You don't need to worry you're going to upset me, Tongshu, because I'm already upset. I'm even scared."

"We shouldn't get too worked up," he said, hoping to allay her fears. "Maybe the party will—"

"Don't be naïve!" She cut him off. "The party doesn't give a damn about you, your music, or us. Do you think the fact that we unselfishly returned to help build a new China means anything to them? They'll throw us away in a heartbeat, if it serves their purposes."

"I understand, Vivian, but . . ."

"You must listen to me. We have a son now!" She pointed to the sleeping boy. "We should consider going back to San Francisco for his sake, if not for our own. I've heard that some people are still able to get out to Hong Kong from Shanghai. Maybe we should try. Will you think about it? Please!" She was almost begging now.

"I will," he said, barely whispering. What he dared not tell her was that his passport, issued by the Nationalist government before 1947, was no longer valid, and that Mao's government would never issue him a new one, so there was no point even dreaming about leaving. That evening, he went to find his old friend at the hospital.

"You look worried," Dr. Song said as they sat down on the front steps of Peking Union Medical College Hospital.

"I've been publicly accused."

"Oh!" Dr. Song gasped. For several moments neither spoke.

"Things have changed since we came back," Li Tongshu finally continued. "All the party's sweet talk about 'united fronts' and 'friendship' were just stratagems to get people like us to return and add luster to their revolution. But now that the Soviet Union is their 'big brother' and America's their enemy, we have no utility except as targets!"

"I understand how concerned you are," said his friend gravely. "More and more, I feel our hopes and expectations were naïve and idealistic. But I also try to remind myself about all the good the party has brought about: the diseases they've brought under control, the medical clinics they've set up in the countryside, the schools they've built, and—"

"Vivian wants to leave, but my passport has expired," interrupted Li Tongshu.

"Tongshu," said his friend, giving a deep sigh, "I want you to listen to me. You must be very careful. It would be the kiss of death for you to be overheard talking about trying to leave. My training in Western medicine gives me some protection—they still need me. But as a Western-trained musician, you're expendable. And then there's your faith. You must be more than careful! We just have to hope things will somehow take a turn for the better—sometimes they do. So be patient." Just then, the hospital PA system summoned him to an emergency. "I have to go," he said, putting a hand on his friend's shoulder. "Be mindful of your family, Tongshu."

Political movements in China always wax and wane as periods of "relaxing" (放) follow periods of "tightening up" (收) to create an ebb-and-flow pattern that becomes clear only in hindsight. In the months that followed his "capping," Li Tongshu was just beginning to feel more hopeful about the future when a telegram arrived via Geneva, addressed to his wife:

VIVIAN: FATHER IN HOSPITAL. INOPERABLE CANCER.
ASKING FOR YOU. COME SOON. MOTHER

A week later, she left by train for Hong Kong. All that Little Li could remember of his mother's departure was her crouching beside him on the train platform, her face streaked with tears, hugging him over and over again as his father stood glumly looking on.

"I'll be back soon," she promised. "I will not forget you, my sweet son! Never! But, for a while, you must wait for me. All right? You must wait!" Then she was swallowed up by a green railway coach, and the whole scene dissolved in a blur of billowing steam and noise. As the engine hooted and chuffed out of the station, Little Li was left suddenly in a gravity-free world.

11

SENT DOWN

ONE AFTERNOON, upon arriving back at Willow Court-yard, Little Li and his father opened their mailbox and found an unfamiliar robin's-egg-blue envelope with dark red-and-blue scalloped edges that was bejeweled with a postage stamp showing a church on a verdant valley floor dotted with cows in the shadow of a jagged, snow-covered mountain peak. At the bottom of the stamp was the word "Helvetia."

"Where's it from?" asked Little Li.

"Switzerland," his father replied.

"Where's Switzerland?"

"In Europe."

"Who sent it?"

"Your mother."

"Is she in Switzerland?"

"No."

"So why is she writing from Switzerland?"

"Americans cannot send mail directly to China, so letters must go via another country to get here." As he spoke, Li Tongshu ran his fingers over the envelope, as if he might learn something just by feel. Once inside their room, he propped the letter against a rice bowl on their kitchen table and left it like an offering on an altar.

"Don't you want to read it?" asked Little Li, filled with curiosity.

"We will wait until after dinner," said his father, as if fearful of what was inside.

After they'd finished eating, his father sat down in his reading chair, put on his spectacles, and summoned Little Li onto his lap. However, he still did not reach for the envelope.

"Let's read Mama's letter!" persisted Little Li impatiently. The faraway look in his father's eyes frightened him. When Li Tongshu finally did take the letter, he opened it very slowly, extracting the sheer onionskin pages from the almost weightless airmail envelope with all the care of an archaeologist handling ancient parchment. Then he touched the pages to his nose, as if they might be infused with some bewitching essence. Little Li, however, could smell nothing special. "Read, Papa!" he goaded.

> *Dearest husband,*
> *My beloved father died one week after I arrived back in San Francisco. Only after we'd laid him to rest and I went to book a passage back to Hong Kong did I discover that my passport would expire in a month. However, when I applied for a new one, I received the disturbing news that, because I've been living in the People's Republic of China, a country to which Americans are forbidden to travel by the U.S. Department of State, my application was being denied. I have filed an appeal, but it will take a while to resolve. In the meantime, all I can do is wait, hope, and pray.*
> *Just know that I am trying everything I can to surmount this unexpected obstacle. I think about you both every day, every moment! Until I can see you again, I will send you letters and packages of treats. And with each one I will also be sending love to my two most precious ones!*
> *Your mother, your Vivian*

"Isn't she coming home?" asked Little Li, trying to imagine his mother stepping back off the train that had swallowed her up at the station.

"Not now, son," his father said in a leaden voice.

Henceforth, each time a letter arrived, they adopted the same ritual. His father propped it up on their table, and only after dinner did he summon Little Li onto his lap, open the envelope, and read it out loud. Often he read so haltingly that Little Li suspected he was leaving things out. However, he didn't ever dare challenge his father, whose total absorption seemed to beg no trespass. And even when he finished, Little Li learned to wait patiently without speaking while his father slowly refolded the letters and slid them back inside their red-and-blue scalloped envelopes. Then he'd gently lift

Little Li off his lap, open the cabinet beside his bed, withdraw the pack of earlier letters, and add the latest arrival. Next he'd take out a sheet of paper, remove the cap of the Parker Brothers pen he'd brought from San Francisco, and begin composing a response. Although Little Li could see everything he was doing, could even hear the scratch of his pen nib, his father's soul seemed to have flown away and left his body in the same trancelike state as when he played the piano. Such moments helped Little Li understand that there were aspects of his father he'd never be able to understand, much less to share.

One day when they arrived home they found a postal notice in their mailbox.

"What does it say?" asked Little Li.

"That we have a package."

"From whom?"

"From your mother." His father was smiling broadly.

"What will be in it?"

"A surprise."

"Will it be for me?"

"Maybe."

"Aiyaaa! Can we get it right now?"

"Well, we'd have to hurry to reach the post office before it closes."

"Let's try," urged Little Li enthusiastically.

As they rode home from the post office on his father's bike, Little Li held the large brown carton tied with twine they'd just fetched.

"What do you think's inside, Papa?" he asked, almost bursting with excitement.

"You'll have to wait and see."

When he cut the twine back in Willow Courtyard and began rummaging through the clouds of crumpled newspaper inside, he was ecstatic to exhume a brightly colored box of cookies, a bulging cellophane bag of salted nuts, a bright can of peaches, a flask of sweet syrup in the shape of a maple leaf, a beveled jar of strawberry preserves, and an oblong tin of sardines. There was also a large red, white, and blue can of Chase & Sanborn coffee with a little metal key soldered to its lid that his father showed him how to use to twist back the steel band around the top until there was a satisfying hiss of air and the pungent aroma of roasted coffee filled the room.

Every month a new package arrived with more treats, each so elegantly shaped and brilliantly colored that they seemed like works of art. And recognizing they'd been sent by his very own mother all the way from San Francisco made them even more thrilling for Little Li. How America managed to produce such fabulous things while China could not remained a mystery. When all the treasures inside a box had been excavated, he lined them up on the tabletop and played with them as if they were a phalanx of toy soldiers, while his father carefully flattened each page of the *San Francisco Chronicle* his mother had used as packing to hungrily scour them for news of the outside world. These occasions were among the most pleasurable in Little Li's life, times when he felt most palpably connected with his departed mother. Not only did the treats lend variety to their spare and monotonous diet, but, once arrayed on their shelf above the sink, their bright labels created welcome mosaics of color in the otherwise drab room.

His father allowed him to open two of these treats a week, and as he enjoyed them, he tried to visualize the beguiling land from which they'd come. For him, California was a place that seemed even more fantastic than the exotic lands along the Silk Road traversed by the Monkey King, Sun Wukong (孙悟空), whose mythic pilgrimage was said to have brought the sacred sutras of Buddhism from India to China. Chronicled in *Journey to the West* (西游记), it was a children's tale Little Li had always loved.

One day, a letter arrived saying that his mother had received hopeful news about her passport application and all during dinner his father was unusually smiling and talkative. But then at bedtime he sat down without a storybook in hand.

"Aren't we having a story tonight?" challenged Little Li.

"We are," his father reassured, "but tonight will be special: I'm going to tell you a story myself."

"What kind of real story can that be?" he asked suspiciously.

"From an opera that's dear to me and your mother, because we first heard it together."

"An opera?" asked Little Li, even more skeptical. "Can't we have a real story?"

"Operas are actually just stories set to music."

"And how did you hear this story?"

"While I was in San Francisco, the great conductor Arturo Toscanini performed Beethoven's only opera, *Fidelio,* for a broadcast that went all across the country."

"And did you like it?"

"I did."

"And did Mother like it, too?" he persisted, ever hungry for details that might help him imagine her.

"She loved it, too."

"Will I like it?"

"I think so."

"What's it about?

"About courage, loyalty, goodness, and freedom."

"All right, but can you make it sound like it's a real story?"

"Okay! Okay!" His father laughed. "Once upon a time, long ago, in Spain, there lived a courageous young man named Florestan, who was unjustly imprisoned by the evil nobleman called Don Pizarro because he'd exposed his many crimes."

"Is Florestan in a real dungeon underground?"

"Yes, he is. And it's dark, cold, and damp."

"Is Florestan scared?"

"Wouldn't you be scared if you were chained to a rock in a dark castle prison awaiting death?" Little Li tried to imagine a European castle, but all he could envision were the great stone churches he'd studied in his mother's book of European cathedrals.

"Yes, I'd be really scared."

"But Florestan never loses faith in his loving wife, Leonore, or in the mercy of God." Although it was too dark for Little Li to see his father's expression, he heard him choke up for a moment. "And . . . even though Florestan's situation seems hopeless, Leonore never stops believing in him and his innocence."

"But what can she do?"

"Well, she devises a secret plan to dress up like a young man called Fidelio. Then she sneaks into Don Pizarro's castle to try and save him. That's what makes her a hero." Li Tongshu repeated the word "hero" (英雄) in Chinese. Little Li was, of course, familiar with socialist heroes who loved the revolution and the party, but the stories about them never mentioned girls or anything about love.

"How does she get into the castle?"

"She convinces the prison guard, Old Rocco, to take her on as his assistant."

"And Old Rocco doesn't know she's a girl?"

"That's right. In fact, Leonore even fools his daughter, Marzelline. And guess what? Poor Marzelline falls in love with Fidelio."

"Even though she's really a girl?"

"She's completely fooled!"

"Aiyaaa! She's in for a big surprise!" laughed Little Li, warming to the story.

"So, when Fidelio overhears Old Rocco say he has to dig a grave for someone, she's terrified it's for her husband, and she convinces him to take her down into the dungeons to help."

"You mean to dig a grave for her own husband?"

"Well, she still isn't sure Florestan's down there, but she wants to find out. Then, as they descend into the darkness, she hears someone in the cell below sing out: 'Oh, come, hope! Let not your last star Be eclipsed by despair.'"

"Who is it?"

"It's so dark Fidelio can't see. But then the voice cries out again: 'Oh God! What darkness is this? What terrifying silence?'"

"It's him, isn't it?" said Little Li excitedly. "It's Florestan!"

"Just wait!" interjected Li Tongshu. "Then the voice sings out again: 'Ah, in the very springtime of my life, All that gave me joy deserted me. Now words of truth too boldly spoken have brought me chains as my reward.'"

"Does Florestan know he's about to be rescued, Papa?"

"No, he doesn't even realize that anyone besides Old Rocco is in the dungeon. He just feels a mystical, uplifting presence, even sees a vision of a liberating angel."

"With real wings?"

"Yes, and he begins singing: 'Oh, do I not feel a soft whispering of air? Who is this figure so radiant and bright? . . . It is an angel, so like my wife, Come to lead me back to freedom and the Kingdom of God!' But as Florestan imagines an angel liberating him, the evil count learns that the minister of justice is on his way and knows he must get rid of Florestan quickly."

"Is the minister of justice a good guy, Papa?"

"Yes. And Count Don Pizarro realizes that if the minister

arrives while Florestan's still alive, Florestan will reveal all his crimes. So, as Fidelio is digging the grave, in the dim light of Rocco's lantern, she becomes sure the man lying on the stone floor is her husband. But just then Don Pizarro marches in and draws a dagger. However, before he can stab Florestan, Fidelio pulls a pistol from her tunic. Then unexpectedly they hear the distant sound of a trumpet. Knowing that the good minister has arrived, Florestan cries out: 'Thanks be to God!' And then . . ." Little Li could feel his father trembling again with emotion. "And then, only then does Florestan realize that the person dressed as a young man before him is his own beloved wife, Leonore, in disguise. Overcome with joy, he begins to sing. And because Beethoven, too, always yearned for someone to rescue him from his loneliness, as Leonore and Florestan embrace they sing a duet to melt the coldest heart! 'Oh Joy, beyond expression, when one heart lost finds another again.'"

"So Florestan gets saved, Papa?"

"Not only is he saved, but the good minister also orders the release of all the prisoners in Don Pizarro's dungeon. And as they emerge into the warm sunlight, they sing a joyful chorus of liberation, celebrating the triumph of good over evil, compassion over cruelty, and loyalty over betrayal."

"And then what?"

"Then Florestan and his wife walk forth together in freedom."

"Is that all?"

"Is that all?" laughed Li Tongshu, stroking his son's hair. "You see, what Beethoven's telling us is that whenever one person is wronged we all have a responsibility to help right that wrong."

"Was Beethoven a nice man?"

"He believed in goodness. He once said, 'I recognize no sign of superiority in mankind other than goodness,' and almost every word and note he wrote expresses that love of goodness."

Sensing how touched his father was by this story, Little Li was sure it had something to do with his mother. But he also knew how difficult it was for him to speak of her. He'd learned that the best time to ask him about her was when the lights were finally turned out at night. Then he would sometimes speak of her, although always in a voice so soft that Little Li often could hardly make out what he was saying.

"Does this story make you think of Mama?" he finally asked.

"It does," his father replied wistfully.

"Maybe, some night, she'll appear, just like Fidelio?"

"Maybe she will," replied his father, but with a weary fatalism. "I suppose everyone yearns for a Fidelio who treasures them enough to stand by them through the worst in life."

"*Do* you think Mama will come back?" Little Li tried to imagine what it would be like if she did.

"I hope so," replied his father softly. "Then the three of us can listen to *Fidelio* together."

"I'll definitely listen with you," responded Little Li, knowing how much such a promise would please his father.

As he fell asleep, his father played the chorale "Rejoice greatly, Oh my soul (Freu dich sehr, e meine Seele)."

The bedtime stories from his father that Little Li liked best were not operas, but tales he told about California's golden hills, towering redwood trees, streets lined with shimmering rows of cars, concert halls with balconies stepping like terraced rice fields up their walls, and magnificent suspension bridges arching over sparkling bays. Whenever his father spoke of San Francisco, he became so rhapsodic that Little Li was sometimes unsure whether he was still awake or dreaming.

Then came another aerogram, and as usual, Little Li's father didn't consent to open it until after dinner when Little Li had climbed into his lap. But this time, after glancing at its contents silently for a few moments himself, instead of reading it out loud, he re-folded it, lifted Little Li from his lap, walked to his bed, lay down and closed his eyes. Not knowing what to do, Little Li just waited. When darkness fell and still his father hadn't gotten up, or even moved, he went to him.

"What's wrong, Papa?" he finally dared ask.

"Your mother's passport appeal was denied," he whispered.

"Will she ever come back?" There was no response. Then his father began sobbing.

That night, when Little Li finally drifted off to sleep, without either a story or a chorale, his mother appeared in his dreams. He wanted to imagine her as comforting, loyal, and noble like Fidelio, but instead she appeared as a deceiving, traitorous hag, and he awakened in a panic.

In the days and weeks that followed, his father hardly spoke.

By 1958, his mother had still not secured her passport, but for Little Li life at Willow Courtyard had otherwise regained a measure of balance. The letters and packages still arrived, his father seemed more reconciled to the ambiguity of waiting, and as the exterior political world grew less adversarial, he was able to take some heart from the fact that, despite his earlier political troubles, some of the Conservatory's most talented keyboard students were again now seeking him out.

"Have you seen this?" a young student from Mao's home province of Hunan asked one morning during a tutorial. She produced a newspaper with the headline: "Can Marxism Be Criticized? It Certainly Can!" Beneath the bold black letters an article explained: "Marxism is scientific truth and fears no criticism. If it did, and if it could not be overthrown by criticism, it would be worthless." Then, even more surprising, the article quoted Mao himself as calling on intellectuals to "let a hundred flowers bloom and a hundred schools of thought contend" (百花齐放百家争鸣). This slogan harked back over two millennia, to the Spring and Autumn Warring States Period (春秋战国), during the Eastern Zhou Dynasty (东周, 770–256 B.C.), when a so-called Hundred Schools of Thought—which included Confucianism, Daoism, Mohism, and Legalism—were all allowed to freely contend in what came to be idealized as a halcyon period of open philosophical debate. And now here was Mao inexplicably encouraging artists and intellectuals to emulate the ancient Hundred Flowers spirit and "air views without reserve," even to criticize Marxism and the party. Although he insisted his new campaign would be conducted with the gentleness of "a breeze or a mild rain," he also half joked (warned?) that he was "not urging people to make disturbances" or "hold riot-promoting conferences."

Was this just another bit of Maoist legerdemain? It was hardly surprising that most of those who'd paid a high price for their dissent in the past—and they were many—remained reluctant at first to speak out, despite Mao's new admonitions.

"It would be prudent to remember that one plum blossom doesn't signal springtime," Li Tongshu reminded his student. But he'd also long since learned not to dismiss such official pronouncements too quickly. As banal and propagandistic as they might seem at first blush, such articles, even slogans, were often signals of changes that grew out of decisions made somewhere inside the black box of leadership politics that were harbingers of the future. Then Deng Xiaoping, the party's general secretary, whom Mao liked to describe as "a pin wrapped in a ball of cotton," added his voice to the clamor: "It would be wrong, just because mistakes are made in criticism, not to dare to speak up," he counseled. "This would be a return to the past, when a deadening spirit of silence and despondency reigned." Something important was seemingly afoot.

After more such exhortations from other high leaders, a few lower-level people finally did dare to start speaking out and when they weren't immediately met with party censure, more and more joined in, until the trickle became a torrent. Indeed, everywhere Li Tongshu turned, he suddenly saw signs of a far more open political environment. Conservatory President Ma Sicong was allowed to celebrate the 130th anniversary of Beethoven's death with a public concert featuring his Fifth Symphony conducted by the East German Werner Gosling, complete with a lecture entitled "Beethoven's Spirit Has Made All Progressive People Join Together." This new openness allowed many who'd chafed under the party's strict controls to dare hope that China's socialist revolution might at last make a place for them. As critiques became bolder, some began calling for a free press, multi-party political elections, and a less worshipful posture toward the USSR. One violinist even criticized Mao for becoming a "dictator," while other students took to the streets to protest the party's suppression of freedom and democracy.

"Chinese seem to be finding their voice again," whispered Dr. Song on one of his visits to Willow Courtyard.

"The irony is that, while they're exercising their freedoms, it's at Mao's command," observed Li Tongshu, wryly.

"Still, I'm hearing young doctors at the hospital say things none of them would have dared even think a few months ago."

"So maybe even here in China there's something innate that makes people want to say what they're actually thinking," responded Li Tongshu, smiling now.

Despite such sentiments, he himself held back. But that May, when a petition calling for greater artistic freedom was jointly circulated by the faculties at the Central Academy of Fine Arts and the Central Conservatory of Music, he felt honor-bound to sign it. The petition had hardly been posted when Mao, incensed by the growing avalanche of criticism, reversed himself and ended the Hundred Flowers Campaign just as suddenly as he'd begun it. Almost overnight, open debates turned into ideological struggle, and critics who'd answered his call to speak out found themselves maligned as "poisonous weeds" (毒草) posing as "fragrant flowers" (香花). As a draconian "rectification movement" (整风运动) began, Mao cynically acknowledged he'd only been using the Hundred Flowers Campaign as a strategy "to lure the snakes of reaction out of their holes," (引蛇出洞) the better to eliminate them.

One evening, while reading an issue of *People's Music,* Li Tongshu came upon an article reviling J. S. Bach as a composer of "dangerously aristocratic music severed from the interests of the masses." The author also lambasted Igor Stravinsky as "reactionary in form and content" and damned Arnold Schoenberg as "reflecting the emptiness and cruel heartlessness of capitalist society." In China, such public statements were never made idly. A week later he was summoned to the Conservatory's party office to meet with Fyodor Fu, who had become party secretary.

When he appeared at Fu's office, the cheerless woman with a bowl haircut who served as his assistant informed him, "Secretary Fu has many pressing responsibilities and important people to see, so you'll have to take a seat and wait." After an hour, he was finally ushered into Fu's reception room. But instead of being invited to enjoy one of the upholstered chairs with lace antimacassars, he was directed to a folding chair, as if he were going to be interrogated.

"So, Li Tongshu, here we are . . ." Fu began with a world-weary sigh as he pushed a document across his desk. Li Tongshu did not need to read more than the first line to know he was in trouble: "Li Tongshu is a Rightist," it charged. "You've taken the wrong path, and you must write a confession in which you hide nothing," said Fu.

"But I'm not hiding anything."

"You must fully criticize your bourgeois outlook and your American wife," continued Fu, clearly enjoying humbling his competitor. "What is more, you must renounce once and for all your hostile intentions toward the Chinese people and the Chinese Motherland."

"My wife, who is not even in China, only had the most noble intentions in returning to Beijing. She never did anything wrong."

"Such self-deception will only harm your case," responded Fu with steely righteousness. "Everyone knows her background."

"What are the charges against us?"

"That you harbor a rightist ideological perspective, are lovers of everything Western, that your wife is an American sent to spy against the Chinese Motherland, and—"

"All untruths!" exploded Li Tongshu.

"Then how do you explain the fact that she shamelessly ran away to hide under the skirts of the Americans and has not dared return?"

"She is trying to return!" he shot back, but knew it was futile to argue.

"You know your errors, Li Tongshu, and it's up to you to acknowledge them." Fu stood up to signal an end to the meeting.

As Li Tongshu left the office, he knew he was stepping back into a world that would henceforth be completely different. Filled with self-blame and worry, he walked all the way home. Although Little Li was still too young to be able to completely understand what was happening, as soon as his father walked through the door, he sensed something wrong. Just how upset his father was became even more evident during the days that followed. He hardly spoke and played the piano for hours at a time. And when the next package arrived from his mother, he would not allow Little Li to line all the treats up on their customary shelf. Nor did he speak of his mother anymore, rendering her more phantomlike than ever. But, strangely, as Little Li's sense of his mother as a person blurred, she seemed to become more real to everyone else around him.

"Who doesn't know that Li Wende is the son of American spies?" an older boy taunted him in the alleyway. "Li Wende is a running puppy of American imperialism!" [美帝狗崽子] jeered another.

When Little Li told his father what had happened, his face turned to stone. "Whatever they say, remember they have no idea who your mother really is."

"But they say such awful things!"

"They do not know what they're saying."

How painful it was for Li Tongshu to watch his only son being persecuted because he, his father, was under accusation, and yet be able to do nothing more than look on helplessly. It was bad enough that politics had severed his son from his mother, but now she was also being cast as an enemy of the state, so he could not even love her from afar. Had Li Tongshu been able to sacrifice himself to right this wrong, he would have done so in a heartbeat. But even this option was now foreclosed to him. For what would his son do if something now happened to his only parent?

Just because a child is unable to comprehend all the complexities of a parent's persecution doesn't mean that he or she doesn't experience that parent's ignominy. And as the Anti-Rightist Campaign gathered momentum, few were willing even to breathe the same air as Li Tongshu. As the presumption of his political impurity inexorably spread, almost everyone kept a distance. Only Granny Sun and Dr. Song refused to observe the quarantine. Because he could see what was happening but did not really understand why, watching his father being shunned was for Little Li as frightening as it was for a person in ancient times experiencing an inexplicable eclipse of the sun. Left to suffer not only his own debasement but his son's humiliation, Li Tongshu felt cast into a profound darkness.

One warm summer afternoon, Little Li awaited his father's return as usual. But when darkness fell and still there was no sign of him, he went to Granny Sun's room.

"Come in, come in, my boy," she urged when she saw how upset he was. "Tell me what's wrong."

"I don't know why my father hasn't come home," he said tremulously, and began to cry.

"Has he gone away?"

"He didn't say anything about going anywhere."

"Well, these are unpredictable times, and your father . . ." She arched her eyebrows. When they'd eaten something and still there was no sign of him, Granny Sun insisted Little Li spend the night.

"That's the way your father would want it," she said emphatically. Lying in bed beside her, he felt abandoned. In the morning, when his father still had not reappeared, she took him to school, promising, "Things will straighten out by the time you're home."

As his teacher droned on, Little Li distracted himself by watching the two acrobatic squirrels that lived in the trees in the schoolyard outside. He'd learned from previous observation that when they were playing, just before they appeared in the square of branches framed by his classroom window, the leaves of the trees would begin to quiver. Then, like trapeze artists, they'd burst into view, gymnastically rocketing through the foliage in daredevil pursuit of each other, never missing a step, much less plummeting to the ground. At recess, he stayed at his desk to avoid being taunted. When he asked his teacher if she knew what had happened to his father, she replied sternly, "You must ask the relevant authorities."

"Who are the relevant authorities?"

"That's not my affair," she replied curtly.

The next morning, still without any sign of his father, Granny Sun peremptorily commanded, "No school or play on Big Sheep Wool Alley today."

Sitting in her gloomy room with its old-lady smell as she puttered about left Little Li simultaneously bored and scared. Then, at noon, there was an unexpected knock, and his heart leapt. No sooner had she cracked the door open than a voice demanded, "Where is the son of rightist Li Tongshu?"

Little Li was so relieved to at least hear his father's name that he rushed to the doorway, where he found Fyodor Fu standing beside a younger man.

"There you are! Come out so you can be properly addressed," commanded Fu, finding no indignity in intimidating a small, frightened boy.

"And be quick about it," barked his sidekick gratuitously.

When Little Li stepped outside, Fu unfolded a document and, as if he were about to give a public address, began reading: "In view of the fact that Li Tongshu is a known reactionary rightist who has brought shame not only on himself and his family, but on the Central Conservatory of Music and the People's Republic of China, he will be 'sent down to the countryside to participate in manual labor' [下放参加劳动] with the broad masses of the peasantry to rectify his incorrect views and attitudes." As Fu read on, his sidekick nodded in obsequious agreement. Although Little Li had no idea what his father's offenses were, through kinship he felt responsible, and his lower lip began to tremble. "I would not shed a single tear for a man like your father," castigated Fyodor Fu.

"What did he do?" queried Granny Sun, whose political innocence made even her most direct question seem guileless.

"What did he do?" repeated Fu, seemingly stunned by the obtuseness of her question. However, since it had never occurred to him actually to catalogue Li Tonghsu's specific crimes, he began spluttering. "It is not just what he did, it's who he is, and who does not know that he is an unregenerated rightist? The first thing you and the boy should do is denounce him!"

"Is he really such an important person?" pressed Granny Sun with an expression that mixed incredulity with awe. "I thought he was only an insignificant musician."

"No, he is certainly not an important personage!" said Fu, offended at the very idea that his explanation might have lent such an impression. "He's just another intellectual who's stubbornly taken the wrong path, opposed Mao's revolutionary line, and . . ."

"Aiyaaa! I didn't know he was someone who makes such a difference!"

"You are turning black into white," rejoined Fu, his patience stretched to the limit by her simplemindedness. "Yes, Li Tongshu is a mere musician, but he allowed himself to be seduced by the West. If one *must* play classical music, far better to play Tchaikovsky and Rachmaninoff than that religious music by Mr. Bach or the reactionary Romanticism of Beethoven!"

"Yes, it is quite beyond belief," agreed Granny Sun, nodding. She'd heard Li Tongshu's piano playing coming across the courtyard for years, but to her it all sounded the same. "Well, Comrade Fu, good luck with your campaign against those two old foreign devils Bach and Beethoven, and all your other political movements." But then, just as she was taking Little Li by the hand to pull him back inside, Fu put his foot in the crack of the door.

"We're not finished," he said sternly. "The boy must come with us."

"But why?" protested Little Li.

"Why?" said Fu, almost indignantly. "Because I'm the party secretary!"

"You must go," coached Granny Sun.

To Little Li's surprise, Fyodor Fu led him not out the gate, but across the courtyard to their room, where, as if it were his own residence, he marched right inside. And there, sitting on his piano bench with his head bowed, was Little Li's father.

"Papa! Papa!" cried Little Li, bolting to him. But as he lunged forward, Fu's sidekick grabbed him by one ear and brought him to a painful halt.

"According to regulations, you will stand here until the renegade Li has said what he has to say," scolded Fu.

"I must go away," began his father, looking up, his eyes heavy with weariness and sadness. "You'll stay with Granny Sun until I return."

"But when will you come back, Papa?" Little Li asked, causing Fu's sidekick to give his ear another painful twist.

"That depends on the rightist Li's attitude," interjected Fu, lighting a cigarette and throwing the match on the floor. "As Chairman Mao correctly teaches, our party's policy is to 'cure the sickness to save the patient.' Your father has a choice: he can persist in his rightism, or he can renounce it and lay bare his bourgeois ways." For emphasis, he chopped one hand down onto the palm of the other. "And you, my little friend, should be grateful to the party for giving your father a chance to reform."

"But—"

"While I am gone," interjected Li Tongshu, raising his hand to pre-empt his son's protest, "I want you to be respectful of Granny Sun and always act in a way that will honor our family." With tears welling in his eyes, he stood, picked up his satchel, stepped over to his son, who hardly came to his waist, and held him for a moment. Then he turned and walked into the courtyard and headed toward the gate, leaving Fu and his sidekick scrambling along behind. Little Li wanted to run after him, but even in his immaturity he knew it was hopeless. So, instead, he just sat there and watched, his insides boiling with a confusing mixture of terror, sadness, and fury that he'd no idea how to express.

Li Tongshu was just one of tens of thousands of "rightist" intellectuals then being denounced, stripped of their positions, and "sent down" to the countryside among "the old hundred names" (老百姓), as China's ordinary peasants were known. Ironically, as the Anti-Rightist Campaign became increasingly extreme, getting sent into rural exile was actually the best, if cryptic, form of protection against further political depredations. But for Little Li, his father's departure was as if a familiar landform that had always been just outside his window had suddenly and inexplicably disappeared. Now he was not only parentless, but because of his "bad family background" (出身不好), he was ostracized. For example, when his class sang songs, he was excluded. One of the most popular songs was about an American black boy called "Li'l Jack," and different students were always assigned each verse as solos. He, however, never got called on, and could only join in on the chorus:

Li'l Jack, oh, Li'l Jack! American black boy, Li'l Jack!
Please tell us, how do you manage to stay alive?
I am just seven, but still I cannot go to school.
Just to survive I must do child labor and suffer torture!
Little Jack, oh, Li'l Jack! American black boy, Li'l Jack!
How thin and weak you are! Why must you still work and toil?

小杰克 小杰克 美国黑孩子 小杰克,
请你告诉我 你怎样生活?
我今年已整七岁, 还不能去上学。
为了活命当童工, 每天都受折磨。
小杰克小杰克, 美国黑孩子小杰克
你这样瘦弱
为什么还要工作?

"America is a land of violence, oppression, and injustice where greedy tycoons heartlessly exploit honest, hardworking people like Little Jack," his teacher authoritatively informed them.

"In America, are children all like Li'l Jack, with nothing to eat?" asked a girl sitting in the next row. Then she turned to stare at Little Li as if he were the cause of the problem.

"We must never forget how lucky we are to live in socialist China, while children of exploited workers in capitalist countries like America go hungry," continued their teacher.

When Little Li tried to envision these unfortunates, he saw waifs in rags like Li'l Jack holding empty rice bowls up to scowling plutocrats with glittering rings on their fat fingers and cigars in their cruel mouths, not the golden land of California evoked by his father's stories. It was impossible to reconcile such malign depictions of America with his father's rhapsodic descriptions. And so

Little Li created separate compartments in his mind for the two very different versions of this phantasmagorical place, America, which had so touched the lives of his parents. As he grew older, however, he became aware of how easily an errant utterance about America could further divide him from his classmates. He learned to be careful and secretive. Little Wang's friendship was one of the few constants in this uncertain universe.

One afternoon several months after his father's exile, Little Li sneaked across the courtyard to their room. The cup filled with chopsticks was still on their table. The pile of newspapers, yellowing now, was exactly where his father had left it, on the stand next to his bed. His bowl of miscellaneous coins still sat on top of the piano. Even his Parker Brothers pen remained on his desk, as if it expected him to return at any minute to write a letter. But, despite all these familiar objects, the room felt alien, eerie, and dead, a capsule where time had stopped.

When Granny Sun came through the gate and discovered him there, she scolded him. "You're a spoiled American child who doesn't listen," she chided. Actually, she need not have done so, for he no longer had any desire to remain in their room.

One day several months later, a letter in his father's elegant hand arrived at Willow Courtyard. Granny Sun read it to him out loud:

> *My beloved son:*
> *I am now working in an apple orchard with the masses in Shanxi Province. I am also collecting songs for the revolution and playing accordion for a rural propaganda team. Life here in the Taihang Mountains takes some adjustments, but at least I still have music.*
> *Do not worry about me. Do not make trouble for Granny Sun. Be kind, respectful, and polite.*
> *Not a day goes by when I do not think of you.*
> *Your father*

"Why did Father go away?" he asked Granny Sun.
"To 'remold himself' [自我改造]."
"How do you 'remold' yourself?"
"It's hard to explain."

"When's he coming back?"

"Only the heavens know!"

When almost a year had passed and Li Tongshu had still not returned, Little Li had begun to get used to life without him. Still, with no bedtime stories or chorales to lull him to sleep each night, he was beset by a dull aching feeling as he lay awake, waiting to be rescued by sleep. And as the months passed and still his father did not return, his ability to recall what he looked like began to fade, as if dusk were settling over memory itself. Little Li could conjure up images of him playing piano, riding his bicycle, or preparing dinner, but, as if a camera lens had been twisted out of focus, the details of his face had begun to lose all their sharpness.

12

KITTENS AND CRICKETS

ONE WINTER afternoon in 1960, after almost two years living in a desperately poor village among the arid Taihang Mountains in China's northwest, Li Tongshu was summoned to the Brigade Office and notified, without explanation or apology, that he could return home. And now, as the sun rose on a frigidly cold morning, he was pulling into Beijing Railroad Station. With Mao seeking to transform China into a "great, powerful, prosperous, and virtuous socialist state" by taking a Great Leap Forward (大跃进) and communizing all agriculture, a famine had begun to sweep the countryside, and he'd eaten little more than rough corn cakes for months. Except for his bedding and a bundle tucked inside his greatcoat, he carried nothing. As he made his way through the cavernous train terminal, out across the esplanade in front, and then finally into the *hutong,* he pulled his collar up against the chill. The familiar gray brick walls, the sloping roofs of the otherwise hidden courtyard houses, the smell of oil sticks sizzling for breakfast, and the thought that he would soon see his son again filled him with a sense of imminence. Before he was able to calm his turbulent feelings, he found himself standing in front of 14 Big Sheep Wool Alley. The red paint on the gateposts was flaking, and one of the protective dragon "gate stones" (门墩子) standing guard at their doorway had been knocked off its pedestal. What would he find inside? Would their room still be unoccupied? Would his piano still be there? Most important, would his son be there? And what would he say to him?

Li Tongshu reached for the gate key he'd worn like a talisman around his neck ever since leaving. He was relieved when it slid smoothly into the lock, the door creaked open, and he was suddenly standing before the old "spirit screen" (影碑) that had for centuries protected their courtyard from meddlesome spirits and prying eyes. A dusty pile of junk heaped on their veranda suggested that no other tenants had yet trespassed. When he reached Granny Sun's door, he stopped and cautiously peered into her window. The gaunt wraithlike visage he saw staring back from his reflection in the grimy pane of glass made him feel like an unwelcome ghost returning to haunt an old home. Finally, screwing up his courage, he knocked. There was no response. He knocked again. A chair scraped inside.

"What do you want?" a voice challenged. Then the door opened a crack and two faces appeared, one above the other. "Who are you?" challenged the top face.

"I am Li Tongshu."

"Who?"

"It's me, Granny Sun!"

Silence.

The door swung open a little wider, and there before him was Granny Sun and a boy holding a rice bowl in one hand and chopsticks in the other.

"My son!" gasped Li Tongshu, falling to his knees.

Unsure who this thin, shaggy, derelict man was, a bewildered Little Li stood with his mouth agape.

"It's your father, foolish child!" rasped Granny Sun, grabbing the boy by the collar and yanking him as if he were a puppet she might levitate into action. "It's him! He's come home, just as I always said he would!"

"My boy!" mumbled Li Tongshu, reaching out to embrace Little Li, but so startling him he dropped one of his chopsticks. Unable quite to believe that the boy standing before him, who was much taller than he remembered, was his son, he turned away so the tears of joy now streaming down his cheeks would not rattle him. Little Li said nothing because this emaciated man looked nothing like the father he'd been visualizing all these months. "I've brought you something. Do you want to see what it is?" asked Li Tongshu. Little Li nodded tentatively. "If you're ready, close your eyes."

Little Li reluctantly shut his eyes as his father unbuckled the belt of his khaki greatcoat, withdrew a cloth bundle, and placed it in his son's arms. Opening his eyes, Little Li pulled back the top layer of cloth, and when he saw the head of a tiny, drowsy orange kitten, he let out such a shriek of astonished delight that the startled kitten shot from its swaddling like a lychee squeezed from its skin. With matted fur and dripping eyes, the scrawny animal wobbled across the floor on unsteady legs.

"What is it?" gasped Granny Sun with a look of distaste.

"A kitten!" exclaimed Li Tongshu proudly, as the animal made an unearthly mewing, like a rusty door hinge creaking open. But Little Li did not care. With an enormous smile, he picked up the scrofulous kitten and hugged her. He named her Whiskers. Dr. Song gave him some boric acid to clean out her infected eyes, and he brushed her matted fur daily until it became soft and fluffy. Never had Little Li adored anything so much.

His father's reappearance and their move back into their old room was more unsettling for Little Li than his departure. Although their dust-covered piano and furniture awaited them inside, their room was like a sealed tomb. And he'd grown so accustomed to living with Granny Sun that being back left him feeling like a guest in his own home. And he didn't know what to say or do when his father was overcome by periods of prolonged silence.

"Where did you go when you went away?" he asked one night after he was in bed.

"To a little mountain village in Shanxi," his father replied, in a way suggesting he wanted to talk.

"What did it look like there?"

"Like the moon, because it hardly ever rained and the mountains were almost treeless."

"Were the people nice?"

"They were very poor and never had enough to eat, but they shared what they had." Little Li did not know what else to ask.

Several weeks later, Fyodor Fu summoned Li Tongshu to his office.

"So, you're back," he said, as if Li Tongshu had only been away on a vacation. "These arrived in your absence." He pointed to a stack of familiar blue-and-red envelopes imprinted with PAR AVION and postmarked from Switzerland. Without replying, Li Tongshu took the letters out into the Conservatory courtyard and sat on the low wall around the rock fountain. As he opened the first letter, his hands were trembling and his heart was beating so fast he could hear it pounding in his ears.

Dear Ones:

Not having heard from you for so many months, I yearn to know if you're both safe. Each day when the postman fails to bring a letter, my heart breaks anew. I can only hope I shall have some news soon.

I am sorry to report some most unwelcome news here: my suit to compel the State Department to grant me a new passport has been rejected again in court. I'm trying to find out what other courses of action are still open to me. But now that the horizon of our being together has again retreated, I wanted you both to know my heart is still filled with nothing but love for my two dear ones.

Life is so uncertain! I hope and pray you are both well and will be able to reply soon.

Your Vivian, your mother

There was not a day in Shanxi when Li Tongshu had not thought about Vivian, and the news that there was still no way for them to be reunited threw him into a pit of gloom. However, several weeks later, he was heartened by a letter from the Conservatory, announcing he'd been reinstated as a faculty member.

"That's good news, isn't it?" asked Little Li.

"It's very good news."

"Why do they like you now, but they didn't like you before?"

Li Tongshu wasn't sure how to respond, but he was, in fact, deeply gratified to have his faculty position back, even though few students had any interest in Bach. He got his piano tuned, and the solace of playing at home for himself helped fill his sense of emptiness. So relieved was he to have regained some version of his old life that, like many others who'd been "sent down," he was only too glad to try to forget the experience. Because he rarely spoke about his time away, past and present soon became so neatly sutured back together that sometimes Little Li himself was hardly aware of the interlude of separation that had actually occurred. Just as before, each morning they again rode together down the Avenue of Eternal Peace on their Flying Pigeon bicycle, dropping Little Li off at the affiliated Preparatory Music Primary School before his father went on to the Conservatory itself. In the evening, they retraced their route, stopping at a state-run store where Li Tongshu lined up with his ration coupons for whatever foodstuff was available that day, while Little Li stole out back to forage scraps for Whiskers in the garbage bins.

"What are you looking for, kid?" an unpleasant man who was already scavenging asked disparagingly one afternoon.

"Something to give my kitten," he innocently responded.

"You're wasting food on a cat when starving peasants are turning to cannibalism?" snarled the man. "Get out of here before I give you a good thrashing!" Little Li hastily retreated empty-handed.

With the effects of the Great Leap Forward becoming more and more extreme, for dinner he and his father rarely had more than a small bowl of noodles garnished with pickled vegetables, or a thin soup made from scraps of cabbage or squash. A roasted sweet potato was a treat, a taste of bean curd or fatty pork a luxury. Although Li Tongshu was teaching again, because he'd been labeled a "rightist" the Conservatory denied him the special ration coupons that made life bearable for other faculty members. Under such a dire regimen, it was perhaps understandable that pets were considered a petit-bourgeois self-indulgence. But because he knew how much his son adored Whiskers, Li Tongshu ignored such prohibitions. Toward the end of each meal, he would put an index finger across his lips, point conspiratorially at Whiskers, and then hand Little Li his own bowl with a small portion of his dinner still uneaten.

"But, Father, you must be hungry," Little Li would always protest.

"No! No! No!" he invariably insisted, waving away the objection. "No arguments!" he persisted, as if at any moment his annoyance might turn to ire.

Despite the meagerness of their daily fare, Li Tongshu still gave thanks each evening, cautioning his son not to mention their ritual of saying grace to anyone. Of all party taboos, religion was still high on the list. Besides Whiskers, Little Li's main pleasure was playing with Little Wang out on Big Sheep Wool Alley. What he liked about his friend was that he always seemed to know what was happening, and when he didn't, he almost always knew how to find out.

"Hey! Little Li," crowed his friend only half jokingly one day.

"You'd better watch out or Whiskers will end up in someone's hot pot!"

"What do you mean?" Little Li snapped back indignantly.

"Some boys over at Liuguan Hutong are trapping and eating cats! One guy even rubs salt on their skins and cures them on his mom's clothesline to make fur hats!" He gave a loud guffaw.

"You're lying!" protested Little Li.

"You wish!" riposted his friend smugly. "Nothing like a savory cat hot pot, I always say!"

"That's not even a little funny!" shouted Little Li as his friend howled with laughter.

If it hadn't been for the food packages, which started arriving again from his mother, Little Li and his father would have had a hard time getting by. Just where the packages went while Li Tongshu was away in Shanxi was never explained, but they both suspected that Fyodor Fu had intercepted them for himself.

Most nights, Little Li went to bed hungry, left to dream of banquet tables laden with platters of crispy roast duck, steamed fish in pungent sauces, strings of glistening red sausage, tureens of fragrant soup, snowy drifts of white rice, and cloudlike piles of meat-filled buns. So alluring were these visions of virtual plenty that he actually looked forward to his dreams. However, in them his father and friends were always prevented from entering the banquet area by a mysterious barrier. As they gazed from afar like helpless mendicants at the platters of food, Little Li frantically sought some way to allow them to cross this invisible frontier. But there was no one to whom he could appeal, and the partition remained inviolable. Unwilling to eat alone as they looked on, he could do no more than hope that providence would somehow deliver at least his father across the divide. Yet, as if his political taint extended even into the realm of dreams, night after night he remained excluded, and Little Li was confronted with the agonizing choice: eat selfishly again and again alone under his doleful scrutiny, or keep solidarity and remain hungry.

One night, he finally gave in to gluttony. However, so remorseful did the forbidden meal make him that he cried out and awakened his father. Unaware of the source of his son's torment, Li Tongshu cradled Little Li's head in his lap and stroked his hair. Then, with a softness that seemed impossible from a piano, he played the chorale "Out of the Depths I Cry to Thee (Aus Tiefer Not schrei ich zu dir)" over and over, improvising different harmonizations as he hummed the chorale's text:

Out of the depths I cry to thee,
Lord God! Oh hear my prayer!
Incline a gracious ear to me,
And bid me not despair

On his eighth birthday, Little Li awakened to find two tan-shelled eggs sitting on their table as a present. They were so precious during this time of scarcity that, for several days after he boiled them, he could not bring himself to break either of their perfect shells and eat them. Simply to know that he possessed them was almost pleasure enough. Only after his father warned that the eggs might go bad if he did not eat them did he finally crack one open, dip its snow-white rubbery end in soy sauce, and begin nibbling. He'd never enjoyed anything quite so much! But, chagrined at having indulged himself alone, he stopped after half of the first egg. That day at school, however, all he could think about was how delicious the uneaten half would taste and, upon returning home, he devoured it in two bites. Then he waited two more days before eating the other egg. Through such experiences, Little Li became acquainted with the perverse pleasures of self-denial.

"You know," said Li Tongshu, amused by his son's meticulous planning, "a friend who studied in France used to joke that the difference between French and Chinese culture was that the lives of Frenchmen revolve around women, while the lives of Chinese revolve around food."

Little Li was puzzled by this remark: with so little food available, he could not conceive how a whole life, much less a whole culture, could be built around eating. As to women, they remained a wilderness as uncharted as the Gobi Desert. As far as he could see, if Chinese life was a cornucopia of anything, it was of political movements. Of course, whenever food did appear, people always fell silent, lowered their heads, and ate with the almost trancelike concentration of cattle. But with Mao's stern emphasis on Spartan living and want now stalking the land, even when a decent meal was afforded, people remained vigilant not to give the appearance of excessive enjoyment. Eating had been reduced to the status of a utility, so when collective mealtimes arrived, diners were expected to treat filling their bellies with no more relish than an industrial boiler being fed with coal to generate power for the revolution.

While at school, Little Li dared not let Whiskers run loose, lest she get boiled and eaten. The minute he returned home each afternoon, he went to find her, and at night he allowed her to climb onto his bed and curl into a purring ball beside him, a small oasis of warmth and pleasure.

One afternoon, he arrived home with a few fish bones scrounged from a restaurant garbage can to find his father sitting on his piano bench, but not playing.

"Come here," he said somberly.

"What is it?" asked Little Li with alarm.

"Whiskers is gone," said his father, his voice cracking.

"Gone? Where?" He ran to his bed to look in her box underneath. "Where is she, Father?" he cried in desperation.

"The Neighborhood Committee came and demanded we give her up. They ordered me to make a self-criticism for 'taking food from the mouths of the masses to feed a useless pet.' "

"Where did they take her?"

"I don't know."

"Whiskers, my Whiskers!" Little Li wailed, throwing himself on his bed and weeping inconsolably. "You must get her back, Father! You must!"

Never had Li Tongshu seen his son so distraught, and never had he felt so powerless. As Little Li sobbed himself to sleep that night, Li Tongshu felt such shame that he cursed the day he'd returned to China.

"I have an idea," announced Li Tongshu one Sunday morning several weeks later.

"What idea?" asked Little Li distrustfully.

"I want to take you to a special place."

"Where?"

"It's a secret," replied his father, trying to project enthusiasm.

"I don't want to go anywhere!" protested the boy.

"I know, but I'm asking you to come anyway."

His awareness that his father was trying to make up for the loss of Whiskers, perhaps somehow even to replace her, made Little Li especially resistant. On the bus, he sat glumly, refusing to look his father in the eye. When they reached Di'anmen (地安门), he grudgingly followed his father to the entranceway of the East Wind Collective Electric Fan Factory, where he rapped on the gatehouse door.

"My boy, I want you to meet a friend," announced his father when an elderly man with a wispy beard and a rabbit-skin hat opened the door. Little Li proffered an unenthusiastic hand.

Before 1949, Old Chu had been a rickshaw puller and had been assigned his present position as gatekeeper after the "liberation" (解放). He was also a cricketeer, and as he and Li Tongshu chatted, Little Li sullenly scanned the clutter of cages, tools, and other cricket paraphernalia strewn around the small room, feeling annoyed with his father for presuming that a lowly insect might ever replace Whiskers. Like many other traditional folk-art forms that had flourished for centuries in China, the once-popular craft of cricketeering was kept alive now only by a few old-timers like Old Chu. Cockfighting and cricket fighting had once been beloved pastimes of Chinese gamblers. Lovers of fighting crickets bet on these ferocious insect gladiators as they were provoked to wage combat in circular clay pots. Equally popular were singing crickets, whose sound is generated when the male insect rubs its serrated wings together. Cricketeers had long amplified this "singing" by putting crickets in special carriers, the most beautiful and elegant of which were made of dried gourds, or *hulu* (葫芦), which acted both as cages and as natural sound-enhancing chambers. In the summertime, as a gourd blossom withered and a young gourd itself was still no bigger than a thumb, craftsmen like Old Chu gently inserted them into sectioned clay molds carved or embossed on their inner walls so that as the gourd grew, it pressed against its walls to become imprinted with a pattern. Then, after the mold was removed, the gourd was hollowed out, dried, etched, and fitted with a carved cap of hardwood, tortoiseshell, or ivory.

"So—you'd like to know about crickets," began Old Chu, speaking with the heavy burr of the Beijing dialect.

"Old Chu knows everything about these little fellows," offered his father gamely.

"How can you like them when they're not even real animals?" he resentfully challenged.

"Fair question," answered Old Chu. He opened a *hulu* festooned with intertwined dragons and capped with an ivory rooster, and shook out two big *guoguor* (蝈蝈), crickets whose feelers were rotating around like radar antennae. "I like them because I'm an old man living alone, and when they sing, I feel among friends—small friends, to be sure, but friends nonetheless." He grinned, revealing a set of cigarette-stained teeth as ancient-looking as Shang Dynasty oracle bones. "They may only be insects, but when they sing, they're beautiful. And they never complain!" He laughed with satisfied finality.

"But don't they die in the winter?"

"Not if you're a good cricketeer."

"How do you keep them warm?"

"Ahhhh! Shall I show you?"

"All right," replied Little Li, warming to Old Chu.

"I put them over my kettle, and if I light the brazier, the little devils warm right up and start singing!" He dropped several pieces of coal into the glowing stove, and as a plume of steam began rising from the kettle spout, the crowded room filled with a chorus of cheerful chirping. "Now, my boy," Old Chu triumphantly continued, "do you know how to feed a cricket?" He posed the question as if he were a teacher giving an oral quiz. Little Li shook his head. "Then you must learn." He tore a leaf from one of the cabbage heads piled near the door, bit off a small piece, and began chewing. Then, after spitting the masticated cabbage out onto one index finger, he removed the top of a *hulu* and, with delight in his eyes, flicked it inside, where the cricket went busily to work on it with its pincerlike mandibles. "Now, on a winter's day, when you take your cricket for a walk, how do you think you keep him warm?" asked Old Chu, as if one of the insects already belonged to Little Li.

"I don't know."

"You carry him inside your jacket, next to your body," he answered, opening his overcoat to reveal a row of *hulu*s hanging from loops sown to its lining, like so many hand grenades on a combat vest. "And what do we do with our little friends at night?" Old Chu's face creased into a broad, expectant smile.

"I'm not sure," replied Little Li, smiling now himself.

"You take them to bed with you!" He beamed. "And what does a cricketeer do if he wakes up one cold morning and his cricket looks dead?"

"I don't know," responded Little Li, wondering what miraculous therapy Old Chu would propose.

With that, the old man shook a cricket out of a *hulu* that had been on the table and held the motionless creature in the palm of one hand. Then, with all the theatricality of a magician, he doffed his hat, put the cricket on top of his bald head, clapped his hat back on, smiled, and rubbed his hands together as if he were warming them. Five minutes later, when he removed his hat with grand flourish, the formerly inert cricket sprang off his bald pate, arced into the air, and landed right in Little Li's lap.

"So—this little fellow already seems to know to whom he belongs!"

"Really?" said Little Li, looking down at the cricket, whose antennae were swinging around drunkenly. "But how did you bring it back to life?"

"He was just cold. As soon as he warmed up, he came around. Now, anyone who's going to become a cricketeer must also have a *hulu*," continued Old Chu, picking up a gourd embossed with an image of the Monkey King topped with an intricate tortoise-shell cap crested by a miniature ivory Buddha. When he had gently coaxed the insect inside, Old Chu proudly handed the *hulu* to Little Li. From that day on, he kept it with him, tucked it under his quilt each night right where Whiskers used to lie, and, instead of sleeping to the sound of purring, now enjoyed the singing of a cricket.

That spring, packages and letters from Vivian Knight stopped arriving. His father said nothing, but Little Li could sense he was growing upset.

"Papa, what's happened to Mama?" he finally asked one evening, as they were eating dinner. For the longest time, there was no reply.

"I don't know," his father finally responded somberly.

The next afternoon, Little Li arrived home alone, opened their mailbox, and found a white envelope posted with foreign stamps he'd never seen before. Unlike the familiar red-and-blue aerograms with stamps showing snowcapped mountains that had come via

Switzerland, this envelope was posted with a single stamp depicting a flock of geese flying over a frozen lake, and bore a return address in Vancouver, Canada. As he gingerly lifted it from the letterbox, there was something about the cold whiteness of the envelope that made him want to set it down quickly.

When his father came home and saw the unfamiliar envelope on their table, he stared at it for several minutes as if he, too, was fearful of touching it.

"Who's it from?" asked Little Li anxiously.

"From your mother's sister," his father replied. Then instead of waiting until after dinner as usual, he opened the letter with trembling hands. When he finished reading it, he sat on his piano bench and buried his face in his open palms. Darkness fell, and still he'd neither moved nor spoken; Little Li finally mustered the courage to go over and put an arm tentatively around his shoulders. His father let out a frightening choking sound. It was then that Little Li saw the tears sliding down his cheeks.

"Your mother wanted so much to come back to you, Little Li. But now, my son, she's left us."

"Left us?" asked the boy uncomprehendingly.

"Gone from us. Forever!" Pressing his son's head against his chest, he sobbed inconsolably.

Taking him onto his lap, his father began swaying back and forth like a mother rocking a baby to sleep. Little Li felt so soothed he became drowsy. He tried to imagine his mother dying, but since he had only dimly been able to imagine her living, it was not easy to understand her as having passed into nothingness. Then he was flying weightlessly through white clouds. Maybe this was what death was like. Perhaps now he would see his mother, discover how she really looked and whether she really loved him.

After they turned out the lights that night, he heard his father whispering, as if there were someone else in the room. Then he heard him choke again with sobs. He longed to comfort him, but there was something ironclad about his father's grief that he didn't feel able to penetrate, as if for him grieving was a solitary matter that no mortal succor could temper.

In the days that followed, Little Li kept wishing he could feel sadder about his mother's death, so he might share more in his father's grief. But for him she'd already died a long time ago, so that her passing now was like a piece of news about another family. So, as his father drew a lonely shroud of grief around himself, Little Li felt anxiety instead of sorrow,. Only when his father sat at the piano, closed his eyes, and played chorales—sometimes the same one over and over, as if his piano was a life-support system—did he seem to be alive.

One day, Little Li came home from school alone, flopped down on his bed, and covered his head with the red woolen Hudson's Bay blanket his mother had brought from San Francisco. He liked it under there, as if shutting out the world with something that had been hers might encourage her to become more concrete. Calmed by the way the threadbare wool transformed the cool white light coming through the windows into a warm crimson glow, he felt it was safer here to pick through the few memories he still had of her: of visiting the Ming tombs and playing on the stone camels, lions, and elephants that lined the Avenue of the Emperors; of her playing the violin with his father at the piano; and of her leaning over him in bed at night after reading a British story about a rabbit family that lived underneath an angry farmer's garden shed. But each time he tried to capture an image of her face, she faded away elusively. The only effective antidote was the photo hanging above the piano. It showed a tall, handsome Eurasian woman holding hands with a younger version of his father wearing a Western suit, necktie, and fedora, standing self-consciously in front of the Golden Gate Bridge, whose two majestic towers limned the rolling hills behind. She had long, dark hair, pale skin, a slightly chipped front tooth, and eyes that were Chinese and Caucasian at the same time, and she wore a dark cardigan sweater over a blouse and a long skirt. She bore a look of surprise, as if in the moment the photo was snapped she'd been poised to ask a question. Li Tongshu's face was frozen in the kind of unnatural expression affected by people as they wait for a camera shutter finally to click.

Because this photo was one of the things he knew his mother had actually touched, it had a relic-like appeal for Little Li. That afternoon, he took it down from the wall and, after studying it with the magnifying glass his father used when reading his classical Chinese dictionary, he unclasped the backing and took the photo out of its wooden frame. There, on the reverse side, was an inscription in his mother's own hand: *"I will lift up mine eyes unto the hills, from whence cometh my help."* He had no idea what these words meant, how help might come from hills, especially those rising so stolidly up behind this distant bridge. However, he memorized them anyway, and henceforth recited them like a magical incantation when trying to imagine what Willow Courtyard had been like when she'd still lived here. As he held the frame, he couldn't help wondering if there was not some minute physical trace of her still on it, or someplace else in their room—perhaps a strand of hair, a few flakes of skin, or some other residue of her corporal existence? Such thoughts helped make it seem less remote that he'd come out of her body. He sometimes imagined that yearning alone might bring her back to life, provoke her to step right out of the framed photograph into their room. Or perhaps she'd beckon him to step into the frame, and then beg his forgiveness for leaving him so stigmatized and alone in a place as unforgiving of foreignness as China.

As Little Li matured, he slowly became aware of the ways she'd left him indelibly marked. Only when he approached adolescence, did he begin to understand that not only was his father's background unlike that of other parents, but his own physical features were different from other children's. When he was playing with Little Wang, both in their faded caps, khaki-colored sneakers, and patched blue jackets, from a distance they were indistinguishable. But as he grew, and his facial features became more pronounced, he appeared ever more like a double exposure that has had the image of one person transposed over another. At the same time that his face was Chinese, it also radiated something unmistakably alien. There was a slight suggestion of redness in his hair, a prominence to his nose, and a hint of an epicanthic fold around his eyes, so that when strangers first encountered him they often couldn't help allowing their gaze to linger on him a little longer than was polite. It was not simply that he was a handsome child, but that his physiognomy conveyed something unresolved, an enigma that begged further deciphering. And this connection to America left him open to unending insinuations that he was not really Chinese. As he shot up faster than other children, he was embarrassed when, to save money, his father asked Granny Sun to keep sewing new cuff extensions onto his trousers. Whereas other children might have one or two such extensions, he often had more, each one a different color (dependent on whatever scraps of spare cloth she had available), so that his ankles looked like geological core samples bored through different-hued layers of sedimentary soil.

"Li Wende gets special pants from America," a rival at school taunted one day, and his clique roared with laughter. On another occasion, after Little Li had spoken out of turn in class, Teacher Jin ordered him to stay in during recess and copy *"Down with American imperialism and its running dogs"* thirty times on the blackboard. Then she left his devoirs unerased, for all to see the next day, making Little Li feel he'd been branded as a plenipotentiary of U.S. imperialism. And after he and several friends accidentally broke a window down the alley throwing stones at a ferret, it was he who got blamed. Doddering out with a piece of glass in his trembling hand, an infuriated old man shook a finger at him alone and screamed, "You little half-breed bastard [小杂种]!" This was just one of the many derogatory terms reserved to describe people of mixed parentage.

"You're growing up to be such a strong, handsome boy!" his father said admiringly one morning. But for Little Li such approbation only made him more self-conscious and aware of his otherness, for his alleged "good looks" were as unbelievable to him as the reality of his mother. When he looked into the cloudy mirror above their sink, what he saw was not a handsome face, but one disfigured by the genetic fingerprints of his errant mother's foreignness. And even as he struggled to conceal his connection to America, his fascination with "Old Gold Mountain" (旧金山), as San Francisco was called in Chinese, was kept alive by his father's irresistible stories.

"San Francisco is such a beautiful city," his father told him excitedly one night. "As soon as you cross the Golden Gate Bridge, you're in a wilderness, where you can wander on beaches, in fields, and through redwood groves without seeing another soul!" Or he described how lovely the University of California, Berkeley, campus was, and how beautiful Point Reyes and the Yosemite Valley were. It seemed amazing to Little Li that such places existed, and that his own father had visited them. As he tried to envision this chimerical world, he understood that if his infatuation was ever revealed he'd only be heaped with more ridicule and censure. There was no way to cleanse himself of his mongrel-like impurity, which had left him so insoluble in the unaccepting Chinese world into which his truant mother had abandoned him.

13

LITTLE LI was doing homework one evening when Dr. Song unexpectedly came by to visit. As the two old friends chatted in hushed voices, he kept an ear cocked to the conversation.

"A medical colleague who treats President Liu Shaoqi told me they'd just returned from a trip to Hunan Province and that 'the old man' was shocked by the severity of the famine they witnessed among the peasantry there," whispered Dr. Song. "He said that both President Liu and Deng Xiaoping are now planning to publicly declare the Great Leap Forward a failure."

"Chairman Mao won't be happy about that," replied his father, shaking his head.

"What is even more surprising, this friend insists he's heard that the famine has made Chairman Mao agree to 'retire from the front lines of party leadership.'"

"What does that mean?"

"Who knows?"

"Well, it's hard to imagine him ever just letting go," continued Li Tongshu skeptically.

"I'm just telling you what I heard."

Fueled by shreds of hearsay picked up from the "back-alley news" (小道消息), it was a typical Beijing conversation. Judging what was going on deep inside leadership circles was like taking a temperature without a thermometer. Nevertheless, over the next few months it did appear that a more levelheaded national leadership had taken the helm. In fact, always sensitive to his father's moods, Little Li noticed that even he was smiling more readily, doing *taiji* (太極拳) exercises each morning in the garden, and practicing the piano almost every day.

"I'm going to start a new project," he cheerfully announced

one morning, slapping his 1938 G. Schirmer, Inc. edition of, *The Goldberg Variations* down on the table. As he did so, something fluttered to the floor.

"What's that?" asked Little Li, leaning over to pick it up.

"Oh, look, it's old Herr Bach himself!" his father said, chuckling as he took the portrait of the composer from Little Li. "I remember the day I cut him out of a magazine in San Francisco; I must have tucked him into this score and then forgotten it." He spoke of Bach as if he were a personal friend. As Little Li studied the clipping, he thought it bore a strange resemblance to the famous rendition of Mao hanging on Tiananmen Gate. Both were torsos with their faces looking stalwartly forward. But while the be-moled visage of Mao reflected an air of imperious, implacable opacity, the bewigged visage of Bach reflected a brooding, clerical rectitude. If Mao projected a temporal invincibility, Bach projected inward contemplation. "You know," Li Tongshu finally said, "I always imagined Bach looked on these variations just like his nineteen children." He smiled.

When Li Tongshu finally sat down to work on the *Variations* again, he was surprised by how organic a part of him they'd become and how many of them he still remembered. He'd always admired musicians who could conduct or play from memory. The idea that whole works, even a composer's complete repertoire, could be stored away in the head of a musician like the entire literary works of a writer in a library, and that they could be played without the notation at any time, impressed him as nothing short of miraculous. And the thought that these archives were then completely erased when a musician died seemed as tragic as the loss of a whole archive in a great library to fire.

Without constant new political shocks, life at Willow Courtyard regained an unexpected equilibrium that allowed Little Li to re-engage in childhood pastimes. Only grudgingly did he yield to his father's insistence that he be coached three times a week by a Paris-trained flutist who'd formerly been on the Conservatory faculty. Professor Liang was a short, thin, seemingly somber man with an aquiline face who at first Little Li found distant and aloof.

"Please, take a seat" was all he said, hardly opening his mouth as he spoke, when Little Li first entered his room. "What have you selected to play?"

"One of Telemann's solo fantasies for flute," he answered halfheartedly.

When he finished and lowered his instrument, Professor Liang remained sitting without speaking for such a long time that Little Li thought he must be displeased.

"Very nice," he finally said, giving a half-smile. It was only then Little Li saw that his front teeth were hideously broken and jagged that he understood that his somber countenance was not owing to a surly disposition, but his embarrassment over inflicting his ruined dentures on others by smiling. Nonetheless, the first time Little Li mastered a new piece, his teacher's face did melt into an unrestrained smile that was all the more rewarding because it was so heartfelt. Professor Liang could no longer play himself, but he treated the triumphs of his students as his own, a trait that made Little Li want to practice all the harder—not for praise, but because he sensed how his own progress uplifted the drought-stricken soul of this good man.

"When did you come back to China?" he asked one day as they were taking a break.

"I left Paris in 1949."

"Did you like it there?"

"Oh yes. It was beautiful," he answered, closing his eyes as if the better to recall the beauty of the city. "Perhaps someday you'll study abroad, just like your father and I did." He gave one of his rare full smiles.

"Would you tell me what happened to your teeth?" Little Li hadn't actually intended to pose such a personal question so bluntly, but it just came out.

"You know," said Professor Liang, looking right into his student's eyes, "you're the first person who's ever dared ask me that directly."

"Were you in an accident?" Professor Liang shook his head. "Then what happened?"

"Well . . ." He took a deep breath. "I got 'sent down' during the Anti-Rightist Campaign, like your father, but my role was to be paraded from village to village to participate in public self-criticism sessions before local peasant associations. At one session, there was a young man who'd been studying physics in Shanghai, and when he spotted the county party secretary with us, he must have decided this was his chance to prove how 'red' and revolutionary he was and maybe get sent home."

"And . . . ?" urged Little Li.

"And I was seated at a table on the threshing floor and had begun speaking about the decadence of Western music when he lunged at me, shook his finger in my face, and screamed, 'You love France more than China!' It was, of course, useless to deny his accusations, so I said nothing. But he became so infuriated by my silence that he grabbed me by the hair and slammed my face down onto the tabletop. When I felt my mouth filled with broken teeth, I knew my life as a musician had ended."

"I am so sorry" was all Little Li could manage.

"Such was my fate." He gave a sad smile. "Fortunately, I am still connected to music through students like you, and for that I'm thankful." Seeing the stricken expression on Little Li's face, Professor Liang reached over and patted the back of one of his hands. "I don't know what I can teach you except to love music and remind you that, unlike human beings, music never betrays us. In fact, somehow it makes us better people. As *The Book of Rights* [礼记] tells us, 'In music the Sages found pleasure and saw that it could be used to make the hearts of people good [樂也者聖人之所樂也而可以善民心].'"

When Professor Liang arranged for him to play trios with a pickup group of older Conservatory students, Little Li wanted to excel as much for his teacher's sake as for his own. And it was in these small groups that he first experienced the glorious sensation of being swept into that state of collective altered consciousness that makes playing with others so thrilling.

By his twelfth birthday, he'd become one of the most promising musicians in his class. But what he loved far more than playing the flute was fooling around with Little Wang and other kids in the neighborhood. The Two Virtuoso Ones attended the same school (where Little Wang played the clarinet without any evidence of talent), and because his parents also had bad "class background" (his father had worked for the Nationalists before 1949 and was a professor of engineering at Tsinghua University) they, too, had been "sent down," given the two boys even more in common. Before their departure, Little Wang's parents had thrust him into the custody of an unmarried aunt who took little interest in his life. And being an innately rebellious boy, he took advantage of her indifference and was soon getting into trouble.

One outgoing, provocative, brash, and cynical, the other shy, measured, studious, and reflective—the Two Virtuous Ones may have been opposites, but under these circumstances they became closer friends than ever. One of their favorite activities was seeing the few foreign movies—from countries like the Democratic People's Republic of Korea and the People's Republic of Albania—that were shown at the Children's Film Theater at Donghuamen. DPRK films invariably depicted Americans as evil imperialists and scheming spies conspiring to sabotage the righteous Korean people's struggle for liberation; those produced in Albania usually featured heroic partisans battling suave Nazi storm troopers. This limited overseas cinematic fare provided Little Li the smallest of portholes into the foreign world through which he could view the noses, eyes, hair, and facial expressions of Occidental women, something he did with all the absorption of an academic researcher doing ethnographic fieldwork.

Some of Little Li's happiest childhood memories were of the two summers spent in his father's "family village" (老家)—Gaozhuang, in Shandong Province's Heze County—where no one ever mocked him for looking foreign. There, a day's travel from Beijing by train, he saw a completely different side of Chinese life through Old Gao, a peasant, and his young son, Big Mountain (大山), who was just Little Li's own age and lived behind his grandfather's family house. Squatting on his haunches outside the doorway of their ramshackle dwelling, scarfing down buckwheat noodles through a mouth of rotten teeth, Old Gao would always ask, "Have you eaten?" Then, beaming broadly, thrust his bowl forward to share his meal.

"Thank you, Big Uncle Gao [高大叔], but my father and I have just eaten," Little Li always responded, knowing how precious each mouthful was to these penurious people, especially during times of want.

"No, no, you must have some!" the old man always insisted, pulling up a tangle of noodles with his chopsticks and forcing Little Li to accept a bowl of his own.

Big Mountain had a round peasant face burned as brown as the tobacco his father smoked in a brass-bowled pipe, and his bean-shaved cranium was etched with a string of ringworm scars that arced like an archipelago of coral atolls across his scalp between his oversized ears. Every day he wore the same threadbare jacket and trousers, onto which so many patches had been sown that virtually no part of the original garment remained visible. And around his neck hung a silver "longevity charm" (长命锁) inscribed with the character for "long life" (寿). Even though rural party cadres had waged relentless campaigns against feudal superstition, Old Gao so cherished Big Mountain that he insisted he wear this protective talisman. After all, every peasant knew the countryside was inhabited by myriad spirits, many of which were inclined to prey on young children. Traditional ways were so deeply rooted in life at Gaozhuang that, no matter how many political mass movements the party launched, or how much propaganda bombarded the peasants, they still clung to their old ways. Little Li was particularly enthralled by Big Mountain's belief in ghosts (鬼), fox spirits (狐狸精), and tutelary gods (门神), to whom he and many rural people still secretly made offerings.

One of Little Li's favorite Gaozhuang stories involved a friend of Big Mountain's who because of rural superstition had been given the unfortunate nickname Pile of Shit Gao (粪堆). Having lost two children before they reached their first year, Pile of Shit's mother was determined to do everything she could to repel predatory spirits from taking him as well. And what better way to protect her son than to give him a truly loathsome name? His mother was also smart enough to know how to convey the appearance of compliance to party demands: she gave Pile of Shit a second name as well, Strong Country Gao (高国强). But the merciless children of the village so reveled in mocking him that, although Pile of Shit Gao was not taken away by otherworldly spirits, he suffered grievously in this world.

Big Mountain's mother had later died in childbirth, so, like Little Li, he'd grown up alone with his father. Even though he spoke only local dialect and there was a vast gulf in education, upbringing, and class between them, the two boys felt instant kinship. As soon as Little Li arrived in Gaozhuang, he sought out Big Mountain and tagged along as he herded goats, weeded vegetables, fished, and shot birds with his slingshot. When traveling propaganda troupes occasionally came through the village, the two boys sneaked backstage to spy on the performers. The highlight of their first summer was a momentary glimpse of the naked breast of a young dancer as she changed costumes.

When they'd had enough spying, they wandered out to the front of the makeshift stage with arms slung around each other's shoulders to sit with the other villagers and enjoy a film, an opera, some revolutionary songs, or a "cross talk" (快板). But what Little Li loved most were Old Gao's tales about the bandits who once roamed the area and the communist guerrillas who'd fought the Japanese there during World War II. Each evening, they had to wait patiently for Old Gao to finish chatting with other village men, all sitting on the work brigade's threshing floor in the light of flickering oil lamps, smoking their brass bowled pipes. When Old Gao was finally ready, the boys were never disappointed in his yarns, especially the ones about the heartless Japanese, who, as far as they were concerned, were the most demonic villains on earth.

It was with great regret that Little Li returned to Willow Court-yard at summer's end where each morning they were awakened by the crackle of static from the tinny loudspeakers on Big Sheep Wool Alley as "The East Is Red" boomed out over the sloping tiled roofs of the neighborhood:

The east is red, the sun is rising.
From China comes a Mao Zedong.
He strives for the people's happiness,
Hurrah, for he is the people's great savior!
Chairman Mao loves the people,
He is our guide
In building a new China
Hurrah, for he will lead us forward!
The Communist Party is like the sun,
Wherever it shines,
Wherever the Communist Party is,
There is brightness.
Hurrah, for only through Mao are the people liberated!

This socialist reveille was always followed by a newscast read in the stentorian tones of revolutionary righteousness. Then, as suddenly as these bombastic broadcasts began, they ended, leaving only a chorus of tin-face-pans scraping on concrete sinks, spitting, and nose blowing, all parts of the neighborhood's morning sonic landscape. Then charcoal braziers were lit, smoke curled over brick walls, and breakfast was eaten before Little Li and his father bicycled together through Tiananmen Square to the Conservatory.

"So"—Li Tongshu loved to jest as they passed Mao's portrait—"the old guy's still up there, eh?" They always had a good laugh, because the portrait had become such a permanent part of the landscape that without Mao gazing imperiously out over Tiananmen Square's vastness this iconic public place would have seemed incomplete. Biking back home in the evenings, Little Li always looked forward to that moment when they finally turned off the broad Avenue of Eternal Peace, to leave the exposed outer world of enormous Stalinist buildings, intimidating squares, and broad socialist boulevards, and reenter the filigree of ancient winding alleys and low-lying courtyard houses where people actually lived. As they entered this maze of *hutong*s, he felt like a small fish leaving the dangerous open ocean for the safety of a sheltering reef. Despite its dilapidation, the satisfyingly diminutive scale of Big Sheep Wool Alley and its familiar sights and sounds were a comfort to Little Li as a boy. He'd come to love the clamorous din of cicadas that, as if secretly directed by an unseen choirmaster, swelled in a collective crescendo before falling away into perfectly coordinated silence; the distinctive cries of street peddlers as they trudged by, hawking their services and wares; the ethereal moan of homing pigeons fitted with hand-carved whistles as they flew overhead in airborne arcs to the commands of unseen earthbound keepers; the gentle clinging of bicycle bells heard over courtyard walls; and the distant chuffing and hooting of steam engines arriving and departing the distant train station.

Sometimes at night, when he went to the public latrine out on Big Sheep Wool Alley, he'd close his eyes and pretend he was blind. With an accuracy as deft as when his father hit just the right key on the piano without looking, he knew how to feel his way across the courtyard with his feet, reach out at exactly the right moment to grasp the cool smoothness of the iron latchkey on the gate, and then navigate the alleyway until he picked up the first sulfurous scent emanating from the public latrine. Like a mariner guided by celestial navigation, he then knew exactly how many steps he needed to take before turning right and mounting the four stone stairs into the latrine itself. The stink in this sepulchral place of communal evacuation was foul, but so familiar that the whole neighborhood would have seemed somehow denatured without it.

One Sunday morning, Little Li awakened to find his father standing beside his bed holding a saw and a coil of rope.

"I think we can save the old willow," he announced excitedly.

"What?" mumbled Little Li, still half asleep.

"The old willow—it just needs to be pruned and watered. So I borrowed a saw and some rope from Old Wu's workshop. Shall we do it together?"

"Do what?"

"Save our lovely willow," he said, beaming. Little Li reluctantly got up and dressed. As they walked outside to survey the tree, which arched its neglected branches over their room, his father announced, "Here's the plan: we'll tie the rope around your waist, and you'll climb up and trim away the dead branches." Because his father's enthusiasm brooked no complaint, Little Li threw one end of the rope up over a branch, tied the other around his waist, and climbed into the tree.

"Get that branch!" his father excitedly commanded. "No, higher! Yes! That one!"

By the time Little Li came back down after scrambling through the skeleton of leafless branches, he had blisters on his hands and his body ached. Still, so infectious was his father's enthusiasm that he pitched in again after lunch, this time to spade up the earth around the old tree's trunk, trim the battered persimmon tree in front of Granny Sun's room, and even prune the feral wisteria vine that ranged on a trellis above their veranda. And then, although evening was falling, he sawed up all the trimmed branches into lengths small enough to burn in their stove.

"Comrades!" announced the chief of the Big Sheep Wool Alley Neighborhood Committee, after calling a meeting of all the residents one evening. "Our committee has been handed down a new policy: residents are now permitted to divide up the garden space into plots in each courtyard for cultivation by individual families."

"You mean we can grow things for ourselves?" asked Granny Sun in her predictably direct way.

"That's the new policy," answered the committee chief.

"Is this idea of private property new communist theory?" she persisted.

"It is not a question of theory," he replied with irritation. "It's a question of eating."

"Oh, I see," said Granny Sun, as if that explained everything.

The change was, in fact, a complete reversal of past policy; however, what was important to the committee chief was not consistency, but that a decision come down from on high now needed to be implemented. Peasants in the countryside were already cultivating private plots, raising chickens, ducks, rabbits, and even keeping pigs. Now urbanitess were being afforded similar privileges. Even tenants of apartment buildings were getting in on the action by cultivating beans, peas, and squash in window boxes, sending vines climbing around window bars and up drainpipes.

As it turned out, except for playing the piano, there was nothing Li Tongshu enjoyed more than gardening, and by summertime his allotment of hardpan in Willow Courtyard had come alive with vegetables and flowers. He even managed to find a potted gardenia at a street market, whose fragrance was so dangerously sweet it seemed positively counterrevolutionary. He and Little Li sometimes bicycled to the edge of the city with a burlap sack in search of manure dropped on the road by the horses and donkeys pulling carts. And after washing dishes, they sprinkled the wastewater onto his beloved plants.

That spring, the old wisteria shot out Medusa-like tendrils that exploded into grapelike bunches of fragrant purple blossoms; the old willow unfurled a new cascade of weeping green foliage; for the first time in years, the persimmon tree fruited; and when Li Tongshu's squash vines discharged flamelike orange flowers, he became childlike with excitement.

"Hey, Professor Li, are you in possession of state agricultural secrets?" an engineer from the next courtyard jokingly asked one day upon seeing his garden.

"Just serving the people," replied Li Tongshu impishly.

No one refused the slender-necked yellow squash, the succulent red tomatoes, or the plump green peppers he generously shared with neighbors in return for their wastewater.

"What are you doing?" Little Li called out one summer evening when he found his father sitting on a stool in the middle of his idyll.

"Just enjoying my little green friends," he responded with a smile. "Even though they'll soon be gone, they neither complain nor surrender. They just keep turning sunlight and water into life, doing something useful, remaining true to their natures without betraying each other."

Months passed without more political drama or upset—as Dr. Song had hopefully predicted, things had settled down. Li Tongshu sought to banish his recurring fears that something dark still lurked just over the horizon. Of course, Chinese politics were still a whirlpool constantly spinning things into their opposites. But for now, the situation allowed a measure of hope and optimism. And Little Li was free to roam the city with Little Wang. They loved to visit the storytellers, acrobats, and seers who congregated in Tianqiao (天桥). Here his friend was most fascinated by the curbside dentists who wore necklaces of decayed molars, had tabletops arrayed with giant tongs, and cast sadistic come-hither grins to passing potential customers. Just being around Little Wang's swaggering cockiness made Little Li feel stronger. One day when they were fooling around on Coal Hill, overlooking the Forbidden City, he began pretending he was a beggar. Seated cross-legged in the middle of the stone steps going up the hill, he made a cup out of both hands, screwed his face up like a palsied mendicant, and chanted, "Give what ya can! Give what ya can!" To Little Li's astonishment, an old woman handed him fifty-five cents. As soon as she left, they repaired to the Forever Red Restaurant (永红 小吃), near Wealth and Power Hutong (富强胡同), for a tasty snack.

As Little Li approached puberty, he began to be powerfully and mysteriously drawn to girls who rendered him speechless. He was most fixated on Feng Yi, a girl in his class with radiant pink cheeks, shiny black pigtails, and nubile breasts just beginning to create a suggestive swell under her tunic. Once, while playing blindman's buff, she'd won the draw to tie the blindfold over his eyes, and when she touched him, she triggered feelings akin to an atomic blast. Little Wang, on the other hand, had an admirably insouciant way of joking with girls until they broke down into fits of embarrassed giggling. And since he was the only person who seemed to have actual information about the mysterious longings now possessing him, Little Li viewed him as possessing the keys to a forbidden kingdom.

"Okay, here's what you need to know about 'chicks' [娘们]," he began with braggadocio as they passed two particularly cute girls coming home from school one day. "The first thing is that, when guys start getting big 'peckers' [鸡巴], they want to use them, and there's only three things peckers are good for: 'taking a piss' [撒尿]; 'shooting down the airplanes' [打飞机]; and 'shooting the cannon' [放炮]. The only other thing you need to know is that, even though every guy wants to 'shoot the cannon' with girls, no one talks about it in public."

"Do the girls want to do it, too?" asked Little Li hesitantly.

"They love it, too, but they'll never admit it. But I've got a cousin who's doing it now to a lot of girls."

"Doing what?"

"Stickin' his thing between their legs!"

Such things were almost impossible for Little Li to imagine. As far as he could tell, adults were asexual beings who never talked about anything related to such topics, much less showed any overt expressions of amorousness toward members of the opposite sex. And it was unthinkable to broach the subject with his father, who seemed to exist on another plane, one ruled by propriety and decorum rather than the riot of passions now beginning to well up inside him. The only manifestation of overt sexuality to occur in Willow Courtyard involved the tiny carved ivory amulet of the Yellow Emperor (黄帝), the mythic grand progenitor from whom all Chinese are said to have descended, which had been given to Li Tongshu by his own father. Because its most distinguishing feature was an oversized erection (an ancient symbol of fertility), his father had kept it in their wardrobe with his American wristwatch and roll of U.S. bills. The day he came home and found Little Li playing with it was one he would not soon forget. His father had snatched it away, and the next time Little Li saw it, the amulet's "jade stalk" (玉杆) was gone.

Little Li would have been surprised to learn that any of the dour teachers at school ever allowed the kinds of lusts that were now inflaming him to overcome them. Though the party clearly did not welcome competition from the libido, Little Li had observed that this most animal of urges sometimes erupted anyway through the carefully scripted surfaces of daily life, and often in embarrassing ways. Little Wang was full of stories about lecherous cadres forcing themselves on young women, or voyeurs peering into people's windows. One afternoon, as they were walking down Water Millstone Hutong, Little Wang suddenly stopped and pointed at a cardboard sign reading "Temporarily Closed" affixed to the entrance of the neighborhood women's latrine.

"This is the place where . . . !" He began laughing so hard he couldn't finish.

"Where?" asked Little Li.

"Check out the roof!" Little Wang managed to get out, pointing to a gaping hole in the latrine's tile roof that looked as if an artillery round had made a direct hit.

"What happened?"

"This horny old guy who used to head the local Neighborhood Committee climbed a tree at the back of the shitter and managed to pry up a couple of roof tiles so he could spy on the ladies doing their business. One night he must have been up in his tree 'shooting down airplanes' and gotten carried away, because he . . . he . . ." Again Little Wang doubled over in laughter.

"He what?" begged Little Li.

"The old 'pervert' [老色鬼] lost his grip, fell through the fucking latrine roof, and landed right on top of an old crone and her granddaughter crouching side by side inside."

"Was he hurt?"

"One of his legs snapped like a wooden chopstick! There he was lying in all that shit and piss, with his junk still hanging out, and he couldn't hightail it out of there because of his leg."

"What did they do to him?"

"The old bugger was accused of 'crimes of counterrevolutionary voyeurism' [反革命偷看罪] and sent off to a 'reform-through-labor camp' [劳改营]. And then there was this other 'moronic egg' [傻蛋] I heard about who kept dreaming about feeling up a girl he liked at his factory. But then he screwed up big-time by telling a friend and soon the whole factory knew about his horny dreams! But that wasn't the end of it, because, some dumb fuck told the poor girl, who'd never even said hello to this creepy guy. Then when she learned everyone else also knew about his gross dreams, she got so embarrassed she committed suicide!"

"Killed herself?"

"Ate rat poison and went off to Western Paradise."

"What did they do to the weirdo?"

"His factory party secretary accused him of having 'counter-revolutionary dreams of rape' [反革命梦奸罪], and he, too, was packed off to a 'reform-through-labor camp.'"

Uncontrollable passion coupling with indiscretion in Mao's puritanical China could lead to tragic consequences. Mathematics Teacher Yao was a slender, reserved woman who taught the fifth grade at Little Li's school. Because she was still single at age forty, everyone assumed she was doomed to remain "an old spinster" (老姑娘). One morning, when she inexplicably failed to show up for class, no one thought much of it. However, the next day, when History Teacher Liu, who was married to a stout, unprepossessing woman who worked in the Conservatory library, also failed to show up, rumors began ricocheting around that a new political purge was under way. Then a boy in the class above Little Li who played percussion and was nicknamed "the Hoodlum Drummer" (流氓鼓手) announced that anyone who wanted to hear the whole story about Teacher Yao should meet at lunchtime under the poplar tree in the far corner of the schoolyard with five cents.

"So here's the straight shit," began the Hoodlum Drummer as a hush fell over those who'd paid up. "One night last week, the Public Security Bureau received a tip from a vice-principal who was angry at Teacher Yao because she wouldn't shoot the cannon with him; he told them that a crime was being committed in the woodwind practice room. When police broke down the door, they found Teacher Liu with his drawers down around his ankles, just about to make some 'clouds and rain' [云雨]. They took photos and told Teacher Yao that if she didn't confess about all the others she'd been 'shooting the cannon' with they'd release the pictures."

"Can we see them?" a boy in the back blurted out.

"Oh yeah! Sure!" mocked the Hoodlum Drummer. "For five cents you want photos?" Everyone laughed at the mortified boy. They were, however, impressed by the raconteur's savvy, even though only a minority in his audience actually understood what they'd just heard.

The story took a more tragic twist two days later. As Little Li was approaching school that morning, he was stunned to spot Teacher Yao kneeling on the sidewalk outside the front gate. Even though it was chilly, she wore only a tattered tan blouse that barely covered her slender torso, and she was rocking back and forth, moaning. A group of girls lugging instrument cases hurriedly passed her by with their gaze downcast, as if they might be done harm by making eye contact. Then a knot of boys gathered across the street to gawk. But no one dared move to help the distraught woman. Finally, an agitated vice-principal appeared.

"It's nothing," he kept tutting nervously, far more concerned with maneuvering Teacher Yao into the gatehouse and out of sight than with consoling her. But just before finally disappearing inside, she looked over to where the stunned boys were standing and let out a plaintive howl.

"Aiyahhhhhhh!" she cried. "I'm no longer among the living!"

Although the boys were not sure what she meant, they could not miss her anguish. Thereafter, no one referred to Teacher Yao again. She simply ceased to exist.

14

WHEN HE was notified that the vice-dean of the Conservatory wished to see him, Li Tongshu feared the worst. It turned out, however, that he was not being called to a self-criticism session, but to provide piano accompaniment for a new revolutionary opera.

"What new opera?" he asked the vice-dean warily.

"A bold new work, *Spark Among the Reeds* [芦荡火种], which celebrates the New Fourth Route Army's heroic struggle against the Japanese occupation of the Chinese Motherland during World War II."

"But perhaps I'm not the most suitable person for such an important production," he demurred, dreading involvement in a propaganda project.

"This is a brand-new opera under Jiang Qing's direction," replied the vice-dean peremptorily. "The schedule has been set, and you've won the assignment as accompanist."

Because Jiang Qing, Mao's wife, was becoming China's cultural tsarina—or, as she liked to call herself, "a plain sentry for the Chairman, patrolling the ideological battlefront"—Li Tongshu knew he had no choice. But during the first rehearsal, all he could think about as he banged out each stultifying number was of that moment when he would not have to listen to another bar of this dreadful score. Then, at the very last run-through, as he was hammering out the finale and looking forward to his liberation, the production manager appeared behind him.

"I bring good news, Comrade Li! Our leadership has decided to extend an invitation to you to attend the opening-night gala." He was beaming.

"I appreciate the honor," began Li Tongshu gingerly, trying to think how best to beg off without giving offense. "But, I'm sure there are others far more worthy of a place at this important cultural event than me."

"Oh, no, no, no!" protested the manager. "You more than anyone appreciate this revolutionary work's true significance, and we wouldn't hear of your being absent."

As it turned out, Chairman Mao himself attended the gala, and as he passed by, Li Tongshu had a chance to study him for a few moments. He looked nothing like his portrait on Tiananmen. His face was white and puffy, what hair he still had was shoe-polish black, and his gait was so shuffling that Li Tongshu wouldn't have been surprised if he'd keeled over into the scrum of fawning subalterns surrounding him. As other audience members spotted him and Jiang Qing, they ceased speaking, moving, perhaps even breathing. It was as if the Jade Emperor had just descended from his celestial realm.

When the opera finally ended, the audience exploded in a storm of ecstatic applause and Jiang Qing stood up to take repeated bows, as if she herself had composed and directed this masterpiece. But it was not the music that audience members were applauding, but the fact that they'd been anointed to sit in the same hall as the Chairman and his wife. They were, in effect, clapping for themselves.

Spark Among the Reeds received an avalanche of extravagant praise. A critic from the *Enlightenment Daily* referred to it as "a sparkling gem in the treasure house of proletarian music," and *Chinese Literature* extolled it as representing "a new dawn" in culture. Mao Zedong had so enjoyed the opera, he ordered that it to be renamed *Shejiabang* (沙家浜), expanded, and enshrined thereafter as part of China's revolutionary repertoire. Unfortunately, the opera was also a harbinger of a new and more militant political climate. Indeed, as the 1960s progressed and as Mao re-emerged from the sidelines, the party began calling on the Chinese people to "never forget class struggle" (千万不要忘记阶级斗争), to wage "permanent revolution," and never surrender to the Soviet "revisionist" (修正主义) policies of cultivating "peaceful coexistence" (和平共处) with America, a policy Mao claimed was "tantamount to believing the U.S. imperialists will lay down the butcher knife and become Buddhas!" As if a seasonal change in foliage were taking place,

Beijing, too, was being etched by a new crimson tide of increasingly militant slogans, banners, and posters.

"Things are moving backward again," Li Tongshu offered in hushed tones to Dr. Song as they walked down Wangfujing together one evening. They had no particular destination in mind, but they knew that the best way to keep a conversation private in Beijing was simply to keep moving.

"At the hospital they've restarted 'political study groups'," added Dr. Song. "Everywhere, the Chairman seems to be pushing things in a more militant direction."

" 'Such is the momentum of history,' " Li Tongshu said with a resigned sigh, reciting the famous lines from the classical novel *All Men Are Brothers* (水浒传). " 'The empire long divided must unite, and long united, must divide [合久必分分久必合].' It's frightening how things keep turning into their opposites, with us left running along behind."

"Did something happen at the Conservatory?" asked Dr. Song, sensing his friend's darkened mood.

"One of our most hotheaded students just wrote Chairman Mao, criticizing the school. And guess what? He wrote back."

"What did he say?" asked Dr. Song in surprise.

"That we should 'make the ancient serve the present and the foreign serve China.' But I read it as a signal to heighten wariness against foreign influences then the *Enlightenment Daily* just ran a piece entitled 'I Was Poisoned by Bourgeois Music of the West,' claiming that listening to Western classical music 'will slowly muddle your class viewpoint and understanding of problems.' And all sorts of other attacks are starting to appear on the Western repertoire, calling it 'yellow music' [黄色音乐], as if it were so much pornography. One of my own students is even turning that dreadful song 'Sailing the Seas Depends on the Great Helmsman' into an opera with a libretto that includes 'Just as fish can't leave the water or melons leave their vines, / So the revolutionary masses cannot from the Communist Party disentwine.' "

"China's own Giuseppe Verdi," said Dr. Song with a bitter laugh.

"But it's no laughing matter," protested his friend. "Remember the Socialist Education Movement a few years ago, when artists and intellectuals began getting sent off to 'learn from the workers, peasants, and soldiers' [学工学农学军]? I ignored it, because it didn't have any immediate impact on me. But now I see it was a warning of something bigger."

"To let hope deceive is all too human."

"I suppose so," responded Li Tongshu wistfully. "The past is never as irrevocably gone as we may like to believe. It just gets buried in the shallowest of graves, ready to rise again at a moment's notice. Just as people allow themselves to hope that the party might finally turn from revolution and allow them to quietly lead their lives, the unwelcome past begins reappearing. That's the logic of Mao's 'permanent revolution' [不断革命]: there may be a temporary slowdown or hiatus, but a resting place is never an end in itself for Mao. 'Our revolutions come one after another,' he wrote. 'After a victory, we must at once put forward a new task.'"

Even as Li Tongshu tried to concentrate on taking care of his son, teaching his students, tending his garden, and practicing the piano, the past hung over him like an unresolved chord. One night, he came home to find Little Li reciting from a recently published essay by Mao entitled "On the Correct Handling of Contradictions Among the People" for school. As he earnestly rehearsed, Li Tongshu kept hearing troubling lines. Intellectuals and artists were described as being "impractical in their thinking and irresolute in action" and not having a correct political point of view was compared to "like having no soul." To escape, Li Tongshu walked out onto the veranda and gazed blankly at his beloved willow tree. He felt blinded by the gathering darkness.

"Son, if there ever comes a time when I must leave again, remember that, wherever I am, I'll be thinking of you," he heard himself say after coming back inside. But when he saw the expression on his son's face, he wished he hadn't spoken.

"What do you mean?" asked Little Li in alarm. "Where are you going?"

"Oh, nowhere," he insisted. "I don't know what I was trying to say."

But Little Li understood perfectly well what he'd meant, and it left him both distraught and annoyed. Why was he always so dour and unenthusiastic about the revolution? Didn't he realize the jeopardy such a bad attitude put them both in? What's more, what excited him just then was not music or gardening, but the political excitement that was building around them in the streets. By 1966, a new struggle was clearly incubating. Everywhere now there were stories about seditious counterrevolutionaries, evil American spies, and dangerous class enemies lurking, maybe even hiding right here on Big Sheep Wool Alley! For the Two Virtuous Ones, the thought that they, mere boys, might play a role in helping uncover such miscreants was thrilling.

When it was reported that Mao had personally addressed a group of young so-called Red Guards at Tsinghua University Middle School to commend their "anger at and denunciation of all landlords, bourgeois elements, imperialists, revisionists, and their running dogs," the boys' sense of excitement only escalated. And when the State Council called on youth to "answer Mao's call" and closed all the schools so students could help "build a new wave of revolutionary youth activity," the Two Virtuous Ones were thrilled. With tens of thousands of students now all imagining themselves as Mao's "foot soldiers" and roaming the streets, the Two Virtuous Ones were only too eager to join in. However, since they were penniless, they had to sneak onto buses and hope the ticket collectors would not spot them.

One afternoon, however, a voice barked over the PA system, "The two 'little devils' [小家伙] in the front must buy tickets or get off the bus!"

When the boys still did not disembark, the surly conductress began wading down the crowded aisle brandishing her ticket punch like a handgun and making menacing clicking noises. Little Li was coiled like a spring, ready to leap off at the next stop, when Little Wang snapped to attention and, in a high-pitched, staccato voice, began reciting: " 'The world is yours, as well as ours, but in the last analysis, it is yours. You young people, full of vigor and vitality, are in the bloom of life, like the sun at eight or nine in the morning. Our hope is placed on you. . . . The world belongs to you. China's future belongs to you.' "

This quote was one of Chairman Mao's most hallowed utterances from the pocket-sized red-jacketed *Quotations from Chairman Mao Zedong,* or the Little Red Book, which was just then sweeping the country in popularity. With the censorious gaze of every passenger now fixed on the conductress, she sheathed her punch in its leather holster, sighed, and, with a look of resignation, returned to her perch. But Little Wang was not about to leave the matter there. When he finished his quotation, he brazenly pushed his way down the crowded aisle until he was standing right in front of the thwarted conductress's catbird seat. Then, turning with military precision to face the hapless woman, he began reciting another Mao quotation with all the sanctimoniousness of a preacher: "We should be modest and prudent, guard against arrogance and rashness, and serve the Chinese people heart and soul."

As she blanched, Little Wang arched his back and, with a mixture of triumph and scorn, clicked his heels together in military fashion, saluted, and marched defiantly back to the front of the bus. Such was the power of Chairman Mao's words, and the boys quickly perfected a routine to use them. Whenever they heard that a "capitalist roader," "counterrevolutionary," or "class enemy" was to be publicly "struggled against" (批斗会) for opposing Chairman Mao's Great Proletarian Cultural Revolutionary line, they jumped on a bus, took up strategic positions near the front door, clasped their Little Red Books reverently to their chests, and began a tag-team recitation of Mao quotations like monks chanting sutras. No conductor ever asked for a fare, much less kicked them off the bus.

When a girl from the Chen family on Dragon Beard Ditch Hutong discovered an incriminating pair of high-heeled shoes under her parents' bed and presented them to the neighborhood Red Guard unit as evidence of her mother's "bourgeois thinking" (资产阶级思想), the boys ran over to watch. They arrived just as the terrified woman was being paraded out of her house with a rope around her neck while her daughter shrieked accusations at her. Instead of feeling sympathy, the Two Virtuous Ones chanted slogans themselves, and felt thrilled to be vicariously participating. In fact, inspired by the slogan "Take up your pen as a weapon and open fire on all black elements!," they even wrote a wall poster of their own:

WE RESOLUTELY SUPPORT COMRADE CHEN YIMING'S
COURAGEOUS ACTIONS IN PURGING HER HOME OF
POISONOUS WESTERN SHOES TO OVERTHROW
THE BOURGEOIS REACTIONARY LINE OF HER MOTHER.
THE TWO VIRTUOUS ONES

In July 1966, when the country was electrified by news that the septuagenarian Chairman Mao had swum across the Yangtze River, The Two Virtuous Ones waited for hours at a news kiosk near the train station to buy one of the many special commemorative issues of newspapers being put out to celebrate the event. When they finally got their copies, they featured a massive blood-red headline: "OUR RESPECTED AND BELOVED LEADER IS SO HEALTHY! THIS IS THE GREATEST HAPPINESS FOR THE ENTIRE CHINESE PEOPLE AND ALL REVOLUTIONARY PEOPLES AROUND THE WORLD."

An accompanying photo showed a framed portrait of Mao draped in ceremonial bunting being towed across the muddy river by a brace of security guards swimming just behind the Chairman's bobbing head. An inscription proclaimed:

> *THROUGH THE MIDST OF THE HIGHEST WAVES AND*
> *STRONGEST WINDS, WE WILL FOLLOW CHAIRMAN MAO.*
> 紧跟毛主席在大风大浪中前进

One morning, Little Li and his father were awakened as usual by "The East Is Red" booming out over Big Sheep Wool Alley. But when it ended, a near-hysterical voice set in to announce that Chairman Mao had written a "wall poster" himself, calling on all youth to "Bombard the Headquarters of the Party" (炮打司令部):

> In the last fifty days, some leading comrades from the
> Central Committee down to local party branches have . . .
> adopted the reactionary stand of the bourgeoisie, enforced
> a bourgeois dictatorship, and struck out at the surging
> movement of the Great Proletarian Cultural Revolution.
> They have stood facts on their head, confused black with
> white, encircled and suppressed revolutionaries, stifled
> opinions differing from their own, imposed a white
> terror on adversaries, and now feel very pleased with
> themselves. . . . How poisonous!

By calling on student rebels to attack the leadership of the party, Mao was, in effect, declaring war on the very apparatus he himself had helped found half a century before.

"Everyone's talking about his call," Little Li excitedly announced to his father at breakfast one morning.

"So I've heard," Li Tongshu replied, trying to be measured in tone. "But you must remember—things are not always what they seem."

"What do you mean?" asked Little Li. "Isn't Chairman Mao trying to defeat all the enemies of the revolution, and shouldn't we support him?" When his father did not immediately respond, Little Li continued: "The revolution is under threat, and you just—"

"I know this is an exciting time for you boys," interrupted his father, putting a hand on Little Li's shoulder. "But you need to be careful. Remember, 'Once on the back of a tiger, it's difficult to dismount' [骑虎难下]."

"Why don't you ever show any enthusiasm?" remonstrated Little Li. "I mean, this is our country's revolution, isn't it?"

"No, it's Chairman Mao's revolution," responded his father, near his wits' end. "His call to young students like you is aimed not at building the nation, but at 'creating great disorder under heaven' [大闹天宫]. He wants to turn everything upside down." The way his son glowered back made Li Tongshu realize there was nothing more he could say.

As the summer progressed, Li Tongshu found refuge only in his dreams, which kept returning to San Francisco, like homing pigeons. These dreams were often accompanied by the *Goldberg Variations,* which made him feel he was watching a film edited to fit a musical score. But then he would awaken, realize where he was, and feel like a character trapped in a story by his favorite writer, Lu Xun, who'd once written, "The most painful thing in life is to awaken from a dream and find no way out."

More and more he felt as if an impenetrable glass dome had been clamped down over China, quarantining its people from the rest of the world. Chinese might still share the planet's atmosphere and oceans with others, but so few connections were left with the outside, they lived in what was essentially a separate universe. Only a small number of international flights left Beijing's Capital International Airport each day, and their destinations were dead ends like Pyongyang, Hanoi, and Moscow. Even if there had been flights to San Francisco, Paris, Tokyo, or New York, Li Tongshu no longer had a valid passport. He could only hope that the political lightning that was starting to strike all around him would not hit them directly. Little Li sensed his father's upset, but knew nothing of the depth of his anguish. And, truth be told, he did not want to know. What he yearned for was to have his father make a clear demonstration that he was on the right side of the great struggle. But by then Little Li was seeing less and less of him because he left home early in the morning and did not arrive back until late at night, weary, distant, and with no stomach to hear about the marches, rallies, and struggle sessions his son had been vicariously attending.

On August 18, Chairman Mao appeared on the Tiananmen Gate rostrum to review the tens of thousands of Red Guards who'd been waiting hours to watch as a pretty young student named Song Binbin (宋彬彬) awarded him a red armband. When he insisted that the characters composing her given name ("Song the Refined") were insufficiently "militant," she immediately agreed to change her name to "Demanding Militancy Song" (宋要武), causing a renaming fever to sweep the country. Little Li, too, had yearned to trade in his own indelibly "feudal" name for one more revolutionary, such as Lover of Struggle Li (李愛斗), Forever Red Li (李永紅), or Oppose Revision Li (李反修), but his father's response was a swift "No."

"But, Papa, the Zhang boy down the alley got permission to change his name from Surpassing Openness Zhang [张启超] to Oppose American Imperialism Zhang [張反帝]," he had tried to argue.

"That boy was named after the greatest turn-of-the-century reformer, Liang Qichao [梁启超], and it's an abomination that his parents allowed him to change it," replied his father angrily.

"But everyone's doing it," insisted Little Li.

"Your mother and I chose your name together, and it's as much a part of you as an arm or a leg," he rejoined. Neither of them said anything more about the matter.

When Little Li spotted Little Wang coming through their gate one September morning, he ran out to intercept him.

"You can't just walk in here," he chided. "My father will see you, and you know he doesn't like us hanging out together all the time!"

"I know, I know!" replied Little Wang impatiently. "But Chairman Mao's appearing again today on Tiananmen Gate to review more Red Guards, and we don't want to miss it."

"All right," responded Little Li, furtively glancing toward their room. "But my father won't be pleased if he finds out, so wait for me in the alley. I'll come out when I can."

"Don't take too long, because security's very tight, but I know a back way in through the old Foreign Legation Quarter."

"What's with your old man?" Little Wang asked when they finally set out for the square.

"I don't know what he does every day, but he certainly doesn't like us messing around at political rallies."

"Well, if he doesn't want to be part of the action, that's his decision!" declared Little Wang dismissively. Little Li was not pleased with his answer, but didn't know how to respond.

As they hurried down Dongjiaomin Xiang, they could already hear the crowd in the square. There were police everywhere, but Little Wang guided them into a passageway past rows of garbage bins until they came out on the edge of the square near a small grove of trees in front of the National Museum of Chinese History. The square itself was packed with exactly the kind of adoring crowd Mao had imagined when, in the 1950s, he'd ordered the area in front of Tiananmen Gate to be expanded and made larger and grander than even Red Square in Moscow.

"Now what?" asked Little Li, seeing that they'd never get through all the police into the square itself, where supporters who'd arrived from their various "units" (单位) had been waiting for hours in organized groups.

"See that tree?" asked Little Wang, pointing to a sycamore in front of the museum. "From the top we'll be able to see everything and maybe no one will bother us."

Little Li went first and pulled his friend up behind him. From their perch they had a good view of the vermilion rostrum on top of Tiananmen Gate. As they waited, a gaggle of teenage girls in red armbands who looked to be from the museum began singing below:

We're the Red Guards of Chairman Mao, our red hearts
steeled in storms and waves.

*Armed with Mao Zedong Thought, we dare storm
mountains and seas of swords and flames.*

After a few hours had passed, Little Wang sang out.

"Hey! I got a problem!"

"What problem?" asked Little Li.

"I've finished all the water in my canteen and I . . ."

"You just gotta hold it in," replied Little Li impatiently.

"I'm gonna explode!" Little Wang called back fifteen minutes later.

"Use your canteen!"

"You're a fucking genius!" gasped his friend. Holding his canteen with one hand, he tried to insert his pecker into its mouth with the other, while simultaneously holding on to the tree.

"Don't fall, like that perv on Water Millstone Hutong!" said Little Li, laughing.

Little Wang was in no mood for humor, because before he could get squared away, he went off like a sprinkler head, sending a shower cascading down through the tree leaves. After one of the girls below looked up and saw what Little Wang was doing, she let out a bloodcurdling shriek completely unlike the cries of adoration being offered up for Chairman Mao. Soon all the girls were shaking their fists and baying up at Little Wang like hounds at a treed animal.

Several hours later, when their aching muscles were reaching the limit of endurance, a tan dot topped by a khaki-colored cap appeared beneath one of the enormous red lanterns hanging over the Tiananmen rostrum. As a great clamor went up, the crowd began thrusting their Little Red Books into the air and chanting over and over, "Long live Chairman Mao!" Then the loudspeakers sprang to life.

"On behalf of the Great Proletarian Cultural Revolution and our Great Helmsman Chairman Mao Zedong, we welcome all revolutionary youth to Beijing and Tiananmen Square." The strident voice of Jiang Qing reverberated out over the square. "Our socialist revolution has reached a stage that affects human beings even to their souls," she continued. "The bourgeoisie may have been dethroned, but the Four Olds have not yet been vanquished. Long live permanent revolution!" The crowd roared like fans at a sports stadium when the home team scores a winning goal. "Respect the initiatives of the masses!" cried Jiang Qing. "Throw away your misgivings! Do not be afraid of disorder! Rely on the masses!" Another roar of acclaim went up.

Then, after a lull, a high-pitched male voice with a heavy Hunan accent began, and the crowd fell completely silent. It was Chairman Mao.

"You should be concerned about important affairs of state, and you should carry out the Cultural Revolution to the end," he intoned, sounding almost drugged.

In anticipation of his continuing, the crowd remained so hushed that Little Li could hear the electronic hiss of the loudspeakers and the flutter of tree leaves in the breeze. But when, to everyone's surprise, no further words issued forth, a perplexed murmur rippled through the crowd. Then a lone voice called out: "Long Live Chairman Mao! May he live ten thousand years!" As if a detonator had triggered a chain reaction, hundreds of thousands of faithful stabbed their Little Red Books into the air and took up the chant: "Long live Chairman Mao! Long live Chairman Mao!"

At that moment, the members of crowd would have done anything Mao asked. However, to everyone's astonishment, this revolutionary godhead who had flooded China with millions of words on almost every subject now, anticlimactically, had nothing more to say. Only after it was evident that his brief revolutionary homily was really finished did they accept that the event was over. Many were unsure whether they'd actually even seen or heard Chairman Mao at all. The Two Virtuous Ones had to wait until the girls who'd been the recipients of Little Wang's cloudburst departed before they dared come down from their perches. When they finally did, they were so stiff and sore it was agony to walk. All the way home, Little Li worried what his father would say if he learned they'd spent the day in the square, waiting for Chairman Mao to utter one sentence. It was after dark when he finally opened their gate, and was relieved to find his father not yet home. But, when 10:00 p.m. passed and he'd still not returned, Little Li began to worry. Had something happened? With guilt eclipsing his earlier irritation, he tried to remain awake but was so exhausted by the day's events, he finally fell asleep. He dreamed of Tiananmen Square. But instead of tens of thousands of adoring, weeping youths, it teemed with fish, like those in one of the Shaanxi Province peasant paintings depicting scenes of smiling farmers netting abundant harvests of fat freshwater fish that adorned the walls of their school library. And when Chairman Mao finally did appear on the rostrum, instead of wearing his usual suit and cap, he was garbed only in a loincloth, and was casting a giant purse seine out across the vastness of the square, as if he himself were a fisherman. But when he pulled it back in, instead of being filled with flopping silver fish, his net was teeming with wet, naked, writhing young bodies that glistened in the sunlight. In their midst was one particularly beguiling girl who slithered sensually among the other buck-naked youths and, seeing that Chairman Mao was grinning in her direction, broke into an ecstatic smile. As he slowly hauled in this harvest, Mao's custodial grin became etched with more than a hint of licentiousness. Then he dropped the net, ripped off his loincloth, and, with his tiny genitals dangling beneath his rotund belly like a sack of coins, he plunged his doughy body into the writhing school of adoring youths and swam toward the pretty girl. As he cupped her breasts in his meaty hands, she lavished kisses on his stony face, held his corpulent body in her slender arms, and rocked him back and forth as if he were an overgrown baby. Weeping tears of joy, she began singing:

> *The golden sun is rising over Tiananmen Square!*
> *The five continents and the four seas shining brightly!*
> *Whenever the Chairman passes and waves,*
> *Brilliant sunshine fills our breasts. . . .*

He was awakened by the door closing. It was his father. As he got ready for bed, Little Li cracked one eye open. Never had he seen him looking so ghostly pale, or his movements so slow and leaden.

15

WHILE PASSING through the Conservatory courtyard one morning, the Two Virtuous Ones were stunned to spot a wall poster headlined "Rightist Element Li Tongshu Thinks He's too Good for the Party!" that charged him with refusing to submit an application to join the party after being chosen to represent China at the 1956 Franz Liszt International Piano Competition in Budapest, Hungary. "Evidently rightist Li Tongshu thinks his American training makes him too good to be a member of the great Chinese Communist Party!" charged the poster. "Such traitors do not deserve to be called 'comrades' or Chinese!"

"Did they really invite him to join?" Little Wang asked in astonishment.

"I don't know," answered a bewildered Little Li.

When he got home, he could not control his upset.

"Did you really refuse to join the party when I was little?" he angrily asked his father.

"Who told you that?" responded Li Tongshu, his face flushing with alarm. Little Li told him about the wall poster at the Conservatory. At first he did not reply.

"Is it true, Father?" pressed Little Li.

"It is."

"You refused to join the party?"

"I did."

"But why?"

"The truth is, they didn't really want *me* to join," he replied, squeezing his eyes shut as if overcome by a sudden migraine. "They just wanted a prize to impress foreigners with the superiority of socialism and hoped that I could get it for them. But I didn't think they deserved it, especially for classical music, so I didn't want to be used as their tool to—"

"But why wouldn't you want to help the country?" interrupted Little Li.

"They didn't want the prize for the country, they wanted it for the party, and I'm not a political commissar." He was trying to mask his irritation. "Some aspects of human life should not be embroiled in politics. As a musician, I can make a small contribution to society, but when it comes to politics, I have no such ability. Anyway, Liu Shikun finally went instead of me, and won third prize for them." Li Tongshu knew that saying anything more would be useless.

Little Li was unable to imagine how anyone could be so foolish as to reject Chinese Communist Party membership, because he would have given anything to be able to join the China Youth Pioneers and then the China Youth League, both precursors to party membership. Exasperated with his father, he refused to answer him in English for the next few days.

"When things finally become more open, you'll understand the importance of speaking English," his father said with the kind of oracular certainty Little Li found irritating.

"You just don't understand, Father," he protested in Chinese. "Always being different just makes trouble for us . . . for me!" Little Li could tell by the way his father stared at the floor without smiling that he was displeased. "Say something, Father! Don't always just sit there silently!" he pleaded.

"What's going on now is not right," his father finally answered solemnly. But what was "not right," as far as Little Li was concerned, was that his father never seemed to end up on the "right" side of things!

When a hand-copied transcript of comments made by Jiang Qing criticizing classical music began circulating among Conservatory faculty, Li Tongshu felt the political noose tightening. He understood her anti-Western prejudices too well, and now she was deriding European opera, saying that soloists sounded "as if they had something in their mouths" when performing, so that their "words came out all garbled"; criticizing Giacomo Puccini for depicting the "degradation of [Asian] women by American imperialism" in operas like *Madame Butterfly;* even attacking the piano as a "foreign instrument." Her husband had once used the piano as a metaphor for effective "methods of work for party committees," urging good communists to "learn to play the piano" figuratively as a way to grasp the discipline necessary to be effective political commissars.

> In playing the piano all ten fingers are in motion; it won't do to move some fingers only and not others. But if all ten fingers press down at once, there is no melody. To produce good music, the ten fingers should move rhythmically and in co-ordination. A Party committee should keep a firm grasp on its central task and at the same time, around the central task, it should unfold the work in other fields. . . . Wherever there is a problem, we must put our finger on it, and this is a method we must master. Some play the piano well and some badly, so there is a great difference in the melodies they produce. Members of Party committees must learn to "play the piano" well.

The idea of viewing piano technique as a pathway to better party organization was absurd, but by the fall of 1966, almost nothing was considered absurd if done in the name of Chairman Mao. Peking Union Medical College Hospital, built with funds provided by the Rockefeller family decades earlier, had changed its name to the Peking Anti-Imperialism Hospital. The color of some traffic lights was being reversed by Red Guards, so that red signified "go" and green signified "stop." Mao had become China, China had become Mao, and Mao was in love with crimson.

Li Tongshu saw how infatuated his son had become with all the Red Guard rallies, marches, and struggle sessions erupting around the city, and knew it was futile to try and restrain him. But at the same time that Little Li wanted to elude his father's critical scrutiny, he also still hungered for his approval. After all, if anything happened to his father, what would become of him? In such a political climate, who'd care for the son of a rightist father and an imperialist mother?

When the knock on their door came, Little Li was almost asleep, and his father was just getting ready to retire. In this increasingly strained atmosphere, visitors rarely just dropped in on friends, lest they be accused of fomenting plots and conspiracies. So, when Li Tongshu saw two faculty colleagues on the veranda, he feared the worst, and before they came in, he turned off the light. As they sat whispering in the darkened room, Little Li eavesdropped.

"Old Qiu's gone," he heard one of the visitors whisper.

"Oh no!" gasped his father. Qiu Xuhua had studied conducting in Germany and returned to become one of the Conservatory's most respected faculty members.

"When he learned his name was on a list to be brought before a struggle session as a 'lover of Beethoven,' he drank insecticide. And when his wife found him, she drank the rest." For a musician to be called on to write a denunciation of Beethoven was like being ordered to write a love letter to the enemy, and for a long time no one spoke. Finally, Little Li heard someone say, "One of us could be next."

After his colleagues departed, Li Tongshu sat on the edge of his bed, to calm himself.

By the time Little Li awoke the next morning, his father had left. Where did he go every day? Wasn't the Conservatory closed, like other schools and academies?

"My old man comes home late every night, leaves early every morning, and always looks so down," he complained to Little Wang.

"You mean you don't know what's been happening to him?" Little Wang asked with more than a hint of condescension. He was always telling Little Li things he ought to know.

"I really don't."

"Have you ever asked him where the hell he goes every day?"

"No, because I didn't think he wanted to talk about it."

"Maybe that's because he doesn't want to upset you!"

"What have you heard?" asked Little Li impatiently.

"That he's been in self-criticism sessions!"

"How do you know?" Little Li was both alarmed and defensive.

"That's just what I've heard, but once someone becomes known as a target, every ass-kissing hack piles on." Little Wang put a forefinger to a nostril and expertly fired some snot at a poplar tree; he hit it dead-on.

"I just wish my father would make more of an effort,"

complained Little Li. "People think he's arrogant, stubborn, and distant."

"Whatever he is, he's going to get it, just like my old man. My mother told me even really famous people, like Lao She, are getting attacked." Lao She, one of China's most renowned writers, had come home from abroad just like Li Tongshu, to help rebuild China.

"What did she say about him?"

"That Red Guards took him to the Temple of Confucius with a bunch of other counterrevolutionary types, made them all kneel on crushed glass in the hot sun to 'beg forgiveness' [请罪], and then beat the shit out of them with a copper-studded belt. And when Lao was finally able to drag his sorry ass home, he discovered that Red Guards had ransacked his house."

"So—what did he do?"

"A wall poster said he went out to Great Peace Lake [太平湖], loaded his pockets with rocks, walked into the water, and drowned himself! And do you know what someone wrote at the bottom of that poster? 'Good Riddance to imperialist garbage'!"

The next day, Little Wang showed up, this time bearing an envelope.

"My father asked me to burn a bunch of papers and photographs last night so they wouldn't fall into the wrong hands, and as I was looking through them, I came across this." He handed Little Li a paper. "It's a reflection Lao She wrote after being in a struggle session ten years ago, during the Anti-Rightist Campaign. Now it's happening all over again":

> Men and women, old and young, one after another came on to the platform to make accusation. When a speech reached its climax of feeling many in the audience would shout, "Beat them!" I myself, like the intelligentsia sitting by me, yelled out involuntarily, "Beat them! Why don't we give them a beating?" As police restrained those who went forward to strike the bullies, my own voice mingled with the voices of hundreds roaring, "They've asked for it! Beat them!" And this roar changed me into a different man! I used to be a man of pretensions to cultivation.

Even as Little Li worried that the Red Guard movement would be his father's ruination, he still wanted to be a part of it. However, no matter what he did, he could not escape his accursed family background. While waiting one morning at a bus stop, the Two Virtuous Ones ran into a rival from a nearby hutong, a scruffy, streetwise kid with whom they often traded insults. Because he had unruly hair that stood up in great tufts, they'd mockingly dubbed him "Big Sheep Wool," after their own *hutong*. His father worked at a cooperative welding-torch factory, so he could afford to be openly contemptuous of children from intellectual families, and when he and his pals spotted the Two Virtuous Ones, they taunted, "There goes Legs of the Imperialist Dog Li Wende!"

"Who will deny he's a foreign spy, just like his American mother and father?" ragged a member of Big Sheep Wool's posse. "Your father loves his American piano so much, I bet his farts smell like the perfume of a foreign devil!" added Big Sheep Wool, sending his buddies into gales of laughter. Little Li burned with humiliation.

"Your hair looks as fucked-up as your mother's crotch after a good night of pounding by the 'honey-bucket man'!" Little Wang fired back.

"If you don't learn to hold your tongue," countered Big Sheep Wool, "I'll knock your teeth so far down your throat you'll have to put chopsticks up your asshole to get 'em back!"

"Oh, go fuck yourself, after you finish fucking your mother!" rejoined Little Wang.

"For heaven's sake!" recoiled a stern-looking woman at the bus stop. "What's become of young people today? Where do they learn such talk?"

Just as one of Big Sheep Wool's sidekicks, an enormous kid with a Mongoloid face, began wading menacingly through the crowd toward the Two Virtuous Ones, a bus providentially pulled up, and they escaped a good drubbing.

Whenever Little Li encountered other kids with "bad family backgrounds," he instantly understood their agony. However, his fear of becoming even more tainted through association prevented him from coming to their defense. What's more, their abject weakness so reminded him of the helplessness he despised in himself that he was sometimes momentarily overcome by an involuntarily feeling of contempt for them. The tendency to look down on the weak and up to the strong was, of course, hardly unique to China. As the ancient aphorism put it, "Bully the weak but fear the powerful" (欺软怕硬). However, over their long history, the Chinese had perfected a uniquely Sinitic version of this syndrome. Mao was a paradox who, despite his egalitarian pretensions and desire to overturn the old order, still expected "the people" to respect their leaders and especially to yield before his own exalted position, just as in the days of yore. And because he now held the scepter of political office, no matter how extreme his rule became, few dared challenge him. Nor did Li Tongshu deign to oppose Mao or the party directly, but neither did he surrender to it. And it was precisely this aloofness that infuriated party secretary Fyodor Fu. If Li Tongshu's stubbornness angered the party, it also infuriated Little Li.

"Why do you keep doing things that make superiors so angry?" he pleaded one night.

"Sometimes one does things simply for the sake of moral clarity," his father numbly responded. He felt trapped, unable even to withdraw into silence in the mountains like a Daoist hermit or a Buddhist monk, the way defrocked officials of old had been able to do. Because the party opposed all forms of religion, temples, churches, and monasteries had all been closed down. As the May Fourth Movement philosopher, essayist, and diplomat Hu Shi had wryly observed after his son was forced to denounce him for going to Taiwan: "We know, of course, that there is no freedom of speech in China. But few people realize that there is no freedom of silence, either."

When Little Li discovered a page ripped from the score of a Bach piano concerto, slashed from corner to corner with a vermilion "X" like the handbill for a common criminal sentenced to death, had been posted on the front gate of Willow Courtyard, his father immediately put on his coat and without speaking left for the Conservatory. He was hastening across the courtyard to his studio when he ran into a colleague who taught violin.

"Sicong's been locked up in a 'cow shed' [牛棚] at the Central Party School, charged with being a 'bloodsucker trying to sabotage socialism,'" he whispered with urgency. Ma Sicong was the famed violinist and founding president of the Conservatory who'd invited Li Tongshu to come home in 1949.

"When was he detained?"

"About a week ago, and . . ." His colleague halted mid-sentence.

"And what?"

"A student of mine gave me another tip."

"Go on."

"Your name is on their list."

Li Tongshu's blood ran cold. He hurried upstairs to his studio, and was frantically gathering his papers together when he heard a hubbub in the courtyard. Edging to the window, he saw a scrum of Red Guards gathered around a just-arrived truck marked "Reserved for Members of the Black Gang." As a man with a rope around his neck was pulled off the back, a Red Guard dumped a pail of glue onto his head and capped him with a cardboard dunce hat inscribed "Counterrevolutionary musician" [反革命音乐家]!

Then three others, with wrists tied behind their backs, were pulled off the truck and herded across the courtyard as a Red Guard flamboyantly conducted them with a chopstick in singing:

> *We are all cow-headed monsters!*
> *We have sinned, we have sinned!*
> *We must submit to the people's dictatorship.*
> *We are the enemy of the people. We must learn always to*
>   *be honest.*
> *If we are not, we must be smashed to bits!*

Li Tongshu hastily stuffed any incriminating papers into a bag, stole out of the Conservatory through a side gate, threw his papers into a fire he passed where some workers were warming themselves around a fifty-gallon steel drum, and then boarded a crowded bus. As it labored down the Avenue of Eternal Peace, the suffocating smell of exhaust, mingled with the stale stench of garlic on the breath of the woman seated beside him, left him gagging back waves of nausea. Darkness had long since fallen when he finally entered Big Sheep Wool Alley. No longer able to control himself, he hunched over and sprayed a bilious shower of vomit out onto a pile of cinders. With the sour taste of puke in his mouth, and feeling as lonely as the last man on earth, he trudged home. When he came through the front gate and spotted his son through the window sitting on his piano bench, he felt relieved. Whatever was to come, he was at least home with his own flesh and blood.

"Where were you?" Little Li asked anxiously as he entered their room.

"I had to get some things at the Conservatory," he said without smiling.

It was as they were washing up after dinner that they'd heard the first muffled beat of a drum and the sound of chanting voices in the alley. Then came a strident pounding on their gate.

"What is it?" asked Little Li in alarm.

"You must put on your coat," ordered his father peremptorily.

There was an explosive sound as the gate splintered open, and then suddenly there were shouting Red Guards rushing everywhere in the darkness of Willow Courtyard.

PART
THREE

16

HAVE THERE BEEN ANY DIFFICULTIES?

LI TONGSHU'S first letter to Little Li at Yak Springs was like a key that involuntarily unlocked the past. Thereafter, he began taking his flute to the quarry, because playing helped him feel more connected to the vanished world that was now suddenly edging back in on him. One lunchtime, while he was at the quarry, a young Golok boy appeared on the road astride a yak and became so absorbed in Little Li's playing that he almost lost his balance and fell from his mount. When Little Li burst out laughing, far from being embarrassed, the boy began giggling.

For most Han Chinese inmates, the Goloks were more part of the indigenous flora and fauna than of the human world. But, unlike the Mongolian gazelles, wild yaks, snow leopards, and blue bharal sheep, the Goloks had had a long adversarial history with Han Chinese. In fact, the road on which Little Li now worked had once been a guerrilla battlefield. One daunting challenge of reunifying China after 1949 was subduing all of the ethnic Tibetan areas that during the last dynasty had occupied a quarter of China's territorial landmass and gained a substantial independence from the central government, with the Goloks being among the most independent, hotheaded, and restive of all Tibetan tribesmen. Sir Charles Bell, British political officer for Bhutan, Sikkim, and Tibet, had sarcastically described them as a people "who trade peacefully for half of the year and rob caravans for the remainder, sending religious offerings to the Dalai Lama in Lhasa every four years." When the PLA arrived in the early 1950s to "pacify" the region, the Goloks fought back tenaciously on horseback with little more than ancient single-shot rifles. But by using the same hit-and-run guerrilla tactics that Mao had made famous, they sucessfully harassed the Chinese troops who'd been assigned to build the very highway across their tribal lands on which Little Li now worked.

Eventually, the Goloks were vanquished, and Qinghai, like other minority ethnic areas, involuntarily became a part of the People's Republic of China. Even though distrust lingered, these nomadic herdsmen now stopped peacefully by Yak Springs to ship their wool and hides to market. But except when manual laborers were needed to build a loyalty wall or erase inscriptions written on the Administration Building wall, Station Chief Wu frowned on Han inmates fraternizing with the Goloks, whom he dismissively referred to as "wild men" (野人). Little Li often spotted their black yak-hair tents pitched on the grasslands, and whenever their horsemen—rifles slung in scabbards from their saddles, and daggers thrust into their sashes—passed by the quarry, he was wary. However, as he mastered a few phrases of their language by hanging around the caravanserai, he discovered they were surprisingly friendly.

"*E dKaa Thal,*" "Have there been any difficulties?," a common greeting, was the first phrase of their language that he learned. Even though the Goloks lived in one of the harshest natural environments on the planet, their response was always "*Ma dKaa Thal,*" "There have been no difficulties," and it was usually accompanied by a broad smile. Given the deficiencies of Little Li's Golok skills, and the fact that most nomads spoke little Chinese, the best he could do was to engage them in tournaments of mugging and grinning, a tactic that was especially winsome with children. And here his interactions would have rested had it not been for his flute. Without sheet music, he was forced to recall meticulously all those pieces he'd once known by heart back in Beijing: a slow Andante movement from a Bach flute sonata he'd played with his father; a few movements from Mozart sonatas whose precise numbers he no longer recalled; a Telemann fantasy, and snatches of other works he still remembered. Then there were all the revolutionary songs burned into his brain, which now served as a junkyard for themes that he could cannibalize for improvisational purposes. Often he'd give up trying to remember a specific work and just string together whatever bits, snatches, and variations that came to mind to create an impromptu patchwork. After all, what did it matter out here in the outback?

One day, while sitting on a rock at the quarry, he became so lost in an improvisation that he closed his eyes. When he opened them again, he was surprised to find an elderly Golok with a fringe of ragged hair framing a weathered face sitting absolutely still about ten meters away. The old man was garbed in a traditional *lokbar* (a robelike garment stitched together from several sheepskins) and Warrior-brand high sneakers onto which he'd stitched traditional Tibetan-style felt leggings; and he had a silver-handled hunting knife thrust into his sash. But there was something so guileless about his absorption in the music that Little Li relaxed, lowered his flute, and smiled. The old man continued to stare.

"Hello," he finally said in Golok.

The old man furrowed his brow as if he were not quite sure what he'd just heard.

"*E dKaa Thal,*" repeated Little Li, and smiled again.

Then he picked up his flute and played a series of cheerful scales. A smile began creeping across the old man's face until his whole mouth was beaming in a broad, toothless grin. As Little Li continued playing and mugging, the next thing he knew, the old man was mumbling something unintelligible in Golok. When Little Li shrugged to indicate he didn't understand, the old man gave a cackle of giddy laughter, raised his staff horizontally to his mouth, and, as if it were a transverse flute, closed his own eyes and began rocking back and forth in a parody of Little Li. Then, as suddenly as he'd begun his pantomime, he stopped, let out a shriek of laughter, pointed to Little Li, sat back down, and cocked his head as if in anticipation of an encore. When Little Li started playing again, he began bobbing his head.

A few days later, the old-timer appeared again, this time accompanied by a younger man with a boy about six years old. When Little Li sat down, they, too, seated themselves, and commenced staring. Little Li stared back, causing the pink-cheeked boy to give a whimper of fright and bury his face in the older man's *lokbar*. But as soon as Little Li picked up his flute, they both began smiling. When he started playing, the old man unexpectedly even began dancing a little jig.

It was not long before more Goloks—including mothers with infants tucked inside their *lokbar*s like kangaroo babies in marsupial pouches, groups of wide-eyed children, and even an occasional

wizened grandmother—were appearing for Little Li's extempora-
neous concerts. But he was mystified by one thing: where did all
these devoted fans come from? Whether he was on the road or in
the quarry, they managed to find him, as if he was under constant
surveillance without knowing it. Nonetheless, he began looking
forward to these recitals, and even prepared for them. As his fame
as a musician and novice linguist spread, more and more nomads
joined the merriment, jockeying for the best seats in the figurative
house. And by managing a few hackneyed words in their dialect,
he was able to melt their stony faces into bewitching smiles. Soon
several of his bolder fans even began correcting his pronunciation;
his efforts to copy them left his audience members in stitches.

One day, after he finished playing, the old man who'd been his
first fan beckoned him to follow. After walking for half an hour,
they came over a rise on the grasslands and there was a settlement of black yak-hair tents (*nag sgar*) completely hidden from the
road. The old man, Thubten Norbu (Precious Stone), lived with
his son, Thubten Lobsang (Precious Disciple) and his family in
this seasonal encampment from which most of Little Li's audience
evidently came. Norbu's tent was guarded by an enormous three-
legged mastiff on a chain, who barked ferociously until Lobsang
threw him an old yak bone. Inside, Little Li was invited to sit on
a sheepskin as Lobsang's young wife, Pema, gave a shy bow and
proffered him some *tsampa,* a traditional Tibetan dish consisting
of roast barley meal kneaded with yak-butter tea. Then, picking up
a goatskin bellows, she fanned the embers of her yak-dung fire to
an orange glow, poured some boiling water into her wooden churn,
threw in a handful of salt, a daub of yak butter, and some leaves
of Tibetan black tea. Although Little Li almost threw up when he
took his first sip, he managed to drink enough of the brackish brew
to avoid mortifying himself before the flock of rosy-cheeked children who had surged into the tent to enjoy the spectacle of a foreign
visitor.

For a Han Chinese there was much about life among the *aBrog
Pa,* or "people of the high pastures," as Goloks called themselves,
that took getting used to. Standards of hygiene were not high.
Pema's hands were so grimy he could not help feeling squeamish
about eating and drinking things she prepared, especially *tsampa,*
that had been kneaded by her bare fingers. Because they rarely

bathed, Golok children's faces were often caked with dirt and snot, and their hair was matted and stringy. But, as unsanitary as things appeared, so high was the altitude, so cold was the air, and so pure was the water that there was little danger of illness. Anyway, the Goloks were not only a devilishly handsome and cheerful people, but also healthy. Pema's cheeks glowed with a rare purity, while her eyes twinkled with good humor and kindness, and her children evinced a winsome, spontaneous playfulness.

One evening, it started raining as he was preparing to return to Yak Springs, and Lobsang was so insistent he spend the night that Little Li finally relented. As he snuggled down among the welter of sheepskins covering the tent floor, one by one the children fell asleep around him. Then, without so much as a "good night," Old Norbu pulled his grizzled head into his *lokbar* and dropped off. A short while later, Lobsang and Pema, too, began snoring, leaving him alone staring into the dying glow of the hearth as raindrops slapped against the tent flaps. He may have been among people with whom he could hardly communicate, but with this happy family he felt accepted. When he told Station Chief Wu he might sometimes stay "nearer the quarry," the better to "serve the people," his superior was dubious. It was all well and good to have Tibetans smile on posters and appear onstage in native dress as expressions of China's ideal of multiethnic diversity, but quite another actually to consort with them. Nonetheless, he finally relented, convinced by Little Li's argument that his absence would not only save the time of walking back and forth, but also save Master Chef Wang from having to feed him.

"We consider our lives a perfection!" bragged Old Norbu. "The rain falls, the grass grows, our animals reproduce and give us milk and we don't have to do anything: we don't plow the earth, plant seeds, or harvest crops!" He laughed exuberantly. "It's a farmer's life that's hard, not ours!"

Goloks were Buddhists, but also clung to remnants of a far older indigenous tradition, Bon, a form of shamanistic animism that predated the arrival of Buddhism from India in the seventh century. It was Bon that gave Tibetans their reverence for the host of spirits and deities that many still believed inhabited the natural world and required propitiation through prayer and other devotional practices. When Buddhism finally reached Tibet from India, it complemented Bon's animism with a very different belief system, one that stressed the impermanence of life, as well as compassion and sympathy, turning Golok folk culture into a contradictory mixture of Buddhist kindness and benevolence and nomadic independence and ferocity. Despite Buddhism's prohibition against harming living creatures, Golok pastoralists were unalloyed carnivores and born hunters. One spring evening, as Pema and Little Li were milking the family sheep and yaks, Lobsang and several fellow herdsmen galloped into camp whooping triumphantly. Slung across the back of Lobsang's saddle was the carcass of a furry animal whose paws bounced limply to the gait of his lathered horse. Only as Lobsang dismounted did Little Li see the animal's bloodied, half-open feline mouth and realize it was a snow leopard. With no small amount of excitement, everyone in the camp dropped whatever they were doing and ran to inspect his trophy. For Lobsang's family, this was a moment of happiness: not only would there be snow-leopard fur to trim the lapels of their *lokbars*, but the cat's bones would bring a handsome price from the East Avenue Bureau for the Purchase of Chinese Medicinal Ingredients in Xining, a state-run enterprise that bought such exotica as the paws of Tibetan brown bears, the horns of Mongolian gazelles, and the bones of snow leopards, which were prized as medicament by practitioners of traditional Chinese medicine. But Little Li could not help feeling a deep sadness at the sight of this graceful, rare creature struck dead. He remembered with wonder the afternoon he'd happened upon the snow-leopard mother and her cub. The thought that the bones of such a magnificent cat would end up in a bottle of wine sold to a Chinese businessman in Hong Kong or an aging party cadre in Beijing seeking the elixir of immortality was repellent.

But no matter how sorry he was to see this dead snow leopard, the more he observed how Goloks treated each other, cared for their animals, and interacted with their natural surroundings, the more admiring he became. Whereas Han Chinese submitted to social and political hierarchies, these herdsmen possessed a defiant sense of individualism and sovereign self-worth. Whereas their Han counterparts masked their feelings and controlled their overt expressions of sentiment, the reactions of Goloks were immediate and irrepressible. They laughed or flew into rages with all the suddenness of the storms that swept down from the mountains into their valley.

Little Li saw Pema as a personification of the tribe's unique combination of simplicity and exuberance. She adorned herself beautifully and with pride. Instead of the revolutionary drabness of baggy mono-colored Han Chinese Mao suits, she and other Golok women boasted an array of colorful hand-woven aprons; bedecked themselves with silver charms, necklaces, and bracelets set with coral, amber, agate, and turquoise; and plaited their shiny black hair into myriad long, handsome braids.

When wintertime approached and pastures became over-grazed, Lobsang culled his herd. Since they grew no barley or other cereal crops and had to buy whatever they used, they were largely dependent on meat and milk for survival, making the slaughtering of livestock unavoidable. Observing Lobsang's tenderness when one of his own herd was to be taken made Little Li recall how cruel he and his friends had been to animals. They liked nothing better than to throw stones at stray cats, dogs, and ferrets just to watch them run, or to shoot birds with slingshots just to see them fall. Lobsang always insisted that each animal designated for slaughter first be smothered with a sheepskin bag pulled over its head, as if this artful dodge could distance his family from the karmic liability of taking life. Little Li quickly discovered that one of the greatest contributions to the family that he, as a non-Buddhist, could make was to do the actual killing for Lobsang. So it often fell to him to slit the animal's throat before its heart completely stopped, as Old Norbu stood alongside, muttering a torrent of prayers. After the animal's body had gone limp, he would take over, to bleed, eviscerate, skin, and then hang the carcass behind their tent where it froze in the winter cold, and was available for months thereafter.

When spring finally brought back the green grass and the winter-starved female yaks could graze, grow fat again, and calve, just as the world was being reborn, Goloks counterintuitively found themselves entering a time of scarcity. To survive, Lobsang's family was sometimes forced to eat "live blood": they would tap into a neck vein of a yak to drain blood out like sap from a tree, and then coagulate it with sour yak milk to make a special nutritious delicacy that Little Li never came to enjoy.

Ironically, the most insurmountable impediment to his fully

integrating himself into nomadic life was not Station Chief Wu, who no longer seemed to care what he did once he left the front gate, or Golok reluctance to take him in, but his own squeamishness about embracing certain parts of their lifestyle. For months after he first drank yak-butter tea and tasted *tsampa,* the ubiquitous smell of rancid yak butter nauseated him. Unfortunately, almost everything among the Goloks seemed to relate to the polymorphous yak, which his fellow Chinese called "hairy cows" (牦牛). These shaggy, lugubrious bovines had evolved an ability to survive the bitter cold, howling winds, and blinding blizzards of the Tibetan Plateau by licking dry grass up off the ground after even heavy snowfalls.

Because they provided an almost full complement of life needs, yaks were the centerpiece of nomadic existence. In Qinghai's barren grasslands, where trees were rare, dried yak dung was used as fuel, and the residual black carbon ash from cook fires was turned into ink, used in monasteries to print sacred Buddhist texts; meat was eaten as a dietary staple in both fresh and cured form; yak hair was woven to makes tent fabric and rope; hide was tanned to make boots, saddles, and leather bags for barley meal; and yak milk was not only fermented into yogurt, cultured into cheese, and dried into curds, but also churned into butter for tea and *tsampa,* as well as for waterproofing, oil for lamps, and even as a skin emollient against the sun and wind. If all that was not enough, these powerful bovines could carry packs weighing hundreds of kilos and were able to survive temperatures of forty degrees below zero Fahrenheit. It was hardly surprising, then, that the word Tibetans used for this all-purpose animal was *nor-a,* meaning literally "wealth," and that prosperity was reckoned in the numbers of head possessed.

To become fully accustomed to the spectrum of yak-based odors that constituted the signature smells of Golok life took immersion. Only as Little Li began overnighting more frequently did he reach a point where he, too, hardly noticed the rancid yak-butter smell. At first, he assumed that his Golok hosts had somehow become less gamey. In actuality, he himself was acquiring their aromatic characteristics, while at the same time his own sense of smell was being numbed. This reality he understood only after returning to the Yak Springs compound one evening after spending several nights with Lobsang's family.

"You smell like a yak in heat!" exclaimed Superintendent Peng, disgustedly grabbing his nose as soon as Little Li entered the canteen. Not even the Tibetan wind was enough to purge the stench from his clothing and hair. It took a long soak in the hot spring and a complete change of clothes to set him right.

If living with Tibetan nomads meant consigning himself to their olfactory universe, it also meant submitting to their gastronomy. But as Little Li spent more time with Lobsang's family, hunger finally compelled accommodation. He'd come to like Tibetan specialties such as *sho,* a tart yogurt made with yak milk and dried yak-milk curds that he began carrying with him on the road as a snack. And because living at such a high altitude quickly dehydrated a person, he also began drinking, then even craving, yak-butter tea. After all, it contained the three key elements needed for survival at high altitudes: water, fat, and salt. It was not long before he was overlooking the occasional yak hair or fleck of manure in his food and drink. Compared to the bilious cabbage, tasteless corn cakes, and wormy rice served up by Master Chef Wang, nomadic fare had its charm.

By helping Lobsang's family with their chores, Little Li came to understand the cycle of seasonal husbandry upon which their delicately balanced lifestyle depended. Because the twice-daily ritual of milking was traditionally performed by women, everyone laughed whenever he helped Pema with her tether lines of sheep and yaks. And they all took great delight in mimicking his clumsy milking technique, calling him *chigye,* "foreigner," a name that, when applied to others, was a term of disparagement. But he wasn't offended, because with him their mockery was done with a playfulness born of affection.

One night, Old Norbu motioned him to the back of their tent and picked up the portrait of Chairman Mao that stood on the family altar between two brass butter-lamps. With a sly smile, he unfastened the cardboard backing and extracted a faded photo of an earnest-looking young man in glasses and monk's robes seated on a throne.

"Who is it?" asked Little Li.

"You don't know?" Old Norbu let out a high-pitched peal of laughter.

"No," said Little Li, examining the young man.

"It's him!" replied Old Norbu with a note of triumph.

"Him?"

Drawing near, as if even the tent might be harboring a listening device, Old Norbu cupped a hand to Little Li's ear. "It is Tenzin Gyatso."

"Tenzin who?"

"Tenzin Gyatso, His Holiness the Fourteenth Dalai Lama!"

"That's him?"

"Yes. We keep him behind the Chairman so that he'll be safe," he explained, letting out another peal of laughter. Then he raised the photo above his head and prostrated himself before the altar, before sliding the photo back behind the implacable visage of Chairman Mao. Even though Mao had forced these nomads into collectivized "people's communes" (人民公社), banned all their religious observances, and closed their monasteries, Goloks still secretly uttered their prayers, circumambulated their sacred sites, and made their genuflections to the Dalai Lama, the Lord Buddha, and their army of protective Tibetan deities.

After the evening meal was finished, Old Norbu, Lobsang, Pema, and their four children nestled under sheepskins around the stove, and, with a single butter-lamp guttering, Old Norbu told stories.

"When I was a boy, each winter we trekked all the way to Kumbum Monastery [塔尔寺] outside of Xining for the Monlam Prayer Festival and to watch the dancing and enjoy the yak-butter sculptures," he recounted wistfully. "When I first saw the great monastery, I couldn't believe my eyes! Never had I imagined anything as grand as its golden-roofed chanting hall, white stupas, and prayer wheels bigger than yaks. And because we knew it was the birthplace of our own Tsong Khapa—the patriarch of the Geluk, Yellow Hat sect—and that nearby Taktser was the birthplace of the fourteenth Dalai Lama, we thought it the most important place on earth!"

Even though Old Norbu often repeated himself, the children never tired of hearing his stories, particularly the one about him being trapped in a blizzard and being so cold he'd warmed his hands by letting a yak piss on them.

"What sweet comfort!" he exclaimed as the children shrieked with delight.

Then he sang his favorite Golok song:

I rebel against those above. I rebel.
I rebel against Tibet. I rebel.
I rebel against the Dharma King of Tibet. I rebel.
I rebel against the sky, and the blue sky is with me. I rebel.
I rebel against those below. I rebel.
I rebel against China. I rebel.
We make our own rules. I rebel.

Little Li understood only snatches of what was sung and said, but sitting among these people as the fire cast dancing shadows on the tent walls and sent wraithlike curls of smoke out the chimney flap into the starry sky above made him feel at peace. As soon as the songs ended, the children tugged on his sleeve until he played his flute; they adored whatever he played. After the first few nights, a pattern was established: Before the smallest child nodded off, he would stop playing and pass his instrument around so everyone could hold it. Sometimes Pema even lit another yak-butter lamp so that they could better enjoy examining this silvery treasure. For the children it was a thing of foreign wonder, but it was the women who were most hypnotically drawn to it. Having a passion for silver ornaments, they stroked the flute's shiny barrel and pressed its gleaming silver keys with only faintly disguised covetousness. Pema's brown eyes sparkled so erotically as she caressed the instrument that Little Li was sure, if he ever left it unguarded, pieces would soon be dangling from her plaits or attached to her belt with her other silver amulets.

After he stowed his flute, one of the children would curl up in his lap and soon be asleep like a purring cat. Without bidding a "good night," the others pulled their heads into their capacious, fleece-lined *lokbar*s like tortoises, or tucked themselves under their sheepskins, and fell asleep. Listening alone to the wind moaning through the tent's guy lines outside, Little Li would sometimes hear rhythmic stirrings from where Lobsang and Pema slept. The soft whimpering, cooing sounds sent shivers through his body. He'd learned many things about Chinese and Western music and culture from his father, and many other things about loneliness, suffering, and endurance from his time at Yak Springs, but he'd never learned anything about the opposite sex. And when he heard these provocative sounds, he thought of Lhamo, a young woman in the next camp, whose braids tumbled down to her shoulders. Lobsang teased him relentlessly about Lhamo, saying how interested she was in him. But Little Li had no idea how to respond to her flirtations. One summer night when the two camps had come together to shear sheep, he'd been sitting alone behind Lobsang's tent, gazing out at the moonstruck mountains and thinking about her, when she magically appeared.

"What are you doing?" she asked in broken Chinese.

"Oh, nothing," he replied.

"Well, can I do nothing with you?" she asked playfully.

"Actually, I was looking at the mountains." He smiled, relieved by her frankness.

"Then can we look at the mountains together?" she giggled.

For several moments, they sat side by side without speaking. Even though they were separated by only a few inches, for him the gap might as well have been a canyon. Then, as if it was the most natural thing in the world for her, she rested her head against his shoulder, so that he could smell the milky, smoky scent that emanated from her body. He desperately wanted to respond. But how did one begin? Of course, she had no sense of his inner turmoil, or how he longed for her, even as he sat stiffly beside her.

"Well, good night, foreigner," she finally said sweetly, stood up, and walked away, leaving him gazing alone at the distant mountains and cursing his ineptness.

Not knowing how to grab the moment, he put his arms around the child sleeping in his lap in Lobsang's tent, amazed that this beautiful, breathing creature was the product of two people he knew, joining together in ways he could hardly imagine.

Sometimes the outside world lanced into the bubble of his existence like a sharp blade. Late one chilly fall night, after four trucks loaded with prisoners stopped at Yak Springs for the night, he stole across the highway to where they were parked and walked around the tarpaulin-covered vehicles in the darkness. The prisoners inside emitted an unsettling symphony of breathing, snoring, sleep talking, and moaning, as their physical stirrings made the trucks rock gently on their springs like boats floating on a rippled lake.

The next morning, Little Li was awakened by shouting. He dressed quickly and ran outside, to find everyone in the parking area and Station Chief Wu in deep discussion with two guards from the convoy.

"What's happened?" Little Li asked Eunuch Liu.

"Last night a prisoner cut through the tarp covering his truck bed, and he's gone."

"Where'd he go?"

"Nobody knows."

"All right!" barked Station Chief Wu. "We have an emergency: a prisoner has escaped. We'll drop our usual work assignments and join the search until he's found."

Little Li was given responsibility for the road to the quarry. As he set off, he began worrying that the escapee might be a dangerous criminal. He was halfway to the quarry when he saw something move behind a bush about twenty meters off the road. Stopping, he crouched behind a boulder. A few moments later, the thing moved again, and he heard a strange, plaintive groan. As stealthily as he could, he crawled toward the bush. There, on the ground, lay a gaunt middle-aged man in a threadbare coat and tattered knit cap with his teeth chattering from the cold.

"My leg's hurt," he said, looking up like an animal caught in a trap.

"I see," said Little Li, not sure what the appropriate response was. But, judging the man to be harmless, he replied, "Let me help you back to the compound."

"But . . ." the man began uncertainly.

"Well, you're hurt. You can't just stay here alone." There was an argumentative tone in his voice that he'd not intended.

"I understand," replied the man resignedly. After helping him up, Little Li had him sling one arm around his shoulders, and they started back toward the compound, the prisoner limping along beside Little Li.

"Where are you from?" he finally asked, to fill the awkwardness of having this other human body so physically close to his own without any kind of communication.

"Hangzhou," the man replied without looking at him.

"And what did you do there?"

"Well," he began, as if he'd been asked to describe a long-ago event. "I was a musician, a cellist."

"Really?" said Little Li in surprise. He was about to say he played the flute, but having such a personal conversation under the circumstances seemed somehow inappropriate, so he said nothing. He did, however, feel a rush of empathy for this poor man. Who knew what his sad story was? He was about to ask him another question when a truck from the convoy came barreling toward them. It stopped in a swirl of dust and two grim-faced guards jumped from the cab. Without a word, they seized the prisoner, bound his wrists, loaded him into the bed of the truck, and headed back toward the compound, leaving Little Li alone on the road.

When he finally reached the front gate himself, the truck was just returning from the other direction. The prisoner was no longer in the back.

17

YANG MING

WHEN TWO trucks pulled in through the front gate of the way station that chilly January afternoon and three young women walked into the canteen, their effect on the inmates inside was akin to having a ward full of patients with chronic heart conditions suddenly administered simultaneous inhalations of nitroglycerin. The women were "barefoot doctors" (赤脚医生), young Chinese who had received rudimentary paramedical training before being sent to remote rural areas of China "to serve the people."

When Little Li got back from the quarry and heard the news of their arrival, he didn't at first think much of it. But when he saw Master Chef Wang decked out in a clean apron with his thatch of hair combed, he knew something unusual was afoot. Nonetheless, once his bowl was filled, he sat down as usual in a far corner and tucked into his dinner. It was only when the canteen suddenly fell silent that he looked up and saw the three young women coming through the doorway, with khaki shoulder bags inscribed with the slogan "Serve the People" slung dashingly over their shoulders. Then, with a solicitude that no inmate had ever before witnessed, Master Chef Wang stepped off his dais and, as if he were a maître d' at a proper restaurant, squired the young women to his wok where he smiled ingratiatingly and gave each a gleaming new tin bowl filled with an extra-generous serving of steaming food. As the girls looked for a place to sit down, every head in the room swiveled to follow their progress. After a moment of hesitation, they headed for Little Li's table. As they sat down, he wanted to say something, but they were chattering away in Shanghai dialect, so he felt awkward about breaking into the middle of their conversation with some inanity in Mandarin.

"How are you all?" he finally asked, when there was a lull in their conversation.

"Not bad," one of them replied without looking at him. The others nodded in agreement.

"And where are you headed?" he continued.

"Not clear," the girl seated next to him replied blankly. Seeing no further way to expand the conversation, he gulped down the rest of his dinner and was on the verge of standing up to leave when the latter suddenly offered, "My name's Yang Ming." She turned toward him so that he was at last able to see her face. Her shiny black hair was not bobbed short in the severe style of the other girls, but cascaded down to her shoulders, limning her handsome face like stage curtains. Her cheeks had been burnished to cinnamon by the sun, her lips were the color of that most delicate species of pink wildflowers that carpeted the valley floor in early spring, and her limpid brown eyes sparkled with a keen intelligence. But in her glance, he also saw more than a hint of sadness.

"Mine is Li . . . Li Wende," he responded. "Where are you from?"

"We're all from Shanghai." She smiled.

"Well, we welcome you all to Yak Springs."

"Thanks for your hospitality." Her smile was bewitching. "And where are you from?"

"Well, originally from Beijing."

"Oh! I've always wanted to go to Beijing! Instead, here I am in Qinghai!"

"I'd be happy to invite you to Beijing sometime; however, first I'd have to find a way to get back there myself. Anyway, we welcome you to our lovely compound." She looked around and rolled her eyes.

"What did your parents do in Beijing?" she asked.

"My father taught at the Central Conservatory."

"Really? And how long have you been out here?"

"Since early 1969," he replied, trying to sound suave.

"That's a long time!" she exclaimed, her eyes widening. By now all the inmates in the canteen had stopped their own conversations, even their chewing, and were trying to overhear what Little Li and Yang Ming were saying.

"Well, if you'll forgive me, I really have to go," he suddenly blurted out. Of course, there was nowhere to go, but he was feeling so exposed that he just wanted to leave.

"Good night, then," responded Yang Ming with a sweet but perplexed look.

Walking toward the door, he felt both liberated from his awkwardness and enslaved by his inhibitions. Why was he always doing the opposite of what he wanted? What was it about young women to whom he was attracted that turned him into such a collision of mutually canceling impulses? As he headed for the barracks, Yang Ming's beautiful melancholy face burned in his mind's eye like a flare. But he imagined her tittering with the other girls at his ineptness back in the canteen. He was a prisoner not only of the state, but also of his own timidity. Perhaps it was just as well he was marooned in a place like Yak Springs, where there could be no disappointments in love. He was about to cry out in frustration when he heard footsteps behind him. Spinning around, he saw a dark silhouette approaching.

"Who is it?" he challenged.

"It's Yang Ming."

"Oh!" he gasped.

"You're so shy, Comrade Li!" She laughed.

"Yes, it's a—what should I call it?—a character flaw."

"Not really," she responded. "I hate pushy boys."

"Well, in that case, you're in luck."

"Indeed," she replied coyly.

"So . . ." Something needed to be said to fill the silence, but he had no idea what.

"I am sorry about how we hijacked your table just now," she continued. "But when I heard you say your father was from the Central Conservatory, I . . . Well, one of the things I've missed most out here is music."

"There are so many things I miss out here," he said, feeling suddenly relaxed by her direct manner. It also helped that they were in the dark, where they could not really see each other's faces; this made him feel somehow comfortable. He was not sure why, but whenever a girl looked at him in broad daylight, he felt as if she was able to see right through him. Being in the darkness was like speaking on the telephone.

"What did your father play?"

"He was a pianist."

"And do you play?"

"The flute."

"Out here?"

"Sometimes."

"And who do you play for?"

"Myself, the Goloks, and the yaks." She laughed. "And where are you coming from?"

"The last place I was assigned was Nagchu Prefecture."

"What was it like there?"

"Oh, even though the bright lights of Lhasa were only a day away, it was still very remote. Lots of beautiful lakes and big mountains. Life there wasn't easy, and most people had never seen a doctor before." She looked at him for a moment. "And what do you do here?"

"I make gravel and fill in potholes on the road to Lhasa, although to me the road feels like it goes nowhere."

"Well, it brought me here!"

"It did!" He smiled, unable to believe he was talking to a lovely young woman right here in Yak Springs.

"I wonder if . . ." she began, and then paused.

"You wonder what?" he asked.

"I wonder if you'd play something for me on your flute before I leave?"

"Oh!" he exclaimed in surprise. "When are you leaving?"

"We go tomorrow." The thought was like a splash of cold water.

"Well, I'd be glad to, but . . ."

"I think you'll find me more appreciative than a yak!"

"I'd hope so." He laughed, unsure how to deliver on her request.

"Where could we go?" she persisted hopefully.

"There's no place in the compound that wouldn't attract attention. And if that old bugger Station Chief Wu ever caught me playing classical music for a girl, he'd call me in for a self-criticism session!"

"Not good!" she replied emphatically. "Still, I'd really—"

"Well, if you're willing," he interrupted, thinking fast, "we could meet outside the gate later on and walk way down the road, where no one could hear us."

"Oh, I'd like that!" she effused, jumping in enthusiasm.

"It'll be cold," he warned.

"That's one thing I'm used to. But I'll have to wait until I can slip away without making the other two girls suspicious."

"All right. Let's meet in an hour. Just remember, once you get out the gate and are on the road, don't pause. Turn left, start walking, and just keep going. I'll find you." She nodded.

Returning to his room, he waited impatiently, warming the mouthpiece of his flute under his quilt. Then, wanting to get across the parking area before the rising moon flooded it with light, he tucked his case inside his overcoat, grabbed his fur-lined hat and gloves, and slid out the gate. As he walked, he was unable to believe this phantom girl who'd swept so unexpectedly into Yak Springs would actually materialize on the dark, lonely highway just to be with him. Perhaps—like one of those "fox fairies" of ancient lore, who appeared as beautiful young women to tempt men, only to transform themselves back into foxes before the moment of consummation—Yang Ming, too, would prove an illusion. But whatever happened, he vowed he was not going to be the one who let this moment slip through his fingers. Wishing Little Wang were with him to give advice, he gazed up at the stars. The notion they were also twinkling down somewhere on his old friend was comforting.

Halfway to the quarry, he stopped and sat down on a flat rock, every molecule in his body supercharged with expectation. An hour later, when there was still no sign of her, he felt overcome with disappointment. Since virtually everything he'd ever really wanted, loved, or hoped for in life had been denied or taken away, why should this assignation turn out differently? Disappointment hardly surprised him anymore. In fact, it seemed the natural order of things. As Granny Sun insisted, every person has a predetermined fate and perhaps his was to be eternally alone. Disconsolately, he started back to the compound. As he was nearing the gate, he heard something. He stopped and cocked an ear. It was the distinctive sound of gravel crunching underfoot. His heart leapt. Suddenly there she was!

"I'm so sorry!" she said.

"Is everything all right?" he asked.

"I had a hard time getting away from the others." She sighed as they walked on. "But I'm so glad you waited. Will you still play for me?" The way she asked melted his heart.

"Of course," he replied.

They didn't stop walking until they reached the flat rock where a short while ago he'd been sitting alone. He put down his flute case, removed his mittens, and took out the head joint to warm it with his bare hands. Then, after assembling his instrument, he stepped into the middle of the road. Imagining the star-encrusted firmament overhead as the dome of a great concert hall, the moon a stage light, and Yang Ming seated on the rock as his concert audience, he put the flute to his lips and began the second movement of Bach's Sonata in E-flat major, a work he'd often played with his father. Even though he could hardly see her face, he felt a sense of urgent expectation emanating from her. For the first time at Yak Springs, he was playing for someone who understood. It so moved him, he didn't want this strange moment of connection to ever end. It was only when he finally came to the last bar, lowered his instrument, and stepped over to her again that he realized she was crying. As she heaved with sobs, he enfolded her in his arms.

"It was beautiful," she finally managed, wiping her tears away with a gloved hand. "It's been so long." Tilting her head back, she looked up at him, went on tiptoe, and kissed his cheek. It sent a pulse of animal energy coursing through his body, as if a long-cramped limb were suddenly beginning to tingle with pins and needles as circulation returned.

"How did you ever end up here, beside me, Yang Ming?" he asked, more in wonder than in the expectation of a reply.

"Don't you think calling me Yang Ming is a bit formal?" she asked playfully. "I realize we hardly know each other, but I did just kiss you!"

"All right," he said, laughing, as he put his flute away. "I'll call you Ming." Then he took her by the arm, and they walked on together, toward the quarry, both lost in their own thoughts.

"What brought you all the way to Yak Springs, with its many comforts, great cultural offerings, and excellent roads?" he finally asked sarcastically.

"Luck, I suppose," she replied with a rueful sigh. "Maybe it's just my turn for some good luck. We Chinese all have such long, sad stories."

"And what's yours?"

"I suppose it's no worse than anyone else's," she said diffidently.

"Will you tell me?"

"Do you really want to hear another tale of woe?"

"From you, yes."

"Well . . ." she said, and gave a long exhalation. "Originally, I wanted to be a doctor, but when the Shanghai Medical College closed because of the Cultural Revolution, I was only able to become a low-level barefoot doctor. After graduation, they sent me off to work at a transfer center outside Xining."

"What kind of a transfer center?"

"It was a depot for political prisoners awaiting assignment to one of the labor camps in the region. Most were from Shanghai, like me."

"How did they treat them?" he asked, thinking of the prisoner who'd tried to escape from his convoy right here in Yak Springs.

"They brought them in on trucks like livestock, treated them like livestock at our transfer center, and then shipped them out again like livestock," she answered gravely. "I don't think I'll ever be able to get their faces out of my mind. Almost everyone suffered from overwork, neglect, and malnutrition, especially those who came in from other camps. They were broken people, and when they got hurt or ill, many were only too glad to die. The sorriest cases were those who tried to kill themselves and failed. And when someone did die, the authorities just ordered their friends to get rid of them, to haul the bodies out onto the grasslands. But most of them were too weak to dig a proper grave in the hard soil, so they just piled up some sand and rocks around the corpses and let the wild animals do the rest."

"Were you there long?"

"Almost two years." She began to sob again and he reached over to stroke her cheek.

"How did you get out of there?"

"One morning, they just announced I was being sent to Nagchu with another girl. There was no explanation. When we got there, I thought we'd die of loneliness! Do you know what saved us?"

"What?"

"The Tibetans! The very people we were supposed to save! They had nothing, but were still generous. In the end, it turned out we needed them as much as they needed us. Do you know what I mean."

"Yes, I do," he said softly, thinking of Lobsang's family. "And where are they transferring you now?" For an instant, he dared hope she might end up someplace nearby, but immediately realized the foolishness of such a hope—for there *was* no other place nearby!

"I think we're being reassigned to the Aba Autonomous Tibetan Region in northern Sichuan Province."

"Are you in touch with your parents?"

"Oh, my poor family!" Yang Ming said with a sigh.

"What happened to them?" For several moments she did not reply.

"You know, I've never spoken to anyone about them."

"Will you tell me?" he asked gently.

"Well," she began reluctantly, "my father taught philosophy at Fudan University in Shanghai, and, like his mentor, the great scholar Feng Youlan, he was a softhearted idealist who just wanted to do his research, teach his classes, and help his country. But, unlike Feng, he didn't understand Mao or how to fit into Mao's political framework, and as soon as the Cultural Revolution began, he was targeted for being a proponent of 'feudal tradition.'"

"How did he respond?"

"He lived in another world, and I don't think he understood what was hitting him. I mean, did any of us really understand what was happening? Then came the 'struggle sessions,' with screaming Red Guards accusing him of supporting 'the Four Olds' [四旧] and demanding he confess. But confess what? Teaching Chinese philosophy? So they locked him up in a 'cow pen.'" Her words were spilling out uncontrollably.

"Where's he now?"

"Gone! And I . . ." She began stammering. "And I didn't even . . . I didn't . . ."

"Didn't what?"

"I wanted so badly to be accepted by them that I . . . I . . ." She grabbed Little Li's arm like a drowning person and began sobbing piteously. "I let them convince me to stand before a crowd at the university and . . . and denounce him. I turned against my own father! Can you imagine how he must have felt . . . to have his only child attack him? How could I have done such a thing?"

"We were so young," responded Little Li.

"I was angry with him for studying such a reactionary subject that brought so much trouble to our family." Again she became so choked with emotion she had to stop. "But I had no idea what they were going to do to him! How could anyone have imagined? And now it is too late, too late to say the things I have felt ten thousand times since. You make a mistake when you're young, and then when the person's gone—you can never go back and make it right again. You just have to live with what you did. Do you understand that burden? It's forever!"

"What did they do to him?"

"They paraded him through the campus wearing a dunce hat inscribed with 'Expert in Reactionary Scholarship' [反动学术权威]." Even though weeping, she was determined to continue, to retch up as much of the poison as possible before she broke down completely. "When he still refused to confess, they beat him, smeared his face with excrement, and locked him in a cage under a staircase. And I didn't help him! Where was my generosity? How could I have betrayed my own father?"

"We were all so scared and lost," he whispered, filled with both sympathy for her and regret about his own father. "None of us knew what we were doing."

"I could have at least shown I cared," she countered, struggling against her emotions. "I was his daughter, but I did nothing! Why?" She cried out this last question as if to the heavens. "Even as they mocked him, saying, 'Before the righteous anger of the people your silence would prove no stronger than a slender reed in a hurricane,' he did not argue. He just refused to speak. They didn't understand such stubbornness. They didn't win, but it was a bitter victory. One night, after an intense struggle session, he gave up, smashed his tea jar and slashed his wrists. As his life was draining away, he wrote a quotation from *The Analects* on the wall with his own blood:

THE SUPERIOR MAN DOES NOT EVEN FOR THE SPACE OF A
SINGLE MEAL ACT CONTRARY TO VIRTUE.

君子無終食之間違仁

Little Li thought of the characters "Save the children!" from Lu Xun that his own father had written on his studio wall.

"When the Red Guards discovered his body, they were furious," continued Yang Ming tenaciously. "Because he'd evaded their torment, they took a fire ax to the wall where he'd scrawled his epitaph."

"And where was your mother during all this?"

"Oh . . . my poor simple mother! She was a devout Buddhist, so when the attacks began she already had a black mark against her! She didn't understand the charges against him at all and kept begging their friends still in high office to intercede. But no one dared help. When they ordered her to denounce and divorce him or be stripped of her job at the research institute where she worked, she just looked at them like they were crazy."

"Did she denounce him?"

"She refused! Then, after he died, no one dared to tell her he was gone. So she just kept bringing clothing and food for him, and the Red Guards kept accepting it. Then, as soon as she left, they ate the food and laughed at her, calling her a 'crazy old lady' [疯老太太]. When she finally learned he was gone, she stopped eating and speaking. Soon she couldn't recognize anyone, even me, her only child! She really did become crazed. One night, I woke up and found her missing from the bed we shared after my father's death. I searched the streets of Shanghai for hours before finding her wandering the Bund with hardly any clothing on, wailing out across the Huangpu River for my father. She'd gotten herself into such a state that not even the Red Guards wanted to bother with her anymore. She was just another person gone mad, and maybe her madness protected her from having to recognize the horror of what had happened. At least, I hope so!" Yang Ming gave a bitter laugh. "In the end, they pronounced her 'ideologically sick,' in need of being 'reintegrated back into the masses' [回到群众当中], and dragged her screaming into a van and drove her away. I heard nothing more until four months ago. Then a letter arrived in Nagchu from a Shanghai hospital saying she'd passed away." Yang Ming fell to the ground and buried her head in her hands.

"I'm so sorry," said Little Li, kneeling down to hold and kiss her. He could taste the saltiness of her tears on her cheeks. Although it was the first time he'd ever kissed a woman, he did it with all the conviction of someone with a lifetime of experience.

"I didn't mean to talk about myself so much," she finally apologized.

"I understand," he answered softly. And he did understand. For her story was his story, was China's story, and it excited such a wave of contradictory emotions in him that, once they had started walking again to keep warm, he was glad when they reached the quarry and he had an excuse to change the subject.

"So—this is where I work," he said, gesturing toward the giant rock face, white in the moonlight.

"You work *here*!" she exclaimed. He nodded. "Well, at least it's peaceful!" In the moonlight, the face of the quarry and the giant boulders strewn across the ground below did convey a ghostly beauty. But for him it was disorienting to be at such a familiar place in such unfamiliar company.

"It's very late," he finally offered. "Aren't you leaving in the morning?" The words "leaving in the morning" chilled him to the bone.

"I don't want to go back until you've told me your story!" she said peremptorily. Like her, he'd never recounted to anyone what had happened to his family. And, having managed to neutralize the past by encysting it in scar tissue made him reluctant to excavate these memories, even for her.

"My story is so similar to yours, you already know it," he protested.

"You must tell me!" she insisted. He did feel a debt of reciprocity, but he was also frightened by what might happen once he began. It was like pulling at the end of a loose strand of yarn on a piece of knitting—he feared he might unravel the whole fabric of his defense system against the past.

"Well, my mother was an American," he began hesitantly.

"Your mother was a what?" she interrupted in disbelief. "An American?"

"Yes, she was a Eurasian from San Francisco, and was studying violin at the Conservatory there when my father arrived from China to study piano."

"So you're half American?"

"I am, although it sounds strange to say so here. My parents got married in San Francisco and came to Beijing in 1950. However, when I was hardly five, my mother had to return to California to see her ailing father, and she never came back."

"You know, I've never met an American, even a half-American, before." She smiled. "So—what happened after that?"

"Because China and the United States were enemies, she was unable to get her American passport renewed. While she was trying to work things out, she got cancer and died."

"So much tragedy," said Little Yang, kissing his neck. "And what happened to you?"

Like a vehicle gathering momentum as it coasts down a steep incline, Little Li had become so swept up in his own narrative that by the time he got to the night at Willow Courtyard with the Red Guards, he was so light-headed he had to sit down. When she knelt beside him, took one of his hands, and rubbed his knuckles against her cheek, years of bottled-up emotion erupted. But even as tears streamed down his cheeks, he, too, tenaciously kept going, as if his life somehow depended on finishing his own story. When he finally came to the end, he felt both emotionally spent and purged. As she stared silently up at him in the moonlight, he reached over and took her in his arms.

"What are the chances of two complete strangers with such similar lives finding each other in a place as remote as this?" she asked.

"As improbable as two random bullets colliding in midair," he replied, and kissed her again. Glancing up at the moon, he saw it now had a white circle around it. "It looks like it might snow, so maybe we should start back."

"All right," she consented regretfully.

Just before they reached the compound gate, she stopped and huddled against him. "Usually, I feel so lost," she murmured. "But tonight I feel found."

"I don't know what to think about my life right now," he replied, stroking a wisp of hair that was hanging out from her cap. "I never thought a person like you would ever like someone like me."

"We've been taught to despise ourselves by being despised," she replied, and for a few moments, neither spoke. "Perhaps we should go now. If I'm not back before the other girls awaken, there'll be trouble."

"Will I ever see you again?" he managed, as she pulled away. The idea of parting forever was so painful, he immediately wished he'd not asked the question.

"I don't know," she said. "We're supposed to leave at sunup." Taking her head in his hands, he kissed her tenderly on both cheeks one more time.

"Goodbye, Yang Ming" was all he could choke out.

"Goodbye, Li Wende. I will never forget you. Ever!"

As he walked back to the barracks, he felt as if the ground beneath his feet had opened and swallowed up his delicately constructed Yak Springs life. As soon as he'd crawled under his quilt and closed his eyes, Yang Ming's face reappeared before him. How inexplicable it was that, after only a few hours, he felt he knew her as well as anyone on earth. The idea that she was still so near, yet would soon disappear as quickly as she'd appeared, seemed as unreal as it was unbearable.

18

WHEN LITTLE LI opened his eyes, daylight had not yet broken, and it took him a moment to recall what had happened the night before. He leapt out of bed, threw on some clothes, and rushed outside. A heavy snow was shrouding everything in white. Electrified with hope that this might mean Yang Ming's convoy would be delayed, he dashed through the snow to the canteen. As soon as he entered, he spotted her sitting with the other two barefoot doctors at the same back table as the night before. When she looked up and saw him, his first impulse was to run to her. But as soon as their gazes met, she withdrew her eyes without registering even a flicker of recognition. It was then that Little Li noticed Station Chief Wu and Eunuch Liu talking with Master Chef Wang by his wok. Knowing he would be immediately suspect if he sat down with the girls, he fetched a bowl of porridge and found a seat alone. It took all his powers of discipline not to look in Yang Ming's direction.

"And now, our station chief has an important announcement," Eunuch Liu proclaimed, unexpectedly standing up to address the room.

"Comrades," Station Chief Wu began grandly, "due to the unfortunate weather conditions, there will be no work details today, and though I know our guests are eager to be on their way, their convoy will remain at Yak Springs until snow levels on the Erla Pass can be checked."

"Are we going to be stuck in this dump till springtime?" exclaimed one of the truck drivers at the next table.

"Relax, Old Shen," another driver replied. "The road is as slick as yak shit, and it's still coming down, so I don't think we want to be out there, sliding around on that mountain!"

As Old Shen scowled, lit a cigarette, and returned to his bowl, Little Li's heart soared. Since the room was still under Station Chief Wu's surveillance, he dared not cast so much as a glance in Yang Ming's direction. But, urgently wanting to connect with her, he began sweeping his gaze around the room like a radar antenna, a tactic that enabled him at least to glimpse her each time his ecumenical glance passed her table. And, each time, he found her more irresistible. But, fearing he might raise suspicions, he forced himself to concentrate on his breakfast. When he finally permitted himself to look up again, the girls had left. As quickly as he could, he, too, departed. Even though they were under whiteout conditions, he headed out the front gate, and there, in the snow, just as he'd hoped, were fresh footprints. He'd gone less than a kilometer when he saw a silhouette.

"I was sure you'd know to look for me here!" she said, rushing toward him with a smile.

"Your convoy's not going!" he gasped.

"It's only a short reprieve."

"Maybe, but what matters is that you're still here." Despite the bitterness of their lives and the frigid remoteness of where they were, as they walked, arm in arm, through the falling snow, Little Li felt the long-frozen core of his being beginning to thaw.

"Will you promise me something?" he asked, in a take-charge tone of voice.

"All right."

"No matter how bad the weather is tonight—one hour after dinner, meet me right here. I have an idea." She nodded. "And, so that we aren't seen together now, you go back to the compound first. If anyone asks where you were, just say you went out for a walk alone. I'll wait and then go back in through a side door." She brushed a few flakes of snow from his cheek and kissed him.

It was still snowing at dinnertime, and in the canteen he sat as far from the three girls as he could. And as he ate, he scrupulously disciplined himself not to cast so much as a glance in their direction. Then, like a commando in one of the Albanian anti-Nazi movies he'd loved as a boy, he anxiously awaited zero hour. In a world where few things had ever worked out in his favor, how had such good fortune now befallen him? When he could restrain himself no longer, he made his way out the front gate and set off down the road. It was still snowing lightly and the road was only dimly outlined as a band of unrelieved whiteness bisecting an otherwise formless landscape. As he walked, he kicked up as much snow as he could, so she'd have a clear track to follow. Only when he reached the rock where he'd played for her the night before did he stop and begin hopping up and down to keep warm. Then he heard the distant sound of boots crunching over snow. Unable to resist, he ran toward the sound.

"Why are you running the wrong way?" she laughed, as they almost collided.

"I'm just running toward the idea of you."

"How sweet!" she said softly. "But where can we go? We can't just stand out here!"

"I said I had a plan, didn't I?" He smiled authoritatively.

"Yes, but what kind of plan?"

"You'll see." Taking her by the arm, he led her slowly back down the road. As they neared the compound, they could hear the truck drivers drinking, singing, and cursing at the caravanserai.

"Are you sure you know what you're doing?" she asked hesitantly as he steered her off the road, through deep snow, and along the outside of the compound wall.

"Yes," he reassured her. When they came to the corner, he guided her down a draw until they saw the dim outline of a shack looming in the snowy darkness. After opening the door, he took a candle out of his pocket and lit it.

"What's this?" she gasped upon seeing steam curling up into the darkness like a phantasm.

"A hot spring."

"Here?"

"Yes, right here." He laughed. "Where do you think the name 'Yak Springs' came from?"

When he'd anchored the candle in a puddle of melted wax on top of a boulder, he took off his boots, sat down, and stretched his bare feet out over a flat stone warmed by the hot water bubbling up around it. She sat down beside him and took off her boots. Never had he imagined that feet could be so beautiful.

"It's like a dream!" she exclaimed as the hot rocks infused both of their cold bodies with warmth.

"What are you thinking about?" he asked after a long silence.

"About our crazy lives," she responded, "how I've always felt my family must have done something very wrong to have deserved its bitter fate, and how I, too, was being punished for those wrongs. Otherwise, things didn't make any sense. Even though I knew that what happened to my parents wasn't right, the idea that we deserved to suffer because of who we were did help explain why so many bad things kept happening. But you make me wonder, Little Li, if I actually deserved such harsh judgment. Why have you been delivered to me now? Are you part of a new, improved destiny [缘分] for me?"

"I don't know about destiny," he answered sweetly. "But I guess sometimes luck does strike!"

"And when it arrives, I'm going to accept it, even if it comes in the form of someone like you, with a 'bad class background.'" Her eyes sparkled with both happiness and sorrow, reminding him that, though gladness and sadness are contradictory, they're also as conjoined as yin (阴) and yang (阳).

"Until yesterday, I, too, always felt I was on a one-way street, always trying to do the right thing, but always getting accused of being politically impure and then being dismissed."

"Well, maybe you are just a 'bad element.'" She chuckled. "After all, being here with a person like me is truly a counterrevolutionary act!"

"Can you imagine what Station Chief Wu would do if he caught us?"

"Don't think about such things!" She grabbed his arm and gave a little shudder.

"You know, up until yesterday, I'd been trying to accept my life here at Yak Springs as it was. Then you crashed through the fragile eggshell I'd managed to build around it, and . . ."

"Aren't you glad?"

"Yes, but it makes everything suddenly seem completely absurd." He was seized by a flush of indignation. "I mean, when you think about it, what did we ever do to deserve being treated like this?"

"Let's not waste time getting upset," she hushed him. "Let's just take what we're being offered now."

Pulling herself up onto her knees, she reached over, took off his hat, and unbuttoned his overcoat, and then, as meticulously as someone peeling a piece of fruit, she removed each of his garments, until he was completely naked. He was too astonished to resist. For a few minutes, she just sat before him and, without any evident self-consciousness, drank in his body the way an art connoisseur might stand in silent absorption before a great sculpture. Then she ran her fingers over the goose-bumped skin of his chest.

"Aiyaaa! What a strong, handsome guy!" She laughed, squeezing one of his calf muscles. The touch of her slender fingers was like a draft of powerful liquor. She seemed so sure of herself, he wondered if she was used to seeing unclothed people as a barefoot doctor, or maybe she'd been with other men. "I don't want you to think that I know what I'm doing!" she said, almost as if reading his thoughts. "I've never been with a boy before, but I am just not as shy as you." She fixed her gaze on his face with such intensity, he had no choice but to look back. There was, he thought, not a single thing lacking in her loveliness. Even the sadness radiating from around her eyes made her more beautiful.

"Do you think that—"

"Shhh! Don't think so much!" she interrupted. We've been allowing people to confuse us for too long. My whole life has been spent doing what others wanted, but tonight there's no one to give me orders, and I'm going to do what my heart tells me."

"And what's your heart telling you?"

"We'll just have to see." She gave a beguiling smile. "Did you really think I didn't notice you in the canteen last night?"

"I've never known what to do around girls. But, then, I've never had a chance to be around them. Chairman Mao says that pure theory is no better than horseshit. When it comes to girls, that describes me: I'm all theory and no practice!"

"You're a funny one. Maybe it's your awkwardness that makes you so lovable!"

"Well, that would be a pleasant surprise," he said, and laughed. He'd never been able to imagine a woman wanting him as much as he always wanted them. After all, who had ever truly wanted him? Certainly not the revolution or China, and maybe not even his mother. But sitting before him now was a refutation of all such self-disparaging presumptions, someone who was enamored of him, even of his reticence. Despite his arousal and nakedness, he felt bathed in an unfamiliar glow of calm, like a hungry man who finds himself about to sit down at a banquet table heaped with delicacies.

With clouds of steam wreathing her, Yang Ming stood up and, in a way that was completely natural, began stripping off her own garments. Beholding her full nakedness was for Little Li like looking at an X-ray and seeing inside someone. Her sinuous body had a compact, taut, simple elegance that he found unbearably erotic. There was nothing exaggerated or wasted about it, not a single protrusion or excess, as if her body had been sculpted with the greatest economy by an artist who understood the power of understatement. Her small breasts, slightly rounded belly, and the V-shaped puff of black between her legs, all now exposed, seemed to say, unapologetically, "They're yours!" It was then that he noticed a nasty line of suture marks like animal tracks running along her inner left thigh. As he ran his index finger along the scar, goose bumps arose on her otherwise smooth skin.

"What happened?" he asked.

"I was attacked one night by a repulsive cadre at the transfer center." She squeezed her eyes closed in revulsion. "So I grabbed a pair of scissors from his desk and stuck that pig right in the you-know-what! That made him so mad, he yanked them out of my hand and slashed me." She spoke with the defiance of someone who has learned how to protect herself.

"And then?"

"Since I'd stuck that old turtle egg right in his private parts, he wasn't in any condition to violate me, or anyone else, for quite a while. Then I got sewn up. But I don't want to think about such repulsive things now." With a smile that was at once innocent and sultry, she rested her head against his chest. Excited by her touch, he was also relaxed by her naturalness. Pressing her cold, hard nipples against his chest, she quivered, conveying not just her chill, but her vulnerability.

"Shall we warm up in the water?" he suggested. Taking her by the hand, they stepped gingerly into the first pool. Gasping, she submerged her body.

"Is this real?" She laughed, splashing his shoulders as he, too, slowly lowered himself into the steaming water. His whole body glowed with warmth, gladness, and gratitude.

"Even in my wildest dreams I never saw anyone like you!" he

said. "I don't think I could even have imagined you!" She took one of his hands and guided it over the skin of her silky, smooth breasts and down to her slender waist. How amazingly sensitive human fingertips are, he thought, even ones that are scarred, toughened, and callused from working with rock. "I really don't know what to think right now."

"Don't think, just be here with me," she said with a beatific smile. "And be kind. Often I wonder where all the kindness in the world has gone. Right now, all I want is to get as warm as I can! Shall we go into the next pool?"

Her feline grace when she stood up made him think of the snow leopard he'd watched in the foothills. As she slowly submerged her body in the next pool, she let out a whimper of joyful pain. The image of her lovely head floating above the water, with her eyes closed, mouth slightly ajar, perspiration beading on her brow, and braids trailing in the water, was one he knew he'd never forget. He stepped in beside her, and the steaming water and her nakedness made him feel invincible. Opening her eyes and finding his gaze fixed on her, she smiled luminously and took both his hands in her own.

"Have you never seen a woman naked before?" she asked, cupping her breasts with his hands.

"Here in Yak Springs, we've had . . . well, a shortage of naked women." He laughed. "As Chairman Mao once said of us Chinese, we're 'poor and blank.' When it comes to naked women, 'poor and blank' definitely describes me."

"You pitiable thing!" she said in mock sympathy. "So poor, so blank, so deprived, yet so selflessly serving the people!"

"You should have respect for such a blank, deprived soul!" Again he laughed. "Remember, our Great Helmsman also said, 'On a blank sheet of paper free from any mark, the freshest and most beautiful characters can be written.'"

"So, Comrade Li, what kind of beautiful characters do you think Chairman Mao would expect us to write tonight on our blank sheet of paper?" He reached over, brushed a strand of wet hair from her cheek, held her face in his hands, and kissed her lips.

"I see," she said, smiling.

Then, as if he'd done it a thousand times before, he took her intoxicatingly wet, slippery body in his arms and embraced her.

She yielded without resistance, clinging to him as if for dear life, transporting him into a state of bliss so sublime he thought he might lose consciousness. When they finally climbed out of the hot springs, he felt baptized anew into life, so that even the clothing he'd been wearing now seemed like dead, desiccated skin shed by some molting reptile.

As they stumbled wordlessly back to the compound through the still-falling snow, he was so relaxed he feared his legs would buckle. When they passed the latrine, they tried not to make any noise, lest they awaken Nikita and Nina. But when Yang Ming accidentally cleared her throat, ever vigilant to any sound that might herald a nocturnal snack, the two pigs roused themselves to a frenzy of grunting and squealing. Hurrying, they kissed one last time. He'd imagined a more extravagant farewell, but they were both so fearful of being discovered, they dared not linger. And since nothing he could think of saying could come close to expressing the ache in his heart, all he said was "Goodbye, Yang Ming."

"Farewell to you, Li Wende. I'll never forget you."

Glowing from her embrace and the warmth of the hot spring, but chilled by the recognition that this dreamlike moment was over, he trudged back to the barracks, wondering how the creator, whoever that might be, came to make human beings so crave members of the opposite sex that they would risk almost anything to be together. Just then, he would have done almost anything to remain with Yang Ming. But there was nothing under heaven that could be done to prevent her inevitable departure.

When he awakened, dawn had not yet broken. He dressed hurriedly and ran outside. The blizzard had ended, and the night sky was filled with giant white clouds that mimicked the rolling snow-covered hills. He rushed to the canteen, but she was not there.

"Leaving today?" he asked one of the drivers.

"Right. The snow's dry, and most of it has already blown off the Pass."

"And not a moment too soon for my taste," another driver said with a derisive laugh. "One more day at Yak Springs and I'd start growing wool!"

Frantic to find her, Little Li searched the compound, but she was nowhere to be found. Not knowing what else to do, he set off down the road toward their nighttime trysting place. How ironic, he thought, that the very road he'd worked so hard to maintain would now take Yang Ming away. He'd just reached the rock where he'd played for her when he heard the distant sound of a truck horn sounding one long, plaintive toot, the signal for departing convoys to form up at the front gate and load passengers. Frantically, he began running, but quickly became so winded by the snow he had to stop and catch his breath. Then came the sound he dreaded— the three long truck-horn blasts that signaled departure. Panting and exhausted, he finally reached the front gate, but not until the last truck was disappearing over the first rise, a giant plume of powdery snow billowing up behind it like the wake of a boat. All that was left were tire tracks ribbing the freshly fallen snow, and a faint smell of exhaust still lingering in the windless air. Helplessly, Little Li watched the necklace of dark beads in the distance inch across the snow-covered valley floor before finally slipping behind a far bluff and disappearing forever.

In the days that followed, there was hardly a waking minute when he did not think of Yang Ming. She'd disappeared just as suddenly as she'd appeared, and taken with her a piece of him that he'd not even known existed. But, even though she was physically gone, he was unable to expel her from his consciousness. She was there, but not there, at the same time. Their few moments together had cracked open the fragile protective cocoon he'd so laboriously spun around his life at Yak Springs to awaken a tumult of unruly feelings that he could not subdue. Yang Ming's advent made it impossible for him to continue ignoring the fact that his life was wasting away, day by day, week by week, month by month, and year by year.

Early that spring, he was once again summoned by Eunuch Liu to Station Chief Wu's office. When the station chief looked up and saw Little Li, he took a deep asthmatic drag on his cigarette and then, as if it were an unclean thing he wished to get as far away from his own person as possible, he pushed an envelope across his desktop. The letter was posted with a stamp depicting a crimson sunrise over Tiananmen Gate, and was addressed in an unfamiliar hand, but Little Li knew exactly from whom it came. So did Station Chief Wu.

"When hosting visiting delegations, all comrades in our unit are expected to exercise discipline over their selfish individualistic urges," he reproached, after a somber pause.

"Of course," Little Li replied, knowing that if he ever hoped to see the letter's contents, he'd have to make "an expression of contrition" (表态). "I will take these criticisms to heart."

"It is not customary, when visitors pass through our jurisdiction, for local comrades to interact in unauthorized ways, so your dossier will show you exhibited manifestations of incorrect behavior."

"I will resolutely strive to improve my outlook," Little Li responded fatuously, willing to say almost anything just then to get the letter that so temptingly sat in limbo between them. After a long silence, Station Chief Wu grudgingly pushed the letter all the way across his desk.

Once outside, Little Li made a beeline for the front gate and ran down the road, as if retracing his route with Yang Ming might somehow bring her essence closer. He stopped only upon reaching the flat stone where they'd sat together. The letter had been posted a month before, in the Aba Tibetan Autonomous Prefecture, Sichuan Province, suggesting that Station Chief Wu had not only withheld it, but opened and read it.

> *My dear Wende:*
> *Our hearts have been broken once and would only be broken a thousand times over if we allowed ourselves to keep hoping we might someday reconnect. Divided by forces beyond our control, we must make do with what fate has assigned us, and we've been assigned separation. But despite this bitter fact, I will never forget our short time together. Will you take care of yourself for me?*
> *Ming*

Although her letter only confirmed what he already knew, he felt stabbed to the quick by the blunt finality of her words. Falling to his knees on the road, he let out a wail of despair. The idea they might be capriciously prevented from being together was unbearable. However, in the framework in which they were being forced to live, her logic was irrefutable, and over the following weeks he

tried to force himself to relegate her cometlike appearance and dis-
appearance to that already extensive inventory of painful experiences in his life for which there were no reasonable responses save
submission and forgetting. His only hope was that, like the scar on
her thigh, he might somehow stitch together the ragged margins of
the wound opened by his brief moment with her and find a way to
go on.

19

AS IT turned out, Yang Ming was only the first of a succession of unexpected outside intrusions into the isolated world of Yak Springs. The compound was stunned again when a passing convoy brought a September 1976 issue of the *People's Daily* emblazoned with an enormous black headline:

OUR BELOVED LEADER CHAIRMAN MAO HAS PASSED FROM THIS WORLD. LONG LIVE HIS GLORIOUS MEMORY!

Station Chief Wu immediately ordered that the paper be posted in the lobby of the Administration Building, next to Mao's portrait, so that all inmates could study the photos of grief-stricken mourners weeping at the mass memorial service in Tiananmen Square and read the testimonials to Mao's eternal greatness.

A month later, another convoy brought a second piece of earth-shaking news: Mao's wife, Jiang Qing, and the three militant allies who'd formed the ideologically extreme core of the Cultural Revolution's leadership, had been arrested and were now being publicly reviled as "the Gang of Four." In Yak Springs, such news had a surreal quality. Whatever happened in Beijing, each day the sun would still rise and fall in Yak Springs, convoys would still come and go, Master Chef Wang would still dish up the same slop, Station Chief Wu would still rule his petty feudatory, and Little Li would still go to work on the highway. As the ancient proverb put it, "Heaven is high and the emperor is far away" (天高皇帝远).

But several weeks later, Eunuch Liu handed Little Li another letter from his father, which made him wonder if fundamental politicalchanges were not, in fact, under way.

My dear son:
  Because of new policy changes, I have been granted
permission to return home to Willow Courtyard. I
am presently awaiting more details and will keep you
informed.
  I do hope you are looking after yourself and are well.
Not a day passes that I do not think of you.
  Your father

The words "return home" (回家) wrenched open that door behind which Little Li had struggled to keep his old life in Beijing locked. But now he could not prevent himself from fantasizing about what it would feel like to walk down Big Sheep Wool Alley again, open the gate to Willow Courtyard, and re-enter his old world. However, when he looked in the mirror now, what he saw looking back shocked him. His skin was burned brown, his body had become brawny, his home-cut hair was like a peasant's, and his clothes were as ragged as a beggar's. Up until recently, whenever he thought of his father, Granny Sun, or Little Wang, they'd appeared inert, as if painted like so many bodhisattvas lined up in a Buddhist cave, who with all this unexpected news, had suddenly come to life to march with impunity through his mind. And although he knew it was folly to try, he could not stop thinking about Yang Ming. Even though he knew she was irrevocably gone, she continued to fill his dreams.

Arriving convoys kept bringing more startling news, such as the mind-bending announcement that Deng Xiaoping, twice deposed from the party leadership as a "capitalist roader," had unexpectedly been rehabilitated and was being restored to all his previous posts. Because these occasional newspapers were the only portholes through which Yak Springs, inmates could peer out at what was happening in the world beyond, each time a batch arrived, so many vied to read them that they were soon in tatters, confronting Eunuch Liu with a latrine crisis. Little Li noticed that Chairman Mao's quotations were no longer highlighted in boldface. Moreover, instead of exhortations such as "Never forget class struggle" (永远不忘阶级斗争), Deng was now urging Chinese to "reform and open up" (改革开放) and to "seek truth from facts" (实事求是). Such a dizzying succession of changes seemed to be so shaking the old revolutionary edifice back in Beijing that even the largely illiterate Goloks sensed a thaw. Whereas Lobsang had hitherto hidden his family's Buddhist practices, now he openly hung prayer flags and genuflected before mani walls. And, when he was trucked out to work on a stretch of highway near Snow Mountain Commune, at the base of Mount Anymachen, Little Li was surprised to find groups of pilgrims openly circumambulating the great peak to earn *sonam,* "merit," for their next lives. Most walked with reverential concentration, but some marked their way around by prostrating themselves over and over on the ground, inchworm-style, in the belief that such genuflections would earn them more favor. And when Lobsang's family returned from their high summer pasture that fall, Little Li was surprised to find that he'd removed Mao's photo from the family altar and allowed the image of His Holiness the Dalai Lama to assume his proper place.

By December 1978, Deng was calling on Chinese to "emancipate their minds" and "develop all productive forces, shake off poverty, build a strong prosperous country, and improve the living conditions of the people." A month later, he shocked the country by announcing he'd go to the United States to visit President Jimmy Carter in the White House. But the day inmates walked into the Administration Building for breakfast to find an enormous blank place on the filthy hallway wall where Chairman Mao had once hung was perhaps the most unforgettable occasion. Whatever was happening in Beijing, shock waves were now reverberating all the way to Yak Springs.

One evening in 1980, just as the grasslands were beginning to erupt in their springtime display of wildflowers, Eunuch Liu appeared in the canteen at dinnertime, clapped his small hands together to silence the assembled inmates and then introduced Station Chief Wu, who was attired in his best gray Mao suit and was proudly clutching a document emblazoned with a large crimson seal.

"As the lead cadre at the Number Six Qinghai–Sichuan Road Engineering and Maintenance Bureau Way Station," he began, "I am proud to announce that high-level officials in the provincial capital have chosen our work unit for a special honor: to collaborate with the Chinese Mountaineering Association to welcome a special delegation of American visitors to our region. Thanks to our country's new and correct open-door policy, spelled out by Vice-Premier Deng Xiaoping at the recent Third Plenum of the Eleventh Central Committee of the Chinese Communist Party, our government has invited a team of American mountaineers to attempt the first ascent of Mount Anymachen. On their way to the mountain, these American friends will honor us by overnighting at Yak Springs!" He stabbed his index finger toward the floor of the canteen, as if Yak Springs had been picked for this honor because of his own stellar leadership, then he gave one of his repellent smiles. "I am sure," he self-importantly continued, "all of you feel as proud as I do to have been selected to host such an important effort to promote friendship and understanding between the peoples of our two great nations." Station Chief Wu, who'd spent his life reviling Americans, now saw no apparent indignity in enthusiastically welcoming them as "friends." Even more counterintuitive was that this out-of-the-way province, whose major industry was its secretive network of penal colonies, was about to open itself to the global recreation industry and international scrutiny.

Whenever "foreign guests" (外宾) came from "advanced capitalist countries" like the United States, host units knew they alone were responsible for assuring that the People's Republic of China be shown in the best light, with no backward parts exposed. It was one thing for Chinese to live in poverty, quite another to reveal this poverty to foreigners. With national face at stake, everyone was expected to assure that no "foreign guest" departed unimpressed by the miracle of Chinese socialism. Station Chief Wu was painfully aware of how difficult it was going to be to turn this disheveled truck stop into a "model unit" capable of impressing anyone, especially Americans. What is more, he had only the dimmest notion of what actually might impress them. But he did know that if he failed in this task being thrust upon him he would be in exile for eternity. His two most distinguishing character traits were his predictable disdain for those beneath him (and at Yak Springs that meant everyone) and his unfailing unctuousness toward those immediately above him (and at Yak Springs meant no one), and now this announcement promised new opportunities for him to both toady before superiors and overlord over inferiors. It was perhaps understandable, then, that a man who'd spent his life being disesteemed, criticized, and persecuted would enjoy the perverse pleasures of turning the tables. For, if those who've been bullied intuitively understand anything, it is the dynamic between master and slave, two roles that, far from being inimical, have the same inverted congruence as sadism and masochism. Little Li always remembered the Lu Xun quote often cited by his father:

> *The simplest and most adequate way of describing the history of China would be to distinguish between two types of periods:*
> *1/ The periods when people wished in vain to enjoy a stable slave condition.*
> *2/ The periods when people managed to enjoy a stable slave condition.*

The upcoming American visit promised to relieve Station Chief Wu of the profoundly galling frustration of being denied the opportunity to perform those rituals of slavish self-ingratiation that can be carried out only in the presence of higher-ups. For example, it had been a long time since he'd enjoyed hosting guests of exalted enough station to warrant using the three stuffed armchairs in his office throne room. Now the American trip promised a fountain-head of high-ranking visitors and opportunities to indulge himself in such sublime pleasures. But he was also aware that these American guests would require special meals, a sanitary place to relieve themselves (with real toilet paper), comfortable accommodations, and a pleasant spot to eat and socialize. If any hint of backwardness was revealed, he would be blamed. He was, in short, being charged with bringing about nothing less than a complete make-over of his dilapidated kingdom at Yak Springs.

Until this unexpected news, Station Chief Wu's daily routine had involved sitting in his office, smoking, shuffling documents, and chatting after hours over bottles of liquor (白干) with Master Chef Wang. Now he was alchemized from torpid bureaucrat to hyperactive but manic straw boss. But the realization that he had to galvanize a very indifferent workforce with great speed filled him with panic. While he anxiously awaited further instructions from provincial authorities, he mobilized crews of Goloks to clean up the refuse that had accumulated over the years in the compound, whitewash walls, and repaint trim, including the rusty flagpole in front of the Administration Building. The frenzy he generated reminded Little Li of his school in Beijing before delegations from other socialist countries visited. Classes were canceled as students were mobilized to clean windows, pick up trash, pull weeds, mop lavatories, write greetings on blackboards, and drape gateways with banners in hackneyed foreign languages:

WARMLY WELCOMING FRIENDSHIP COMRADES FROM THE NAW-ABSHAH BALL BEARING FACTORY IN THE ISLAMIC REPUBLIC OF PAKISTAN TO PRIMARY SCHOOL ATTACHING WITH CENTRAL CON-SERVATORY OF MUSIC FOR A FRUITLY VISIT.

Little Li could have told his school's teachers their English was off . . . if they'd asked. But they didn't, and, not wanting to be accused of harboring a covert love for America, he remained silent. Then, as soon as the visiting "fraternal comrades" returned to whichever benighted Islamic republic or socialist paradise they hailed from, his school slumped back to its normal state of dereliction and slovenliness. These spasmodic efforts succeeded in accomplishing only one thing: deceiving the visitors into thinking that China was a great success, and sending them home depressed about the relative state of haplessness of their own socialist revolutions or Islamic republic. Of course, they were doing the same thing to visiting delegations from China. The outcome was that whoever toured another, fraternal country returned home thinking that socialism was far more successful abroad than it was at home, a syndrome that created a giant daisy chain of inferiority complexes.

One of Station Chief Wu's main aspirations now was to upgrade the appearance of the compound's main gate, an unprepossessing gap in the undulating Tibetan-style sod wall, bookended by two concrete columns that had been hit by so many trucks that rusty rebar stuck out like skeletal bones emerging from shallow graves. On the Richter scale of Chinese entryways, which was usually grand indeed, Yak Springs hardly registered, and Station Chief Wu was determined to rectify this sorry state of affairs. His plan was to distract attention from the sagging wall by erecting two large stone gateposts crowned with electrified red stars—embellishments that were perplexing, inasmuch as Yak Springs lacked power. But then a truck unexpectedly arrived from Xining and, to everyone's astonishment, brought not only a brand-new portable Japanese generator, but two electricians, who began stringing up electrical lines. That evening, when Little Li returned from the quarry, he was stunned to find a lighting fixture dangling over his own sleeping platform. Alas, his gladness was short-lived. Several nights later, Eunuch Liu informed him that, "until further notice," he was being banished from the newly electrified barracks to the very ramshackle shed across the road that had precipitated Little Liang's unceremonious departure. Since then, herdsmen had been using it to store uncured yak and sheep hides awaiting trucking, and it smelled accordingly. The arbitrariness of the move filled Little Li with rage, but, unlike Little Liang, he was acutely aware of the retribution that would be visited on him if he dared protest, and so he restrained himself. Nonetheless, Eunuch Liu reported him to his boss as having an "attitude problem" (态度问题), and the next day he was assigned to refurbish the latrine.

Having decided it would be indecorous to subject the visiting Americans to the indignities of two ravenous hogs snapping at their private parts as they relieved themselves, Station Chief Wu ordered Little Li to round up a team of Goloks and erect a sod wall to quarantine the two pigs from ground zero. Next he was commanded to excavate a pit beneath the platform and landscape the perimeter with ornamental native grasses, an assignment that won him the compound sobriquet of "Honey Bucket Li." Then Station Chief Wu issued a third decree: instead of waiting until New Year's to slaughter the Khrushchevs, as had been the compound custom for years, he announced that they'd be dispatched just before the arrival of the Americans, so their pork could help "build an iron bridge of friendship between the U.S. and the PRC." The new order not only made the pigsty wall Little Li had just built superfluous, but fomented a near rebellion among inmates who'd always passionately looked forward to their New Year's pork festival.

"Fuck all this claptrap about 'building friendship,'" Road Superintendent Peng suddenly screamed one night in the canteen. "And fuck the Americans, too! What are we Chinese going to do come Spring Festival? Eat more dead yak meat?"

His tirade enraged Station Chief Wu. "If anyone wishes to criticize the decisions made by the high leadership of this unit, they can—"

"They can what?" snapped the road superintendent with uncharacteristic cheekiness. "What are you going to do? Send us off to Qinghai?"

If the imminent arrival of the Americans was reducing Station Chief Wu to near hysteria, it had the opposite effect on Master Chef Wang. Whereas previously he'd run his galley with stubborn sullenness, now, like the victim of a head injury who after years of living in a coma suddenly returns to sentience, he became a paragon of initiative, energy, and congeniality. For the first time in anyone's memory, he started uttering complete sentences that were neither commands nor insults. Without any prodding, he set about scrubbing off the velveteen film of dust and grease that had built up on the canteen's windows, brushing away the beardlike growths of oily cobwebs that drooped from the ceiling over his Stygian kitchen, even washing the canteen's filthy walls. Then he lugged all his pots and woks down to the hot spring and scrubbed them with sand. As a final touch, he even dusted off the cans, bottles, and jars in the glass-topped display case that served as the compound store, some of which had been at Yak Springs for as long as Little Li. His resurrection from surly lord of a gastronomical Hades to smiling public servant did not become fully understandable to Little Li until one morning when he found himself squatting beside Eunuch Liu at the privy.

"What's gotten into our leadership?" he asked, to break the awkward silence.

Only after a prolonged peristaltic grunt did Eunuch Liu reply. "You don't think those two are doing all this just to build socialism, do you?" he said, squeezing out a disdainful fart. "They know the Americans are their best ticket out of Yak Springs. If the Motherland doesn't lose face when those imperialist playboys come through here, they might get sent home."

Little Li was surprised by his vehemence. Before Yang Ming's appearance, he'd come close to shutting the door on the past; now the door was being repeatedly yanked open, and this time he'd have to confront both real Americans and that part of himself he'd managed to keep closeted for so long. Lying awake in his hovel, he found himself involuntarily retracing his passage from Beijing to Yak Springs, only in reverse. But his overheated mind was unable to stop in Beijing. Instead, he was swept all the way to San Francisco, the forbidden land of his mother, whose disinterment he'd so long resisted. And the nearer the visit of the Americans drew, the more California entered his dreams, as if it had just been queued up outside his consciousness, waiting to be let back in.

Station Chief Wu had heard somewhere that Americans liked to take daily baths, a revelation that sent him nearly into nervous breakdown. How was he going to prove that Chinese were not unlaundered primitives without running water? Even though no one had ever seen him actually bathe, he now became dedicated to bathing in theory, even as the question of bathing in practice left him flummoxed. Then Little Li reminded him that they actually had a ready and abundant source of warm, running water at Yak Springs, which could easily be repurposed as a communal bathhouse. Station Chief Wu's relief was so immense that he actually thanked Little Li, before ordering him to do whatever was necessary to slick up the hot springs for "foreign use." Once again Little Li set his Golok team to work, hauling away the piles of sun-bleached yak bones, discarded sneaker soles, smashed liquor bottles, bits of leather tack, rusty tin cans, and old pieces of plastic that had lain strewn around the hot springs unnoticed for years. Then he relined the pools with smooth stones and repaired the collapsing shack. As he worked, he kept seeing Yang Ming with pearls of water dripping down between her lovely breasts.

As news that Americans would visit Yak Springs spread among the Goloks, whole families began appearing and pitching tents around the compound so as not to miss the upcoming carnival of foreigners. Each morning, they clustered in front of Station Chief Wu's imposing new gateposts like pilgrims at a holy shrine, waiting and watching with a patience that seemed infinite. Even Lobsang came, so he could join Little Li's work team, make some cash, and enjoy the fun.

When the Friendship Dormitory, from which Little Li and Little Liang had been expelled, was finished, a brace of Chinese and American flags miraculously materialized to reconsecrate its entryway. No one was quite sure where such affectations were coming from, but, like so many other things that were now inexplicably appearing at Yak Springs, they just showed up on one of the many special trucks arriving almost daily, with everything from gourmet foods and instant coffee to Western cutlery, electric lights, iron-framed beds and mattresses, washstands and towels, and plastic tables and chairs. A cheerful-colored set of tablecloths with matching curtains even appeared so that Master Chef Wang could decorate his freshly laundered canteen windows. Such cargo underscored the seriousness with which officials were taking this visit, but they also further excited Golok expectations. Although repeatedly disappointed each time an incoming truck failed to produce any actual foreigners, the Goloks continued to monitor every arrival. And, like the birdie in a Swiss cuckoo clock, so did Station Chief Wu, who kept popping out the door of the Administration Building onto the stoop to check on what was being unloaded. Wearing an expression that mixed fear with self-congratulation, he gazed down on the arriving goods as if he was a potentate accepting tribute-bearing missions from vassal states. When something arrived that particularly thrilled him—a collection of new thermos bottles emblazoned with the model soldier Lei Feng's smiling face; a case of Yellow River beer; a record album featuring the waltzes of Johann Strauss—his normally tightly clenched jaw lost all discipline and he broke into a self-satisfied smile. But soon enough, when subalterns incorrectly unpacked things or Goloks crowded too tightly around a truck to see what treasures they'd brought, he quickly regained his scowl.

One afternoon, a truck arrived engorged with bales of gray Mao suits, and at dinner, Station Chief Wu proudly announced that each inmate would be issued a new pair of trousers and a jacket. However, this did not end up being quite the giveaway for which inmates initially hoped. The next day, he decreed that the suits could not to be worn until the day the Americans arrived, and then, as soon as the guests departed, they'd have to be repatriated to the Mountaineering Association. What is more, the suits all turned out to be the same size—namely, large—leaving most of the Yak Springs dramatis personae with trouser cuffs a foot too long and jackets hanging off them like tenting. Because all the suits had to be returned "to the people" at the end of the charade, permanent alterations were out of the question. So Eunuch Liu ended up being designated as tailor-in-chief. Armed with Station Chief Wu's office stapler rather than a scissors and a needle and thread, he set himself up in the back of the canteen to make temporary alterations by turning up overly long trouser cuffs, folding back lengthy sleeves, taking in bulging waistlines, and then stapling the fabric together so the alterations could be reversed after the Americans departed. Eunuch Liu proved amazingly well suited to be head couturier. No sartorial detail was too small for his attentions.

Somehow Eunuch Liu also got his hands on several sheets of stick-on lapel badges imprinted with two pandas dancing on the Great Wall and the English felicitation: HI! I AM NAMED: . . . . *WE SO PLEASING TO WELCOME YOU!*

"Our American friends may find it inconvenient to remember our Chinese names, so we must each choose an English name and write it on our badge," he explained one morning at the compound's now daily breakfast briefing. "Because this trip is being viewed with such importance by our central government, we must strive to make our guests from afar feel our special hospitality," he continued. "So each comrade will wear his lapel label on his new suit at all times."

Taking the lead, Station Chief Wu chose the name "Wendell," because he liked the sound of the alliterating "W"s in "Wendell Wu." However, even after endless coaching, the best he could manage was: "Herrow, I name Wender Wu."

Little Li had always thought the idea of adopting a Western given name was pretentious, but now, because he loved the story of Camelot and King Arthur's court that his mother had sent him as a boy, he chose the name "Lancelot." Master Chef Wang, on the other hand, refused to pick a name.

"Because these foreign devils will be hungry, I wager they won't have trouble finding me even without a ridiculous English name stuck onto my front," he pronounced, patting his potbelly. But Station Chief Wu was insistent, so, after consulting a passing trucker who'd driven an American sedan in Shanghai's French Concession before 1949, he adopted the name "Buick." Little Li bit his tongue when he heard this choice, but because the last thing he wanted to do was to remind anyone of his own American provenance, much less that he spoke English, he said nothing.

One bright, sunny morning in April 1981, a week before the Americans were scheduled to arrive, the Khrushchevs broke out of their new confinement area, and just as Road Superintendent Peng and a crew of Goloks were trying to corral them, three jeeps unexpectedly turned in through Station Chief Wu's new gate. Believing that the foreigners had at last arrived, the Goloks mobbed their vehicles, preventing the unannounced visitors from disembarking. When the front window of the lead car wound down and the corpulent face of a scowling, middle-aged official wearing dark glasses and a pug-nosed Mao cap peered out, the Goloks, seeing that he was not a white-faced "foreign devil," immediately began pressing their faces up against the dusty windows of the other two vehicles. Little Li heard the ruckus from the canteen, ran outside, and reached the parking lot just as the lead official was finally managing to get out of his car.

"Where the hell are we?" he asked Little Li with irritation.

"Yak Springs," he responded lamely.

"Where's your unit leadership?"

"Perhaps they were not advised of your visit."

"That's the whole point!" answered the irritated official.

Eunuch Liu had, in fact, already alerted his boss to this unannounced inspection. However, instead of coming out immediately to greet the guests, he'd run back to his office to don his new Mao jacket. And now, just as Little Li was squiring the irritated visitors up the steps of the Administration Building, he came bursting through the door, almost colliding with them. Unfortunately, he was unable to reach out and shake his surprised visitors' hands, because his own arm was stuck in the sleeve of his new ceremonial jacket and some malefactor had stapled it shut. Try as he might, he could not get his hand out and finally just ripped the new jacket off and flung it at Eunuch Liu, who had providentially appeared with a scrap of paper bearing the names of the two unannounced guests. They were officials from the Chinese Mountaineering Association and the All-China Sports Federation whose hands Station Chief Wu immediately commenced shaking as if performing this ritual with extra vigor might make up for his earlier dereliction of duty. Then he thrust both his hands up into the air to silence the Golok tumult. When no one paid him any attention, he was forced to begin his formal welcome anyway.

"When those leading our country and revolution come from afar, who is not inspired by their resolute service to the party and the people?" he began with pompous grandiloquence. "So, on behalf of the Yak Springs Way Station Number Six Qinghai–Sichuan Road Engineering and Maintenance Bureau in the Golok

Tibetan Autonomous Prefecture of Qinghai Province, we warmly welcome . . . uh . . ." Here he had to look at the folded scrap of paper just handed to him by Eunuch Liu. "Uh . . . We warmly welcome Director Gao Xin from the All-China Sports Federation and . . . uh . . ." Again he halted, unable to decipher Eunuch Liu's handwriting. "Uh . . . Director Mu Jianmin from the Chinese Mountaineering Association, who—"

"Wrong!" interrupted a dyspeptic voice. "It's Su Jianmin!"

"Of course," muttered Station Chief Wu, gamely forging on. ". . . who are boldly implementing the Central Committee's policies on reform and opening to the outside world and . . ."

Rather than paying any attention to his welcome, the visiting officials were glowering at the Goloks, who were still crowding around their jeeps—just in case some Americans lurked inside after all. Upon finishing his welcome, Station Chief Wu had hoped to usher his guests into his throne room for a high council on his ceremonial armchairs. But they refused, wanting instead to inspect the compound's state of readiness and then be gone as quickly as possible. However, just as they headed for the Friendship Dormitory, the Khrushchevs rounded the corner of the Administration Building and, perhaps dreaming of a snack, grunted along behind the visiting delegation. Repeated orders hissed by Station Chief Wu to Eunuch Liu to deal with this embarrassing situation produced only an episode of bloodcurdling porcine shrieking when Superintendent Peng sought to restrain Nikita by grabbing his tail. Seeking to repair the damage done by the appearance of the unruly pigs, Master Chef Wang was ordered to expropriate several tins of sliced donkey meat from the compound store and prepare a last-minute repast for the visitors. Alas, by the time these first culinary offerings made their way out of his wok, the dignitaries had already bidden an impatient farewell to Yak Springs. Crestfallen, Station Chief Wu watched their motorcade turn out between his new gateposts and speed away. He'd not even had a chance to fire up his new generator and turn on his beloved crimson stars.

20

WATCH OUT FOR THE FOREIGN GUESTS

THE DISASTROUS inspection tour pushed Station Chief Wu to the brink of nervous prostration. His fears that the team of American mountaineers might now be billeted elsewhere, and that all his labors to beautify the Yak Springs compound would come to naught, caused the clouds of smoke issuing forth from under his office door to reach industrial levels. After a week of thrashing about sleeplessly at night, he finally wrote a letter to Director Gao that mixed shameless self-promotion with obsequious apology. He boasted of the "high state of readiness of our Yak Springs team" and promised to "hold high the banner of reform" (高举改革大旗) while simultaneously "boldly resisting 'wholesale Westernization' [拒绝全盘西化]" during the visit of the Americans. But the ordeal of awaiting a response left him a physical wreck. Indeed, a reply never came, for after checking every alternative to Yak Springs, Director Gao concluded there was no other conceivable stopping place in the area for the U.S. mountaineers.

Quite surprisingly, the Yak Springs compound was by then starting to look quite presentable. The derelict areas between buildings that had been wastelands of litter were now clean. The tufts of grass, thistles, and weeds that had taken root on top of the sod wall and in broken roof tiles had been pulled. Cracked adobe walls had been spackled with mud and whitewashed; desiccated doorways and flaking window frames had been scraped and painted; grimy windows had been washed and cleaned; and political posters had even been hung, adding a dash of political rectitude and color to the compound's otherwise dour palette. There was even a massive new poster in the lobby, featuring a beaming Shanxi peasant with a towel wrapped around his head. But, the most impressive part of the compound's makeover was the Friendship Dormitory. It boasted metal beds with new mattresses, neatly folded quilts, toothbrushes sealed in plastic envelopes, and tin face bowls on washstands accessorized with bright-red thermos bottles inscribed with the model soldier Lei Feng's smiling face and the admonition: TEMPER YOURSELF IN THE FURNACE OF REVOLUTION SO AS TO BECOME A REVOLUTIONARY FIGHTER LIKE LEI FENG!

Then Little Li was given an unexpected new assignment. To minister to the needs of the Americans as a kind of socialist concierge at the Friendship Dormitory, so that by the time they left they'd have concluded that everyone in this people's republic was treated with just as much deference as they. Although he'd never revealed to anyone except Little Liang that he spoke English, his new assignment made him sure Station Chief Wu had learned about his linguistic skills from his dossier. However, he hadn't spoken English for a decade, and the thought that he'd now be called on to use it filled him with such anxiety that he started practicing in bed at night.

The day before the Americans were due to arrive, Station Chief Wu ordered Master Chef Wang to sharpen his knives, and to catch, slaughter, and then hang the carcasses of Nikita and Nina in the coolness of the tool shed behind the canteen, in readiness for the gustatory pleasure of the visitors. But when the cook and his knife-wielding acolytes showed up at the pigsty, the Khrushchevs, now weighing almost two hundred pounds each, instantly sensed an assassination plot, and as soon as the gate to their pen was opened, they bolted past their would-be slayers and fled a second time. When Station Chief Wu heard the shrieks of the two hysterical pigs as they streaked past his office with a ragtag phalanx of amateur butchers in breathless pursuit, he almost had apoplexy. As a precaution, he ordered Eunuch Liu to pay two Goloks to stand guard at his new front gate, in case the truant animals made a run for freedom. When by afternoon, they'd still not been caught, he threatened the team of butchers with a stint in a real reform-through-labor camp, if they didn't complete their assignment by sunset. But every time they got one of their prey cornered, the pigs charged their pursuers and, with a crescendo of bloodcurdling squeals, easily breached their defenses. The closest anyone came to getting a hand on either was when Master Chef Wang succeeded in slicing a piece of one of Nikita's ears off as he streaked by like a torpedo. When darkness fell and neither pig had been caught, a despondent Station Chief Wu ordered his Golok guards to sleep in the gateway and the chase be resumed as soon as the sun rose the next morning.

It was not until midday that the drama ended, when Nina became so stressed that she keeled over dead in front of her beloved latrine. A panting Nikita, his head smeared with dried blood, ended up being not so much slaughtered as stabbed to death like Julius Caesar.

Determined not to miss his chance this time to give a formal welcome, Station Chief Wu hired two more Goloks as scouts to camp out on the bluff several kilometers down the road and light a bonfire as soon as they sighted the first telltale puffs of dust on the horizon. When the column of smoke appeared that afternoon, Station Chief Wu ran into the canteen to order Master Chef Wang to toll the kitchen gong, and all other inmates to suit up and rally on the road in front of his new gate. Little Li had been designated to hold one end of a banner proclaiming: "YAK SPRINGS WARMLY WELCOMING OUR FOREIGN FRIENDS FROM SO AFAR." As members of the honor guard took their places, the roadside also flooded with nomads. In a state of high anticipation, they took up a position behind Station Chief Wu and Master Chef Wang, like an opera chorus behind soloists. With their elaborately braided hair, manly *lokbar*s, exotic hats, and colorful jewelry, they provided a stark contrast to the gray blur of Han Chinese in stapled-together Mao suits in front of them.

When three khaki-colored Liberation trucks finally pulled up in front of the compound's new gateposts, this time the red stars actually lit up on cue. So did the Goloks, who, despite Station Chief Wu's best efforts to maintain order, surged expectantly around the vehicles, cutting him off from his honored guests. As he and Eunuch Liu flailed through the melee, a procession of tall, bearded Americans began disembarking. Completely oblivious of protocol, they fraternally began reaching out to shake the hands of the jubilant nomads, whom they assumed to be their welcoming committee. What immediately impressed Little Li about them was not just their size, but the gaudiness of their attire. Their riotous palette of different-colored hats, parkas, wind pants, and scarves all made with glossy fabric stood out with all the starkness of spring wildflowers on the just-greening grasslands. What surprised him even more, however, were two female climbers, one a statuesque young woman with blond hair cascading down her back like a waterfall, the other short and chunky woman with a halo of brown curls framing her pleasant face, who was wading among the milling Goloks crying out in comically atonal Chinese, "We are Americans! How are you? [我们是美国人.你好]" Every time she repeated the phrase, the Goloks cheered.

Little Li watched with fascination as a tall climber advanced toward an elderly nomad who stood alone spinning a small prayer wheel, and draped an arm clad in bright-blue Gore-Tex around his shoulders.

"Hey, Chuck!" he yelled to a nearby friend. "Get a Polaroid snap of me with this old-timer, will ya? The kids and the little lady'll love it!"

As the camera shutter snapped, the old man sprang back as if stuck by a pin. To reassure him that the camera was harmless, the American held it up for his inspection.

"Okay, now, listen up," he said, pulling the still-blank Polaroid photo out of the bottom of the camera. "You take this, you wait, then you see a picture of yourself." He pointed right at the old man's face, causing him again to recoil reflexively. "No, no!" the American remonstrated earnestly. "You wait. Savvy?" Holding the blank, moist Polaroid shot in one hand and his prayer wheel in the other, the old-timer looked in puzzlement at the mountaineer towering over him. "Just watch!" insisted the American, pointing at the print. By now, the crowd had fallen silent, and even Station Chief Wu and Eunuch Liu had stopped struggling to watch what was happening. When the old Golok saw the image of himself standing alongside this American giant slowly emerge from the milky blankness, his face morphed from bewilderment into a full-blown, toothless grin. Then turning to his expectant fellow tribesmen, he raised this bit of technological wizardry triumphantly above his head. The effect was catalytic: the crowd began mobbing the climber with the miraculous American camera in hopes of getting their own souvenirs.

Only after several other Goloks had received Polaroid snapshots was Station Chief Wu finally able to reach the leader of the American expedition, a short, middle-aged man with long brown hair tied in a ponytail, and officiously begin his prepared remarks.

Although the moment for a formal welcome had long since passed, nothing was going to deter him this time, and on and on he went, extolling the virtues of "building friendship and mutual trust between the U.S. and China." The young interpreter attached to the Mountaineering Association was repeatedly forced to interrupt him so he could translate. However, his English was so poor that even those Americans within earshot understood little of what was being said. When Station Chief Wu finally finished, only Eunuch Liu and the American leader clapped.

"Hi! The name's Carl, Carl Dempsey. And you are?" a tall American in a red parka called out as he reached over to shake Little Li's hand. Bald, with a bushy red beard, he seemed to have decided that since he couldn't grow hair on the top of his head he'd settle for growing as much as possible at the bottom, on his chin. It was an affectation that left the impression that his head was on upside down.

"I am Li Wende, but you can call me Little Li." It was the first time he'd shaken the hand of an American.

"Whoa there, cowboy!" said Carl Dempsey. "You speak good English!"

"I can get along," responded Little Li.

"Tibet is a dream come true!" enthused Carl, pronouncing it "Ty-bet."

"Compared to America, Yak Springs must be quite different," replied Little Li.

"Well, roger that!" said Carl with a laugh. Then he called out, "Hey, guys, this dude speaks serious English!" Turning back to Little Li, he asked, "What'd you say your name was? Little what?"

"Little Li."

"Got it. Want to give us a hand with our gear, Mr. Little?"

"Sure." With easygoing camaraderie, the visitors all pitched in to unload their trucks as Station Chief Wu, Eunuch Liu, and Superintendent Peng stood by, watching.

Later, after he'd received his ration of braised pork from Master Chef Wang's spanking-clean kitchen, Little Li seated himself at the far end of the canteen at one of the new plastic tables.

"Hey, Mr. Little, can me and my posse join you?" asked Carl, spotting him.

"Okay," he responded, unsure what "posse" meant, or what

the protocol was for sitting with these foreign guests. But, in a matter of minutes, his table was filled with other Americans, and the heads of all the inmates in the canteen had swiveled to focus on them as the mountaineers peppered Little Li with questions. The realization that one of their own was able to converse with these barbarians led to much furtive whispering, and Little Li felt dangerously exposed.

"Where you from? How did you ever get to Yak Springs? Why are you here? Where did you learn English? Who are the Goloks? Why do they have an autonomous prefecture? Have you ever been to Anymachen? Are there any snow leopards around?" With Little Li as the object of so much attention, it was not long before even Station Chief Wu and Eunuch Liu drifted over.

"Hey, where'd you ever find this guy?" asked Carl, clapping Little Li on the back.

"Shit, we oughta take him up the fucking mountain!" said one of the other climbers.

"Yeah, he's a lot stronger than you, Wayne!" chimed in another.

"You got that right," said Wayne, stroking his protruding belly. "That's why I've come to Tibet. Gonna leave the love handles on the mountain!"

Eager to bask in the glow of his minion's newly revealed linguistic skills, Station Chief Wu began smiling with eccentric vigor every time Little Li answered a question. As he tried to tune in to the vernacular English banter through the Mountaineering Association interpreter (who was understanding very little of it himself), Station Chief Wu kept bobbing his head, as if agreeing with everything that was being said.

"No! I mean it!" insisted Carl, putting an arm around Little Li. "Waddya say, Chief? Will ya let him come with us?"

"We can all take pride in Comrade Li's high technical level," offered Station Chief Wu, not so much to compliment his inferior as to take some credit for his being Yak Springs' own. "We hope he'll build even stronger bridges of friendship." His sudden custodial pride made Little Li want to stop speaking, if for no other reason than to deprive his overlord of the undeserved pleasure of any credit.

Following dinner, Little Li stayed on in the canteen with the Americans long after the other inmates had left. It turned out that

Wayne taught biology at the University of California, Berkeley, and was particularly interested in the regional fauna of the Tibetan Plateau, especially Tibetan brown bears, snow leopards, Mongolian gazelles, and blue bharal sheep.

"They're all considered endangered species, and we want to see if we can get an assessment of their remaining numbers," he explained.

"I've seen a few snow leopards," Little Li allowed innocently, "even one that was shot."

"Shot?" interjected Wayne indignantly. "You gotta be fuckin' kidding! Killed? By whom?"

"The local nomads. They're really poor, and make a lot of money from one leopard."

"Whoa!" said Wayne censoriously. "Who do they sell them to?"

"To state-run stores that buy animal parts for traditional medicine. Snow-leopard bones are supposed to enhance longevity and sexual potency. Sheep and gazelle horns are prized in other Chinese medicines. Bear paws are considered a great delicacy at official banquets."

"Holy shit!" exclaimed Carl. "That's why they're all endangered!"

"Do you have children?" Little Li asked Carl, attempting to change the subject.

"Here ya go," replied Carl, taking out his wallet and extracting a dog-eared color photo of a smiling auburn-haired woman sitting in a sailboat with two small blond children on her knees. "That's Rory, that's Alice, and that's the little lady, Gina."

But Little Li hardly heard what Carl was saying, because in the background of the photo he spotted the outline of a red steel superstructure arching over a channel toward a high bluff.

"What's that?" he asked, trying to sound casual.

"Oh, you're looking at the Golden Gate Bridge, my friend. Beautiful, isn't it?" Carl gazed dreamily into the photo.

"That's the Golden Gate Bridge?" gasped Little Li.

"None other!" Carl nodded. Suddenly Little Li could neither see nor hear. As the canteen disintegrated around him, he was back in Willow Courtyard, kneeling on his father's piano bench, gazing up at the photo of his parents standing in front of this same bridge. During all his years at Yak Springs, he'd told no one but Little Liang and Yang Ming about his mother and father's connection to San Francisco. But now this forbidden part of his life was suddenly being exhumed.

"My mother was from San Francisco," he haltingly explained.

"You're kidding!" replied Carl. Then, turning to his friends, who'd been chatting together, he exclaimed, "Hey, my guy here says his mother was from the Bay Area!" Little Li immediately regretted having divulged this potentially dangerous secret. "So—how the hell did you get out here?" asked Carl.

"It's a long story." He had no idea how he could ever explain to these curious strangers the tortured odyssey of his family.

"Yeah, I can dig it," said Carl, nodding sympathetically. Fortunately, just then the woman with the long blond hair materialized with a guitar.

"Okay, sports fans," she said with a laugh. "It's showtime here at the very lovely Yak Springs Spa Resort!" As she began singing a cowboy song, Little Li found the sweetness of her voice as lovely as the softness of her blond hair. After a few more songs, she came over and sat down next to Carl.

"Hey, Mimi, meet Mr. Little," introduced Carl. "You'll never guess where he's from."

"Where?"

"He's from the Bay Area!"

"No way!" said Mimi.

"Well, I don't actually *come* from there," Little Li corrected. "My mother grew up there."

"Far out!" she said guilelessly. "And how the heck did you get out here?"

"I'd really be interested, too, in hearing how you got here," pressed Carl.

"Absolutely!" agreed Mimi.

"I mean, it's hard to know what to make of this place!" Carl added, nodding.

Exile had not changed the reality that sharing one's past with others, especially outsiders, was risky. Horrible things had happened to everyone, but publicly acknowledging them, especially before foreigners, was considered traitorous. Thinking quickly,

Little Li rationalized that the dangers of being open with these Americans were relatively small, because no other inmate at Yak Springs spoke English, and these visitors would soon be gone.

As he told them about his life, their faces registered the same kind of spellbound enthrallment that comes over small children who become absorbed in a riveting story. They found it difficult to comprehend why such suffering and privation should have been meted out so unnecessarily to so many. Indeed, as Little Li continued, even to him his story sounded bizarre, senseless, arbitrary, and vindictive. Yet it had happened, not only to his family but to millions of other families. In this weirdly inverted world, the absurd and inexplicable had become the ordinary and expectable, a circumstance that clearly befuddled these straight-grained Americans.

"Yours certainly is an unusual story," Carl ventured diplomatically when Little Li paused.

"Actually, it's quite a common story," he replied. "And mine's hardly the most extreme."

"Dude!" exclaimed Carl, shaking his head.

"What alarms me is not just learning that such things happened here, but that they happened while we were in our American bubble," said Mimi, shaking her head.

If they were drawn to the drama and tragedy of his story, Little Li was equally drawn to their infectious directness and openness, and they did not leave the canteen until long after the compound's new generator had fallen silent. As Little Li walked back to his shack under the starry sky, he had the sensation of a great weight having been lifted from his shoulders. Rather than ducking and weaving down the Chinese obstacle course, past endless sensitivities and taboos that compel one to speak warily and untruthfully, with these strangers he'd felt able—in fact, obliged—to speak openly, freely, and honestly, and the experience left him tingling with a heady sensation of relief. Once he'd curled up under his quilt, his head exploded with long-suppressed visions of San Francisco that had now involuntarily reconnected him to this mystical place that had been crouching in his subconscious, just waiting for permission to spring forth again.

Since childhood, he'd always understood that expressing overt interest in things Western was an invitation to ruin. Now, as if a long-banked ember had been fanned back to life, he wondered anew about America. What would it be like to live in this land of liberty, unburdened by all the limiting strictures of life here in China? Falling asleep, he dreamed of towering redwood trees so old they were alive during the Tang Dynasty; buildings so tall their top floors were lost in the clouds; bridges so majestic they spanned whole harbors; and lines of shimmering automobiles so long they stretched endlessly to the curve of the earth. Just as he'd dreamed as a boy of being able to step into the framed photo of his parents, and to fly away like the Monkey King, Sun Wukong, to the magical land of his mother, now in his dream he flew past glistening glass-and-steel skyscrapers through bevies of floating naked girls who had skin as white as parchment and hair as flaxen as Mimi's, as Bach played in the background.

The next morning, he rose at dawn, fetched hot water from the spring for the mountaineers, and then directed them to the canteen. All the way, they plied him with more questions.

"Damn, it's good to find a guy like you, who knows where the hell we are," Carl Dempsey said, laughing and slapping Little Li on the back.

After breakfast, a single truck horn sounded, and the mountaineers assembled in the parking area to reload their multicolored duffel bags and knapsacks onto their trucks.

"Hey, Mr. Little!" yelled Carl. "Maybe we'll catch you in San Francisco!"

"Maybe," Little Li called back, but he felt as if he were underwater, unable to hear, see, or think clearly.

When three horn blasts signaled "all ready," the ebullient Americans shouted their thanks and enthusiastically waved. As engines roared to life and the trucks turned out through Station Chief Wu's new gate, the red stars lit up on schedule. Little Li waved numbly goodbye.

Everyone was pleased by how things had turned out. Cadre Wu won a certificate of praise from the Chinese Mountaineering Association and a letter hinting that other foreign trekking expeditions might be entrusted to Yak Springs. And, because Little Li's English skills had reflected well on the whole effort, he was authorized to move back into the Friendship Dormitory. However, the move hardly returned things to the status quo ante.

A month later another letter arrived from his father:

My son:

   Though my health has been generally acceptable, for some time I've had a respiratory problem, and I've received permission to return home earlier than anticipated. I am otherwise fine, so please do not worry. The best medicine for what ails me will be Willow Courtyard.

   I hope you're well and that the future will hold more welcome surprises.

   Your father

As he returned to work on the road, vivid memories—of summer evenings on Big Sheep Wool Alley, when everyone poured out of their suffocating houses to sleep on reed mats in the alleyway; the old men pulled their undershirts up over their fat bellies and their trousers up their hairless shins to play chess and drink tea; streetlights cast dappled shadows through dusty leaves; and cicadas serenaded drowsy children held by chattering parents—kept flooding in on him. He thought of Granny Sun, churning the turbid summer air with her chicken-feather fan as he sat in her lap. He'd always felt deprived of that most elemental right of possession small children can feel only for their own mothers. Nonetheless, it was with fondness he now recalled sitting with Granny Sun, being lulled by the familiar sounds of their neighborhood as he slowly succumbed to drowsiness.

He had just returned to the compound after overnighting at Lobsang's when he was again summoned to Station Chief Wu's office. There another letter awaited him. This one bore a Beijing postmark.

My dear son:

   I have arrived back in Beijing where I received a letter from Wu Zuqiang, the vice-president of the newly reorganized Central Conservatory informing me that, in line with current policies, my case was being re-evaluated by the Ministry of Culture and that he was hopeful the school would rehire me. It would be gratifying to have the good name of our family restored. He also told me that,

because I'm a veteran professor with a disability who has
only one child, I am entitled to request that you, too, be
allowed to return to Beijing. I have already made such a
request.
   Your father

Although Little Li was glad to read this news, he did not feel the kind of ecstasy at the prospect of finally being able to leave Yak Springs for "home" that he'd always imagined he would. If the idea of at last escaping the compound was welcome, it was also unexpectedly terrifying: for him, the outside world had become little more than a distant memory, frozen in time past. While he'd been chipping gravel, the world had been going on its way without him. How would he ever catch up to it and reintegrate himself into its irresistible flow?

A few weeks later, he was summoned again to Station Chief Wu's office. This time, a large brown envelope sat on the desk, and he looked more disapproving than usual. However, when Little Li reached to take the envelope, he did not protest. Then, instead of walking outside to open it, Little Li did so right there. It was a permit from the Beijing People's Government complete with a vermilion seal approving the transfer of his "household registration" (户口) from Qinghai back to the city of his birth.

"I'll be going home" was all he said to Station Chief Wu. He looked crushed. After all, over the past decade, no Yak Springs inmate had been repatriated, and since the visit of the American mountaineers, he'd allowed himself to hope that he might be the first to win such a reprieve.

Three days later, Little Li arose before dawn, tied his possessions inside his quilt, and stuffed them into the rice sack in which Granny Sun had packed them so long ago. Then, after breakfast, he walked out of the canteen for the last time and climbed into the back of an awaiting truck. However, when the lead driver gave the familiar first warning toot on his horn, instead of feeling elated, he felt almost as uncertain as he had when he'd first arrived at Yak Springs. Only Eunuch Liu had come out to see him off, and he stood almost motionless beside the road, looking very old, small, and sad. Little Li did not know what to say to this person whom he neither liked nor disliked, but with whom he'd shared a whole chapter of life. He'd spent so many days here at Yak Springs, each one with a morning, an afternoon, and an evening when something had happened. But now, as he looked back on all these days, weeks, months, and years, they were marked by so few memories of distinction that it was hard to distinguish one from another. Except for Little Liang, his encounter with Yang Ming, and Lobsang's family, life at Yak Springs was just a succession of endless immemorable scenes, like those one observes while driving that are perfectly vivid at the moment but, once passed, almost instantly become erased from memory.

In old China, there had been myriad rituals and ceremonies for leave-taking, "seeing" (送) friends to the city gate. But since then, such traditions had been attacked by the revolution as backward, and there were no longer clear-cut forms for marking endings and beginnings, much less for expressing deep sentiment upon meeting or parting. When he'd bid Lobsang and his family farewell, he didn't know what to say. And they'd just looked at him quizzically, as if they did not quite comprehend what was happening.

The sun was just rising over Anymachen when the final three horn blasts sounded and engines coughed to life. All that Little Li could summon up by way of a farewell to Eunuch Liu was a wave with one hand. But it was, in truth, intended as much for Yak Springs as for this faithful retainer of Station Chief Wu, who hadn't deigned to emerge from his smokehouse to say farewell. Perhaps he deemed it beneath his station, or perhaps the departure of this far younger inmate left him feeling so old and forgotten he could not face Little Li's departure. It was the equivalent of one person's managing to overcome death. And then there was the bitter reality that, because Little Li was the youngest Yak Springs inmate, his repatriation overthrew the whole hierarchy of power and privilege on which Station Chief Wu's vision of things depended. Little Li's reprieve made the last first and the first last, an order of things not in his playbook.

As the convoy started to move out, Eunuch Liu waved mechanically, then turned and, with weary resignation, trudged back through Station Chief Wu's star-crowned gateposts into the compound. Knowing that this was the last time he'd ever see him, these mountains, these hills, and these grasslands, Little Li wished he could have stopped to look more carefully one last time. Indeed, if he'd been alone, he would have pulled over, perhaps even knelt down beside the highway to acknowledge the curious love he'd acquired for this unlikely place. But, like the rest of his life in which events just keep happening, the convoy kept going, and all he could do was stand in the truck bed gazing out at the strangely beautiful landscape around him and feel an unexpected sense of loss.

PART
FOUR

21

HOMECOMING

DURING HIS years in exile, Little Li had tried to avoid dwelling on the past. However, now, as he stared out the train window, even though they were still far from Beijing, his soul was already home and walking down Big Sheep Wool Alley. He tried to imagine his father in Willow Courtyard, as if a concrete mental image might help prepare him for the actual moment of reconnection. But instead of being able to see him as a flesh-and-blood person with a face, body, arms, and legs, he kept seeing only a nebulous, auralike emanation. As the world around him had raged out of control, scorning, abusing, and finally physically assaulting him, in his own quiet, steadfast way his father had remained unyielding. A model of restraint, courtesy, and uprightness, he was the antithesis of all those state-sponsored "artists" with long lists of official titles on their name cards that only bespoke of their readiness to keep realigning themselves opportunistically with whatever changing lines the party's latest leaders handed down. Little Wang had mocked such people as belonging to "the wind faction" (风派), a derogatory term derived from the ancient saying "The grass on top of the wall always bends in the wind" (墙头草风吹两边倒). But, like so many older Chinese who were grounded in traditional culture and values before going abroad to study, his father was deeply Eastern and Western at the same time, what his hero Lu Xun—himself torn between Chinese tradition and Western modernity—had mordantly referred to as "something stuck in between." On the one hand, his father venerated J. S. Bach, insisting that his music was fundamentally democratic because his many voices were always as independent and equal as "two persons of the same rank" in dialogue; on the other hand, he venerated Confucius for embracing the universal values such as "benevolence" (仁) as fundamental parts of the moral order.

It seemed absurdly misplaced to be thinking about J. S. Bach and Confucius while on a Chinese train filled with snoring people who'd never heard a note of the German composer's music and had spent the last decade reviling the Sage's humanism. But Bach and Confucius were his father's godheads, he was his father's son, and now here he was going home to meet whatever was left of this man who, even when assaulted by Mao's revolution, continued to esteem these two men for trying to bring some order to the chaos around them. One had codified the rules of harmony and polyphony, the other the rules for human relations, both searching for some grand concordance, or "great unity" (大同), to bring everything "harmoniously" (和谐) together. Perhaps it was not so strange, then, that his father loved the works of both of these two very different men.

The sound of the train's steel wheels rhythmically slapping over the rails was so hypnotic that, even as his head was inflamed with all these thoughts, Little Li was often unsure whether he was awake and thinking, or asleep and dreaming. But he also knew that sooner or later the image of his father's bloodied hands raised over his head and his eyes filled with horror would reappear. And yet, despite all that had befallen him, his father had never shown either resentment nor disappointment. He was a man of quiet endurance and private sadness. With slumber and wakefulness, thinking and reverie, and past and present all spinning in a whirlpool, Little Li involuntarily cried out from his half-sleep: "Father! Oh no!" His seatmate sat bolt upright, stared at him as if he were deranged, and then inched as far away as he could get on the seat before closing his eyes again.

He changed in Xian and they snaked through the barren "yellow-earth" (黄土地) hills of Northwest China, a landscape as leafless and desolate as the mountains of the moon. As they passed by one gray, smoggy industrial city after another—in one, ash was heaped on factory workshop rooftops as deep as gray snow—the crystal-clear air and azure skies of Qinghai seemed light-years away. In the remaining time before he arrived in Beijing, Little Li felt an urgent need to rally himself for that moment when he would, at last, step across the threshold of their old gate into Willow Courtyard. After all these years, what would his father look like? And how should he greet this man whom he'd not seen for a decade? Nod, shake his hand, embrace him? And what should he say?

Exhausted, he finally fell asleep, and did not awaken until the train engine hooted out the same plaintive sound he'd heard so often from Willow Courtyard. Groggy and almost nauseated from thirst, hunger, fatigue, and cigarette smoke, he sat up, rubbed his eyes, and looked out the window. It was early morning, and they were just passing Dragon Well Lake Park, at the southeast corner of Beijing. Then the train slowed and lurched to a stop. As he walked down the platform, every nerve ending in his body jangled in anticipation. Although the familiar burr of Beijing dialect suddenly being spoken all around him was welcoming, he was not sure if he still belonged here. Indeed, anyone seeing his dark, suntanned face, unshaven chin, shabby clothing, tufted hair, and dazed look might have mistaken him for just another "yokel" (土包子) arriving from the provinces to seek his fortune in the capital.

The terminal was at once reassuringly familiar and disturbingly changed. When he'd left as a boy, it had impressed him as huge, grand, and modern. Now it seemed unimposing and rundown. And the low-lying shops with tile roofs around the ellipse just outside were grimier and more disheveled than he recalled. In fact they were so drained of color they looked as if they'd been photographed in black and white. The only thing that broke this monochromatic tableau was a single crimson flag fluttering over the domed station. Who could blame the party for loving crimson? Amid such drabness, it was a breath of fresh air let into an oxygen-starved room.

While he was still at Yak Springs, the abstract idea of homecoming had filled him with a confusing sense of expectation, but now he felt only off balance. Lobsang believed that with death one's spiritual essence, or "soul," departed the corporeal body to wander in a nether region called *bardo* before finally becoming ready to be reincarnated in another newborn creature. As Little Li left the station, he felt like just such a disembodied spirit, adrift in limbo, awaiting an uncertain rebirth in a new life form.

Once he'd entered the familiar maze of *hutong*s, things seemed far smaller and more claustrophobic than he'd remembered. The piles of trash, crumbling gray walls, and disheveled houses made everything more neglected than he'd recalled. Peeking through an occasional open gate, he saw that shacks had been thrown up in many of the courtyard gardens, and sloping tile roofs had cracked and been patched with tarpaper anchored with hunks of broken concrete. After the towering peaks, pristine glaciers, blue skies, and brilliant wildflowers of Qinghai, these alleys seemed drab, sullen, and unkempt. As he rounded the last corner before Big Sheep Wool Alley, a rooster crowed and three pigtailed girls skipped by on their way to school. But it wasn't until he caught the first sulfurous whiff of the public latrine that he felt truly home. Then, as if a musical score had been composed for his homecoming, the matinal "The East Is Red" started blaring forth from neighborhood loudspeakers. At least some things were constant.

No matter how lowly one's birthplace, it would always make the heart beat faster. Just as certain types of metal are said to possess "shape memory," allowing them to bend when heated, only to regain their original shape when cooled, so humans retain an innate longing for those places where they were shaped as children. Because Big Sheep Wool Alley was that place for Little Li, he did not now judge it according to normal standards of beauty or utility.

Then suddenly he was standing in front of Number 14. The paint on their gate, which to his surprise had been left ajar, was faded, chipped, and lusterless and for several minutes, he just stood staring in front of it, hardly daring to move.

"What's your business?" a voice challenged, as if he were an itinerant peddler, even a burglar. An unfamiliar woman was glowering suspiciously at him from a window across the alley.

"I am just visiting," he stammered, not feeling he yet had the prerogative to say he lived here. She scowled and disappeared. His heart was beating so hard he could hear it in his ears. He knew that as soon as he passed through this gate the bubble of vivid remembrance in which he'd been living for so long would be burst by reality.

As he stepped inside, Little Li saw him. His father was in the middle of the garden, beside the old water faucet, filling a battered tin bucket. Little Li recognized his father long before he recognized him. But his father's body was so stooped, his hair so drained of color, and his face so ghostly pale that he looked nothing like the man who'd been living in his mind's eye.

Upon hearing the gate close, Li Tongshu turned off the faucet, took out a pair of spectacles, methodically opened them, and put them on. Only after peering through their thick lenses as if through a dense fog did he finally realize who'd entered.

"Son!" he gasped.

"Father!" cried Little Li, dropping his pack and running toward him. Surprised by his suddenness, Li Tongshu raised his hands as if to defend himself, so that, instead of connecting with his son in an embrace, Little Li awkwardly collided with his father's outstretched arms.

"Son!" Li Tongshu exclaimed again, sensing his son's disappointment and reaching out.

"Aiyaaa! Father!" said Little Li, seeing his father's gnarled, deformed knuckles, as hard as a rooster's spurs. "Look what they did to you!"

"No, no!" demurred his father. "It's not important."

"I'm so sorry!" Little Li repeated, unable to take his eyes off his father's clawlike hands. "If only . . ."

"Please!" pleaded his father. "Bygones are bygones. But how good it is to see you, my boy! Have you eaten? You must be hungry and tired after your trip. Come inside, and I'll fix us something."

"I'd like that."

Despite his hunger, thirst, and fatigue, what Little Li really craved was the kind of catharsis he'd long imagined homecoming would trigger. Although he understood that his father's restraint masked deep feelings, he was nonetheless shaken by how they'd managed to evade the poignancy of the moment.

"And, look, as a welcome home, I've made a special place for you." His father pointed proudly to a metal cot placed against the wall where their piano once stood.

"Thank you, Father," said Little Li as enthusiastically as he could. "It is so good to see you again. How has your health been?"

"Oh, it's really not worth worrying about," he replied. "We must eat!"

As his father moved with slow deliberation to fetch things for a meal, Little Li surveyed their old room. Without the piano, wardrobe, and bookshelf, and with one broken window still boarded up, it hardly seemed the same place in which he'd grown up. Across from his narrow cot was a larger bed and a small wooden table set with two stools he'd never seen before. In fact, the only thing recognizable in the room were the cracks on the plaster ceiling that still formed a rough outline of the continent of Africa. Otherwise, their room was devoid of any of the attributes he'd been envisioning as part of "home." And the sight of this old man shuffling around preparing a simple repast of steamed buns and pickled vegetables on two mismatched plates so filled Little Li with melancholy that he had to avert his gaze to hide his sadness. How the passage of time had ravaged Willow Courtyard and his father! The windows were filthy, screens rusted, lacquer peeling, the roof tiles sprouting weeds, the old willow looked all but expired, and except for a few green weeds around the leaking faucet, the garden was a wasteland.

"It's good to be back," he said softly. "I still can't believe we both managed to make it!"

"Nor can I." Even though you were far away, just knowing you were somewhere helped me endure." His barely audible voice was quavering now and his eyes were brimming with tears. "You're a good son. But how about you, my boy?" Li Tongshu switched to English, trying to affect an air of more jaunty cheerfulness. "Tell me about your life up there."

Not quite knowing where to begin, especially in English, Little Li thought his father might at least enjoy hearing about his "recitals" for the nomads, and, indeed, he did. He smiled and chuckled as his son regaled him with tales about playing in the quarry and Lobsang's tent. But as Little Li began describing other parts of life at Yak Springs, it sounded so uninteresting and unlikely, he finally stopped.

"I'd rather hear about what happened to you at your May 7 Cadre School," he said as his father finished eating.

"I don't really know what to say," he began and sighed, no better able to bridge the divide than his son. "Every day was almost the same, like being asleep in an ever-repeating dream."

"What's happened is all so . . ." Little Li began.

"I know how upsetting you find it," interjected his father in a way that was both calming and peremptory. "But it's over now, and we'd better just put those troubled times aside and focus on what's still beautiful in the world and can still be changed." He smiled wanly. "The future's the thing."

"Maybe," said Little Li, although just then he was having a hard time imagining the future.

"I'll tell you one good piece of news," his father offered. "I was told that Ma Sicong managed to escape to Hong Kong right after being dragged around the Conservatory courtyard."

"He was one of the lucky ones."

"And Granny Sun's still here." A smile flickered across Li Tongshu's face.

"For me, Willow Courtyard is unthinkable without her," said Little Li, laughing and looking out the window toward her room.

"Indeed," said his father softly, his eyes misting over. "You must go to her."

"I will," he said, glad to have a reason to disengage.

As he walked across what had once been their garden, it was difficult to believe anything could ever have grown in this hard, dusty patch of ground. And yet he could still vividly recall how he'd skipped down this very path as a child to proudly deliver flowers and vegetables to Granny Sun. Just then, two swallows arced overhead and dived into a nest under the eaves of her veranda. Even if they were not the same pair he'd watched as a boy, they were reassuring reminders that, despite everything, some creatures still managed to maintain their habitual routines. He'd almost reached her doorway when something made him stop and look back. His father was standing on their own veranda, gazing wistfully after him. Seeing this frail, good man looking longingly after his only son left Little Li so overcome that he hurried back and, without thinking what he was doing, embraced his father, who yielded in a way that was almost feminine.

Granny Sun's windows were so thickly covered with grit and cobwebs that her room looked unlived in. He knocked. No response. He knocked harder. There was a stirring within.

"It's me, Granny Sun!"

"Who?" rasped a voice. The door cracked open, and a narrow slice of a wizened face appeared.

"It's Li Wende!"

"Who do you say you are?"

"It's Li Wende!" he said more insistently. "I've come back, Granny Sun, all the way from Qinghai. I've come back to see you!"

"Who?"

"I'm Li Tongshu's son, Li Wende!"

"Li Wende?" she croaked incredulously.

"Yes!"

"But how can it be?"

"It is!" he insisted impatiently, as she opened the door wider.

"Aiyaaaa!" she exclaimed. "So it *is* you!" Although she was older, he instantly recognized the kindness in her eyes. "Have you been a good boy?" she asked, taking one of his hands in her own. They both laughed at the preposterousness of putting such a question to a man now six feet tall and almost thirty years old.

"Let's just say I've tried, but out on the Tibetan grasslands that's not much of a challenge!"

"How often I've thought of you, my child," she said, reaching up to touch his face as if to reassure herself he was real. "So much trouble! I didn't believe I'd ever see you, or your father, again! But now here you both are! As the old saying goes, 'The road to happiness is strewn with obstacles' [好事多磨]. Come in. Come in!" she said, pulling him inside. Even after all the years, they quickly reestablished their old sense of closeness.

"Have you seen much of my father since his return?" asked Little Li.

"Your father is a good man, child, but hardship turns people in on themselves!" She closed her eyes and shook her head. "So much regret! Now you're all he has. He wants to care for you, but it's really your time to care for him."

As he and his father slowly knitted their lives back together, Granny Sun's admonition kept ringing in his ears. But, having always looked up to his father as a source of counsel and authority, he found it hard to accept that the man was now on the downhill slope of life. Nor did he find it easy to live again under the same roof with him. After all, over their many years apart both had become accustomed to bearing their troubles in solitude. On his part, after the openness of the grasslands, Little Li found it difficult to feel comfortable in the claustrophobic place where he'd grown up. And during his first few weeks home, he kept searching for the key that could unlock a door through all the walls within walls that now divided him and his father. But whenever he tried to coax him into talking about what had happened that night, right here in Willow Courtyard, and then during his years in exile, his father's answers were evasive and unsatisfying. So Little Li concentrated instead on repairing their broken window, setting up new shelves for all the books his father had started buying, finding a desk and comfortable chair for him to read in, and helping him revive a small part of his old garden. But with his mangled hands, gardening went slowly. Besides, he seemed to find it hard to catch his breath, and had to stop frequently to rest. Nonetheless, their life slowly regained a more normal flow.

They were uplifted when the Conservatory granted them a stipend and Li Tongshu immensely enjoyed his old friend Dr. Song Shaoming's weekly visits on Sundays. The two old friends were so similar in their tastes, courtly manners, and decorousness, they almost seemed like brothers. Both had suffered through much and, now that they'd been given chances to lead quasi-normal lives again, even if the price was forgetting how much they'd been wronged, it was a price they were willing to pay. Little Li felt differently. With nothing pressing to do and his future blank, he could not help dwelling on the injustices of the past. As he observed his father's truncated life and thought of his own impasse, resentment welled up. How had such injustices been allowed to happen? Would anyone ever be held responsible? When he started thinking this way, he not only became incensed, but swore that if he ever managed to slip free of China, he'd never make the error of returning out of misguided love of country. Li Tongshu showed no such indignation.

"Son, I have a request," he said very tentatively one morning.

"What is it?" inquired Little Li, eager to oblige.

"Would you accompany me to church?" he asked with a childlike sweetness.

"To church?" asked Little Li in surprise.

"Since returning, I've sometimes started attending church on Sundays."

The idea that his father was openly going to church made Little Li wary. After all, the party's own constitution forbade members from being believers, and, as anti-Western sentiment crescendoed during the Cultural Revolution, churches had been shut all across China, clergymen arrested, stained-glass windows smashed, crucifixes torn down, and sacristies desecrated with Maoist slogans. If someone now attended a church, even one of the newly opened party-sanctioned "patriotic churches" (爱国教堂), who knew what might happen?

"Couldn't attending church services cause you more trouble?" he asked cautiously.

"I doubt it," replied his father. "Since Deng Xiaoping's return, they've allowed hundreds of churches to reopen. Anyway, what more can they do to a toothless old tiger like me?" He smiled wanly.

"Well, I was just . . ."

"It's all right," rejoined his father. "I've already attended several services, and there's been no problem." Little Li hadn't seen his father quite so definite, animated, and determined since his return. "You know, when I first met your mother, we used to go to Grace Cathedral on Nob Hill in San Francisco and listen to organ recitals," he continued. "How she loved the way the huge pipes of that magnificent instrument reverberated in that cavernous space! To hear Bach there made us feel we were connected to the heavens." He smiled with a faraway look in his eyes.

"Didn't our old book on the cathedrals of Europe belong to Mother?"

"It did." He paused for a moment, as if considering whether to put his next thought into words. "Perhaps I never told you how religious she was."

"Was she more religious than you?"

"She was. What made me religious was music, especially the music by my friend Herr Bach!" He smiled. "But your mother was the daughter of a preacher."

"All I knew was that her father was a missionary in Shanghai."

"Yes, and your mother was his favorite."

"Why didn't you ever tell me more about her?"

"When your mother left us, I missed her too much to speak of her, even to you. If I had, I feared I would have been overcome, and you were still just a little boy."

"I've often wondered how you managed all alone."

"Playing the piano was my way of talking to her. Now I go to church to speak to her."

That Sunday morning, they biked down Front Gate Avenue to the South Cathedral (南堂) with Little Li pedaling and his father riding side-saddle behind him. As they approached, the church's gray brick ramparts were beginning to be bathed in the warm yellow light of the rising sun. Just the short walk from the bike park left Li Tongshu short of breath.

"Are you sure you're okay?" Little Li asked.

"Oh yes," his father replied stalwartly. "No problem."

They sat down in the shaded churchyard on a bench next to a dusty glass case filled with pocket-sized Bibles and prayer books whose green plastic covers made them look like siblings of what had previously been China's most popular sacred text, Chairman Mao's Little Red Book of quotations. Considered apostasy only a few years ago, Little Li was surprised to see these books of scripture now so openly displayed. Even though South Cathedral, or the Cathedral of the Immaculate Conception, was Catholic, and Li Tongshu was Episcopalian, he sometimes came here anyway, because he liked the idea that it had been founded by the Italian Jesuit Matteo Ricci, the first Western cleric allowed to reside in Beijing, who'd brought the Wanli Emperor a clavichord in 1601.

Inside the cathedral, they took a pew behind several dozen elderly worshippers. Little Li reflected that perhaps his father was right: as people advanced in age, maybe the party did view them as increasingly irrelevant, and thus allowed them more freedom. It was an ironic form of inverted progress!

As a boy, Little Li had often leafed through his mother's book on the great churches of Europe and been awed by their magnificence, and while bicycling that morning, he'd been anticipating that South Cathedral would share some of the same grandeur. But—with its clear-paned windows, columns finished with simulated marble veneer, a very modestly vaulted ceiling, and an altar adorned with a rendering of the Virgin that looked as if it had been painted by a revolutionary committee at an electrical machinery factory—the cathedral was disappointingly unimposing. And when music began playing, it came from a small electronic instrument that pumped out saccharine renditions of hymns with heavy vibrato, the antithesis of the chorales his father used to play. Still, as unprepossessing as it was, the church nonetheless did invite worshippers to lay down their burdens and be alone with their thoughts, souls, and God. And Little Li was caught off guard when his father unexpectedly fell to his knees, closed his eyes, and pressed his mangled hands together.

When he was a small boy and his father became lost in prayer, playing the piano, or writing letters to his mother, Little Li had always felt so alone. But watching him now, he felt touched. Although he didn't really understand religion, in Qinghai he'd admired the devotion that Old Norbu and Lobsang had shown to Lord Buddha. And in the presence of the mountains there, he, too, had felt an unexpected communion with a force greater than himself. If the spirit of God had ever touched him, it was while walking among the wildflowers, gazelles, snow leopards, and eagles in the shadow of those majestic peaks. And now an unexpected feeling of peace came over him. He took a deep breath, knelt beside his father, and closed his eyes.

22

DEMOCRACY WALL

LITTLE LI was just on his way to find his old friend Little Wang when he spotted someone in front of him with long hair and a scraggly beard whose shambling gait looked familiar.

"Hey! Is that you?" he impetuously cried out.

"It *is* me!" shrieked Little Wang, and upon turning around realized who was hailing him. "I was just talking about you, Li Wende, and here you are! 'As soon as one speaks of Cao Cao, Cao Cao appears' [说曹操曹操到]!" he cried out, reciting the old aphorism about the ancient general. Then he threw an arm around Little Li's shoulders, just as when they were boys.

"I've missed you!" exclaimed Little Li.

"Ah, don't bullshit me! But tell your old buddy what's up." Little Li remembered his friend as a scruffy, impertinent, and sometimes uncouth teenager whose knowledge of worldly things had always surpassed his own. Now his face was so pale, and his rakish mustache and beard so shaggy, that he was almost unrecognizable, but he still possessed the same cheekiness.

"It's a long story," said Little Li, laughing.

"Aren't they all, but just give me the straight shit! Like, have you been doing the no-pants dance with any 'little sisters' [小妹妹] out there in the Beautiful Country?"

"Well, although I still lag far behind the party's ambitious Five-Year Plan targets for building friendship with the members of the opposite sex, I am able to report statistical progress in upping my production quota." They both guffawed as if nothing had changed.

"Damn, it's great to see you!" cried Little Wang, laughing and clapping his friend on the back again.

"And what have you been doing all these years?" asked Little Li.

"That's another story, too," replied his friend, taking a long drag on his cigarette.

"I want to hear it all. Shall we get something to eat?"

"For sure!"

As they seated themselves in one of the many private dumpling restaurants that had sprung up in the city, Little Wang dived right in.

"So—where'd they send you? I heard some shit about Tibet?"

"I ended up out in the middle of nowhere in Qinghai."

"That place is one big prison camp!"

"And where did you get 'assigned'?" There was a pause as Little Wang took another long drag on his cigarette. "Do you mean, where'd they lock me up?" He gave a scornful chuckle. "And are you inquiring about my first or second term in the 'pen' [牢里头]?"

"You went to prison twice?" asked Little Li in surprise.

"I'm a real star!" Little Wang smirked. "You want the full catastrophe?"

"Yeah."

"Well, my first term was spent as an 'educated youth,' like you: they sent me off to Ulan Suhai, in Inner Mongolia, where I spent seven years serving the people by harvesting reeds for a pulp mill, eating potatoes, and sucking in a lot of cold wind! If you think it's freezing here, try Ulan Suhai! By comparison, Beijing is Hainan Island without palm trees!"

"And after Mongolia?"

"After that, the party's leaders started showing me some real respect as an enemy of the people." He stuck his chest out boastfully. "Along with Qincheng, Banbuqiao Detention Center is one of our country's most prestigious prisons. They are the Peking and Tsinghua universities of our glorious party's penal colony. The very top of the top!" He gave a mocking laugh.

"And what did you do to deserve such an honor?"

"Ahhh! So now the question of honor arises. Well, to be sent to Mongolia, I didn't have to do shit except get born. To get sent to Banbuqiao, well, that took some doing. Not just anyone gets in there, you know! They only admit 'the elite of the elite' [精英尖子]!"

"You sound like you expect congratulations."

"Why not?"

"I thought they only put the worst criminals away in those prisons."

"Only the worst . . . or the best, depending on your political perspective," responded Little Wang with a smirk. "The point I'd like to underscore here is this: You're eating dumplings with someone who has real standing in our great people's republic! In the party's view, I am ranked among the gentry . . . of the imprisoned!"

"Aiyaaa! So you were actually in a real prison!"

"Yes, but let's pause a moment here, Comrade Li, for a little critical self-analysis. Sure, I did real time, but before you start viewing me as some kind of super-con and you as an innocent civilian, let's think things through a little. Now, where did you say you got sent?"

"To the Yak Springs Number Six Qinghai–Sichuan Road Engineering and Maintenance Bureau Way Station, Golok Tibetan Autonomous Prefecture, Qinghai Province."

"So you got your sorry ass sent off to Qinghai, the Motherland's labor-camp central? Okay. Not bad. Not bad at all!"

"Well, it wasn't exactly a 'labor camp,' and I wasn't a real prisoner, with—"

"Whoa! Slow down, big guy!" interrupted Little Wang. "You insist you weren't a real prisoner. Well, perhaps you'd care to tell me what you were and what the precise difference is between where you got sent and my elite prison? They may have called you an 'educated youth,' but they didn't have you researching Ming Dynasty texts or writing poetry out there in Yakville, did they?"

"No." Little Li smiled.

"So perhaps you'd like to share the kinds of genteel jobs they had you doing?"

"I was working in a quarry."

"How delicate and refined! But no doubt you were also practicing calligraphy each morning and . . . ?"

"No, I was making gravel."

"Oh, how absolutely marvelous! So—why don't you admit it? You were a prisoner just like me! Or does that thought rob you of your dignity?"

"All right! You win!" said Little Li, smiling at the intensity of his friend's argument. "Allow me to confess: my bourgeois tendencies have made me erroneously view myself as superior to other prisoners."

"Okay! Now that we got that straightened out, would you care to know how I got busted the second time?"

"The people cry out to hear your tale of oppression," replied Little Li, laughing.

"Well, all I had to do was to put up posters on Democracy Wall in 1979 and hang out with guys like Wei Jingsheng, Xu Wenli, and—"

"Who are they?"

"Damn! You really are out of it, aren't you?"

"It's hard to get any farther out of it than the Golok Tibetan Autonomous Prefecture."

"Okay. So here's the short course: Wei Jingsheng was an electrician from the Beijing Zoo who had a Tibetan wife, so you'd probably like him. Xu Wenli was a lowly Beijing factory worker and both ended up leading a political protest movement after Old Deng came back to power in 1978."

"But didn't Deng start all the reforms?"

"Yeah, and at first we all liked his reforms. However, we still criticized him for being undemocratic. Wei even called him an 'autocrat' [独裁者]." As Little Wang said the word, he cast a wary glance around the small restaurant. "I like Wei, because he's always truthful. He never just goes along. Like the Grand Historian, Sima Qian, he believes that 'The refusal of one decent man outweighs the acquiescence of the multitude' [千人之諾諾,不如一士之諤諤]. He also believes that 'Marxism, Leninism, and Mao Zedong Thought have poisoned the ability of Chinese people to think,' and that 'China will never become a truly modern nation without democracy.'"

"But things are so much more open now than they used to be, how can you . . . ?"

"Sure, Old Deng allows us to come back from exile, to get rehabilitated, to take English classes, to go to discos, and even to get rich. But try asking the 'old warlord' [老军阀] to let us speak our minds. He'll lock you up before we can squeeze out a good fart."

Listening to his friend, Little Li suddenly felt that his own life was small, self-absorbed, and irrelevant. Little Wang was concerned with noble issues—freedom, justice, and the future of

China—whereas his concerns centered on his father, girls, and his future.

"What finally happened to your dad?" asked Little Li, recalling that during the Cultural Revolution he'd been accused of spying for Taiwan and then vanished.

"What the hell do you think happened to him? He got 'sent down,' and, of course, they never bothered to tell us where! And that was the end of him."

"So what are you going to do now?"

"You'll probably think I'm mad, but, like Chairman Mao and the Monkey King, I want to make 'great disorder under heaven' [大闹天宫]. I mean, they're the mad ones. Look at what they did to us! So whatever my future is, it won't be on the side of that cunt of a party! I'll be in the streets. Sure, I could become an obedient little Leninist capitalist, selling Jockey shorts and bell-bottom trousers off the back of a cart in the street and then sing karaoke at night! That's what they'd like us to do: forget what happened and become petty merchants who keep our traps shut, quietly sell useless shit, and hope to get rich while we leave the politics to the very party that's done such a great job screwing everything up! But that's not for me! I'm going to become a hawker of freedom and democracy and a supporter of a marketplace of free thinking. How about that?"

"Well, good luck!" said Little Li. He admired his friend's pluck, but at the same time doubted things would end well.

"Remember what Xunzi said thousands of years ago: 'The rulers are the boat, the commoners are the water, and the water that carries the boat can also capsize it' [水可載舟亦可覆舟: 君子者舟也庶人者水也水則載舟水則覆舟]."

"And Mao also likened the PLA to fish and the people to water?" added Little Li.

"He did, and it just shows how unoriginal he was."

Little Wang's rebirth as a political dissident had paradoxically developed just as Deng Xiaoping's program of "reform and opening up" (改革开放) was creating a heady new sense of possibility. Deng's goal to turn China into "a great, modern, and powerful country within this century" did, at first, seem far-fetched. But who could say what the Chinese people were capable of doing once their incredible discipline and tenacity were freed from Mao's straitjacket?

Being jobless, the Two Virtuous Ones began roaming the city together just as they had when they were younger, and Little Li was impressed by the rapidity and magnitude of the changes they saw in the streets. Able to farm their own plots, peasants were now also able to sell their surplus produce in "free markets" (自由市场). At the same time, millions of urbanites were "plunging into the sea of commerce" (下海) and setting up their own small "private businesses" (个体户). Food stands, clothing stores, nightclubs, beauty parlors, repair shops, and restaurants were popping up everywhere, filling the streets with people selling everything from knock-off foreign fashions, fake Swiss watches, and purloined electronics, to illegal copies of music cassettes, and pirated books.

One day, while trolling through a row of "book stalls" (书摊儿), that were now proliferating the streets, he and Little Wang came across a bilingual copy of George Orwell's *1984;* in it they found a passage that Little Wang liked so much he bought the book and pasted a paragraph onto the cover of his journal:

> To know and not to know, to be conscious of complete truthfulness while telling carefully constructed lies, to hold simultaneously two opinions which cancelled out, knowing them to be contradictory and believing in both of them, to use logic against logic, to repudiate morality while laying claim to it, to believe that democracy was impossible and that the Party was the guardian of democracy, to forget whatever it was necessary to forget, then to draw it back into memory again at the moment when it was needed, and then promptly to forget it again, and above all, to apply the same process to the process itself—that was the ultimate subtlety: consciously to induce unconsciousness, and then, once again, to become unconscious of the act of hypnosis you had just performed. Even to understand the word "doublethink" involved the use of doublethink.

Managers of state-owned enterprises were discovering they could make more profit with less effort by simply leasing out space to private entrepreneurs. One such business was Uncle Meng's Dumpling Palace, where the Two Virtuous Ones often ate, because, unlike dreary state-run restaurants, it offered tasty food and was clean and efficient. Uncle Meng had been accused of "counterrevolutionary rightism" in 1958 and sent off to a "reform-through-labor camp" (劳改营) as a coal miner. Upon being released and "rehabilitated," he leased a room in the Number 6 Foodstuffs, Native Produce, and Animal By-Products Export and Import Company building and opened a tiny restaurant. In the beginning, he did everything himself. A year later, Uncle Meng had a staff of twenty, and was renting the entire first floor as well as an adjacent brick wall that had once been covered with Mao quotations. He wasted no time in turning his new wall into a second profit center by leasing it out as a billboard. Now it featured a rendering of a Western woman with ruby-red lips touting Yves Saint Laurent's Opium perfume. The alchemical powers of Deng's reforms had managed to transform even the Opium Wars, long a quintessential symbol of European imperialism at its most rapacious, into an acceptable luxury brand.

"Any Chinese who can sell the idea of opium as an acceptable perfume brand in the People's Republic of China is a true revolutionary!" pronounced Little Wang facetiously as he stuffed a capitalist dumpling into his mouth. "When it comes to squaring circles, few in history have equaled the audacious inconsistency of the Chinese Communist Party!" he continued. "Under Deng, capitalism is now rescuing communism, living proof that Chairman Mao's theory of the unity of opposites is correct!"

For party overseers, history was an infinitely malleable narrative. Because they saw themselves as the "makers of history," they believed that they alone had the prerogative to rewrite it so that even when they had been manifestly wrong they could end up appearing right.

"Our past history is always changing, because the party's always always rewriting it," noted Little Wang acidly. "Only the present is certain, because you can see it in front of your face. The only reason people are still inspired by the future is because the party hasn't yet discovered a way to get there ahead of them and screw it up!"

"So—what's the party going to do about young people like us?" asked Little Li.

"Old Mao thought that everyone he 'sent down' to the country-side would just quietly give up and 'take root for the rest of their lives' [扎根一辈子] wherever he sent them," scoffed Little Wang. "But who wants to stay in a dump like Ulan Suhei or Yak Springs? And now all of us returned 'educated youths' are being joined by the older generation, guys like your father. With millions of unemployed [无业] staring him in the face, now Old Deng's come up with a less embarrassing term for us: 'waiting for employment' [待业]! And what's the easiest way to get people off the waiting list? Allow them to create their own jobs! The hypocrisy of it all makes me want to throw up!"

Despite his antipathy for the CCP, Little Wang was one of the few people who still faithfully read the *People's Daily*. "Know the enemy and win every battle," he insisted, bowdlerizing the ancient strategist Sunzi's (孙子) aphorism (知己知彼 百戰百勝). Once filled with blandishments about "class warfare" and stories lionizing proletarian heroes, the party's official mouthpiece was now touting capitalist entrepreneurs. One day, Little Li found an article about a peasant who'd started a private dog-meat restaurant and had made so much money his family was off on a vacation at a gambling casino in the Portuguese colony of Macau. "Where have all our Lei Feng–type heroes gone?" asked Little Wang with mock indignation. "Suddenly 'ten-thousand-yuan households' [万元户] are being extolled as 'the vanguard' of reform, and Old Deng is calling for 'some to get rich first' [让一部分人先富起来] to show the way for the rest. It's like the members of the Politburo have all gone out and had sex-change operations!"

"Well, isn't that better than how they were?" countered Little Li.

"Sure, if the Communist Party doesn't mind becoming the biggest exponent of counterrevolution and capitalism the world has ever known."

"Granny Sun loves to say, 'When you have money, you can get even the devil to turn your grindstone' [有钱能使鬼推磨]."

"And getting the devil of capitalism on board is just the beginning of it," scoffed Little Wang. "Now we'll really be able to develop some world-class corruption."

When Little Li had left Beijing in 1968, except for buses, a few Shanghai sedans, and an occasional Red Flag limousine, the streets had been filled with bicycles and animal carts. Now there were a growing number of shiny foreign cars. Young women were abandoning their Mao suits for European-style dresses and high-heeled shoes, while young men were turning to double-breasted pin-striped suits, neckties, and aviator sunglasses adopted from the hero of the first American TV series shown on Central Chinese Television, *Man from Atlantis.*

"There are those who say we should not open our windows, because open windows let in flies and insects," Deng declared when queried on the dangers of "spiritual pollution" (精神污染). "They want the windows to stay closed so that we will expire from a lack of air. But we say, 'Open the windows, breathe the fresh air, and at the same time fight the flies and insects!'"

Now all sorts of "flies and insects" were swarming into China. Returned youth were starting magazines, writing bold investigative pieces for newspapers, playing classical music in the hotel lobbies, dabbling in modern art, and holding "political discussion salons" (沙龙) at universities. Neon-lit discotheques and raucous karaoke bars abounded. Chinese who'd been punished for playing mah-jongg, wearing makeup, or gambling were now free to indulge, even to bet on the horses at newly opened racetracks; ogle bikini-clad women at bodybuilding competitions; play golf at newly opened links; enjoy the sexual services of peasant girls at barbershops; blaze away with .50-caliber machine guns and rocket-propelled grenade launchers at commercial firing ranges; even get plastic sur-gery—eye, nose, and breast jobs—at private clinics. And, having spent the first part of his life longing to erase all physical signs of his Eurasian heritage and hide his ability to speak English, Little Li now unexpectedly found himself in a world where his height, prominent nose, and epicanthic eye folds had become so much the rage that young Chinese were seeking makeovers to look like him. Was it possible for a society to reverse itself so suddenly and com-pletely without sowing deep confusion? With China in the throes of another epic twentieth-century effort to negate its past and rein-vent its future, it was unclear whether one was supposed to believe in communism or capitalism.

"Son of a bitch!" exclaimed Little Wang one night, when he and Little Li came upon a red neon heart pulsing on a signboard outside a hole-in-the-wall shop carved out of a state-run plumbing-supply outlet. Instead of finding a window display featuring pipe elbows, wrenches, and toilet flanges, The Red Star House of Marital Bliss boasted an array of rubber vibrators lined up on purple velvet, like so many toy rockets.

"If someone in Yak Springs had told me I'd be coming home to bikinis, racetracks, and vibrators," said Little Li, laughing, "I'd have thought they'd lost their mind!"

"And my buddies tell me a hot new café just opened at the old Peace Hotel, and—"

"The Peace Hotel?" queried Little Li, finding it hard to believe that this staid courtyard hotel had become part of the counterculture.

"It's said to be a hangout for Beijing's cool new 'hoodlum culture' [流氓文化]."

Several nights later, as they walked down Goldfish Alley (金鱼胡同), they spotted a ghostly fluorescent glare radiating up into the distant darkness. Drawing nearer, Little Li saw that the gray brick wall that once sequestered the hotel from the *hutong* was gone, turning its courtyard into a sidewalk café, whose clientele was a scrum of exotically clad youths who lounged on lawn furniture, sipped instant coffee, drank beer, ate ice cream, smoked, and listened to pop music from Taiwan. Most of the girls wore makeup, and the boys sported mustaches, beards, and had hair tumbling down over their eyes. Little Li was fascinated by one in a cape and a beret who was ostentatiously kissing a girl wearing bright-red lipstick, a tight black turtleneck sweater, and hip-hugging jeans.

Sitting down, the Two Virtuous Ones ordered Coca-Colas from a young woman in a black body stocking. Though Little Li found the idea of this iconic American beverage exciting, it tasted like herbal cough syrup. When he noticed something in the shadows of the alleyway, he began watching closely. To his surprise, he saw that a foreign man was loitering suspiciously behind a tree.

"Oh yeah," said Little Wang, following his glance. "Foreigners come here for girls."

Sure enough, before long the man was approached by two young women smoking cigarettes. The prettier one whispered something in his ear; he nodded, looked furtively around, and slipped something into her hand. A moment later, both were gone.

Everywhere, the raw, forceful influence of the outside world was rushing in. Even the party's new general secretary, Hu Yaobang, seemed to have become enamored of its "wealth and power" (富强), telling Chinese they should "learn from all who know," from whichever political, social, or economic system, including that of the United States, had the most effective answers. But the Western fashion consciousness evinced among Peace Café habitués made Little Li feel utterly out of step in his faded Mao jacket.

"Don't be too impressed by all the flash," Little Wang said and smiled. "Just because Old Deng has waved his wand and declared a new 'correct line' that allows everyone to dress up, that doesn't mean the poison from the revolution will all magically disappear. Mao may be dead, but he'll be in our bloodstream a lot longer than we want to imagine. As long as we don't change this fucked-up system, we're sitting ducks for the next two-bit tyrant who comes along, fancying himself an updated version of Mao's big leader culture."

"And what about all the reforms that are happening? Won't they make a difference?"

"They're only skin-deep. All these fashions and free markets don't mean we're headed to democracy. Deng's offering us a bargain: 'Leave the politics to the party and we'll leave your private lives to you.' "

"So—you going to take the bargain?"

"Fuck, no!" he replied contemptuously.

When Little Wang showed up with his activist friend Pei Heli, with whom he'd been sent to Mongolia, Little Li did not at first recognize him. He'd last seen Pei as a teenager, and he was now a tall, studious young man. As they walked around Beihai Park together, Pei and Little Wang reminisced about how crowds of people had started holding political debates, giving speeches, and plastering an unprepossessing brick wall around a bus yard at Xidan with political posters. It ultimately became known as Democracy Wall and for the first time in decades party leaders were forced to hear the uncensored voices of "the people" in whose putative name they claimed to rule.

"And so—what happened?" asked Little Li.

"The crowds kept getting larger and larger and at first nothing happened because Old Deng needed us in the streets to help him topple his political rivals," replied Little Wang. "But as soon as he won out over that turd-brain Hua Guofeng, whom Mao had appointed his 'successor,' he threw us all in the can."

"And, as the party slogan goes, 'First the verdict, then the trial'

[先判后审]," said Pei with a wry laugh. "It's a system built for efficiency. Your arrest is also your indictment and verdict. Three in one!"

"They sent Old Pei away for two years," exclaimed Little Wang. "He was a sophomore with a bright future in the philosophy department at Peking University. Now he's an ex-con, selling underwear off the back of a bicycle cart."

"What was your crime?"

"Ah yes, my crime," began Pei. "Well, I worked on a publication called *Exploration* [探索] that a bunch of us edited, printed, and sold it around the city."

"What was in it?"

"Oh, poetry, articles about democracy, exposés on political prisons, and things like that," he explained matter-of-factly. "I know it doesn't sound like much, but it proved, as Lu Xun put it, an 'unsettling clap of thunder where silence reigns' [于无声处听惊雷]. And our editor was Wei Jingsheng, who Deng hated because he charged that party leaders were drunk on power. So he put Wei away for fifteen years."

"Aren't you afraid they'll put you back in prison, too?" Little Li asked.

"Sure, but even if you slit the throat of every rooster, dawn will still break," he replied, lighting a cigarette. "I mean, if the first thing you worry about is prison, then they've won. They accused me of 'counterrevolutionary propaganda' [反革命宣传]. After they locked you up, of course, they always boasted that they've sentenced you 'according to law' [依法]."

"We used to have two choices," interjected Little Wang. "We could either shut our mouths and survive, or speak out and get locked up. Either way, we were going to be poor. Now, with Old Deng, we have new choices: we can shut up, survive, and get rich, or we can speak out, get crushed, and stay poor. Who says there's been no progress!"

"I met a Russian guy at Democracy Wall who gave me a translated chapter from Alexander Solzhenitsyn's *The Gulag Archipelago*, and one part really made me laugh," chimed in Pei. "So, this Russian guy arrives at one of Stalin's labor camps in Siberia with a bunch of other prisoners, and the commandant orders each of them to step forward and announce the length of his prison term.

The first guy steps forward and says, 'Sir! I got twenty-five years.' 'Twenty-five years?' exclaims the commandant. 'For what?' 'For nothing at all,' answers the prisoner. 'Aha!' rejoins the commandant. 'I know you're lying!' 'How do you know that?' asks the insulted prisoner. 'Because everyone knows the sentence for doing nothing at all is only ten years.'"

"Chinese are the most patriotic people in the world, and we keep eating the party's shit in the name of patriotism, as if opposing it was a disloyalty to our country," added Little Wang.

"Take it easy, Comrade!" said Pei, laughing at how indignant his friend had become. "Nobody gets as worked up over political things as Little Wang. He reads too much!"

"What's he reading?"

"All kinds of stuff that just makes him crazier!" Pei chuckled.

"You should read more, too, and get out of your Yak Springs bubble!" said Little Wang.

"What should I read?" asked Little Li.

"You can start with this." He extricated an envelope from his book bag. "And never forget what our Great Helmsman told us: 'To rebel is justified' [造反有理]." He gave his best bad-boy smile.

When Little Li opened the envelope that night at home, he found a hand-copied essay entitled "Democracy or New Dictatorship" by Wei Jingsheng, from the March 1979 issue of *Exploration*.

> Everyone in China knows that the Chinese social system is not democratic and that its lack of democracy has severely stunted every aspect of the country's social development over the past thirty years. . . . According to the principles of democracy, any authority must give way to opposition from the people. But Deng Xiaoping does not give way. When the people demand a widespread inquiry into the reason for China's backwardness over the past three decades and into Mao Zedong's crimes, Deng is the first to declare, "Without Mao there would be no new China. . . . Anyone forgiving such a criminal would be indirectly guilty of crimes against the people."

Little Li was dazzled by the essay's unflinching clarity and honesty. Wei's indictment of China's leaders as self-appointed "dictators working without restraint" was unchallengeable. Had his own family, and millions of others, not been victims of just such unrestrained authority? And yet, he'd never heard anyone so much as whisper that a high Chinese leader might be guilty of "crimes against the people." But here, in bold, unrepentant language, was an ordinary worker calling the whole system of one-party rule into question. As shocking as his conclusions were, there was not a single one with which Little Li could disagree.

> We cannot help asking Mr. Deng what his idea of democracy is. . . . When there are no divergent opinions, no discussion, and no publications, then it is clear that there is dictatorship. . . . The crux of the matter is not who becomes master of the nation, but that the people maintain firm control over their nation. This is the very essence of democracy. People entrusted with government positions must be controlled and must remain responsible to the people. . . . We can only trust those representatives who are supervised by us and who are responsible to us, and such representatives should be chosen by us, not thrust upon us.

Curious about Democracy Wall, Little Li went to Xidan the next morning to have a look for himself. However, all he could find was a low, undistinguished brick wall surrounding a municipal bus yard, now plastered with advertisements for ductile steel pipe, machine tools, and DC electrical generators. Nowhere was there any hint of the historic events recounted by Little Wang and Pei Heli. It was amazing how completely the party could expunge the record of all visible reminders of unwelcome events. Just as it airbrushed the faces of purged leaders from official photos, it had also removed all physical traces of the namesake movement from Democracy Wall. Then they'd rewritten the historical record to make sure all objectionable voices were also expunged. And to remind any pilgrims who might return to this street corner to commemorate the Democracy Wall Movement, just to show them who was still boss, the party had erected an enormous billboard across the Avenue of Eternal Peace and emblazoned it with the Mao quo-

tation: "STRENGTHEN THE SOCIALIST ROAD, STRENGTHEN THE DIC-
TATORSHIP OF THE PROLETARIAT, STRENGTHEN THE LEADERSHIP OF
THE COMMUNIST PARTY, AND STRENGTHEN MARXISM-LENINISM—
MAO ZEDONG THOUGHT."

As Little Li was waiting at the bus stop to go home, he heard
the sound of sirens. Moments later, a flotilla of police cars plowed
up the traffic-crowded avenue like icebreakers ramming through an
Arctic floe. Once they'd cleared a channel, two Red Flag limousines
with lace curtains sped through the busy intersection with sirens
howling and lights flashing. An old peasant riding a bicycle loaded
with two rattan baskets filled with cabbages was already weaving
precariously when one of the police cars blasted its horn. The sound
so unnerved the old man that his bike capsized and spilled its cargo
of cabbage heads out onto the broad avenue where they rolled like
so many oversized marbles. He frantically started trying to gather
up his cabbages, even as they kept tumbling out of his arms. Unable
to decide whether to rescue his cabbages, himself, or his bicycle,
the old man froze. Then a large truck maneuvering to get into the
traffic-free slipstream behind the motorcade flattened the desperate man's bike as if it were made of a wire coat-hanger. As vehicles
swerved to avoid hitting him and horns honked, a policeman swag-
gered over from his traffic island. However, instead of helping the
old man, he began cursing and ordering him to clear away his flattened bike so as not to further obstruct traffic. Defeated, the old
peasant dragged his mangled bicycle to the sidewalk. Slumped on
the curbstone right in front of Democracy Wall, he watched as, one
after another his cabbage heads were crushed under the wheels of
passing vehicles. Touched by this individual human drama, Little
Li sat down beside him.

"Can I help you?" he asked.

"It's all gone [都完了]," the old man moaned.

"I'm so sorry" was all he could think to say. Not knowing what
else to do, Little Li dropped a ten-yuan note into his lap. It was all
he had.

Instead of getting off the bus at his usual stop, Little Li kept
right on going down Jianguomenwai Avenue until he reached the
Qijiayuan diplomatic compound near the foreign embassy district. He always loved walking here because it was so peaceful and

orderly. Each mission was set back from the street behind a high iron fence, shaded by tall trees, and marked by a glass display case out front filled with photos depicting scenes from each country's national life. The Embassy of the Republic of Finland showed grinning Laplanders in fur suits standing in snow with herds of reindeer. The Democratic People's Republic of Korea featured Great Leader Kim Il-sung saluting a parade of missiles. The Republic of France displayed photo portraits of its great cathedrals.

Just past Ritan Park [日坛公园], he passed a crest affixed to a wrought-iron gate depicting an eagle holding a clutch of arrows in one claw and an olive sprig in the other. It was the American Embassy. In front were cases filled with color photos of a smiling Deng Xiaoping and President Jimmy Carter in front of the White House and of Deng riding in a Western-style stagecoach wearing a cowboy hat. Whereas most diplomatic missions were almost tomb-like, the entrance to this embassy was traversed by a steady stream of businessmen in pressed suits, spotless white shirts, and shoes that gleamed like polished metal; women decked out in corporate pant suits with hair swept back like manes; and dumpy tourists wearing flip-flops and tentlike sports shirts over protruding bellies. All were striding in and out as if it were their own home. But what intrigued Little Li most was the line of Chinese clutching sheaves of documents that stretched down the sidewalk.

"What brings everyone here?" he asked a young man.

"You don't know?" he replied nervously, glancing at the PLA soldiers guarding the mission.

"No," said Little Li, feeling foolish, because he was, after all, half American, and this embassy theoretically represented part of him.

"Well, most of us want to study in America," said the youth, lowering his voice and gesturing toward the long line behind him.

"Is it easy to get a visa?"

"No. But it's easier now that Old Deng and Carter made their deal. This is the new Gate of Heavenly Peace!" He chuckled guardedly.

Deng had visited Washington, D.C., early in 1979 to re-establish diplomatic relations and now Chinese were flocking to the U.S. Consulate with applications for visas to study at American universities. At the same time, American tourists were flooding into China. For Little Li, the thought that those in line would soon be setting foot in this once-forbidden land was electrifying. Just then, a tour bus pulled up and several Americans inside opened their windows and began snapping photos of the visa applicants in front of the U.S. crest. A bald man stuck his head out, clenched a fist, and shouted, "U.S.A.! U.S.A.!" One youth in line smiled, gave a double thumbs-up, and shouted back, "I'm like America good, too!" Everyone on the bus cheered.

Of course, wherever and whenever Chinese interacted with foreigners, there was surveillance. Here, a whole squad of Chinese soldiers stood guard. But their khaki uniforms, canvas sneakers, and weapons held provocatively at the ready made them seem strangely out of place. Little Li was about to leave when a black car drove up and a voice with a southern drawl boomed out, "Hey, son, is this the Commercial Section?" Although it was obvious the Chinese guard didn't speak English, the American persisted, enunciating each word with the exaggerated clarity of someone addressing a small child. "Can—you—please—tell—me—if—this—is—the— Commercial Section—of—the—U.S.—Embassy?" Trying to be helpful, Little Li translated the question for the guard.

Almost instantly, a Chinese officer appeared, raised an admonishing hand, and screamed, "No, no [不不]!"

"All right," said Little Li, backing off. "Just trying to help!"

"What's your unit?" challenged the officer, reaching toward his sidearm. "Where're your papers?"

As Little Li fumbled for his registration card, three laughing American men stepped out the door of the embassy, and as soon as the soldier saw them approaching, he snapped to attention. "If you don't want trouble you'll get moving!" he hissed.

Walking away as fast as he could, Little Li headed down a side street behind the Beijing International Club, a socialist edifice erected by the party in the 1950s to give foreigners a place to socialize without mingling with local Chinese. As he walked, he passed a brass plaque: BEIJING AIR CATERERS FRENCH RESTAURANT. Drawn by the pleasing sound of Vivaldi and the tantalizing aroma of roasting meat issuing from an open window, he peered inside. Two foreign men were just being squired by a young Chinese in a tuxedo through a carpeted dining room filled with tables set with white cloths, gleaming silverware, and long-stemmed wineglasses.

Unlike crowded Chinese restaurants, this French counterpart was so spacious, clean, orderly, and stylish that Little Li felt he was gazing into a picture. There were no dirty windows, shabby chairs, stained uniforms, or the usual pall of cigarette smoke mixed with vaporized kitchen grease that characterized most Chinese restaurants. As a chef wearing a white toque and a snow-white smock came through a swinging door, for a fleeting moment, the image of Master Chef Wang sullenly dispatching his unappetizing "cuisine" flashed through Little Li's mind, a memory seemed as if it was from a dream world. But perhaps he had it wrong. But then, he thought, maybe it was this scene of a European chef politely greeting guests as they readied themselves for a refined French meal that was the dream world.

Before he'd left for Yak Springs, foreigners had been few in Beijing, but now they were everywhere, and the front of the Beijing Hotel, the only high-rise building constructed in the capital during the Mao era, had become an especially lively place. The parking area out in front had turned into an outdoor stage on which businessmen, diplomats, journalists, students, and tourists visiting Beijing provided a free, nonstop performance of foreign exotica for locals. And as these often provocatively clad guests—dressed in everything from powder-blue trousers to bright plaid shorts topped with canary-yellow knit jerseys and skimpy T-shirts—came and went in their late-model cars and buses, they attracted audiences of passersby, who tarried on the sidewalks to gape through a screen of cedar trees. It was the women who were the real attention-getters, for far from shrouding their figures, as most Chinese still did, these Americans seemed to delight in sporting tight garments that accentuated the prominence of their hips, breasts, and V-shaped crotches. And in warm weather they seemed to vie for ever more sartorial minimalism. Some contestants appeared to have their clothing no more than spray-painted on their bare bodies so that to Beijingers they looked more outlandish than the most exotic tropical birds at the Beijing Zoo. Little Li enjoyed studying these foreigners, many of whom elicited little of the litheness of their Chinese counterparts. However, they moved with a distinct absence of inhibition, always laughing, touching, even hugging one another.

As he was watching one afternoon, a blond girl wearing a red-

and-white-striped blouse and blue shorts stepped out of the hotel and, spotting the frieze of rapt Chinese faces peering through the hedge, walked over. She raised the camera hanging around her neck, and began snapping photos. The gawkers scattered as if someone had aimed a gun at them, but Little Li held his ground.

"Jumpy, aren't they?" she said cheerfully.

"Yeah, they get nervous around foreigners," he answered in English.

"Wow!" she said, a look of surprise registering on her pretty face. "You speak English?"

"I do," he replied, enunciating as correctly as he could.

"Stick with the group, Laura!" a man shouted from a bus waiting at the hotel entryway.

"Oh, okay," she called back with more than a hint of irritation. Just then, a man coming down the avenue on a battered bicycle became so transfixed by the sight of a Chinese speaking to a blond-haired foreign girl that he piled headlong into a signpost. "Jeez! What came over him?" she asked, as the still-grinning rubbernecker picked up his bike and, without taking his eyes off her, remounted and pedaled away.

"Oh, it's nothing," said Little Li, embarrassed at how his countrymen sometimes deported themselves.

"I didn't think Americans were that interesting," she said, laughing.

"We haven't seen that many of you."

"Laura! Let's pick it up!" yelled the man at the bus.

"Shit! I'd really like to chat, but I gotta go. We're off to something called the Friendship Store for a little gift-shopping."

"Oh, that's just down the street," he offered.

"Well, maybe we could meet there and have a cup of tea together?"

"Good," he said, electrified by the idea of talking with an actual American girl his age.

"Okay, see ya there in a little."

As she ran back to her bus, he could not help noticing the tantalizing jiggle of unrestrained breasts beneath her sheer blouse.

It took only twenty minutes to walk to the Friendship Store, an emporium built by the Chinese government for the exclusive use of foreign diplomats and visitors. But, as he approached its main entrance, one of the two uniformed police standing guard challenged him.

"Your papers?" he harshly demanded. Little Li took out his household registration card.

"You cannot be here," said the policeman peremptorily. "This store's for foreign guests."

"But I'm here to meet a foreign friend," he stammered.

"You cannot be here," repeated the police as the bus pulled up and the blond girl stepped off.

"Far out!" She smiled, walking over to where Little Li stood. "You're actually here!"

"Yes, but I don't think they—"

"I hear there's a café inside the store," she interrupted, oblivious of what was going on. "Let's go in and sit there. You can tell me about Beijing."

"Okay, but this police guard insists that Chinese are not allowed inside."

"Just come with me," she said insouciantly. However, no sooner had they started up the steps than the two policemen lunged at Little Li and grabbed him by the arms.

"What's going on?" screamed the startled girl as members of her tour group turned in alarm.

"We've already told you that this store is only for foreign guests!" the policemen snarled at Little Li in Chinese, as the other twisted his arm behind his back. "No troublemakers!"

"Why are you doing this?" shrieked the girl, rushing toward the policemen herself.

"Not permitted," he kept repeating, but in Chinese. "Not permitted."

"Stop! Stop!" she cried hysterically. "This is completely unjust!"

"They don't allow Chinese inside," Little Li managed to call out. The American tour group stood motionless on the steps of the Friendship Store, watching in horrified bewilderment. Humiliated, Little Li could do nothing as the policemen dragged him off to a small Public Security Bureau guardhouse.

"You've broken our laws and caused the Motherland to lose face," steamed the ranking policeman.

"How can Chinese be excluded from a Chinese store?" asked Little Li bitterly.

"You're violating regulations and causing social unrest," replied the policeman. Knowing that his troubles would only be compounded by talking back, Little Li did not reply.

After interrogating him, they demanded he sign a confession admitting he'd illegally sought to enter an off-limits building and had "resisted the legitimate guidance of security officers." And, added the ranking guard, "Let us give you a friendly warning. The next time you violate the law, you won't be treated with such politeness."

Little Li was fuming. Why were foreigners, who'd been reviled for so long as predatory capitalists and exploitive imperialists, now treated with such deference and given such privilege? What justification was there for going to such lengths to shield them and exclude Chinese? He went home boiling.

While at the Xinhua Bookstore on Wangfujing a few weeks later, he came across another American tour group, this one poring over sets of silk embroideries featuring the stony visages of Marx, Lenin, Engels, Stalin, and Mao.

"You gotta love 'em!" one beaming American man exclaimed. "I mean, where else are ya gonna get world-class tyrants and mass murderers done in the feminine softness of silk!" He laughed and waved some bills above his head to get the attention of the harried clerk, who was being forced by these souvenir hunters to climb up and down a tall ladder to the very top shelf, where these revolutionary fossils had been slumbering in undisturbed repose. Just as revolution-weary Chinese were rejecting such communist iconography, foreign tourists were embracing it, imagining that these pieces of memorabilia, especially images of Mao, represented the hidden essence of China and its fabled revolution. With Chinese pleased to rid themselves of these retrograde artifacts and foreigners eager to buy them, and with hard currency, tourists had turned China's vast lode of vestigial Mao buttons, banners, busts, books, and baubles into an unexpected bonanza. And since every tourist had family and friends back home expecting some memento from this Holy Land of Asian revolution, what better gift than some Mao kitsch? It was a latter-day marvel of commercial yin and yang.

23

MUSIC RETURNS

NEARING HOME one day, Little Li spotted a man out on Big Sheep Wool Alley peering through a crack in their gate and immediately feared that his father was under surveillance. But, as he drew closer, he saw that the man had snow-white hair and wore wire-rimmed glasses.

"Can I help you?" he asked warily.

"Perhaps you can," replied the man, speaking in soft, elegant Beijing dialect. "I'm looking for a certain Professor Li."

"Do you mean Li Tongshu?"

"Yes, just so. And you are?"

"I am Li Wende, his son."

"Ah! I am very pleased to meet you," said the man, proffering his hand. "You must be wondering why I'm here, so allow me to introduce myself. I am Professor Lian Zushi, a mathematician who came to know your father in the Henan countryside. I would have simply knocked and presented myself, but I was apprehensive, lest I make trouble for your father, a man for whom I have only the highest regard."

"Won't you come in for a moment?" offered Little Li tentatively.

"Oh, no, no, that won't be necessary," protested Professor Lian, waving off the idea with a nervous laugh. "But would you be so kind as to convey something to your father for me?" He extracted from his jacket a small package wrapped in newspaper and tied with twine. "Knowing how much your father appreciates music, I wanted to share this with him, something that a colleague who recently returned from the U.S. shared with me. I have already derived immense pleasure from it, and, knowing that your father's appreciation will be far greater than my own, I want him to have it."

"Thank you," said Little Li, touched by such generosity of spirit.

"And will you please offer my best regards to your father. He is the finest of men." With that, he gave a half-bow, turned, and walked away.

Wanting to know what the gift was before he gave it to his father, Little Li untied the twine. Inside he found a small rectangular plastic case containing a cassette with spools of tape at each end. A handwritten label read:

Johann Sebastian Bach
The Goldberg Variations
Played by Glenn Gould
1981

"This piece was written for music lovers to refresh their spirit."
J. S. Bach

Little Li hastened to Little Wang's house. Although it was already afternoon, when his friend finally answered the door he looked like a hibernating animal just disturbed from a deep winter slumber.

"You don't know what this is?" he asked incredulously, taking the plastic case. "It's a recording on a tape cassette."

"Oh," responded Little Li, feeling woefully uninformed.

"Wait here," ordered his friend, and disappeared out the door.

He returned half an hour later carrying a battery-powered Sony portable radio–cassette player studded with buttons, knobs, dials, and gauges. "Borrowed it from a pal!" He smiled triumphantly.

"To play a tape, you just insert the cassette here, press 'play,' adjust the volume, and you're off!" explained Little Wang. "It's yours for two days!"

"Amazing!" exclaimed Little Li, feeling as if he were just emerging from the Stone Age.

"These babies are all the rage, because everyone wants to listen to pop music from Hong Kong and Taiwan." Little Wang lovingly stroked the plastic cowling of the borrowed player. "Everything people want these days is made abroad."

Before Little Li had left for Qinghai, Chinese aspired to own what were then known as "the five big things" (五大件): a watch, a bicycle, a radio, a sewing machine, and a television. Now that more and more people were traveling abroad, their aspirations had expanded to include such things as cassette players, VCRs, and even refrigerators and air conditioners.

Touched by his friend's solicitude, Little Li hurried home. Because his father had played the *Goldberg Variations* for his final recital at the San Francisco Conservatory in 1949, he was sure he'd be pleased.

"Father," he announced excitedly upon entering their room. "A Professor Lian Zushi came by with something for you. And—"

"Ah yes! Professor Lian," said Li Tongshu, his face warming. Then he began coughing. "And did Professor Lian not want to come in?" he asked, when he finally stopped.

"I think he worried he might cause you trouble." Li Tongshu nodded and took the package. But his crippled fingers made opening the cassette case difficult.

"What is it?" he finally asked with bemusement.

"It's the *Goldberg Variations* recorded on a tape cassette."

"How nice," he said, cocking his head quizzically to one side with an unconvinced smile.

"Shall we play them?" urged Little Li, gesturing to the cassette player.

"Did you know that Bach is said to have composed these variations as an exercise for a student, Johann Gottlieb Goldberg, who worked for an insomniac Russian count who was said to have used them as a sedative for his sleeplessness?" asked his father. It was just like his father to know such things.

As Little Li slipped the cassette into the spring-loaded door of the player, his father sat down and waited without seeming to hold much expectation. However, when the delicate opening aria on which the thirty subsequent variations are all based took flight and filled their room with its ethereal sweetness, he tilted his head back, closed his eyes, and smiled. Hearing these jewel-like pieces again, each as distinct in its crystalline structure as an individual snowflake, was like unexpectedly reencountering a series of dear but long-lost friends. As a new variation burst buoyantly forth, Li Tongshu wished he could somehow slow them all down, the better to savor each. But Gould's tempi were as relentless as a racing heartbeat, and they kept galloping toward one climactic conclusion after another. The way the voices in each variation intertweined, mirrored, and answered each other made it sound as if they were talking to each other. Knowing every note of each canon, fugue, and dance by heart, he was suddenly aware of the loneliness with which he'd been living all these years without their company. And to be listening again with his own son back beside him made all the difference in the world.

Little Li, too, was transported by this glorious cascade of music. As the *Variations* rained down on them one after another, he had the sensation of being caught in a downpour of sharp needles that were at once freezing cold and burning hot. Over and over, Bach managed to create something that had not previously existed by weaving one voice together with another to create a series of perfectly well-tempered and seamless tapestries of sound. Whenever it seemed that the deceptively simple opening aria might have been exhausted of its potential, Bach somehow managed to spin out another miniature perfection. Some were soft, tentative, and gentle; some uncertain, moody, enigmatic, while others raged with motion, fire, even bellicosity. Although each had its own distinctive personality, yet they all still belonged irrevocably together. How mysterious, thought Little Li, that something so abstract and indirect could also be so filled with feeling.

When he'd first studied this great work, Li Tongshu had liked to imagine Bach as a brilliant scientist and the *Goldberg Variations* the output of a laboratory in which he conducted musical experiments to create bursts of sizzling new energy out of nothing. Bach changed keys, shifted tempi, skidded into a chromaticism bordering on dissonance, and set so many centrifugal parts in motion against each other at the same time that sometimes a variation seemed to teeter on the edge of chaos. But before allowing them to implode from sheer exuberance, the grand ringmaster always regained the upper hand (if, in fact, he'd ever lost it!) to reduce the intense flame beneath each before the beaker boiled over.

As these beloved pieces now re-entered Li Tongshu's soul, they transported him back into a universe he'd feared gone forever. Swaying at the waist as if he himself were again at the piano, he felt reborn. The beauty and truth in each variation was, he thought, akin to what mathematicians must experience when, with heart-stopping perfection, they finally work out a complex equation.

How fitting that it was Professor Lian, a mathematician who'd brought them, so that even with his hands crippled he could still fly away once more to what Bach had lovingly called his *Himmelsburg*, or "castle of heaven."

As one variation after another broke like new waves on a beach, Little Li, too, closed his eyes. Then, like a film scripted to a musical score, visual images began unfolding. At one moment, he was reprising the ballet of those gymnastic squirrels that had amused him when he was a boy staring so distractedly out the window of his classroom as they ran pall mall after each other through the trees. In their playful almost recklessly competitive way, they were, he thought, just like his father's hands chasing each other up and down the keyboard when they played Bach. The next moment, he was back in the quarry at Yak Springs, with the sun suddenly eclipsed by rain as a squall swept out of the mountains and down onto the valley. Then into this fantasia came the old prisoner who'd smiled so beatifically on that Qinghai road to quench his thirst with ladles of cold, clear water.

Presiding over this crazy-quilt masterwork was the Canadian pianist Glenn Gould, who, like a disembodied spirit crying out of the whirlwind, hummed and moaned as he played almost as if he were making love to the music. For Li Tongshu this intrusion was not off-putting, because in it he recognized the ecstatic sounds of another artist lost in his craft. Indeed, hearing Gould's voice helped the music penetrate the scar tissue with which he had become armored, so that by the last few variations he felt that something elemental might snap inside him. But just before the whole serial experiment threatened to explode like a chain reaction, Bach subdued it by simply restating the sweet, fragile opening aria.

"Ah well!" he thought. "Bach the Lutheran true believer is reminding us that in the end all things return to their beginnings. We may think we're making progress and going someplace, but in the end we all come back to where we began." Just as he and his son had returned from exile to Willow Courtyard, Bach returned his variations to their initial starting point.

Little Li was about to turn off the cassette player when a male voice with an English accent surprised them by beginning to speak.

"We will end this program of Johann Sebastian Bach with

'Now I Go Before Thy Throne' [Vor deinen Thron tret' ich hier-
mit], the last of the composer's eighteen great chorale preludes,
reputed to have been dictated by him as he lay blind and dying," it
said. "Now often referred to as the 'Deathbed Chorale,' it draws
from a Lutheran hymn by the same name":

> *"Before Thy throne I now appear,*
> *O Lord, bow down Thy gracious ear*
> *To me, and cast not from Thy face*
> *Thy sinful child that sues for grace . . .*
> *Grant that in peace I close mine eyes,*
> *But, on the last day, bid me rise,*
> *And let me see Thy face fore'er—*
> *Amen, Amen, Lord, hear my prayer!*

"Bach so loved this chorale melody," continued the voice,
"it was sung in Leipzig the day he was buried at his beloved
Johanneskirche."

As a reedy pipe organ began playing, what followed was a
far cry from the gymnastic virtuosity of the *Goldberg Variations*.
Instead of fierce contrapuntal energy racing to and fro, this chorale
prelude was constructed around the simple line of the lovely, sad
chorale melody that entered and re-entered as a bass line marched
on with determined resolution beneath. And instead of exultation,
these voices were freighted with so much weariness that, each time
the piece might have gathered the strength to crescendo, it faltered,
as if Bach himself was unsure he wanted to continue his own earthly
struggle. But, seemingly determined to keep hope alive, at the end
came a long sustained G, which hung in the air like a match glowing for a few tantalizing moments after its flame is extinguished.
Then, as if it was too much to struggle on after all, a last resigned,
resolving chord sounded and was sustained for several measures
before finally fading away until all that was left was the windlike
hiss of blank tape.

Not wanting the moment to end, Little Li rewound the cassette and as they listened to the chorale prelude again in the darkened room, he tried to visualize the ailing Bach fighting against
the recognition of life's impending completion. Knowing that each
measure was bringing them closer to the end of this transcendent

moment, he stepped behind his father's chair. Fiercely determined not to miss the promise of this moment, he placed his hands gently on his stooped shoulders. As a child, Little Li had often climbed into his father's lap when he was reading, even playing the piano. But it had been a long time since he'd actually touched this man for a sustained time. Feeling the warmth of his body now made him dizzy with a sense of time past and opportunity lost. Then, as the last mournful chords died away, his father reached back and, with a clawlike hand, pressed Little Li's palm to his cheek. It was wet with tears.

"Bach makes me believe again, although I'm not sure in what," said Li Tongshu softly. "All I know is that everything one ever needs to know about music and life is here. Do you remember what Gustav Mahler said, son?" He squeezed Little Li's hand. "He said, 'In Bach, all the seeds of music are found, as the world is contained in God.'"

"Is Bach your god, Father?"

"I suppose he is," Li Tongshu answered meditatively. "His music begins where language leaves off and is as close to the eternal as a work by man can get. I've always imagined he turned to composing because he couldn't say what he wanted to say any other way. And, he used his music against death to gain consolation to live." He paused and smiled. "Do you know what the greatest miracle of Bach is, son? It's the sheer volume of extraordinary music he left us. It just flowed out of him like a bubbling spring. Sometimes it's filled with such sadness one cannot help weeping, but just as often it's filled with utter joy and playfulness. If one of us was able to compose even one of his works, it would be a monumental accomplishment. But he composed hundreds and hundreds, each of them proof that God must exist!"

For several minutes, Li Tongshu fell silent. "Do you know how Franz Schubert started his song cycle *Winterreise*?" he finally continued.

"I don't," responded Little Li.

"'I came here a stranger, as a stranger I depart.'" Little Li didn't know how to reply. Over all these dark years, there had been no one with whom his father could share his love of music—or love of anything, for that matter. To think of him severed from everything for which he cared and now to be ready to depart "a stranger" was unbearable. "How kind of Professor Lian to bring us this tape," Li Tongshu finally said in an almost inaudible voice.

"How did you know him, Father?"

"We shared a room. He was the only person with whom I could ever really talk. But we had no music. Now he's given us this. It's so like him."

If this gift irrigated Li Tongshu's parched soul with gladness, it also presaged a new phase of life for Little Li. Until then, he'd been hanging out with Little Wang and Pei Heli and living in a state of limbo. Now he resolved to start a new regimen of practicing the flute, and even asked his father to coach him in harmony and theory. The old man was immensely pleased.

Several months later, a letter arrived from the Conservatory. Li Tongshu's infirm hands made opening the envelope a torturous process. But when he was finally finished reading the letter, he set it down on the table, lowered his head, and just sat without moving. Fearful the letter had brought bad news, Little Li reached over to read it himself: it was an invitation to rejoin the Conservatory faculty.

Looking up and smiling broadly, Li Tongshu said in English, "The Lord giveth and the Lord taketh away." It was the first time since coming home that Little Li had seen an expression of such unalloyed happiness on his father's face.

"Is any part of you reluctant to go back and serve an organization that betrayed you?" Little Li asked him several nights later.

"It wasn't the institution or even socialism that betrayed us," replied his father without rancor. "It was our leaders."

"You're still an idealist, aren't you, Father?"

"I suppose I am. Anyway, there is no path forward except to try and keep our ideals and protect the next generation."

Though he admired his father's stoicism, Little Li had a hard time understanding how, after all the indignities he'd suffered, he was still able to accept the past with so little bitterness. He could not help thinking about Little Wang's challenge to stand up and refuse to be as accommodating as their parents' generation. Whether his father was a sad, deluded old man who'd had all the fight crushed out of him, or an evolved sage who understood that struggle only leads to more struggle and violence, Little Li did not know.

Whatever the answer, twice a week Li Tongshu started going

off without complaint to teach. One morning, when his cough was acting up, he asked Little Li if he would show a young pianist from Wuhan around the Conservatory campus for him. Little Li was surprised to see that there was now a new high-rise classroom building going up and new energy pulsing throughout the campus. As they passed through the old courtyard, where the familiar sounds of practicing again spilled out of every window, a wave of primal nostalgia hit him. Closed down during the Cultural Revolution, the Conservatory had reopened in 1973 as the Central May 7 Arts University, admitting students on the basis of class background and political views to be trained to join so-called "song-and-dance troupes" run by the Central Propaganda Department rather than for symphony orchestras. However, after Deng Xiaoping's return to power, the school reorganized yet again. When it reopened in 1978 as the Central Conservatory of Music, it received eighteen thousand applications for one hundred spaces. All students were to be admitted on the basis of musical ability alone.

"You know," his father said one morning, "you've developed a good ear, son. Maybe you should apply to the Conservatory yourself."

Little Li had been quietly mulling over the same idea. But to hear his father propose it was an enormous encouragement. When he decided he would, in fact, apply, his father was ecstatic, and they started working together each day in earnest to prepare him for his audition and six months later, another letter arrived from the Conservatory. This time it was for Little Li. He'd been accepted. Upon registering, he was assigned a shared practice room in Building 2, just one floor below where his father had been detained, a proximity that only goaded him on to practice more diligently.

"Why do you want to become an effete artist playing irrelevant classical music when, with a little help, China might still become a normal country?" joked Little Wang as they caught up one day at a noodle shop.

"Because I don't know anything else," said Little Li, smiling. "You may be a politically liberated man of the people, but I'm a prisoner of my bourgeois mentality."

"Fuck you and all your damned facetiousness!" his friend cried with a laugh. "But don't forget, a 'bourgeois mentality' doesn't give you a pass on politics."

That winter, the Conservatory was electrified by news that the Shanghai-born pianist Fou Ts'ong (Fu Cong, 傅聪) would return from Europe to give master classes and a concert. Fou came from a distinguished literary family. His mother, Zhu Meifu, was a classical pianist; his father, Fu Lei, a well-known translator of French literature and lover of the Chinese classics who had taught at the Shanghai Academy of Fine Arts. While living in Paris, Fu Lei was so moved by Romain Rolland's biography of Beethoven, he said he felt as if he'd "been enlightened by a divine light." It was hardly surprising, then, that at his 1952 Shanghai debut, his son played Beethoven's *Emperor* Concerto. Later, Fou attracted the Chinese musical world's attention when, after studying in Warsaw, in 1955, he won third prize at the Fifth Chopin International Piano Competition, behind Adam Harasiewicz from Poland and Vladimir Ashkenazy from the Soviet Union, to become one of the first Chinese to place in a major European piano competition.

After winning, Fou stayed on in Europe to study. However, when the Anti-Rightist Movement erupted in 1957, he was ordered back to China, and it was then that Li Tongshu had gotten to know him. But their friendship was interrupted when Fou's parents came under political attack, and fearful of being criticized himself, Fou quietly escaped back to Europe.

"Life outside China is so very different," he wrote his besieged father. "Conditions here are so much more conducive to genuine artistic achievement. Life is so much richer, and one can give one's imagination free rein. Artists need this freedom in order to live. Without it they simply wither and die. . . . I can't abide all this ideological struggle."

In London, Fou married the daughter of the celebrated violinist Yehudi Menuhin, and then stunned the Chinese cultural world by seeking political asylum. Even while under attack back home, his father continued writing his son, and during a short period of openness his collected letters were published as *The Family Letters of Fu Lei* (傅雷家书). However, when the Cultural Revolution began, Red Guards stormed their home, and Fu Lei and his wife were forced to stand for hours on a bench in their front doorway wearing dunce caps. When they could endure no more, they took poison, joining the epidemic of political suicides among China's intelligentsia. When Fou Ts'ong learned of his parents' deaths, he was so devastated that he vowed never to set foot in China again.

It was not until Mao Zedong died, the Cultural Revolution ended, Deng Xiaoping regained power, and the party finally permitted his parents' remains to be laid properly to rest that he consented to return so he could bury their ashes under a tombstone inscribed with his father's own epitaph: "The loneliness of an innocent heart leads to the creation of a new world." Perhaps only someone like Li Tongshu could understand the full complexity of emotions Fou Ts'ong had for his homeland for he knew how stubbornly patriotism lingers in the hearts of most Chinese and how deep the yearning is even among its victims to see their natal land flourish and regain greatness.

"If I returned to China, I knew my situation would be impossible," Fou told a European journalist in reflecting on his departure. But, he explained, "I've always felt full of regret and anguish. After all, I am one of millions of Chinese intellectuals in China. They all suffered terribly in the Cultural Revolution, but I escaped. It seemed so unfair. I felt uneasy, as if I owed something to all my friends."

No matter how much abuse was heaped on his generation, love of country often won out, as it had when Li Tongshu and Song Shaoming had decided to return home in 1950. Even the violinist Ma Sicong, who'd invited Li Tongshu to teach at the Conservatory, was said to have wept when told that Zhou Enlai had confided to Henry Kissinger that one of his greatest regrets was that persecution forced Ma to leave China.

Whether such a tenacious love of country was a national flaw or a strength was hard to say. But just as Mao's early revolution had inspired many of Li Tongshu's generation to "return to the Motherland" (回归祖国) to "build the nation" (建设祖国), Deng's reforms were once again rallying the Chinese diaspora. Now even Fou Ts'ong was returning.

When a letter from London written in "long-form characters" (繁体字)—the script still used outside China, which looked strangely antiquarian beside the "shortened-form characters" (简体字) used on the mainland—arrived at Willow Courtyard, Li Tongshu was surprised.

My dear Tongshu:

It has been so many years since we last met, and I was gratified to learn from Wu Zuqiang that despite your travails you are back at the Central Conservatory. Now, after a long and difficult interim, I, too, am coming home. After all, no matter how I look on the past, finally I, too, am a Chinese artist.

Will you be my guest for my concert in Beijing? I have reserved tickets in your name.

Your colleague, Ts'ong

Li Tongshu had often struggled with the all-too-human inclination to dwell on what might have been. In the Henan countryside, where he was just another physically damaged soul, he'd been able to put distance between himself and the past. But now he would meet a colleague who inexorably raised the upsetting question: what would his own life have been like if he and Vivian had not returned to China?

As the line inched forward outside the auditorium for Fou's concert, Li Tongshu felt self-conscious and out of place. This was the first time he'd appeared at a public event in over a decade, and when a former student bounded over to greet him, he was hardly able to manage a civil hello before turning away in awkwardness. The rebuked student had no way of knowing that what his old teacher feared was not being reacquainted, but that inevitable moment when he would be required to shake his hand. For Li Tongshu alone understood that anyone who took his twisted hand in theirs would immediately be so overwhelmed by pity that no further normal interaction would be possible. Some scars left by the revolution would never heal.

Of course, he yearned to once again hear the long-banned works of Chopin, Schubert, Beethoven, and Bach played by a musician of world stature, but there was also the question of his nagging cough. What if, in the middle of the recital, he started coughing and couldn't control himself? Even more upsetting, what would he do when the concert ended? Of course, he'd be expected to go backstage to greet his old colleague. But with his clawlike hands, how could he ever shake those delicate fingers that had just rippled over a keyboard? What he wished for most just then was to be ignored, to be able to slip into the hall, listen quietly, and then leave unobtrusively.

When Fou Ts'ong strode onstage and the audience erupted in applause, because he could not clap, Li Tongshu sat with his hands in his lap. The enthusiasm of this audience was no doubt real, but what were they acclaiming? Certainly not Fou's artistry, because they'd never been allowed to hear him play before. Nor was it likely they were celebrating his courage in defecting. After all, it was in this very concert hall, only a few years before, that many of them had declaimed Western classical music and physically attacked musicians who refused to submit to Mao's class-based version of culture. So perhaps they were simply acclaiming him as an ethnic Chinese, another "son of the Yellow Emperor" (炎黄子孙), who'd managed to win fame abroad and confer honor on the Chinese escutcheon. The irony was that despite all their attacks on the West, winning foreign respect was still something party leaders insatiably craved.

Although Fou was Chinese, there was something about the way he moved his lanky frame, confidently smiled, and then seemed to stroke rather than strike the piano keys with his long slender fingers that marked him as indelibly European. As soon as the last note of Beethoven's *Appassionata* Sonata sounded, the crowd leapt to its feet and clapped ecstatically. But when he played Bach's first *French Suite,* the audience applauded with far more reserve. While for them, Bach was too formal, abstract, and unemotional, each note cut into Li Tongshu's heart with razorlike sharpness. It was not until Fou concluded with some Chopin mazurkas, milking them for every drop of Romantic effect, that the audience regained its state of delirium. Standing to acknowledge their thunderous ovation, Fou bowed again and again, his long hair flopping down over his brow with such bohemian panache that it was hard to imagine such a debonair musician had grown up right here in the People's Republic of China.

"What did you think?" Little Li asked his father.

"It was beautiful!" was all he said, as a single tear sliding down his cheek glistened like mercury in the stage lights. But when the hall began emptying, he did not move.

"Don't you want to go backstage?"

"There will be so many people, I think it would be inconvenient for Fou," he responded with a formality that did little to mask his agitation. Having naïvely supposed that reconnecting with Fou would help infuse his father with life and hope, Little Li was confused.

"But I thought you wanted . . ." Then his father began to cough.

"Perhaps we will find another time to pay our respects," he said summarily. Then, holding a handkerchief to his mouth, he began making his way down the now almost empty aisle.

24

TWO-PART INVENTION

EVERY TIME Little Li walked past the studio at the Conservatory where his father had been held, he paused. While it seemed almost grave-like to him, he wondered if the current occupants had any idea of what had transpired inside. He doubted it. The past was now something to be avoided and forgotten. Even for him, the idea of Red Guards frog-marching professors across the courtyard, much less of his own father slumped on the floor of his studio, clashed with the hopeful dynamism now pulsing through the campus. As they hurried to class, students didn't even notice the old Maoist slogan—"Never Forget Class Struggle" (永远不忘阶级斗争)—fading away on the wall of the administration building. And instead of the tomblike silence of Building 2 when he and Dr. Song had found his father there many years ago, it now swelled with such a jubilant cacophony that Little Li found it difficult to concentrate on his own work. But when the bell rang for lunch, it was as if an orchestra had suddenly fallen silent in the middle of a very contemporary work. As most students stopped playing, only those who appreciated the tranquillity of the noon hour continued practicing. One of the instruments Little Li was then able to hear was a *yangqin* (洋琴), a classical Chinese stringed instrument whose strings are sounded with bamboo "beaters" tipped with leather, producing a sound that sparkles with the same icelike clarity as the harpsichord. So enthralled did he become with the sound that he often ceased playing himself just to listen. What intrigued him was how, halfway through a piece of traditional Chinese music such as "Springtime on Dinghu Lake," the musician would elide into a Western minuet, like a radio suddenly tuned to another station.

One warm evening when students had opened their studio windows to let in the balmy spring air, he heard the *yangqin* begin.

While the other instruments sounded like so much noise, it alone possessed a crystalline purity. As it grew later and other instruments dropped away, the *yangqin* became clearer, the way a light grows brighter as darkness deepens. And when a two-part invention by Bach began playing, the two sinuous lines so gorgeously intertwined that Little Li put his flute down to listen. Then, because the music seemed somehow directed at him, he stepped out into the unlit corridor and began walking toward it, ascending the stairs to the Traditional Chinese Music Department on the floor above. As he drew nearer, he could almost feel the sound on his skin. Then he found himself standing in front of a doorway from which a dim orange glow radiated through a pane of frosted glass set just above a card listing the names of three female students who'd been assigned to the practice room. The thought that he was eavesdropping like a stalker made him feel so exposed that he was about to tiptoe away when, unexpectedly, the music stopped, a chair scraped, a shadow appeared behind the glass pane, the door swung open, and there before him stood a surprised young woman. She cocked her head to one side and, with an expression that merged a frown with a quizzical smile, asked, "Can I help you?"

"I was just . . ." he stammered, trying to think of some explanation for his presence. She was in her mid-twenties, slender, with long, glossy hair tumbling down to her shoulders and eyes that sparkled even in the half-light. He felt at once foolish and bewitched.

"Well?" she said, arching her eyebrows.

"I just stopped outside your studio to see who was playing, and . . . ," he began, feeling that even looking directly at her face was the equivalent of groping her. What possible justification could he give for lurking outside her door like an intelligence agent?

"I'm not sure I understand," she responded.

"Please forgive me," he blurted out. Then, because something had to be said and he couldn't think of any other credible alibi, he told her the truth. "Actually, I play the flute." He held his instrument up as if evidence of his own musicianship might help disarm her. "I practice downstairs and I keep overhearing you. And . . . , and, you play so beautifully that I . . ."

"Well, thank you." She proffered her hand. "My name is Hong Hui [洪慧]."

"And I am Li Wende and I apologize for disturbing you." With that, he turned and retreated.

All the way home, he burned with such embarrassment and excitement that by the time he reached Big Sheep Wool Alley he felt feverish. Every day, he saw hundreds of young women who, like neutrally charged particles, were bereft of any power of attraction, and sailed past without leaving any impression. But Hong Hui played so beautifully and was so intoxicatingly lovely that as soon as he'd laid eyes on her, he felt he'd been captured by an invisible force.

That night, he dreamed of long, shiny black hair intertwining with inky black notes and tossed so violently that at one point his father shook him awake. When he opened his eyes and saw his perplexed face, at first he thought he was a small child again, being soothed after a nightmare.

Over the next few weeks, the first thing Little Li did upon reaching the Conservatory was to pause in the courtyard outside Building 2 and, like a hound sniffing the breeze for a familiar scent, listen for the sound of Hong Hui's *yangqin*. Once he got to his practice room, he often just sat with his flute across his lap, straining to hear whether she was playing. Soon he had cultivated an ear so sensitive he was able to pick her out of even the loudest din, just as a conductor can hear even the subtlest instrument playing in an orchestra. And to know she was upstairs filled him with such a delicious sense of presence, he never left until she fell silent. Then he'd pack his things and rush to the gatehouse, hoping to encounter her as she rode off on her bicycle. She was, however, frustratingly elusive.

In the mornings, Little Li would occasionally catch sight of her out the window as she crossed the courtyard, and through such vicarious sightings imagined he was even coming to *know* her. She preferred skirts to trousers, wore her hair loose, and walked with a fluid gait that perfectly matched her playing. He would have streaked out and intercepted her like a heat-seeking missile, but she was always with other female classmates.

He was now spending so much time at the Conservatory that his father began wondering if something was wrong. And sometimes he felt something was wrong, for the mere sound of her playing triggered uncontrollable chain reactions of desire-soaked fantasies. Yet, if he was a prisoner of desire, he was also a prisoner of timorousness. Perhaps his paralysis could be blamed on the oppressive Chinese behavioral norms, which prohibited the display of personal emotion as fiercely as the expression of dissenting political views. China was most assuredly a land of walls, but he was also imprisoned by the walled kingdom of his own insecurity, and there was no small indignity in the recognition that he was still so inexperienced in male-female relationships that all he could do around women was fantasize. Try as he might, he could hardly imagine what it would be like to touch this goddess who made such heavenly music. Yes, he'd been with Yang Ming, but had long since concluded that what had happened with her was a fluke. After all, at Yak Springs he was the only Chinese male her age for several hundred square kilometers. Anyway, the experience was now so distant, he wasn't sure it had even happened.

When he finally did come face-to-face again with Hong Hui, it was by happenstance. He'd just left his studio and was unlocking his bike when there she was, heading toward him.

"Hey, Mr. Flute, is that you?" she asked, flashing a beguiling smile.

"It is me," he replied. "Forgive me for intruding on you the other night, but . . ."

"It doesn't matter," she said, dismissing his apology with a wave of one hand. Her elegant fingers reminded him of Granny Sun's maxim that one can tell young women of good breeding and intelligence by the slenderness of their fingers and toes. "Do you remember my name?" she playfully continued.

"I do," he replied, hoping the intensity of his interest was not evident.

"What is it?"

"Hong Hui."

"Not bad at all!" she said, nodding her head in approval. He would have liked to ask her if he could accompany her as she went home, but he dared not, for he knew that if a young woman was seen alone with a single man it was tantamount to announcing a match. Like a machine stripped of all but its lowest and highest gears, courtship in China still had no middle range. "I should be getting home," she said, turning around so quickly that centrifugal force sent her hair flying around her shoulders in an almost perfect semicircle. While any trend-conscious women were racing to newly opened beauty salons to perm their hair, hers remained naturally straight.

In the days that followed, Little Li continued listening for her *yangqin,* and when he played himself, he did so only for her. Even if she never heard him, he was at least getting some practicing done. Indeed, in one week he mastered Handel's Flute Sonata in E minor, dumbfounding his teacher. It was several weeks later before he ran into her again. He was just fastening his flute case onto the back of his bike when she unexpectedly pedaled by.

"How are you?" he called out.

"Good. Heading home?" she asked with a disarming directness.

"Yes."

"Me, too."

"Where do you live?"

"The East City, past the train station."

"Oh, that's on my way home. Let's ride together."

"I'd like that."

As they pedaled side by side, she asked whether he'd been "sent down," what year he'd entered the Conservatory, and what his musical interests were. He was enjoying their conversation so much that when they reached the turnoff to Big Sheep Wool Alley, he decided just to keep pedaling and see her all the way home. However, as they passed the new Jianguo Hotel, she unexpectedly swerved, and, like dance partners, each of whom is trying to follow the other's lead, they collided.

"Where are you going?" she cried, jumping off her bicycle and grabbing onto him as it fell over.

"Well . . ." he replied, "I was following you."

"What?" She gave a squeal of delight. "I was following you!"

"So we're both heading nowhere!" He helped her pick up her bike, marveling at the absurdity of their situation.

"All right, Mr. Flute, it's ten p.m. Here's what we're going to do: I'm going to go this way, and you're going to go that way." She pointed north with her right arm and southwest with her left.

"And tomorrow night, shall we ride home together again?"

"Not if you're going to lead me astray," she said, laughing. "But why not?"

As he made his way home, the cicadas in the trees were in full throat, and their rising, falling chorus seemed to sing for him and Hong Hui alone. Although it was certainly not what the Chinese Communist Party meant by "liberation" (解放), he felt he now understood some deeper and more personal aspect of that notion.

They left the Conservatory earlier the next evening, and as they were passing through Tiananmen Square, he suggested they stop to enjoy the sunset from the plinth of the Monument to the People's Heroes (人民英雄纪念碑), the ten-story obelisk situated at the center of the square and inscribed, in Mao's own hand, with gold-leafed characters proclaiming, "Eternal glory to the people's heroes" (人民英雄永垂不朽). As they sat on the balustrade, watching the orange sun set behind the Great Hall of the People, he could not help thinking back to the Red Guard rally he'd attended there with Little Wang. Even though Mao was now gone, he still refused to relinquish his grip on this symbolic heart of his revolution. With the technical assistance of an elite fraternity of socialist taxidermists whose specialty was putting dead communist titans like Vladmir Lenin and Ho Chi Minh on public view, Mao's embalmed remains now lay on permanent display in a crystal sarcophagus inside his mausoleum, just behind them.

Not sure how to begin a courtship, Little Li proposed a stroll. As they chatted about the Conservatory and friends, he was as impressed by her self-possession as her musical talents. But when they paused in front of the white marble Bridge Over Golden Waters, where he'd stood to pledge allegiance in front of Mao's portrait before leaving for Qinghai, she fell suddenly silent.

"Are you all right?" he asked.

"He worked there," she finally said, gesturing toward the vermilion walls of the Forbidden City.

"Who?"

"My father."

"Doing what?" When she did not at first reply, he had a terrible premonition of what was coming. The recurring sameness of people's tragic stories in China made them so predictable, all one needed to hear was the first few lines and the rest almost wrote itself.

"He was an archaeologist working on bronze inscriptions in the

Palace Museum," she finally continued, pointing to the Forbidden City. "When the Cultural Revolution hit, younger staffers attacked him as a 'useless old antique' [没用的老古董] and beat him."

"And where is he now?"

"We never saw him again."

"And your mother?" For several long moments she did not reply.

"I came home one day . . ." she began to sob. "And, there was a crowd milling around outside our building. When I asked a bystander what had happened, a stranger told me someone had jumped out a window. It was her."

"Oh, Little Hui!" he gasped, thinking of the man he'd seen on the sidewalk at Iron Lion Tomb. "How did you ever manage?"

"I had to go and live with my father's unmarried sister."

"Did she want you?"

"She did, and I adore her to this day." She looked imploringly at him. "I don't feel comfortable here right now. Can we go?"

As they walked away, she didn't speak. Then he spotted a woman selling popsicles from a wooden cart incongruously parked beneath a giant propaganda portrait of Joseph Stalin, that along with Marx, Lenin, and Engels the party put up each May Day along the Avenue of Eternal Peace where they reigned like a pantheon of visiting foreign deities come to pay tribute to China's Zeus, Chariman Mao.

"Would you like to get a popsicle?" he asked hoping to cheer her up. She nodded and smiled thinly.

"Do you think, now that Mao is dead, movements like the Cultural Revolution are gone forever?" she asked tentatively as they crossed the street.

"I'm not sure I know what to think about anything anymore," he muttered. "How have we managed to inflict so much hurt on ourselves? Birth, marriage, childbirth, and death don't seem to be enough for us Chinese. It's as if we can't consider our short lives complete without adding an extra dose of 'eating bitterness' [吃苦]."

"I understand your pessimism, but still try and think of things as always changing—for the better, I hope," she offered unconvincingly.

"The fact that these portraits still go up makes me wonder," he replied. "I mean, how does it happen that these guys with European beards, nineteenth-century suits, cravats, and big noses who scream 'wholesale Westernization' get lionized, while our fathers, who were Chinese, got villainized?"

"It's both weird and unjust, but there's nothing to be done," she replied, shaking her head dolefully. "We just have to let it go, so maybe we can at least have a little peace."

"That's what I tried to tell myself in Qinghai," he rejoined. "Then I came back, saw my poor father, and got manhandled by police for no reason myself and I find it impossible just to forgive and forget the past in which we did such horrible things to each other!" Little Li felt he was unwittingly channeling the voices of Little Wang and Pei Heli, but he couldn't stop. "Of course, I'm glad Deng started his reforms, but are we just supposed to say, 'Oh my! That stretch of history with Chairman Mao at the helm was a bad patch! So sorry it happened! Let's just write ourselves a free pass and move on'?"

"Well . . ."

"My father's always urging me just to let go of the past, but how can we? Look at his hands! And look what happened to your father! I mean . . . Sometimes I just want to walk away from the whole mess, even go abroad!"

"But not everyone can run away!" she retorted, almost fiercely. "Somehow we have to find a way to live here. For better or worse, it's our own country, our home!"

"I know!" he replied defensively. "But don't you ever wonder what it would be like to live in a place where there aren't so many political campaigns, so much self-inflicted misery?"

"I never have," she responded with a sudden coolness.

"You're not even a little curious about what it's like outside?" he continued, pleadingly.

"Maybe you wonder about such things because your mother was American."

"She probably did leave a few rebellious foreign genes behind," he said, and laughed, trying to allay some of the rising tension.

"Besides, who in the U.S. would ever want to hear me play the *yangqin*?" she continued. Then, in a much softer tone, "You'd never really leave China, would you?" Because he didn't want to disappoint her, he did not immediately reply. He'd been so certain that, if he could only get to know this beautiful and talented young woman, she'd prove congruent with him in every imaginable way. However, she was clearly not one of that growing group of Chinese youth infected with curiosity about the outside world, and was certainly not interested in politics. "It's almost ten o'clock," she finally said, as if reconciled to not getting a reply. "I should be getting back."

As they headed up the Avenue of Eternal Peace, he felt rebuked and deflated. If at that moment he'd been told that, even as she was alarmed by all his talk of politics and going abroad, she was also still deeply smitten by his combination of smartness, shyness, and good looks, he would not have believed it.

25

ALL AFTERNOON, Little Li listened for the sound of Hong Hui's *yangqin*. When, by late afternoon, he still hadn't heard it, he slipped a note under the door of her practice room, proposing they meet at the Monument to the People's Heroes the following evening. The next day, his father's cough was more persistent.

"Your staying here won't help me," he stoically argued. "Anyway, Dr. Song brought me some cough syrup, and I'm sure I'll shake this thing soon. There's no need to worry."

Little Li reached the monument early and distracted himself by watching a boy fly a bat-shaped kite with his father, a reminder that, despite all the turmoil and suffering, ordinary life stubbornly continued. When he turned back toward the museum, he saw her. She was striding toward the monument, her long legs and boyish hips swinging her blue skirt from side to side. Whereas some women used their good looks as bait, she appeared oblivious of her feminine powers. But he could not help imagining what lay beneath the thin wrapping of garments shrouding her graceful body. But, because things he'd always most wanted had invariably been snatched away, he would not have been surprised if he'd blinked only to find she'd been an apparition. Then, she waved.

"Are you hiding from me?" she called out as she bounded up the steps.

"I was just looking," he answered with a foolish grin.

"I guess there's no party regulation against looking." She smiled.

"I'm sure there's a document somewhere spelling out the party's line on ogling women." He laughed. "Central Document Number Sixteen from the CCP's Fifth Plenum of the Thirteenth Central Committee, 'On the Question of Ogling with Chinese Characteristics'!"

As they strolled around the square, they passed one of the photography carts that were fixtures, and she proposed they take a snapshot together. "But let's not take it in front of Tiananmen like everyone else—let's use the Monument as our backdrop. It's where we started."

He liked the idea that she believed they'd "started," and as they stood stiffly, waiting for the shutter to click, he wondered if a child of theirs might someday study this snapshot, just as he'd studied the photo of his parents in front of the Golden Gate Bridge. The notion that he could actually create a child with this lovely young woman sent shivers down his spine. When he paid the photographer, he gave her address, so she would receive the print in the mail when it was developed and printed. Then they walked along the moat running up the east side of the Forbidden City until they got to the Gate of Divine Pride, where they sat on a marble bench across from the spot where musicians congregated on warm summer nights to practice outdoors. From one end of the moat came the voice of a soprano singing an aria from *Madame Butterfly;* from the other, a lugubrious horn player bleated out a solo he couldn't identify. From directly across the moat a fiddle player was sawing out the solo part from the first movement of Beethoven's violin concerto. Only when all the other instruments momentarily rested did they hear the delicate sounds of a *pipa* (琵琶), a traditional-style Chinese plucked instrument.

"Which do you like the best?" he asked.

"Guess."

"The *pipa*."

"How did you know?"

"It's both classical and Chinese. Obvious!"

"Huh!" she huffed, miffed at being considered so predictable. "And you?"

"It's your turn to guess."

"The Beethoven, because it's as close as we'll get tonight to Bach."

"Of course," he said, and laughed. He told her about the tape of the *Goldberg Variations,* and how touched his father had been to hear them again. "You know," he added, "it would be amazing to hear you play some Bach on the *yangqin*."

"East and West are not yet quite that commingled," she replied, giving his prominent nose a tweak. "Anyway, I doubt anyone has transcribed them."

"Why don't you?"

"Maybe," she said elusively.

When it came time to say good night, he desperately wanted to kiss her, but was made too self-conscious by the crowd standing at the bus stop. Several days later, however, as they were strolling together, she suddenly stopped, looked up at him, gave an enigmatic smile, and said, "You know, I like you."

"And I like you, too," he replied, and then astounded himself by kissing her.

"Are you my boyfriend?" she asked, wearing a foolish smile.

" 'From the beginning to the end' [开天辟地]," he said, his heart soaring. It suddenly seemed so easy!

"Can I ask you a question?"

"Sure."

"Why did you wait so long to kiss me?"

"I had my reasons," he responded, as if he had some inscrutable master plan of conquest.

"Very mysterious, you are!" she rejoined.

They agreed to meet every Friday in the square, and he so looked forward to each rendezvous that his father wondered if something was wrong. But Little Li was unsure how a son broached the subject of a girlfriend with a straitlaced parent like his father.

"Do you really want to go to America?" she asked him unexpectedly a week later in a way that suggested it had been on her mind. She wrinkled her nose up. "It's so far away!"

"It's a question mark," he replied. "Technically, I'm half American. So . . ." Her face darkened.

The more time they spent together, the harder it was to hide their relationship from others. One evening, as they were walking hand in hand down Wangfujing, two of Little Hong's girlfriends, an oboist and a *pipa* player, appeared, coming the other direction. As soon as the oboist saw them, she grabbed her friend's arm and whispered something in her ear. Little Li knew that gossip about them would soon be circulating around the Conservatory.

In Beijing, couples had few places to be alone. Young people could not find seclusion in their cramped dorm rooms or family apartments and there were virtually no cafés in which they could sit together undisturbed. The Peace Café notwithstanding, couples were left to wander in public spaces. Parks afforded the few quiet spots without gawkers. But policemen were infamous for rousting lovers, because couples seeking such solitude were ipso facto considered bent on hiding something illicit. The best refuge was to stay in motion. As they walked, Little Li always scanned their route for any place where they might grab a few moments together away from prying eyes. Recalling his two nights with Yang Ming, he even became nostalgic for the bittersweet solitude of the road at Yak Springs.

One warm October evening while waiting for her outside the latrine at the northeast edge of Tiananmen Square, he noticed that behind a screen of shrubbery at the far end of the reviewing stands flanking Tiananmen Gate there was an iron ladder bolted to the wall. He climbed up it and vaulted the guardrail, and found that if he lay down on the front bleacher, he was hidden from both pedestrians and vehicular traffic along the busy Avenue of Eternal Peace.

"I think I've found a perfect place for us!" he reported excitedly when she returned.

"What kind of place?"

"I just climbed into the reviewing stands, and it's quiet, even scenic!" he replied—this last flourish added in the hope that a little aesthetic enticement would help cancel out any doubts she might have.

"Where they watch all the big parades?" she asked skeptically, pointing to the stands. "Are you crazy?"

"Why not?"

"Because it's forbidden!" she protested. "What if the Public Security Bureau catches us?"

"But . . ."

"Anyway, I don't like being so near the Forbidden City. You know how . . ." She did not finish, but he understood.

Several weeks later, when they found themselves again walking past the stands, he could not resist proposing the idea once more.

"Let's at least try!" he insisted, determined to find a private sanctuary.

"But what if we get caught?"

"Where's your spirit of adventure?" he pleaded, as she looked dubiously over her shoulder at the reviewing stand. Finally, she reluctantly consented. Fortunately, there were few pedestrians that evening, and the shrubbery did hide them as they climbed up. "Lie down quickly!" he urged, once she was over the rail.

"This is not Yak Springs, it's the dragon's lair!" she protested.

"I don't think anyone saw us," he reassured her. This was the first time they'd been alone, and he didn't want to be thwarted. Anyway, with a beautiful orange moon rising, and squadrons of bats flying acrobatics overhead, she finally relaxed. In the weeks that followed, she began to look forward to their new sanctuary. One evening, she even sang him a verse by the poet Wang Wei that she'd set to music:

> *After rain the lonely mountain*
> *Stands autumnal in the evening,*
> *Moonlight in its grove of pines,*
> *Stones of crystal in its brooks.*
> *Bamboos whisper of girls bound home from washing,*
> *Lotus leaves give way to a fisherman's boat.*
> *What does it matter that springtime has past,*
> *While you are here, Prince of Friends?*

Unexpectedly, she began to cry. He reached over to hold her. But instead of yielding, she stiffened with resistance.

"What is it?"

"Oh" she gasped. "I'm afraid." She flung her arms around his neck.

"Afraid of what?"

"Of losing you . . . To America." Whereas her talent and beauty had always made her seem so composed and inviolable, her upset now lent her a sudden air of vulnerability.

"It's all right," he said, taking her by the shoulders and cradling her taut body in his arms. She exhaled a long, deep sigh, as if all she'd ever wanted was to be held this way.

"I love you," she whispered. "I've loved you since I first saw you outside my studio."

Instead of replying, he caressed her cheek and neck. Then, as if it had a will of its own, his hand began wandering, finding its way through the layers of her clothing to the warm skin of her belly, sending shivers through her body. When he brushed a finger

lightly over one of her nipples, she gasped as if touched by a freezing object.

"No, don't . . . You can't . . ." she cried.

"It's all right," he soothed.

"I am afraid! Please, I . . . !"

"But why?"

"Because you're going away! I feel it, and . . ."

"No, no," he whispered disingenuously, so drunk with desire
that nothing mattered just then except his animal nature. Having
learned to expect denial, he could not bear the thought of being
denied now. So, as if soothing a distressed child, he tried to calm
her while at the same time trying to excite her. With her gasping
breath pumping in his ear, he sensed the tide turning, even as he felt
himself heading to the edge. Then, like a cat arching its back into
a stroking hand, she leaned into him, let out a long sigh, and fell
limply into his arms.

"Don't leave me," she pleaded.

It was while rocking her back and forth in his arms like a frightened child that he heard a voice. A beam of light menacingly raked
the railing in front of them, probing as if it hadn't yet found what
it was looking for. Then, suddenly, it came to rest right on them.

"Who goes there?" a voice challenged. Shielding his eyes from
the blinding brightness of the beam with one hand, Little Li made
out a silhouette at the top of the stands. Too agitated to be frightened, he bent over her.

"Quick—roll down onto the deck!" he ordered, trying to steady
his voice. "I'll distract him. But when you hear me yell, 'Broken leg,'
scramble down the ladder and run! No matter what, don't stop!"

"But what about—"

"There is no time!" he shot back. Then, ostentatiously, he leapt
up and began running toward the other end of the stands.

"Stop!" the voice yelled as Little Li jumped from bleacher to
bleacher, trying to get as far away from her as he could. Then he
pretended to fall.

"Broken leg!" he cried out.

"That's doesn't matter to me, you hoodlum [流氓]," shrieked
the guard, lunging at him.

"You can take it easy," Little Li groaned. "My leg's hurt."

"I'm not gonna take it easy on a punk like you!" cursed the

guard, raining blows down on Little Li's head and back with the butt of his flashlight. He was so close that Little Li could smell the spicy odor of tobacco exuded by his body. Instead of resisting, he just lay with his hands over his head to shield himself. Little Hong could hear the dull chopping sounds of the steel flashlight coming down, but good sense prevailed, and she crawled to the railing. Just as she was clambering over it, however, the guard spotted her.

"Halt!" he yelled.

"My leg! My leg!" Little Li cried out again.

"Shut up, or I'll send you off to see your ancestors!" screamed the guard, whirling around again to beat Little Li on his legs.

"I'm not going anywhere," he croaked, raising his hands in surrender. "But all the others are getting away."

"All the others?" exclaimed the guard. "If you're bullshitting me, here's what you're gonna get!" He delivered another series of cracks to the ribs that took Little Li's breath away. Then, spinning around, he bounded toward the place from which Little Hong had just disappeared. To distract him, Little Li jumped up and bolted in the opposite direction. The confused guard hesitated for a moment before running after him. He waited until the guard had gotten halfway to him before leaping over the guardrail himself. It was a long way down, but a hedge broke his fall. Fired by pure adrenaline, he picked himself up, and though pain shot through his bruised body, he began running. He did not slow down until he reached a streetcar stop. As a bus pulled up, he turned around one last time. Several flashlights were now raking the bleachers with menacing beams.

Knowing that it would be folly to seek out Little Hong at her aunt's apartment, he limped home. It was almost midnight when he reached Willow Courtyard. Fortunately, his father was already asleep. But after he'd collapsed on his cot, his aching body and anxiety over Little Hong conspired to rob him of any slumber. The next day, he was able to walk only with difficulty. Insisting he'd been in a bicycle collision, he resisted his father's entreaties to go to a clinic, because anytime anything untoward happened, clinics and hospitals were the first places Public Security Bureau agents searched for suspects. He was greatly relieved when, that afternoon, a note appeared in their letterbox:

Wende:
  I want you to know I did manage to get home safely last
     night.
Will you somehow tell me if you're all right?

And . . . you must promise we'll never do anything like
     that again!

  I want a peaceful life!
  Hui

When he saw her at the Conservatory the next night, she threw her arms around his neck, and he felt chastened.

Over the next few weeks, it continued to be painful to walk that they just sat in Ritan Park and talked. But even though he still looked forward to seeing her, a subtle change had transpired in the chemistry between them. He was disturbingly aware that their night in the stands had somehow been a dividing line. Whereas before he'd been unable to imagine getting enough of her, now he was surprised by an almost blasé aspect infecting his spirits, as if, now with the absence of untraversed territory beckoning him onward, he was suddenly left somehow denatured. He even found himself wishing he could hang out more with Little Wang and Pei Heli. At first he could not pinpoint the exact cause of his diminished ardor, but there was something about the way she'd finally surrendered that now blunted his appetite. Without the heady sense of her elusiveness that had once so stirred him, he was divested of that unique kind of longing only thwarted or unreciprocated desire can generate. With no distance between them remaining to be overcome, no uncertainty left to resolve, and no challenge still to triumph over, the fuel that had stoked his yearning was gone. Perhaps, he argued to himself, his new absence of zeal was due to her habit of always arriving at the right place on time, indifference to the allure of going abroad, or her willingness to acquiesce to the Chinese world as she found it. Whatever the cause, a new dusting of ambiguity had been sprinkled on their relationship, denaturing his previously urgent sense of desire, demonstrating how quickly intense yearnings can evanesce when finally slaked.

There was one other cloud that also began casting a shadow. He began experiencing her determined expectations about their togetherness as pressure. Now that she'd physically relented, she assumed they'd marry, settle down, and even have children. While for him California remained an alluring unanswered question, for her America did not beckon. Even to raise the subject with her made him feel unkind and lacking in fidelity.

"Where have you been?" Pei Heli asked when they ran into each other next.

"Oh, around."

"I hear you have an 'old lady' [婆子]." Pei used a slang term for "girlfriend" with an edge of derision.

"Kind of," answered Little Li with an evasive smile. "And what mischief have you and Little Wang been up to?" he countered, trying to change the subject.

"Well . . ." said Pei, lighting a cigarette. "Unlike you, I don't know how I fit into all the shit that's going on now." He laughed. "There are only two things I do know: First, I don't like the way our so-called leaders still boss everyone around. Second, I don't want to go back to prison. But if I shut up, I'll piss myself off. If I complain too loudly, I'll piss the government off and will end up back behind bars."

"Real prison?"

"Once you graduate from an elite Chinese prison, you're always an honored alumnus." He laughed. They walked silently for a few moments. "Hey!" Pei suddenly piped up. "Ever read that essay we gave you by 'the electrician'?"

"Oh, that!" replied Little Li. "Yes."

"And . . . ?"

"It was a relief to read someone who dares say what we actually think!"

"Yeah, that's Wei Jingsheng. A straight shooter. If you have a piece of paper, I'll give you something else he wrote. In prison, we had to memorize everything important, because they wouldn't let us write things down, and I still remember this paragraph of Wei's." Little Li took a tablet of music paper out of his book bag and handed it to Pei, who wrote across the staves: *The leaders of our nation must be informed that we want to take our destiny into our own hands. We want no more gods, emperors, or saviors of any kind. We want to be masters of our own country, not the modernized tools for the ever-expanding ambitions of dictators.* The Electrician.

Several nights later, as they sat in the park, he read Wei's lines to Little Hong.

"You'll never win looking at things this way," she responded, almost sternly. "They're too powerful. 'A slender arm can never twist a stout leg' [胳膊拧不过大腿]."

"But why should we always be such cowards?" he argued, thinking how much her fatalistic acceptance of things sounded like his father. "Nothing is permitted in this infernal country. No matter how badly they treat us, we don't dare to object. We have so many ways to justify biting our tongues and waiting for them to loosen our chains. And when they do, we just gratefully say, 'Oh! Thank you very much!'"

"But be realistic!" Her voice had taken on a sudden pleading tone. "They'll crush you!"

"When the party gives orders, even when leaders have gone mad, we obediently follow?"

"It may not be right, but it's the way things are." His indignation frightened her.

"They killed your father and maimed mine, and yet we still crawl around on our hands and knees, hoping they'll give us a little more breathing room."

"You can't rage against heaven!"

"Do you know what Marshal Peng Dehuai said when Mao purged him during the Great Leap Forward?" he shot back. "He said, 'Chinese prefer death to waking up.'"

He was shocked by the vehemence of his own argument. She took it as a reproach and for the rest of the evening said almost nothing. Thereafter, they didn't talk about politics. But he could feel an invisible wall rising between them. One night, as they walked by Zhongnanhai, the parklike compound in which the party leadership lived, she suddenly stopped, turned to face him, and asked, "Do you really know what you want from life?"

"What do you mean?" he asked, thrown off by her abruptness.

"I mean, what would make you feel really contented with your life?"

"I'm not sure," he replied, realizing he'd better respond with caution. "What about you?"

"I dream about becoming a better musician and having a real home, with a father, mother, and children, something like the old ideal of 'four generations under one roof' [四世同堂]."

"Well, of course, I'd like that, too, but sometimes . . ."

"Sometimes what?"

"Sometimes I just want to vault over the walls we're so fond of building around ourselves, get away from all our mistreatment of each other and all that stuff about foreigners being poisonous."

"Oh?" she exclaimed. "So you really would like to leave China?"

"Well, yes!" he replied defensively. "In fact . . ." But he didn't complete his thought, because he saw the disappointment on her face.

"If you went abroad, would you come back soon?" she asked, her voice filling with alarm.

"Well . . ."

"Does your mother still have relatives over there?" she pointedly asked.

"A few. But aren't you curious about what it's like over there, too?"

"Me?" She pointed to herself. "I just don't think that way. I don't speak a foreign language, and there isn't much I could learn on the *yangqin* from 'foreign devils' [洋鬼子]." She tried to laugh at her slang. "Also, I need to take care of my aunt."

Suddenly he felt regretful. After all, didn't he, too, have an elderly father to worry about? At least she acknowledged her familial obligations.

"Maybe it's just a dream," he said and sighed. "But sometimes I feel so suffocated here."

"Well, maybe it's just something you have to do," she said fatalistically. He put an arm around her, but her body was stiff with resistance.

In the days that followed, there were more and more long, awkward gaps in their conversations, with many important things left unsaid.

26

DECISION

AGGRAVATED BY the dust, cold, and dry air of winter, Li Tongshu's cough grew more persistent. Little Li had hoped that with time it would cure itself, but now he was beginning to worry. His father rarely left home except to teach, and Little Li felt obliged to stay with him most evenings. Although Little Hong was uncomplaining, he sensed how dispirited she was. He, too, was dismayed, but as much by the mystery of his own growing ambivalence toward her as by her disappointment. One evening, she appeared unexpectedly at their gate with some traditional medicine for his father. Because he'd said nothing to him about their relationship, Little Li was anxious about how he'd react.

"Father, I'd like to introduce you to . . ." he began.

"Oh, I'm so pleased to at last meet you," he exclaimed, standing up before Little Li had even finished his sentence, and engaging Little Hong in such a spirited conversation that it was impossible for her to leave. While Little Li was relieved that they took to each other so easily, he was also irritated, because her visit had let her escape the containment vessel in which he thought he'd confined her.

"She's obviously a person of character and refinement," his father effused when she finally left. "And you say she has musical talent?"

"She does," replied Little Li sullenly.

"It makes me proud you've chosen so wisely," he added, as if a match had already been struck.

The party's new policy of "opening up to the outside world" (对外开放) had left students at almost every academy and university buzzing with excitement about prospects for foreign study. Though at first it seemed impossible that he, too, might be able to go abroad, almost every day brought word of more startling changes in China's relations with the outside world. A voice student he knew had won a fellowship to the San Francisco Opera's Merola Program for young singers; a violin player was admitted to the Eastman School of Music; and a pianist was going to study at the New England Conservatory. Swept away by hopes of connecting with kindhearted American tourists who might sponsor them, Chinese students were now trolling hotel lobbies, antiques stores, and tourist sites to "practice English" and score the sponsorship necessary to procure a U.S. visa. Students who homed in on such foreigners became known as "silkworm missiles," an allusion to the PLA's medium-range guided ballistic missiles. And then there was the clarinet player from Canton who'd become famous by teaming up with a tenor from Shanghai to give performances at the Temple of Heaven.

"We, being Chinese classical-musical students, are wanting the practice of English with your American friends, so who will make partners with us?" went their barely intelligible English pitch.

Tourists were delighted to oblige these penurious young buskers, and in no time they'd made so many "foreign friends" that they were passing extra names off to classmates for ten renminbi a head. Soon they set up a matchmaking agency with separate departments specializing in German, Japanese, and French, as well as English.

"Right now, it's easy to get out," Zhang Dan, the voice student, told Little Li.

"How easy?"

"The government's loosened up on passport requirements, and they're giving exit permits to almost any applicant with relatives or friends abroad who are willing to guarantee private financial support for their studies. Officials view this as a way of getting free foreign training."

"Do you think the policy will last?"

"The party's as unpredictable as the weather," said his friend, laughing. His comments set so many wheels spinning in Little Li's head that he was unable to sleep.

"Does Mother still have relatives in San Francisco?" he asked his father one morning.

"Why do you ask?"

"Just wondering," he replied, as vaguely as possible.

"Well, your aunt lives there, but I never really knew her. She wasn't like your mother, and then she married a guy named Woo I never cared for. You probably don't remember, but they were the ones who wrote us about your mother's death."

"Oh yes," muttered Little Li, remembering the bone-white envelope addressed in unfamiliar script that had arrived from Canada.

"I suppose she's still alive," added his father.

"It would be nice to go abroad," said Little Li, trying to sound as if he were only musing.

"On the other hand, things here are now changing so fast that—" began his father.

"But didn't you go to America?" interrupted Little Li, feeling a twinge of annoyance at his father's lack of enthusiasm. Where had loyalty and love of country ever gotten him and his generation?

"Indeed, I did," he acknowledged, realizing he was infecting his son's enthusiasm with his ambiguity. "Maybe you should go, too. As the poet Li Bai wrote:

Despite the high winds and breaking great waves,
One still must hoist one's cloudlike sail and cross the
*   mighty ocean.*
长风破浪会有时,直挂云帆济沧海.

The more Little Li asked around, the more he encountered students who'd already gotten both their Chinese passports and U.S. visas. And for every student on an official exchange program, many more were getting out privately. After being so scornful of the bourgeois West, the party was now shamelessly encouraging students to use wealthy overseas relatives and friends to secure educations abroad. Foreign study, whose stigma had so tainted his father's life, was now alchemizing into an asset.

Entering the Conservatory's front gate one afternoon, Little Li spotted an unusual poster:

The First American Ballet Company to Visit China
Since Liberation!
THE BEIJING ACADEMY OF DANCE
AND
THE HOUSTON BALLET OF TEXAS

Present
A JOINT DANCE CONCERT
To the music of Richard Strauss and J. S. Bach

To see the names of J. S. Bach and Richard Strauss in this city that was ony recently in the throes of Mao's Cultural Revolution was the kind of cognitive dissonance that Deng's new "New China" had made common. The Philadelphia Orchestra under Eugene Ormandy, the Boston Symphony Orchestra under Seiji Ozawa, and the Vienna Philharmonic under Herbert von Karajan had all given concerts in Beijing, and, knowing how popular such performances had been, Little Li went immediately for tickets. However, fearing his coughing would disrupt the performance, his father urged him to invite "that nice girl" in his stead. So, on a lovely April evening, as the sycamore buds were beginning to unfold along the Avenue of Eternal Peace, they biked to the Beijing Exhibition Center. He was excited to be going to a foreign performance, but Little Hong was subdued, and lagged so far behind him that he had to keep turning around to make sure he hadn't lost her.

As they waited for the concert hall doors to open, the sprinkling of older people—men in white sleeveless shirts and nondescript trousers and women in severe bobs, plain dresses, and dowdy shoes—looked like a different species compared to the younger men and women who were attired casually in blue jeans, T-shirts, and brightly colored skirts and stylish blouses. Since returning from Yak Springs, Little Li had watched with astonishment as fashions, hairstyles, and pop-music tastes changed. Although many of these changes were imitative of the West, they were also buoyantly rebellious and inspiring.

To stand now in the shadow of the gingerbread tower of the Beijing Exhibition Center was to be reminded of an earlier era, when China's leaders were enamored not of the West but of the USSR under Joseph Stalin. The errant progeny of that "friendship" included this fantastical building that had been constructed during the beginning of the Cold War, when the newly established People's Republic of China began "leaning to one side" (一边倒), toward its putative "Soviet big brother" (苏联老大哥).

However, by 1960, all that remained of those heady times of Sino-Soviet fraternity were these architectural throwbacks—such as the Beijing Train Station near Big Sheep Wool Alley—that still dotted the landscape like so many Stonehenges left over from international socialism's paleontological past. As a child, Little Li had found the Exhibition Center's stiletto-like steeple topped by a star and flanked by minarets as exotic as the color plates in his mother's book of great European cathedrals. When his father had taken him, as a special treat, to its Moscow Restaurant for ice cream, he'd been dazzled by the dark wood paneling, plush velvet curtains, and crystal chandeliers. One of the few places in Beijing that served "foreign" food—Russian borscht, chicken Kiev, vodka—the restaurant was for him the personification of the outside world, insofar as that forbidden universe could be divined at all from Beijing. Now, however, as he stared up at the Exhibition Center's steeple, it seemed preposterously out of time and place, and as pretentious as a piece of oversized costume jewelry. And, having fallen into seedy decline, the Moscow Restaurant was a far cry from the glittering Western-style hotels going up around Beijing, with their all-you-can-eat buffets, marble lobbies, health spas, and luxury shops, which were becoming China's new post–Mao-era cathedrals.

When the doors finally opened, the stone columns ringing the hall inside—each embellished with a hammer and sickle chipped into their stone capitals—gave it a sepulchral, Stalinist dowdiness. In this reform-inspired era, with a new generation of Chinese striving for wealth, power, and style, such retrograde symbols left the auditorium reeking of revolutionary failure.

"Are you all right?" he asked Little Hong, who'd hardly said a word.

"Fine," she said. But she was not fine. She was caught in a clash between China and the promise of a fresh start in the United States. When Little Li spotted the poster for this ballet, the thought of catching an American performance with his father had excited him. And since the Houston Ballet was the first American dance troupe to visit China, as the house lights finally dimmed he was filled with expectation. When the sequined curtain finally rose and the audience saw that the stage was set with nothing more than pieces of diaphanous white fabric hanging from the loft like cumulus clouds, they murmured in bewilderment.

"What is it?" a young woman behind them asked her boyfriend.

"It's modern art," he whispered back with unconvincing authority.

"Huh?" she retorted.

But Little Li loved the otherworldly way the footlights made the hanging fabric iridescent, so that for the moment one forgot the hammers and sickles. As the hall filled with the first of Richard Strauss's *Four Last Songs,* composed as meditations on the transcendent power of love over death at the end of his life, and as dancers in skintight leotards revealing every contour of their bodies floated across the stage in a way that made them look almost windblown, he was transported. However, he knew that if his enjoyment was too overt, she would only interpret it as further evidence that his heart was taking flight. So, when the first song ended, he clapped only tepidly. But he found the third song, "Upon Going to Sleep," so unbearably beautiful that he could not restrain himself. Beginning with a low growl from the cellos and basses, which slowly swelled to meet the voice of a solo viola, the song filled the stolid hall with a sound so heartbreaking, the audience was tranquilized into a mystified silence. Just as an ink brush in the hands of a master calligrapher covers a sheet of rice paper with strokes that are graceful and continuous, dancers painted their fluid way across the stage, holding, touching, and caressing each other in ways that allowed the audience to feel they were witnessing the kind of tender, intimate acts from which decorum might normally compel them to avert their gaze. And, with each gorgeous bar and every masterly step, Little Li was pulled a little further to the edge of that powerful force field that had been holding him so resolutely in China's orbit. By the time the French horns gave way to the final chimelike tolling of a bell, he'd been pulled far away from the shoreline like a swimmer caught in a powerful current.

Feeling his ineluctable drift, Little Hong had the sensation of being left alone to drown. She was losing him, and not to another woman, but to a force she neither understood nor knew how to resist. It was a force that did not even afford her the dignity of being wronged by infidelity, so she could soothe the pain of separation with blame. Instead, she was left to explain his ambivalence as her own failure. Why wasn't she more adventuresome, eager to go abroad, and open to transforming herself into an exciting, contemporary person? Why was she so willing to accept things as they were, play traditional music, remain in Beijing, get married, and lead a conventional life? Compared with him, she felt unadventuresome, one-dimensional, and flat.

Because bilateral cultural exchanges with the PRC and other countries required at least a simulacrum of equality, it was unacceptable for most visiting foreign arts troupes to perform alone. So, after the intermission, the stage was turned over to the Beijing Dance Academy, and the audience's mood changed from puzzled reservation to the kind of raucous enthusiasm that greets athletic competitions. Whereas the abstract choreography of the *Four Last Songs* suggested no discernible plot and employed no florid costumes or props, *Young Woman Washing Clothes for the People's Liberation Army* left nothing to the imagination. With a frenzy of Slavic flourishes, six male dancers sporting handlebar mustaches, red uniforms, high patent-leather boots, and black lambskin hats burst from the wings to help a young maiden who was washing clothes in a nearby stream. Rebuking them with a proletarian serve-the-people dedication to her calling, she clasped her lavage to her chaste bosom. The number concluded with her doing a flamboyant grand jeté to offstage right, with the soldiers swarming in hot pursuit. The audience exploded into applause.

The Houston Ballet was allowed to close the performance and as the hall plunged back into darkness and a piano began playing the allemande from Bach's first *French Suite,* Little Li was a small boy again in Willow Courtyard listening to his father play this very piece. But now, as two dancers in white glided across the stage, floating like underwater sea creatures, and as Bach's music rained down like a shower of ice crystals, he felt so transported that, when the lights came back up and the hammers and the sickles revealed themselves again on the pillars, he felt more determined than ever to reach the shores from which such artistry had come.

"What did you think?" he asked Little Hong.

"Lovely," she replied, a misty sadness in her eyes. "But it's hard to know what they intend." As they pedaled home, she said nothing more.

Several days later his friend the voice student came up to Little Li again at the Conservatory.

"I've a favor to ask," he said in a conspiratorial whisper, "but you have to keep it a secret."

"I promise!"

"I'm leaving in two weeks for Boston University."

"They're letting you out?" gasped Little Li incredulously.

"Yeah, but I need help filling out a few forms in English."

"Of course, but how did you do it?"

"Relatives."

"And you got a passport?"

"If you get admitted to an American school, our side is issuing passports and the U.S. is giving visas."

"And how did you get a guarantor?"

"My father has a brother in Boston."

"My old man says I have an aunt in San Francisco!"

"You should write her."

"Are you sure our government will approve a passport with such a letter?"

His friend picked up his black plastic portfolio and extracted a gleaming new maroon passport embossed with China's national seal. He flipped through its pages until he came to a stamp showing the crest of an eagle in bright red with the words "The United States of America Non-Emigrants Visa. Issued at the U.S. Consulate, Beijing, China."

All that day, Little Li was so excited he could not concentrate. But when he arrived back home and found his father standing with his battered watering can in the small bed of chrysanthemums he still managed to cultivate, he looked so old and stooped that Little Li couldn't imagine leaving him.

"What is it?" his father asked gently, as they went inside, and he filled two cups with hot water from their thermos.

"Nothing," replied Little Li. Suddenly even dreaming about going abroad felt like a violation of his filial obligations.

"Is it something at school?"

"Not really."

"Is it that you want to go abroad?" Little Li was stunned by his father's acuity in divining what was bothering him. "Of course, I don't want to lose you," he continued, "but if it's really possible for you to go, it would be as good for you, just as it was for me."

"Oh, Father!" exclaimed Little Li, flooded with relief. "I'd like to go, if you'll be all right?"

"Don't worry about me. I've managed this long on my own.

And, if there's ever a need, you could come back." For several minutes, they sat staring at the steam rising from their cups as the clock ticked on the counter and a train locomotive hooted in the distance. "To catch a big fish, one must cast a large net [撒大网捞大鱼]," his father finally said smiling. "I'll write your aunt and ask if she'll invite you to America in your mother's memory." He reached out and took one of his son's hands. The feel of his shattered, bony knuckles broke Little Li's heart.

27

WHEN AN envelope plastered with stamps depicting the Statue of Liberty arrived at Willow Courtyard, Little Li's heart jumped. Inside was a letter written in loopy longhand on stationery embossed with two cuddling poodles, one limned in baby blue, the other in pink. The letter was from his mother's sister, Aunt Crystal, and her husband, Dudley Woo:

> Dear Tongshu:
> We were surprised to receive a letter from you after all these years! With things being so upside down over there in Red China, we're glad to know you're OK.
> About your request to help the boy: We're sending a letter from Heald College, which just opened here in Frisco, where P.K. knows someone. It may help with his visa. And we've signed the affidavit of support, although with P.K. retired and all, we're not in a position to get financial right now. So, even though we've signed as "guarantors," if the boy comes, make sure he understands he'll be on his own.
> As you probably heard, our mother passed away in '77 and is at rest in Colma, beside your blessed wife, Vivian.
> Both P.K. and I hope things are OK over there for you and the boy.
> Yours, Crystal and P. K. Woo

Like a salmon whose brain is encoded with a primal memory of a distant spawning ground to which it is instinctually programmed to return, Little Li was driven to reach America. He was also determined to cease being such a passive receptor for whatever came along, to begin to shape his own destiny more actively. So, when his passport arrived, he went immediately to the U.S. Consulate, and three days later he had a visa. Now came the moment he'd been dreading: speaking to Little Hong. He decided to leave a note asking her to meet him at the monument in Tiananmen Square. Only after he'd pushed it irretrievably under her door did he realize his cruelty: he'd asked her to meet him at the very place they'd first come together, making the monument the alpha and the omega of their relationship.

"Did you really think I wouldn't know why you wanted to meet here?" she asked when he finally told her he'd gotten a U.S. visa. "I've known you were leaving for months. From that first night when you told me your family story, I feared things would end this way."

"Oh, Little Hui!" was all he could say.

When things go awry, it is not uncommon for a person to want to find someone else to blame. Hong Hui was not such a person. She bore her distress with a stoic dignity that only made Little Li feel the selfishness of his decision more acutely. How could he hurt someone he had so ardently courted and to whom he'd become so attached? He was no Fidelio. At that moment, he felt he was hardly less a betrayer than all those hypocritical party leaders who, after enticing patriots like his father home with rosy promises, turned against them. When he tried to comfort her, she turned away, her limpid eyes brimming with tears. Long ago, when he'd been required to memorize parts of Chairman Mao's essay *On the Correct Handling of Contradictions Among the People* (关于正确处理人民内部矛盾的问题), he'd become acquainted with Mao's theories on "the struggle between opposites" and the need to distinguish between what he called "contradictions among the people" (人民内部矛盾) and "antagonistic contradictions" (敌我矛盾). The former could be resolved through negotiation and compromise, but the latter could be resolved only through confrontation, struggle, and violence. Little Li knew he was now ensnared on the horns of an "antagonistic contradiction," and it was Little Hong to whom violence would be done. And for what? So he could pursue his wild dream of an American escape.

When they finally reached her aunt's building, he was at a loss to know how to say goodbye, and just stood staring at his feet. The thought that two flesh-and-blood human beings who'd held each other in their arms might voluntarily dissolve their togetherness seemed surreal. And because it was he who was willing this separation, it felt almost like a form of suicide. For Little Hong it felt more like an execution.

"Oh, Wende!" she finally gasped, then pressed her head to his chest so he could smell the animal earthiness of her scalp and feel the warmth of her cheek. "Why is it this way?"

Huge tears slid down her cheeks, making dark stains on his shirt. He wanted her to know how much he still cared for her, but was aware that any such expression might only inflame her sense of hurt. Moreover, he knew that if he stood there much longer he, too, might break down and lose his resolve. He could not turn back on his American dream without annihilating himself, so taking her head between his hands, he kissed her cheek.

"Goodbye," he murmured. "I . . ." He could not go on. She went limp, like a distressed child yearning to be comforted by a parent. Fighting back tears, he turned and walked away. But as soon as he rounded the corner, he was so overcome, he doubled up against a poplar tree and wept.

As Little Li made preparations for his departure, his father's cough became more persistent. Although he refused to acknowledge anything wrong, he was eating less. The morning when Little Li made his airline reservation to San Francisco, he returned to Willow Courtyard to find his father slumped on his bed, a handkerchief soaked with bloody sputum in one hand.

"I'm just fine," he protested.

"I'm going to call Dr. Song," insisted Little Li.

"Oh, no, no!" protested his father, even as he succumbed to another attack.

When Dr. Song arrived, with his physician's bag clamped to the back of his bicycle, he listened to his old friend's heart and lungs with his stethoscope and tapped with his knuckles on his back, as if he were sounding a melon for ripeness. Watching these familiar fingers with their carefully trimmed nails and bleached skin go about their work, Little Li recalled that wintry day when even as others were betraying their friends, Dr. Song had come to his father's aid.

Now everything about his father spelled decline. His cheeks were unshaven, his head was sprouting tufts of unruly gray hair, and instead of looking outward with his usual intelligence, his gaze was fixed inward.

"It would be prudent for you to come in for an X-ray," Dr. Song announced as he folded his stethoscope.

"Is there anything unusual?" asked Little Li, trying to hide his anxiety.

"I'd just like to take a closer look."

Several days later, they set off for Peking Union Medical College Hospital, where Dr. Song had practiced since returning to China in 1950. Established in 1917 by the philanthropies of the Rockefeller family, the hospital had been buffeted by upheaval, occupation, civil war, and revolution ever since. As they entered the lobby, Little Li had the sensation of passing irretrievably from one universe to another. The hospital's overcrowded waiting rooms brimmed with anxious patients standing, sitting, and sprawling wherever they could find space and the lobby looked like a train station, except that there were people in bandages, on crutches, in wheelchairs, on stretchers, and hobbling along with the support of family members. Everyone was waiting for something: admission, diagnoses, treatment, results of surgical procedures, prescriptions. . . . So many sick, broken people. As they made their way to the radiology department, Little Li was painfully aware that, once the X-ray negative was rendered, unlike all the verdicts of counterrevolutionary crimes that were now being overturned, this machine's verdict would allow no such reversal. When an X-ray froze the image of a tumor onto film, it delivered a dictum that not even the Standing Committee of the Politburo of the Central Committee of the Chinese Communist Party in all its omnipotent perversity could overturn. Evidence of a tumor would matriculate his father into a new system of despotism even more unforgiving than the party's. Under the dictatorship of terminal disease, there was no reprieve or rehabilitation.

After the X-rays had been developed, Dr. Song summoned them into his office.

"I have unwelcome news, Tongshu," he began. "You have a cancerous lesion on your left lung's top lobe, and we should get it out as soon as possible." He picked up a large negative from his

desktop, clipped it onto a light box, and pointed with an index finger to a milky white splotch that looked more like a swirling nebula
of gas and dust in outer space than anything organic. "It's quite
large. I've scheduled surgery for next week. I hope we can take care
of it with one operation."

"I see," responded Li Tongshu. "How long will I be in the
hospital?"

"Less than a week, I hope. I'll arrange everything, so don't
worry."

When his father excused himself to go to the lavatory, Little
Li stood up to accompany him, as if the news they'd just received
had already rendered him an invalid. But Dr. Song motioned him
to stay.

"This will not be an easy operation," he began after Li Tongshu
had left. "We won't know if it's spread until we can examine his
lymph nodes, but, whatever the case, you will have to delay your
trip to San Francisco."

"Of course," responded Little Li as evenly as he could, although
he felt the earth had just given way beneath his feet.

Five days later, Li Tongshu packed a pair of pajamas, a toothbrush, and his copy of *The Dream of the Red Chamber,* a book he
knew as well as an experienced conductor knows a great score and,
like a great work of music, one he loved more each time he read
it. After all that had happened to him, the world depicted in this
literary work had come to seem a more livable one than the actual
world. As they walked out of Willow Courtyard, Li Tongshu
paused at the gate, turned, and gave a bow in the direction of their
room. Then they took a public bus to the hospital, an inglorious
way to start the beginning of the end of a life.

Once admitted for surgery, Li Tongshu was put on a gurney
and wheeled away.

"Goodbye, Papa," Little Li said, addressing him as he had as a
boy.

"Goodbye, son," his father answered, squeezing his hand.

Not knowing whether he'd said goodbye for a few hours or
forever, Little Li sat down in the hallway outside the operating
rooms to wait. What had caused those first errant cells within his
father's lungs to mutate and begin their murderous multiplication?
Was it exile during the Anti-Rightist Campaign, hunger during the

Great Leap Forward, banishment during the Cultural Revolution, the polluted air of Beijing, or just the collective litany of insults that had been inflicted on him over the decades? All that mattered now was the hope of ridding his body of these savage colonizers so he could enjoy a few more years of life. But each time the door to the operating rooms opened and a white-gowned surgeon came out and it wasn't Dr. Song, Little Li's pessimism deepened. When, finally, Dr. Song did emerge, he looked tired and somber.

"The operation was successful," he began. "But the cancer has spread. There is nothing more to be done surgically. We can try chemotherapy, but I am afraid it would only be palliative." He said the word "palliative" in English, and Little Li wasn't sure what it meant. However, the fact it was preceded by the adverb "only" conveyed the dire nature of the situation.

When Little Li left the hospital that night, his father was still in an anesthetic stupor. Back at Willow Courtyard, their room seemed empty, cold, and uninviting, and he couldn't help thinking of Hong Hui. How he wished she was there. Sitting in his father's reading chair, he closed his eyes and tried to distract himself by conjuring up the room as it had been when the piano and bookcase were still standing side by side, the wardrobe was against the opposite wall, and the kitchen shelf was laden with bright-colored jars, boxes, and cans from America. Although these things were now long gone, they were so palpable in his memory that he would not have been surprised to open his eyes and find them all magically back in their places. But if his father died, all these recollections would then reside in his memory alone.

Because he knew it was what his father would have done, he washed the few bowls and cups in the sink, took the dishwater outside, and tenderly poured it on the old wisteria vine. Then, sitting at his father's desk, he began searching for his "household registration," which the hospital required. As he rummaged through the piles of papers and books his father had recently bought from the street stalls he loved to frequent, he found a slender, yellowing volume in English entitled *Socrates, Buddha, Confucius, Jesus: The Paradigmatic Individuals,* by the German philosopher Karl Jaspers. Its binding had become so dry and brittle that when he opened it, it cracked like ice, open to a passage that his father had underlined:

Where the superior man is concerned with justice
and where the inferior man with profit, the superior
man is quiet and serene, and the inferior man is full of
anxiety. The superior man is congenial, though never
stooping to vulgarity; the inferior man is vulgar without
being congenial. The superior man is dignified without
arrogance; the inferior man is arrogant without dignity.
The superior man is steadfast in distress while the inferior
man in distress loses all control of himself. The superior
man goes searching in himself; the inferior man goes
searching in others. The superior man strives upward; the
inferior man strives downward. . . . He is slow in words
and quick in action. He is careful not to let his words
outshine his deeds; he first acts, then speaks accordingly.

How had his father ever stumbled onto a text on the moral
aspects of the Confucian "superior man" (君子) written by a German philosopher, translated into English, and sold in China? As
he read on, he thought he finally understood something about the
expression "To allow the spittle to dry on one's face without wiping it off," which Granny Sun had tried to explain years before:
Even when publicly reviled, by not deigning to acknowledge such
an insult, the "superior man" maintains a posture of dignified,
unapologetic, unflinching rectitude. Little Li vividly recalled how
his father had refused to wipe his own cheek after being spat upon
by Red Guards. The incident still made him flare with resentment
and shame, but now he suddenly saw a new dignity in it. He set the
book down and stepped out onto the veranda. Seeing that Granny
Sun's light was still on, he went to knock on her door.

"Tell me the news?" she asked as soon as she saw him.

"The cancer's spread."

She squeezed her eyes shut and shook her head. "Have you
eaten?" she asked in her motherly way.

"No," he replied, suddenly aware of how hungry he was.

"Where's your father now?"

"In the hospital."

After setting a bowl of soup before him, she sat down herself
and put a hand on his forearm. "I want you to listen to me, my son.
Whatever happens, never forget what a fine man your father is."

"I know," he said in a choked voice. "But I don't think I've been as good a son."

"No need for such talk," she shushed, putting an index finger to her lips. "You've been a 'filial son' [孝子], but there is no negotiating with the will of heaven. Remember: 'Efforts are in the hands of man, but accomplishments are the hands of heaven' [谋事在人成事在天]. We can only do our best."

Five days later, Li Tongshu returned home in a car arranged by Dr. Song, but was so weak that, even with Little Li's help, he could barely make it across the courtyard.

"Don't be sad, son," he said through eyes drowsy with pain and morphine as he lay down on his bed. "I've been ready to meet my maker for a long time."

Little Li covered him with the same quilt he'd used ever since arriving back in Beijing more than three decades ago. Of course, it had been washed, had its cover changed, even its cotton batting fluffed and supplemented by the roving quilt restorers (弹棉花) who plied the *hutong*. But the fact that it was the "same" quilt was strangely comforting.

"You're a good son," his father whispered. Little Li had to turn away to hide the anguish that was etched on his face.

The next morning, Dr. Song came to clean and dress his incision.

"How does it look?" asked his friend.

"I think you're doing all right. I want to give you some more pain medicine. And because Beijing's so dry, I want to put you on a drip to keep you hydrated." He hung a pouch of intravenous fluid on a metal stand. "You must also drink more."

After Dr. Song departed, Little Li watched his father sleep as drops of fluid slowly formed at the mouth of the plastic pouch, then gained enough mass to drip down and flow through the plastic tubing into his father's veins like a liquid hourglass slowly emptying. With mouth ajar, his wispy hair aswirl, his knees drawn up, and his arms akimbo, his father looked more like a sleeping child than an adult. When he was a boy, it had never occurred to Little Li that he himself was important to anyone, much less to this proper, aloof man. Nor had he ever imagined what deep subterranean aquifers of emotion and sadness might lay pooled up unexpressed in the depths of his father's private being. Now he felt the pathos of his life.

When he at last himself fell asleep, he dreamed he was a small boy again exploring an unknown *hutong* with Little Wang when they stumbled upon an iron door. On the other side was an underground passageway hung with dripping roots that opened onto a quaint village shaded by trees hung with fruit and surrounded by lush pastures ablaze with wildflowers. Everywhere, cheerful naked people were unself-consciously going about their affairs. He and Little Wang began playing with some children in a stream of clear, warm water, while a smiling woman weeded a bed of crimson tomatoes next to a man under an arbor playing an ebony grand piano. Then, suddenly, this sylvan scene changed. The man turned into a horseman and the piano into a black stallion that pranced over to the woman, the rider swept her up onto the steed and galloped off across the verdant pasture. Then this luxuriant reverie turned black and white, and he found himself staring into a huge X-ray where tumors bloomed like ghostly white peonies. But before his dream could progress any further, he was awakened by one of those moments of unexpected stillness as when for a brief instant, waves lapping against the side of a boat skip an interval, he felt something go missing. Jolted awake, he realized that he could no longer hear the rasping of his father's breathing. When he bent over him to listen, his father uttered a sound that was more like a groan than a breath. Then he opened his eyes.

"Son!" he exclaimed.

"Father!" gasped Little Li.

But instead of saying anything more, he just dropped his head back down onto his pillow, shut his eyes, and resumed his troubled breathing.

Having taken a leave of absence from the Conservatory, Little Li traded his life as a student for that of an orderly changing dressings, preparing meals, doing laundry, reading aloud, shopping, and keeping vigil at his father's bedside, as one indistinguishable day passed after another. Little Hong sent a note saying how sorry she was to hear about his father and asking how she could help. He'd been missing her profoundly, but felt no right to torment her further. But one night he felt so lonely, he could not resist writing her a note suggesting that they meet.

As he waited for her on the monument balustrade several days later, he wasn't sure what was making him more ill-at-ease, his truancy from his father's bedside or this rendezvous with his ex-girlfriend. When he finally saw her walking toward him, there was something so seductively beautiful about the way she waved and picked up her pace at the sight of him that threw him completely off balance. The last thing he wanted was to be reminded of her loveliness, yet there she was, sashaying toward him and threatening to stampede right back into his heart. As she ran up the steps, she was smiling so radiantly, he wanted to take her in his arms, renounce his shattered dreams of going abroad, beg her forgiveness, accept her as his wife, and settle down here in Beijing.

"How's your dad?" she asked. "You know I'll do whatever I can."

"Thanks for asking, but there's really nothing more to be done."

"I'm so sorry," she said sweetly. An uncomfortable silence ensued.

"And what have you been doing these last few months?" he finally asked.

"Well . . ." she said, but then paused.

"How are things going at the Conservatory?" he pressed, trying to kindle a conversation.

"Oh, fine," she said in a strangely offhanded way.

"And what's new?"

"Not much, except my new part-time job."

"Oh! Doing what?"

"Well, I needed money, and a professor at the Central Academy of Fine Arts asked if I'd do some work there, so . . ."

"Some kind of office work?"

"Well, not exactly," she replied, registering a flicker of uneasiness. "They asked if I'd be willing—for pay, of course—to pose for a life drawing class. So I . . . Well, after pondering it, I thought, 'The pay's good, the hours are short, so why not?'"

"You're working as an artist's model?" he asked incredulously.

"Yes."

"You're posing?"

"Yes."

"In the nude?" he erupted, unable to control himself.

"Well, yes, that's the whole point. But don't be so concerned," she added quickly, sensing his upset. "It's actually very straightforward, all part of the new fascination with European art and the classical human form that's sweeping the art world here."

"But . . ."

"It's not what you might think. Anyway, now that I'm used to it, I don't mind."

He felt as if his brain had been firebombed. The thought that a whole roomful of randy art students were now enjoying the privilege of gaping at her lovely body, one that not even he had ever seen completely unclothed, so inflamed him with envy and jealousy that he couldn't speak. Imagining her standing before an enthralled classroom, her raisin-tipped nipples at attention, and the fuzzy cleft between her legs exposed for every horny guy to ogle, ignited a paralyzing wave of lustful resentment. But since, by his own choice, she was no longer "his," what right did he have to say, or feel, anything? What a fool he'd been, to blithely imagine she'd chastely pine away when he left! Now not only had he failed to make his escape, but he was being drawn back into her orbit via an unexpected storm of envy and desire.

"I just wanted to say goodbye to you one more time," he blurted out. Then, not quite knowing what he was doing, he turned and stumbled down the steps of the monument.

"Little Li! Wait!" she cried out. But he did not stop.

28

MORTALITY

LI TONGSHU'S cancer kept eating away at his body and enervating his soul, until his only enjoyment was reading. He often sent Little Li out to look for new books in which his still-lucid mind could escape the corporeal ruin overtaking him. One evening, he asked his son to read aloud from Lu Xun's "My Old Home" (故鄉), a story he'd always adored about the well-known author's return as a grown man to a childhood home in search of his past. Little Li, too, loved Lu's bittersweet recollection of arriving back in his hometown one winter day, years after becoming a celebrated writer, and looking forward to reconnecting with a local companion he remembers fondly from their days of mischief and adventure as boys. But when his childhood friend reappears, Lu finds not the plucky boy engraved in memory, but a cowed, deferential peasant. Li Tongshu so loved the description of their agonizing reunion that he could recite whole paragraphs by heart. So, when he unexpectedly started delivering a section of the story from memory, Little Li stopped reading. It had been months since he'd seen his father so animated.

> He wore a shabby felt cap and just one very thin padded jacket, with the result that he was shivering from head to foot. . . . Nor was his hand the plump red hand I remembered, but coarse and clumsy and chapped, like the bark of a pine tree. . . .
> He stood there, mixed joy and sadness on his face. His lips moved, but not a sound did he utter. Finally, assuming a respectful attitude, he said clearly:
> "Master . . . !"

I felt a shiver run through me, for I knew then what a
lamentably thick wall had grown up between us. . . .
. . . I only felt that all round me was an invisible high
wall, cutting me off from my fellows. . . .

"Such divisions are the heartbreak of China," said his father
when he became too choked with emotion to continue. Little Li,
too, was still feeling the difficulty of breaking through all the barriers. The Chinese did love their walls! The Great Wall of China,
Beijing's City Wall, the wall around the Forbidden City, the wall
around the Yak Springs compound, and the wall enclosing Willow
Courtyard—a place was hardly considered of consequence without
a proper wall. As Lu Xun had plaintively written:

I have always felt hemmed in on all sides by the Great
Wall; that wall of ancient bricks which is constantly being
reinforced. The old and the new conspire to confine us all.
When will we stop adding new bricks to the Wall?
The Great Wall of China: a wonder and a curse!

As long as life had no obvious approaching end point, one
could keep hoping that eventually something might yet happen
between two people to bring about a moment of grand epiphany, a
moment when such walls would finally be breached. But the prospect of death changed the nature of walls, because the deferred
promise of someday being able to vault over them perished forever
with a person's passing. Little Li tried to imagine returning to Willow Courtyard knowing that his father would never come through
their gate again, that henceforth there would be no more walls to
scale, not even anyone through whom he could gain access to their
shared past.

When his father drifted off to sleep that night, Little Li began
thumbing through the preface Lu had written to this famous story
collection.

When I was young I, too, had many dreams. Most of
them came to be forgotten, but I see nothing in this to
regret. For although remembering the past may make you

happy, it may sometimes also make you lonely, and there is no point in clinging in spirit to lonely bygone days. However, my trouble is that I cannot forget completely, and these stories have resulted from what I have been unable to erase from my memory.

Although his father was still able to get up to take meals and relieve himself in the chamber pot kept under his bed, even modest exertions left him breathless and wheezing. Then after attacking his lungs, renegade cancer cells opened a new front, haughtily attacking his skin and disfiguring his face, neck, and torso with scaly, discolored lesions that grew like lichen. Little Li found it unbearable to watch, knowing there was nothing he could do to arrest their advance. Alarmed by his father's deterioration, but knowing how difficult it would be to transport him to the hospital for consultation, he decided to call Dr. Song. But the only phone was near the Red Star Restaurant at the end of Big Sheep Wool Alley, where a fierce woman sat behind a table on the sidewalk with a blue plastic phone, collecting ten cents a call. As Little Li got in the line, a man in a dirty blue factory smock was screaming into the receiver.

"Wei, Wei! Hello!" he kept yelling, as if he'd no confidence in the telephone's ability to transmit the human voices electronically.

When he finally reached the head of the line and got through to the hospital switchboard, Little Li, too, had to embarrassingly bellow over and over, "Dr. Song Shaoming! Please connect me to Dr. Song Shaoming!" When he finally came on the line, Little Li announced through the crackling static, "My father seems sicker."

"Your father's what?"

"He's worse," he repeated, several decibels louder. "Could you come by and see him?"

"Of course," Dr. Song finally responded. "I'll come this evening."

As soon as Li Tongshu saw his old friend come through the door, he rallied to create an appearance of normality.

"Oh! How good it is to see you!" he said, getting out of bed.

"Please, sit down," insisted his friend, tactfully surveying him. "How've you been feeling?"

"Oh, a few aches and pains," he replied with a forced smile, but a moment later began coughing and had to sit down.

"Let's take a look," suggested Dr. Song. After examining the lesions on his friend's face and neck, and studying the incision down his chest, which was failing to heal, he listened with his stethoscope to Li Tongshu's lungs. They sounded like leaky bellows. "Are you sleeping all right?" he asked, furrowing his brows.

"So-so."

"I'll send some sleeping pills around." He smiled. After the two old friends had chatted awhile, Dr. Song stood and said, "Take care of yourself, Tongshu. I'll look in on you again very soon." He picked up his satchel and gestured for Little Li to follow him outside. There all his simulated good cheer fell away. "Your father's cancer is very aggressive," he said, unable to hide his distress. "It looks like the metastasis has entered the other lung and spread throughout his body. For the time left, there's little to do except keep him comfortable."

"Is it that bad?" asked Little Li, feeling he'd just had a blow to the head.

"He's quite sick," Dr. Song said, his voice cracking with emotion.

"How long do you think he has?"

"A month or so," he replied, turning to face Little Li directly. "I've known your father since San Francisco, and there are three things he loved: your mother, music, and you. When he lost your mother, he was left only with you and music, and when he lost music, you were all that remained. He took care of you; now you must take care of him, for both of us. And never be tempted to mistake your father's distant nature for lack of love." He reached over and cupped Little Li's cheek with his hand.

After Dr. Song departed, Little Li remained on the dark veranda, staring up into the night sky. Just as in Yak Springs, the constellations were in their fixed positions in the firmament. But human life afforded no such permanence. Only the great works of literature and music had the capacity to resist the merciless erosion of time. After two and a half centuries, the *Goldberg Variations* remained uncorrupted, providing a sliver of reassurance that somewhere, in all of life's transience, there were still things capable of resisting the unstoppable forces of change.

"What did our friend say?" his father asked as Little Li stepped back inside.

"Oh, he says you should get a lot of rest and eat and drink as much as possible," he replied in that tone of voice adults reserve for allaying the fears of small children with half-truths.

When his father finally fell asleep, Little Li gazed around their dimly lit room, his eye stopping on that place on their wall where the photo of his parents had once hung. Now all that remained was a small square of paint that was lighter in color. While he'd still been able to gaze at the photo, it had been difficult to imagine his parents as being "in love"—even to say the word "love" (爱情) in Chinese was shocking. So nakedly direct was it in its appeal to raw sentiment that it threatened not only traditional rules of propriety, decorum, and rectitude, but the equally rigid puritanical taboos of Chinese communism. The recognition that this dignified man asleep beside him had been denied love for so much of his life and was now at the end of his journey seemed unbearable. What is more, his balding pate and face had now become as transfigured by weeping sores as his life had been transfigured by inhumanity. In fact, the only thriving parts of his body now seemed to be the cancerous lesions themselves. It was agonizing to contemplate so much defeated tissue and it left Li Tongshu suffering as much from the indignity of his decay as discomfort. His face had been so embarrassingly eroded, he insisted that colleagues no longer come to visit.

Because he knew how much his father had always savored Big White Rabbit candy, a taffylike confection he himself had loved as a boy, Little Li kept a bag at his bedside. If sucking on these small white treats provided a rare moment of pleasure for Li Tongshu, so deeply had the habit of thrift been instilled in him that he never allowed himself more than a single piece a day. That a human being so well educated, who had traveled the world and once made such heavenly music should have his sensory life narrowed to a single piece of Big White Rabbit candy each day was unspeakably sad.

Whenever he pondered the idea of death as a child, Little Li had always thought of it as an abrupt, tragic shock that would leave everyone breathless with a sense of loss, not a slow-motion decay. He'd imagined death as culminating in a dramatic moment with everything peaking in a final cathartic moment when a person's accomplishments would be catalogued and celebrated. But his father's worth as a person, a musician, and a teacher would not be so acknowledged. Nor would all the wrongs that he'd been done to him ever be righted, or even acknowledged. His sacrifices and useless suffering would receive no explanation, apology, or reparation. And there would be no dramatic last-minute trumpet call, much less a moment of liberation, as in *Fidelio*. For Li Tongshu, there was only the slow, difficult business of dying.

One night, as Little Li was cleaning up after dinner, his father beckoned him to his bedside. "My father gave this to me before I left for America," he said, holding the thumb-sized ivory carving of the Yellow Emperor (黄帝) that Little Li remembered from childhood. "He's yours now." He squeezed his son's hand closed around the charm. "I am not a superstitious man, but, no matter how modernized we Chinese get, we still have a weakness for old habits, and my Yellow Emperor has always given me a sense of being watched over."

"But he didn't do a very good job of protecting you."

"Well, I can't argue there," said his father with a bittersweet smile. "Still, I like him, so take care of him for me, will you?"

"I will."

One afternoon, Granny Sun hobbled breathlessly to their door.

"There's a girl here!" she whispered.

"A what?" challenged Little Li.

"A girl's waiting outside!"

Assuming it was someone sent by Dr. Song from the hospital, Little Li went to the gate. There was Hong Hui, in a bright-red jacket, her hair braided with blue ribbons.

"I've been thinking about your father," she said, holding a thick envelope out to him.

"What's this?" he stammered.

"For him." She smiled, and then, before he could say anything more, she turned and walked away. He was shocked, not just by her unexpected appearance, but by the discipline with which she'd done what she'd come to do and then departed. Such decisiveness made him want to run after her. But how could you run after someone from whom you were running away? A note inside the envelope read:

My dear Wende:
  This is for your father, in recognition that he'll appreciate it more than anyone.
  It's so beautiful, and we must somehow make a place in our lives for such beauty.
  Hui

The note was wrapped around another tape cassette, this one imprinted with the image of a Renaissance altarpiece showing Jesus on the cross, his head wreathed in a crown of thorns and his eyes downcast in agony. Handwritten in German: "Cantata, BWV 82: *Ich habe genug,* mit Dietrich Fischer-Dieskau." Little Li went immediately to Little Wang's house.

"What happened to you?" asked his father when he burst back into their room with the cassette player.

"Father, I have some more music!" he said excitedly.

"How nice!" he replied, as if the mere mention of music was deliverance enough.

"Hong Hui knows you love Bach and brought you this." He handed his father the cassette.

"Where did she get it?" he asked.

"I don't know."

"I seem to be a magnet for musical offerings of Herr Bach's works!" He looked both mystified and appreciative.

"Shall we listen?" His father nodded.

Little Li slipped the cassette into the player. The reedy sound of an oboe over strings began filling their room, then a plaintive tenor voice entered and began weaving in and out around the oboe as if in antiphonal prayer. Li Tongshu smiled and closed his eyes. As Bach's first melancholy aria filled their room, it seemed impossible that such monstrous things had once happened right here in this very space. The tenor sang:

I've had enough,
I've taken the savior, the hope of righteousness
Into my eager arms . . .
Now I wish with joy even today,
To depart from here.

Little Li followed the text in the liner notes and was calmed by Bach's portrayal of death not as terrifying, but as a restful culmination to the arduous process of living. At the same time that the music was deeply resigned and tragic, it was also joyously uplifting, bent on removing the sting of regret and fear from life's conclusion:

Ah! Would that from the bondage of my body
The Lord might set me free.
Ah! My departure, were it now:
With joy I would say to you,
Ah, world! Now, I have had enough.

Then their darkening room filled with an angelic lullaby, beckoning all in travail to heavenly rest:

Slumber now, your eyes so weary,
Close into soft and sweet repose!
World, I will not remain here any longer,
I own no part of you
That could matter to my soul.
Here, I must with sorrow reckon,
But there, yes, there, shall I witness
Sweet repose and quiet rest.
My God! When will the lovely "now" come?
When will I journey into peace
And into the cool soil of earth,
And there, near You, rest in Your lap?
My farewells are made,
World, good night!

As the cantata ended, Li Tongshu reached over and squeezed his son's hand. Little Li had been waiting for an epiphany of words since returning home. Now such a moment had crept up on them through music, and neither of them had said a thing.

29

DEATH IN SLOW MOTION

AS WINTER winds blew down off the Mongolian steppe and engulfed Beijing in frigid clouds of yellow dust, Li Tongshu's skin became as parched and sheer as rice paper. So chapped did his lips become that Little Li had to daub them with a writing brush dipped in cooking oil. At night, his father made an ominous phlegmy rattle as he breathed. Being completely confined to bed, most of the quotidian chores he'd once performed without thinking he'd now done for the last time. Because he had such trouble swallowing, Little Li scoured markets for any soft nutritious foods, such as bean curd, yogurt, or almond jelly. Each day, Granny Sun hobbled over with a steaming bowl of soup. But Li Tongshu's brain had already signaled his body to get on with the task of dying, crying out like Bach: *"My God! When will the lovely 'now' come?"*

"When I eat, I feel I'm only feeding my disease!" he complained. One morning, as Little Li was coaxing him to eat some rice porridge, he asked point-blank, "Am I the first person you know who's died?" The question caught Little Li off guard.

"You're the first," he said hesitantly, as his mind darkened with the recognition that this man before him, his own father, would soon vanish and be irrevocably gone. The thought almost immobilized him with its finality.

"There's no pleasure in growing old and becoming ill, but here we are, so we'll go through it together," continued his father, as if proposing they go for a stroll. "Do you know what I most regret?"

"What?"

"That I'll be leaving you."

"Please, don't talk that way, Father!" protested Little Li.

"It's all right," his father soothed. Then, after a pause, "Will you fetch that lovely cricket *hulu* with the carved ivory Buddha cap that Old Chu gave you?"

"Certainly, but why?"

"I'd just like to hold it." When Little Li finally found the old *hulu* and gave it to his father, he stroked it, appreciating it as much by feel as sight. "I like it because it makes me think of you as a boy!"

Little Li vividly recalled the day they'd brought the *hulu* home, after the demise of Whiskers. Then he had an idea. During the Cultural Revolution, the markets that once sold plants, pet birds, and crickets were all closed as "relics of China's feudal past" (封建老古董). Even goldfish, once cultivated in courtyard ponds, and pigeons trained to fly with hand-carved whistles attached to their tails, which made ghostly sounds, had disappeared. However, since Deng's return, old-timers had begun to congregate again on Sundays to sell birds, crickets, and pigeons in places like Dragon Well Lake Park.

When Little Li arrived at the park early that Sunday morning, devotees were already squatting on the bare earth with their wares arrayed around them on drop cloths, watching as a grizzled peasant in a padded coat was throwing pieces of dried corn into the air for his trained magpie to fly up and grab. These aficionados were not the middle-aged bureaucrats who'd come up through party ranks or the fashion-conscious youths who gravitated to the Peace Café, but were from the older generation, who'd come of age before 1949 and still found pleasure in traditional hobbies. And no matter how inclement the weather, they spent their Sundays on their haunches, trading and selling whatever relics of these folk crafts they could find.

Spotting an old fellow with a weather-beaten face showing off his *hulu*s to a pale-complexioned man with a small boy in tow, Little Li stood unobtrusively against a tree, listening as they jabbered away in his burry Beijing dialect.

"How about this lovely pot?" the old man asked, producing a clay bowl in which fighting crickets traditionally waged combat as onlookers placed their bets.

"I'm not interested in fighters," said the pale man dismissively. "I like singers and *hulu*s."

"Ah, so that's the way it is," replied the old man. However, every time he produced a new *hulu,* the pale man shook his head and waved it away.

"Don't you have any that are older?"

"Well, perhaps we can find something!" said the old man coyly, his unshaven face breaking into a grin that revealed several missing teeth. Then, looking warily around as if he were about to commit an illicit act, he reached inside his patched greatcoat and triumphantly extracted a long-waisted *hulu* delicately etched with flowering plum trees and capped with a rooster carved in mahogany.

"Ahh!" exclaimed the pale-complexioned man, reverently inspecting it. "Not bad at all!"

"Let me see, Papa!" exclaimed the excited boy.

"Is this going to be for our little friend?" asked the old-timer, winking at the child in a way that reminded Little Li of Old Chu. The pale man nodded. The old timer reached back into his greatcoat, took out a glass jar, and shook a pair of singing (蝈蝈) crickets onto the palm of one dirt-encrusted hand. "These are for you, little friend!" He thrust a thumb up in approval.

"Papa, can I have them?" asked the boy as the two diminutive pets swung their antennae searchingly around.

"How much for the crickets and the *hulu*?" asked the pale man.

"Oh . . ." The old man sucked in a long, meditative breath. "For the boy, the crickets are free. Just give me sixty yuan for the *hulu.*"

"Here you go," said the pale man, handing over a fistful of ten-yuan notes with an eagerness suggesting he feared the old-timer might be about to reconsider the deal.

"These crickets are worthy of this *hulu*," the old man said, dropping the two insects inside and handing them to the boy. "And remember: keep them close to your heart when it's cold. If you have trouble, come back. Everyone here knows Old Meng. I never miss a Sunday."

How ironic, thought Little Li, that the man was paying for this very traditional art form, which Mao had tried to destroy, with banknotes featuring his likeness!

Only after the father and son had departed did Little Li step forward.

"Aiyyo!" the old man exclaimed when Little Li showed him his *hulu.* "One rarely sees such nice ones nowadays!"

"I'd like to buy some crickets for my father, who's ill," he announced.

"Yes, yes, when my time comes, I want to go to the sound of singing crickets," Old Meng muttered as he shook two more out of his jar. "Just take them! For such a beautiful *hulu*, crickets should never be sold."

By the time Little Li neared Big Sheep Wool Alley, body heat from his pedaling had warmed the crickets inside his coat to full voice. At home he found his father staring blankly up at the ceiling, but as soon as he heard the singing of crickets, his mind sharpened.

"Aha!" he exclaimed with a smile. "Have we some new friends?"

"How did you know?"

"I may not be able to play piano, but I can still hear. So, you don't . . ." Unexpectedly his voice trailed off, like the fading signal of a distant transmitter. He'd fallen asleep.

As spring approached, Li Tongshu had to be spoon-fed. Desperate to coax more fluid into his parched body, Little Li bought a box of plastic straws. However, his father did not even have the strength, or perhaps it was the will, to suck fluid all the way up the stem. Caring for him in such intimate ways made Little Li feel almost physically linked to his father, as if their circulatory systems had been conjoined. Every time his father winced or uttered a half suppressed moan of pain, Little Li felt as if an ice cold dagger had been plunged into his heart.

One night, while sleeping fitfully, Little Li was awakened by the sound of singing crickets and was surprised to see his father's slender arms waving in the air above his supine body, as if they were conducting a phantom orchestra. "Listen!" he pronounced with penetrating clarity. "Never forsake it, my son!"

"Never forsake what, Father?"

"Music. Listen, there's music everywhere!" His eyes glowed with rapture. "Shhhh! Don't tell anyone about our crickets. They might take them away!"

"Oh, Father!"

"Aren't you going to America, my boy?" he asked, looking his son straight in the eye.

"Yes, but I . . ."

His father gave an ecstatic smile and resumed his phantom conducting. But then, like birds shot out of the air in mid-flight, his hands dropped, his head sagged back onto his pillow, and his mouth fell ajar. Little Li grabbed one of his father's clawlike hands and squeezed it, as if pressure might coax him back from the abyss.

"Father, are you still here?" he cried out, frantically shaking him as if just trying to awaken him from slumber. "Come back! Don't go! Not yet!" He pressed an ear to his father's chest, but all he could hear was the systolic pounding of his own heart in his temples. Letting out a wail of anguish, he threw his arms around his father's bony shoulders. How could it be that only a moment before there'd been life and now there was none? Where did it go? How could such a monumental thing become extinguished so suddenly, completely, and eternally, leaving only an inert body behind?

It took him a few moments to realize that this morning would be different from all the other mornings in his life. Leaning over his father's still-warm body, he kissed his waxy brow. Then he felt a sudden fierce thirst, and poured himself a cup of hot water. It seemed unfair that the water in their thermos would stay warm longer than the body of his father. Possessed by a sudden need for human company, he stumbled across the courtyard to Granny Sun's room.

"He's gone" was all he could get out when she opened the door.

"So . . . his time finally came," she said, drawing him inside.

"What do I do now?"

"In *The Analects,* Confucius tells us:

> *When parents are alive, observe the proper rites and*
> *serve them. When they die, observe the proper rites. In*
> *burying them, observe the proper rites. In sacrifices later*
> *observe the proper rites.*
> 生事之礼死葬之以礼祭 之以礼

"How does one *'observe the proper rites'* now?" he asked numbly.

"A son must first mourn his father, and then strive to follow the path of his uprightness. It will not bring him back, but it will help keep his memory part of you."

Holding her arm, he led her across the courtyard. From the old wisteria vine his father had so lovingly cultivated back to life, he plucked one of the first grapelike bunches of purple blossoms just then beginning to open. When he'd helped Granny Sun up the steps, they entered the room and stood arm in arm in the stillness beside Li Tongshu's bed.

"Go to him," she said.

Little Li leaned over and clasped his father's ruined hands in his own one last time. They were so unnaturally cold and stiff that after crossing them on his chest he was glad to let them go.

"We must say goodbye to the soul of this good man," said Granny Sun. Kneeling down with great effort, she began chanting a Buddhist sutra. Then Little Li gently laid the lavender wisteria buds across his father's gnarled knuckles.

30

BURIAL

AS HE, Dr. Song, and Granny Sun approached the gray brick smokestack of the Babaoshan Crematorium, Little Li looked forward to having the tumors and disfiguring lesions that had ravaged his father's body consumed by fire, and the purified ashes placed in the lacquer box that was Dr. Song's parting gift to his friend. On its shimmering black top he'd written the Latin inscription "*Sunt lacrimae rerum et mentem mortalia tangunt.*"

"Where does this come from?" asked Little Li.

"One day in California we visited the UC Berkeley campus, and your father and mother found a copy of Virgil's *Aeneid* in a used-book store," remembered Dr. Song wistfully. "After they'd read it aloud together, they gave it to me, and your father had copied out this line inside the back cover."

"What does it mean?"

" 'There are tears at the heart of things and the burdens of mortality touch men's souls.' "

Little Li tried to imagine his parents in that California bookstore. Instead, he saw them in a swirl of clouds, as if in heaven. Perhaps his father's religious belief did have some benefits: at least he could be reunited with his wife in heaven. Still, unlike all those years when his father was just in exile, now—even though his clothes still hung in the wardrobe, the jar in which he'd saved soap scraps still sat above the sink, his shoes still waited by the door, and several half-read books still lay beside his bed—he'd never use them again. They were all accessories now, as useless as objects in a museum.

Because Li Tongshu had been designated a patriotic "returnee to the Motherland" (回归祖国), he technically had the right to be laid to rest in the third tier of Babaoshan Revolutionary Cemetery

(八宝山革命公墓), the PRC's most honored place of rest. However, Little Li could not find the document necessary for burial there, and instead decided to take his father's ashes to their family home in Heze County, Shandong Province, and bury them beside his own father who'd studied in Germany in the 1920s and become a professor at Shandong University in the provincial capital. But after being attacked during the Anti-Rightist Campaign in 1958, he was sent in disgrace back to his village, Gaozhuang. Elderly and alone, he'd survived there until the Cultural Revolution, when he was attacked anew by Red Guards and died of neglect there in a "cowshed." Li Tongshu had not learned of his death until a year later, and was filled with remorse at being unable to say goodbye. Now death would reunite father and son.

When he'd packed the lacquer box, his cricket, and a few articles of clothing in a shoulder bag, Little Li headed to the train station. Since Mao's agricultural "people's communes" were being disbanded, peasants freed from collectivized rural life were flooding Chinese cities in search of work. Known as "the floating population" (流动人口), these internal migrants jammed terminals, so that the only places not packed with travelers were often those small circumferences immediately around the green-and-yellow cast-iron waste receptacles comically cast in the shape of cuddly pandas with mouths yawning open. Despite tireless official appeals against public expectoration, peasant fusiliers found these open-mouthed pandas irresistible targets, and as they passed, they fired endless projectiles at them, as if they were spittoons. By and large, they displayed the accuracy of well-trained snipers. However, sometimes even the deftest rural marksman missed the bull's-eye, and the result was a slippery no-man's-land around each smiling panda that begged a wide berth.

As he joined the unruly crush of passengers surging down the platform for his train, Little Li passed the lace-curtained windows of a first-class "soft sleeper" (软卧) coach, the top tier of China's three-class rail system, which had endured even through the most fevered periods of class warfare. Inside, a group of party officials were peacefully sipping tea and gazing impassively out at the "people," whom they purported to represent, as they stampeded past. The adjacent first-class compartments were filled with foreigners absorbed in observing the tableau of ordinary Chinese struggling by them toward the lower-class coaches. Only when he heard a conductor cry out "Number Three!" did Little Li realize he'd arrived at his own coach, a "hard sleeper" (硬卧), in the middle tier.

When he finally lay on his wooden bunk, with his shoulder bag under his head and his father's ashes and crickets beside him, he couldn't help thinking about Little Hong. He tried to distract himself by recalling his childhood trips to Heze, where everything but the blue sky and green fields partook of some tonal variation of the region's yellow-brown earth. Even the muddy waters of rivers and ponds came in the same hues. The dun color of the Yellow River, the burnt umber of the tamped-earth walls, and the dusty brown of roof tiles all bespoke of ancient earthbound China, where soil, dust, and mud were constant human companions. In wintertime, when the rutted earth froze as hard as steel, the land became so bleak it was difficult to imagine it would ever give forth life again. And yet, each spring, it somehow revived, and fields of colorful peonies, for which Heze was famed, sprang forth from the exhausted earth in a florid profusion of pinks, reds, whites, and yellows.

Although Little Li was only nine when he last visited, he knew that the way into the hearts of locals was to say things like, "Oh yes! In the capital, everyone's heard of how Heze's famous peony roots fortify health." He'd quickly figured out how to add a little extra authority to his voice by saying "in the capital," as if he were speaking for all Beijing. In Beijing, adults didn't bother heeding a boy, but out here, when he described the Great Hall of the People, the Forbidden City, the Summer Palace, or even the Beijing Railroad Station, people were so enthralled that he could imagine himself as of some importance. Such nostalgic remembrances made it seem right now to be bringing his father's ashes back here.

After a sleepless night, at dawn his train pulled into Zhengzhou. Little Li boarded a local bus and instantly nodded off. He did not awaken until they were laboring up a dike along the Yellow River. On treks in Qinghai, he'd loved to throw sticks into small mountain streams, knowing they were tributaries of the mighty river and would eventually be carried downstream through Mongolia, northwestern China, and across the North China Plain to the sea. But when he looked across the muddy, serpentine river now, it was not easy to conjure up those sparkling freshets that cascaded down from the Tibetan Plateau's snowcapped peaks. And as they drew nearer to Gaozhuang, everything looked much more run-down than he remembered riding from there on a donkey cart as an excited boy.

Suddenly the bus squealed to a halt at a roadside snack shop. He disembarked and asked an elderly woman manning the shop how to get to Gaozhuang.

"There!" she croaked, pointing an arthritic finger toward a path through a wheat field.

"How far is it?" he asked. She waved him off as if this were privileged information.

Not until he actually entered the village did he recognize anything. But the old town well had not changed at all. And then there he was, standing before his grandfather's house; it had a large hole in its tile roof and the front door drooped from its frame. Just behind it was Old Gao's house. If it hadn't been for a single sway-backed sow asleep in a pigsty out front, he would have assumed this, too, was abandoned. And, when he knocked, there was no response. He gave a louder knock and called out. The only sound was that of the oinking sow.

"Big Uncle Gao! [高大叔]!" he cried out.

"Eh?" someone muttered inside.

"Big Uncle Gao!"

"All right, all right! My ears are no good!" a voice wheezed. A latch drew, the door creaked open, and a face with a wispy beard appeared.

"It's me! Li Wende, son of Li Tongshu!" Old Gao peered suspiciously out. "I'm the boy from Beijing who played with Big Mountain. My grandfather was Li Deming (李德明)."

"Ahhhh!" Old Gao finally replied, his face dissolving into a toothless grin. "I'm remembering now! Big Mountain's little friend, is it?"

"Is he still here?"

"He hasn't yet found a wife." Old Gao sighed. "It's hard for us poor peasants."

"Then he and I still have something in common," replied Little Li, forcing a laugh as the old man opened the door. He was now so stooped that he barely came to Little Li's shoulders.

"I must look at you," Old Gao announced, surveying Little Li from head to toe with milky eyes. "So—you've become a man, eh, Young Master Li [李少爷]?"

"No, no! Call me Little Li, like before," he protested.

"A handsome young man you've become, too, Young Master Li," said Old Gao, chuckling, and disregarding his protest. "And how's your father?"

"He passed away, and I've come to bury his ashes." He took the lacquer box from his bag and held it in both hands.

"So he's gone," he said and sighed. "Ahhh well . . ."

"Will you help me?" Little Li continued without allowing him to finish expressing his condolence.

"Of course," replied the old man. He took the lacquer box to the dusty counter at the back of the room, which had once served as their ancestral altar, and set it down next to a brass chalice filled with sand and sticks of burned incense. "Come in and have some 'white tea' [白茶]!" he urged, using the peasant euphemism for hot water. Even though the house was ramshackle and dark, Little Li found it welcoming.

Dusk was falling by the time Big Mountain came through the gate with a mattock over his shoulder. He'd grown into a tall, wiry man, but had the same bean-shaved, ringworm-scarred scalp, patched pants, and peasant straw hat hanging around his neck. But when he saw someone in city clothes inside, he hesitated in the doorway.

"It's your old friend from Beijing, Li Wende," said Old Gao. His son stared blankly. "Don't be so simpleminded! Have you forgotten those times you spent together as boys?"

"Oh!" he finally gasped, becoming even more self-conscious.

"What a 'dumb egg' [笨蛋] I have for a son! Old Gao chided. "Come! Come inside!"

"Young Master Li," Big Mountain finally mumbled, putting his hands together and giving a bow that sent a shiver of sadness through Little Li.

"How have you been all these years?" he asked, trying to sound jovial, even though he was pierced to the quick by his childhood friend's timorous deference.

"We're all right, Young Master Li," replied Big Mountain, continuing to stand in the doorway. "Now, with apologies, I must feed the pig." He backed out, as if turning around to exit might constitute an insult to Little Li's exalted station. All Little Li could think was how sad it was that, half a century after Lu Xun's melancholy story about the dynamics of China's class system, things were so little changed.

After they'd eaten, Little Li borrowed Old Gao's pocketknife and whittled a cross from a tree branch he found outside. They slept on the same "heated platform" (炕) he'd used as a boy, but, with Old Gao snoring beside him, Little Li hardly caught a wink. In the morning, the old man mumbled something in local dialect to his still-speechless son, who went out the door without replying. He returned with two bruised apples, a can of mandarin oranges with a faded label, three white cloth armbands, and a pack of "spirit money" (纸钱) burned to aid the souls of the deceased to pass through the courts of hell on their way to Western Paradise. Once he'd delivered these to his father, he resumed his place at the doorway.

"All right, we'll go," Old Gao finally pronounced. Big Mountain shouldered a mattock and a spade and they set off single-file along a narrow path through a wheat field that, against the cool, gray sky, was so intensely green it almost hurt Little Li's eyes. The windblown snatches of disco drifting out from the village were an ironic musical epitaph for Li Tongshu. When they reached a small copse of poplar trees that stood like an island in the middle of the surrounding ocean of green winter wheat, Old Gao stopped.

"This is your grandfather's grave," he said, pointing to a mound covered with weeds. "When he died, your father could not come, so we summoned a yin-yang master from the next village to find the most auspicious site to bury him."

Little Li knelt and began pulling up the weeds that had overgrown the grave mound. Then Big Mountain began swinging his mattock into the unyielding clay. Little Li was filled with gratitude for the goodness of these two steadfast people, for to have had to dig his father's grave alone would have been agonizingly lonely.

"Enough!" Old Gao finally commanded. Big Mountain grunted, set down his mattock, and wiped the sweat from his brow with the back of his sleeve. It was starting to rain when Little Li knelt again to place the lacquer box in the freshly dug hole. As its perfectly polished top became flecked with jewel-like drops of water, he pushed the lead-heavy clods of earth over it with his bare hands, feeling that each one severed him a little more irrevocably from his past. When the last black edge of the box had disappeared, Old Gao knelt and began chanting in the guttural local dialect:

When you were alive, you attended your father's grave.
Now your son will attend to yours.
When you were alive, we did not weep for you.
Now we lament your passing.
We pray to Guanyin for mercy,
And for your safe passage to life beyond.
May your spirit soon rest in peace.

Then he set the two apples and the can of oranges before the grave and, using his plastic cigarette lighter, lit the spirit money.

"Your father never much cared about money, did he?" said Old Gao, smiling. "But we're sending him to the afterlife with some anyway. Who knows what he may need there?"

Little Li stood the wooden cross he'd carved on top of the mound and then kowtowed (磕头), weeping not just for his father, but for the uncertainty of his own life and China.

Little Li recalled almost nothing about his trip home. Numb with grief and loneliness, he arrived back at Willow Courtyard and collapsed into bed, where he fell into a troubled sleep filled with phantasms of a teasingly naked Little Hong watching him coquettishly from on high.

When a strange tap-tapping interrupted his reverie, he opened his eyes. It sounded like a windblown branch knocking against the window. Still not sure whether he was asleep or awake, he lay there listening. The tapping sounded again. He got warily out of bed and tiptoed to the window. In the darkness, he saw a silhouette outside on the veranda.

"Little Li!" came a voice that sent a prickle of fear down his spine.

"Who's there?" he challenged fearfully.

"It's me."

"Who?"

"Hong Hui!"

As soon as he opened the door, she threw her arms around his neck and kissed his face. "I am so sorry about your father," she said. "So sorry!"

Still unsure whether he was dreaming or awake, he fell with her onto his bed.

Afterward, as they lay silently side by side, he was on the verge of telling her about his trip to Shandong when she slid out from under his quilt and started to dress, the paleness of her naked body glowing in the darkness like a marble statue. Unsure what to do, he just watched. Then she leaned over, kissed him, and, as quietly as she'd come, she departed.

PART
FIVE

31

ESCAPE

WHEN LITTLE LI arrived at the Pan Am check-in counter at Capital International Airport, an exasperated agent in a powder-blue uniform was begging the scrum of anxious San Francisco–bound passengers to form a line.

"There's no need to worry!" she pleaded. "Everyone gets an assigned seat!"

Although she had Asian features, her spoken Chinese was so halting that most passengers could hardly understand what she was saying and continued anxiously pushing toward the counter. So much adversity had dashed so many hopes for so long, few trusted any promises.

"Jeez, this is just like the proverbial last flight out of Shanghai!" a voice complained in English behind Little Li. "If these people ever get loose on the world, watch out!" He turned to see a bulky Caucasian woman wearing the kind of conical straw hat favored by southern Chinese peasants; she was marooned beside an enormous pile of luggage with her husband, who wore a blue Mao jacket festooned with a brace of Mao buttons pinned to his chest like so many flies hooked onto a fisherman's vest.

When Little Li finally stepped onto the Pan Am jumbo jet, he had the sensation of crossing a forbidden international frontier. The plane's air-conditioned cabin, with its rows of bright-colored seats accessorized with linen headrests, pillows, and blankets wrapped in plastic, made crowded, dusty Beijing seem already far away. But once he'd taken his seat beside a window, he could not stop worrying that something might still intervene to prevent him from getting away. It even seemed to him that the two podlike engines hanging beneath the plane's silver wing were too tenuously attached to the plane's aluminum skin to ever get it off the ground.

To calm himself, he shut his eyes until he felt the huge aircraft jerk and begin rolling backward. As its engines started and they began taxiing, he felt that his own consciousness was somehow required to assist the enormous machine to get airborne. It was not until it finally roared down the runway, trembled, and climbed into the sky that he was able to believe he was, at last, winging toward "America," "the Beautiful Country" (美国). The use of these two Chinese characters had always struck him as ironic: even though the party disparaged America, it continued to use this admiring Chinese translation.

As they flew over Beijing, Tiananmen Square, the Great Hall of the People, Chairman Mao Memorial Hall, and the Forbidden City had all been shrunken to such a toylike scale that he was, at last, able to believe he'd broken free of the fierce gravity of this labyrinthine city's tenacious grip. A short while later, he saw a flash of light below: it was the sun reflecting off the Yellow River as it debouched into the Yellow Sea, after carving its way across the North China Plain like a giant vein of quicksilver. As the shadow of their plane glided across the river and lanced over the coastline to the open, white-capped ocean, the recognition that he'd finally escaped his natal land filled him with unexpected pangs of sadness.

Just then, the steward came down the aisle with a cart of newspapers, offering dailies from Hong Kong, Japan, and the United States, but none from China. The *People's Daily* was admittedly a turgid propaganda organ, but wasn't reading it nevertheless essential for understanding the most populous nation on earth? The closest thing was the English-language *South China Morning Post* from Hong Kong. He took a copy, but was immediately struck by how un-Chinese it was. Many "Hong Kong fellow countrymen" (香港同胞), as the party proprietarily referred to residents of the British colony mentioned inside, had adopted Westernized given names: Sidney Wow, Z. Greenstreet Kan, Tweety Yuk, Bosco Peng, Ringo Yip, Nectar Dong, Adonis Chew, and even a Rimsky Kwok, the latter presumably the offspring of a Russian-classical-music enthusiast. Such emphatically Occidental names were a far cry from those he'd wanted to adopt during the Cultural Revolution. But now he wondered if he, too, shouldn't have fortified himself against anonymity in America by adopting such a name. When his father was in the United States, he'd taken the name Franklin, after Benjamin Franklin and Franklin Delano Roosevelt, but he'd dropped it upon returning home in 1950, lest he be accused of having become a "fake foreign devil" (假洋鬼子). And he'd temporarily taken the absurd name, Lancelot, in Yak Springs.

When Little Li visited the plane's lavatory, it smelled so unnaturally sweet that he felt embarrassed by China's filthy squat toilets, with their broken water fixtures and trails of muddy wetness streaming out into carpeted hallways like river deltas. Glancing in the mirror, staring back at him he saw an expectant young man with a square jaw, slightly sad but penetrating brown eyes, a prominent nose, and a high forehead crowned by a shock of unruly dark hair. His ragged haircut, tentative expression, and shapeless suit jacket made him feel insoluble in this new American world. While trying to smooth out some creases in his trousers, he felt the key to Willow Courtyard in his pocket. He took it out and turned it over several times. The years of use had worn the five stars on its round brass head almost smooth. Even in Qinghai, he'd faithfully kept this key as a kind of amulet, and when he arrived back home and found it still fit their gate lock, he was overjoyed. But now that his father had died, he'd left China, and their house assignment had been voided, what further use did this key have to him? Indeed, might it not just serve as an irksome reminder of a place he wanted to forget? Noticing a slot above the sink marked "Razor Blade Disposal," he impetuously pushed the key in. It made a satisfying clinking sound as it fell.

"How're we doin' today?" a flight attendant pushing a beverage cart inquired when he'd regained his seat. "Coffee, tea, Sprite, or Diet Coke?" she asked, with the flat intonation of a chanting monk.

"I beg your pardon?" he asked.

"You must be from China, so let me get you some nice hot tea?" she interjected wth synthetic cheerfulness. Before he could respond, she'd poured steaming water into a foam cup, plopped a tea bag into it, unlatched his tray table, and set the drink before him. As she moved on to the next row, she left a lingering scent in her wake that was even more intensely sweet than the lavatory. A short while later, she returned pushing a meal cart, and unceremoniously set a lunch tray on his table. With its little plastic compartments for each food item, it was a masterpiece of organization, but the food was not very tasty. He took out his *hulu* from the inside pocket of his suit jacket and was reassured to see that his diminutive friend was still expectantly waving its antennae around. Although he'd originally not intended to bring his cricket, when he left Willow Courtyard he hadn't known what else to do with this singular pet that had so faithfully serenaded him through the last days and nights of his father's life, so at the last moment he tucked it into his pocket. Now he masticated a bit of lettuce and dropped it into the *hulu*, then watched as this last living link with his homeland grabbed it with its mandibles. At that moment, he heard a buzzing above the whine of the engines that sounded like an electrical short. A fly, careening around in drunken loops, landed right on the seat facing an American man sitting just across the aisle. Shaking his head with distaste, he rolled up a newspaper and swatted it dead.

"And they told me there were no flies in Red China!" he said, looking at Little Li as if he were somehow responsible for this Chinese intrusion into American airspace.

When they circled over Tokyo, there were so many pinpricks of light in the darkness below, it looked as if someone had kicked an open fire, showering the ground with sparks. Unlike Beijing's airport, the tarmac here was crowded with rows of colorful jumbo jets from all around the world. The only plane from China bore a lackluster inscription on its grime-streaked fuselage, "C.A.A.C." (Civil Aviation Administration of China).

Inside, the airport's escalators and glittering duty-free stores were a far cry from the somnambulant airport shops in Beijing. But what impressed him most were the Japanese toilets, each with a little motor pulling a sanitized plastic cover around its seat after every use and its own dashboard of buttons and dials that, when pressed, sent jets of warm water squirting up one's crack. Alas, once on, he couldn't figure out how to turn the jet off, and when he stood up to get a better look at the control panel, the geyser continued shooting into the air. Only after he indiscriminately pressed every button was he able to subdue the mutinous gusher, but he was already drenched.

After his next flight took off, an attendant confusing him with someone else set a steaming cup of coffee down on his table. Although he did not like its bitter taste, the sensation of drinking something hot felt good. However, ten minutes later, he experienced a feeling akin to being electrocuted so that even when the cabin lights dimmed, he was unable to fall asleep for the longest time.

The next thing he knew, he was awakened by a noise sounding like a squeaking wheel. It took him a few moments to realize that it was his cricket. Warmed by the heat of his dream-addled body, it had begun to sing. The businessman in the seat across the aisle had also awakened and was looking at him suspiciously. Embarrassed, he unbuttoned his jacket so his cricket would cool off and quiet down. Then, unable to fall back asleep, he raised his window screen. Dawn was just beginning to streak the eastern sky with robin's-egg blue, turning the plane wing a ghostly silver.

As the cabin lights blinked back on and meal carts reappeared, Little Li had no appetite for breakfast. And when the pilot announced they'd be landing in half an hour, rather than looking forward to arrival, he now wished only to remain suspended forever in this airborne cocoon, gliding serenely over the pastoral California coastline etched by a bank of fog rolling in from the sea.

"Ladies and gentlemen, if you look off the port side you'll see two red ears sticking up through the fog," the pilot announced. "Those are the towers of the beautiful Golden Gate Bridge and we here at Pan Am want to welcome you to lovely San Francisco. We'll be touching down in about fifteen minutes, so please buckle up."

Rolling languorously like a great whale in the ocean, the huge 747 banked, and did not level off again until it was gliding over yacht harbors and housing developments bejeweled with aquamarine swimming pools set in emerald lawns like turquoise stones. As they descended, he felt as unstable as a chemical compound that loses its solid state at sea level. Then there was a sudden thumping and the plane's wheels hit the runway. Even as other passengers prepared to disembark, Little Li stayed seated. Only after almost everyone else had filed past did he stand up, fetch his satchel from the overhead bin, and step out of the plane into America.

On the way to passport control, passengers were directed down a narrow corridor flanked by a plate-glass wall behind which a throng of people stood waiting to greet new arrivals. As silent as marine creatures in an aquarium tank, they peered expectantly through the partition, coming alive with smiles and waves when they spotted their loved ones. Just as Little Li passed, a pretty young woman with a blond ponytail sticking out the back of a

San Francisco Giants baseball cap broke into a glowing smile. She placed both of her hands flat up against the glass as a bearded passenger in blue jeans and a red parka ran over, slid his own palms up the glass until they matched hers. Then, with comic panache, she pressed her lips to the pane and kissed him. All that was left behind after they'd both turned to go was the red lipstick imprint of her kiss. If the sight of these lovers went unnoticed by others, it did not go overlooked by Little Li. There would be no one to greet him, because not a single person in San Francisco knew he was arriving to start a new life.

32

JUST AS a passport-control agent signaled Little Li to approach, his cricket began vocalizing. His first impulse was to drop out of the line, but before he could do so, the agent impatiently commanded, "Okay, pal, let's keep the line moving."

"Hello," Little Li said, his lips trembling as the chirping grew louder.

"Documents, please!" demanded the agent without looking up. After studying Little Li's visa for a moment, he furrowed his brow, looked up, and called over to his colleague. "Hey, Manuel! You hearin' somethin'?"

"Yeah!" muttered the other agent. "Probably having trouble with the A/C system again."

Reaching as unobtrusively as he could into his jacket pocket, Little Li gave his *hulu* such a vigorous shaking that he could feel his cricket's chitinous body smack up against its walls; mercifully, it fell silent. Why had he brought along this relic that could sabotage his entry into the New World? Hadn't his whole intention in coming here been to put his past and China's backwardness behind him?

"What countries you comin' from, sir?"

"China."

"And how much money you bringing in?"

"Eight hundred dollars." The agent looked up as if in surprise.

"And what brings you to San Francisco?"

"Relatives and school." Telltale beads of perspiration were forming on his brow.

"Okay, buddy," the agent announced, stamping his passport and sliding it back across the counter. "You're good to go."

He walked out of the customs area under a red, white, and blue banner over the doorway:

WELCOME TO THE UNITED STATES OF AMERICA
We hold these truths to be self-evident, that all men are
    created equal,
that they are endowed by their Creator with certain
    unalienable Rights,
that among these are Life, Liberty and the pursuit of
    Happiness.
The U.S. Declaration of Independence, July 4, 1776

Were these rights guaranteed to visitors and immigrants as well as citizens? Until the automatic steel door that ushered arrivals out to the lobby snapped shut behind him, Little Li had been tempted to imagine that if he could only *get* to this fabled land, like a magic elixir, America would bring about an instant change in him. But now that he was actually here, his scuffed shoes, shapeless suit jacket, battered satchel, and synthetic-leather wallet with so few U.S. dollars in it that even the passport agent had looked askance made such a transformation seem far from automatic. Outside, where others were queuing up for taxis, he set his things down and consoled himself that at least he spoke English. He was trying to decide what to do next when a tall, red faced man, as large as a walking side of beef, came up beside him.

"Could you tell me how to get into San Francisco?" Little Li asked.

"Y'all in the right spot," said the man, who was wearing a white shirt, a purple necktie, and a blue blazer with a jaunty red handkerchief blooming from his breast pocket. He pointed to a metal sign, "s.f. airporter," and then stared at Little Li for a moment. "Now, I'm jus' guessin'," he continued in a drawl, "but are y'all from Japan?"

"Well, no, actually . . ."

"So—where ya from, son? Veetnam?"

"Actually, China."

"China? Which one?"

'What do you mean?"

"Well, don't you guys have two Chinas over there, one goin' for Chiang Kai-shek and one for Mao Zedong?" He pronounced the latter, "Mousey Dung."

"I'm from Beijing."

"Red China, huh?"

"I guess so."

"Well, howdy anyway!" He rocked back on the heels of his Western boots and broke into a laugh that triggered a phlegmy cough. As he lit a cigarette, he kept looking at Little Li as if trying to make up his mind about something. Then, squinting against the smoke curling out of his mouth, he said, "Ya know, I fought you guys over there in Korea, Yalu River, 1951."

"You mean the People's Liberation Army?" corrected Little Li.

"Whatever y'all wanna call 'em," replied the side of beef with a sudden hardness. Just then, a black Town Car pulled up. "Well, welcome to the Free World, partner!" he ended.

When the S.F. Airporter bus finally pulled up, only three people got on and Little Li sat alone. As they merged onto the freeway, they joined bumper-to-bumper traffic that stretched away in both directions as far as Little Li could see. Whereas in China buses were crowded but the streets were empty, here the opposite was true. And whereas in China cars came in subdued shades of gray, green, or black, here they shimmered in every color of the rainbow, looking almost as if they were freshly painted each night. As tired as he was, he found every detail fascinating, especially the illuminated commercial billboards and signs along the freeway that towered over gas stations, fast-food restaurants, and hotels like garish long-stemmed flowers.

And then, as they crested a hill, there was San Francisco. The sun was just emerging across the bay from behind a soft white bank of morning fog, turning the city's high-rise buildings a fiery orange. Connecting the city's chimerical center to the rest of the country, like a giant vascular system, was a tangle of freeways, overpasses, and off-ramps that were humbling because he knew there was not one Chinese city that could compare with this second-tier American urban center. Nor had China recently produced anything of enduring cultural or spiritual significance. Yet all across the country were monuments to its "greatness," to the "Great Leader," "the Great Helmsman," "the Great Teacher," and all his "great" political movements, like "the Great Leap Forward" and "the Great Proletarian Cultural Revolution." But, then, Chinese leaders were omnipotent enough to call things anything they wanted. As the ancient expression went, high leaders could even "point at a deer and call it a horse" (指鹿为马). It was true that when foreigners walked on the Great Wall, toured the Forbidden City, or visited the entombed terra-cotta soldiers outside Xian, they left with a new respect for the greatness of China's millennial civilization. But what among China's recent accomplishments truly deserved the adjective "great" (伟大)? He could think of nothing.

At the seedy Greyhound bus terminal, Little Li stepped down into a roar of traffic and construction. Unlike in China, where pedestrians often shuffled lackadaisically through public spaces with their hands clasped behind their backs, here Americans were striding purposefully forward, their arms churning, like competitive runners. So lost did he suddenly feel that he reluctantly decided to seek out his aunt, not because he felt any real kinship with her, but because, like a freezing man, he knew he had to keep moving or perish. He hadn't been in touch since thanking her for the affidavit of support, but he could, at least, express his appreciation in person and inform her of his father's passing. In anticipation, he'd brought a piece of his father's calligraphy: 无中生有, "To make something out of nothing." The phrase came from *The Thirty-six Stratagems* (三十六计), a series of ancient strategies each involving a story in which some kind of deceit, deception, or artifice was used to gain advantage, if not victory, over an adversary. Little Li had never been sure what his father meant to convey in calligraphing this particular scroll, but he suspected that he was alluding ironically to the duplicitousness of Mao's revolution, which had sought to create the appearance of leadership, purpose, strength, and accomplishment where there was little but bravado, illusion, weakness, and absurdity. Whatever his father's intention, Little Li was glad he'd brought something as a gift. After all, his aunt was his only living relative, and he'd be mortified if she viewed him as just a penurious family member arriving from Red China to beg for charity.

With everyone speeding by so resolutely, even asking somebody for directions seemed like an imposition. One man was reading a newspaper as he plowed down the crowded sidewalk; another had his head lowered, as if he were bucking a strong headwind. Finally, he saw a stylishly dressed woman carrying a shopping bag, waiting for a traffic light. But just as he was about to approach her, she sped across the street, leaving him feeling as sluggish as a logy carp among sleek trout.

"Excuse me," he finally asked an unshaven man hawking newspapers at the corner. "I'm looking for Vallejo Street. Could you . . ."

"Yeah, it's near Chinatown," the man replied without looking up from the handful of bills he was counting. "Go up to Union Square and through the Stockton Street Tunnel."

When Little Li emerged from the tunnel, he unexpectedly found himself back in an Asian world full of shoppers laden with bulging plastic bags. As he walked, he passed through myriad different field of smell, of frying fat wafting from restaurant fans, the overripe sweetness of fruit-and-vegetable stands, and the reek of seafood emanating from a sidewalk fish market that displayed all manner of marine creatures on beds of crushed ice. The streets were crowded with double-parked trucks unloading crates of greens, bins of fruit, cages of live poultry, and wooden boxes of goods from Singapore, Taiwan, and Hong Kong imprinted with "long-form characters" (繁体字) used only outside of China.

"Can you tell me how to get to Vallejo Street?" he asked in Mandarin of an elderly Chinese gentleman basking on a stoop in the morning sun like a lizard; the man erupted in an unintelligible southern dialect. Next he tried a man emerging from an antiques store who was wearing a double-breasted suit and a fedora that made him look as if he'd just stepped out of a 1940s Shanghai spy film. But this man just stared at him and walked on. Even the faces of the Chinese here were different. The window display at the Yuk Fat Realty Co. featured a poster for "The Miss Chinatown U.S.A. Beauty Pageant," which showed four smiling contestants decked out in rhinestone-studded tiaras and form-fitting, sequined *qipao* (旗袍), a traditional style of dress long banned in Beijing as too sexually provocative. Each contestant listed a hobby: "Michelle Gee: Ballroom dancing"; "Brenda Chuck: Young Christians Club"; "Doreen Yap: Playing the clarinet"; and "Suzanne Leandre Chew: Football cheerleader." With their stylized smiles, glossy red lips, and heavy makeup, these beauty queens were the antithesis of the beaming, pink-cheeked, pigtailed female comrades joyously driving tractors or clutching sheaves of golden wheat to their chaste proletarian bosoms on posters back home. Though these young women of the diaspora were "Chinese," there was something about their "Chinese-ness"—the way they spoke, dressed, held themselves— that hardly seemed to come from the same culture and race at all.

As he walked on, the files of gleaming parked cars, some still radiating an almost animal warmth from under their hoods, modern-day steeds just waiting to be ridden off again. The idea of someday owning such a vehicle struck him as more than sublime.

Before calling on his aunt, he paused at Vallejo Street, outside the August Moon Bakery. The fog had lifted, a refreshing breeze was blowing off the bay, and a sun-filled sky was bathing the street in a pristine light that made San Francisco seem every bit the fabled city of his childhood fantasies. Suddenly he had an intuition that he was being watched, and he turned around. Several customers inside the bakery were, in fact, staring at him, out the front window, as if they suspected his loitering was a prelude to an antisocial act. Hoping to appear less derelict, he moved to where a huge four-tiered wedding cake was on display, to examine it as if he were a prospective groom. This meter-high confection was made up of four layers supported by plastic Doric columns set on crystalline sugar capitals, each rising layer progressively smaller in diameter. The bottom layer was ringed with waves of fluffy pink frosting dotted with white lotus blossoms, while the top layer featured two small figurines—the bride resplendent in a flowing wedding gown, the groom decked out in tails and top hat—both standing ankle-deep in a snowfield of white frosting inside a miniature Chinese pagoda made of meringue. Some attentive soul had rendered their ambiguous facial features more Asian with a felt-tipped pen. Suddenly he felt imbecilic for wasting his time staring at this cake and unzipped his satchel, took out his father's scroll, and started up the hill to his aunt's building. He'd decided that, after extending a greeting, informing his aunt that his father had passed away, and then presenting the scroll, he'd simply take his leave. It was a matter of face that his relatives not conclude he'd come because he wanted or needed something. His plan was to get a job for a few months, make some money, and then apply to a music school.

Spotting a nameplate, "The Dudley Woos," on an outside brace of mailboxes, he rang the bell. Once they buzzed him in, as he approached their first-floor apartment he could hear the muffled sound of a TV. He knocked. A high-pitched yapping erupted.

"That's a good girl," a rasping female voice crooned as the door opened—secured by a gold-plated safety chain inside, so it could open only a few inches. This was just as well, for as soon as the small white poodle saw a stranger outside, it exploded in an even more frenzied seizure of yapping. "That's all right," the voice reassured the hysterical dog. "Mommy's not going to let anything happen to her Coco-kins. No, no, no!" The barking subsided into a peevish whining.

"Is this the home of Dudley and Crystal Woo?" Little Li asked, able to see only a slice of face through the crack.

"Yeah." He saw an eye look down to his satchel.

"We've never actually met, but . . ." The face vanished.

"Hey, Dud, there's a guy here with a satchel!"

"Find out if he's selling something, Crystal," a male voice replied as the TV emitted a burst of canned laughter. Little Li was about to introduce himself, but was interrupted by more yapping.

"Did you tell some guy to come and fix the TV?" she called back.

"No!" came an impatient reply.

"You with that church in Utah?" the woman asked, pointing at his scroll.

"No, actually . . ."

"What's he want?" the male voice demanded.

"Maybe somethin' religious." The poodle gave a mistrustful growl. "I don't think we're interested, mister," said the face.

As the door closed, Little Li experienced weariness so deep he felt ill. Without even a place to stay that night, he began just walking. It was not until he smelled the pleasing aroma of food wafting out of the Old Gold Mountain Noodle King that he realized how famished he was. As he took a seat at the counter, the heads of other customers silently swiveled. From their cool expressions, he wondered if they were not thinking: "Oh, here's another of our benighted brethren from Red China, seeking their fortune in America, a place their government always runs down! You can tell these guys by their shapeless suits, peasant haircuts, clunky shoes, and the way they're always so hungry!"

A cook in a white cap and a soy-sauce-splattered apron who made Little Li think of Master Chef Wang slapped a paper napkin folded around a set of plastic chopsticks down on the counter and said something in Cantonese that sounded more like a challenge than a question. Little Li pointed to the characters for "beef noodles" (牛肉面) on the dog-eared menu. For a Mandarin-speaking northerner, southern dialects were not only unintelligible, but unsonorous. The disputatious inflections in Cantonese, and the way speakers allowed sentences to trail off into nasal whines, made even pleasantries sound like complaints. To Little Li, Cantonese sounded like angry ducks quacking at each other. The couple sitting at the table behind him may have been talking about nothing more than the weather or the price of vegetables, but in Cantonese they sounded as if they were having an argument. And what sweet endearments whispered during courtship might sound like in this abrasive dialect, he dared not imagine. Arrogant northern Chinese liked to imagine themselves the progenitors of "high" (雅) culture and southerners of "low" (俗) culture. But this was no time for cultural smugness. The simple fact was that he could not understand what these Chinese compatriots were saying, interpret their expressions, or gauge their personalities. Once again, he was in exile.

33

GRACE CATHEDRAL

ARMS ACHING and head swimming, Little Li spotted a sign on Broadway for "THE HOTEL SAM WONG: ELECTRIC KITCH-ENS, TELEVISION (WEEKLY RATES)." He entered, to find himself in a narrow lobby decorated with potted palms positioned between traditional-style rosewood-and-marble Chinese chairs that were occupied by a gauntlet of elderly Chinese gentlemen. A Chinese landscape painting hung between a gleaming red, white, and blue Pepsi machine and a wall-mounted TV set tuned to a professional-wrestling match. A reception desk enclosed in a birdcage-like construction was staffed by a Chinese man wearing a Hawaiian shirt affixed with a plastic badge announcing him as "LIM POON, MAN-AGER" who quacked something in Cantonese without looking up from his abacus as Little Li approached.

"I'm sorry, but I don't speak Cantonese," Little Li replied in Mandarin. "But I'd like a room." A murmur went up from the old-timers.

"You wanna room, no problem," Lim Poon replied in English. "Twenny-fi' dolla' one night for one people." He thrust a registra-tion form under his barred window with one hand, while continu-ing to click away on his abacus with the other. Little Li filled out the form and peeled twenty-five dollars off his roll of bills.

"Aiyaaa!" Lim exhaled after studying the form. "You comin' Red China!" Then he said something in Cantonese that caused the old-timers to smile. "No sweat," he said, laughing, when he noticed Little Li's frown. "Every kind of peoples okay at Sam Wong."

A small elevator labored to the third floor, where Little Li walked down a low-ceilinged hallway through the reek of burned cooking oil and boiled cabbage. His room looked out on an air-shaft filled with drying laundry and was furnished with a washbasin stained with weeping rust marks, a swaybacked bed covered by a faded pink spread, and a brown shag carpet with so many pockmarks singed into its synthetic fiber by hot cigarette ash that it looked as if it had been hit by a meteor shower. Even the plastic veneer on the bedside tabletop was scarred with craters from unattended cigarettes. When he'd removed his jacket, he put his cricket and Yellow Emperor amulet on the bedside table, washed his face, and lay down. More than anything, he wanted an exit from the intensity of his dead-end arrival, but the din of voices, TV sets, and whooping sirens outside made slumber impossible. Then, just as the first welcome ether of sleepiness was coming over him, his bowels sprang to life, as if they grudged his efforts to make the transition from one side of the globe to the other. Wearily he padded down the unappetizing carpet. As he flushed the toilet, it occurred to him that this was a milestone: the last time his alimentary tract would expel food from China!

When the pale-gray glow of dawn was just beginning to fill the airshaft, he was awakened by the clatter of metal garbage cans being dragged over concrete. Still drugged with jet lag, he was just about to pull his head back under the covers when the realization that he was in America sent a fatal shot of adrenaline through his body. Irrevocably awake, he got up, washed, dressed, and went downstairs, where the TV was playing white noise and Lim Poon was asleep on a folding cot in the back of his cage. A neon sign across the street featuring the silhouette of a salaciously grinning nude woman with bright-red nipples was still blinking on and off. Having no sense of San Francisco geography, he just started walking uphill.

A half-hour later, he arrived breathless in a small park on the top of Nob Hill and sat down on a bench beside a fountain depicting four naked boys holding up a stone cauldron full of turtles. He was watching the sun rise like a giant bubble of molten metal over the fringe of hills across the bay when the park's irrigation system came on, spraying delicate fan-shaped jets of water out over the neat beds of flowers and well-groomed lawns. It wasn't until he stood up that he noticed the steeple rising from the rampart of a massive church behind him. As he approached it, he was seized by a feeling similar to what he'd felt when approaching the mountains in whose shadow he'd lived at Yak Springs. At first, he'd thought of them as remote, foreboding places, but the longer he was in their presence, the more he fell under the spell of their stately snow-clad peaks with massive glaciers cascading down their slopes. In the midst of all the uncertainty and tragedy in the world, their immutability and purity allowed him to believe that unsullied beauty still did exist and helped him understand how Tibetan Buddhists might believe them to be the sacred abodes of deities.

Drawn now by the grandeur of this cathedral, he made his way up the stone steps in front leading to an immense bronze door, where a plaque identified the church as Grace Cathedral and the door as a replica of a set made in the fifteenth century by Lorenzo Ghiberti for Florence's Duomo, known as "The Gates to Paradise." So this was Grace Cathedral, the church to which his mother and father had come years ago. When he stepped cautiously inside, he found himself standing before an immense mandala-like pattern inlaid in the marble floor, a labyrinth serving, perhaps, as a reminder that the pathway to God is neither obvious nor easy. Beyond was the towering nave flanked by stately stained-glass windows, which marched sentinel-like down the cathedral walls under the ribbing of Gothic arches soaring above.

Little Li started tentatively down the white marble aisle toward the bank of organ pipes that rose over one side of the altar. As he sat down in a pew, he tried to imagine his parents walking arm in arm down this aisle, his mother in a white organdy wedding gown and his father in a topcoat just like the couple on the wedding cake at the August Moon Bakery. This vision was interrupted by a creaking sound followed by a curious wheezing, as if a wind had suddenly begun to blow through the church. Then the great organ came to life, filling the cathedral's vastness with music. It was then that he noticed a flyer slipped into the rack on the back of his pew, announcing a recital featuring the organ works of J. S. Bach scheduled for that evening. Evidently, the organist was here to practice, and his first piece was the chorale prelude "O Man, Bewail Thy Sins So Great" ("O Mensch bewein dein Sünde Groß"). As the prelude's simple chorale melody sounded, he felt he'd stumbled into a memorial service for his father, and closed his eyes.

When he next opened them, several other worshippers had entered the cathedral, and one of them, a woman seated several rows in front of him, had turned to stare, as if to admonish him for perhaps sleeping in the house of the Lord. But as he watched her, he realized her gaze was actually drawn not by him, but upward, to something else. He turned, too, and saw that the large rose window behind the choir loft at the very back of the cathedral was ablaze with color, as the rising sun was turning the enormous window into a celestial prism. Then, as if on cue, the organ broke forth into the "Little" Fugue in G minor. With its voices entering obediently one after another—the smaller pipes trilling calliope-like, the middle-range pipes like bagpipes, and the enormous bass pipes issuing throaty rumbles—Little Li moved forward to hear better. He seated himself beside one of the pillars that rose up like the trunk of a giant tree from the cathedral floor to support the towering Gothic arches above, as the fugue galvanized toward its epic finale and he thought how much his father would have enjoyed this magisterial recital. As the bass pipes rumbled out the fugal statement one final time, they made the whole cathedral tremble. Then, as quickly as the piece had begun, it ended, leaving only the sound of a distant car horn and the clang of a cable-car bell outside.

Mao Zedong and Johann Sebastian Bach, what a collision of different sensibilities! Mao had been filled with paranoia, infatuated with contradiction, in love with struggle, dedicated to temporal power, and fixated on writing himself across the sweep of history. "A revolution," he proclaimed, "is an insurrection, an act of violence by which one class overthrows another." Bach, on the other hand, had been filled with a quest for peace, reverence for God, concern for the spirit, in love with music, and focused on readying the souls of men for eternity. Mao believed the world needed to be remade by outward politics and violent revolution, whereas Bach believed in the curative powers of music to help people accept life's travails and the inevitability of death. "The aim and final end of music," he said, "should be none other than the glory of God and the refreshment of the soul."

Whatever preternatural force had brought him here to Nob Hill, Little Li was glad it had. Maybe there was some kind of fate at work after all? How else could one explain that he, like his father, had been mysteriously drawn up to this hilltop, this cathedral, to hear this organ play this music? Tears began splashing down, leaving jagged splotches on the white marble floor. Whether he was weeping because of the music's beauty, the calamity of his father's life, his own loneliness, or the tragedy of China, he wasn't sure. But how had his country, the self-proclaimed socialist savior of mankind, ever ended up inflicting so much suffering and hardship on so many innocent people? Only his father's favorite writer, Lu Xun, seemed to understand the full depths of China's self-destructiveness:

> Our Chinese civilization, so highly vaunted, is nothing but a feast of human flesh prepared for the rich and powerful. What we call "China" is merely the kitchen where this stew is concocted. Those who praise us are to be excused only in as much as they do not know what they are talking about, like those foreigners whose high positions and pampered lives have rendered them completely blind and obtuse.

In his "Diary of a Madman" Lu Xun had described a fictional society where there was a "murderous gleam" in the eyes of people who'd become so perverted they'd become "eaters of human flesh." When the story's hero alone rejects the "etiquette of cannibalism" (吃人的礼教), he is deemed "mad," causing Lu to cry out in despair: "You must change from the bottom of your hearts! You must know that in the future there will be no place for man-eaters in the world. . . . Perhaps there are still children who have not eaten men. Save the children!"

But Lu Xun was wrong. In Mao's revolution, there had been plenty of room for cannibalism and myriad other cruelties.

"Excuse me, but can you recommend a less expensive place to stay?" he asked Lim Poon back at the Hotel Sam Wong.

"You like cheapo hotel renting by month, you betta off try Hotel Asterix in Tenderloin District. Okay?"

"Indian guy," said Lim, scrawling a name on a piece of paper and shoving it under the bars of his cage.

"Is it far?"

"Maybe far. You take numba-thirty bus. You betta off at Sam Wong," he chided. "But alla same for me." He held up an admonitory hand. "Tenderloin cheaper, but lotta bad guys and too many porno."

"Well, thanks." Little Li nodded fatalistically.

"No sweat!" said Lim, smiling perfunctorily.

Before going upstairs to gather his things, he bought two post-cards showing the Golden Gate Bridge from the rack next to Lim's cage. He addressed the first to Little Wang and the second to Little Hong, whom he missed with piercing poignancy.

> *Dear Hui:*
> *This is an amazing place! I am sure you'd enjoy it!*
> *I do hope you're well.*
> *Wende*

On Little Wang's card he wrote:

> *Hey buddy:*
> *Greetings from the land of American imperialism!*
> *I don't know how this whole adventure will work out,*
> *but each time I think of you, I hope your path isn't as*
> *uncertain as mine.*
> *Long live the Two Virtuous Ones!*

By the time he reached a mailbox, he was so disgusted with the disingenuousness of what he'd written to Little Hong, he threw the card into a curbside trash can.

When he stepped off the bus at Golden Gate Street, he found himself in the middle of an encampment of homeless people that reeked of urine. Two blocks later, where the Hotel Asterix should have been, he found only an aging building identified on a side brick wall as the Hotel Colon. The Tenderloin certainly was down-and-out, but that it might have a hotel named after the lower intestine seemed really peculiar. He paused in front of a bar called Club 2:00 AM from which a zephyr of sour, smoky, beery air wafted out onto the sidewalk as a jukebox pounded.

"The name's Wooster. Are you lookin' for somethin'?" a scruffy man loitering outside asked with boozy good cheer.

"Can you tell me where the Hotel Asterix is?"

"Well, it so happens you've arrived at the right place," replied Wooster grandiloquently. "They change its name so often, only us natives can keep track of it."

"Is that the Asterix?" Little Li asked, pointing at the Hotel Colon.

"You got it! Talk about piss-in-the-sink hotels!" Wooster accidentally inhaled some port while swigging from a bottle in a brown bag and went into a fit of coughing. Then, swaying so close to Little Li that he could smell the stale sweetness on his breath, Wooster added, "That joint's run by Indians, an' I don't mean guys with tomahawks and tom-toms."

"Thank you for the warning," said Little Li, unable to resist smiling. Wooster may not have been San Francisco's finest, but he'd extended the most effusive expression of hospitality Little Li had yet been afforded in America.

34

THE NEW WORLD

LITTLE LI was so dispirited that, without even looking at the room, he forked over three hundred dollars to Patel, the turbaned clerk at the Hotel Asterix's front desk, for a month's rent. Room 24 was furnished with a dinette table whose wobbly metal legs were plated with flaking chrome, and whose plastic top was scarred with rings from so many hot pans that it looked like a parody of the Olympic Games logo. Other furnishings included a folding metal chair with bent legs, and a mattress on the floor hemorrhaging stuffing and covered by a faded floral-pattern quilt. In the coating of dust covering the bedside table someone had written "Fuck you, Rhonda!" The room's single grimy window propped up with an empty Diet Coke can looked out over a dumpster to the Club 2:00 AM. Hoping to make this forlorn space his own, Little Li took his father's scroll out of his satchel and hung it above the mattress.

As he tried to fall asleep that first night, his room came alive with a procession of intrusive noises: the repeated clump-clump of footsteps, then the slamming of a door, the clicking of a latch, and the clap of a toilet seat slamming down as another "guest" entered the adjacent lavatory. Then, after a brief silence, came a fusillade of bassoonlike crepitations, an obbligato of tinkling piss, and a rush of water, a soundscape that truly bespoke the name Hotel Colon.

From across the street came another nonstop cacophony of clinking glasses, drunken voices, and the percussive thumping of a jukebox. Each time a customer came or left and the door opened, the volume swelled as if a radio had suddenly been turned up. And even with the ripped window shade down, the Club 2:00 AM's neon sign—a bright-blue smiling olive impaled on a green toothpick that danced in a pink martini glass—filled Room 24 with oscillating pulses of gaudy color. But the most provocative audio drama to contend with was a moaning sound that turned out to be the sounds of a woman in ecstasy in the room next door, that only served as a painful reminder of how alone Little Li was. The only competitor with this quadraphonic racket was the small, reedy voice of his cricket.

For the next few weeks, Little Li did little but sleep, eat one budget meal a day at the Duc Pho restaurant, a Vietnamese dive down the street, and stroll the derelict neighborhood, past the other "residential" hotels, strip clubs, bars, cheap Asian diners, adult bookshops, and porno shops. Besides Wooster, who stood like a carnival barker in front of Club 2:00 AM, hailing passersby with drunken good cheer, he spoke to no one. He considered returning to his aunt's, but felt so humiliated by his initial reception that he rejected the idea. He had, in effect, disappeared. Even to think of the word "home" (家) made him feel dejected, because he was no longer sure he still had one. From the Hotel Asterix, his escape from China seemed like a cruel joke, one he'd played on himself. What upset him most about his attacks of nostalgia was the recognition that, even though he'd finally arrived in the promised land of California, he was still not free of China's sway. Instead of being able to savor his getaway, he was pining for Willow Courtyard, his father, and especially Little Hong. It all made him wonder if the party was not, in fact, correct in scorning those Chinese who naïvely fantasized that the moon is rounder in America than in China.

It was not long before he began welcoming the noises bombarding his room. They were, at least, reminders that there was a living world outside, even if he hadn't figured out how to join it. When the Club 2:00 AM closed on Sundays, far from granting Little Li surcease, the silence only made him more eager to be intruded on by his neighbor's moaning. Like a theatergoer expectantly awaiting for the curtain to go up on a performance, he lay awake, hoping not to be cheated of this bit of real-life drama that allowed his troubled mind to sink into waking reveries of American girls shamelessly satisfying themselves. He may have managed to enter geographic America, but no passport could assure him entrance into the universe of American hedonism.

One night, while out walking aimlessly, he spotted an aurora borealis of light bleeding up into the foggy San Francisco sky. As he drew closer, he saw it came from floodlights illuminating the exterior of an all-night Cala Foods supermarket. The minute he stepped through the store's automatic doors, he experienced a mood change so profound, it felt almost chemically induced. Everything about the supermarket—its hangarlike vastness, brightly lit interior, soft music, drifts of perfectly complexioned vegetables and fruits, shelves of gleaming products, and aisles of refrigerated cases—justified its name. So entranced was he by this all-night American emporium that, after picking up the few things he could afford, he lingered for the simple pleasure of being surrounded by such abundance. Roaming the aisles, he tarried over each section as if the bins, shelves, and cases were exhibits in a great museum. The supermarket was, indeed, a far cry from the state-run stores he was used to back home, where surly disinterested clerks watched as truckloads of cabbage, turnips, or squash were dumped unceremoniously on dusty sidewalks like loads of gravel. Here an attentive Japanese American manager presided over the produce section like an emergency-room nurse, carefully stacking his apples, pears, and oranges in neat pyramids and spritzing his lettuces and legumes with invigorating mists of water. And whereas Chinese butcher shops often looked like execution grounds, here the meat-and-seafood section was as spotless as a hospital examination room, and the smocks worn by the butchers were as white as the gowns of medical orderlies. And he loved the forceful product brand names: Miracle Whip, Challenge Milk, Comet Cleanser, Cheerios, and Wonder Bread. But what most entranced him was a life-sized cardboard cutout of a shapely young blonde in a scarlet bikini who stood watch over the detergents in Aisle 4. Sporting a tricornered hat and a snare drum hanging around her neck, she held a plastic container of aquamarine-tinted Minuteman Toilet Bowl Magic in one of her delicate hands. Little Li tried to imagine the effect of such an ad in the Wangfujing Department Store, but he knew it would assuredly be removed as a form of "spiritual pollution" (精神污染). Such come-ons might be base, but they were, at least, a demonstration that even companies here in America were obliged to court "the people" in a form of commercial crypto-democracy.

Since Cala Foods was always open, whenever Little Li was lonely or unable to sleep, he headed over, grabbed a shopping cart, and trolled its aisles. Late at night, when customers were few, he sometimes played a version of his old boyhood game of shutting his eyes and trying to navigate his way by touch, sound, and smell. It took him no time to map the supermarket's interlocking fields of fragrances, sounds, and temperatures. There was the sweet, cinnamon aroma of the baked goods in Aisle 1; the pungent fragrance of roasted beans around the coffee section at the end of Aisle 2; the pleasing smell of roast chicken and barbecued ribs near the deli department; the low-tide smell around the seafood cases; and the raw, almost sexual odor of cut meats that lingered around the butcher counter. Then there was a damp feeling in the lettuce section and a miniature weather system of frigid arctic air around the frozen-food cases. But ruling over all these separate sensory domains was the overpowering chemical pungency emanating from Aisle 4 next to the Minuteman Toilet Bowl Magic girl, where the air fresheners, detergents, household pesticides, and toilet-bowl cleaners were shelved. This aisle's nostril-tingling chemical signature had such authority that whenever Little Li lost his way he knew he could always reorient himself simply by homing in on it, like the North Star.

He was, of course, aware that drunkenly pushing a shopping cart around with his eyes shut made him look quite daft. But because there was no chance he'd run into anyone he knew, he didn't care. What's more, there were so many other deviants in the store late at night, he was hardly out of place. In fact, as he shuffled along with his nose held high like a hunting dog on point, he sometimes half wished he were blind. At least then he'd have a proper excuse for being so inept and insoluble in this impregnable land.

One night as he arrived at Cala Foods, he heard the sound of a violin. Next to the main door, beside the ice-vending machine, stood a young man with a beard and a top hat playing a Mozart sonata. A hand-lettered sign around his neck announced: PENURI-OUS MUSIC STUDENT: HELP ME GET THROUGH THE SAN FRANCISCO CONSERVATORY!

Little Li stopped to listen to this talented busker.

"Hey, man! Where ya from?" the violinist asked when he came to the end of the movement.

"China," replied Little Li.

"Far out! Do you like music?"

"I do."

"You play?"

"Yes, the flute," he answered, but immediately felt regretful, because, having come all this way to the United States to study music, he'd not yet made any progress in that direction.

"You should come out to the Conservatory some time," the violinist said. "We've got a lot of foreign students." Then he tucked his fiddle back under his chin and sawed out the next movement.

The words "San Francisco Conservatory" jolted Little Li. After all, this was where his parents had both studied and met. He dropped a dollar into the violinist's open instrument case, and as he walked back to the Asterix, he resolved that as soon as he made some money, he'd investigate music school.

That night, he put his *hulu* under his quilt, hoping his cricket would sing. But when, after a while, there was still no sound, he turned on the light and twisted off the carved top. His cricket was lying on its back, its paper-clip legs sticking up in the air and both its antennae were broken.

When Grace Cathedral's bells tolled at 6:00 a.m., Little Li was already in Huntington Park. As dawn broke, he dug a hole in a bed of primroses, shook his dead cricket out onto the palm of his hand, laid its weightless body in the miniature grave, and gently pushed the earth back in around its body. It was only an insect, but it had been alive, traveled with him all the way from China, and was the last living tie to his homeland. Its death left him feeling even more friendless and lost.

A few days later, when several houseflies appeared in his room, he almost welcomed their company. At least, when it came to insects, he was not alone! But during a hot spell, the number of flies being spawned by the dumpster below began to increase. When it was dark and cool, they stayed hunkered down on the walls and ceiling. However, as the sun warmed his room, they came to life and, like a squadron of tiny fighter planes commanded by crazed pilots, began dive-bombing the panes of his window. And as they multiplied, their collective buzzing so aggravated him that he began stalking them with a rolled-up newspaper.

Long before arriving in America, Little Li had become a master fly-slayer. He was only eight when the government initiated a mass campaign "to eliminate the four pests" (除四害) (mosquitoes, rats, sparrows, and flies) and he'd been assigned to his school's "Fly Extermination Brigade." Every morning, students lined up in front of Teacher Yang's desk to present their previous day's catch so she could tabulate the body count and solemnly enter the tally on her blackboard. Each Saturday, the top three achievers were awarded certificates proclaiming them "Champions of Extermination" (除四害能手) and made class monitors. So for Little Li killing flies was already more than pest control: it was a competitive sport promising social mobility.

Painfully aware of how the meager resources he'd brought from China were dwindling, he regularly checked the classified ads in the *San Francisco Chronicle*. However, work permits were required even for most menial jobs such as door-to-door salesmen, night watchmen, and parking-lot attendants. One category that seemed hopeful was "domestic service." One ad read:

HOUSEHOLD DOMESTIC WANTED
LIVE-IN MANSERVANT SOUGHT
MUST BE PRESENTABLE
NO COUPLES
BOARD AND LODGING OFFERED
CALL: 415 559-9789

The fact that the job provided free board and lodging interested him. When he called the number, a woman with a demure voice asked how old he was, if he was single, whether he smoked, and . . . she continued with some hesitation, "exactly what persuasion are we?"

"Persuasion?" he asked in confusion.

"Well, yes," she said coolly. "What ethnic background are we talking about?"

"Chinese and American?" he answered, not sure how best to describe himself.

"Of course, we'll require a personal interview," she said archly.

"I'd be glad to come by anytime."

"Shall we expect you, then, at about four p.m. today? You'll find us on Washington Street. Do you know Pacific Heights?"

"No, but I'll find it."

As he walked up Washington Street past a row of mansions, he tried to imagine what it would be like to live in one of these grand homes. Whereas in China even new buildings often looked old before they were completed, these houses were so well maintained it was impossible to tell how old they were. Even more impressive than their size and elegance was the almost complete absence of human activity around them. Besides a single Hispanic gardener blasting the sidewalk with a leaf blower, there was no one else in evidence. Pacific Heights was so well manicured and tranquil, it gave the air of being a place from which all human care had been banished, where even the cloudless sky above seemed part of its man-made perfection.

The house was an immense white woodframed mansion with a wrought-iron gate on the sidewalk. He opened it and walked up a flagstone path past a row of porcelain cauldrons filled with pink petunias. At the top of the steps he found an imposing double door affixed with an engraved brass plaque: "THE MILES VAN CAMPS." Feeling he was about to step out onstage, Little Li took a deep breath and pressed the bell. A distant gong sounded. The door opened. A uniformed black maid looked out distrustfully and asked, "Can I help you?"

"I'm here to be interviewed."

"Oh yes! If you'll come this way." She motioned Little Li down a hallway to a drawing room with a picture window overlooking San Francisco Bay. Facing this natural panorama was a small black-and-white television set built into a bookcase that, instead of broadcasting regular programming, featured the image of a slumbering bulldog over a caption: "Argyle McSnutt." Little Li was digesting this curious image when the dog's snout quivered and its lubricious jowls twitched. Then, moments later, the dog's image vanished and was replaced by an ad:

DOG-GONE IT
CALIFORNIA'S FIRST DOGGIE-TEL
WE'LL TAKE ROVER WHEN YOU GO ROVIN'
SPECIALISTS IN CANINE HOSPITALITY
PRIVATE KENNELS
24/7 VETS AND CANINE-CAMS
RANCHO MIRAGE, CALIFORNIA

When the slumbering bulldog unexpectedly reappeared, a canine reverie was making its sloppy jowls puff in and out.

"Will we see you tomorrow, Tyrena?" came a woman's voice from the hallway.

"Yes, you will, Mrs. Van Camp."

Little Li heard the front door close, the padding of slippers, and a tall, middle-aged woman in a white terry-cloth robe with a bath towel wrapped around her head like a turban swept into the room. Even though she'd evidently just emerged from her bath, her face was already made up.

"And you are . . . ?" she asked, extending a regal hand.

"I am Li Wende," he replied stiffly, feeling utterly out of place in his shapeless Chinese suit jacket.

"Li what?"

"Li Wende."

"Indeed," she said, surveying him, her gaze starting at his face and slowly moving down his body to his feet. "Have you a name like . . . Frank or Bob?"

"Not yet. But you can call me Li." He regretted not having chosen an English name, and thought better of using Lancelot.

"Of course. And, so Mr. . . . ."

"Li. Mr. Li," he prompted.

"Mr. Li, do you care for dogs?" she asked, gesturing toward the TV set.

"Well . . ." he stammered, thinking of Lobsang's three-legged mastiff.

"McSnutt there"—she pointed to the screen—"goes with our winter home, down on the desert at Rancho Mirage," she explained, her expression softening. "My former husband named him after the Right Reverend Argyle McSnutt, a pastor at the church down there where we sometimes attended services. The Reverend wasn't a looker like you, Mr. Li, but, being in the clergy, I don't suppose he cared much? Anyway, after the divorce, I was convinced by a nice young man at the Doggie-Tel in Rancho to sign up for their Canine-Cam Option, so I could watch McSnutt when I was back up here in the Bay Area." She smiled at the image on the screen. "And where do you call home, Mr. Li?"

"Beijing."

"Oh, how absolutely marvelous! I'll be joining a museum tour to China with the Brundage Collection this spring to see your Great Wall, Shanghai, and visit those life-sized figurines from Marco Polo's time," she enthused, crossing her legs in a way that left one thigh exposed up to a well-tanned buttock. Her long, shapely legs were both tempting and terrifying.

"Oh, you mean Xian," he offered, not bothering to correct her confusion between the Qin and Yuan dynasties, which were actually separated by more than a millennium.

"So much history!" she continued, raking his body again with her gaze. Then, taking a tube of L'Occitane Creme Ultra Riche Corps out of her robe pocket, she squeezed a wormlike extrusion out onto the palm of one hand and began rubbing it onto her exposed leg. "One's skin gets so dry after a long, hot bath," she said, looking suggestively at him. He felt paralyzed by her glance, the elegance of her house, and the weirdness of her Doggie-Tel broadcast. "Perhaps you'd come over here for a moment and help me with your strong hands, Mr. Li." She said this with the matter-of-factness of someone accustomed to having subalterns do her bidding. But just as she was proffering him the tube and easing her robe back to expose her shoulders, the phone rang.

"Oh, Mimi! How lovely to hear your voice!" she said, waving Little Li away. Relieved, he retreated to the hallway. Then seized by an overpowering urge to be gone, he tiptoed to the front door, exited, threw the tube of lotion into a cauldron of petunias, and hurried down the path.

It was on one of his aimless peregrinations around the city that Little Li stumbled on Out of the Closet, a thrift shop in the Mission District, where he immediately became enamored of its "As-Is Department." This consisted of a cavernous back room overflowing with second-hand clothing, bedding, drapery, books, toys, kitchenware, tools, sports equipment, and electrical appliances that had been judged "below standards." The things had been sorted into huge piles to be sold at cut-rate prices by a team of clerks, many of whom had some form of autism. Little Li quickly discovered that most things there had nothing wrong with them other than superficial dents or stains. And whereas most customers didn't have the patience to look through more than the top layer of each pile, he had unlimited time, and was thus able to explore a pile the way an archaeologist methodically excavates an ancient midden.

His first deep dive was into a pile of castaway kitchen appliances, from which he quickly unearthed an array of treasures costing no more than a dollar each. As he was musing over a small but heavy mechanical contraption, one of the handicapped clerks lumbered over and plugged it in to demonstrate how an electric can opener works. When he thought of the few canned treasures guarded by Master Chef Wang at Yak Springs, the idea that here in America a person might consume such a volume of canned goods that an electric-powered device was required to open them all seemed surreal. But it cost only fifty cents!

In another pile, he came upon a three-dollar TV (minus knobs) that came to life when he plugged it in, albeit with a very fuzzy picture.

"This way! This way!" the same clerk shrieked. Rushing to the rescue again, she grabbed a wire clothes hanger from a nearby pile, bent the hooked end straight, and rammed it into the broken antenna stub causing the TV's reception to suddenly clear. Her face lit up with a triumphant grin.

His next two finds were a ten-cent pair of pliers (to turn on his knobless TV) and a set of fifty-cent REJECT bedsheets imprinted with clowns boasting enormous red noses, tufted blue hair, and oversized purple shoes. Although he now had only $300 left and no idea how he was going to earn more, the catharsis of trading a few grimy bills for this bounty of things was irresistible.

On his next trip, he chanced on a pile of vacuum cleaners in a snarl of suction hoses, power cords, and assorted attachments. Since China was still in the broom age and he'd never actually seen, much less used, one of these appliances, this vacuum cleaner reliquary entranced him. And his room needed a good cleaning! Spotting a compact Eureka Mighty Mite, he plugged it in, and it immediately roared to life. However, instead of sucking up the dust bunnies at which he'd aimed its nozzle, it exhaled a nest of dust and hair. He yanked the plug from the socket and was about to put the refractory machine back when his favorite clerk again materialized.

"Not like that!" she shrieked with jubilant urgency, and deftly disconnected the hose from one end of the machine and rammed it into the other. When she turned the vacuum back on, it obliged by sucking up all the debris it had just expelled, like a film projected in reverse. Victoriously, she raised both hands above her head and smiled as joyously as an Olympic gold medalist.

Little Li was about to leave when a fly unexpectedly zoomed by. Reflexively, he thrust the end of the suction hose at this kamikaze and, to his astonishment, sucked the fly right out of the air! The girl gave a thrilled yelp. He paid three dollars and with the hose of his newly purchased weapon slung rakishly over his shoulders like a bandolier, he returned to the Asterix. Where, brandishing its nozzle like Excalibur, he vanquished every fly in his room in a few minutes.

With the arrival of the Mighty Mite, Little Li's fly-hunting days underwent a Great Leap Forward. As his stalking ritual grew more elaborate, he developed a rating system for his "kills." The easiest flies to dispatch were those caught copulating, because once they landed for their fatal moment of conjugation, it was impossible for them to decouple and get airborne quickly enough to avoid his nozzle of death. A close second were flies that streaked uncontrollably toward the warmth of his sunlit window, where, buzzing helplessly against a pane of glass, even a novice could dispatch them. But, like a sportsman refusing to shoot ducks on a pond, Little Li usually prodded such benighted prey back into flight before beginning his duel to the death.

By far the most challenging category were those hyperactive flies that flew endlessly back and forth across the room without landing. Because the Mighty Mite's nozzle was only an inch in diameter, it took lightning reflexes to suck one of these daredevils out of the air in mid-flight. After trying to repeat the maneuver he'd executed so effortlessly at Out of the Closet, he concluded that his initial triumph was beginner's luck, a recognition that was reinforced when, while watching PBS late one night, he saw a Japanese film in which a samurai reached out with chopsticks while eating dinner and plucked a fly right out of the air.

Although Little Li's life seemed to have lost all direction, it still went on. To maintain any optimism, he liked to imagine himself as a silkworm pupating in a chrysalis in preparation to emerge reborn. But he was starting to doubt that anything so impressive would come from his tortured metamorphosis. In this new land where everything was supposed to be possible, maybe he would prove the exception to the rule. Perhaps, like those unfortunate Chinese silkworms that end up getting boiled alive so their cocoons can be spun into silk, he'd never emerge resplendent as a moth. Perhaps the promise of rebirth in America would for him prove to be just one more insidious piece of Western propaganda.

35

TREADING WATER

IN HIS SOLITUDE, Little Li found American television addictive, and he became particularly fascinated by two local anchorwomen. The first was Emerald Yeh, a Chinese American who appeared on Channel 4 News. Though she was genetically more purely Chinese than he, her manner was completely American. Such Chinese immigrants who'd become Americanized helped him understand the actual gulf that existed between "Chinese-ness" and "American-ness." What impressed him was the stylishness with which Yeh dressed, her poise on camera, and her flawless English. Evidently, immigrant families of her parents' generation desired nothing more than for their children to become absorbed in the great American melting pot. Yeh's meticulous makeup and stylish wardrobe of svelte suits and silky scarves all seemed calculated to de-emphasize her Asian-ness. Even when reporting on a subject like homosexuals or sex-change operations, she remained cool and poised, whereas young women at home were inclined to giggle and avert their gaze when confronted with even slightly embarrassing topics.

The second TV personality who fascinated him was Kate Kelly on Channel 5 News. Tall, blond, blue-eyed, and with a classically lovely face and figure, she was the incarnation of his vision of American pulchritude. Watching her made him feel he was looking into the heart of the American Dream. What he liked about her was that on camera she radiated a hint of vulnerability that allowed him to imagine himself as her savior. To possess Kate Kelly would surely be to sip the elixir of American immortality!

Little Li's only other vicarious connection to the outside was the Duc Pho All-You-Can-Eat, a Vietnamese dive owned by "the Major," who'd served in the Army of the Republic of Vietnam before the fall of Saigon. Little Li allowed himself a single daily meal at his buffet. However, his dining habits changed radically after he added a toaster oven to his growing inventory of Out of the Closet appliances and then discovered Louie's House of Dented Cans. With no regular aisles, promotional displays, soft music, bright lights, or even shelves, Louie's was a warehouse outlet that sold "distressed merchandise" at rock-bottom prices. Its surprising variety of products was matched only by the diversity of its clientele, many of whom were as bruised by life as the cans, bottles, boxes, and sacks of food they came to buy were by the marketplace. What Little Li particularly enjoyed about Louie's was figuring out what imperfection had destined each item to this commercial twilight zone. There were rusty cans of vegetables; bottles of ketchup with stained labels; boxes of cereal that had been crushed; jugs of fruit juice that were off color; bags of potato chips past their expiration dates; jars labeled in undecipherable languages; and rolls of toilet tissue containing paper in different colors, making them look like oversized party streamers.

For Little Li, the most exciting things came from what staffers referred to as the Big Bin, an enormous wire basket chock-full of cans without labels, some of which looked as if they'd been dropped from the top of a tall building. What attracted Little Li to the Big Bin was not just the low prices—five or ten cents per can—but the thrill of gambling. He could hardly wait to get his purchases back to his electric can opener to see what he'd won. Most cans contained fruit, vegetables, or soup. Occasionally, he got tuna fish or chicken; one mystery can turned out to contain roofing tar.

Of all the delicacies at Louie's, there was none that could quite compare to the Sara Lee frozen coffee cakes, stacked like cordwood in a stand-up freezer at the very back of the warehouse, each affixed with a bright-green sticker: THRIFT!

DUE TO MINOR MANUFACTURING OR PACKAGING IMPERFEC-TIONS THIS PRODUCT DOES NOT MEET OUR HIGH STANDARDS FOR GENERAL DISTRIBUTION AND IS MARKED AND SOLD AS "THRIFT." WE WISH YOU TO BE INFORMED IN ORDER TO AVOID DISAPPOINT-MENT IN YOUR PURCHASE.

THE KITCHENS OF SARA LEE.

Whatever fault American quality-control inspectors found with these cakes created no "disappointment" for Little Li. In fact, the cloudlike undulations of golden pastry covered with pecans and swirls of white icing that nestled in each aluminum tray brought him as close to ecstasy as he was going to get just then. Slight deformities—an albino intrusion of dough without cinnamon, a spot where the icing machine had misfired, or a deficit of pecans— might, under marketplace rules of advanced capitalism, consign a cake to "thrift" status. However, for a refugee from socialism, under which inspectors of baked goods, if they existed, would not have batted an eye at such deficiencies, these "cripples" were living proof of the superiority of market systems.

Louie's was in a tough neighborhood, and one evening, while waiting outside with a bag of groceries for a traffic light to change, Little Li suddenly felt a forearm clamped around his windpipe and something hard jabbed into the small of his back.

"Okay, Mr. Chinaman, don't pull no fast shit!" hissed a menacing voice, as a second youth with bushy hair that glistened like plastic grabbed him by the lapels.

"We gonna aks you one motherfuckin' time," he snarled. "You gonna give us yo' motherfuckin' wallet, or we gonna put a cap in yo' motherfuckin yellow ass. Unnerstand, motherfucka?" "Motherfucker" was an epithet that he kept hearing, but these guys were able to construct whole sentences out of it!

When the youth in front of him suddenly ripped his suit jacket open and grabbed his wallet, Little Li reflexively executed a martial-arts maneuver that sent his assailant flying over his shoulder and right on top of his younger partner. As cans and bottles exploded from his paper bag, a snub-nosed pistol skated across the sidewalk. Lunging for the gun, Little Li hurled it onto the rooftop of a garage behind them. When he turned around again, the muggers were halfway down the block, his wallet with them. The fifty dollars in his pants pocket was now all he had left.

In China, Little Li's acquaintance with blacks had come primarily from Communist Party Youth League propaganda posters extolling socialist solidarity between the PRC and Third World peoples in Africa. In rosy scenes of revolutionary solidarity, hammer-and-sickle-toting Chinese workers and peasants stood shoulder to shoulder with other oppressed dark-skinned peoples, such as U.S. blacks, Arabs, Eskimos, Malays, East Indians, and Africans around the world. However, when real Africans actually appeared in China from "fraternal socialist countries," their experiences bore little resemblance to these idealized scenes. Instead, they were often looked down on as wild, music-besotted, sex-crazed savages. Worse, it was generally assumed that all these dark-skinned visitors cared about was playing drums and finding devious ways to insinuate their enormous black male organs into the private parts of innocent Chinese girls. The only black Little Li had ever encountered in the flesh was a likable young man from Angola named Innocent Savimbi, who landed at the Central Conservatory to study percussion but quickly became so homesick that he petitioned to leave. However, since he'd been awarded a two-year government scholarship dedicated to "building friendship" between the peoples of the People's Republic of Angola and the People's Republic of China, his embassy forced him to soldier on. Then, one night, he was found in a state of incriminating undress in a practice studio with a female violinist from Tibet. Without even giving him a chance to stop at his dorm, police hustled Innocent off to the Angolan Embassy.

"We all knew what these guys from Africa want!" snorted the indignant oboist who'd stumbled on the trysting couple. "Now we know Tibetans are no better." Little Li was acquainted firsthand with how Han Chinese regarded dark-skinned Tibetans, as backward, polyandrous primitives steeped in superstition, but this was his first experience with Africans. Neither Innocent nor the violinist was seen at the Conservatory again.

"Mr. Li, I must be reminding you, your rent is due," said Patel in his singsong voice as Little Li passed the Asterix front desk one morning. In desperation, Little Li decided to try playing his flute in front of Cala Foods. He took up a position beside the ice machine, opened his battered case, twisted together the sections of his instrument, and began playing a traditional Chinese folk song. Most shoppers just hurried past, but one older couple stopped. When he finished the piece, the woman came forward hesitantly.

"Oh my goodness!" she exclaimed. "You wouldn't be from China, would you?"

"In fact, I am."

"Well, Walter and I just got back from a cruise to your country and . . . what was the name of that German city we stopped at, Walter?" she asked, turning to her husband.

"You mean Qingdao?" he rejoined impatiently.

"Yes! That's the one, And we have some lovely slides. Perhaps you'd like . . ."

"Oh, for Christ's sake, Beverly!" exclaimed the man, his voice tinged with exasperation. "The guy grew up in China! Why the hell would he want to see our slides?"

"Well, I was just thinking . . ." she stammered.

"I've never been to Qingdao," said Little Li, trying to come to her rescue. "But . . ."

"Anyway, you seem like such a nice young man, and you play so beautifully," she said, her voice trailing off as she took out a five-dollar bill from her oversized purse and dropped it into his open flute case.

When he left that night, he'd netted only $16.27. Desperate, he bought a *San Francisco Chronicle* to peruse the classified ads again. One caught his eye: "Janitor Wanted. $4 @ hour. Grecian Fitness Club. Call: (415) 452-7864. Ask for Milo."

"Grecian, this is Stephanie," answered a saccharine female voice when he called from the pay phone at the Club 2 A.M.

"Mr. Milo, please," he said, forming his words carefully to remove any hint of an accent.

"Hold, please." There was a beep, and some disco music came on. After a wait, a recorded voice announced: "I'm sorry. Your first three minutes are up. Please insert another twenty-five cents." Reaching into his pocket, he accidentally dropped his change and when he stooped to retrieve it, the cord connecting the receiver to the coin box was too short, so he had to let it dangle while he lunged for the coins. Just as he managed to cram another quarter into the slot and grab the receiver again, a loud voice said, "Hello. Grecian. Vuccovich."

"Yes," Little Li replied breathlessly. "You've listed a job in the—"

"Who's this?"

"My name is Li."

"Can you vacuum and mop?"

"Yes."

"Can you start work today?"

"Sure."

"All right. The club's at the Stonestown Shopping Center, under the Emporium. You can't miss it."

As Little Li stepped off a J-line tram, a thick fog was rolling in off the ocean. He wandered the mall for twenty minutes before, finally spotting a sign that pointed down a subterranean stairway to the Grecian Fitness Club. At the bottom, a white plaster statue of a muscle-bound Greek god, naked except for a fig leaf over his private parts, stood in a bower of synthetic bamboo. A placard around his neck read:

NOW'S YOUR OPPORTUNITY! GET STARTED ON THAT BODY
YOU'VE ALWAYS DREAMED ABOUT!
AND AT SUCH AFFORDABLE RATES, TOO!
THE GRECIAN FITNESS CLUB.

As Little Li stepped into the lobby, he was hit by a tropical zephyr of moist air redolent of chlorine, sweat, and the unnaturally pungent fragrances of shampoo and deodorant. At the front desk sat a blonde in a white T-shirt with "Fitness First" inscribed across her ample bosom.

"Hi. I'm Stephanie." She smiled. "You already a Grecian member?"

"No, and actually . . ."

"Well, perhaps you'd be interested in learning about the annual 'membership bonanza' we have goin' on right now, which means that, if you subscribe for one month today, we here in the Grecian family can give you another full month free, absolutely free! And . . ."

"Thanks, but I'm here to see Mr. Milo about the janitor's job."

"Oh yeah, you called, dincha?" Her voice lost its earlier enthusiasm. She picked up the phone and drummed her lacquered nails on the countertop as she waited. "Hey, Milo, the guy who called about bein' janitor is out front." She turned back to Little Li. "He's on the phone, so take a seat."

Little Li sat down on a leatherette couch in front of a glass-topped coffee table displaying a fanlike array of brochures featuring a young woman with a perfectly proportioned body clad in a sheer black-and-white-striped leotard.

A GREAT BODY! GET IT! SHOW IT!
A great body is no free gift!
You've got to earn it! You've got to trim it! You've got to shape it!
If you're serious about your body, make the move to Grecian!
Put your body first and see one of our experienced trainers now!

"Ya know maybe you better just go in," said Stephanie after a while. She gestured toward a half-open door. "Milo might talk forever."

When Milo saw Little Li in his doorway, he gave a friendly wink and motioned for him to take a seat. On the mirror behind his desk was the cover of a *Sports Illustrated* swimsuit issue alongside a lenticular 3-D postcard of Pope John Paul, who winked when you changed vantage points. The office was small, but because its walls were mirrored, it seemed far more spacious.

"Just tell that moron to go fuck himself!" said Milo, and slammed down the receiver. Then, turning to Little Li, he added, "'Scuse my French."

Milo Vuccovich was a short, balding brick of a man in his fifties who wore a sleeveless "Fitness First" T-shirt over a torso that had once been ripped but was beginning to balloon and sag. To restrain his now ample belly, he wore a leather weight-lifter's belt carved with his initials. Whereas the bodies of Chinese men were usually hairless, Milo's was covered with a mat of dark curls.

"Okay. What's your name?" asked Milo.

"I am Li Wende. Call me Li."

"So—what can I do you for, Li?"

"I am interested in becoming your janitor."

"Oh, you're the guy who called. Ever work health spas?"

"No."

"Just get here from the old country?"

"Yes."

"So—where d'ya hail from?"

"China."

"Well, welcome to America."

"Thanks."

"Hey, you got quite a build. Take your shirt off so old Milo can see your stuff."

Not exactly sure why he was being asked to disrobe, Little Li slowly removed his jacket and shirt, until he was standing naked from the waist up.

Milo whistled. "Where'd you get a bod like that?"

"Working on a road."

"You work construction?"

"Sort of," Little Li demurred, unsure how to explain the disparity between American "construction work" and Chinese "forced labor."

"If all Chinese roadworkers are as pumped as you, I'm guessing you got some good roads over there!" He laughed. Little Li was glad his Qinghai experience was finally proving to pay some dividend. "Okay. So—here's what I'm gonna do. I'm gonna try ya as janitor at four fifty an hour. You on board?"

"Thank you so much," said Little Li, flooded with relief.

"Well, don't be so fuckin' polite, 'cause it's a seriously shitty job! But if you've got the stuff, I'll move you up, even make you an 'initiator,' where you'll get five bucks an hour, plus a twenty-five-percent commission on every 'potential' you turn into a 'kill.'"

"A 'kill'?"

"A 'kill' is what we call new club members. 'Initiators' are the trainers who work new 'potentials,' which is what we call the folks we're trying to turn into 'kills.' This 'kill' shit is some sickness my 'initiators' started as a joke, and I oughta wash their mouths out with Mr. Clean. They should be talkin' about 'Joining the Grecian Family.'"

"I see," responded Little Li, though he was confused by all the terminology.

"Anyway, you'll get the hang of the place real quick, 'cause you're gonna get a lot of on-the-job training!" Milo laughed congenially. "You get here by eight p.m., so that when the joint closes you can begin. You gotta pick up all the crap left around, put the towels in the washer, mop both locker rooms, clean the frigging hair out of the shower drains, fill the soap dispensers, dump the trash baskets, clean the toilets, put paper in every stall, and then hose down the steam room and sauna, stick chlorine in the Jacuzzi, and vacuum the carpets. It's a soup-to-nuts type of deal." Then, Milo ushered Little Li out to the exercise room, where club members were toiling away on Nautilus machines to throbbing disco music.

"Okay, Comrade? So—let's do it to it!" Milo put a fatherly arm around Little Li's shoulders. "My folks were from the old country, too. My pops was from Yugoslavia, and my mother from Italy. Jesus, Mary, Joseph, when the old guy arrived here after the war, he didn't have a pot to piss in, couldn't even say 'Fuck you!' in English. But, he worked his ass off! Then he brought over Mama, and now the old guy owns two Leaning Tower of Pizza restaurants, drives a Lincoln Town Car, and has a lovely home in Redwood City. That's the way it works here, son. You start off moppin', and who knows where it goes? Look at me!" He flexed his not inconsiderable biceps and laughed. "Come on, I'll show you the janitor's closet."

As members straggled out each evening, Little Li donned his "Fitness First" coveralls, switched the club's sound-system from disco to classical music, and began work. One night, while mopping the women's locker room to the strains of Tchaikovsky's *Swan Lake,* he got into pushing his mop around in rhythm with the music. Then, as if his mop had become a prima ballerina and he was doing a pas de deux with her, he began making comical little stylized steps across the tiled floor. The sheer absurdity of the idea of dancers in tights and tutus doing a ballet with a fitness-club theme set in a shower room to Russian tsarist music made him laugh out loud.

Working alone in an underground health club might have dispirited others, but he was glad just to be employed, even when doing the most repellent parts of his job. One of those came around every Friday when he had to take up the grill-like rubber mats covering the locker-room floors to clean up the foul slurry that had collected underneath during the week. In the men's locker room, he confronted a mush of pubic hair, toenail clippings, athlete's-foot powder, old Band-Aids, buttons, toothpicks, and once even a condom, all steeped in a broth that had dripped off members as they left the shower room. In the women's locker room, he confronted snarls of multicolored hair, artificial fingernails, bobby pins, dirty Q-tips, Tampax strings, and false eyelashes. After squeegeeing these gender-specific slurries into repulsive piles, he used a child's beach trowel to shovel the glop into a plastic bag. Then he scrubbed the tiles with Mr. Clean and hosed them down. This travail had one perk: he usually found some spare change that had fallen irretrievably through the holes in the mats.

When he became bored, he distracted himself by calculating

exactly how much he was earning. There was something deeply satisfying about knowing that, every time the big hand on the electric clock in the aerobics-room swept past twelve, he was $4.50 richer, or $.075 richer each minute. This was the addictive genius of capitalism: no matter how low-paying a job, even the most oppressed proletarian could find relief in the notion that every time another hour passed he was a little richer.

It was not long, however, before the thrill of simply having a job began to wear off, and Little Li found himself experiencing flashes of panic about his life. Where was he headed? Would he ever get to his musical studies? How would he ever acquire a social life? Because he came to work so late, few others at the club knew he even existed. He'd escaped China, but become a prisoner of American oblivion.

"Hey, Li!" began Milo, putting an arm around his shoulders several months after he'd started work. Although Little Li appreciated his friendliness, he could not help recoiling from his caterpillar-like furriness. "Something's come up."

"What?" asked Little Li anxiously.

"An immigration guy came around asking if we had anyone working without papers."

"Well, I have a student visa that allows me to work," he started defensively.

"But you're not in school."

"I'm working toward it."

Milo did not immediately reply. Then: "Never tell anyone you're on a student visa until you're in school, or you're gonna get shipped back to Chairman Mayo," he warned. "But because every morning when I come in the club's so clean I could eat my Egg McMuffins off the locker-room floor, what I'm thinkin' in my mind is this: I'll pay you in cash, so there won't be any tracks. And"—he raised an index finger to signal he wasn't finished—"even though you're an illegal, I'm gonna let you start subbing at the front counter when Stephanie's off."

"Aiyyo! Thanks!" replied Little Li, elated at being given a second job despite his visa status.

The front desk offered one new benefit: from this perch, he was able to observe everything going on in the club. One of the first things he noticed was how the exercise room underwent an atmospheric change as soon as an attractive young woman entered. As she moved from machine to machine, male heads synchronously tracked her, as if they were sports fans following a ball up and down a field. In China, he'd been no less curious about the bodies of girls, but since Chinese girls had until recently worn regulation Mao suits, it had been difficult to ascertain their physical contours. To compensate, he'd had to rely on what he thought of as "Granny Sun's Unified Field Theory of the Human Physiognomy and Character," which postulated a correlation between the length of a girl's fingers and her level of refinement. Now, after considerably more fieldwork here at the reception desk, he was ready to expand this theorem to postulate a correlation between finger length and body type as well. Long, slender fingers correlated with lithe, narrow waists, long legs, and modestly breasted torsos, whereas short, stubby fingers correlated with heavyset, blocky bodies, stumpy legs, and large-breasted torsos. Each time a young woman stepped to the front desk, he was presented with an opportunity to do more survey research, and after a few weeks of data gathering, he found that his theorem held up with a high degree of precision. That Granny Sun was a fox!

In China, it was unimaginable that people would work as hard as they did here just to perfect the shapes of their bodies. Chinese physiques were naturally sculpted through unavoidable and exhausting physical labor and even famine, while in America people overate and then toiled on their bodies as if on proprietary works of sculpture. They had, in effect, invented their own recreational equivalent of "reform through labor."

From the front desk, Little Li also quickly discerned that club members were divided physically into a virtual class system.

At the top of the male class structure were people like Lance Prince, a handsome "initiator" with curly blond hair, pearly white teeth, a spectacular physique, and an ingratiating manner, whom Little Li often saw pausing in front of a mirror to give a self-admiring twitch of a biceps or a flex of his abs. Lance took the Grecian Fitness Club's motto, "A GREAT BODY! GET IT! SHOW IT!," literally, and went about the task of bodybuilding with all the dedication of a "model worker" meeting a party-set production quota. But instead of producing tons of pig iron or kilos of sorghum for the state, his target was more muscle mass for himself.

At the other end of this class structure was a group of men as determined to deflect attention from their unprepossessing physiques as Lance was to attract it. Only after switching into baggy sweatshirts and oversized jogging suits did this group dare emerge from the locker room to face public scrutiny.

Then there were a few who marched to their own drummers, and by far the most eccentric of these was a spry sexagenarian known as "Spider-Man" who rarely missed a day at the club. His usual getup consisted of an old pair of high-top Converse sneakers (no socks), faded chartreuse jogging pants held up by a black leather dress belt, a limp Diet Pepsi cap worn backward, and a Spider-Man sweatshirt featuring the web-faced superhero crouched in arachnid-like readiness. Spider-Man was at the top of Milo's "Wackos List," and the first time Little Li saw him he'd just burst through the swinging doors from the men's locker room and, like a deranged dancer, started flinging himself pyrotechnically around the exercise-room floor. Then he began snapping his fingers in rhythm with the disco music and doing his version of jumping jacks, which involved clapping his hands over his head twice, like a cheerleader, each time he jumped. Finally, he doffed his Diet Pepsi cap, did a headstand, and began pedaling in the air with his feet like an overturned insect. Whenever he sensed he was losing people's attention, he would ratchet up the theatricality of his act.

One day, he sprang from the floor with a whoop, hopped onto a Lifecycle, pedaled for a few minutes, gyrated completely around on the seat, and then did a dramatic roll across the carpeted floor to the side of a young blond girl doing stretching exercises. There he began a set of push-ups that involved exaggerated pelvic thrusts, until an outraged matron stormed into Milo's office.

"Hey, you! *Spider-Man!*" Milo barked when he saw what was going on. "Knock that crap off or you're going to S.F. General for observation!" Suspended in the middle of one of his obscene push-ups, Spider-Man gave a lascivious leer, nimbly sprang to his feet, and retired to the locker room. "That weirdo drags down the tone of the whole club," grumbled Milo.

"You don't have to be Alfred Einstein to see that!" chimed in Annette DiSalvo.

Little Li found Annette, the club's most successful "initiator," intimidating. In her signature skintight silver leotard and black tights, she looked as sleek as a shark. Her ruby-red lips were almost always in constant motion, thanks to a two-pack-a-day sugarless Dentyne habit, and she chewed her gum so vigorously that it snapped like fat in a hot wok. Her signature expletive was "Naw! Get outta town!" For example, when Milo announced the club was having a new Jacuzzi installed, she stopped chewing gum long enough to exclaim, "A new Jacuzzi, Milo? Naw! Get outta town!"

As Little Li manned the front desk by day and performed janitorial duties by night, it was difficult to prevent his mind from running wild with fantasies involving some of the girls who paraded by him all day. Americans seemed to know how to bridge the gap between everyday chitchat and the bedroom. For him, this divide remained wider than the ocean he'd just spanned to come from China.

36

YEARNING

WHEN RIDING BACK to the Hotel Asterix one night, Little Li's bus stopped at a traffic signal on Diamond Heights where a lone couple stood in a pale circumference of light cast by a streetlamp. As wisps of windblown fog eddied around them, the woman turned to her lover, encircled his neck with her arms, and kissed him. Even as the bus pulled away, Little Li could not tear his eyes from them, for in this scene he felt he saw the whole universe of what was eluding him. It was one thing to have been deprived of such companionship at Yak Springs, where there were no possible mates, but quite another here in San Francisco. By concentrating on work, he was sometimes able to override his loneliness. However, a passing glimpse of such a couple together was often enough to overrun his flimsy defenses. In Chinese life, every sentiment, emotion, and desire required a mask, especially in politics, where almost every interaction demanded the use of some form of indirect "polite language" (客气话) or "ritual behavior" (礼节). One of the few times in adult life when men were permitted to engage in impulsive expressions of unrestrained emotion was with small children. But as soon as a child neared puberty, the holding, caressing, and kissing stopped, with a totality matched only by the extremism of Chinese politics. Fathers then retreated to postures of aloofness, and children were expected to start suppressing overt expressions of their own feelings and act with propriety. In this traditional scheme of things, the passions were viewed as needing to be restrained by etiquette (礼), lest, like wild beasts, they break loose, create disharmony, and disorder human affairs. Little Li wondered if he'd ever escape the confinement of such behavioral proscriptions to wrest a new life from this New World? Maybe he'd been foolish to dismiss Little Hong's instinct for a peaceful and harmonious Chinese life. What sort of imbecile would leave a woman like her for this uncertain, fickle, and uncaring land?

"Hey, Peking Man, c'mere!" Milo called out one day as he sat at the front desk. "You're the best, so I'm gonna promote you to 'initiator.'"

"You're going to what?" asked a stunned Little Li.

"Whatsa matter? You don' wanna move up, or what?"

"No, no," Little Li protested. "I appreciate your concern, Milo, but—"

"So—here's how I'm thinkin'," he interrupted. "The Asian market's gettin' stronger, and those Orientals are young and got bucks, and since you're one of 'em, maybe getting that irresistible Asian bod of yours out on the floor will turn some of those Asian dollies into 'kills'!" He looked up hopefully. "I'm gonna let you be the janitor, too. But just don't let the goddamn 'potentials' know you're the poor fuck who pulls the pussy hair out of the shower drains at night!" He gave Little Li a slap on the back. "Hey, Annette!" he called out. "Meet our newest 'initiator'!"

"Naw! Get outta town!"

"Yep," said Milo, putting one arm around Little Li's waist and the other around hers, as if they were about to take a group photo. "Now, Annette here's gonna rub some of her magic off on you, Li, and teach ya how it's done."

Milo may not have been able to pen elegant calligraphy or play Bach, but he had a good heart, and his kindness helped drown out the nagging voices of despair raging in Little Li's head. For now, he'd concentrate on making more money, escaping the Asterix, and then seeking to resume his musical studies.

Little Li spent the next several days following Annette around, never correcting her when she introduced him to "potentials" as "the new guy from Japan," a country she was convinced was more or less synonymous with his own. Watching her exploit her female wiles to convince male "potentials" to buy expensive memberships was like watching a skilled martial artist drop adversaries with a single deft blow. Before she went to work on someone, she tucked her wad of gum into one cheek, and then only after warming up a "potential" with a few personal questions and showing him (and it was almost always a man) around the club did she begin her rap about how "everyone deserves to give themselves a great body."

When she finally felt sufficient interest had been incubated, she maneuvered a "potential" toward the front desk, where, without breaking eye contact, she picked up a pre-positioned clipboard with a contract conveniently at the ready.

"Now, would you prefer to pay the modest yearly fee in low monthly installments or economical semiannual increments?" she would ask, slyly avoiding the question of whether the "potential" had decided he wanted a membership or understood how much membership actually cost. Dazzled by her rap, her body, and her resolve, few argued with her, and at the end of each month her name invariably appeared at the top of the sales ladder Milo kept on the mirror behind his desk.

Chairman Mao may have believed in anti-imperialism and class struggle as powerful engines of human motivation, but when Little Li watched club "initiators" sell memberships, such socialist incentives seemed to him dull tools compared with capitalist inducements. Whereas in China sexual attraction existed only as a hum beneath the surface, here it intruded overtly into almost every aspect of life, even commerce. As Little Li contemplated his future as an "initiator," he felt far from assured that, if he just "put his body out on the floor," the "Asian dollies" would come running. In fact, when he finally got his first "kill," it was not a beautiful young Asian girl, but Mrs. Mona Hughtower, whose membership had nothing to do with his prowess as a salesman.

Mona was led into the club by her sullen husband, Eddie, who, before Little Li could even begin his pitch, demanded, "How much is it?"

"For how long?"

"What's the longest period?" he'd countered. "What's forever cost?"

"Well, people usually sign up for a year at a time," Little Li began, immediately regretting he had not proposed a five-year membership. "But some people sign up for longer; you just have to . . ."

Eddie was not listening. Unsheathing an American Express Gold Card from a gallery of credit cards in his wallet, he snapped, "Mona here will take two years!"

Mona stood silently behind her husband, clutching a satchel like a refugee awaiting transshipment from a displaced-persons center. As soon as Eddie had signed the credit-card slip and stuffed the receipt into his wallet, he left. Although Little Li felt deflated by having to take custody of this dispirited, overweight woman, because she was his first "kill," he felt a proprietary responsibility. But when she emerged from the locker room in a leotard that still had the price tag hanging off it, he couldn't help thinking it was highly unlikely she'd ever find the resolve to lose enough weight to regain her dignity, much less Eddie's affections.

"Are you from the Orient, Mr. Li?" she asked.

"From China."

"Oh my, my! Don't you miss your home?" She seemed relieved to have found a reason to be able to express concern for someone else. When he started her on a Lifecycle, she hadn't pedaled for more than three minutes before she was puffing so hard she had to stop. Each time she came to the club thereafter, she was delivered by Eddie like a parent dropping a child off at school, and usually went right into the Jacuzzi. For him, Mona Hughtower was a reminder that even here in America there was failure.

As soon as he received his first "initiator's" commission, he opened a bank account, went to Chinatown, picked up a copy of the overseas edition of the *People's Daily* at the Eastwind Books, and treated himself to a northern Chinese meal at the Yenching Restaurant on Kearny Street. Looking through the paper, he was stunned to see a front-page headline proclaiming "Deng Xiaoping: Economic Reform and Opening to the Outside World Is the Unshakable Path of the Future" and an article below quoting him as saying, "We must not fear adopting the advanced management methods applied in capitalist countries. . . . Socialism and market economies are not incompatible." Another headline reported Premier Zhao Ziyang as having declared "Democracy Must Be Deepened!" But for him the most stunning thing was a photo showing a peasant woman standing with her family beside a new Toyota sedan under the headline "Party Leaders Praise Private Entrepreneurs." An article extolled her as a "new model" for having started a private chicken farm and becoming prosperous enough to be able to buy her own car. The recognition that in China farmers were acquiring cars, while here in America he was still taking public buses, hit Little Li hard. He'd dreamed of owning a car ever since riding into San Francisco from the airport, and often since had stopped to gaze into the windows of parked cars, trying to imagine what it would be like to own one. The interiors were so unbearably inviting, especially compared with Shanghai sedans, People's Liberation Army trucks, and boxy Soviet-built Ladas back home. He felt sheepish about how easily his materialist desires could eclipse other aspirations. But even if he tried, he knew he'd be no more successful at suppressing this longing for a car than at extirpating his desire for women. And since it seemed unlikely he'd soon be satisfying his urges for the latter, he decided that the moment he accumulated eight hundred dollars in commissions, he'd buy a car.

"By the way, you know you need a license to drive, don't you?" Milo asked when he heard the news. Seeing Little Li's crestfallen look, he added, "Tell ya what I'm gonna do. I'm gonna teach you how to drive, okay?" Little Li felt a rush of gratitude. But then, wagging an admonishing forefinger in his face, Milo added, "But put one scratch on the Town Car and I'm gonna send you back to Chairman Mayo, COD!"

"Don't worry," Little Li assured him. He hoped he was right.

Several weeks later, Milo drove him down to the DMV on Fell Street for his driving test. When he passed, Milo took his success as a triumph for both of them, which in a way it was.

"Now we come to step two, getting you some wheels," said Milo. "Here's the address of my pal Chuck Malavenco, at De Anza Used Cars."

The next day, Little Li took a bus to Redwood City, and walked down El Camino Real until he spotted a giant banner DE ANZA AAA USED CARS: HOME OF MIRACLE E-Z FINANCING: ASK FOR A PRICE!!! Stretching across the entire car lot were steel wires strung with bright-colored plastic pennants that snapped in the breeze like Tibetan prayer flags. Below were gleaming rows of cars, each windshield inscribed with a price and a cartoon face etched with an expression of amazement. He headed for a trailer on cinder blocks with a sign on the door saying: OFFICE.

"What can I do for you?" cheerfully asked a heavyset man sitting inside behind a desk with only a calculator on it.

"I'm looking for Chuck Malavenco."

"Is this something personal with Chuck, or are we talking a business type of deal?" asked the man, with considerably less good cheer.

"I want to buy a car," Little Li announced proudly.

"Well, Chuck's no longer with us here at De Anza, but if you want a fine used car, you've arrived at the right place!" He reached into his shirt pocket, took out a plastic wallet, and extracted a name card. "The name is Reddy, Al Reddy." Leaning back in his swivel chair, Reddy flipped on an air conditioner that made two strips of plastic tape tied to the grill flutter in the jets of cool air like fishing lures in a fast-moving stream. "You're Mr. . . . ?" He looked up expectantly.

"Mr. Li."

"Diet Coke, Mr. Li?"

Without waiting for an answer, Reddy opened the door of an old refrigerator behind his desk, took out two cans, expertly snapped their pop tops with the thumbs of each hand, and proffered one to Little Li. His first sip left his mouth ringing with an unpleasant aftertaste.

"Lemme ask you this," began Reddy with cheery unctuousness. "What price range are we're talkin' here?"

"Well, I have about—"

"Just give me a ballpark, so I know what part of the lot we'll be workin'," interrupted Reddy impatiently as he pulled his calculator closer. "Are we talkin' a coupla grand? What?"

"Well, actually, I only have seven hundred dollars."

"Okay . . ." Reddy's voice trailed off into a disappointed sigh.

"But I have cash," interjected Little Li, extracting his roll of twenties, hoping that a visual display would reignite Reddy's interest.

"Well, to be quite frank, Mr. Li, seven hundred dollars puts us almost off the lot and into the junkyard." He tapped a Marlboro out of a pack and lit up.

"Well—" began Little Li.

"So let's just head out back," interrupted Reddy

As they stepped outside, Reddy put on a pair of wraparound sunglasses, so that all Little Li could see when he looked at him was a distorted reflection of himself in the lenses. They'd walked only a few minutes when another car turned into the lot.

"Okay, my friend, ya see those babies in the last row? Anything behind 'em's in your range, and because you're Malavenco's pal, I'm gonna let you look 'em over by yourself. And if you feel any love from one of 'em, I'm gonna let you steal it from me!" He gave a smile lacking any hint of sincerity.

The back row of cars was bounded by a chain-link fence topped with coils of concertina wire, whose main purpose seemed to be to catch plastic bags as they blew across the lot like tumbleweeds. Once snagged, the bags fluttered in the breeze, slowly fraying into ghostly tatters as the plastic broke down in the bright California sunlight. Unlike the shining cars up front, those at the back were so dusty it was hard to tell one from another, much less to see inside. But Little Li liked their names: Mustang, Bronco, Barracuda, and Cougar suggesting the prowess of wild animals; Monte Carlo, Malibu, Eldorado, and Riviera, redolent of romantic places; and Gran Fury, Cutlass, Charger, and Marauder, conveying dashing martial qualities. The first vehicle in the row was a Plymouth Fury with its hood open and engine ripped out like an eyeball gouged from its socket. Behind it was a Buick Regal listing to one side on deflated tires, which reminded him of Master Chef Wang's choice of names for the visit of the American mountaineers to Yak Springs. In the next row sat a faded burgundy Oldsmobile Cutlass Supreme with automatic transmission, an AM-FM radio, a tape deck, a bumper sticker boasting an American flag and claiming THESE COLORS DON'T RUN! and a flaking leatherette-veneer roof that looked as if it had contracted a dermatological disorder. Even though it was a far cry from what he'd been dreaming about, the idea that he could just hand over his wad of cash and drive one of these cars away was still thrilling. He was about to open the Cutlass's door when Reddy reappeared.

"Once you get one of those Chinese sweethearts in the back seat, you're gonna start battin' home runs!" he said, slapping the car's dusty front fender. "So—what'll it take to put you in this baby?" Reddy's voice had suddenly turned as earnest as a preacher's.

"Well," said Little Li hesitantly, "how much is it?"

"C'mere, kid. I wanna show you something," responded Reddy, reminding Little Li of how "initiators" at the club avoided mentioning the full price of membership for as long as possible.

Reddy jerked open the door, dusted off the driver's seat with a Jack in the Box bag that he found lying on the floor, slid behind the wheel, and rammed a key into the ignition. Instead of the engine starting, however, the radio came on. "Slick as shit!" yelled Reddy over the hyperkinetic commercial that boomed forth. "I'll let this beaut out the door for seven even." He dangled the car keys in front of Little Li as if they were a magic charm. "If you want to trade up, that'll move us into the front of the lot."

"Let's see how this one does," replied Little Li.

"You got it!" Reddy pounded his foot down on the accelerator and twisted the key again. As the radio lost half its volume, the engine turned over a few times, then trailed off into a series of unenthusiastic clicks. Grimacing, Reddy pumped the accelerator a few more times and gave the key another twist. This time, the car coughed miraculously to life, belching out a cloud of gray exhaust.

"Like a charm!" said Reddy, cleaning the dirty windshield with the Jack in the Box bag and sliding over to the passenger side so Little Li could drive. As he eased the shift lever to "D," the car shuddered, but with gratifying smoothness began gliding forward. Long before Reddy told him to head back, Little Li had fallen in love with this Cutlass Supreme.

"Okay, let's do it!" exclaimed Reddy, putting a hand on Little Li's shoulder, as if he thought he might try to escape, and squired him back into the trailer. When he'd dropped into his swivel chair and lit up another Marlboro, Reddy pulled out a stack of forms and began filling them out. "Okay, as soon as I see some green, *amigo,* you're good to go!" he finally announced. When Little Li handed over his wad of twenties, Reddy licked his thumb, counted the bills, and then stuffed them unceremoniously into his pocket.

"Thank you," said Little Li, hardly able to wait for the moment when he could drive away alone.

"Roger that!" said Reddy, handing over the keys and showing no interest in prolonging the moment with any further ceremony.

As he cruised down El Camino Real, with one arm draped out the window and the wind blowing his hair, Little Li flicked on the radio and turned to KKHI, San Francisco's classical-music station. An announcer was just introducing Yo-Yo Ma playing the first of Bach's cello suites. With the volume cranked up so high he could almost feel the music on his skin, he sailed past fast-food restaurants, doughnut franchises, filling stations, and patio-and-pool-supply outlets invigorated by the blaring music and thought that he could now go wherever he wished whenever he wanted.

With the promise of America made a little closer, he headed up into the hills. As he wound along Alpine Highway, even the forest seemed to bespeak the differences between California and China. Chinese venerated ancient cypress and cedar trees whose twisted trunks and gnarled branches had been purposely deformed for aesthetic reasons, like the bound feet of girls, whereas Americans admired strong, tall, straight-grained redwood and fir trees that refused to bend for anyone, just like those towering over this highway. He thought of the old Chinese saying, "It's better to stand up and die rather than to kneel and live (宁可站着死 不愿跪着生)."

As he finally wound his way back downhill, he pulled over under a spreading oak in Burlingame just to enjoy the moment. His battered Cutlass was completely out of place among the gleaming BMWs and Audis that whizzed by, but he was soothed by the vista of the grand estates arrayed around him and didn't care. Just the knowledge that there were such lovely places with verdant gardens, aquamarine swimming pools, and white-fenced paddocks filled with sleek horses was somehow comforting. And it was strangely calming to follow the progress of a lawn-tractor with its tumorous bag ballooning from one side as a Latino driver navigated it back and forth across a vast sward, sucking up every last grass cutting, lest the well-manicured perfection of the lawn be marred by a single unruly blade. Across the road, fountains of water arced up from underground sprinklers, bathing another lawn in wreaths of rainbow-flecked mist, and throwing out so much surplus water that it sheeted out across the driveway and gurgled down a gutter into a storm drain. Like so many things in America, water was so limitless, people didn't even seem to notice it.

As a program featuring excerpts from various choral requia came on the radio, Little Li headed his Cutlass back to El Camino. But seeing that his fuel gauge was low, he pulled into a gas station that offered a free car wash with every fill-up. He was just rolling up his windows to enter the wash tunnel when the chorus "Dies Irae," "Days of Wrath," from the Verdi *Requiem* began thundering forth. It was the perfect score for the assault by robotic high-pressure nozzles firing jets of soapy water and the automated sponge mop with its foam-rubber tentacles that began engulfing the car:

Day of wrath and doom impending,
David's word with Sibyl's blending,
Heaven and earth in ashes ending!

And then, as if a programmer had personally scored a special sound track for his first American car-wash experience, as the Cutlass moved to the dry-and-buff cycle, Brahms's heartrendingly beautiful setting of the Eighty-fourth Psalm, "How Lovely Is Thy Dwelling Place," from his own requiem began:

How lovely is thy dwelling place, O Lord God of hosts!
My soul longeth, even fainteth, for the courts of the Lord!
My heart and flesh crieth out for the living God.
Blessed are they that dwell in the house of the Lord:
They will be ever praising thee.

He didn't return to his senses until an irritated Latino worker began banging with a squeegee on his windshield, demanding that he restart his engine and leave the tunnel. When he finally emerged out into the blinding California sunlight again, his Cutlass still did not exactly gleam, but it was at least clean. Milo's father had "made it" with a chain of pizza restaurants, maybe he'd make it with a chain of Requiem Car Washes: "Each cycle of your wash experience scored to a part of a great requiem mass!"

Several weeks later, he was driving up Jackson Street, near Chinatown, when he passed a group of men in dark suits milling about on a sidewalk. At first he thought he'd happened upon a congregation waiting to enter a church, except it was not Sunday, and the way these pilgrims clasped their hands behind their backs and stood like a flock of penguins unmistakably marked them as visiting Chinese. Pulling the Cutlass curbside, he watched from across the street. For Little Li, there was something morbidly fascinating about studying his fellow countrymen from afar. He watched as a middle-aged man hiked up the tails of his suit jacket, grabbed the end of his long belt, unbuckled it, and cinched up his trousers until they were pleated around his waist like a laundry bag pulled tight by a drawstring. Left over, however, was a foot-long piece of surplus belt hanging down over his fly like the tongue of a panting dog. This sojourner's solution was to blithely thread it back through the loops of his trousers, for safe storage.

Why were men's belts always too long only in China? Was this some sort of perverse fashion statement, or were the Chinese simply victims of a centralized Ministry of Belts that had commanded all state-owned enterprises in the belt sector to produce one uniform-length product for simplicity's sake? But why didn't men just lop off a hank and adjust their belts to their own waist sizes? Some things about his homeland were unknowable.

When he realized that this gaggle of men were Chinese, his initial impulse had been to stroll over and find out where they were from. But the longer he watched, the less inclined he became to do so. Because their boxy shoes, ill-fitting suits, provincial hairstyles, and absurd belts made them seem so undissolvable in this American world, he wanted to avoid them. They made him feel he was looking at himself. So, instead of walking over, he just rolled down his window and eavesdropped. He couldn't hear everything they were saying, but he could catch snatches of their conversations: "Oh, she'd love a tape recorder"; "Don't you already have a VCR?"; "No, no, the Wangs already have two cordless phones"; "How about a TV set for . . . ?" Then he saw the reason they'd gathered. Over a doorway hung a yellow sign:

YIP'S ELECTRONICS:
WALKMANS, VCRS, TVS, STEREOS, PHONES AND MORE!

This was a visiting Chinese delegation's last day in the United States, a time when members were given a chance to buy a "big item" (大件) that customs officials now allowed to be brought home duty-free from a trip abroad. Little Li knew they'd all been hoarding their per-diem allowances so that they'd have sufficient foreign exchange to make this purchase.

His meditation was interrupted when a Chinese man with pomaded hair emerged from the shop, unceremoniously pushed the waiting group against the wall and then opened a set of double doors. To Little Li's surprise, out of the store came a different delegation, each member lugging a large carton or bag. Yip's was like a bordello that sold electronic goods rather than sex.

Little Li waited until after the new delegation had entered Yip's. Then he crossed the street to peer into the store through the front window. Everyone inside was far too preoccupied with poring over the stacks of New Orleans–style decorator telephones, Sony Quasar color televisions, Dream Machine bedside radios, and Samsung Galaxy ghetto blasters to pay him any heed. He understood perfectly the conflicted feelings a place like Yip's aroused in his visiting fellow countrymen: their craving for electronic gear collided head-on with the party's earlier prohibitions against expressing overt cravings for anything foreign. What's more, Yip's would only make it more difficult for these comrades to fully accept their lives back home—unless China, too, someday turned into a big shopping mall. It seemed a distant dream, but who could say where this endlessly energetic country was headed now that so many conflicting forces had been unleashed.

For now, however, these visitors were left to "Look at the flowers from a galloping horse" (走马观花), so perhaps it was just as well they were on their way home. Why infect them with too much enticement? And if any of them did somehow manage to stay on in the United States, wouldn't they just end up like him: toiling in a fitness club and living in a skid-row hotel among a jumble of castoff appliances?

Such thoughts made him want to cry out a warning! But what kind of warning? Against staying in America, or going back to China? Given the magnitude of tragedy that most had suffered, it was understandable that some might idealize life in a more promising land. Hadn't he himself had such dreams? And even if this dreamland held no guarantees, a person here could, at least, buy a car, collect secondhand appliances, and binge-eat "crippled" Sara Lee coffee cakes. Wasn't that consolation enough? Of course, Mao had never placed much stock in such private dreams or individual wealth, much less in household appliances. His had been a far grander collective dream of a great, reunified, powerful country, of national "rejuvenation" (复兴) and "wealth and power" (富强) regained, not of tape decks and cordless phones.

Not quite sure what came over him, Little Li got back into his Cutlass, drove across the Golden Gate Bridge, and did not stop until he reached Muir Beach. There he sat down on the sand in the fog and watched the waves break. He'd been in America only a year, but it already seemed like an eternity, especially since an impermeable membrane still separated him from the world into which he'd arrived.

37

"WE GOT a 'potential' on deck for you," Stephanie sang out from the front desk as Little Li entered the club lobby.

"Thanks," he replied. "Let me change first."

When he emerged from the locker room, he found a young woman with a look of despair on her face waiting on the leatherette couch opposite the front desk.

"When I start gaining, the pounds go down there and not up here," complained Pam Keller, moving her pale hands from her hips to her modest breasts.

"I think we can devise a training program to help you," Little Li responded as clinically as possible. As she began exercising, Pam Keller, who worked at the Yes Burger upstairs in the mall, began exuding the aroma of fried onion rings. As much as he wanted another "kill," he was having a difficult time concentrating. It was while staring vacantly across the aerobics room that he first caught sight of *her*. She was tall, wore a purple leotard over black tights, and was effortlessly bending over at the waist and touching her palms to the floor in cadence with the music. Among other club members, she stood out like a graceful yacht sailing through a flotilla of barges.

"Okay. Now what, Mr. Li?" Pam Keller was suddenly at his side again.

Reluctantly, he turned his attention back to her. But as soon as he'd shown her how to use the double chest machine, he tried to relocate his quarry. She was lying on her back now with her hands behind her head, slowly arching her body up in undulating rhythms that were so graceful they looked choreographed. Then his concentration was interrupted again by the aroma of fried onion rings, and he had to guide Pam Keller to a Lifecycle and get her pedaling.

When he was next able to spot the phantom woman, she was at the barre, doing a series of pliés. Lance Prince was also staring at her. But instead of basking in his attention, she seemed to neutralize it, as if she was accustomed to being in the public eye.

"Is the old one-eyed weasel talkin' to ya?" Milo unexpectedly asked, sidling up and sliding a furry arm around Little Li's shoulders. "You won't have to do all your lookin' today, chief, 'cause—guess what?—old Milo just hired her as our new aerobics instructor."

"Good work, Milo!" exclaimed Little Li, enjoying this moment of male bonding. Then, unexpectedly, Milo grabbed him by the arm and towed him over to the barre.

"Hey, Juliette. Meet Li here," he said with a broad smile. "He's the best. Since you two will be working together, you need to connect." Milo winked and obligingly returned to his office.

"Quite an introduction," she said, brushing a wisp of hair from her perspiring brow.

"Milo's known to overdo things," replied Little Li, trying not only to mask his breathlessness, but to speak unaccented English.

"Well, to cut to the chase, my name is Juliette Shaw."

"And mine is Li Wende," he replied, shaking her hand.

"Say that again?" she asked, wrinkling her brow.

"Li, like 'Lee' in the jeans. Then Wende, like 'wonder.' It's Chinese."

"Oh, really," she said with surprise. "Have you been working here long?"

"A little while."

"How is it?" she asked, leaning toward him as if to make sure they would not be overheard. The refreshing fragrance of gardenias hung in the air about her, providing a welcome counterpoint to Pam Keller.

"It's okay," he replied. "But there are some pretty strange people here."

"And do you do anything else besides this?" She gestured around the club.

"Yeah, I play the flute," he replied, glad to establish himself as more than an "initiator."

"Really?"

"And you?"

"I dance. Ballet. Just need to make a few bucks, so it's the aerobics class for me."

"It was difficult to find much dance in Beijing," he offered, thinking of his outing to the Houston Ballet's performance.

"Oh, so you're actually *from* China!" she exclaimed, her eyes studying him as if she now felt the need to make a more complete assessment.

"Yeah."

"Wow!" she replied. "Ever since I saw that over-the-top ballet, *The Red Detachment of Women*, with all those rifle-toting ballerinas hurling themselves around the stage, I've been interested in China."

"That ballet was a favorite of Mao's wife, and . . ." Alas, before he could finish, a perspiring Pam Keller reappeared.

"Well, nice to meet you," he interjected. "I've got a client to take care of, so . . ."

"At least I'll be seeing you around the club, no?" she said, giving him an inviting smile. Then she raised one long leg effortlessly and rested it on the barre. The shape of her calf was so riveting he had a hard time tearing his eyes away.

Juliette Shaw's 5:30 aerobics class quickly became the talk of the club, but he did not see her again until several days later, when she came running into the club late for the class.

"Could you call this number at the San Francisco Ballet and ask for Anna?" she asked breathlessly. "Tell her that Juliette got stuck in traffic and she's sorry she missed her appointment." She grimaced and ran into the locker room.

"Sorry I'm late everybody," she announced to her waiting class when she re-emerged. "Okay, to get going, everyone down on the floor, please!" She lay on her back to lead leg-raising exercise. "And—one, two, three, four," she called out in rhythm to the music pounding over the PA system. "All right. Give me another set," she continued. Her tights adhered so perfectly to her body that, except for the color, she seemed all but naked. Again and again she raised and lowered her own graceful legs, as if they were immune to gravity. Compared with the class members struggling to keep up, she was a swan among geese.

After he'd locked the door behind the last departing club members that night, he wrapped a towel around his waist and headed for the comforting solitude of the steam room. But as he padded down the hallway, he was astonished to find Juliette still in the aerobics room in ballet slippers doing positions at the barre. He hardly dared breathe as he watched. But then, as if she'd known he'd been watching, she suddenly pirouetted across the floor and came to a stop right in front of where he stood.

"Hi!" She smiled.

"What are you doing here so late?" he asked.

"Practicing. I have a performance coming up."

"Where?"

"The Marin Ballet."

"Where's Marin?"

"Across the Golden Gate Bridge." She looked at him for a moment without speaking, as if a thought was still forming in her mind. "You should come," she finally added.

"I'd love to," he replied, hoping he didn't sound too eager.

"Forgive my nosiness," she said, cocking her head quizzically to one side. "But, how does a musician from communist China end up a muscle man in a California fitness club?" The question caught him off guard. He was, after all, clad only in a skimpy towel, and the way she allowed her gaze to fall away from his face to the rest of his naked body made him feel very self-conscious.

"It's a long story," he said.

"I'm sure it is." She laughed. "But sometime I'd like to hear it."

"I'll be glad to tell you . . . sometime. But I'll let you get back to practicing now. I'm going to have a quick steam bath before closing the place up."

"Bye," she said, waggling fingers on one hand in the gesture people reserve for bidding farewell to small children.

It was inside the steam room, after everyone else had left the club, that Little Li felt most at ease. And now, he closed the door, drew in a long inhalation of hot, moist, aromatic air, and then climbed to the highest ledge to lay down. As he became drenched with sweat and condensation dripping down like tropical rain from the overhead tiling, he couldn't stop thinking about Juliette, standing on one leg at the barre like a flamingo. But even though he knew she was just outside, she was as chimerical as a "fox spirit" in an ancient Chinese story, who was said to materialize as a beautiful woman to tempt naïve men, only to vanish just before the anticipated moment of consummation. Maybe, he thought, it was his fate just to be a bystander, a vigil keeper for whom fantasy never becomes reality, no matter which side of the Pacific Ocean he lived on.

As the steam machine tripped on like a hissing locomotive, he closed his eyes. In the warmth and wetness, a vision of Juliette's smiling face blossomed before him. That was so real, he even allowed himself to imagine he could feel her skin brushing his, her lips pressing against his own, and could smell the aroma of her gardenia scent.

"Are you . . . ?"

"Shhhhhhh," the rushing steam whispered in reply.

But then something seemed to caress his chest, and he wanted Juliette with a fierce desire. But could one embrace a desire as real? He felt he had fallen into the great Ming Dynasty play, *The Peony Pavilion,* in which the heroine's passion allows her to dream up an imaginary lover, Liu Mengmei, and then to fall irretrievably in love with him. After all, wrote the author, Tang Xianzu, "What a thin line divides reverie and reality. Who can say what is real and not?"

As slippery breasts seemed to slide up his chest, a wiry nest to press against his thighs, and lips to kiss his face, he no longer knew if he was only dreaming.

"I've been watching you," a voice whispered through the hissing steam.

When he opened his eyes, Juliette's face hovered in the misty half-light above him. Not wanting to break the spell, he reached out and pressed her slippery body to his own. She melted without resistance. Whenever he'd imagined seduction, it had always involved design and artifice. But now everything was suddenly effortless, weightless, exhilarating.

When Juliette arrived at the club the next afternoon, she was again late, and the hallway outside the aerobics room was filled with milling members waiting for her class to begin. She rushed into the locker room without seeing Little Li standing by the squat machine. He didn't have a clue what protocol was here in America after such an assignation, which still seemed as fantastical to him as a dream. Was he naïve in assuming that some ongoing connection was forged during such an encounter? What would she think if she knew that, in hopeful anticipation of another night of abandon, he'd stopped by the Emporium that morning and spent twelve dollars on a tube containing three new pairs of bright-red Calvin Klein jockey shorts?

For all he knew, after these unpredictable American girls made love to someone, maybe they just went on their way as if nothing much had happened. Nothing he'd learned in China had relevance for a circumstance like this. Of course, he understood that one plum blossom didn't mean springtime, and that, when it came to foreigners, allowances had to be made for boundless unpredictability.

All his uncertainties were only heightened as male club members flocked around Juliette after her class was over. Watching as she chatted and smiled with them, he felt as powerless as a defendant awaiting a court verdict. What was most unnerving was his wanton hunger for her. He had to remind himself that she was her own independent person, not a prosthetic device to be strapped on by him so he wouldn't have to hobble around America like a cripple. He was on the verge of abandoning all hope when she looked up, spotted him, and bounded over with an expectant smile on her lovely perspiration-streaked face.

"Well, Initiator Li," she asked with the kind of playfulness enjoyed by those with an inborn expectation of being responded to in a favorable manner. "What've you got to say for yourself today?"

"I am speechless," he replied. Although he was intending to be humorous and suave, his rejoinder also had the virtue of truthfulness.

"You're a strange one," she said, smiling, her chest still heaving from her class. "Will you give me a lift home tonight?" She went up on tiptoes to kiss him.

"Of course," he replied—not too eagerly, he hoped, but he felt near a boiling point.

"Your place or mine?"

"If you could see my place, you'd definitely say yours." He smiled.

"When you see mine, you might change your mind." She let out a peal of laughter. "Just tell me when you're ready. I'll be in the aerobics room."

Never had he done his chores so quickly. Hoping that Milo would not notice, he neither vacuumed the carpets nor mopped the floors. As he was unlocking his Cutlass in the parking lot, she stepped back as if to contemplate the vehicle like a great work of art.

"A chariot fit for a queen!" she exclaimed.

"Well, we Chinese are accustomed to treating our honorable guests grandly," he joked.

No sooner had they stepped into her street-level studio than her phone rang. As she ran to answer it, he surveyed the cavernous space. She lived in an old Laundromat so heaped with piles of things it looked a little like the As-Is Department at Out of the Closet. Because he could find no other place to sit, he repaired to her bed, which consisted of a mattress on a box spring. He could not miss the aerosol canister of contraceptive foam that sat on the overturned milk crate that served as her bedside table—obviously, he was hardly the first man to make landfall in her singular boudoir. The notion that he was just another male playmate whose spawn would need killing by this curbside fire hydrant in order to satisfy her evidently boundless sexual appetites made him cringe. He'd just picked a copy of *Dance Magazine* up off the floor, and was trying to distract himself by reading an article about the Bolshoi Ballet Theater, when she finished her call, spun around, and leapt onto the bed. Slithering up to him, she shed her clothing like a snake molting its skin, unbuckled his belt, yanked off his trousers. Moments later, they were locked together again.

Afterward, she asked if he wanted to stay over. He did not hesitate to accept, and for the first time had a real chance to look around the ex-Laundromat she called home.

While most people live in spaces divided into separate sections reserved for eating, sleeping, entertaining, bathing, and working, in Juliette's "studio" such separations were blurred. Other than her kitchen, which occupied one corner of the large room, and the bathroom, which consisted of a sink, a shower stall, and a toilet lined up against one wall with a shower curtain around them, the rest was common space. Even after growing up in the land of the people's communes, where privacy was considered counterrevolutionary and individual toilet stalls a bourgeois affectation, he found her studio overly communal and chaotic. Clothing, appliances, junk mail, dishes, paintings, plants, photographs, and useless furniture were strewn around helter-skelter. One defunct washing machine served as a repository for ballet slippers, another for old music tapes, and a third for empty jars and bottles. The couch was heaped with laundry and the bed was a snarl of clothing, blankets, sheets, and pillows that never got "made." When he asked why a floral-print bedspread hung on a coatrack by the front door, she insisted it served as a reminder to do the laundry. And when he inquired about the provenance of certain other piles of things, she waved the questions off, protesting that they belonged to the landlord. Whatever the case, Juliette had clearly made her own substantial contribution to the disorder. Only against one wall was there a clearing where a ballet barre had been affixed to the wainscoting below a large mirror.

Throughout this repurposed Laundromat roamed Petit Paws, a long-haired cat named after the nineteenth-century St. Petersburg choreographer Marius Petipa, who, as soon as anyone sat down, started purring like a small engine. Juliette adored Petit Paws.

"Perhaps I should get a second cat in your honor," she offered playfully one night. "I could name it Chairman Meow."

"I'd be honored," he said and laughed.

So enchanted was Little Li by Juliette just then that, if her cavalier attitude toward outer order bespoke of any deeper character flaw, he was more than willing to overlook it. For since arriving in America, this was the first time that he'd felt he was actually living; it was hardly surprising, then, that whenever he found himself impatiently wondering why she did not organize her clothes, wash the dishes, clean the bathroom, or do the laundry, all it took was her bewitching touch to override his urge to criticize.

"Do you know what I think?" she asked unexpectedly one evening as they were leaving the club.

"What?"

"Your clothes don't measure up to your bod! They're a bit . . . clunky!"

"Clunky?" he asked. Although he was unsure what the term meant, he was under no illusion that his wardrobe, a combination of garments from China and Out of the Closet, constituted much of a fashion statement.

"You definitely need a makeover!"

"A what?"

"A makeover! We're gonna slick you up!"

"I'm in," he replied, using a Milo-ism.

So off they went to the Gap one Sunday, and an hour later he emerged decked out in a new pair of gray slacks, a tight-fitting green sports shirt, and a zippered black jacket.

"Not bad! Not bad at all!" she said, laughing as she inspected him. "There's only one problem: now I won't have such a strong impulse to undress you!" She slid a finger down under his new belt.

Now that he was better dressed and had an American girlfriend, Little Li decided he also needed better grooming habits. After he washed his hair, which he did almost every day at the club, it had the unfortunate tendency to stick up. What was worse, if he went to bed with a wet head, he woke up looking as if a typhoon had hit him. At Yak Springs, no one but Station Chief Wu worried about such tonsorial matters, and around the Asterix he could have dyed his hair green and no one would have batted an eye.

"With a can of Crisco," Juliette joked one morning as she ran her hand through his disobedient hair, "I could turn you into Beijing's first punker!"

But he was distrustful of her fascination with the bizarre, for where she seemed to aspire to be part of the rebellious avant-garde, he aspired to fit in. To tame his hair, he considered not shampooing so often, but since showers were one of the most enjoyable luxuries of American life, he was unwilling to forgo their pleasure. The idea of hair tonic repelled. Finally, he discovered that if he used Juliette's jojoba-bean shampoo and wore a hat after showering, he could tame his hair. As part of this new hair-care regimen, he bought a shovel-billed cap at Out of the Closet, embossed on the crown with "God Bless John Wayne!" He had no idea who John Wayne was.

38

AMBIGUITY

AS SHE waited for him to finish vacuuming the club, Juliette sat on the carpeted aerobics-room floor, legs spread, with a copy of *The New Yorker* open in front of her.

"What are you reading?" he asked.

"Oh, some article on China by someone I heard talk on NPR."

"On China?" he asked, flattered to find her curious about his country.

"Yeah, I'm really interested," she replied, bending her supple body forward until her chin touched the open magazine.

"Who wrote the article?"

"Some American guy who did a series for the magazine about all the changes going on over there that ended up as a book entitled *To Get Rich Is Glorious*."

"You don't expect to learn anything about China from a white guy, do you?" he challenged. "They never let foreigners see what's really going on." She looked at the magazine's cover, which showed a row of persimmons on a windowsill, and then back at him.

"Well, if I can't read articles, how am I going to understand you and the mysteries of the East?"

"Just hang with me." He smiled.

"God, when you talk hip, it turns me on!" She reached out and goosed him. He jumped back, still wielding his vacuum-cleaner nozzle.

"But, seriously," he persisted, "you can't expect a foreigner to know what's going on in China, because the party lies about everything, especially to outsiders."

"Why do they tell so many lies?"

"Because if they told the truth they'd look bad and lose face."

"So—tell me something: would you read a book about America written by a Chinese?"

"Are you kidding?" His voice dripped with scorn. "If I wrote a book, would you read it?"

"I probably would."

"Why?"

"Because I'd be curious to see what a Chinese guy like you makes of this place."

"Did you Americans always find us Chinese so interesting?"

"I did."

"Why?"

"I don't know, but maybe because we Americans couldn't go to China for so long and we love places where we're not wanted! That's why as a kid I always loved the idea of Tibet. It was a forbidden mystery. You're a little like that, too, my friend. I have a hard time seeing into you." He sensed she was saying something important about herself, him, and China, but he had to get back to work or they'd never get home, so the conversation ended. When he finished cleaning up, she was in the pool. It was only when she pulled herself up dripping wet onto the ledge beside him that he realized she was stark naked.

"Were you ever in love with a Chinese girl?" she asked, sweeping some wet hair from her eyes.

"Well, sort of," he said tentatively.

"Sort of?" she exclaimed. "What the hell does that mean?"

"Well, there was someone at the Conservatory who . . ."

"What did she look like?"

"She was . . ." He halted.

"Why won't you tell me?" she persisted.

"Why do you want to know?"

"Because I can hardly imagine what girls are like over there and it turns me on to think of you with some lovely little Chinese girl in a Mao suit."

"Turns you on?"

"Yup! So tell me."

"You're strange!"

"Strange or not, I want to know."

"Well, she played a traditional stringed instrument called the *yangqin* and was . . ." He immediately felt he was betraying Little Hong, especially by talking about her in the past tense.

"Was she beautiful?"

"I thought so."

"And did you sleep with her?" Juliette looked right at him. "Or don't you people do that sort of thing over there?"

He was both offended and impressed by the unperturbed way she could probe something so personal. He would have preferred to detect a flicker of jealousy in her curiosity, but all he sensed was prurience. Then before he could respond, she slipped back into the water. When she surfaced again, before he could get away, she'd grabbed his ankles and pulled him, clothes and all, into the pool.

"And, how about you, Juliette?" he asked as they drove back to her studio. "Have you ever been in love before?"

"There've been a few people," she said evasively. "But, frankly, I don't think you want to know about them." She was right. Whereas she'd seemed titillated by the idea of his lovers, he was not excited by the idea of hers.

One night, she suggested they eat at a nearby Chinese restaurant, and he was at first pleased. However, while Juliette loved the neon-red sweet-and-sour pork that came laced with big chunks of Day-Glo yellow canned pineapple, he found the food at The Dragon and Pearl—which advertised its "specialties" as "Hunan, Sichuan, and Mandarin"—execrable.

Whenever he'd felt critical of her, he'd reminded himself that things were going pretty well. However, when he looked into the future, all he saw were question marks that he tried to write off as owing to his own innately distrustful disposition.

"What's going on?" she asked when he fell suddenly quiet.

"Oh, nothing," he replied, hardly knowing how to respond.

"Something," she insisted.

"Sometimes everything about you puzzles me," he replied.

"About me?" she countered, staring at him with a sudden intensity. "You, sir, are also a bit of a mystery, if I may say so. I let you into my pants every night, but I'm still wondering: Who the hell is this guy? Where does he come from? What's his trip? I mean, how did I get involved with such a character?"

"Well, if it's any consolation, I ask myself the same questions."

"And another thing," she continued. "There are always so

many wheels turning in your head. What are you always thinking about?"

"Life."

"Life? Whoa! That's really deep! Let me know if you make any sense out of it, because I sure can't."

"My life didn't make any sense in China, either, but there we didn't expect it to make sense. Difficulties felt normal! However, here . . ." He wasn't sure how to finish his thought.

"Well, my mystery man, here's a question for you: are you a real communist?" She had a mischievous glint in her eyes.

"No! No!" he protested. "I never joined the Communist Party. They wouldn't let me!"

"Too bad. I've never slept with a real communist, even anyone from a communist country. I've always liked the idea of being ravished by a real communist revolutionary."

"I'm sorry to disappoint you," he said unenthusiastically. "It seems that anything you don't understand excites you."

"Sort of. You excite me because you came out of nowhere and seem to go nowhere."

"What do you mean?"

"I mean, you're sitting right in front of me, but your past vanishes around so many corners, I can't see where it comes from."

He'd never really talked about himself, perhaps because he couldn't imagine her ever truly understanding his life. As she ate her sweet-and-sour pork now, he tried to give her the outlines of his life. But the more he told her, the more bizarre it sounded, even to him, almost as if he were telling an unlikely tall tale. For some reason she was most interested in the Goloks.

"I wish I could have met you in your native habitat and seen those nomad guys up there in Tibet!" she gushed.

"Well, it wasn't exactly *my* native habitat," he countered. "I didn't go there voluntarily!"

"When I was little, I read this book about an Austrian mountain climber who was a Nazi and escaped from a British detention camp in Pakistan during World War II and trekked all the way to Lhasa to become the Dalai Lama's tutor. I think the book was called *Seven Years in Tibet*. Anyway, ever since, I've wanted to go there. Oh, Little Li, would you take me up there to Tibet sometime? Please!" she squealed with delight, as if they could just sally forth to Tibet like characters in a Tintin comic. Americans were like that. As soon as they impulsively thought of something, they wanted to run off and do it, the more exotic the better. "Why are you smiling?" she asked.

"I am trying to imagine you up there, but I really don't think you'd like a place that's so backward." He was having difficulty visualizing this white-skinned American ballerina in the Yak Springs canteen, much less in Lobsang's tent.

"But Tibet's so strange and romantic!" she effused.

"Tibetans do have their charm, but their lives are really hard."

"Well, I just like the sound of the name!" As she said "Tibet" she squeezed her eyes closed, as if she was being possessed by a sudden vision.

"Okay!" He laughed. "So—someday we'll go to Tibet together." The last thing he wanted was to put himself at cross-purposes with such delightful, if naïve, enthusiasm. A little "barbarian management," he reminded himself, was always advised when dealing with whimsical, unpredictable foreigners.

"Your life is like two parallel universes!" she continued. "There's the Little Li who's sitting here in front of me, and then that other, shadow Little Li I can't see."

"Sometimes I feel I do come from two parallel universes," he replied, realizing that there was a lot more going on inside her head than he'd originally supposed.

"So, if you had that sweet little Tootsie Pop over there in Beijing, why did you leave?"

"Well . . ." He gave a deep sigh. "My mother was from here, and my father studied here, and so I felt this piece of me needed some exploration."

"And, what have you found?"

"I'm still looking."

"Do you think you were right to leave home?"

"I don't know." The word "home" rang in his ears.

"It's almost like you've been reincarnated into a new body in a new place, just like a Tibetan lama!"

"Maybe," he responded, impressed by her analogy, for that was exactly how he often felt. "Sometimes I think my body got here but my soul didn't, that it's still wandering around over the Pacific Ocean someplace, trying to catch up."

"Well, you have a really nice body, so at some point I'm sure your soul will want to reclaim it!" She grinned and reached under the table to squeeze his thigh.

"So—now it's your turn," he said. "Where did you come from?"

"Ahhh, yes!" she said evasively. "Me."

"Well . . . ?"

Without great enthusiasm, she explained she was from Vermont, had gone to college in Boston, come to San Francisco four years ago to study dance, and was now, as she put it with an elusive smirk, "in between transitions."

"But that doesn't tell me very much," he protested.

"My life is dull compared to yours. Let's just go back to my place and make the monster with two backs!" As they drove home, he had a sense that she was just as divided and enigmatic as he was.

Back at her studio, she pirouetted to the sink, grabbed her toothbrush, brushed her teeth, and shed her clothing in another few perfectly choreographed steps. Then, like a beaver plunging into its underwater lodge, she dived buck-naked into the tangle of blankets and sheets on her bed.

"Betcha can't find me!" she playfully cried out.

As he sat down on the edge of the mattress to undress, a hand reached out and snapped the elastic on his jockey shorts. Then two arms grabbed his waist and pulled him into the tangle of bedding. He was surprised by her strength. Little Hong's body had been soft and delicate, but Juliette's was muscled and firm. Grappling playfully with him, she rolled him over onto his back and perched triumphantly on top of him like a wrestler.

"If you don't surrender, Comrade Li, I'm going to do unspeakable things to you!" She rolled her eyes salaciously.

"Like what?"

"Like . . . !" She slid her breasts down his stomach to his crotch. Then, as a bus lumbered up the hill outside, she grabbed his erection and, as if she were the driver shifting gears, rammed it forward into first, then sharply backward, as if into a higher gear, all the while making sounds of an engine revving at high rpms, like a child at play. He knew he could not be dreaming, because who—especially a Chinese—was capable of dreaming such a scene? Flushed with strength and confidence, he kissed her through a cascade of hair.

Juliette articulated what she wanted without fear of rebuke.

She made love the same way she taught aerobics, danced, kept house, cooked, even undressed—namely, unrepentantly. Just as Petit Paws rubbed herself against any living thing to satisfy her insatiable craving for physical contact, Juliette sought gratification. How uncomplicated life must be, he thought, for someone who did not always fear being denied! As he contemplated her beside him now, he hoped some of these qualities would be contagious and inoculate him, too, against the purgatory of wanting and waiting.

The next morning, when he awakened, she was already at her makeshift barre, wearing nothing but ballet slippers. With one arm gracefully arced overhead and the long dancer's muscles of her thighs and buttocks articulating with feline grace, she did one plié after another. Then both arms swept up over her head as she did a port de bras, the sinuous muscles across her back rippling like taut vines. Moving on to a développé, she raised one left leg slowly and elegantly through the various positions until it was high over her head. Whereas she seemed almost reckless in so many other aspects, in dance she was disciplined. Then, suddenly, she was bounding across the studio with her breasts bouncing.

"Banzai!" she yelled, grabbing her perfume atomizer and squeezing off one fusillade of gardenia-scented L'Air du Temps perfume after another. He finally managed to subdue her by grabbing one of her wrists and pulling her into the tangle of bedclothes on top of him.

"You shameful seducer!" she cried when they'd finished. "I'm late again for rehearsal!" With that, she sprang out of bed, dressed, and ran out the door.

Whenever an appealing idea came to her, Juliette immediately wanted to change plans. One Sunday, they were already at a Laundromat with a pile of wash when she saw an article in a stray newspaper about the African-cat exhibit at the San Francisco Zoo; with unalloyed joy, she insisted they go. "Maybe we could even take Petit Paws," she said with a laugh, pressing one of his hands to her breasts, as if his consent could be influenced by the hint of a payoff. It was impossible to resist such enthusiasm, so they lugged the unwashed laundry back to her studio, dumped it unceremoniously inside the front door, and took off for the zoo.

Then one night as they were on their way to the store for provisions so he could cook a Chinese dinner when she spotted a new Vietnamese-French restaurant called La Nouvelle Saigon.

"Oh, let's eat here!" she exclaimed, seeing tables set with checkered cloths and a chef in a white toque in an open kitchen. "It's so cute!"

He'd been looking forward to cooking a real Chinese meal for her and was disappointed to have the opportunity snatched away. But, because her spontaneity was not susceptible to any known antidote, he yielded. And the Vietnamese-Chinese chef served them a wonderful dinner. When Little Li found he spoke Chinese, she gazed at him as if he was a linguistic prodigy.

"I could never learn such a language!" she said in wonder.

"Well, over a billion Chinese have, so I'm sure you could, too," he replied, smiling.

Little Li came to love Juliette's neighborhood. Unlike the dark, claustrophobic Tenderloin, Noe Valley was clean and light, with a breeze off Diamond Heights so fresh it made him feel tipsy just to walk down the street. And there was one house he always enjoyed passing, because piano music often spilled forth from an open window. At such moments, he felt a sense of rebirth, and in certain ways he was being reborn and Juliette was the midwife. Only a short while ago, life had seemed quite hopeless, but now the portals of this land of milk and honey had opened. Nonetheless, he often felt that China was still somehow lurking—waiting for him to falter so it could reclaim him? After all, as every Buddhist knows, nothing lasts forever.

As he spent more time at Juliette's studio, he continued to be amazed by the things he discovered. Like an archaeological dig, in which new artifacts keep being exposed as new strata were excavated, unexpected finds kept revealing themselves. For instance, one morning he was astounded to discover the end of an upright piano peeking out from a pile of what looked like old drapery.

"Oh, it belongs to my predecessor," she said offhandedly, and threw some draperies back over it.

When making tea one morning in what passed as her kitchen, he spotted a box of outdated birth-control pills on a shelf, between a jar of jam and a box of cornflakes. Then he found a can marked "Mixed Nuts" that contained a welter of scratch-and-sniff perfume samples torn out of glossy magazines. When Juliette caught him examining them, she laughed, extracted a Guerlain Shalimar sample, scratched it, and daubed herself daintily behind each ear.

"A bit of extra refinement is something no young woman in today's competitive world can afford to be without," she warbled. Then, closing her eyes, she theatrically thrust her face toward him and said, "Kiss me, my prince." He needed no excuse.

Perhaps the most emblematic demonstration of Juliette's challenged skills as a homemaker was her ancient refrigerator. Its compressor motor was so weary that when it switched on the studio lights momentarily dimmed. But even more notable was what lay entombed inside this ancient appliance. For want of defrosting, the freezer compartment had turned into a brick of ice in which Little Li could dimly make out a carton of Häagen-Dazs ice cream and a box of Birds Eye peas. They reminded him of those ancient hominids who'd been frozen into glaciers centuries ago, only to emerge as the ice underwent oblation. In the refrigerator's main compartment, the food toward the front of each shelf was usually more or less identifiable. However, the farther back one ranged, the more primordial the finds became. Behind the front tier of still-edible items was a twilight zone of things just passing the point of no return: wilted vegetables, wrinkled fruits, dried-out English muffins, cans of cat food sprouting gray beards, and containers of half-eaten yogurt growing archipelagoes of mold. Deeper excavations exhumed progressively more antediluvian generations of things, some left undisturbed for months, possibly years. There were cheeses that had become as hard and creviced as the surface of the moon, plums that had become prunes, and unidentifiable vegetables so desiccated they looked like the handiwork of Amazon tribesmen skilled in the sacramental practices of shrinking human heads. There were also Ziploc bags swollen with gases emitted by the biological digestion taking place inside. And, finally, there was a small army of opened jars, cups, and cans left forgotten for so long that not even a forensic inquest could identify their original contents. Like a scientist relying on carbon-dating techniques, Little Li learned to perform his own tests before even thinking about consuming anything. On one occasion, he wondered out loud to Juliette whether it was not time to dispose of an unrecognizable item in a plastic container that looked like a petri dish run amok.

"It belongs where you found it!" she tersely snapped.

Her cutlery was a mishmash of engraved knives, forks, and spoons from United Airlines, Laguna Honda Hospital, the U.S. Navy, and the Hilton Hotel. The only matching cups were two from Denny's, and her collection of dinner plates included ones emblazoned with portraits of California Governor Jerry Brown and Linda Ronstadt, and another showing a freeway overpass inscribed with: "I ♥ San Jose!" Since the tableware was always scattered around the studio, whenever they wanted to have a cup of tea, much less an actual meal, they first had to set off like children on an Easter-egg hunt to round up a quorum of cups, plates, and bowls.

No space was in a more provocative state of disarray than her so-called bathroom, where colonies of mildew flourished on the shower walls and great snarls of hair nested in the drain. Rather than hanging towels on the rack after showering, she wadded them up in damp balls and left them composting on top of the toilet tank. And instead of squeezing the toothpaste at the bottom, she grabbed it in the middle, so that tubes always looked as if someone had tried to strangle them. Then there was her antiquated answering machine, which had the annoying habit of turning on in the middle of the night without being called and playing back its outgoing message at full volume, as if talking in its sleep. Nonetheless, each morning Juliette somehow managed to find what she wanted to wear, to dress stylishly, and to get to most of her dance rehearsals, aerobics classes, and other appointments. But her unreliability put Little Li on edge. The idea that someone might unnecessarily throw things into disarray seemed as counterproductive as Chairman Mao's self-induced revolutionary disorder. But because she also embodied an important aspect of his idealization of American spontaneity, he held his tongue.

However, hardly had he adjusted to his new state of contentment than a subliminal sense of something awry began to incubate. He was most aware of this dissonance when they were together, for that was when he felt most acutely that she held whole parts of herself aloof. However wantonly she might throw herself into his arms, she never allowed her being to become completely his. In fact, sometimes he felt almost like a mere accessory to her pleasure seeking, and wondered if one of her former lovers might still possess an important part of her heart.

Juliette's favorite coffeehouse was the Flore, on Market Street, where writers, musicians, actors, and other counterculture figures lingered over espressos as rock music pounded. At the café they almost always ran into friends of hers who, when they learned he was from China, looked at him with sudden new curiosity, as if his presence with her begged further explanation. Though such scrutiny made Little Li uncomfortable, her friends were far more interesting than the "family" at the Grecian Fitness Club. One afternoon, a tall young man dressed in black with hair in a ponytail approached their table while they were both reading.

"How have you been, Juliette?" he asked coolly.

"Oh! Okay," she replied, with an uncharacteristic air of disquiet. "And . . . You?"

"Good. Real good, actually," he replied, still very coolly. Then, gesturing toward Little Li, he asked, "And, who's . . . ?"

"Oh yeah. So—Victor, meet my friend Li," she said with no great enthusiasm.

The way the unsmiling Victor shook his hand and then immediately turned to leave unnerved Little Li. A few minutes later, Juliette excused herself, too. When he spotted her with him at the back of the café, he was seized by a spasm of jealousy. He tried to distract himself by picking up the book she'd been reading, a collection of Franz Kafka's writings she'd left open to a "Fragment":

I loved her and cannot talk to her.
I lie in wait for her in order not to meet her.
I loved a girl who loved me, but I had to leave her. Why? I
*   don't know.*
It was as though she were surrounded by a circle of armed
*   men holding their lances pointing out*
Whenever I approached, I ran into the points, was
*   wounded, and had to fall back.*
I suffered much.

Suddenly Juliette was behind him.

"Let's go," she said abruptly, grabbing back her book.

Neither of them spoke as they drove away. After dropping her off at her studio, Little Li returned to the Hotel Asterix feeling that something, he did not quite know what, had chemically changed.

39

JEALOUSY

LITTLE LI had just gotten out of his Cutlass at the Stonestown Shopping Center, when he saw a Caucasian man about his age walking hand in hand with his Eurasian daughter. The little girl had long, dark hair and fawnlike eyes, and was so strikingly lovely he could not tear his eyes from her. He paused to watch as her father unexpectedly stopped and, engaging in one of those acts that beg nothing in return, knelt beside her, smoothed her hair, and kissed her cheek. Not fully appreciating what she'd been given, she wiped away the kiss. But when her father kissed her again on the nose, after wriggling impishly, she leaned forward and kissed him back. The sight of this radiant child who knew she was loved touched Little Li. He tried to recall what it had been like when he was small, but couldn't. Then he wondered if he'd ever have a child. Given his present circumstances, the idea was preposterous. But the thought that he and Juliette were themselves capable of creating such a small creature struck him with such force that, even after the little girl and her father had driven away, he remained frozen on the sidewalk. During their bouts of lovemaking, it had never occurred to him before that they had the power to bring forth such a child themselves. Anyway, for her sex was recreation, not procreation. Nor had he ever viewed their couplings as anything more than simple pleasure.

"Have you ever wanted a child?" he asked as they were getting ready for bed one night.

"Never," she answered without a moment's hesitation, peeling off her dress to reveal that she'd been wearing no undergarments.

"Haven't you ever wondered what a child of yours would look like?" he persisted. He would have said "of ours," but intuitively sensed this would not have been well received.

"Not yet," she responded coolly. Then, with businesslike efficiency, she reached for the can of contraceptive foam.

"Well, I was just wondering."

"No harm in wondering, but just don't start asking so many deep questions that you confuse Mr. Happy!" She reached under the covers and gave the eponymous Mr. Happy a yank. Although he quickly lost himself in her wiles, her retort rang in his ears. In truth, the last thing he needed just then was a child, but the quickness with which she'd rejected the idea felt like a rebuke.

In China, young women drew boundaries with men not by denying commitment but by withholding physical contact. Here, women did not place limits on physical intimacy, but resisted encroachment by fending off incursions into other parts of their lives. Juliette had a strict notion of territorial sovereignty: she might be visited, but could not be claimed or occupied. Perhaps because he wanted her so much, he found it difficult to fully accept how critical independence was to her. But for him there was also a paradox: the more independence she sought, the more elusive and erotic she became. What an irony that he, the progeny of the great revolutionary sage Chairman Mao, who had immortalized the motto "Dare to rebel," should end up seeking constancy and stability, while she, the child of a reactionary, bourgeois, capitalist society, should end up embracing the idea of "great disorder under heaven."

Could one fall in love with ambiguity, aloofness, even rejection? Little Li was infatuated because she excited that part of him still trying to make a successful transmigration from China to America, and she was his passport. As soon as she came into the club with her satchel hanging jauntily over one shoulder and sashayed up to the front desk to kiss him, as every male eye in the club followed her progress, he felt anointed. However, as soon as they parted, the covetous glances of other admirers gained menace. Then, instead of feeling proprietary pride in the way other envious suitors raked her body with their eyes, he was gripped by a sense of defenseless jeopardy. He even began to wonder if she was as unaware of the covetous looks of admirers as he'd initially supposed. Sometimes she seemed not just to tolerate them but to provoke them, flashing a smile here or making a flirtatious gesture there. The more he watched from behind the front desk, the more he suspected that the interest she stirred in these predatory fans was as titillating to her as it was arousing to them.

"Do you enjoy it when guys leer at you?" he asked one night.

"It's just a game," she replied dismissively. "Guys are so horny and predictable! That's why I like you. You have Oriental restraint."

Perhaps, he thought, he was for her little more than an exotic interim plaything, a glamorous foreign creature with a nice physique, similar to one of those African cats at the zoo she so adored. Was his virtue that he sprinkled a little foreign glitter on her life, the way a chef might add an extra zing to a dish with an exotic spice? Such doubts began to eat at him, and each time he caught another man gazing longingly at her, it made him more unsettled. Was he just one more soul destined to be bested in a never-ending Darwinian combat of the fittest? He tried to banish such fears, because they made him worried, homesick, and tempted him to think that, despite all its faults, at least China did not force one to contend with such a supercharged competition at every level of life. Yes, there were prohibitions on courtship, regulations on marriages, and stipulations on who could have a child, but at least one knew the terms of the game. Watching Juliette strut into the aerobics room as if making a stage entrance made him miss Little Hong's modesty and constancy. Sure, at the time he'd wished she'd been less predictable and more adventuresome. However, she'd never made him feel uncertain of her devotion. But, had he journeyed all this way to America just to founder on nostalgia?

When he arrived at the club several days later, she was warming up on a Lifecycle before her class. He was about to go over when, unexpectedly, Lance mounted the adjacent machine. He was normally a habitué of the free-weight room and Little Li had never seen him on a Lifecycle before. But as they both pedaled away, they began talking. At first Juliette just nodded and kept looking ahead, as if she were on a real bicycle and feared taking her eyes off the road. Then she began gesturing and smiling. Little Li could feel the tide slowly turning as her resistance ebbed and she allowed herself to be lured into Lance's web.

"Stop!" he wanted to cry out. "He's not interested in talking, he wants to seduce you!"

Of course, no such words came out of his mouth, for to have said anything so overt would have been humiliating. Instead, he just sat behind his counter, feeling as defenseless as a small country under imminent threat of invasion by a brazen great power.

Because the weekend intervened and they'd made no plans to get together, Little Li would not see Juliette in the natural course of events until the next Monday. Even though it was not uncommon for them to be apart for several nights at a time, an inchoate sense of dispossession now gripped him. His yearning to be with her was so powerful he could hardly restrain himself from rushing to her studio and banging on her door. But what would he say? "I'm fearful of losing you"? "Please, reassure me"?

The only thing constraining him was pride. Despite his paranoia, he understood there were latitudes in human relations into which reckless trespass was fatal. Yes, they'd shared each other's bodies, but there was no formal agreement that gave him rights to protest over imagined mistreatment. She was not a country committed to him by treaty obligations! If he was going to be so churlish and encumbered by Old World suspicions, how would he ever make his way in this new land?

That Monday morning, when he arrived at the club for his usual stint behind the front desk, his job was only made tolerable by the awareness that at 5:00 p.m. Juliette would appear for her aerobics class. But when 5:15 p.m. came and she still hadn't shown up, he feared the worst. Then, suddenly, the door burst open, and in she swept, her long coat almost knocking the Greek statue off its pedestal.

"Where've you been?" she protested, making a beeline for him. "You didn't call or come over!"

"Oh, I've just been busy," he said disingenuously as she leaned over the counter to kiss him.

"Hey! Will you keep these for me?" she said breathlessly. She dumped her things beside the counter and ran into the locker room. He was flooded with a sense of relief, and when they made love that night, his connection to her again seemed so indisputably concrete, he chastised himself for ever doubting she was his. However, as soon as they were apart again, his faith wore off like a drug, and the undefined nature of their relationship began conspiring with his own insecurities to again reinfect his optimism with the poison of doubt.

To build a future that was not so dependent on her, he began a rigorous new practice regimen each morning after she left, working on Bach's Sonata in E-flat major, the score of which he'd found in a used-book store. He'd played its second movement, the Siciliano, for Yang Ming at Yak Springs, a time that now seemed long ago. As he thumbed through the tattered score, he saw that someone had scrawled Richard Wagner's exclamation on the inside cover: "Bach is the most stupendous miracle in all of music!"

Little Li's first real altercation with Juliette began over the matter of her untidiness. At his suggestion, they'd agreed to clean up the sleeping area by vacuuming the floor with his Mighty Mite, washing the sheets, and even hanging a curtain in the half-window. But his custodial attitude toward the project made her bridle, especially at his insinuation that her homemaking needed improving.

"Let's not worry so much about being orderly," she declared testily. "I don't want to spend my life neatening up!" When she caught him throwing out some of the most repulsive relics from her refrigerator, she dismissively said, "I suppose busy hands are happy hands." He could think of no rejoinder that would not sound hopelessly defensive.

"How do you look at the future?" he finally asked her, as they drove back to her studio one night.

"Well, I try not to," she replied indifferently.

"Aren't you concerned about where your life is headed?"

"Why worry about the future when you can't do anything about it? The future's going to happen all on its own."

"But what do you want for yourself?"

"I want to become a better dancer and enjoy myself," she said peremptorily. He felt as if he'd been slapped. He'd hoped to ask her about "them," perhaps even raise the question of actually living together. After all, if he was going to spend so much time with her, why should he keep his dreary room at the Asterix?

As they were fixing something to eat one evening, he finally asked her point-blank: "What do you think will happen to us, Juliette?"

"What do you mean?" she asked, whirling around.

"I mean our future together." He immediately regretted raising the topic.

"Sometimes I just don't think you understand me," she said. "I like you, but I don't want to be completely tied down right now. I need my freedom! Can you understand that?"

"You think I can't understand wanting freedom?" he exclaimed indignantly.

"When I say 'freedom,' I'm not talking about the same thing as you!" She looked pained. "I don't mean barbed wire, walls, dictators, and all that. I'm an American, for Christ's sake! What I mean is the freedom to explore! I really don't know what I want to do with my life." Her voice had a pleading tone now. "I mean, do you really know what you want? You may think you want me, but I can tell you I'm not the answer. Anyway, I'm not ready to be anyone's answer!" She was on the verge of tears. He knew he'd overstepped the bounds of what she could bear.

"Oh, Juliette!" was all he could say. But, he was thinking, "How suffocating neediness can be when it masquerades as love!"

After she fell asleep that night, he remained awake. Petit Paws jumped onto the bed with a little chirrup. He didn't normally welcome her, but now, as she commenced making a nest with her paws, he sentimentally recalled the morning his father had appeared with Whiskers like a phantom in Granny Sun's doorway. How passionately he'd loved that scrawny kitten! As quickly as these memories flooded in, they faded away, almost as if they knew they didn't belong here in this faraway city, in this strange bed, with this alien woman, and this infidel cat. Anyway, he thought, such memories would only make it harder for him to escape the turbid waters of China and swim out into the deep, clear, refreshing currents of American life. As he stroked Petit Paws, she arched her back to his touch and purred. Cats were such elemental creatures: you patted them, they purred, and all was well. With humans there were no such simple formulas. He had no idea how to satisfy Juliette, much less how to fit the disparate pieces of his own disjointed life together with hers. He wasn't even sure if he possessed the fortitude to keep trying. He began to sob quietly. Feeling his body tremble beside her, she reached over and wordlessly put her arm around him.

"It's all right," she whispered, as if she knew exactly what was going on. "None of us knows what will happen. It's all a great mystery. I just try to take each day as it comes."

As much as he wanted to be reassured by her touch, long after she fell back asleep he remained awake, chilled by a fear that he would be expelled from the world in which he'd been so innocently luxuriating. How naïve to entertain the illusion that Juliette was the answer, that as a couple they'd march happily into a neat American future like those figurines standing in their meringue pagoda on that August Moon wedding cake. Was it not a similar scenario that had made him reject life with Little Hong and leave Beijing? What had happened to his fierce dreams of freedom and studying music? Had some involuntary autoimmune reaction set in, causing him to reject the very things he'd once wanted?

Whatever happened now with Juliette, he vowed two things: first, to resist surrendering his independence, and second, to resist yielding to the siren song of the "Chinese Motherland" (祖国) calling him home. Gullible Chinese were always looking for saviors. China had lured his father back over three decades before, and look how his efforts to help "save the country" (救国) had ended. But he could not deny that, just as the Chinese had allowed Chairman Mao to become their "great saving star" (大救星), now he'd allowed Juliette to become his. What is more, just as the CCP saw 1949 as the year demarcating "before liberation" (解放以前) from "after liberation" (解放以后) for China, he had now come to see his own life as divided into Before Juliette (B.J.) and After Juliette (A.J.) periods. If the months in the 1950s "after liberation," when Mao's new government was just being established, had glowed with halcyon promise, so his early A.J. days had been filled with hopefulness. But then in both cases ambiguity all too quickly began to set in.

Why couldn't he just accept things as they were and take life "one day at a time," as she'd suggested? He closed his eyes, tried to turn off his overheated mind and just appreciate the fact that she was by his side. A garbage truck devoured its way up the street, tires hissed over fog-dampened streets, a distant car alarm went off, and Juliette sighed. He hungered to touch her, but on some deep and terrifying level, he understood how far beyond his possession she actually was. He was beside her, but still apart.

The next morning, she leapt out of bed, hastily pulled on a pair of black tights and some pink leg-warmers, and raced out the door for a rehearsal at the Opera House. He was just getting ready to practice when the door burst open again and she rushed back in.

"Can't find my fucking keys," she growled in a way that seemed aimed as much at him as at herself.

"Where did you last see them?" he asked. She didn't reply.

Lost things were not uncommon in Juliette's life. He'd given her a key chain from the U.S.-China People's Friendship Association with a pendant featuring two pandas with inebriated smiles holding crossed American and Chinese flags inscribed with the characters for "friendship" (友好), a notion the party tirelessly flogged in its artless propaganda war to win over gullible foreigners. But if he hoped the garishness of the two communist pandas would make her keys harder to lose, he was wrong.

At first he'd viewed her penchant for misplacing things as a charming aspect of her unpossessive, carefree personality. But recently he'd come to view her absentmindedness as also part of a repulsion mechanism designed, like the quills of porcupines or the stink of skunks, to repel intruders. The anarchy she deployed around her appeared ever more as an unconscious stratagem to keep him—and perhaps others—from coming too close. After all, she danced with discipline and dressed with style, demonstrating she was hardly out of control. As to the keys, he'd learned that offers to help her find things usually only engendered more resistance. While she hunted now, even dumping the contents of her purse out onto the floor in frustration, he said nothing. But, because finally it seemed wrong not to help, he began searching the kitchen, and quickly found the truant keys on top of the refrigerator.

"Perhaps you should put them in a special place each time you come in," he suggested, trying to expunge any hint of judgment from his voice. But as soon as he'd spoken, he regretted it.

"Don't be so fucking uptight," she barked, snatching the keys from him and storming out.

In an attempt to alleviate some of the pressure he felt building, before leaving her studio that morning he put a note on the door:

J.: I have some things to take care of.
Let's hook up again next week. Love, L.L.

It was a Friday and he hoped that a weekend of separation would help cleanse both their palates. Anyway, in the natural course of events, they'd see each other again on Monday at work.

But even though this moratorium had been self-imposed, he immediately began missing her. And with his neighbor giving full throat next door, and the Club 2:00 AM's jukebox pounding away, the Hotel Asterix was hardly a therapeutic environment.

On Monday, he waited impatiently all day for her arrival at the club, but at the last minute she called in sick, and Annette had to take over her class. Since Tuesday was his day off, he would not run into her for two more days—not a long separation, but he nonetheless felt alone and rejected. He thought about the agony his father had endured, waiting helplessly month after month and year after year for his mother. Short of a death, or knowing that the person one loves is in the embrace of another, there are few things more agonizing than such indeterminate sentences. How had his father ever so stoically borne this lifetime of partition first from his wife, then his son, and finally his music?

At midnight, when a bell struck in a distant church steeple, it was as if a fuse blew in his head. Throwing on the jacket Juliette had chosen for him, Little Li ran down the hotel stairs and out through the lobby, jumped into his Cutlass, and sped to her studio. After double-parking, he ran to her vestibule and put his ear to her door, but could hear nothing. Dispiritedly, he retreated to his Cutlass, and had almost reached the Asterix again when, without knowing quite what he was doing, he made a U-turn and headed back. After parking in a spot from which he could see her doorway, he waited, imagining her with a handsome American like Victor, doing unspeakable things. To calm himself, he flicked on the radio. The predictability of the Haydn symphony that came on so annoyed him that he turned it off.

He must have fallen asleep, because it was 2:30 a.m. when he next looked at his watch. Had she returned while he slept, been inside all along, or was she still out? He was on the verge of abandoning his vigil when a red Volvo pulled up at her door, and she got out with her dance-class satchel slung over her shoulder and went inside. He didn't know whether to rejoice or cry. Where had she been until so late? He felt spurned and angry, but, infuriatingly, he still yearned for her, and began running toward her doorway. But what possible excuse could he give for showing up at such an ungodly hour? It would be mortifying to claim he'd just been passing by.

Embarrassed by the powerful grip this compulsion had on him, he stopped in his tracks, turned, and trudged back to the Cutlass. Perhaps he was just culturally and psychologically allergic to the very spontaneity and freedom that had drawn him both to her and to this infernal country. In China, he'd always imagined that, with the proper measure of freedom, he'd be transformed, that, once liberated from the shackles of the socialist fallacy, he'd finally be emancipated to become himself. But now here he was, in the early hours of morning, stalking an American girl to whom he'd become enslaved by a torrent of neediness. Enraged with himself, he turned the key in the Cutlass's ignition and drove back to the Asterix.

40

"URGENT CALL for Li," yelled Patel as he pounded on Little Li's hotel-room door.

"All right," he answered, a surge of adrenaline shooting through his sleep-benumbed brain as he threw on a jacket and hurried downstairs. The rotund Tongan who seemed to live in the lobby looked up without smiling as Patel handed Little Li the telephone receiver.

"Hello," said Little Li, trying to sound as cool as possible.

"Is that you, Li?" a male voice asked. "It's Milo here, at Grecian."

"Oh, hi, Milo," responded Little Li, crestfallen not to hear Juliette's voice.

"We got ourselves a little situation," Milo began without any of his usual jocularity. "My new janitor's mother's in surgery, and he can't clean up tonight. I know it's your day off, but you're the only one who knows what to do. Can I count on you? Waddya say?"

"Okay, Milo," replied Little Li, his spirits lifting at the thought that, if he went in to the Club a little early, he might run into Juliette after her aerobics class.

"Hey, you're all right, Li. I'll make it up to you."

"Thanks, Milo."

"You bet. And, hey, remember me to the emperor of China!" Milo's raucous laugh was cut off by a dial tone.

As Little Li was driving up Diamond Heights, his Cutlass's engine suddenly died. He managed to back into a parking space and then had to walk all the way to Mission Street to find a garage willing to tow his car in for repairs. By the time a mechanic had finished installing a new alternator, Juliette's class was long over, the club had closed, and the Stonestown parking lot was almost empty. A chill rain started just as he left his car. At the head of the stairway, the spotlight that usually illuminated the Greek statue in its bower of plastic bamboo was already off. He unlocked the door and stepped inside. Without the steady beat of disco music, the club was ominously silent, and although the humid air inside was not pleasing, its familiarity was comforting, like certain smells recalled from childhood. Minus the rush of air that usually issued forth from the ventilation system, the little cardboard discs proclaiming "Be Trim! Ask Us How" that hung from the ceiling vents were now unnaturally still. Except for one lone cone of light shining outside the aerobics room, the club was dark.

In the janitor's closet, the dog-eared *Playboy* Bunny foldout featuring a blonde with enormous bovine breasts pinned to the back wall, the battered clipboard used to check off the night's tasks, the red canister vacuum cleaner, and the emerald-green tub of chlorine sticks for the Jacuzzi and pool only enhanced his sense of despondency. He was just putting on his old coveralls when he heard a sound. Although he couldn't imagine anyone breaking into a health club after hours, the thought of being trapped alone in this underground catacomb with an intruder made him immediately tense up. When he heard the sound again, a muffled cry, he grabbed a mop handle and tiptoed down the hallway. As he edged slowly along the wall toward the aerobics room, the sound grew both louder and more rhythmic. When he was finally able to peek through a crack in the doorway, he was stunned to see a naked female body spread-eagled on the carpeted dais where Juliette conducted her classes. With her head hanging over the far edge and her legs dangling over the other, the woman looked almost like a human sacrifice on a pagan altar. But instead of a dagger-wielding shaman priest looming over her, a blond man wearing a bright-blue tank top was kneeling, with his back to the door, between her spread legs. Little Li's heart was pounding so furiously that he feared at any moment he'd be heard, and was about to pull back when the man turned. As their eyes met, Lance Prince froze. Then, he glanced in alarm down at the woman. Like someone coming back to life from a near-death experience, she raised her head and opened her delirious eyes. When she saw Little Li in the doorway, she sat bolt upright, clutched her hands to her forehead, and, as if seized by a sudden skull-splitting migraine, cried out: "Oh no! My God! No!" It was Juliette.

As if her cry was a round discharged by a deadly weapon, Little Li reeled backward. He ran down the hallway, out the door, up the stairs, and across the rain-streaked parking lot as her anguished cries continued. How he managed to make it back to the Asterix, he did not know. As he lay on his mattress, such a firestorm of emotion engulfed him that he felt on the verge of combustion, with no idea what time it was, whether he was asleep or awake, mad or sane. Without the sound of a TV blaring down the hall and the thump, thump, thump of the Club 2:00 A M's jukebox, he might have just floated away like an untethered balloon.

He tried to re-anchor himself by thinking of home. China may have been an elaborate prison, but at least its walls had given him boundaries and generated fantasies of escape. Here in America, that the tenuous roots he'd started to plant had now suddenly and ruthlessly been ripped out. All he craved just then was unconsciousness. But whenever he closed his eyes, he was immediately assaulted by nightmarish re-enactments of Juliette's treachery.

When great losses had befallen him as a child, he'd always believed that, if he'd only been a better, stronger, or cleverer child, he might have prevented his misfortunes. If only he'd been more dutiful, his mother would not have left; if he'd taken better care of Whiskers, she would not have been taken; and if he'd dared to rush from Granny Sun's room, his father's hands might not have been crippled. So, despite his fury, it felt quite natural for him to turn the onus of fault for what had happened back in on himself. Wasn't that how Confucian "gentlemen" (君子) had for centuries been taught to comport themselves? When things went wrong, first look within oneself and address the deficiency through the age-old virtue of "self-cultivation" (修身). If he could claim responsibility for some part of the calamity that had just befallen him, then some capacity to rectify the problem still lay within his hands. Over the millennia, such habits had sunk deep roots into the Chinese psyche.

Desperate for surcease, he went to the shower room and, as if pain could be washed away, let hot water cascade over him. But the steam filling the shower stall only summoned up that first mystical night with Juliette. Desperately wanting to vomit her up, he dressed and went downstairs. Outside, it was still raining, and the toothpick-skewered blue olive was still dancing away in its pink martini glass over the Club 2:00 AM, making the rain-slick street pulse with flashes of gaudy color. From inside the bar came muffled sounds of music, clinking glasses, and bursts of boozy laughter. Not knowing where else to go, he walked in. As soon as the three regulars perched on bar stools saw him, they stopped talking.

"Greetings, son, whoever you are," a balding man with a nose like a giant ripe strawberry finally offered.

"Can we drink to ya?" asked the second, gray-haired man in a slurred brogue, who was wearing a green T-shirt inscribed with, "God invented whiskey so that Irishmen would never take over the world!"

"Shit, Martin! You'd drink to the goddamn health inspector if he walked through the fuckin' door to bust the joint!" rejoined the bald man.

"That's correct, Eddie, I'd drink to Hitler, I'd drink to Stalin, I'd even drink to Mao Zedong . . . if he was buying Irish whiskey!" He laughed. "I'm a drinkin' Irishman!" He hoisted his shot glass.

"Oh, don't bother with Martin," said a middle-aged redhead woman who had a cigarette clamped between fingers with long, lacquered red nails.

"You tell him, Darlene!" chimed in Eddie.

"What can I get you, my friend?" asked the bartender, a tall man with a protruding stomach.

"How 'bout a beer?" suggested Eddie, seeing Little Li hesitate.

"Jesus, Mary, Joseph!" yelped Martin, leaning over so close that Little Li could see the veins in his bloodshot eyes. "If there was ever a fella who looked like he needed a good stiff shot of Irish whiskey, 'tis you this night!" When Little Li didn't reply, he added, "Ya wouldn't turn down a wee drink o' real whiskey with a real Irishman, wouldja?"

"I wouldn't," replied Little Li, not sure what he was in for. When a shot glass arrived on the bar, he followed Martin's lead and threw it back. He felt he'd just taken a draft of industrial solvent.

"So—where ya from, anyway?" asked Eddie.

When he didn't immediately respond, Martin charitably offered, "Well, he looks like he's got a Romanian count for a father and a Japanese princess for a mother."

"That works for me," said Darlene, twirling the ice in her glass with an index finger.

"In that case, let's drink to royalty," piped up Martin. "It's on me!" Everyone cheered as the bartender set up another round. A welcome numbness was beginning to dull Little Li's pain.

When he awoke the next morning, he had a pounding head-ache, a sour mouth, and a raging thirst. He turned on the tap and drank straight from the sink faucet. Then he must have fallen asleep again, because the next thing he knew, the sun was beam-ing through the window and a lone suicidal fly was dive-bombing a windowpane over and over. As he recalled what had happened, he was stabbed by pain so fierce it momentarily eclipsed his aching head. Separation from Juliette felt as if some part of his own body had been ripped away, leaving a gaping contusion. Was there any geographic place on earth that could help alleviate his throbbing sense of loss? If someone had offered him an airline ticket back to China, he would have taken it, not because he wanted to return, but because it would, at least, enable him to fly away from the epi-center of his hurt. How could a person who'd been so palpably present in someone's life become so rapidly and completely extir-pated? The only impulse competing with his grief was his rage—at Juliette, at himself, and even at America. And yet, despite his rage at her faithlessness, if she'd suddenly appeared and expressed willingness to reconcile, he knew that even now he'd be powerless to resist.

Maybe conservatives were right to resist the hybridization of cultures. And perhaps there was some logic to the party's historical fixation on protecting the "purity" of China's "national essence" (国粹), what they liked to call "Chinese characteristics" (中国特色), from being corrupted by the impure outside world. Of course, as a Eurasian, he was himself already a physical embodiment of this contradiction. And just as China remained torn between adoring and despising the West, he was riven between loving and hating Juliette. She was both his savior and his nemesis. But the more he tried to tar her infidelity as a foreign defect, the more he despised himself for sinking into the very victim culture that lay behind the party's penchant to blame the West for everything, that had made him want to flee China. But like a colony that, after an epic strug-gle for self-determination, continues to run back under the skirts of its mother country in times of travail, Little Li still humiliatingly longed for his deceiver's embrace.

When he glanced at his watch, he saw that he was already late for work, but the thought of returning cuckolded to the Grecian Fitness Club "family" horrified him. However, since he could not survive without his job, he set off anyway, arguing with himself the whole way there: Perhaps he was responding too hysterically. So what if Juliette had had an affair? She'd never pretended to be virginal. What's more, from an American perspective, such extracurricular activities seemed to have little significance. Hadn't the *San Francisco Chronicle* reported that 60 to 70 percent of all couples engaged in extramarital affairs? Besides, having sex did no physical harm, much less killed anyone. It was just a ritual act of hardly greater significance than shaking hands or kissing. So why should he, who'd come all the way from Beijing in search of a more open, libertine lifestyle, recoil so strenuously from an American who'd done nothing more than exercise her God-given right to pursue happiness? How could he, a rigid Chinese who'd come to America to break out of precisely such confinement, ever expect someone here to live up to his expectations of correct behavior? Maybe he was just "making a big deal out of a small matter" (小题大作).

For a moment, such rationalizations convinced him that he was overreacting. But then, as he started across the mall parking lot, the thought of all the times he'd walked over this very stretch of pavement with Juliette, basking in the glow of having a lovely young American woman at his side, overwhelmed him. Suddenly there was a screeching of rubber on asphalt and a furious salvo of honking, as a Mercedes skidded to a stop a few feet away. He'd been so absorbed in his thoughts, he'd stepped out into the path of an oncoming car.

When he passed the Greek statue at the bottom of the stairs, pushed open the glass door to the club, caught the first whiff of the fetid tropical air, heard the sound of disco music, and saw Stephanie at the front desk, he felt he'd stepped into the mouth of a blast furnace. Spinning around, he ran back up the stairs and across the parking lot. He did not stop driving until he came to a gas station, where he called Milo.

"Stephanie saw you hightailing it up the stairs like you'd just seen a ghost!" said Milo.

"I'm leaving," was all he could get out.

"You're outta the club?"

"Yes."

"But you're my best guy!"

"I appreciate all you've done for me, Milo, but I just . . ." Fighting back tears, he couldn't finish.

"Are you in trouble?"

"It's nothing. I've got to get back to playing music, and—"

"Oh, fuck that shit!" Milo interrupted. "Is it because of Lance fooling around with Juliette?" Little Li felt a flash of molten indignation. But Milo went right on: "Just remember the first rule of life, Li: a stiff prick has no conscience, so don't take it personally. You're a good kid, and this is a big, bad world." A sudden softness had entered his voice. "You gotta take care of yourself, kid. Okay? You . . ."

"Yeah. Okay. Thanks, Milo," replied Little Li, and hung up.

The next morning, he was awakened by another pounding on his door at the Asterix.

"Something delivered to you," Patel's guttural voice announced. "That dancing girl came with a letter, in great urgency."

"Okay," said Little Li, immediately opening the door.

"No sweat."

The envelope was the kind used to mail in payments for utility bills. Juliette had crossed out Pacific Gas and Electric's address and written in, "Little Li, Asterix Hotel." He realized that, after all these months, she still didn't know his full name. If she'd come to the door herself, he would have ripped the letter into pieces. But since such a demonstration of outrage was futile with Patel, he took the envelope, closed the door, and sat down on his mattress.

Dear Little Li:

I am so deeply sorry I've hurt you. I've loved getting to know you, being with you, and hearing all your incredible stories about places I'll never know myself. You are one of the most faithful, loyal, decent people I know, and you're also unbelievably handsome. Although you may not be able to believe me right now, I did love you. But it was never my intention to settle down with you, or anyone. I simply do not yet know enough about myself or what will

become of me to do that now. I guess this is what I've been
indirectly trying to tell you. But, feeling how much you
did not want to hear it, I made the mistake of remaining
mostly silent. Now I've chosen the worst possible way to let
you know.

You are too fine a person to have been treated this way!
Goodbye, Juliette

What pierced Little Li's heart most savagely was how easily she seemed able to surrender any ongoing claim on him, as if
leaving him was no more difficult than changing tenses. Though
he'd allowed her to become an essential part of him, she seemed no
more thrown off course by his loss than by misplacing a set of keys.
He tore up the letter, opened the window, and let the pieces flutter
down into the dumpster in the alley below.

41

DURING THE following weeks, Little Li was rent by so many contradictory emotions, he feared something inside him might snap like the mainspring of a watch wound too tightly. By quitting his job, he'd avoided confronting Juliette in person, but he found no such evasion in his own imagination. As if hooked up to a VCR gone berserk, her betrayal kept replaying itself in ever more lurid variations in his mind. He wished that, like a party censor air-brushing purged Politburo members from official photos, he could excise the contorted faces, horrifying sounds, and mind-searing body parts that kept floating through his memory, but, no matter what he did, he was unable to arrest the procession of upsetting images.

One morning, he spotted something blue that had slipped down between his mattress and the wall, and used the coat-hanger antenna from his TV to claw it out. It was a pair of Juliette's bikini panties. The thought that, after surrendering herself to him, she'd walked out of this very room wearing nothing under her skirt seized him with an unwelcome spasm of desire. It was so like her that he had to smile. Then the recognition she was no longer his hit, and left him aching.

He got into his Cutlass and began driving. As long as the crisp, clear San Francisco air was blowing through the open window, and the rows of neat houses were flying past in the morning sunlight outside, he felt he might outpace these pursuing memories. Then he unexpectedly found himself at the corner of Vallejo and Powell Streets and saw the August Moon Bakery; he pulled into an empty parking space. The Alp-sized wedding cake in the bakery's front window had been replaced for the Fourth of July by three lesser confections plastered with red, white, and blue stuccolike coatings of shaggy coconut frosting, sprinkled with tiny white sugar stars. He went inside, and even though everyone in the bakery was speaking Cantonese, for old times' sake he ordered a doughnut in Mandarin.

"You betta off speak English," responded the clerk. "Hong Kong people no saying Mandarin."

As he ate his doughnut out on the sidewalk, he could not help thinking about his aunt up the street. "What do I have to lose by trying them once more?" he thought to himself. "At worst, they'll slam the door in my face again."

He walked up the hill to his aunt and uncle's building. When he rang the buzzer, this time it was Dudley Woo who answered and opened the apartment door.

"Mr. Woo, I'm Vivian Knight's son from Beijing," Little Li announced.

"Hey, Crystal," Dudley Woo called out. "It's Vivian's kid from China."

"Oh Jeez!" a distant voice responded. "So . . . I guess we should tell him to come in."

"Come on in," said Woo, but with little enthusiasm as Crystal appeared in the hallway holding the furiously yapping miniature poodle.

"If it's not inconvenient," he replied.

"No, no! I mean . . ." As they ushered him down the hallway into the living room, the agitated dog stopped yapping and started growling.

"Oh, shush!" she soothed. "No one's going to hurt you."

The Woos' living room looked out over a small garden, and would have been cheerful if the shades had not been drawn.

"I'm glad to be able to meet you at last," began Little Li, trying to break the ice.

"For sure," she said, sitting down on the couch with the dog on her lap. "And what did you say your name was?"

"Li Wende."

"Got it." She turned to her husband. "Hey, Dud! Will ya get the boy something to drink?"

"Tab or juice?" he asked. Little Li chose juice.

"So—what brings you our way?" began Crystal, studying his face.

"Oh, I'm here to study music . . . at some point."

"Just like Sis, huh? She loved her violin! And they say she was okay at it, too. When she went off to Red China, just when the communists were coming in and all, none of us could figure it out." She shook her head mournfully and lit a cigarette.

"Your grandfather sure wasn't pleased when your dad took her back there," chimed in Dudley.

"I mean, you had to be nuts to trust that guy Mao!" added Crystal. "But that's young people for you." She shook her head. "But, hey, you look like a nice boy! Too bad your mom isn't still here to see you. When she came back and got that damn cancer, she was in such a state over you, always talking about her 'beautiful boy,' writing letters, and sending packages. You know, I used to go with her to the super to buy all that stuff, and she'd only pick the very best things for you both."

"Really?" said Little Li, thrilled to have a door into his mother's life suddenly thrown open.

"Oh! She couldn't stop talking about you! And all she had was that one photo. I thought she'd wear it out, the way she showed it to everyone and cried over it."

"Were you close to her when you were young, Aunt Crystal?" he asked. He was glad to be able to say her name, because he was fearful she might stop talking if he didn't goad her on.

"Well, we weren't the same type of person, don'cha know." She squinted as a plume of smoke drifted up past her eyes. "She took after Dad's interest in the church and music, while me and Dud were more into business and a little golf. Being younger, I didn't get as much of the China deal as she did when Dad was over there preaching in Shanghai."

"Hey, Crystal?" Dudley suddenly interjected. "Where the heck's that old photo anyway? Didn't Vivian give it to you when she was on her last?"

"Oh yeah! What did we do with that thing?" Crystal's face lit up as she laboriously got up, put the dog on the floor, padded over to a desk, and began rummaging through its drawers. "Hey, Dud!" she cried, suddenly standing upright. "Found it!" Triumphantly, she handed Little Li a small, bent, black-and-white photo with scalloped edges. And, there she was! His mother, a shock of hair falling over her forehead, smiling proudly and crouching next to him between the two stone "door guardians" (门墩儿) that protected the Willow Courtyard entryway. He was about four; wore a white shirt, short pants, and high-top sneakers; and had one hand raised to shield his eyes from the sun. She looked beautiful, and the recognition that this photo had not only belonged to her but had been taken of them together just before she'd departed from Beijing left him overcome with emotion. Holding it made him feel as if a mythical person had suddenly appeared in physical form. Seeing that he was choked with emotion, Crystal summoned Dudley.

"Hey, Dud! Get the boy another drink," she said softly.

"Roger," he replied obediently.

"You know, I might never have looked for that photo, if Dud hadn't mentioned it just now," continued his aunt, as Little Li regained his composure. "I'm real glad you could see it. It's what our Vivian would have wanted. And, now that I'm thinking on it, you know what? A few days before she passed, she gave me something she wanted saved in case you ever showed up. At the time, I thought, 'We'll never see that kid! No way! He's trapped by the communists!'" A faraway look crossed her face. "But now, here you are!" She smiled.

"What are you talking about?" asked Dudley.

"Don'cha remember, Dud, that thingy Vivian left for the boy? Gimme a moment and maybe I'll find it, too." She got up again and opened a cupboard door under a bric-a-brac shelf.

"What was it?" asked Little Li.

"Some kind of an amulet deal," she said as she rummaged. "Oh, look!" she suddenly exclaimed. "Here it is!" She handed Little Li a yellowing envelope. "You see, it says right here: 'For My Boy.' Gosh, I'm glad we thought of it."

"Thank you," Little Li responded, not knowing quite what else to say.

"So—go ahead, son! Open it," urged Crystal with real enthusiasm now. "She wanted you to have it!" The glue on the envelope was so dry he was able to open the flap without ripping the envelope. Inside was a silver "locket" (长命锁) on a chain, inscribed with the character "longevity" (寿). "Isn't that lovely," cooed Crystal. "Must of been somethin' she got in Shanghai in the old days. But now it's yours."

Holding it gingerly, Little Li noticed a tiny clasp on one side. When he unlatched it, the back sprang open like a pocket watch, and inside was a small piece of tightly folded paper, the same kind of sheer onionskin on which she used to write him and his father. He unfolded it slowly, and there, in his mother's familiar script, were the words "For My Dearest Son." Unable to read on as his eyes blurred with tears, he refolded the paper, tucked it back into the locket, snapped it shut again, and then he sat in stunned silence just staring at his aunt.

"That's all right, son," she soothed, and walked over to place a sympathetic hand on his shoulder. "It must have been real hard for you over there."

"Aunt Crystal, if you'll pardon me," Little Li began, when he was finally able to get a few words out, "I think I need to go, so I can read this note from Mother alone." The word "Mother" choked him up again.

"Of course." She nodded. "Maybe you'll let us know what happens to you."

It is mystifying how a wandering person can without intention end up arriving someplace that at first appears to have no great importance, only to discover that, like a homing pigeon, they've actually been drawn to a spot of enormous significance. This had happened to Little Li on his first morning in San Francisco, when he'd unintentionally found his way to Grace Cathedral. Now, driving aimlessly through Park Presidio, past rows of nineteenth-century brick military billets, a cemetery filled with white headstones stepping up a green hillside, and lines of cream-colored barracks under arching cypress trees, he made a quixotic turn into a parking area overlooking Alcatraz Island and San Francisco Bay. It was only when he stepped from his car and out from behind a clump of trees that he saw it: the Golden Gate Bridge. With fog billowing in through its sinuous suspension cables, and a distant foghorn bleating out baleful tubalike warnings, it was a scene of such ethereal beauty that he sat down on the low stone wall rimming the observation area to drink it in. The water, sky, and fog were gray, but the coast beyond was lit by sunlight, making the scene before him look like a photo printed half in black and white and half in color. As he unfastened the clasps on the locket and extracted the onionskin, he felt as if he were opening a miniature tomb. The sheer paper shivered in the wind as he began reading:

My dearest son:
  I don't know if you'll ever see this, but somehow I believe it's God's will you shall.
  I was snatched from you by fate and politics. How agonizing it was to only be able to love you from afar. In writing you and your father, I always feared saying more than he could bear. What an upright man! Despite all the hardship, never did I doubt his goodness or integrity, traits I'm sure you've inherited. How tragic I could not reunite with you, but life is filled with disappointment and bitterness as well as gladness and joy.
  Were you thinking of me in Beijing all those years, my dear sweet boy? I was thinking of you. Always! Most agonizing was never being able to tell you how much I cared about you.
  I was never a political person, but the poison injected into the veins of China—and, remember, I am half Chinese—was so unspeakable that perhaps it was best I never knew the full measure of suffering you and your father endured. It would only have broken that small part of my heart not already shattered. Now my only consolation in death will be that I won't have to endure an endless broken heart over you and your beloved father.
  If you ever read this, know that, in whatever afterlife we're allowed to pass, I'll be cherishing you as only a mother can cherish her only child. And if you read this, will you do something for me, dear one? Will you choose somewhere that is a sacred place and say a blessing for your dear father for me? Know that, as you do so, I'll be watching.
  In eternal love, Mother

Little Li wasn't sure how long he sat with his head in his hands. But when he finally stood up to see that the two steel towers of the bridge had just emerged for a moment from the windblown fog, he realized he was sitting almost exactly where his parents had stood decades before as they'd posed for the photo that had hung above their piano in Willow Courtyard. Transfixed by the scene, warmed by his mother's letter, stunned by the recognition that his own parents had once stood together in this very place, he fell to his knees and prostrated himself before the bridge. Each time he touched his forehead to the ground, a different image of his father appeared: sitting at his piano; standing in his garden; slumped on the floor of the dark practice room; walking through the Conservatory courtyard; lying in bed with *The Dream of the Red Chamber* open on his chest; and conducting his fantasy symphony as he lay dying. That these memories were all that was now left of this man who'd been his father sucked the breath out of Little Li with such ferocity that he was left gasping. When he finally opened his tear-filled eyes, a platoon of camera-draped Japanese businessmen in dark suits were just trooping past. Their faces registered not bewilderment or disdain, but respect, as if they sensed in his devotions some Confucian aspect of themselves.

When he awoke the next morning, he had little sense of how much time had elapsed since his ordeal began. Lying in bed, he turned his radio on and rifled through the cacophony of frenzied commercial talk shows, sportscasts, and pop-music stations until he found KKHI, where, miraculously, Bach's *Well-Tempered Clavier* was being played by none other than Glenn Gould. As the forty-eight jewel-like preludes and fugues, set in every major and minor key, filled his drab room, for the first time he felt that he might survive the anguish of his betrayal.

At the end, the program host announced that a chamber-music concert featuring some of the last works of Franz Schubert was scheduled that night at the Herbst Theatre, in the Veteran's War Memorial Building. He decided to go, certain that if his father and mother were looking down on him, they'd be despairing over the way he'd allowed his life to career out of control. His father had lost his wife and much more, but had defiantly kept going, rejecting victimhood, resentment, and self-laceration. Feeling impatient with himself, Little Li dressed and went out to the Duc Pho restaurant for a bowl of noodles. Then he drove to the Civic Center and parked near the concert hall, between a bright-red BMW and a shiny black SUV that made his Cutlass look as forlorn as the homeless man lying beside an overloaded shopping cart in a nearby doorway.

"Hey, ma good man!" said the derelict, coming to life as Little Li locked his car door. "Myself would be willin' to watch yo short so nothin' gonna be happenin' while you 'way," he offered, smiling and putting out his hand.

"Thanks for helping out," said Little Li. Although he had a hard time imagining what further indignity could be inflicted on his Cutlass, he gave the old gent a dollar.

At Herbst Theatre, he bought an inexpensive seat in the back of the orchestra, glad to be shrouded in half-darkness. The program included Schubert's Quintet in C major, which the program notes explained was never performed before the composer's agonizing death at age thirty-one and that the pianist Arthur Rubenstein had so loved he'd asked to have its second movement played at his funeral, to help him "enter death resigned and happy."

Was there anything sadder than someone like Schubert, who'd been deprived of the pleasure of his creation? Just as death had deprived Schubert of the satisfaction of hearing his own masterwork performed, death and politics had denied Little Li's mother and father the pleasure of each other; forced separation had robbed his mother of the joy of her child; and political savagery had deprived his father of the ability to make music. If Schubert's life was a tragedy, his mother's was a misfortune and his father's a travesty.

As the five musicians strode onstage, Little Li felt possessed by an unexpected sense of serenity. The opening movement of the quintet was like being splashed alternately with hot and cold water—sweet and gentle one moment, assertive and brooding the next. But it was the deeply meditative next movement, the Adagio, that overwhelmed him emotionally with its tremulous uncertainty and raw soulfulness. As love seemed to be conversing with suffering and Schubert with God, the musicians filled the hall with a sound so rich and affecting that Little Li was hardly able to breathe.

The final piece in the concert, "The Shepherd on the Rock," was composed by Schubert for a piano, clarinet, and soprano in the very last months of his life. The notes explained that he'd written it for the Viennese soprano who'd first sung the role of Leonore in the premiere of Beethoven's *Fidelio*. His father's love of this opera, compounded with the fact that the trio was written on Schubert's deathbed, helped Little Li to put his own melancholia in perspective. The work evoked a shepherd sitting high on a mountain, gazing into a "dark and deep" valley while thinking of his lover. As the soprano conversed with the mournful clarinet, they sounded like two Swiss yodelers echoing back and forth across an Alpine chasm. The next moment, the music turned inward and more despairing:

> *I am consumed in misery.*
> *Happiness is far from me,*
> *Hope has on earth eluded me,*
> *I am so lonesome here.*

But then, as if, even while Schubert lay dying, he wanted to remind himself that life was still beautiful and worth living, everything suddenly brightened, became dancelike and joyous.

> *The Springtime will come,*
> *The Springtime, my happiness,*
> *Now I must make ready*
> *To wander forth.*

The thrall of Schubert's trio in which gladness overpowers sadness uplifted Little Li. The ability to find succor in great music had given him something to love when humans failed, and now Schubert was reminding him that, despite the abyss into which he'd fallen, there were still powers that could help him regain admittance to life. How something as abstract as music could touch a human heart and help heal even its gravest wounds was a mystery. But, thanks to Schubert, Little Li felt this mystery now at work on his own heart.

As he approached his Cutlass after the concert, the homeless man began chanting, "Give whatcha can! Give whatcha can!" Little Li handed him everything in his wallet. "God bless ya, brother," said the old man, smiling broadly and bowing. "God bless your kindness!"

42

REBIRTH IN A LAUNDROMAT

WHEN LITTLE LI woke up the next morning, he attacked the clutter in his room, as if rectifying some part of everyday life might help restore his dignity. Within an hour, he'd collected all the empty aluminum Sara Lee cake trays, bottles, newspapers, and trash that had accumulated, and in a moment of grand catharsis heaved them out the window into the dumpster below. Then he piled all his unwashed clothing, towels, and his clown sheets into a garbage bag and hauled them to the Spin City Wash Center. The idea of harvesting something concrete and measurable—a pile of gravel or a stack of clean laundry—had undeniable appeal.

But at the Laundromat the empty rows of open-mouthed washers and dryers only reminded him of the vestigial machines in Juliette's studio and the industrial-sized versions at the Grecian Fitness Club. Though his life in America had offered him limited social intercourse, it certainly had provided an abundance of washing machines, dryers, and household appliances!

Trying to put Juliette out of his mind, he set his things down on one of the bright-orange plastic chairs that lined the back wall and began stuffing laundry into a machine. Then he punched in some quarters and sat back, watching as his wash sloshed around behind the machine's TV-screen-like window. Not unlike his own thoughts that had been churning for days, the machine kept going around and around without going anywhere. Quickly bored with Laundromat TV, he rummaged through the pile of dog-eared magazines heaped on a window ledge. A story in a *Cosmopolitan* promised to explain "How to Handle *That Affair with Another Woman*!" He'd have preferred an article addressing the question of "that other man," but flipped anyway through the article by Rhonda Pinsky, Ph.D., who was shown in an author's photo to be blond, well coiffed, with very white teeth and a cleavage definitely in excess of academic norms.

"First things first," began Dr. Pinsky. "When you discover your hubby's been cheating on you, you have to ask: is this fling a one-off or is my guy a chronic Lothario? If you answer that he's just gone off the tracks this once, it may be time for a little forgiveness. And why not a little marriage counseling as well to ease your pain? Remember, if he really is Mr. Terrific he'll agree to counseling and can't be all bad! And . . . Maybe you can turn this into a growth opportunity for both of you."

In their relentless pursuit of freedom and pleasure, Americans seemed to have become habituated to excusing such transgressions, even cheerfully turning them into "growth opportunities," "learning experiences," and the like. Little Li had been surprised by how people here were so readily able to find virtue in failure, as if setbacks were really only hidden positive lessons waiting to be repurposed as pathways forward to a better future. Indeed, one of Juliette's friends loved to bang on about how the two Chinese characters that form the compound for "crisis" (危机) separately mean "danger" and "opportunity." In this guy's treasure chest of Oriental wisdom, every catastrophe was just another hidden opportunity for personal growth. That textual readings like this were hackneyed didn't seem to bother such self-anointed authorities, who rarely brooked correction, even from a Chinese. In any event, Little Li remained unconvinced that his train wreck with Juliette would ever become a stepping-stone to greater success. Right now, failure was just plain failure, and, quite frankly, he'd had enough of it! Even though he still aspired to become more modern and more American, he doubted he'd ever attain a high enough level of enlightenment to confer absolution on a friend or lover capable of such a brazen betrayal as Juliette, and then view all the agony it had caused as a cheery prelude to a higher stage of being. Disgusted by the whole subject, he threw the *Cosmo* back onto the pile.

When he looked up, a Chinese man had come in and was reading the Chinese-language *World Journal* as he waited for his laundry. Little Li caught his eye, and he smiled.

"Where you from?" he asked.

"Beijing."

"Really? Me, too."

"How long have you been here?" asked Little Li, in Chinese.

"Couple of years."

"What do you do?"

"I work at UCSF's hospital, but I like to keep up with what's happening back home, where things really seem to be moving." He slapped a headline, "Premier Zhao Ziyang Says Reform Is Inevitable," above a photo of him and other Chinese leaders decked out in natty Western suits and ties, smiling and waving to foreign reporters. "And here's an article quoting Hu Qili, who's a Politburo member, calling for 'the creation of a more democratic, harmonious, and mutually trusting environment.' Pretty amazing!"

When the man stood to put his clothing into a dryer, Little Li looked at the paper. Another headline reported on the arrival in the United States of the well-known journalist Liu Binyan who'd been writing bold investigative pieces in the *People's Daily* unmasking party corruption. He was quoted as saying that now "you can express yourself more easily in China than in the Soviet Union." Was it possible, he wondered, that while he'd been preoccupied with Juliette, his homeland had actually been breaking free of its destructive revolutionary past?

"What do you make of it all?" he asked the man.

"The heavens only know!" He shrugged. "Chairman Mao used to tell us to embrace contradictions. The party's certainly doing that right now." He laughed.

After the man left, Little Li picked up his discarded newspaper, and no matter where he glanced in it, he found surprising items. The liberal political theorist Wang Ruoshui was even quoted as asserting that "Marxism is but one school in the history of human thought that can neither end the search for truth nor monopolize truth."

When Little Li next glanced up from the paper, a young woman in her mid-twenties had entered the Laundromat. She had brown hair falling to her shoulders and wore a pair of faded jeans topped by a man's button-down shirt. Not statuesque like Juliette, there was something sweet and straightforward about her face and diminutive body that he found appealing. Glad for the distraction, he furtively watched as she sorted through her basketful of pillowcases, sheets, towels, blouses, and undergarments. When she stuffed a set of pink sheets into a washing machine, he found himself wondering what it would be like to caress her body on her freshly washed linen. Just being able to entertain such a thought served as an antidote to the defeatist venom coursing through his veins, providing a welcome reassurance that his own capacity for desire was still intact. However, he was still not up to just walking over to her, as he imagined the shameless Lance Prince would. Then, unexpectedly, she spun around and caught him staring, but instead of a reproving glance, she gave an open smile.

Anyone watching this brief encounter might have dismissed it as inconsequential. After all, people smile at strangers all the time. But just as listening to Schubert had helped ground him, this young woman's smile supercharged him with a new confidence. Hoping to position himself better for a conversation, he walked over to the detergent machine, as if interested in purchasing a mini-box of Tide. Then it dawned on him that his clothes were already in the dryer, and that pretending to buy detergent would be absurdly transparent. To make matters worse, just then his dryer suddenly stopped spinning, so he couldn't just go back to his seat and continue watching a motionless machine like an imbecile. Opening its door, he felt his laundry, and then punched in another quarter. She'd have no way of knowing that his laundry was so hot it was nearing its kindling point. On the other hand, if it spontaneously burst into flame, he'd at least have an ice-breaking moment!

By the time she finally stood up to remove her own things from the dryer, he knew he had to move or lose his chance. But, just then, she turned, smiled again, put her hands on her hips, and playfully asked, "Hey! What are you drying over there, horse blankets?"

"Actually . . ." He began laughing. "I was just trying to think of some way to start up a conversation with you."

"No kidding?" she replied, a slight flush in her cheeks. Then, cocking her head coyly to one side, she added, "And do you know what I was thinking? 'How the hell am I going to get that mysteriously good-looking guy to talk to me before his clothes catch on fire?' Anyway, my name's Lisa Singleton." She proffered her hand with a charming matter-of-factness.

"And my name is Li Wende."

"Oh boy!" she exclaimed. "I kinda knew you weren't going to be a Buster or a Chuck!"

"I'm actually Chinese, at least mostly."

"And what's the rest of you?"

"My mother was half American, from San Francisco, and my father was from Beijing."

"Interesting!" she said.

Lisa, he learned, was twenty-six years old, had grown up in Iowa, come to San Francisco to get away from the small town where her father taught music at a local high school and she worked in the administrative offices of the San Francisco Conservatory of Music. What's more, she played the piano. "And here's a fun fact," she added. "My grandparents were once missionaries in China."

"Really?" he said with surprise. "Where?"

"Up the Yangtze River somewhere, in a town with a name that's impossible to pronounce. My dad was born there. We even have some old photos of him going downriver on a junk! Think of it! If your Chairman Mao hadn't chased us all out of town, I might have been Chinese, too."

"My apologies. Everyone here seems to know about our Chairman Mao. You honor us!"

"I think you're pulling my honorable leg."

Little Li told her that his American grandfather had been a missionary, too, and they quickly became so engrossed in conversation that they kept talking long after both of their dryers had ceased turning.

"Oh, wow! It's getting dark," she finally exclaimed. "But it's been such fun talking with you." She stood up, opened the door of her dryer, and began pulling her laundry into her hamper.

"Hey! Could I drive you home?" he impulsively offered.

"Oh!" she responded, caught off guard. "I live nearby, but why not?" As she got out of his car, she hesitated, smiled, and said, "You know, if you're free, I could fix us a cup of tea."

"That would be nice," he responded, trying to sound casual, even though the thought that you could meet a lovely stranger in a Laundromat and moments later be going up to her apartment for tea had him electrified. Breaking the ice had turned out to be so easy that he felt foolish for ever having imagined it was difficult.

Lisa's apartment consisted of a small vestibule, a tiny kitchen with a table and three chairs, a compact bathroom, and a bedroom with a single stuffed chair, a small desk, and a large bed set with four aquamarine pillows arranged against the headboard. As cramped as her apartment was, it was welcoming.

"If you like, I could cook us some dinner," she offered after they'd talked for a while at her table.

"I'd like that," he replied.

Lisa knew exactly where everything was in her kitchen and how to do things with a minimum of effort and fuss. Her compact body moved with efficiency and adeptness, telegraphing that she was in charge without being peremptory. After washing some lettuce and laying some chicken drumsticks in a frying pan, she set the table with matching black plates. On those few occasions when Juliette had "cooked," the kitchen had quickly become a battlefield of spilled ingredients, shredded packaging, crudely opened cans, unwashed pots, and dirty implements. Even though she was in evident need of help, she brooked no assistance, leaving him to observe from the sidelines as her chaotic preparations unfolded. Lisa, on the other hand, went about cooking with all the cool effortlessness of an experienced aircraft pilot. When he asked if he could help, she smiled as if he'd quaintly offered to hold the door open for her.

"Why don't you grab some salad dressing from the fridge," she finally suggested.

He opened its door to find a gleaming white interior occupied by an array of yogurt, milk, and juice containers all lined up as neatly as a regiment of toy soldiers. A second shelf was reserved for bread and eggs, each in its own little nesting place in a plastic tray. And the two drawers at the bottom were filled with plastic bags of vegetables and fruits, all of which looked fresh and edible. Her shipshape fridge and apartment were as different from Juliette's sprawling ruin as San Francisco's broad, straight streets were from the mazes of winding, disheveled *hutong*s in Beijing.

After dinner, they stretched out on her bed, she lying against the headboard and he sprawled across the foot, and for several hours she listened with absorption as he told her about his life in Beijing and Qinghai. China may have become a land obsessed with forgetting, but Americans seemed to want to know everything. As he regaled her, she gazed unflinchingly at him with a look that mixed fascination, incredulity, sympathy, and admiration. Like him, she was wondering how she'd ended up here, on her bed, next to a curious stranger from a Laundromat who was telling her fantastic tales about Tibetans in charmingly accented English.

"How do I know you're not just making all this up?" she asked when he was recounting what it was like to live with the Goloks in their yak-hair tents.

"The best proof is, if I hadn't actually lived it, I couldn't have dreamed it up."

"Okay," she said, and laughed. "You've convinced me!"

By 10:00 p.m. he was beginning to feel presumptuous in lingering. But there was something so open and accessible about Lisa that he quite unexpectedly found himself leaning over and stroking her hair. He'd never before acted with such spontaneous conviction around a woman he hardly knew, and the way she yielded to his touch announced she was already his. With a sigh, she curled up beside him. Like one of those cartoon figures that hurl themselves against a closed door only to have it unexpectedly open at the last minute, so they fly right through the doorway out to a swimming pool or into a wall, he was put off balance by her receptivity.

"I don't even really know you, but already I feel comfortable," she said with a guileless grin. As they lay together in the dark, listening to the sounds of the city, the warmth of her body made him tingle, as if circulation were finally being restored to a long-benumbed limbs. "Shall we get under the covers?" she sweetly suggested.

"Sure," he replied, and kissed her, hardly able to believe how things were unfolding.

"But, please, know that I'm not accustomed to bringing strange men home every time I go to the Laundromat!"

"Well," he replied, "I'm not even accustomed to going to Laundromats!"

"Don't you have them in China?" she asked, wide-eyed.

"I'd never heard of a Laundromat before arriving here."

"Oh, you poor, benighted boy!" She kissed him.

"So," he thought, "when impulse replaces fear, is this what life is like?" Then, as if it were the most natural thing in the world, he began unbuttoning her blouse. Unlike Juliette, who always undressed herself and flung her garments on the floor, Lisa waited for him, seeming to enjoy being disrobed as, one by one, he popped open the buttons as if unwrapping a gift. When she lay down on her freshly washed sheets, he felt reborn.

"Thank you, Lisa," he whispered.

"Oh my goodness!" she responded with a quizzical expression. "I haven't even given you anything . . . yet. Anyway, who's to say who should be giving thanks to whom?" She laughed.

"It's just . . ." he began. "Actually, I don't think I can explain. It's just so nice being with you." She leaned her head back against his chest.

Whereas Juliette had been defiant, unpredictable, and exciting, Lisa was sweet, reliable, and reassuring, leaving him feeling as soothed as he was aroused. It was simpleminded of him ever to have assumed that Juliette somehow represented the totality of America, and that their breakup meant he was destined to be cut off from this new land. Lisa was American, too, but opened a very different door into this elusive country. So beautiful was she in her nakedness that he almost wanted to stop right there to freeze-frame the moment. Her white shoulders had a delicate elegance; her modest breasts were so perfectly shaped they hardly seemed real; and her hips had a provocatively boyish slenderness that gave them an appealing androgynous cleanness of line. Nestled against him, she looked almost too delicate to be embraced by his own strong, dark-skinned body.

"Gently," she said, and then kissed him again, but not so much in passion as in vulnerability. Juliette approached sex like a competitive sport she was bent on winning, while at the same time holding whole parts of herself aloof, so that even the most ecstatic moments ended up feeling somehow incomplete. But Lisa seemed all there; he felt she was both his and satisfied before they'd begun.

As they lay together, watching shadows from the headlights of passing cars play across the ceiling, he marveled at how suddenly life's fortunes could change. Just when there appeared to be no way forward, a pathway opened. Already he could feel his shattered bones knitting back together. Of course, though he was elated by the sudden draft of new optimism, he had to remind himself that this harsh and unpredictable land was still just as filled with false promises and cruel illusions as before, and that in the end Lisa, too, might prove just another tantalizing false horizon dangled before him by a perfidious America.

Gradually, he began spending more nights with Lisa, even driving her to work at the Conservatory. When her father, Hank Singleton, who taught history and directed the high-school band in Storm Lake, Iowa, visited San Francisco, he took an instant liking to Little Li, joking that he, too, was "Chinese," because he spoke some Chinese and had been born in a Methodist mission in Changsha, the capital of Mao Zedong's home province.

"They used to call me Hunan Hank," he joked in a comical Hunan accent.

Hank introduced Little Li to the bandmaster at a nearby public high school, who arranged for him to give individual music lessons to woodwind students after class. Though he was thrilled to have some income that didn't embroil him in visa issues, he found the music dull, the students lacking in promise, and the job boring. One evening when Lisa mentioned that the cellist Yo-Yo Ma was scheduled to give a master class at the Conservatory and that he could come as her guest, he jumped at the opportunity. Ma was, after all, not only one of the world's most renowned musicians, but also Chinese.

43

MASTER CLASS

WHEN LITTLE LI walked in through the main door of the San Francisco Conservatory of Music's hacienda-style main building, on 19th Avenue and heard the familiar din of practicing instruments coming from every corner, he felt instantly at home. He was also filled with a piercing sense of regret that he'd allowed himself to become so entrapped by Juliette's and the Grecian Fitness Club's field of gravity and forsaken his pursuit of music. Wasn't an environment like the Conservatory at the center of the dream that had lured him to California in the first place? An oboe was bleating out long tones, a bass was singing a Mozart aria, a violin was sawing out arpeggios, and a pianist was practicing the cadenza from Bach's Fifth Brandenburg Concerto, starting over and over again at the same place, as if a phonograph needle had gotten stuck on a scratched record. And a hallway bulletin board was festooned with so many flyers that from a distance it reminded him of the Conservatory in Beijing during the Cultural Revolution, when every vertical surface was shaggy with Red Guard wall posters. These posters, however, were not political attacks and diatribes but benign celebrations of music competitions, summer camps, and festivals.

The morning of Yo-Yo Ma's master class the line was so long that by the time they got into the auditorium, there were only a few empty seats available. So Little Li let Lisa take one up front and repaired to the back, where he stood behind the last row. As the students hummed with excitement he tried to envision his father here as a young man.

Having expected Yo-Yo Ma to appear, the audience applauded only politely when the director of the school walked out onstage instead.

"We're here to celebrate great music and learn from a great musician," he began in a very soft voice. "We all feel classical music gives us something special, but just how an art form so abstract can make us feel so intensely is part of the enigma of art and being human. And someone who understands this mystery as well as anyone is our friend Yo-Yo Ma." The audience started clapping. "But before our guest comes out to do his master class, I want to speak to you for a few moments about how music connects us to the rest of our lives, and how another great cellist, Pablo Casals, who had a profound influence on Yo-Yo, saw himself, his music, and the world.

"Casals played for Queen Victoria, and then again, for President John F. Kennedy, to whom he introduced Yo-Yo as a little boy. While Casals had the deepest reverence for music, he revered free expression and democratic values just as much. He even went into self-imposed exile to oppose General Francisco Franco's fascist rule in his own country, Spain. He said it was a 'lack of humanity' that was 'at the core' of his 'argument with music today.' Though he was a devout Catholic, he insisted that it was not the church but church music that claimed his loyalty and that if he had a patron saint it was J. S. Bach, whom he called 'the supreme genius of music,' a man who 'cannot write one note, however unimportant it may appear, which is anything but transcendent.' Casals was awed by what he called the 'magic and mystery' of Bach, especially his Six Unaccompanied Cello Suites, which he played throughout his life."

Even though the director's talk was standing between the students and Ma's master class, there was something so direct and sincere about his delivery that the hall had nonetheless fallen completely silent.

"Let me read what Casals said of his first encounter with the cello suites as a boy: 'All I could do was stare at the pages and caress them. I hurried home, clutching the suites as if they were the crown jewels," he said. "Then, I read and reread them. I was thirteen at the time, but for the following eighty years the wonder of my discovery has continued to grow on me. Those suites opened up a whole new world. I began playing them with indescribable excitement. They became my most cherished music.'

"When Casals he was ninety-seven, he summed up his love of Bach's music this way: 'For the last eighty years I've started each day in the same manner. I go to the piano and I play two preludes and fugues of Bach. I cannot think of doing otherwise. It is a sort of benediction on the house. . . . It fills me with awareness of the wonder of life, with a feeling of the incredible marvel of being a human being.'

"So," continued the Director, "I hope you, too, will come to see music not just as notes and technique, but as Thomas Mann described Casals, as a 'symbol of the indissoluble union of art and morality.' And there are few living musicians who better exemplify the spirit of Casals than Yo-Yo Ma. That's why we're so pleased to welcome him here today."

As Ma stepped out onstage, the students broke into a thunderous applause. He wore baggy gray flannel slacks, a tweed jacket, a white shirt, a striped tie, round wire-rimmed glasses, and had his hair parted down the middle, just as Li Tongshu had as a young man.

"I really don't know how to respond to such a kind introduction," he said, patting his heart. Then, as if conversing with friends, he leaned toward the audience and said: "To be mentioned in the same sentence as Pablo Casals . . . Well . . . As a child, he was my idol. He was, of course, a cellist of extraordinary talent, but he was first a human being, only second a musician, and third a cellist. What was most unique about him was that he always believed there was something bigger than each of us connecting us all together. But"—he clapped his hands together—"we're here today not just to talk about the past, but to celebrate the next generation of musicians. You! So . . ." He looked expectantly toward the wings. When no one materialized, he ran offstage, and reappeared leading a reluctant young woman holding a cello.

"It's so good to be here with you," he said, giving her a deferential bow. "What are you going to play for us today?"

"The prelude from the first Bach suite?"

"Ahhh! One of my favorites," rejoined Ma with a beatific smile. "Hey!" he called out to the audience. "Anybody happen to have a copy of the suites?"

"I do!" a girl in the third row excitedly cried out, thrusting her score forward.

"Excellent!" He beamed. "And what do you play?"

"Cello, of course!" she replied breathlessly.

"Bingo!" he rejoined, like a game-show host when a contestant answers the jackpot question correctly. The girl gave a little shriek of delight. Turning back to the nervous young cellist on stage, Ma gave her an avuncular wink. "I know you'll be great!"

"We'll see," she murmured, blushing.

When she sat down in a chair center stage, Ma stepped back beyond the circle of illumination cast by a spotlight. As she began playing, he stood with hands clasped as if praying. After a moment or so, he jumped off the stage and strode down the aisle to listen from farther away. The young cellist sensed that something was happening, but, unable to see exactly what, sawed away with fierce, if wooden, determination. Then, suddenly, Ma was beside Little Li, his head lowered to listen. Wary of disturbing his concentration, Little Li tried to focus on the music, too. The girl was technically good, but lacked confidence and feeling.

"Hey! Do you play cello?" Ma suddenly whispered to him. There was something about the way his hair flopped down over his brow, his boyish grin, and his self-deprecating manner that put Little Li instantly at ease. His open face seemed to say, "Yes, I'm famous, but can't we just forget this annoying fact for a moment so I can be a regular guy like you?"

"Actually, I play flute," he whispered back.

"Oh, wow! Great!" replied Ma, as if he'd just heard a piece of very good news. Then, giving another wink, he resumed listening.

Never had Little Li imagined that someone of such repute could behave with such childlike enthusiasm in public. In China, where most people relied on their prescribed rank in a well-ordered pyramid, it was considered unseemly for someone of senior position or exalted reputation to consort in a way that was too informal or familiar with persons of lesser standing. But here was Yo-Yo Ma, one of the world's great solo musicians, seemingly bent on dissolving the differences between himself and young students. It was as if he viewed this master class as an opportunity not just to teach music, but to dismantle the very notions of hierarchy and celebrity.

There was something else about Yo-Yo Ma that struck Little Li. Though he was obviously an ethnic Chinese, those features were not what one noticed first about him. In China, there was always such a self-consciousness about what was foreign and what was Chinese, and Little Li had this contradiction so embedded in his own being that he'd always felt irrevocably split. But here was one of the world's best-known musicians, who, while ethnically Chinese, was born in Paris, and raised in America, but seemed completely comfortable with all the different constituent pieces of his being. His virtuoso talent projected an image that was neither Chinese, American, nor Chinese American, but universal. Was this perhaps the genius of the U.S. melting pot? Foreigners from wherever threw themselves into this pot and were smelted into more vigorous hybrid "Americans."

As the young girl bowed out the last chords of Bach's prelude, Ma ran down the aisle, leapt back up onto the stage, and raised his hands above his head.

"Wonderful!" he effused. "You play so well! But let me ask: what do you think Bach is trying to tell us in this prelude?" He clutched his hands to his chest.

"Well, I guess it's . . ." the young girl began haltingly.

"It's what?" he goaded her, gesticulating like someone urging a player on in a game of charades.

"Well, isn't it kind of melancholy?"

"You got it!" He raised a forefinger, spoofing a comic-book moment of illumination. "You play beautifully, but we want more melancholy and resignation. When you get to D minor, we want you to turn us into emotional wrecks, to reach our hearts! I know you can do it!"

"Okay, but . . ." she responded hesitantly.

"May I show you?" chirruped Ma, rolling up his sleeves.

"Oh, well, sure!" she replied, handing him her cello, a look of surprise spreading across her smiling face.

When he took her instrument, he crouched without a chair in a way that was hauntingly reminiscent of how Little Li's own father had continued playing the night Red Guards had ripped his piano bench out from beneath him in Willow Courtyard. Even in this awkward position, the instrument became part of his body and Ma bowed out a sound that was celestial. When he finished the last bar, his eyes remained closed, and he held the bow motionless for an extended moment, as if reluctant to part with the last, sustained note. The crowd broke into another delirious applause.

"Okay, now this time I want you to really lose yourself in the music!" He smiled. "But before you begin, you have to decide mentally what you're going to do to make us feel how the different blocks of the piece build into something. And remember: we're all always still learning! It took Casals twelve years playing these suites before he felt ready to perform even one in public. And do you know what he said when asked why he kept practicing them at age ninety-three?" The young girl shook her head. "He said, 'I do it because I'm beginning to notice some improvement!'" The audience roared.

Relaxed by Ma's levity, the young girl composed herself and began playing again. This time her body posture was less rigid, and her sound more expressive and soulful.

"Yeah! Much, much better," Ma unexpectedly interrupted. "But what we want is that heartfelt quality that is deep in the music, that is at once subtle and moving. Remember, even though Bach was a very proper ecclesiastical man, he was surrounded by death, and had deep feelings! Your job is to enable us to feel those feelings ourselves."

"Uh-huh," she replied uncertainly. Fearful he might have discouraged her, he grabbed his own cello from under the piano.

"Let's try together?" he suggested with an impish grin. She nodded enthusiastically. As she began, he plucked pizzicato, like a backup jazz bassist, and she played with a sudden new warmth and feeling. "Wonderful! Wonderful!" he said, jumping up when she'd finished. "Isn't she great?" he asked the audience. The girl beamed with pride.

The next master-class student was a Eurasian in that twilight period between still being a girl and becoming a woman. Although beneath her gangling awkwardness a radiant beauty was beginning to bloom, she was so self-conscious, she kept averting her gaze as if that would help her escape the scrutiny of both her teacher and the audience.

"So what do you have for us?" asked Ma cheerfully.

"Elgar" was all she said before settling awkwardly in the onstage chair as an accompanist seated himself at the piano. Then, hunching over her instrument, she began the Adagio from the Elgar Cello Concerto in E minor, bowing with a forcefulness completely at odds with her awkward body language. Although her eyes never left the floor and her shoulders remained hunched, she filled the hall with a sound so sensuous it made Little Li's scalp prickle. It hardly seemed possible that such a mature sound could emanate from such an immature, gawky girl. As she concluded the movement, Ma grabbed his hair and shook his head in theatrical disbelief.

"That's really just . . . , just fantastic!" he enthused. The girl blushed and lowered her chin even farther. "You were just great!" he added, leaning down to force eye contact.

"Thank you so much!" she said, stifling a giggle that was all the sweeter for its hesitancy.

"But I should thank *you*!" he insisted. "You play *so* beautifully!" Then, after standing for a moment in reflection, he suddenly added, "All right! I have an idea." He scrubbed his hands together conspiratorially. "Could you start again, but this time, follow me with your eyes wherever I go? No matter what I do, you just *follow me*. Okay?" She nodded, biting back a smile.

As soon as she started, Ma jumped offstage again. However, instead of moving to the back of the hall, this time he began climbing like a monkey down a row of seats. The student audience members laughed, and as the young cellist followed his antics, she, too, began giggling. Then, with her head higher now and her shoulders back, she opened up and played with such riveting sovereignty, power, and sonority that Ma stopped his clowning and moved to the side of the hall to just listen. Never had Little Li heard someone so young play with such feeling, command, and richness of tone. Then, as if she were a diver on a high board, who suddenly looks down and becomes panicked by the height, just as the music should have reached a grand climax, she faltered and, reinfected by self-consciousness, let her bow drop. The scattering of nervous titters that rippled through the hall doubled her mortification. But, like a medic wading into a firefight to rescue a wounded comrade, Ma was already running toward the crestfallen girl. Almost tripping as he leapt up onto the stage, he opened his arms.

"You were so wonderful!" he said, his voice raising at least an octave as he hugged her. Thawed by his generosity, she let slip a grin. Like a gospel preacher calling a congregation to response, Ma turned to the audience, raised his arms above his head, and cried out, "Wasn't she great? Couldn't you guys hear the difference?" The audience gave an affirmative roar. Ma turned back to the girl, who was now squirming with delight. "When you guarded the space around you, we were kept outside of the music. But then you reached out and engaged us. Bravo! Now, details. You got carried away by the accelerando and rushed. Whenever you speed up, you must do it with bodily feeling to make it move." Grabbing his own cello, he sawed out the accelerando with such vigor it seemed almost unthinkable that he, too, had once been a beginner. Then, fingering down the neck in a rapidly descending arpeggio, he made an obvious mistake. "Never mind!" he cried insouciantly, continuing to play. "When you perform, you can't afford to worry about your fingers. Your technique must just be there! What matters is that you get the feeling and energy right." Little Li wondered if the mistake had not been a premeditated ploy designed to manifest his own fallibility, just to set his young student at ease.

"Now," he pronounced, "I'm going to sit on the floor, and you're going to keep your eyes on me, play for me, and melt my heart . . . and theirs." He gestured out to the audience and sat down cross-legged onstage. She played like an angel. When she finished, the audience's entusiastic applause was directed not just at their talented classmate, but at the generous master who'd opened her up to Elgar and herself. As she walked offstage, Little Li felt he'd just seen two skillfully performed one-act plays that had changed the whole way he looked at the world.

44

LIKE AFTERSHOCKS that continue to pulse long after an earthquake subsides, the master class reverberated in Little Li's life until he finally decided to apply to the San Francisco Conservatory himself. Sitting at Lisa's kitchen table as she drew in her sketchbook, he filled out an application. An audition was, of course, the most critical admissions hurdle, so, with music Lisa borrowed from the Conservatory library, he began a strict schedule of daily practice. On weekends, when she was able to book rehearsal rooms, he played trios, with her on piano and a friend on cello. For his audition selection, he chose the Bach Sonata in E-flat major, which he'd played for Yang Ming at Yak Springs, but as the audition approached, he felt as nervous as one of the young students he'd seen in the master class. After all, his musical life had been punctuated by long interruptions that had left him feeling like a pretender to the title of "musician." Nonetheless, when he walked into the studio to meet his committee—a tall, bearded oboist; a plump, mustached bassoonist with a bald head; and a slender woman flutist with frizzy hair—their friendliness set him at ease.

"And you come from China?" asked the bassoonist, looking up from his application.

"I do."

"And how did you hear about the Conservatory?" he continued, pulling at his mustache.

"Well, actually, my father studied piano here in the late 1940s."

"Far out!" exclaimed the oboist. "That was back in the day!" For a few moments they discussed when the Conservatory was founded.

"Well, we welcome the family back!" said the bassoonist, smiling. "We don't get all that many second-generation students . . . especially from China." They all laughed.

"So what will you be playing for us?" asked the flutist.

"Bach's Flute Sonata in E-flat major."

"You know some people think that was written by his son," offered the flutist.

"So I've heard, but I like it anyway."

"Well, that's the right answer," replied the bassoonist, chuckling.

"Let me know when you're ready," cued the accompanist at a piano.

Little Li stood up, understanding that his future hung in the balance. As he began playing, he closed his eyes and imagined himself back on the road at Yak Springs. But when he finished the last bar, opened his eyes, and saw his three judges just sitting expressionless behind their table, his heart sank.

"Well, thank you so much," the flutist finally offered, in a tone evincing little enthusiasm. After an awkward silence, the oboist looked up from his folder, furrowed his brow, and said, "So . . . that was very nice, but what's all this about Tibet?"

"Well, it's a long story." As always, Little Li was unsure how to give a short, convincing explanation of his time in Qinghai.

"I mean, why would a classical musician want to go way out there?"

"Actually, it wasn't a question of 'wanting' to go," he answered warily. "I was assigned there, and when the party 'assigns' you someplace, you want. You had no choice."

"How old were you when you went?" The bassoonist looked vexed.

"About sixteen."

"And you couldn't leave?"

"No. We were all stuck with whatever assignments we got, and I got a Tibetan ethnic area out in the middle of nowhere."

"And how long were you there?" pressed the oboist.

"Over ten years."

"You gotta be kidding!" exclaimed the flutist, almost indignantly.

"That's just the way it was." Little Li shrugged. He had to admit that, from the vantage point of San Francisco, where everyone was free to do whatever they wished, such a system of compulsory assignments sounded draconian, even bizarre. But, because he could tell that the committee members were engaged by his story, he decided he'd better keep playing along with them.

"I mean, how could you play music out there?" asked the oboist.

"Well, I did take my flute."

"To Tibet?" she pressed incredulously.

"Yes."

"And . . . who did you play with?"

"There was no one, so the best I could do was give outdoor recitals for the nomads. I'm not sure how much they liked the music, but they love silver and had never seen anything like my flute. Maybe some came to hear me play, but probably a lot more came to admire my flute!" Recalling the covetous looks Lobsang's family gave his flute as they held it made him smile.

"Guess my ax wouldn't cut it out there!" laughed the oboist, holding up his ebony instrument.

"The Chinese have a woodwind instrument within a double-reed called the *suona* (唢呐), and the Tibetans have a version called the *gyaling*," he replied. "But they don't have silver keys. If they did, I don't think they'd last long, because those nomads love silver ornaments so much, they'd probably all end up as jewelry." Everyone laughed.

"And were the people up there all Buddhists?" asked the flutist, smiling and playing with one of her silver hoop earrings.

"They were."

"But didn't Mao see Buddhism and other religions as 'the opium of the masses'?"

"He did, but the nomads remained secretly devoted to the Buddha anyway. And since they were pastoralists and always moving around, the party wasn't able to control them well."

"And you were just out there living with them?" queried the disbelieving bassoonist.

"My situation there is hard to explain."

"But we'd love to hear more." Everyone nodded in agreement.

"Well, I was on a road crew that maintained part of a highway to Lhasa, and I . . ."

"Lhasa!" exclaimed the oboist. "Whoa! That's a place I've always dreamed about!" By now, all of the members of the audition committee were staring at Little Li with the same kind of unalloyed wonder as the Goloks when he played his flute.

"What kind of music did you play for those guys?" asked the now wide-eyed flutist. "Tibetan stuff?"

"No. Although they chant and sing, the nomads didn't have instrumental music. So I'd just play them anything. Sometimes I'd do classical, even this Bach sonata. But since I had no sheet music, I could only play pieces I'd memorized before leaving Beijing. It was very frustrating, because if I'd forgotten a whole movement, or just a few bars, there was no way to get it back, so I quickly ran out of stuff to play."

"Then what did you do?" she persisted.

"Improvised."

"You mean like in jazz?" asked the oboist.

"You could say that. For instance, I'd take a revolutionary song and start fooling around with it. I didn't know what else to do. And the nomads would listen to anything!"

"Fascinating!" exclaimed the smiling bassoonist.

"Hey! Maybe you'd do some of that improv for us?" suggested the flutist.

"Right now?" exclaimed Little Li, caught off guard. It was a long way from Bach to one of his improvisations of "Chairman Mao Is Together with Us" or "Without the Communist Party There'd Be No New China."

"Do you think it's strange that a bunch of American classical musicians are attracted to such an out-of-the-way place as Tibet?" asked the bassoonist, sensing Little Li's confusion.

"Well, I must say that it's not easy to understand why a country as modern as the U.S. is so interested in a place so remote, traditional, and backward as Tibet," admitted Little Li. "But you're not the first ones who've seemed interested."

"The whole Tibetan Buddhism thing is very trendy these days!" offered the oboist.

"I'm not sure if our little encounter group on Tibet is helping explain anything to Mr. Li here," interrupted the bassoonist with a whinnying laugh. "But . . . I think we'd all love you to treat us to some Tibetan improv."

Little Li sensed his candidacy at the Conservancy now depended as much on the oddity of his Qinghai exile and ability to now come through extemporaneously with some improvisation as on his formal interpretation of Bach, so he began trying to think which revolutionary song would be most suitable for them.

"Okay," he finally suggested. "How about some variations on a theme from 'Sailing the Seas Depends on the Great Helmsman'?"

"Far out!" exclaimed the bassoonist enthusiastically.

"So—the first thing to understand is that 'the Great Helmsman' [伟大舵手] refers to Chairman Mao, and 'sailing the seas' to his navigating the world, spreading socialist revolution. Here's the first verse:

"Just as sailing the seas depends on the helmsman,
Life and growth depends on the sun.
Just as rain and dew nourish the crops,
Making revolution depends on Mao Zedong Thought.
Just as fish are unable to leave the water,
Or melons to escape their vines,
Neither can the revolutionary masses
Ever do without the Communist Party.
Mao Zedong Thought is the sun that never sets.

"Far out!" exclaimed the bassoonist again.

"Okay, from here on you have to think: the *Goldberg Variations* collide with the Great Proletarian Cultural Revolution!" They all smiled. "So—I'll start, how do you say . . . ?"

"Jamming?" offered the flutist helpfully.

"Something like that," he agreed, trying to imagine Bach sitting at his harpsichord and making his *Goldberg* aria undergo mitosis into thirty separate variations. But as he began to play, it was not Bach he saw, but his Golok fans arrayed around him on their stone seats in the Drogyu Quarry.

When he finished, the three judges sat spellbound. Then the flutist began clapping, and soon they were all applauding. The bassoonist even gave a wolf whistle.

"Quite a country you got over there, Mr. Li!" said the oboist.

"If you were admitted," added the bassoonist, "you'd be our third student from China."

"And the only one who plays Tibetan/Maoist jazz!" exclaimed the flutist enthusiastically. "You could join the Conservatory jazz combo!"

"Well, Mr. Li, I'm sure we could sit here talking to you all day, but . . ." The bassoonist looked at his watch and then reached out to shake Little Li's hand.

"Yeah, for sure!" said the flutist, also reaching over to bid him goodbye. "It's been fun getting to know you and something about your unusual background."

Little Li left the Conservatory arm in arm with Lisa, flushed with hope. His exotic Tibetan pedigree had at last mattered to someone.

"Thick envelopes are good news!" a smiling Lisa announced when, several months later, a fat envelope from the Conservatory's admission office arrived. As he opened it, she kissed him.

When Conservatory classes began that fall, he felt he'd come back from a near-death experience. The course he enjoyed most was the History of Western Music, which started with plainsong and early polyphony and moved up through the Baroque, Classical, and Romantic periods to the advent of contemporary and atonal music. Getting a fuller sense of the sweep of classical music's historical development made him realize how fractured the teaching of history was in China. Whole periods were distorted, and others were completely erased from the record as culturally oppressive. As he began studying under the flutist with the frizzy hair, he was quickly won over, not just by her talent but by her friendliness and humor. Then, one day, she introduced him to her female "partner."

"Sabine plays harp for the San Francisco Symphony," she said cheerfully. "We'd both really love it if you'd come over for dinner some night and tell us more about China." Back in China, there'd always been rumors of homosexual relationships, especially in arts troupes. But they were alluded to only in the most veiled ways. The idea of two lesbians living openly together as a couple and inviting friends to dinner was unthinkable.

While Lisa was lovely, had a steady job, and truly cared for him, Little Li's limited life experience had ill-prepared him to understand how freighted with unanticipated ambiguity fulfillment can end up being, especially for those long accustomed to deprivation. As they went about their lives together—practicing, working, shopping, going to movies, attending concerts, and sharing meals—he found himself feeling both at peace and strangely becalmed. On weekend excursions with her to museums, he came to see how Western art and music shared the same arc through history. And the fact that it was Lisa who'd brought this kind of insight into his intellectual life made him all the more appreciative of her. One afternoon, as they were walking through a wing at the Legion of Honor, she paused before a Degas painting of a ballerina.

"I love the way Degas's dancers always seem so absorbed in themselves," she mused, slipping an arm around his waist. But the painting had involuntarily triggered a very different vision for him: of Juliette at the barre. Who was sleeping with her now? Immediately he felt stabbed anew by her betrayal. Lying in bed that night, when Lisa kissed him and then snuggled closer, he felt obliged to reciprocate, because she'd given him so much. But his mind was elsewhere. Over the last few months, a gnawing but elusive sense of something missing had slowly been growing within him. But what was this absence?

One fog-embroiled evening, after finishing a particularly uninspired session with a high-school band student, he'd had a sudden impulse to return to Grace Cathedral. As he took the same oak pew he'd sat in the day after arriving in San Francisco, he felt calmed by the church's magisterial tranquillity, especially the stately stained-glass windows that flanked the nave, each a miraculous convergence of hundreds of tiny fragments of colored glass, all brought together to form luminous islands of reassuring permanence and order in an otherwise disaggregated world. These windows were the antithesis of his own disjointed life. No matter on which side of the divide he landed, China and the United States remained grinding tectonic plates that could tear apart at any moment and throw his fragile world into chaos. Sun Yat-sen had once described his country as "a plate of loose sand" (一盘散沙), a perfect metaphor for Little Li's own fragmented self. And into this disarray had stepped Lisa Singleton, to help him be reborn a second time in America. This narrative even had its own quaint creation myth, a Bethlehem-like beginning set in a lowly San Francisco Laundromat. Because his inborn instinct was to show appreciation, he dropped to his knees on the green prayer cushion before him and wept in gratitude.

"You know, Little Li, I've been thinking," Lisa said with a shy impishness as they drove to the Conservatory one morning.

"What have you been thinking?" he asked.

"That you should move in with me." She looked expectantly at him.

"Oh!" was all he could gasp. He hadn't raised the subject, not because the thought had not occurred to him, but because he deemed his own commitment insufficient to warrant asking.

"You need to get rid of that room at the Asterix!" she added, wrinkling up her nose.

"You're such a nice person that sometimes I don't think I deserve you," he responded.

"But you will move in, won't you?"

"I will." He smiled.

For all that anyone on the outside could tell, her invitation represented a higher stage of convergence in their relationship. And for Little Li, moving in with her certainly would place him closer to the idea of his American dream. However, as he began packing his things, he was surprised by how ambivalent he felt about vacating his old room at the Asterix. Just as a prisoner can grow unexpectedly attached to the confinement of a cell and have complex feelings about leaving when parole is finally granted, Little Li discovered a bond that went deeper than he'd ever imagined. As tawdry as the Hotel Asterix was, it had still been his beachhead in America, his Plymouth Rock. And now, as he contemplated giving it up, he experienced a sense not only of time's passage, but of unexpected loss.

And there was one other problem, which neither he nor Lisa had foreseen: how to integrate all his possessions—especially his accumulation of secondhand appliances—into her small, well-ordered apartment? For him, these castaways were his American patrimony, and the thought of leaving them behind made him feel like a refugee ordered to abandon all worldly possessions as a condition of safe passage from a war-torn homeland. For her, what she dismissively referred to as his "dowry" was just alien clutter. Indeed, when she visited the Asterix to help him sort through his things, he sensed no small amount of impatience.

"You know, Little Li," she began in an overly restrained tone that signaled trouble, "my apartment is so small, maybe we should bring along only some of these things."

"But they work perfectly well," he remonstrated.

"But it's just junk!" she protested.

"Junk?" he exclaimed, and for the first time they found themselves arguing. Only after much back-and-forth did she manage to convince him to triage his TV set, electric can opener, and toaster oven. However, he refused to part with his vacuum cleaner. As if it were a sword and shield that had seen him through many a perilous military campaign, he felt fraternally bonded to his Mighty Mite. And, being the kind of person who, even when indisposed, is capable of wanting another person's happiness as much as her own, Lisa relented. Moreover, at the last minute, she gave his electric can opener a reprieve as well. Nonetheless, as he gathered up his other acquisitions to drop them out the window into the yawning mouth of the dumpster below, he felt faithless. He was about to let a final pile of things go when he spotted the ill-fitting suit jacket he'd brought from Beijing.

"No!" he thought. No matter how wrinkled, gray, and shapeless it was, he'd keep it! Trolling through its pockets, he was surprised to find a crumpled piece of paper: Unfolding it, he saw that it was the note Little Hong had written when she'd brought the Bach cantata to Willow Courtyard for his father. Flooded with nostalgia, he wondered what had become of her, and whether she ever thought of him.

As he walked away from the Hotel Asterix for the last time, the recognition that he'd never return here again left him unexpectedly melancholy. The irony was that whenever he left somewhere, even places from which he'd long yearned to escape, the actual moment of parting was bittersweet. He thought of his departure from Yak Springs, and how even that strange, barren place had managed to wend its way into his heart. He was tempted to blame his feelings of loss as the predictable result of the American dream: first it beckoned, but then, by finally delivering, it left the dreamer alone with the strange emptiness that can come only at the end of striving. Living with Lisa, he'd entered a state that was novel for him: equilibrium. He'd begun gaining a little weight, and they'd even discussed trading in his Cutlass for a smaller, neater Japanese car.

"Can I tell you something?" Lisa whispered one night as he was drifting off to sleep.

"Of course," he responded gently.

"I think Miss Lisa Singleton has grown to love Mr. Li Wende."

"Oh, Lisa!" was all he could manage. Even though he could feel her hoping for a more heartfelt declaration, he could not bring himself to say the words he knew she wanted to hear. Actually, since he was not sure what real love felt like, to say he loved her would have been untruthful. "You're such a lovely person, Lisa," he finally whispered instead. He was going to say, "But . . ." However, he caught himself at the last moment, because he knew how wounding it would have been. The truth was, he did not experience her with as much urgency as she experienced him. Lying beside her now, he felt a puzzling sense of absence, as if a mysterious but close companion was still somehow missing. Just as he should have been celebrating a new chapter in his American progress, a mutinous part of him was in a state of resistance leaving him chilled with a sense of ambiguity.

Had his dreaming deceived him into thinking he knew what he wanted, when he didn't? But then, he'd never anticipated the ways in which deprivation leaves ineradicable footprints, so that when old scarcities are finally addressed, a confusing sense of loss follows. And if his previous life had been marked by anything, it was certainly by inexhaustible reservoirs of deprivation. By finally being figuratively granted entrance into the forbidden banquet hall he'd so often dreamed of as a child, he was now missing the bittersweetness of gratification withheld and enjoyment withheld. This new world, in which everything was both offered and delivered, was yearning's antithesis. What he missed now was the intoxicatingly primal feeling of being denied.

If being deprived had become so deeply ingrained in his being that he could not escape equating the kind of disturbing excitement that was its byproduct with being fully alive, how could he ever love a Lisa Singleton, who unwittingly deprived him of the very thing from which he'd thought he was running, but which he actually needed to feel complete? It was terrifying to think that need for strife might have become so embedded in his DNA that he could feel fully alive only when dispossessed. Had he become so twisted that he'd turned into a microcosm of a China suckled at the poisoned breast of Mao's revolution? Of course, he said nothing to Lisa of such convoluted thoughts, because he did not want to alarm or hurt her. But she sensed his torment.

"You know, even when you smile, I see hesitation," she said with resignation one night.

"Oh, it's nothing," he tried to reassure her. But at that very moment, he'd been thinking about Little Hong and Qinghai's strange, stark beauty. Even when he and Lisa were in bed together, China was there with them. He tried to rationalize such nostalgia as natural. After all, had he not spent his whole life in China?

Feeling the warmth of her body, he drew her to his side. However, he knew he did so more out of sympathy than out of passion. She'd helped break his spell of despair, ushered him back into the world of the living, and he did love her. And yet . . . sometimes she seemed less a lover than a nurse into whose steadfast care he'd been entrusted, like a wounded soldier.

When things became too confusing, he got in his Cutlass and escaped across the Golden Gate Bridge to Muir Beach. Driving over the imposing bridge with the radio cranked up, he was able momentarily to blot out the background noise of life and convince himself, for that instant, that the growing distance between them was due to the fact that there was no way a person like Lisa could ever be expected to comprehend fully, much less share, a Chinese life like his. For he was coming to appreciate that, even when ignored, one's homeland slumbers on stubbornly within one, bound to reawaken sooner or later and demand its due. And the Chinese imperium never let claims on those it viewed as its own lapse easily. Even after being abroad for years, ethnic Chinese were considered eternal "sons and daughters of the Yellow Emperor," and only temporary "sojourners" in their adopted lands. Chinese Americans, who'd lived and worked in mines, laundries, restaurants, and on the railroads in California for generations, were still viewed only as "longtime Californians," not as complete Americans. China might be out of sight, but for the Chinese overseas, it could never be considered completely out of mind. One might try running away, but just as a person imagined he'd escaped the orbit of this homeland, it pulled one back again. As the Chinese aphorism beloved by Granny Sun put it, "One may get the monk out of the monastery, but never the monastery out of the monk" (跑得了和尚跑 不了庙).

Now, even with a loving American girlfriend and entrance into the San Francisco Conservatory, Little Li could feel China mocking his escape efforts. In truth, he'd no idea how to put China in a comfortable angle of repose within his new life. Like one of those tattered books circulating in Yak Springs that had been torn into sections so several people could read it at the same time, his life was in disconnected chapters. The first parts, lived in China, were now blank to everyone here, so that when he looked back at them through the portholes of memory, he was alone. The two brief nights he'd spent with Yang Ming may have been no more than the blink of an eye, but because she was Chinese and had experienced the same bitter life as he, she understood him without words. And because Little Hong had been similarly dispossessed, she, too, instantly understood. Dispossession was his generation's bond, a common currency in which they all could trade. But here in America that currency was worthless.

Sometimes his internal torment threw Lisa so off balance she said things she later wished she hadn't.

"Where do you go when you drive off?" she resentfully asked one evening.

"For rides."

"Why do you love that old junker so much?"

"Maybe because it's all I have," he replied, irritated by the challenging edge in her voice.

"But . . . you have me, don't you?" she countered, her voice filled with hurt.

"I do. Yes, I do." He nodded, trying to summon forth the look of affection she needed for reassurance. And, yes, he did "have" her . . . whatever it meant to "have" someone.

Feeling an urge to reconnect with his old life, he bought another postcard of the Golden Gate Bridge and sent it to Little Wang. He was surprised when, two weeks later, a return letter arrived, regaling him with all the ways China was opening up and changing.

> *Old buddy:*
> *What a surprise to get your card. You ask what I've been doing. Well, here goes: I've been working with students setting up free-speech "salons" on university campuses to promote open discussion about China's future. You'd be astounded by what can be said now in public. This famous astrophysicist, Fang Lizhi, has been electrifying*

us with the non-bullshit way he speaks out about things
like democracy and human rights. He once told students
in Shanghai that "the socialist movement from Marx and
Lenin to Stalin and Mao Zedong has been a failure." And
when he showed up at Peking University, he blasted all
the timid academics, telling them to "straighten out their
bent backs." He even let the party have it, saying, "A great
diversity of thought should be allowed in colleges and
universities. For if all thought is narrow and simplistic,
creativity will die."

But more amazing than what he says is the fact that so
far he's gotten away with it! Although I hardly dare say it,
sometimes I wonder if this infuriating place isn't, at last,
changing.

When are you coming home?
The other half of the Two Virtuous Ones

Reading the characters 回家 ("coming home") and 二德 ("the
Two Virtuous Ones") jolted Little Li right back into his former life.

"You've been so quiet," Lisa whispered that same night. He'd
thought she was already asleep.

"I'm all right," he replied, not knowing how to begin explaining what was agitating him.

"I sometimes have the sense you aren't really here beside me,"
she said wistfully.

"Sometimes I'm not really sure where I am myself, much less
where I ought to be," he replied, squeezing her hand unconvincingly. For several minutes, they lay side by side. Then he kissed
her, despising himself for not being able to love her as much as she
seemed to love him.

PART
SIX

45

THE YIN AND YANG OF DREAMING

"BUT WHY are you leaving?" a disconsolate Lisa half asked, half begged, when he finally found the courage to tell her he was going back to China for a visit during the 1988 winter holidays.

"I haven't been home for so long, and I need to confirm whether the other side of me still exists," he tried to explain.

"But isn't your life here in San Francisco now?" she protested. She had wanted to say "with me," but she dared not.

"I'll be back soon," he prevaricated. But he'd been slipping away bit by bit with each new letter from Little Wang.

"It'll be hard to be in the apartment with your things, but not you," she responded. "It was mine, but now it's become ours."

He did not know how to reply. The truth was, he couldn't fully explain even to himself why he was so determined to return. But as Little Wang had catalogued the changes gripping Beijing in his letter, he wanted to see for himself what was happening. And then, at the end of one letter, his friend had offhandedly noted that he'd just run into Little Hong and she looked "very cool" (很帅). That night, Little Li had dreamed he was standing back on the monument in Tiananmen Square, watching as she ran toward him. But as he waited, she just kept running and running without ever getting any closer.

When Lisa drove him to the airport that rainy December morning, she'd wanted to come inside and bid him a proper farewell. However, feeling awkward about leaving, he'd insisted that she just drop him off. As they pulled up at the curb, she was unable to restrain herself any longer and burst into tears.

"Oh, Lisa!" he said, giving her a hug that did not last as long as she'd hoped. "You're such a wonderful person." He kissed her. "I'm only going for a visit." Then, unable to face her sadness or his own conflicted heart, he shouldered his things, turned, and walked into the terminal. Although he didn't dare to look back, he kept seeing her in his mind's eye, standing alone next to his Cutlass, looking utterly bereft.

The same kind of tadpole-shaped blue-and-white Pan Am 747 that had brought him from Beijing was waiting at the gate to take him back. However, instead of the excitement he'd felt upon departing from China he was now besieged by an avalanche of qualms: why was he leaving Lisa and his newly established life to return to the very place he'd struggled so hard to vacate? Four decades ago, his father had optimistically returned to Beijing, and look what had happened. Now, just as in 1949, China again appeared to be in a process of rejuvenation, and here he was, overriding his own resolve never to consign himself back into its careless embrace. To calm himself, he swore he'd stay only long enough to become reacquainted with what was going on, and then return to San Francisco and Lisa.

When he landed, all the new and unfamiliar buildings that had gone up in his absence along the new highway into Beijing made it seem as if he'd landed in the wrong country. It was not until his bus reached the Railroad Station and he saw the two familiar clock towers with their pagoda-like roofs that he felt any sense of homecoming. As he walked across the esplanade in front of the terminal, he recalled with perfect vividness the day he'd left from this very place for Qinghai as a lost sixteen-year-old boy. But it was only as he headed into the maze of *hutong*s in which he'd grown up—among the familiar gray brick walls crowned with shards of broken glass, faded red gateways, and small ragtag shops encrusting the intersections like barnacles—that he felt the first wave of real homecoming nostalgia. As he walked on, he remembered how, upon returning home from Yak Springs, their front gate at Willow Courtyard was ajar so he had been able to walk in unannounced to find his father weeding their garden. And because this memory was still so real, he half expected to be able to walk in again through their vermilion gate, step back in time, and find him still there, watering can in hand.

When he spotted the metal street placard for Big Sheep Wool Alley, with its familiar white characters on a red background, he realized how indelibly imprinted he still was with these surroundings, and regretted having so cavalierly disposed of his gate key on his flight to San Francisco. How would he get into Willow Court-yard now? And what would he find inside? Who was in their house? Would Granny Sun still be there? He quickened his step.

It was not until the first primal whiff of the sulfurous public latrine on Big Sheep Wool Alley hit his nostrils that he felt irrefut-ably home. He had to smile at such a perverse form of welcome. His step quickened. However, when he turned the corner, his sense of anticipation was jolted to an abrupt halt. Where the gray brick wall enclosing Willow Courtyard should have stretched along the narrow alleyway, there was now only a chain-link fence, and where sloping tile roofs and trees should have been silhouetted against the clouds, there was now nothing but a smoggy gray stretch of open sky. Making the scene unfold before him even more disori-enting was a long piece of polyethylene sheeting stretched along the fence, imprinted with a sylvan mountain landscape scene and the inscription *"Yosemite Apartments—Coming Soon"* (优山美地). On the other side of the fence lay a rubble-strewn wasteland of broken bricks, splintered beams, and crushed plaster walls with a triumphant yellow Komatsu bulldozer parked in the middle. Like front teeth missing in a set of dentures, some twenty-five meters of wall, and everything that had once been protected behind it, had been razed. Only by surveying the houses on the opposite side of the alley was Little Li able to approximate where their gateway had once stood. But now all that remained of their old courtyard was the willow tree he and his father had saved, its battered trunk now inscribed with the character for "demolition" (拆) in whitewash. Whatever else he'd been expecting as a homecoming, it was cer-tainly not this.

Little Li was unsure how long he'd been standing in the dusty alleyway, gaping at the emptiness before him, when an old man hobbled past.

"When did they demolish Willow Courtyard?" he asked him.

"A few months ago," the man replied laconically.

"And where did the people go?"

"The old lady had passed on. The others got sent to a high-rise in the suburbs."

"Ah, so that's the way it is" was all Little Li could think to say.

"That's the way it is," repeated the old man, sighing, and then trudging on.

Little Li, too, walked robotically away. Perhaps he should just return to the airport, board the next flight for San Francisco, and pick up the thread of his life he'd left behind there. Maybe he belonged with Lisa in California after all. As he passed the latrine again, he was glad that it, at least, was still as he remembered it. Walking up its worn stone steps, he stood over one of its familiar shit-encrusted slits and took a piss. At least some things were eternal! Then, desperately needing to ground his homecoming in some concrete destination, he set off for Little Wang's. When he knocked on his door, there was no response. Noticing that the door was actually unlocked, he stepped inside where he found the familiar clutter of overflowing ashtrays, piles of newspapers and magazines, and shelves groaning with books. Approaching the door to what used to be Little Wang's minuscule bedroom, he called out, "Wang Dehua! It's me, your old buddy!" No response. He gingerly opened the door and poked his head into the darkened space, which reeked of cigarette smoke and bad breath. "Anyone here?"

"Unhhh!" someone groaned.

"It's me," Little Li cried out.

"Who?" a groggy voice growled.

"Li Wende."

"No fucking way!" Little Wang jumped up from under his quilt. He looked as if he'd been up all night. "Am I dreaming?"

"No, I'm actually here."

"Son of a bitch! It *is* you! So—sit down!" Little Wang pushed a stack of newspapers off a chair. "I thought I'd never see you again."

"Well, here I am," said Little Li, laughing. "So . . . what's the other Virtue been up to?"

"Still messing around with politics and trying to help the old Central Kingdom become a modern country!" He laughed, lit a cigarette, and studied his friend's face. "You look just like a fucking American movie star!" he exclaimed. Although they hadn't seen each other for several years, Little Li was sure of what would follow and it warmed his heart to know this person so well that he could still predict his next move. And, sure enough: "So . . . been getting much action from those luscious blond girls over there in the Beautiful Country?"

"I think Comrade Wang would be pleased by my progress in

exceeding party production quotas by generating ever more friend-ship and fraternal relations between the Chinese and American peoples," he said and laughed.

"Glad you still have some bullshit left in you," said Little Wang with a grin. "Mao would be proud."

"I stopped by Willow Courtyard," continued Little Li, becom-ing more serious.

"Yeah, I know. They turned those old 'chicken shacks' [鸡窝] to rubble. They're tearing down the *hutong*s. Why don't you stay with me?"

"Where's your mother?"

"She left this world a year ago. After my father went, she was never the same."

"I'm sorry to hear it," mumbled Little Li.

"You can sleep in her room, though the housekeeping's a bit subpar since she went." He gave a self-deprecating smirk.

"Thanks! And, what have you been up to?" asked Little Li as they sat down at his cluttered table.

"Well, as I wrote you, I'm working with this crazy astrophysi-cist, Fang Lizhi [方励之]."

"So it's still politics for you?"

"Yeah, but things have been getting pretty exciting! At Peking University there's this history student, Wang Dan, who's been hold-ing 'democracy salons' [沙龙] and inviting all kinds of people to speak out. He's had Professor Fang, U.S. Ambassador Winston Lord, and his Chinese wife, Bette Bao Lord, as well as other well-known Chinese writers, like Dai Qing [戴晴], come and talk."

"Why hasn't the government closed him down?"

"They hold their meetings outside, so it's difficult for the uni-versity to stop them."

"So—what's with this guy Fang?"

"Well, he's an odd one, a scientist who believes that open inquiry, logic, and reason are as necessary in politics as in science. He speaks out as naturally as he breathes, and says things most others don't even dare think. And by taking advantage of the recent openness, he's gotten invited to campuses all over China so that his ideas have spread like wildfire."

"How did you meet him?"

"I heard him one day at Peking University, and I just went up and offered to help out."

"You're still a bold fucker, aren't you?" exclaimed Little Li with a laugh. "What do you do for the old guy?"

"Oh, research, answer mail, arrange travel, anything. Sooner or later, they'll shut him down, too, so I've started a little project of my own." He pushed across the table a small blue book, entitled *The Quotations of Ex-Vice-President Fang Lizhi.*

"It's just like Mao's Little Red Book, but in blue!" exclaimed Little Li.

"You got it, Comrade. Think of it as Chairman Mao's Little Red Book turned inside out and upside down! The whole idea is to stick it to Mao just the way he stuck it to us!"

"The party must love Fang!" said Little Li facetiously.

"They tried to blame him for all the student demonstrations two years ago by throwing him out of the party and firing him from his position as vice-president of the University of Science and Technology. But that didn't shut him up. In fact, he's planning to write a really bold public letter to Old Deng himself on the upcoming anniversary of the PRC protesting how Wei Jingsheng got locked up for exercising his free speech." Little Li vividly recalled the essay by Wei that Little Wang and Pei Heli had given him before he left China, "Democracy or New Dictatorship." "Until Fang came along, everyone's been content to let Wei just rot in prison. Here's a draft of what he plans to send." Little Wang thrust a paper across the table.

> *Dear Chairman Deng:*
> *1989 is both the 40th anniversary of the People's Republic of China and the 70th anniversary of the May Fourth Movement. Surrounding these events there will no doubt be many commemorative activities. But beyond just remembering the past, the many of us who are even more concerned with the present and future will look to these commemorations to bring with them new hope. Therefore, I would like to sincerely suggest that a general amnesty be declared, and what is more, that Wei Jingsheng and all other political prisoners be released. Regardless of how one might view Wei Jingsheng, to release someone such*

as him, who has already served nearly a decade in prison,
would, in my view, not only constitute a humanitarian act,
but would have a beneficial effect on the atmosphere of our
society.

This year also happens to be the 200th anniversary of
the French Revolution. From any perspective the ideas
of liberty, equality, fraternity, and human rights that the
French Revolution symbolizes have won the respect of
people all over the world. In this light, let me again express
my earnest hope that you will consider this suggestion,
and thus demonstrate even more concern for the future.
Sincerely and with best wishes, Fang Lizhi

"Aiyyo!" exclaimed Little Li. "Is he nuts?"

"In a crazy world, sometimes it's the seemingly mad people who are the most sane! Remember Lu Xun's 'Diary of a Madman'? Well, I look at it that way: Fang's refusing to engage in cannibalism in a cannibalistic society, just like Lu Xun's hero."

"Mad or not, they'll make him pay."

"They will, but still, there are times when one shouldn't compromise."

The more Little Li heard about his friend's activities, the harder it was for him to make overall sense of what was happening in China. On the one hand, things were loosening up and becoming politically more open, while on the other hand most of the old Soviet structures of control were still firmly in place and functioning, leaving a glaring contradiction between the party's Leninist roots and its reformist aspirations to become more open, modern, and democratic.

"How did you ever get all these quotations together?" asked Little Li, thumbing admiringly through his friend's Little Blue Book.

"The answer to your question brings us to a part of the story you really won't believe: the party did most of the work for me."

"What do you mean?"

"Those morons in the party wanted to put out an 'internal document' [内部文件] attacking Fang's 'erroneous bourgeois liberal line,' so they assigned a pack of researchers to gather all his writings, interviews, and speeches together in a master collection for distribution to every party branch around the country. The absurdity of their project was that, before people saw their 'internal document,' most had never heard of Fang. But after they were forced to study all his writings, many began to think: 'Hey! This guy makes sense!' So the party ended up doing Fang's hard propaganda work for him, and made it really easy for me to slap my book together!"

As his friend threw on some clothes, Little Li studied his handiwork. Instead of being divided into categories like *"Classes and Class Struggle," "Socialism and Communism," "People's War,"* and *"Revolutionary Heroism,"* as Mao's crimson-covered counterpart was, Little Wang's collection of Fang's utterances was divided into sections on *"Democracy," "International Human Rights," "Student Demonstrations,"* and *"Enlightened Foreign Thinkers."* Most astonishing was Fang's uncompromising tone. Almost every quotation was like a gunshot in a quiet room:

> *If you really want to promote respect for learning and do something about our backwardness, then you have to address Comrade Mao's mistakes, which were many.*
> "THOUGHTS ON REFORM," ZHEJIANG UNIVERSITY,
> MARCH 24, 1985

> *Without democracy, the academic community will make no progress.*
> QUESTION-AND-ANSWER SESSION AT THE CHINESE
> JOURNALISTS ASSOCIATION, SEPTEMBER 3, 1986

> *If foreigners are no more intelligent than we Chinese, why, then, can't we produce first-rate work? The reasons for our inability to develop our potential lie within our own social system.*
> PEKING UNIVERSITY SPEECH, NOVEMBER 4, 1985

The more Little Li read, the more impressed he was. But where did Fang, who could have remained gazing peacefully up into the heavens through a radio telescope, find the audacity to go around evangelizing for democracy? A section entitled "The Silence of Intellectuals" suggested some answers.

*Some of us dare not speak out. But if we all spoke out,
there would be nothing to be afraid of. . . . In fact, it is
our duty. If we remain silent, we will fail to live up to our
responsibility.*
PEKING UNIVERSITY SPEECH, NOVEMBER 4, 1985

*Right now there's talk about "loosening up," but
this very phrase suggests something bestowed on us by
superiors. . . . Loosening up is not democracy, because
democracy is not something that can be bestowed from
above.*
SESSION AT THE CHINESE JOURNALISTS ASSOCIATION,
SEPTEMBER 3, 1986

"Fang refuses to recognize fear," explained Little Wang proudly.
"How did he get that way?"

"I don't know how, but there's the result." Little Wang lovingly
slapped the cover of his book. "In this long-subdued land, the fact
that there's at least one person still clearheaded and courageous
enough to use his standing to speak out against this autocratic system keeps me going."

As they were getting something to eat several days later, Little
Wang casually asked, "Hey, after all those American babes you've
been scoring, I don't suppose you still care about that pretty little
yangqin player who used to give you such a fever."

"You mean Hong Hui?" stammered Little Li.

"Was that her name?"

"Where'd you see her?" He tried to sound only casually interested, but in truth he hadn't been able to get her out of his mind.
Since arriving in Beijing, he'd been telling himself that she was
from an earlier chapter in his life and best left entombed in the
past. Moreover, given that it was he who'd left her, how could he
now just show up back on her doorstep?

"I ran into her on the street and when I called out to see if she
remembered me, she immediately responded, 'Of course, I remember you! You're Li Wende's friend! Do you ever hear from him?'
When I told her I'd just gotten a letter from you, she became very
quiet. Maybe she never got over you, brother. But I didn't tell her
you were coming back. I wasn't sure you still had a thing for her."

"Did she say where she lived or worked?"

"No, but she's probably back at the Conservatory, because I saw her near there. But, hey, didn't you ditch her to run off to America?"

The next day, Little Li set off alone for the Conservatory, but there were so many new buildings along the way, he hardly recognized the neighborhood. When he asked the guard at the back gatehouse to check the faculty register for a Hong Hui, without looking her up, he responded, "Department of Traditional Chinese Music."

As Little Li made his way through the familiar courtyard to the school's new administrative offices, it seemed impossible that so many tumultuous things had happened right here in this familiar peaceful setting. How could it be that at one moment a courtyard like this could be engulfed in violence and chaos, and the next filled with students calmly strolling with instrument cases as if nothing had ever happened? Did they even know what had taken place here years ago? The party was always trying to bury the past. And perhaps it was just as well. Why pick scabs off barely healed wounds? Indeed, as he strolled across the peaceful campus now, what had happened then seemed so chimerical, it was hard to know what had been real and what had not. But China was like that. The lines from his father's favorite novel, *The Dream of the Red Chamber,* still said it best: "When the unreal is taken for the real, then the real becomes unreal. When nonexistence is taken for existence, then existence becomes nonexistence."

Only after he insisted that Miss Hong Hui was a friend of his departed father, a former faculty member, was he able to convince the surly administrative clerk to give him her place of residence. As he left, the slip with her address on it felt positively radioactive in his hand. He wanted to see her, but felt completely unprepared for the moment, so, instead of taking the bus down the Avenue of Eternal Peace, he walked all the way across the city. As he went, he thought about Lisa. The chasm between the United States and China was suddenly symbolized not only by two different geographic places, languages, histories, political systems, values, and cultures, but also two women.

As he passed Xidan, he saw that Democracy Wall, just like Willow Courtyard, had been completely demolished, replaced by a shopping mall. Beijing had become a city he hardly recognized.

It wasn't until he reached Tiananmen Square and caught sight of Mao's famous portrait that he felt on familiar ground. But if things kept changing, how long would Mao remain hanging there on Tiananmen Gate, like an altarpiece in the PRC's paramount place of worship? Little Li had recently read that the Italian journalist Oriana Fallaci had asked Deng Xiaoping if Chairman Mao's portrait would remain there forever. "It will," he'd replied, "forever." Then he added, "It's true that he [Mao] made mistakes in a certain period, but . . . what he did for the Chinese people can never be erased. In our hearts we Chinese will always cherish him as a founder of our Party and our state."

As Little Li left the square, he reminded himself that even this iconic center-of-the-center of Beijing and the nation was not immutable. Mao had himself changed the square in the 1950s, greatly expanding it and then hanging his own portrait on the same storied gate where Chiang Kai-shek had displayed his. To his chagrin, Little Li had to acknowledge that he'd feel dispossessed, if Mao's famous portrait ever came down.

As he approached Little Hong's apartment block, the sudden feeling of having unfinished business with her made him increasingly agitated. What did she look like now? Would she be glad to see him? Might she be married? Would she want to talk to him? He walked around her block three times before finally climbing her concrete stairway. When, outside her third-floor door, he saw two pairs of shoes, one larger than the other, he almost retreated. Instead, he took a deep breath and knocked. The door opened and there stood a little girl in pigtails who looked as if he'd seen her someplace before.

"Mama!" she called out. "Someone's here that we don't know."

"Just a moment," came a voice from the back.

"But, Mama, he's waiting!" All Little Li could think was how beautiful this child was.

"All right, I'm coming!" Then there she was, walking down the narrow hallway in an apron, holding a wooden spoon. Seeing Little Li, she froze like a startled wild animal.

"It's you!" she gasped and cupped a hand over her mouth. As the girl recoiled in alarm, Little Hong knelt down to put a protective arm around her shoulders. "It's all right, Xiaomei."

"I've come back," said Little Li.

Little Hong looked up as if she was trying to decide something. There was a more mature quality in her face now, a certain sadness around her eyes that made her handsome as well as beautiful. Only slowly did she stand up and give a half-smile.

"So . . . you've come back to your old home," she said, gazing at him.

"To my old home!" he nodded.

"Mama! What's happening?" the girl asked anxiously.

"It's all right," soothed Little Hong, crouching down again to stroke her hair.

"How old are you?" asked Little Li, also kneeling.

"I'm only five," the girl replied, her big eyes staring distrustfully. "Who is he, Mama?" she asked, turning to her mother.

"It's all right, Xiaomei. This man's a friend."

"But who is he?" she persisted.

"He's . . . he's your father." She looked up at Little Li with a melancholy smile.

"Oh," he gasped.

"She's our daughter," Little Hong said, kissing the girl's neck. For several minutes, Little Li stared down at his daughter, who stared back in wide-eyed incomprehension.

"She's really ours?" he asked incredulously.

"She is. It was that night you came home from burying your father's ashes. I only found out after you'd left for America, and I couldn't see any good in bothering you. Anyway, I didn't know how to get in touch." As Little Li reached out, she fell into his arms. "But I've always believed that someday you'd return," she said and sighed. "I always remembered you telling me how your father waited for your mother and loved *Fidelio,* so I was sure such loyalty was in you, too. Now here you are, and here's our daughter, Li Mei [李美], named after you and America." Little Hong's eyes sparkled with tears.

"What's going on, Mama?" asked Li Mei, knowing that something beyond her comprehension was happening.

Indeed, it was also almost beyond Little Li's comprehension. While Little Hong's sense of loyalty to their daughter had endured, his loyalty to her had failed. From where did such loyalty come, especially in a land that had known so much betrayal? Perhaps it was true that suffering tempers, clarifies, even purifies devotion, at least for those strong enough to survive its corrosion. But at this moment, Little Li felt so overwhelmed that he did not know what to think. When Little Hong asked if he'd stay for dinner, he agreed, wondering if this was just the first meal of a completely new life. After dinner, while Li Mei practiced calligraphy, he listened while Little Hong recounted what had happened in his absence.

"After learning I was pregnant, I quit the job at the Central Academy of Fine Arts, left the Conservatory, and quietly moved to Shanghai," she began in a voice so soft he sometimes could hardly make her out. "There I rented a small room in a professor's apartment in the old French Concession, and a friend found me a position tutoring *yangqin* students at a high school."

"And who was with you when you gave birth?"

"No one."

"How did you manage?"

"While I waited for Xiaomei to be born, I felt lonelier than I'd ever imagined possible. But then, afterward, because she needed me to care for her, I had no time to worry about such things."

"And how did you explain being a single woman with a child?"

"It wasn't easy, because everyone wanted to know where my husband was. So, I told them he was a student from Beijing who'd gone to study in America." She laughed.

"Did they believe you?"

"Probably not. But in its way, it was true enough. At least it allowed me not to be looked down on as a 'fallen woman' [破鞋]."

"How did you ever manage all alone with Xiaomei?" he asked, using the diminutive, Little Mei.

"I don't know. Sometimes, at night, I'd play Bach two-part inventions very softly and think of you. I guess it was her who pulled me through." She nodded toward their oblivious daughter. "Even though China can be an unforgiving place for a single mother, I've never once regretted having her."

"How did you get back here to Beijing?"

"When Xiaomei was three, I landed a job as an adjunct back at the Conservatory, through my old teacher."

"And where did you live?"

"With my aunt, until she got us this space from a friend of hers who is now teaching in Boston."

"And what did you tell people here about Xiaomei?"

"I used the same story, only I said my husband came from Shanghai and was overseas studying. But now look! Her once-imaginary father has become real and returned home just as I said he would!" Her eyes darted around his face as if she was searching for something. "So . . . that's the end of my long march. What kind of march have you been on?"

As he told her about San Francisco, the Hotel Asterix, the Grecian Fitness Club, the Conservatory, Grace Cathedral, the Golden Gate Bridge, and even Out of the Closet and Louie's House of Dented Cans, she took it all in with a faraway look in her eyes. He said nothing about Lisa or Juliette, and she did not ask about his private life. It was as if America was for her still a distant planet, and she wanted to keep it that way. Indeed, as he continued to narrate his American saga, California seemed increasingly far away, even to him. When she got up to put Xiaomei to bed, he might have left. Instead, he stayed sitting at her kitchen table. As he waited, he kept thinking about Lisa at the San Francisco Airport, looking small and forlorn. The thought that his Cutlass, Mighty Mite, electric can opener, and modest wardrobe were all of him that remained for her, made him wince. But he was calmed by Little Hong's voice, softly reading from *Journey to the West*, the same classical tale his father had once read to him, about the magical Monkey King, Sun Wukong, who journeyed to India to bring Buddhist scriptures back to China.

"Can you believe it?" she asked, after Li Mei fell asleep. "I used to be your Little Hui?"

"And I used to be your Little Li?"

"And who are you now?" she teased. "Are you Winston or Hugo Li of San Francisco?"

"No, I'm still Li Wende, Li the Literate and Virtuous, who never adopted a foreign devil's name!" They both laughed. The crow's-feet radiating from the corners of her eyes bespoke a life that had not been easy. Her skin was less radiant now, and she wore her hair in a conservative bun. If other men had passed through her life in his absence, he did not care to know about them, because, whatever had happened, she still had about her an air of complete fidelity. She leaned against him, and he took her in his arms, astonished by how easy it was to pick up where they'd left off. It was as if each still held a secret title to the genetic code of the other.

"You'll stay tonight, won't you." She said it as more of a statement than as a question.

"I will," he answered.

She led him by the hand to an alcove hardly bigger than the bed in it, and there, on a side table, in a wooden frame not unlike the one that had held his parents' photo above their piano, was the snapshot they'd taken together in Tiananmen Square on their first date. As he held her, he felt it was as if, without knowing it both of them had been unconsciously preparing for this moment during their long separation.

Two weeks later, he moved in with Little Hong and Li Mei. However, almost immediately, his daughter became standoffish, even resentful, of the way he'd barged into their lives and claimed a part of her mother's once undivided affections.

"Why's he always here now?" she asked one morning, as if Little Li weren't in the room.

"Because he's your father," responded Little Hong, but Li Mei was hardly convinced by her mother's answer. He tried to imagine how he would have felt if his own mother had returned years later to disrupt the fragile balance of life that he and his father had finally managed to achieve in Willow Courtyard. But slowly, Xiaomei warmed to him, especially after he started reading her bedtime stories. Just like him, what she adored most was hearing tales of distant California.

"Have you really been there, Papa?" she'd ask, staring at him in bug-eyed wonder.

"Yes, I really have lived there."

"Doing what?"

"It's hard to explain." He laughed.

"Is California far away?"

"All the way across the Pacific Ocean."

"What color is the water?"

"Blue."

"Did you go in an airplane?"

"I did."

The thought that her very own father had been in an airplane and flown all the way to the "Beautiful Country"—after which she herself was named—thrilled her. The night he told her the story of Leonore in *Fidelio,* he added, "You see, some people are just fated to be together. When Leonore married Florestan, they became bound to each other by loyalty, just as I am now bound to you."

"Loyalty?" she asked. "What's that?" He had to think for a moment how best to describe it.

"Loyalty's when people become so attached, they'd give up their lives for each other."

"Would I give my life for someone when I grow older?"

"I hope you'll never confront such a situation, but I also hope you'll be a loyal person."

"Would you give your life for me?"

"I would."

"Why?"

"Because you were fated to be my daughter, just as I was fated to be your father. And it must have been 'heaven's will' [天注定] that sent me back to you, all the way across the Pacific Ocean. But I'm so glad fate was on our side, because now I'll always be your father . . . forever." He said the last sentence in both Chinese and English.

"It's funny when you speak English," she said, hunching up her shoulders and giggling. "Will I ever speak English?"

"If you'll let me teach you."

"Will I like it?" she asked after thinking for a moment.

"I think you will."

"Will it be hard?"

"No, because we'll do it together."

Her eyes danced with delight at the idea that this father of hers, who'd dropped out of the heavens, would teach her English, and her delight filled Little Li with a joy he'd never been able even to imagine before. The knowledge that not only had Hong Hui given birth to this nymphlike creature, cherished and raised her alone, but that she was now willing to share her without any blame for his truancy, touched him to the quick. At last, he'd live in a family with a father, a mother, and a child all under one roof.

"I have a present for you, Xiaomei," he told her one night, after he'd read her a story.

"Just for me?" she asked excitedly.

"Just for you." He took the locket that his mother had given him out of his pocket.

"What is it?"

"It's a 长命锁 and if you hang it hang him around your neck, it'll bring you good luck."

"Why are you giving it to me?"

"Because you're my daughter, my mother gave it to me, and I want you to have good luck, too." As she smiled and turned the locket over and over with absorption, he saw in her lovely face not only a reflection of himself, but of Little Hong, his father, and even his mother. Here, in this one small being who'd so unexpectedly fallen into his life, was, at last, a composite of all the disparate pieces of his life, a living stained-glass window. The thought that he'd helped give her life, that her blood was his blood, and that her genes were his genes made him dizzy with devotion. Perhaps this was why innocent children were put on earth: to teach adults how to experience selflessness.

"We as fathers should shoulder the falling gate of darkness and guide our children out to a vast land full of brightness to live happy lives as normal, upright human beings," Lu Xun had urged fathers over half a century before. How often had his own father repeated this admonition, "Save the children!" And now, no matter how much his father's tragic life had forewarned him against coming home, here he, Li Wende, was back in China. After trying to leave Hong Hui, Beijing, and China to chase the fickle mistress of America, he'd finally returned home, just like his father, perhaps guided back by some divine hand to help this little girl become one of those blessed enough "to live happy lives as normal, upright human beings."

Bathed in the sheltering warmth of this family, during the weeks and months that followed, Little Li experienced a contentment that sometimes frightened him with its intensity. To hear his daughter speak her perfect child sentences, drink in the guileless light of her eyes, listen to her practice the *yangqin,* and feel the warmth of her small, flawless body in their bed at night was as addictive as opium. Even dropping her off at school and taking her to the zoo left him floating. And Little Hong, too, was elated by how things had worked out and they'd taken to each other.

Upon arriving back in Beijing, he'd imagined himself as only a visitor. But after the revelation of Li Mei and his move in with her and Little Hong, each passing day sent him drifting farther from the shores of California and his old life. He kept meaning to write to Lisa, but didn't because he did not know what to say. Then, one day, a letter arrived at Little Wang's house.

My dear Little Li,
　I miss you every day. Will you write and tell me what you're doing?
　I keep trying to imagine what things are like in Beijing, but I cannot. I see only blankness. Above all, can you let me know when you will come back?
　I can hardly wait!
　Much love, Lisa

He was so unnerved by the letter that he showed it to Little Wang.

"You're a fucking polygamist!" he exclaimed. "You go from not having a clue about the ladies to being a bicontinental lady killer. Where'd you learn stuff like that? From those polyandrous Tibetans?"

"Oh, cut the bullshit and give me some advice," begged Little Li.

"How would I know what to do? I'm an expert on politics, not women!"

"But what should I tell her?"

"Well, you can tell her that the evil communists have sent you back to Qinghai for a refresher course in forced labor and that she shouldn't expect you back in California anytime soon." He gave a bitter laugh.

"Lot of help you are," complained Little Li.

Finally, he wrote Lisa, saying only that he'd become "involved in some complex family matters" and would have to stay in Beijing longer than planned. But just printing her name and address on the envelope felt like chalk screeching on a blackboard. The truth was, he had no idea how to explain to her what was happening to him. More upsetting, how could he explain his own duplicity to himself?

"Are you asleep?" Little Hong whispered one night, as he lay in bed wide awake.

"What is it?" he asked, sensing her seriousness.

"When you think about Xiaomei, me, and the future, what do you think?" The suddenness and pointedness of her question caught him off guard. He thought of Lisa, but then he was hit with blinding clear recognition: this was where he belonged and this is where he should be after all. He reached over and put his arms around Little Hong.

"Have we just been waiting for each other all this time without knowing what we were doing?" he whispered.

"Maybe so."

"Well, then, Hong Hui, will you marry me?"

"I will, Li Wende," she replied after a long exhalation.

"And will you stay with me forever?" For once the word "forever"—made up of the two characters meaning "perpetual" (永) and "far away" (远)—didn't sound ominous to him, as in "gone forever." Instead, staying together "forever" with Hong Hui and Li Mei seemed not only right, but predestined. Several days later, they went together to register for a marriage license.

"You know, even without a license, I felt married to you," she said on their way home.

"And now that we've actually married, congratulations are due!" He kissed her, wishing that his devotion had always been the equal of hers.

Having no job, Little Li was now challenged with inventing a new life. Sometimes he and a few of Little Hong's friends got together at the Conservatory to play music. But it didn't take long for him to realize that his talents were outmatched by those of the upcoming generation, who'd suffered none of the disruptions he had. As much as he loved music, he could see he'd never make it as a musician. And he'd been spending more and more time helping Little Wang and his friends organize their political salons, edit their articles, and recruit students returning from abroad to lobby for faster political reform. Because he knew English, they tasked him with reading foreign newspapers, magazines, and journals, to pick out pertinent essays, articles, and reports and then translate the salient parts for others to read in Chinese. And at night he gave private English lessons to earn some money. Without intending it, he was becoming an important part of their dissident network. This work helped him realize just how deep the craving among his generation was to see the reform movement succeed and for China gain the respect of the very democratic world that the party had spent decades denouncing. Change was in the air, and the more he learned, the more hopeful he became that it was just such political reform that would end up making China safer for his wife and daughter.

Little Hong remained as dubious of politics as ever, and would have far preferred him not to hang out so much with Little Wang and his political buddies. But recognizing that such concerns had become important to her new husband, she said nothing. He was, however, aware of her misgivings, and even as he became more involved, he rarely went out to eat with his activist comrades after hours.

Even though things in Little Li's own life had gained an unexpected new stability, China was still in an undeniably confused state of uncertain self-reinvention, and the fault line between his inner world of family and the outer world of politics remained tectonically active. When the United States and China exchanged diplomatic recognition in 1979, Deng Xiaoping and Jimmy Carter had hoped that more engagement would serve as a solvent to help dissolve the antagonism that had so divided the two countries during the Cold War. And, for a while, the two dissimilar societies did now seem to be evolving on more convergent glide paths. Historically, Chinese and Americans had been drawn to each other by powerful forces of attraction, at the same time they were also divided by other powerful forces of repulsion. And although Little Li had now found a new and welcome point of connection to his homeland, the fundamental contradictions that had always divided his life remained far from resolved.

46

INTO THE FLAME

"SO—HOW'S THE family man?" Little Wang facetiously asked as they sat around his cluttered table one afternoon.

"I admit, things turned out in a way I wasn't expecting, but I . . ."

"You've ended up like one of those white guys who gets a wife from a mail-order catalogue with a name like *Cherry Blossom Special*, filled with preening Chinese girls willing to sell their asses to fat bald guys from the Beautiful Country with wallets full of credit cards. I have a friend who sent her photo in to one of those catalogues just to see what would happen and she got all these letters, from guys with tattoos, rings in their ears, big stomachs, and pickup trucks. Talk about imperialists exploiting our Chinese natural resources! But you did 'em one better, brother." He slapped his friend on the back. "First you scored yourself some of those imperialist babes, then you came back to the Motherland and not only snagged a nice Chinese wife, but also got a kid thrown into the deal, all without even a fucking catalogue!"

"Have you ever had an old lady?" Little Li gently asked, for once feeling superior to his friend.

"Politics is my mistress," replied Little Wang dismissively, grinding his cigarette out in an already brimming ashtray. "The ladies find me too. . . . Well, I'm not handsome like you, and politics scares them. Chinese girls these days want a guy with a boring job, an apartment, a refrigerator, and a motorbike, not a risk-taking political train wreck like me."

"I'll keep my eyes out for a catalogue of American girls," laughed Little Li, trying not embarrass his friend too much. "Maybe we can find you a nice 'foreign devil' for a wife!" Then, as if the conversation was getting too close to a tender spot, Little Wang turned the focus back on Little Li. "You may have your sweetheart now, but when you got back from the Beautiful Country three months ago, you were a mess to behold!"

"I know, I know!" admitted Little Li, shaking his head. "It's pretty bewildering! Still, you can't imagine what it's like to have a child until you actually have one."

"You sound like someone who's just become the proud owner of a new TV set or air conditioner," said Little Wang, with a snort of laughter, sending images of the delegation at Yip's Electronics flashing through Little Li's head. "Those American girls will just have to wait till after the counterrevolution, for this guy. Speaking of which, what are you doing Sunday? Before you get any more henpecked, you should come with us on Sunday!" He guffawed.

"Where?"

"I borrowed a video camera, and we're going to shoot Fang Lizhi talking about getting kicked out of the party."

"Let me talk with my wife."

"Okay, but just don't forget that your new model family lives in a country that's having an identity crisis!" taunted Little Wang. "At one moment we're in love with Confucianism and scholar's robes, the next with Stalinism and Mao suits, and then it's on to Michael Jackson and Western suits and ties. You may think that everything's just going to keep on opening up and getting better, but people are getting pissed about low salaries, inflation, corruption, the slow pace of reform. I can feel the dissatisfaction with the party in people's reactions to Fang's speeches. Frankly, I don't think our leaders have any idea where we're headed."

Little Li was excited by the prospect of actually meeting the outspoken astrophysicist that he'd been hearing so much about. Even though the official media were now filled with articles exhorting people to "liberate their thinking," decades of bitter experience with the party still kept most Chinese from speaking out freely. Fang, however, appeared immune to such political pressures.

"Where're you going?" Little Hong asked him as he put his jacket on to go out the next morning.

"Just out with Little Wang," he replied evasively.

"Papa, Papa, can I go with you?" asked Xiaomei, jumping up and down.

"Not this time."

"Why not?"

"Because I've got some things to do."

"Like what?"

"Like . . . I can't explain."

"But I want to go, too!"

"It's not for kids!"

"Remember, you're a father now," admonished Little Hong. "We lost you once and don't want to lose you again. Whatever things were like in America, they're different here. You still have to be careful!"

"I understand!" he demurred, feeling both rebuked and frustrated by her lack of interest in what was going on around them.

As he got off the bus near the Great Wall Sheraton Hotel, his suspicions were aroused when two black-suited men stepped off at the same stop and then remained behind him as he walked toward the hotel. The recognition that he was probably being tailed by Public Security Bureau agents sent a prickle down his spine. When he reached the hotel portico, he ducked behind a parked tourist bus to see if he could shake them. As they rounded the front of the bus to enter the hotel, he slid around its back, successfully staying out of their line of sight. Once inside the lobby, they looked anxiously around and, not finding their quarry, walked disconsolately back outside to the taxi stand, where they began arguing. As a perverse impulse came over Little Li, he slid slowly up behind them, stopped ten meters away, and just waited, enjoying the pleasure of having transformed himself from prey into predator. Then, when one of his shadows finally sensed a presence behind them, turned, and saw Little Li standing statuelike, staring at them, he furtively whispered something to his partner. Both spun around like dancers and hurried away.

As Little Li triumphantly entered the hotel lobby, he was flabbergasted by the polished granite floors, shimmering stainless-steel support columns, elegant furniture, and abundant bright lighting. China did seem to be emerging from its Spartan revolutionary cocoon. When he knocked on the door of the room upstairs whose number Little Wang had given him, Fang Lizhi was about to begin his interview.

"Dehua Wang tells me that you've just returned from America," he said, standing up and courteously welcoming Little Li as he entered. "I'd enjoy talking with you sometime."

"Of course," replied Little Li, wondering what he could possibly tell this renowned scientist. What most immediately impressive about Fang was his unpretentiousness: he was hardly the scheming, diabolical subversive depicted by the party. His tan windbreaker, knit polo shirt, permanent-press slacks, and tortoiseshell glasses all gave him a nerdy, owlish, unthreatening look.

"Why, after so many party warnings, do you still keep speaking out?" Little Wang asked him when the shooting finally began.

"Well"—he smiled—"asking questions is the most natural thing for scientists, so we are sometimes the first to become aware of emerging social crises. And when we do, I believe that it's our responsibility to speak out, otherwise our silence makes us accomplices."

His commitment to facts and truth put Fang completely at odds with the party's mendacity. By repeatedly speaking the unspeakable and doing so in public, he'd begun creating a new corpus of thought beyond the party's propaganda apparatus. What particularly infuriated leaders was the belated recognition that by expelling him from the party and dismissing him from his posts, they'd only made him a more renowned and influential figure.

"Is it true you've gotten a lot of mail lately?" Little Wang asked.

"Yes, I was surprised when I suddenly began getting a flood of letters, many addressed simply to 'Fang Lizhi, Beijing,' and yet I still somehow received them."

"How do you explain it?"

"I think people in the post office were making a special effort!" He gave one of his signature laughs, an infectious, open laugh that spiraled spontaneously into a mirthful whinny. "My wife and I were particularly touched by one postcard on which the sender not only expressed outrage at my ouster, but then openly wrote his name and address."

"Meaning?"

"They were refusing to be cowed. Then something else happened that really mystified us. After the first batch of letters tapered off, a whole new wave began arriving. This time, they didn't simply express sympathy over my expulsion, but contained long comments on what I'd actually been saying about free expression, democracy, and human rights. I couldn't figure out how they knew so much about what I'd been saying. Then it dawned on me! Their letters were triggered by the party's own distribution of my speeches for criticism! Maybe now I'll get a third wave from your little blue book of quotations." He winked at Little Wang.

One of the most unusual things about Fang was that, although he'd been politically persecuted most of his adult life, he showed no hint of bitterness or resentment. What he stood for seemed to so transcend what he was against that there was no place for denigrating enemies, retribution, or revenge. His outspokenness made Little Li almost instinctively want to urge him to be more careful. Yet, though such warnings had already come from many quarters, Fang seemed impervious to them.

"I've got nothing to hide," he said, shrugging. "Since I've already said everything I believe many times before, what's the point of trying to hide now?"

"But how could your iconoclastic views, especially on Marxism, Leninism, and Maoism, not trigger a party counterreaction?" pressed Little Wang.

"Well, they already have."

"But it hasn't silenced you."

"Truth is truth," he replied. "That Marxism no longer has any worth is a truth that cannot be denied. Marxism is a thing of the past, like a worn-out dress that should be discarded. If Party General Secretary Hu Yaobang can be quoted in the *People's Daily* saying, 'Marx and Lenin can't solve our problems,' why can't I? Back in 1980, when I first started saying that socialism was past its prime, Fang Yi, vice-premier for science and technology, called me in. 'How could you say a thing like that?' he asked. I replied, 'I say it because I believe it.' And he said, 'Well, I might even go so far in private as to agree, but one can't just come right out and say such things in public!' " Fang gave another of his whinnying laughs. "If we all spoke out, you know, we'd have great strength."

Little Li found it stunning to hear a public figure speak with such frankness. During a break, he struck up a conversation with Fang's wife, Li Shuxian, who was also a physicist.

"I don't think we're going to end up friends of the party anytime soon," she offered with a sigh. "The party talks about friendship, fraternity, equality, trust, mutual respect, cooperation, and reciprocity, but friendly compromises are rare, because the party always has to be right. For them, 'reciprocity' means that critics must give up their views and do the party's bidding. It's a bad habit."

"What do you think the party leaders fear most about your husband?"

"They think Old Fang can send students into the streets at a moment's notice. It's their conspiratorial mentality!" She laughed. "So, when he made his cross-country tour in 1986, speaking out about freedom and democracy, and students started demonstrating, they blamed him. For them, it's one thing to allow a few intellectuals to discuss democracy in the abstract on campuses, but quite another to permit students to engage in public protest, especially in Tiananmen Square."

Over his lifetime, Little Li had become so accustomed to hearing people speak in code that it was shocking to now hear Fang describe things as they actually were. It was no small wonder that members of the foreign press corps had started calling him "China's Sakharov."

For Little Li, Fang Lizhi was yet another reminder that there was a public universe spinning beyond the confines of the new family in which he'd found refuge. When he was younger, Little Wang had always been his guide to this outer world, and now he was playing the same role again. And in recognition of their long-standing friendship, Hong Hui tried to indulge her husband. However, even the mention of dissidents like Wei Jingsheng and Fang Lizhi filled her with trepidation.

"I know politics excites you, but it makes me afraid," she said one morning,

"You really shouldn't worry," he tried to reassure her. "When it comes to politics, you and I have always been different. But if things are ever to be set right for Xiaomei's generation, we must—"

"But," she interrupted, "look what happened when our parents tangled with politics!"

"I know," he responded impatiently. "Just don't forget, 'Lies written in ink can never disguise facts written in blood. Blood debts must be repaid in kind: the longer the delay, the greater the interest.' [墨写的谎说, 绝掩不住血写的事实]"

"Did you make that up?"

"No. That's Lu Xun."

"But such talk about 'blood debts' is exactly what scares me."

"But we can't just walk away from history and pretend it never happened!" He was channeling Little Wang now. "Whether we like it or not, it's there and will keep biting us if we ignore it."

"But isn't history moving in a promising way now? So why can't we just . . . ?"

"Because when the party cracks down again it will be too late."

"Oh, Wende!" She heaved a sigh of exasperation. "I've waited so long for you!"

"I know, I know, but . . ."

"Will you at least be careful for me and Xiaomei?" She was almost pleading now.

"I will," he promised, wanting to end the discussion before it escalated any further.

On April 15, 1989, former Party General Secretary Hu Yaobang died of a heart attack. As head of the Communist Party, Hu had gained the reputation of being quirky, open, and sympathetic to those who'd been politically persecuted during the Mao years. However, in 1987, when student protests kept erupting across the country, he was forced to resign.

"Something's brewing, and we Chinese love a good funeral as an outlet for our frustrations," announced Little Wang with oracular certainty.

"But things seem so much more open, even normal, now," countered Little Li, his wife's argument still ringing in his ears.

"Sure, but in our country nothing's ever what it seems. While you were off in the Beautiful Country, chasing all those American babes, you missed most of Old Hu's reign. Things were even more open then than now. You could say almost anything, go anywhere, publish anything, run for local assemblies, even protest in public. But when students started taking to the streets, all ginned up on things that critics like Wei Jingsheng and Fang Lizhi had said, the party spooked, and Old Deng sacked Hu as chief! And now, with so many problems worsening, people have started missing Hu and are criticizing Deng. This piece of 'doggerel' [顺口溜] says it all:

Chairman Mao was like the sun,
Roasting us morning, noon, and night.
Deng Xiaoping is like the moon.
Ever changing what is right.

That night, when the Two Virtuous Ones went out to the Peking University campus together, they found it buzzing with activity. "The star of hope has fallen [希望之星在坠落]!" proclaimed a huge banner draped from a dorm window. Another featured a quote by the writer Bing Xin, who'd marched in China's first mass protest, the May Fourth Movement in 1919, against the Great Powers' unfair treatment of China in the Treaty of Versailles: "The One Who Should Not Have Died Is Dead, While the One Who Should Have Died Remains Alive" (该死没死不该死却死). Something did, indeed, seem to be brewing.

The next few days, Little Li stayed home in deference to his wife. But, unable to resist turning on the TV, he was stunned to see that thousands of people had, in fact, been spontaneously spilling into Tiananmen Square to commemorate Hu's death, laying so many funeral wreaths, placards, and banners demanding his rehabilitation on the plinth of the Monument to the People's Heroes that it was completely buried. While he felt supremely frustrated to be stuck at home, he did not want to break his promise. Then on April 18 thousands of protesters staged a surprise sit-in on the Avenue of Eternal Peace, right in front of Xinhuamen, the gate into the party leadership's compound, that police finally broke up with arrests. The mayor of Beijing darkly warned that these demonstrators were like "a match thrown into a barrel of waiting gunpowder." Every fiber in Little Li's body wanted to go out and see what was happening. Then, several nights later, well after midnight he was awakened by a tap-tapping on their door.

"What's gotten into you?" he demanded when he found Little Wang standing outside.

"We've got to go to the square!" his friend breathlessly exclaimed. "Something big is up, and we don't want to miss it!" He got as excited over politics as other young men did over sex.

"But it's two a.m.!"

"Never mind—history's being made!" his friend persisted.

Little Li felt a hand on his back. It was his wife.

"I want you two to quiet down and not wake Xiaomei!" she said icily. "And remember what you promised me, Li Wende." Then she turned and walked away.

"Tomorrow there's going to be an official memorial service for Hu Yaobang inside the Great Hall of the People," the incorrigible Little Wang continued as soon as she'd gone. "The party's so fearful of more protests, they've ordered the police to close Tiananmen Square early in the morning. So student leaders are calling on demonstrators to sneak in tonight, before police cordons can be thrown up. Tomorrow they want to hold a people's funeral outside, in the square, while party leaders hold their official funeral inside!" His friend's infectious enthusiasm reminded Little Li of the day he'd shown up at Willow Courtyard just as excited about going to Tiananmen Square to see Chairman Mao review his Red Guards. "This could be one of the most momentous things that's ever happened in the square, and you can't let your wife—"

Before he could finish his sentence, Little Li raised a hand to cut him off. "Please! Don't say anything more about my wife."

"All right, all right!" demurred Little Wang. "But we need to be there before the police realize what's happening." For a few moments, the only sound in the hallway was the ticking of the clock Little Li had bought for his daughter, which featured a plastic butterfly twitching back and forth on its dial each time a second ticked. "So—what's your decision?"

"Do you think there's any danger of a crackdown?" Little Li asked after a long pause.

"Not now, because the party's too off balance."

"Okay," he relented. "Let's go!"

"Once a buddy [哥儿], always a buddy, right?" said Little Wang, putting an arm around his friend's shoulders. "The Two Virtuous Ones ride again."

Little Li quickly wrote his wife a note:

Hui:
   Little Wang is my oldest friend, and I need to honor that and go with him.
   Please don't worry. It's only a funeral!
   Wende

As they drew closer to the square, the streets became filled with people silently drifting through the darkness, all drawn by the same magnetic power of this symbolic space, Tiananmen Square, the sacred terminus for almost every national celebration and remonstration in modern Chinese history. The last time demonstrators had spontaneously filled it was to protest against Mao and the Gang of Four, when Zhou Enlai died, in January 1976. Now they were gathering again around the Monument to the People's Heroes, which was bedecked for the occasion with an enormous black-and-white funeral portrait of Hu Yaobang bearing the inscription "Whither Has Your Soul Gone? [何处招魂]"

Once in the square, the Two Virtuous Ones ended up standing beside a youth carrying a sign proclaiming MR. SCIENCE AND MR. DEMOCRACY: WE'VE BEEN EXPECTING YOU FOR SEVENTY YEARS. As they listened to impassioned appeals, songs, and chants delivered from a podium hastily erected on the monument's plinth, almost exactly where Little Li had first rendezvoused with Little Hong. He felt deeply conflicted about defying her to come here, but there was something about the game being acted out between "the people" and their putative "leaders" that was addictively exciting. After so many years of being thwarted, people's outcries for justice and democracy were being given voice, at last, and he didn't want to miss it.

Daybreak brought a beautiful spring morning. Fuzz from budding poplar trees drifted languorously through the warm air as thousands of "mourners" gazed up at the windows of the Great Hall of the People, where party leaders inside kept pulling back the draperies to catch furtive peeks at the spectacle outside. Each time they did so, protesters outside cheered.

"I don't think the leaders of this 'people's republic' have ever confronted such a public display of people power," chortled Little Li, awed that the balance had for the moment reversed itself.

"Not since Mao attacked the party during the Cultural Revolution have these guys been forced to deal with such opposition," chortled Little Wang. "And, frankly, I don't know what they're going to do. But if history's any judge, such a monumental loss of face will require retaliation. Never forget the expression 'Appear outwardly strong, even when inwardly weak' [外强中干]. The party can never tolerate having its weakness put on public display."

What made this official memorial service so bizarre was that party leaders inside the Great Hall of the People had been summoned to commemorate a man they'd deposed and defamed, while the demonstrators outside were the ones who harbored the truest feelings of respect for Hu and felt the greatest sense of loss. Indeed, when loudspeakers crackled to life so that the eulogies inside could be heard outside, those memorializing Hu had to balance precariously on that razor's edge between extolling and declaiming his leadership.

"There is nothing like having to praise someone you've just purged, although I suppose it's an improvement on just executing them and airbrushing their photos from the historical record." Little Wang sardonically laughed.

The irony that Hu's real supporters were shut out while his detractors were locked in did not escape the veteran revolutionary writer Ge Yang. As she peered out a window at the cordons of police struggling to hold back demonstrators from the stairway leading up to the Great Hall's main doorway, she composed a wistful elegy she later entitled "This Side and That Side":

A single land split
By a wall of brute force.
On one side lies an iceberg,
Chilling those who dwell therein.
On the other side, a warm sea.
Here lies Yaobang's body,
And there his soul. . . .

When all the official eulogies had ended inside, the crowd outside began chanting, "Dialogue! Dialogue! Dialogue [对话]!" Then three students approached the main stairway to the Great Hall with a scroll calling for a free press and better conditions at universities and held it solemnly above their heads, like petitioners of old "genuflecting" (跪谏) before the imperial throne. Needless to say, the latter-day emperor, Premier Li Peng, did not appear to receive it. One could hardly blame him, for with Tiananmen Square boiling with protesters, his dream of revolutionary masses obediently yielding to the party's "democratic dictatorship of the proletariat" (人民民主专政) must have seemed far away. Not only had much of

Mao's revolution been undermined by Deng's reforms, but now the revolution's most hallowed ground was filled with thousands of rebellious free thinkers mocking him and the party. The Two Virtuous Ones went home exhausted but euphoric.

Little Hong said nothing until Little Li was back in her arms. "You went to the square, didn't you?" she said.

"I did," he replied. "It was peaceful, even joyous."

"I'm relieved, but still . . ."

"Don't worry, there were too many people for them to do anything."

"Still, I beg you, be careful. Opposition only creates more opposition."

"I understand," he replied, relieved that she'd not reacted more vehemently.

The protests might have quieted down thereafter if, just as Little Wang had predicted, party leaders hadn't felt obligated to retaliate. On April 26, after he dropped Li Mei off at school, Little Wang passed a kiosk where newspapers were posted that had scores of people clustered around.

"What's going on?" he asked a young man.

"Old Deng's warned students against 'making trouble' [捣乱]."

"Have those students lost their minds?" chimed in a middle-aged woman carrying a sack of leeks. "Everyone knows you don't argue with the party!"

Scanning the papers himself, Little Li saw that the *People's Daily* prominently featured a *Commentary* entitled "It Is Necessary to Take a Clear Stand Against Unrest," attacking demonstrators for seeking to "poison people's minds, create national turmoil, and sabotage the nation's political stability." It warned that, "If the party were to take a lenient attitude toward this turmoil, chaos would emerge." Little Li found the *Commentary* so ominous that, instead of returning home, he went to find Little Wang, who was just leaving for the square.

"You on board today?" he immediately asked.

"For what?"

"The march against the *People's Daily* editorial leaving from the university quarter. We can go together."

There was something about the way his friend assumed their old fraternity was indissoluble that Little Li found irresistible, and he nodded his assent. As they walked down the *hutong* together, he felt just as he had when they'd set off on their many adventures around Beijing as young boys. Something in him was still made more alive by the kinds of struggles to which Little Wang was drawn. Perhaps it was just such struggle that had seduced Mao, too, to the idea of "permanent revolution." For people like Mao, the more elusive the object of desire, or the more challenging the goal, the more alluring they became.

"Do you think Fang Lizhi will show up?" he asked Little Wang as they rode together on his bike.

"Fang won't go near students or the square, because he knows that if he does the party will brand them as his puppets."

It was a supreme irony that, having laid absolute claim to representing "the people," the party now felt threatened by these self-same "people" as they found their collective voice. In the party's judgment, "the people" ceased being "the people" as soon as they chose opposition. Carrying placards declaring PEACEFUL PETITION IS NOT TURMOIL, PATRIOTISM IS NO CRIME, AND WILLING TO DIE FOR DEMOCRACY, they found protesters already spilling out of the gates of Peking University that lovely spring morning to march past tens of thousands of well-wishers who stood along their route to the square. The Two Virtuous Ones had been marching for almost an hour when they suddenly heard a loud roaring swell of voices coming from up ahead.

"Get on my shoulders and see what's up," urged Little Li.

"Police have locked arms and made a chain across the street ahead, to block the march," reported Little Wang with excitement. "Now marchers are colliding with the police, and—"

"Can we get through?"

"It's hard to see, but I think the lead marchers are being forced to pull back. No, wait! They're pushing forward again!" announced Little Wang like a sportscaster. "Now the line is starting to bulge! And . . . it's breaking! The marchers have pushed through!" A loud roar went up, and suddenly the seething procession was spilling down the street again toward the square, like a river that's breached a dam.

When the march confronted yet another police cordon, it, too, was quickly breached, and again a triumphant roar went up. As marchers streamed down the Avenue of Eternal Peace past Xinhuamen, where only a week before fellow protesters had been beaten and arrested, they defiantly chanted, *"We are not afraid!"* Their repeated successes had given them a sense of dauntlessness. By the time they surged into Tiananmen Square, the sanctum sanctorum of Mao's revolution, they were viewing themselves as the rightful heirs of the May Fourth Movement's traditions of nationalism, egalitarianism, democracy, and public remonstration, the very standards under which the Chinese Communist Party itself had once marched.

"It's hard to imagine that the government would dare suppress such a movement," said an elated Little Li. "Maybe we are at a turning point."

"Maybe." His friend smiled enigmatically.

47

HOPE

"I REALIZE that, with a new family, it may be inconvenient for you to die right now," said Little Wang sarcastically. "However, I assume you still subscribe to the 'right to know.'"

"You always did have a delicate way of putting things!" responded Little Li, who would have been offended had he not known his friend so well.

"Well, since here in the Motherland we rarely dare say what we think, the truth can sometimes seem rude!"

To celebrate the seventieth anniversary of the May Fourth Movement, student leaders announced an even grander march, for when Little Wang had been elected a member of the organizing committee. In preparation, he'd made two headbands—one for himself, proclaiming "We Are Willing to Die for Freedom," and one for Little Li, declaring "People Have a Right to Know." As Little Li tied on his headband, he felt conflicted. He was leading a double life: as husband and father at home, and as comrade-in-arms to his intrepid friend in the streets. At the same time he loved his wife and child, he felt drawn to this protest movement in an almost animal way. He said nothing to her about the other side of his divided life, because he didn't want to worry her, but he could sense her apprehensiveness. As he and Little Wang set off on that lovely warm morning for the May Fourth march, he felt almost as if he were slipping out for an affair with another woman.

The march was both far larger and more laid-back than its predecessors. The Two Virtuous Ones walked with a smiling Buddhist monk in a saffron robe, a young woman wearing a green foam rubber Statue of Liberty crown, and a newspaper editor carrying a placard declaring, "The *People's Daily* Speaks Nothing but Nonsense," and their collective euphoria made it almost impossible to imagine that anything untoward might happen. The fact that so many marches had met with so little governmental resistance had had a kind of narcotic effect on participants, allowing them to imagine that maybe China was undergoing an almost mystical change that was finally transforming the party into being able to accommodate itself to the popular will. So, when, once more, they reached Tiananmen Square unobstructed, and a rising movement leader, Wu'er Kaixi, mounted the steps of the monument to congratulate the marchers for having revived the "May Fourth spirit of science and democracy," the Two Virtuous Ones felt both proud and indomitable.

As it happened, there was a reason why party leaders had been so restrained: Russian General Secretary Mikhail Gorbachev was scheduled to arrive in Beijing soon for a long-awaited summit at which China and the Soviet Union planned a dramatic reconciliation. However, student leaders cleverly recognized that, because the meeting was slated to begin with a twenty-one-gun salute on the square and a state banquet in the Great Hall, if they were able to motivate large numbers of demonstrators to remain in the square until the Russian leader's arrival, their protest movement would be essentially immune to counterattack.

"We have petitioned, through a series of peaceful actions, for a direct and open dialogue with the government on the basis of full equality," declared a handbill. "The government has delayed answering our petitions, and we will no longer tolerate such a deceitful attitude, with one delay after another. To make a determined and forceful protest, we have decided to hold a hunger strike."

By the time Gorbachev's plane touched down, several hundred fasters wearing "hunger striker" (绝食) headbands had gathered around the monument to begin a fast, where they immediately captured the attention of the international journalists who were arriving in droves to cover the summit. What is more, as word of the fast spread around the city, tens of thousands of ordinary Beijingers, many wearing "support" (声援) headbands, also poured into the square out of curiosity and in solidarity.

Although Little Li was determined to keep his vow to his new wife and not surrender to the siren song of the protest movement, because everything seemed so peaceful, he rationalized a last visit to the square. Rushing to Little Wang's house, he found a note on his door:

> *Gone to Tiananmen Square until further notice!*
> *This is our country.*
> *Its people are our people.*
> *Its government should be our government.*
> *If we do not speak out, who will?*

When Little Li reached the square himself, it was packed with demonstrators flushed with a heady sense of liberation reminiscent of the spirit during the 1920s and '30s in Mao's "liberated zones" (解放区), "soviet" areas that were beyond the reach of either Nationalist or Japanese control. Fears about saying what they thought had evaporated, and the protest movement was pervaded by an almost millenarian feeling of expectation that made it possible to dream that, through selfless example, these idealistic hunger strikers might actually help the Chinese people be reborn as what the great turn-of-the-century reformer Liang Qichao (梁启超) had heralded "new citizens" (新民). People were so awed by the size of the crowds, charmed by the good cheer, and stunned that the movement had lasted so long without government intrusion that few were able to imagine a return to the status quo ante. A few even dared imagine the end of the Chinese Communist Party. The unthinkable had become thinkable, and as Little Li made his way through the buoyant crowds, he, too, felt uplifted to be even peripherally involved in something transcending his own immediate needs and wants.

Noticing that a long canvas tent fly had been strung up to provide shade for hunger strikers, he walked over to the entrance where an earnest young woman stood reading out loud from the declaration written by the fasters, as tears slid down her cheeks:

> "In this bright sunny month of May, we are on a hunger strike. In the finest moment of our youth, we must leave behind everything beautiful about life, no matter how reluctant and unwilling we are. The country has reached an impasse. . . . History demands it: we have no choice

but to die. . . . So—farewell, mothers; farewell, fathers. Please forgive us if your children cannot remain loyal to their country and act in a filial manner at the same time. Farewell, people! Please allow us to use these means, however reluctantly, to demonstrate our loyalty. The vows written with our lives will brighten the Republic's skies."

Inside the fasting tent, Little Li found his old friend sprawled on newspapers amid scores of other hunger strikers beneath a banner: "We Sacrifice Ourselves to Rejuvenate the National Spirit."

"Nice bed you have there," Little Li whispered.

"At last, the *People's Daily* has a use," replied Little Wang, barely opening his eyes.

"You feeling all right?"

"Lousy. This starving business stinks. But at last we've found a way to force those 'old turtle eggs' to listen!" He gestured toward the Great Hall. "If they don't hear us now, they never will."

Although he kept complaining about how hungry he was, Little Li had never seen his friend quite so defiant, and he would have joined him if obligation didn't still trump impulse. When younger, he'd been constrained by his father; now he was constrained by his wife and daughter and still destined to watch from the sidelines while others acted. As they chatted, out of the corner of one eye Little Li watched a girl who lay nearby with closed eyes as her father spooned broth into her mouth from a thermos cup and pleaded with her to come home. Steadfastly, she refused. So overcome by emotion did her father become that he dropped his thermos and shattered its glass vacuum tube inside.

"My generation never dared speak up, much less act out what we believed," he said, half sobbing and half laughing, as Little Li helped him clean up. "Now she's acting for me. How can I not be moved?"

As the tent flap undulated in the soft spring breeze reminded Little Li of the set for the Houston Ballet and made him wonder what Bach would make of such a scene. Might he have joined the students? The idea of J. S. Bach, with his stern Lutheran countenance, marching through Tiananmen Square under a banner, "Kappelmeisters United Against the Dictatorship of the Proletariat," made him smile.

"Hey, Little Wang, I've got a question for you," he said as his friend lit a cigarette. "Do you think liberty, freedom, and justice are things that people gravitate toward naturally, or do they have to be taught to appreciate them?"

"How the fuck do I know?" Little Wang blinked.

"I really want your opinion," insisted Little Li. "I mean, if there's no fundamental goodness in people, then what's the point of trying to appeal to their better natures?"

"Well, if you're going to insist on dragging me into a deep philosophical discussion while I'm starving, I'll go with Confucius, who believed that people are fundamentally good but need moral leaders and teachers to help them cultivate their innate sense of goodness, so they don't turn to shit."

"And do you think history has a determined direction that is irresistibly leading us toward more openness and freedom?" Little Li continued tenaciously. "I mean, do you believe we are part of some bigger historical force flowing in an already determined direction?"

"What the hell's gotten into you?"

"I just want to know what you think—do you believe a protest and hunger strike like this will actually lead to anything better? I mean, are these demonstrations the expression of some larger historical trend with a motion of its own, or just random acts of no special historical significance?"

"Man! You really are overheating!"

"I feel history has a direction, that we're all part of it, and that we can help nudge it along in a good way. But my wife insists that history's dumb and nothing good comes from opposition and politics, especially when it leads to violence."

"Okay! Here's the way I look at it: Germany gave us both Hegel and Marx, who believed history had a positive, determinist direction. That's what good communists are supposed to believe, right? But, then, look what happened to the Germans! The Führer was more than a bump on Hegel's nice road of dialectical evolution, and those bandits Stalin and Mao were more than potholes in Russia's and China's supposedly inevitable progressions to a socialist utopia. So how can we ever dare to say history has a positive direction? Where did such naïveté ever get us?"

"So maybe Little Hong's right."

"Maybe. But even if history is directionless and amoral, we still have to fight."

"Why?"

"Because it's the right thing to do!" Despite his enervated state, Little Wang had become quite animated. "The trouble with you, my friend, is that you're one of those 'fools' [傻瓜] who like to believe people have noble natures. Maybe there are a few who are noble, loyal, and true, but even they need watching and cultivation. It's just like the 'Three Character Classic' says in its first lines: 'While men at birth may be naturally good, and their natures may be the same; their habits soon become different and without teaching, their basic natures deteriorate.' Humans may not be complete monsters, but what really counts is power, and occasionally wealth and sex. There are a few men of conscience, but there are many more inclined to tyranny and the relentless quest for power. That's why we're starving ourselves! It gives us power. Moral power, but power nonetheless."

"Thanks for sharing," Little Li said and laughed.

"You're welcome. And now, having brought enlightenment to the benighted, this martyr's going to take a nap." Crossing his arms over his chest, he pulled his headband down over his eyes. Just when Little Li thought he'd nodded off, Little Wang opened his eyes again. "Okay. Now I have a question for you," he suddenly piped up. "Do you know how many demonstrators were involved during the May Fourth Movement, in 1919?"

"Oh . . . maybe twenty-five thousand or so?"

"Only three thousand."

"So few?"

"And do you know how many of them died?"

"Fifty or so?"

"One. Compared with our present leaders, 'warlords' [军阀] of old were positively backward in their killing power! It took a foreigner, Vladimir Lenin, to teach us Chinese how to get organized and oppress ourselves in a truly modern and efficient way."

"So—bravo to the Communist Party!" Little Li chuckled.

"Indeed," said Little Wang with the hint of a smile. "You know, speaking of tyrants, a friend just told me that lately visitors have been allowed to go up on Tiananmen Gate just like Mao. I'd go up if I wasn't on this fucking fast." He rubbed his belly. "God, I'm hungry!"

The idea of standing on top of the Gate of Heavenly Peace, where Mao had so often stood, intrigued Little Li. As soon as his friend drifted off, he made his way through the crowds to the base of the fabled gate. On his way, he passed an elderly woman with an ancient clay water-cooler strapped to the back of her bicycle, dispensing free drinks. As he thirstily downed several cups of water, he thought of the old man on the road in Qinghai with his water pail. Maybe there still was some goodness left in the world that came from the hearts of well-intentioned souls. Then he thought of Lisa and felt seized with guilt. He resolved to write and tell her . . . But, tell her what? He still didn't know.

As he stepped out onto the Tiananmen rostrum, it was impossible not to think about the larger-than-life role Mao had played on China's historical stage. Like that of Napoleon, Stalin, and Hitler, Mao's "greatness" had little to do with his good character or humanity and everything to do with his charisma and will to power. All these men were tyrants, but one nonetheless grew so accustomed to them as national icons that it was impossible to imagine history without them. For better or worse, Mao had become an ineradicable feature of the modern Chinese landscape.

Mao had built this one-hundred-acre public square that now stretched out before him for regimented parades celebrating loyalty to him and the party. Now, however, instead of worshipful minions marching in lockstep past his portraited gate in adoration of his communist dynasty, his square had become a roiling cauldron of what he would have viewed as disrespectful, disloyal, and disorderly adversaries, each with his or her own grievances and reasons to sympathize with the protest movement. There was so much unresolved injustice littering the landscape, China was a tinderbox. In his youth, Mao had written about a similarly inflammatory situation he'd uncovered in the countryside in the 1930s as being so incendiary that "a single spark can light a prairie fire" (星星之火可以燎原). He'd been referring then to peasant unrest, which he compared to "a child about to be born moving restlessly in its mother's womb." And now "moving restlessly" within Tiananmen Square was a new incipient movement. No wonder the party was worried.

From the top of the gate, there was no visual evidence that inexperienced student organizers, who'd frantically been trying to impose some semblance of order on this inchoate multitude, were being successful. However, a rudimentary city within a city was, in fact, slowly trying to take form. Arrayed around the "fasting tent," protesters had created a patchwork of cordoned-off areas dedicated to different universities, academies, institutions, and special functions. There was a communications area (where volunteers maintained generators and sound systems so leaders could have some pretense of "governing" the amorphous multitude); a printing area (where speeches, statements, leaflets, and press announcements were duplicated and distributed); a food and drink area (where contributions were received and redistributed); a finance area (where the growing number of cash donations were collected, tallied, and disbursed); and even a sanitation area (that managed trash collection and the portable toilets). Physically dividing all these areas were access lanes marked with plastic crime tape, constantly being navigated by ambulances ferrying hunger strikers to the hospital, their wailing sirens only heightening the sense of drama that hovered over this unprecedented, spontaneously generated human colony.

When Little Li got back to the fasting tent, he found two protest-movement organizers looking for him, to ask if he would serve as translator for some interviews between the newly arrived phalanx of foreign correspondents and the hunger-strike leaders. The invitation excited him, but as he headed home late that night, all his suppressed guilt about betraying his promise to Little Hong began welling up. He let himself into their apartment as quietly as he could, and tiptoed to Xiaomei's bedside to look at her sleeping figure in the half-light. How miraculous that he'd played a part in creating this perfect small being. No sooner had his father died than she'd been conceived. Perhaps she was his reincarnation. The thought made him regret spending the whole day in the square without once thinking about her. Then he heard a sound he could not identify. Cocking an ear to listen, he stopped breathing. It was music, but playing very softly. As he tiptoed down the hallway he realized the sound was coming from their sleeping alcove and was the taped Bach cantata that Little Hong had brought to Willow Courtyard during the last weeks of his father's life. He undressed quietly, slid under their quilt beside her, and let the loveliness of this musical prayer wash over him. She did not move.

> *Slumber now, you eyes so weary,*
> *Close into soft and sweet repose!*
> *World, I will not tarry here any longer,*
> *I own no part of you*
> *That could matter to my soul.*

Although his version of the human "soul" bore little resemblance to Bach's, Mao had once written, "Not to have a correct political point of view is like having no soul." Could he, other party officials, or even the student protest leaders understand the "soul" of this cantata? He'd heard that Adolf Hitler liked Bach's Teutonic discipline and orderliness and even played some of his works at rallies. As he felt Little Hong stir beside him, he put an arm around her.

"While you were in America, I listened to this cantata almost every night," she whispered.

"How did you get it?" he asked, stroking her cheek.

"I made a copy before I brought it over to your father." He tried to imagine her alone with Li Mei while he was lusting after Juliette and collecting used appliances. And now he was being unfaithful to her again, this time with the square. As he listened, even the music seemed to be crying out: "Enough with political demonstrations! Choose Bach, not Mao. Choose your wife, not protest movements. Choose your daughter, not abstractions of justice! Above all, do not choose the deformed world of politics!" Then came the line that had so moved his father:

> *My God! When will the lovely "now" come?*
> *When will I journey into peace*
> *And the cool soil of earth . . .*

He thought of his father lying in the cold Shandong earth, Little Wang lying prostrate in the square, and Lisa lying alone in her San Francisco bed, and felt dizzy with regret.

"Is Mr. Bach your hint that you've had enough of politics?" he asked. Instead of replying, she kissed his forehead and he swore to himself that he'd be more faithful to his oath not to endanger himself. However, because he'd already agreed to translate the next morning for Wang Dan at an important interview that the CBS News correspondent Charles Kuralt was doing with him, he felt honor-bound to return to the square this one last time.

The next morning, he waited until Little Hong had left with Li Mei before setting out. The square was more crowded, chaotic, and littered than ever. Unruly piles of plastic bottles, newspapers, handbills, foam clamshells, and discarded clothing made it look like a disaster area. At the fasting tent, he found Little Wang lying motionless, his pale, haggard face hardly a beacon of the idealized struggle that had initially animated the hunger strikers. He'd already been taken to the hospital once. Fortunately, strike protocols took no position on cigarette smoking. Sometimes it seemed that nicotine was all that kept his friend running.

"An empty belly saws at your gut twenty-four/seven," he croaked when he opened his eyes and saw that his friend was sitting beside him. Smiling thinly, he took a draft of water.

"How long are you going to continue with this?" asked Little Li with concern.

"Who knows? But, as soon as we stop, we lose. I still dream of big changes, but my pessimistic side suspects these bastards will never change. Remember what Old Deng said a year ago: 'We cannot do without dictatorship. We must not only affirm the need for it, but exercise it whenever necessary.'"

"That's the kind of talk that makes Little Hong worried."

"Of course she's worried. She's got a kid." For a moment, neither spoke, but Little Li felt miffed by the imputation that he did not also have some responsibility for their child. He was about to object when Little Wang suddenly interjected, "Can I give you something?"

"Sure."

"Because I'm in the hands of fate, I want you to take this." He handed Little Li a sheet of paper.

"What is it?"

"A will."

"A what?"

"My fucking will!"

Little Li had heard that many hunger strikers had started writing wills, but he'd viewed their "Give me liberty or give me death" rhetoric as being overly melodramatic. Now, however, things were changing. At the far end of the fasting area, a dozen students from the Beijing Drama Institute were refusing to eat or drink; they lay under plastic sheeting, each with a red rose across their necks, so they looked like corpses. Because the last thing he wanted to do was to excite Little Hong's fears, he'd stubbornly resisted the idea that anything untoward could happen to either of them. But now, with an air of ultimate sacrifice hovering over this once-jubilant, youthful protest, it was impossible not to take Little Wang's will seriously.

"Because there's no one left in my family to miss me, I'm appointing you my designated mourner!" He smiled ruefully. "Whatever I have, it's going to you, old buddy!" He'd never seen his old friend quite so sentimental.

When Little Li reached the communications area, scores of recently arrived foreign correspondents were milling around, scrawling on pads, clicking away with cameras, thrusting microphones in the faces of any Chinese willing to try a few words in English. The irony was that, just when the party most needed to control the narrative, satellite links approved for the Gorbachev summit now made it impossible to staunch the hemorrhage of TV reporting pulsing out around the world. Tiananmen Square had turned into a giant global television soundstage.

Charles Kuralt was a heavyset, affable man decked out in a khaki jacket enhanced with shoulder epaulets that made it look like a cross between an army officer's uniform and a vintage British Empire explorer's tunic. He was trailed by a retinue that included an officious woman producer with a clipboard and a face etched with worry, and a cameraman and a soundman, the latter two both boasting world-class stomachs under fishnet vests draped with lanyarded press credentials. When Little Li introduced himself, Kuralt immediately began extolling the selfless spirit of the hunger strikers.

"It's just such a moving experience to be here in your square that I'm finding it hard to be dispassionate!" he rhapsodically declared, shaking Little Li's hand as if he were an official plenipotentiary for the whole movement. "I mean, what you've got going here is something, a cross between the Free Speech Movement, Woodstock, and an anti–Vietnam War love-in!"

"We Chinese have surprised even ourselves," offered Little Li, impressed by how involved this American correspondent had become in their far-flung drama.

"I think what draws us foreign reporters to this sort of thing is our emotional attachment to the idea of American justice," replied Kuralt, as if the movement were a U.S. inspiration. "Or maybe it's that you guys live in a communist country and are just coming to your senses about autocracy." He gave a burst of uncertain laughter, as if he thought he might have overstepped and given offense.

After a century of being bullied and looked down on by superior foreign powers, China was finally doing something worthy of international acclaim and respect. Even though he was playing only a small part, Little Li felt gratified to hear this famous American correspondent wax so admiringly about the protest movement.

"Hey! Here's an idea," Kuralt suddenly exclaimed, turning to the woman with a clipboard. "This guy's English is fantastic! Why don't we put him on camera?" The producer nodded enthusiastically, and before Little Li could protest, the camera was on and Kuralt was asking him, "So, tell us, what do these demonstrations mean to you as a young, idealistic Chinese?"

"Well . . ." he stammered, not sure he even wanted to be on American television.

"I mean, why are you all out here?" goaded Kuralt, leaving a silence that begged filling.

"Well . . . our government's always been telling us what to do, but never listening to us, and here's the result!" He gestured across the square. "People are just fed up with being ignored and pushed around."

"How does it feel to not only challenge the Communist Party, but to be so successful?"

"It's unfamiliar territory."

"And where do you think this movement's headed?"

"We hope it leads toward greater reform, but nothing like this has happened before."

"Absolutely! And the whole world is watching!" Then, turning to his producer, Kuralt said: "Hey! You know what? While we wait for Wang Dan, why don't we get this guy to set up some interviews with ordinary people for us? What do you say?"

"Sure," nodded his producer enthusiastically. "Nothing like a little vox pop." Just then, Little Li saw a *People's Daily* reporter passing by and flagged him down. To his surprise, he agreed to speak on camera.

"Do you feel the Chinese media has at last found its conscience here in Tiananmen Square?" Kuralt asked pointedly, with Little Li translating.

"It is not that we Chinese reporters lacked a conscience," he replied, "it's that we were never our own masters."

"And how are things different now?"

"Look around at all the people who've turned out!" he continued. "We've come alive!"

"And, how does it feel to pull off such a grand caper?"

"If you want to know how people are feeling, let me read you something." He took a newspaper out from under his arm. "This is a poem from my own paper, *People's Daily,* entitled 'Looking Forward to Spring.'"

"Fantastic!" replied Kuralt, beaming like a big-game hunter who's just drawn a bead on a trophy animal. "Good to go?" he asked his crew.

"Rolling." His cameraman gave a thumbs-up.

"Okay. We'll let this guy read in Chinese, then you'll translate, okay, Li?"

"They'll eat this up in New York!" enthused the producer.

Standing stiffly at attention, the reporter began:

Standing on the edge of winter,
Looking forward to spring,
I feel spring so close to me.
Reaching out I can touch it,
Its fragrant aroma intoxicates me and compels belief
That this vast life of ours can suddenly turn many
*   splendored. . . .*

By the time he'd finished reading, a throng of curious bystanders had gathered, including two students dressed up as "Mr. Science" (赛先生) and "Mr. Democracy" (德先生), characters made famous seventy years before, during the May Fourth Movement; an elderly man in a wheelchair; two lovers, arm in arm; and a worker with a ragged haircut and a placard announcing "The Ordinary Folks Have Arrived! [市民来了]" As this gaggle of onlookers grew, the *People's Daily* reporter became more nervous, until he finally waved off further questions from Kuralt.

"Well, as you all make history, the world needs to know what's happening," Kuralt declared. The reporter nodded hesitantly and melted into the crowd.

Because this colorful, larger-than-life pageant had also been playing uncensored over CCTV, people were now pouring into Beijing from the provinces to participate, and foreign tourists were giving up trips to the Great Wall and Summer Palace to "experience the protest movement." The atmosphere in the square had become so festive that Little Li even decided to try to persuade Little Hong to bring Li Mei for a family outing.

"I know how wary you are, but won't you at least have a look?" he pleaded in his most temperate tone of voice. "If you could see what's going on, perhaps you'd stop worrying so much."

"That may be, but politics never leads anywhere except tragedy," she replied in such a peremptory way that he suspected she'd been harboring this retort for just such an occasion.

"Can I read you something?" he asked her that night, after a story with Xiaomei.

"What?" she asked distrustfully.

"Something by Ba Jin [巴金] that's been circulating in the square." Ba Jin was one of the twentieth century's most celebrated Chinese writers.

"All right," she grudgingly consented.

" 'Seventy years ago,' " he read, " 'during the May Fourth Movement, a group of patriotic students demonstrated for the cause of science and democracy in our Motherland. Now seventy years have passed, and we are still a backward country. I believe the students' demands are completely reasonable. What they are doing now is completing the task we were unable to finish. They are the hope of China. Now I am a sickly and decrepit old man, but I feel deeply encouraged by the example of these young people.' "

"Ba Jin is a man of conscience," she acknowledged softly when he finished reading. "If . . ." She halted. "If we come with you to the square, will you make me a promise in return?"

"What kind of a promise?"

"That hereafter you'll always put your family first?"

"Yes. I promise."

"Ever since that night in the reviewing stand, I've not trusted your good sense." He wished she might have chuckled indulgently here, but she did not.

"I understand," he said solemnly.

"I'll come only because I know it's important to you. But I ask you to also understand what's important to me."

"All right." He smiled.

"And what's important to me is us."

Since there was no longer bus service down the Avenue of Eternal Peace, they hailed a cab. But as they reached the Second Ring Road, there were so many pedestrians in the street they had to give up the car. When Little Li handed the driver some money, he waved it away.

"Forget it," he said with a smile. "If you're supporting the students, it's on me." Beijing cabdrivers were famous for their ill-temper, but even they seemed transformed by the spirit of the protest movement.

"Why are there so many people here?" Li Mei asked anxiously, riding on her father's shoulders and holding on to his forehead as they set out on foot for the square.

"They're here to ask the government to listen to them."

"What do they want to say?"

"They want to say they aren't satisfied with how they're being treated."

"Oh," she replied. It wasn't an easy question to answer to the satisfaction of a five-year-old.

In the crowd around them were marchers with banners from every imaginable profession and organization—the National Volleyball Team, the Beijing Industrial Boiler Factory, the Capital Department of Sanitation, the Central Party School, the Bank of China, the Ministry of Foreign Affairs, even a contingent from the feared Ministry of Public Security—all laughing, singing, and chanting.

"Where are they all going?" asked Li Mei restively.

"To Tiananmen Square."

"Why?"

"To protest government injustices."

"What's an injustice?"

"When someone is treated unfairly."

"You mean like when Teacher Guo is mean to us at school?"

"I guess you could say that." He laughed.

By the time they neared the Beijing Hotel, just before the Avenue of Eternal Peace debouches into the square, the roar of the crowd was like that from a sports stadium. Adding to the cacophony was the growling of two large backhoes that belched great plumes of black diesel exhaust as grinning workers stood in their front loaders and boisterously chanted, "Rule by old men must end!" There was even a Red Flag limousine, incongruously driven by a wild-eyed youth with a drooping mustache, boasting a placard hanging from its red-flag hood ornament: "Why Take a Benz?"

In this carnival-macabre atmosphere, for the first time Little Li felt an unfamiliar undertow, something new, dark, and even threatening. Those now being drawn to the square were not just idealistic students, intellectuals, and professionals, but ordinary workers and thousands of new arrivals from the provinces, whose enthusiasm for protest grew not out of an affection for democratic niceties but from a raw, lumpen excitement for disorder. And like a frightened wild animal, Li Mei had become wide-eyed and fallen silent. When an ambulance whooped by, she put fingers in her ears and squeezed her eyes shut.

"Papa!" she cried out. "I don't think I like it here."

"What's wrong?"

"It's too loud and scary!"

"It will be quieter in a moment," he tried to reassure her.

"But I want to go home!" she cried.

Little Hong was staring grimly ahead, as if to say, "I knew it wouldn't work!"

As they walked home, against the flow of people, Little Li was crestfallen. He'd lost his chance to bridge the gap between his family and this movement. But Li Mei's reaction had been strangely preternatural: with more workers and outsiders pouring into the square, the movement was becoming increasingly leaderless and angry, and the heady, hopeful sense that had prevailed was clotting into antagonism. Even protest imagery was changing. Instead of idealistic banners proclaiming freedom and democracy, there were more and more personal attacks on party leaders. One long-haired youth held an effigy of Premier Li Peng dressed in a Nazi uniform. Another brandished a placard depicting Deng Xiaoping with blood dripping from his lips. It read "Your Brain Is Addled! Retire and Go Back to Playing Bridge!"

If the demonstrations were reaching a point of no return, so was the tolerance of the party that over the past weeks had been forced to suffer one humiliation after another. Not only had they been compelled to move the official welcome ceremony for President Gorbachev from the square to the airport, but then to endure a gauntlet of embarrassing banners as his motorcade finally made its way into the city. *"IN THE SOVIET UNION THEY HAVE A GORBACHEV. WHAT DO WE HAVE IN CHINA?"* read one. *"WE WELCOME THE INITIATOR OF GLASNOST!"* read another. Adding insult to injury, at his farewell press conference, Gorbachev had blithely proclaimed: "All communist countries are headed toward greater freedom of expression, democracy, and human rights. The processes are painful but necessary."

No sooner had his plane taken off for Moscow than the skies over Beijing darkened, and as if the heavens themselves were bent on displaying cosmic upset, they poured down an apocalyptic deluge, transforming the already bedraggled encampment of hunger strikers and protesters in the square into a sodden mess. Banners that had once fluttered proudly were now drooping limply, defiant handwritten messages on placards were blurred, and the square's paving stones were covered by a fetid black slurry that gave this celebrated place a pestilent feeling. Concerned for his friend's health, Little Li had managed to win his wife's consent to once more return to the square with the express purpose of convincing his friend to give up his fast. But no sooner had he reached the now sodden fasting tent than an organizer from the Hunger Strike Committee made a beeline for him.

"You've been designated to join a televised meeting that Premier Li Peng has just agreed to hold with us in the Great Hall of the People," he breathlessly announced.

"With whom?" Little Li asked incredulously.

"The premier."

"But why me?" he stammered.

"Because we need a trustworthy English speaker to take notes and then interface with members of the foreign press and translate for strike leaders after the meeting."

As news of the impending meeting swept the square, many viewed it as a sign that the party was, at last, ready to compromise. Ever the skeptic, Little Wang, who'd become weaker and more enervated with each passing day, remained unconvinced. "That old pirate Li Peng always has tricks up his sleeve," he warned. "Men like him only compromise when they're trapped, but that's also when they become most vicious."

Having stared from afar at the Great Hall of the People's hulking presence since childhood, Little Li found the notion of actually going inside, much less attending a meeting with the premier, unreal. But as their ragtag delegation climbed the broad bank of stone steps to one of its gates, they were filled with hope. As they were received by liveried doormen in an enormous marble lobby, festooned with decorative vases as large as people and hung with artwork larger than movie-theater screens, an awed hush came over the group. If the party understood anything, it was how to use grandiosity to intimidate. The experience only became more surreal when Wu'er Kaixi, the protest leader from Beijing Normal University whose disregard for authority had made him famous, stumbled in directly from the hospital, where he'd been taken after fasting. He was clad in a pair of hospital-issue striped pajamas that he wore with all the panache of a warrior just returned in a bloodstained uniform from the front. Topping off this already bizarre outfit was a khaki oxygen pillow, which he sucked on like a bagpipe player. His rumpled pajamas, pouting lips, tousled hair, and swaggering gait marked him as someone who, although only twenty-one years old, understood political theater. But, it was clear that the weeks of demonstrating and fasting had also taken their toll. He looked tired, puffy, ill, and dyspeptic.

As attendants ushered the protest delegation upstairs to the Xinjiang Hall, a grand salon representing the province of Xinjiang that featured an enormous painting of a snowcapped mountain with flocks of sheep grazing in the foreground, Little Li was reminded of Qinghai. However, the fact that Li Peng had chosen to hold this unprecedented meeting in a hall dedicated to Wu'er's home province did not seem to impress the young protester. Brashness had been so deeply bred into him that even the prospect of being received by the premier in a hall named after his home province did nothing to temper his bravado. Instead, he harangued his colleagues to remain firm, so that when the dialogue was televised, ordinary Chinese would, as he put it, "finally have a chance to see ordinary citizens standing up to their officials."

When Premier Li finally entered, everyone stood. As he went down the line and greeted each protester, an aide read off the requisite name from a printed list. This ritual may have been designed to show personal concern, but it sent a chill through the room. In China, one rarely welcomed the discovery of one's name on any official list, especially that of the premier.

"I am delighted to meet you all," he began, though no delight registered on his dour face. Indeed, he had the air of a man so accustomed to acting out public roles that the question of what he actually thought and felt had long since become excised from his comportment. Nonetheless, hoping to bond with his interlocutors, he began talking about his own children, gratuitously declaring that they were not involved in "corruption" (官倒). As Little Li watched from his back-row seat, what most impressed him was the premier's look of undistinguished ordinariness. He wore a shapeless gray Mao-style jacket and trousers and beige slip-on shoes.

"We look on you as if you are our own children, our own flesh and blood," he continued.

"We don't have much time," interrupted Wu'er impatiently from an armchair in which he'd slumped, theatrically inhaling from his oxygen pillow. "We feel uncomfortable sitting here, knowing that our classmates are starving outside. So—please pardon me for interrupting. . . . The fact is that it is not you who invited us to come here for a discussion, it is us who, on behalf of all the people in the square, invited you! So the topic for discussion should be decided by us!" After his demonstration of brashness, neither side seemed to know how to proceed, and so for a moment there was silence.

"I would like to take this opportunity to clearly state once again our demands," interjected Wang Dan who was dressed in a leather jacket, a blue T-shirt, a headband, and baggy trousers soiled from his days in the square. "First, the current student movement should be re-evaluated as a democratic, patriotic movement, not as 'unrest' [动乱]. Second, we should establish a dialogue."

Little Li felt much more comfortable around the cerebral and understated Wang, a twenty-year-old history major from Peking University and one of the movement's main leaders, than the ostentatious Wu'er. But as he watched, he could see that Li Peng was affronted equally by both rebels, who, having humiliated the party for weeks, were now refusing to manifest any deference to him as premier. Instead, they and their fellow activists were sprawled out disrespectfully on chairs normally intended for heads of state, ministers, and royalty and defying him. The whole exercise made Li Peng look as if he'd just bitten into a particularly astringent piece of unripe fruit.

"In the past few days, Beijing has basically fallen into a state of anarchy," he charged. "Creating turmoil may not have been the intent of most people, but in the end, turmoil is what has occurred. So it is impossible for us to sit idly by, doing nothing."

"Okay, okay. Let's avoid endless quibbling," Wu'er interjected petulantly. "Please, respond quickly to the conditions we have presented, because our fellow students in the square are suffering from hunger right now. If we continue to quibble, then, in our view, the government doesn't have the slightest sincerity about solving the problem. In that case, there is no need for us as representatives of the students to remain sitting here any longer."

With Li Peng offended by their insolence and the protesters bridling at being lectured to, the meeting ended inconclusively. As they left the hall, the earlier élan of the protesters had vanished. As he translated for several interviews afterward, it was clear to Little Li that the moment for compromise, if there had ever been one, had now passed. Something elemental had changed. For the first time, he felt frightened.

He said nothing to Hong Hui about his experience in the Great Hall. But as she was cleaning up the kitchen after dinner the next evening, he turned on the TV and was stunned when a replay of the dialogue flickered on the screen and there he was in the back row, pen in hand, mouth slightly ajar, a slightly perplexed look on his face. Seeing himself inside the Great Hall of the People with the premier, while he was sitting in his own home, was as disturbing as being at a movie theater and suddenly seeing oneself appear in the middle of a film. When he heard Little Hong's footsteps in the hallway, he snapped the TV off just as she walked in.

"What are those crazy students up to now?" she asked skeptically.

48

TURMOIL

WHEN THE government-controlled loudspeakers in the square crackled to life and the voice of Premier Li Peng began speaking, just before midnight, Little Wang was asleep on his cardboard pallet, his face so sallow it looked almost necrotic.

"Comrades, anarchy is becoming more and more serious; law and discipline are being violated," intoned Premier Li as everyone in the tent fell silent. "If we do not promptly bring this standoff to an end, but instead let things go on, a situation that no one wants to see develop will very likely emerge. It is becoming clearer and clearer that an extremely small handful of people want to achieve their own political goals of negating the socialist system . . . undermining the leadership of the Chinese Communist Party, overthrowing the government, and totally negating the people's democratic dictatorship through turmoil. . . . To protect the leadership of the party and the socialist system, the government is now forced to take resolute and decisive measures to put a swift end to this turmoil."

Because the word "turmoil" implied that demonstrators had no regard for the country's welfare, the weary hunger strikers began jeering, but with none of their earlier bravado. Then, since it was a song whose words they all knew, they began singing "The Communist Internationale." Its words did befit the occasion, if in a cryptic way:

> *Arise ye prisoners of starvation*
> *Arise ye toilers of the earth*
> *For reason thunders new creation*
> *'Tis a better world in birth.*

Never more traditions' chains shall bind us
Arise ye toilers no more in thrall
The earth shall rise on new foundations
We are but naught, we shall be all.

Just as the anthem was ending, a young man on a motorbike, part of a flotilla of bikers known as the Flying Tigers Brigade (飞虎队), drove right into the tent.

"Troops are mobilizing at the Diaoyutai Guest House and getting ready to enter the city!" he shouted, like a town crier. Little Wang opened his eyes and laboriously sat up.

"What does that mean for us?" asked a confused young girl who was also fasting.

"It means the beginning of the end," answered Little Wang wearily. "We were naïve to have ever imagined any other outcome." Then he wrote a note to Little Li asking him to come and help him go home and asked a friend to deliver it for him.

"What are you going to do now?" asked an agitated Little Li when he arrived at the tent.

"Stop fasting and go home," he said diffidently.

"You're going to give up?"

"The writing's on the wall."

"I'll help you back and then cook something for you."

"Thanks, buddy," said Little Wang. "I'm all used up." He closed his eyes, held his aching forehead, before he began to get up. He was barely able to stand alone.

After seeing his friend safely home and preparing him something to eat, Little Li went home himself. On the bus, he swore that out of deference to Little Hong, henceforth he'd stay away from the square. With things hurtling toward an uncertain conclusion, he knew he'd made the right decision. But at the same time, he was swept by a conflicting sense of loss. The square and the protest movement had become such an integral part of his new life in Beijing that it was hard to imagine being severed from them.

When he slid into bed, Little Hong did not move. Then he whispered his decision in her ear, and she gave a long exhalation of relief, put her arms around his neck, and pressed her breasts against his back, so he could feel the thumping of her heart. Then there was a stirring in the corridor; he looked up to see Xiaomei standing in the doorway, holding her Sun Wukong monkey.

"What is it?" he asked.

"I'm frightened, Papa."

"Why?"

"When you're not home, Mama's so worried."

Without speaking, he pulled her into their bed, where, snuggled against him, she quickly fell asleep. When he, too, finally nodded off, he was beset by fevered dreams of the square. But this time it was filled not with democracy protesters, but ecstatic youths gazing adoringly up at the Gate of Heavenly Peace. However, as a roar of approval went up, it was not Chairman Mao who stepped out onto the rostrum, but a slender young man with a forelock of tousled hair falling over his "Hunger Fast" headband. Wang Dan gazed out across the vast square for a moment without speaking, as if the crowd had cast a spell on him. Then as a hush descended, Mao's fabled portrait began to slide in slow motion from its famous hanging place on the gate, until all that was left was a dark square where the painting had once shielded a square of vermilion from the sun, like the telltale place on their wall at Willow Courtyard where his parents' photo had once hung above their piano.

"A new day is dawning!" Wang finally began, his thin but penetrating voice reverberating out across the square. "I stand here as a voice of China's new citizenry, who will tolerate no more autocrats, big leaders, or portraits glorifying them. Hereafter, we will keep this place, on this gate, in this most revered of public spaces in China, empty, as a reminder for future generations that when the voice of despotism replaces the voice of freedom, a nation becomes endangered." Again and again the crowd chanted, "May Wang Dan live ten thousand years!"

The next day, Li Mei's school was closed, so they all stayed home, but Little Li felt marooned. Unable to bear not knowing what was going on in the square, he turned on the television, just in time to hear Li Peng declare martial law:

> They stir up trouble, set up secret ties, organize all kinds
> of illegal associations, and try to force the government
> into recognizing them. We must be firm in exposing this
> handful's political conspiracies bent on stirring up trouble,

spreading rumors, confusing the people, and escalating the turmoil. . . . We must now take resolute measures to stop them once and for all.

Because most protesters had already voted to vacate the square, the movement might well have quieted down on its own if it hadn't been for this new provocation. But, humiliated by the effrontery of the demonstrators, Deng Xiaoping and Premier Li Peng felt compelled to bring this "disturbance" to a clear and uncontestable end by declaring martial law and retaking the square with troops. However, as rumors spread that army units were on the march, tens of thousands of ordinary people spilled out into the streets. By the time the first convoys actually entered the city, there were such enormous crowds blocking the way that their trucks were brought to an ignominious halt. While confused commanders awaited further orders, troops gazed with bewilderment out at the sea of people obstructing their way and chanting: *The People's Liberation Army is an army of the people's own sons and brothers! How can you attack your own family?*"

As more units vectored in on the square, thousands more Beijingers rallied to throw up barricades made out of concrete traffic-lane dividers, hijacked public buses, commandeered trucks, piles of sand and rubble—anything they could get their hands on. When one military unit after another was brought to a grinding halt, "the people" began offering the paralyzed troops food and drink. For party leaders, this was their greatest humiliation yet: the People's Liberation Army had been thwarted by the very people in whose name it purported to serve.

Mao Zedong had idealized the relationship between "the people" and this "people's army" as one in which "the former were likened to the water, and the latter to fish that swim in it." Bogged down in this fickle ocean of protesters, Mao's proverbial "fish" were now perversely being drowned in the very waters of "the people" that were supposed to sustain them. As one man declared to a CCTV reporter: "Forty years ago, when the PLA entered Beijing, our fathers rushed into the streets to welcome it. Today, the PLA is again entering Beijing, but the people are opposing it. Such is the difference between winning and losing the hearts of the masses."

When the Flying Tigers Brigade brought news to those protesters still huddled around the monument in the square that the PLA's advance had been arrested, they broadcast Beethoven's "Ode to Joy." The movement had been like a serial drama, constantly reinvigorating itself by creating new, self-generated episodes, one after another. Now, after almost foundering again, it had once more rejuvenated itself, and in the process thrown party propaganda organs into such disarray that they'd lost control of even official state-run media outlets. Journalists had begun to report what they were seeing rather than what propaganda officials were telling them to report, so that listeners and viewers all across China had grown accustomed to turning on their radios and televisions, or opening their newspapers, and getting relatively truthful coverage. However, with the declaration of martial law, a new shroud of censorship fell back over the media.

As Little Li watched these events unfold on television, he felt like a caged animal. He was accustomed to being at the center of things, and chafed now at being sidelined at home during this moment of historic popular triumph. The closest he was able to get to the action was when Little Hong asked him to go out and buy some food, and a troop convoy—the same Liberation trucks he'd ridden in Qinghai—sped past him.

"I know you want to see what's happening out there," she sympathized when he told her what he'd seen. "But I am so relieved you're here with us! Thank you, my husband."

"It's all right," he said, giving her hand an unconvincing squeeze.

Sitting just behind their TV set was his tattered flute case. Since arriving back in Beijing, he'd taken his instrument out only a few times, once to serenade the hunger strikers. Nonetheless, because it was one of the few things that had traveled with him during every chapter of his life, it was a comforting presence: like Little Wang's friendship, his flute helped tie his life together. When Little Wang showed up at their doorstep several days later, Little Li was glad to see him. Even Little Hong, who no longer felt so threatened by his presence, greeted him cordially, and then took Li Mei to the park so the two could be alone.

"Have all troops really been withdrawn?" asked Little Li, eager to know every detail.

"All gone!" replied Little Wang. "It was amazing, and for now things are on hold. But what's up with you? Has your old lady grounded you?" He wore a bemused smile.

"I've grounded myself," Little Li replied defensively.

"Why?"

"Because she's worried something bad will happen."

"Well, she's not wrong. Things appear peaceful now, but there are rumors Old Deng's assembling a far more powerful military-force, led by fresh commanders from outside Beijing who, unlike the last local bunch, will have no friends and children in the square."

"But, I still can't quite believe that ordinary people stopped the PLA."

"If you'd been there, you'd have wet your pants!" chortled Little Wang. "But, because it turned into such an embarrassment, there's now a larger score than ever to be settled. And you know the old saying, 'All debts get settled after harvest time' [秋后算账]. It's going to get nasty."

"So why are people staying in the square?"

"Most of us veterans think that with the hunger strike over, it's time to leave. However, the new arrivals from the provinces want to have their own protest experience, so they want to stay. Their new leader who thinks she's China's Joan of Arc, Chai Ling—even calls herself 'Commander in Chief.' So things can't end."

"Shall we go out and get something to eat?" suggested Little Li with a sigh.

"You certainly know the way into a lapsed hunger striker's heart," smiled Little Wang, who was still thin and anemic-looking. As they ate, he recounted some of the things that had been happening over the past few days. "Students from the Central Academy of Fine Arts built a huge foam and papier-mâché statue called *The Goddess of Democracy* [民主女神] and set her up in the square just in front of Chairman Mao's portrait, so it looks like she's going to whack him right in the kisser with her torch of freedom! In retaliation, the party turned on its loudspeakers and blasted out all sorts of crap about how 'Your movement's bound to fail, because it's foreign!' and 'This is China, not the United States!' But all they did was help fan the protest movement back to life."

When Little Li went out for a walk with Xiaomei a few days later, and they passed the Jianguo Hotel, one of Beijing's first foreign hotels, he was surprised to see it draped with a new banner: SUPPORT THE GREAT, GLORIOUS, AND CORRECT CHINESE COMMU- NIST PARTY!

"The wind's shifted," declared a young man standing next to them with a bicycle, when he saw Little Li staring at the banner. As the stranger mounted his bike and headed toward the square, Little Li had the unsettling sensation of someone riding innocently toward a nuclear reactor heading toward meltdown.

"I don't feel any wind," Li Mei innocently observed.

"There's no real wind," he explained. "The boy meant that things are about to change politically, just like the weather."

"Oh," she answered. "Can we get a popsicle?"

Her request came as a relief, because, unlike demands for more freedom and democracy, this was one that could be met. As she sucked on her treat, Little Li gazed at her, still unable to quite believe she was actually his own daughter. What could a politi- cal demonstration add to such flawlessness? He stooped down and put his arm around her, but she was so engrossed in her popsicle, she didn't even look up. How reassuring that a child could still become absorbed in a small pleasure and shut out all the world's other intrusions.

Walking home, Little Li found it difficult to make sense out of what had happened since he'd arrived back in China. During these few months, he'd discovered that his old home was gone; found out Granny Sun was dead; Little Wang was still involved in poli- tics; and that he had a daughter. Then he'd gotten married and became part of an epic political movement. And yet all the while Lisa Singleton, his Cutlass, and his Mighty Mite were still wait- ing for him over the horizon in America. Every time he thought of her, he cringed. How could he be so duplicitous? She and Little Hong were emblematic of his divided state, disparate pieces that fit together no better than the United States and China. He wished that there was some cosmic clock whose hands he could simply turn back, so that he could then select out those events from the past he wanted to keep and disregard the rest, just as the party did when it manipulated its own historical record.

As June began, rumors were spreading like wildfire, creating a sense of imminence that was only heightened by the *People's Daily* calling on everyone "to act without hesitation" to thwart the "small handful" of malcontents "plotting to overthrow the Communist Party's leadership and the socialist system."

Then, the Flying Tigers began reporting that new PLA units were bivouacking outside the city, and protest leaders began urgently organizing Dare-to-Die Squads. But when nothing happened, many began wondering if another military assault would actually ever come.

"Trust me," assured Little Wang. "These old guys won't give up. I've heard they're just delaying while they bring in more undercover forces into the city through secret tunnels, even disguised as joggers and bicycle riders."

On the afternoon of June 2, Little Wang showed up at Hong Hui's apartment so excited he was almost incoherent. "It's starting!" he blurted out. "You've got to come!"

"What are you talking about?" asked Little Li, worrying that his wife and Li Mei, who'd gone shopping, would return at any moment and catch them.

"Things are coming to a head!" Little Wang continued breathlessly. "The Taiwan rock star Hou Dejian, some stuttering professor from Beijing Normal University named Liu Xiaobo, and two other senior intellectuals have launched a hunger strike of their own at the monument, to show protesters that the older generation still supports them. They've even written a new declaration, and now people are streaming back into the square." He thrust a leaflet at Little Li.

"In the face of the high-handed military violence of the irrational Li Peng government," read their declaration, "Chinese intellectuals must bring to an end their age-old propensity that has been handed down over the millennia of being spineless and merely speaking, but never acting." What China needed, the declaration continued, was "not a perfect savior, but a sound democratic system." The four senior intellectuals were fasting, they claimed, because they preferred to "have ten devils who check and balance each other than one angel who holds absolute power."

"How dangerous is it?" asked Little Li, thinking of his pledge to Little Hong, but also not wanting to miss the next chapter of whatever drama was about to play itself out in the square.

"Who the hell knows, but history's being made!"

Just then they heard voices in the stairwell.

"All right," Little Li responded impetuously. "I'll go."

"Bravo!" His friend beamed.

"But I . . ." Before he could complete his sentence, his friend had run upstairs to hide on the fourth floor until the coast was clear to leave. Little Li had just enough time to shut the front door before Little Hong and Li Mei reached their landing. As her key turned in the lock, he was overcome with self-reproach. He didn't want to betray her, but couldn't deny the call of the square.

By the time they finished eating dinner, he'd decided he'd run down, have a quick look and then come right back. He read Li Mei a story, hugged her good night, and walked over to Little Hong at the sink, put a hand on her shoulder, and said, "I think I'll get a little air."

"But don't you . . ." she began, a troubled look in her eyes.

"I need to get out for a while." With a pained resignation, she went back to the dishes.

It was a muggy, moonless night, and he felt both elated and conflicted.

When he was still blocks away from the square, he started hearing the government loudspeakers: "For the sake of our country's prosperity and to prevent one-point-one billion people from being martyred on the altar of a new White Terror," they boomed out, "there will be no softness in dealing with thugs!"

Only as he drew nearer was he also able to make out the far weaker broadcasts of the protesters' sound system: "Tiananmen is our square, the people's square, and should never be surrendered to despotism. We call on the entire population to take action. Students, workers, people of Beijing: go on a general strike! Resolutely resist the ruthless rule of Li Peng!"

This jousting match of amplified verbiage ended suddenly when a protester managed to find and cut the master cable to the party's speaker system. But the silence was short-lived. A while later, even larger speakers on the roof of the Great Hall of the People sprang to life. "You will fail!" they warned. "You are not behaving in a correct Chinese manner! This is not the West! This is China! Go home and save your lives!"

When Little Li reached the communications tent, there was no sign of his friend. A harried colleague said he thought he'd been assigned to coordinate the Flying Tigers Brigade in front of the

Museum of History. Making his way across the chaotic, trash-strewn square, Little Li finally spotted Little Wang addressing a throng of motorbikers all trying to speak at once.

"Let's talk one at a time!" he was urging them.

"They're moving in from the West!" shouted a frantic youth of no more than seventeen, astride a bright-red bike. "Thousands of them armed with AK-47s and led by APCs and tanks!"

"And they're shooting!" cried out a scruffy boy with a head-band proclaiming "Freedom or Death!" "It's not like before."

"People are building barricades near the Military Museum and need help!" hollered another biker in a sweat-stained T-shirt. "Who's willing to go?"

"No motorbike should leave here without at least two passengers," ordered Little Wang peremptorily. Then, spotting Little Li, he waved him over. "Look who's here!" he sang out, and slung an arm around his shoulders. "Ready for the final struggle?"

The next thing Little Li knew, he was on the back of the red motorbike, holding on to Little Wang, and their Flying Tiger was dodging around tents and through piles of rubbish heading west toward Xidan, where it seemed like half the city was in the streets. In the distance, an ominous orange halo flickered up into the humid night sky, as if the whole city was burning. Images of Little Hong and Lisa lying asleep flashed through his mind, and he was seized by a spasm of regret. What was he doing?

"This is as far as I go," said the Flying Tiger as they neared Muxidi Bridge [木樨地桥], where a line of disabled trolley buses and dump trucks had been parked bumper-to-bumper across the broad boulevard. A distant popping noise that sounded like kernels of dried corn exploding rent the air. "Rifle fire," said the Flying Tiger. "They'll be here soon." With a birdlike beep of his horn, he turned, threaded his way back through the crowd to pick up more reinforcements in the square.

While the Two Virtuous Ones were making their way through the swirl of people to the front of the barricade, three young men ran into the middle of the broad avenue and, as if rallying fans at a sporting event, began waving huge crimson banners. It was not until the cheering crowd fell eerily quiet that Little Li looked up. A column of soldiers marching in lockstep was just cresting the distant bridge. As they drew closer, he was surprised to see how young they were and that their facial expressions reflected not anger or defiance, but uncertainty and apprehension.

"A people's army doesn't oppose the people!" screamed a young protester.

"Never oppose the people!" echoed the crowd, cursing the soldiers. Then they began hurling bricks, rocks, bottles, and rubble. Soon a rudimentary supply chain had spontaneously formed, to pass whatever people could get their hands on as ammunition to a front line.

"This one's for Li Peng," screamed Little Wang, flinging a jagged piece of concrete with all his might. "And this one's for anyone else on the Politburo!"

It was as if all the grievances that had been pooling up for decades were now seeking an outlet at once. Overcome by the same primal urge to resist, Little Li, too, began hurling projectiles.

"Bandits!" taunted the crowd as a lifetime of restraint fell away. "Fascist dogs!"

"Charge, you cowards!" a military officer screamed at his troops through a megaphone. "Sweep away this trash!" There was a ripping, like the sound of a zipper opening under amplification, as soldiers in the front line began firing their automatic weapons into the air. A strange sizzling sound arced overhead and then a concussion grenade went off. People began running, colliding, tripping over debris, bicycles, and even fallen comrades. Then the firing ceased, and a phalanx of foolhardy souls edged back out onto the boulevard again, to pelt the advancing soldiers at closer quarters.

"Advance! Advance against these hoodlums!" the frenzied commander screamed. But even as he tried to rally his troops, they began breaking ranks and falling back. A buzz of disbelief rippled through the crowd. The banner wavers leapt joyously out into the middle of the debris-strewn boulevard as a triumphant cheer went up.

"What now?" Little Li asked, turning to his friend.

"It's just beginning," replied Little Wang, wiping the sweat from his brow and lighting a cigarette.

By midnight, things were so quiet that Little Li wondered if this was the end of the confrontation. Then a murmur rippled through the crowd and in the shadowy distance he saw that a fresh column of helmeted troops led by several armored vehicles was just coming over the bridge. Emboldened by their previous success, the indignant crowd began jeering and shaking their fists at the advancing soldiers. Then a few surged out onto the boulevard to launch another barrage of projectiles.

"Bastards! Dogs! Lay down your arms!" they shrieked, faces contorted with outrage.

But no matter what they hurled this time, the column kept coming. As an APC neared the barricade, a young man in overalls sprinted out, stuffed a gasoline-soaked rag down the fuel tank of one of the disabled buses, and lit it with his cigarette lighter. The vehicle erupted into a wall of flame and he was just running back toward the refuge of the crowd when there was a series of loud snapping sounds. He pitched forward mid-step and fell on his stomach. With his arms and legs flailing, he looked like a drowning swimmer desperately trying to reach the shore.

"Live fire! [真弹真弹]" someone screamed, as automatic weapons chattered in the darkness.

"Oh no! Please, no!" a young girl screamed as the boy next to her grabbed his head, spun, and fell. Cries of agony mixed with taunts of derision. Panicked people began fleeing.

"Make way!" an urgent voice yelled. "Emergency!"

A flatbed tricycle cart pedaled by a young man wearing a bloodstained shirt and with a sweat-streaked face burst from the mayhem. Sprawled on its fantail was the blood-soaked body of a young man, one arm hanging limply down, as the desperate cycler pedaled through the chaos. Then a second cart appeared, carrying a girl vomiting blood, cradled in the arms of a young man whose face was etched with terror. When the cart hit a brick, it tipped over, so that both passengers spilled down onto the asphalt. Standing over the girl's crumpled body, the boy pressed both hands to his temples and cried out to everyone and no one, "Someone help!" he wailed. "She's been hit!"

By this time, many onlookers had become so unhinged they'd lost all concern for their own safety, and two young women rushed to the wounded girl's aid. As the boy took her arms, each girl tookone of her legs, and somehow they managed to drag her body from the battlefield.

Little Li's every instinct was to flee, and yet he didn't move. Horrified, he watched as two mustached young men peeled a soldier at the edge of the advancing formation away from his cohort and then savagely pummeled him with lengths of iron rebar, while the bloodthirsty crowd roared with vengeful, animal approval. Enraged soldiers began firing directly into the surging crowd. When someone handed him a soda bottle filled with gasoline, Little Wang flicked his cigarette lighter, lit its rag wick, and, as a tongue of flame sprang to life, he hurled it with all his might at the soldiers. The flaming bottle arced up into the hellish, smoky darkness and for a moment looked as if it might extinguish itself in flight. But then it landed in the middle of the oncoming troops and slowly petals of orange flame began blooming up from the street, like a paper flower slowly unfolding from one of those clamshells dropped into a glass of water. As soldiers scattered, the cuff of one who'd been splattered with gasoline burst into flame. The desperate soldier tried to pat out the blaze with his bare hands. When that failed, he started running, as if he might somehow outpace the flames now licking hungrily up his pant leg. At that precise moment, Little Li's sightline was blocked as an APC thundered past, rammed headlong into the burning barricade, sending showers of sparks swirling up into the dark night sky like swarms of angry insects. Because it had failed to break through, the immobilized vehicle was quickly set upon by an angry mob. One youth, wielding a steel pry, leapt on top of it and began trying to pry open the hatch. When it finally sprang open like a pocket watch, a soldier inside made the fatal mistake of sticking his head out. He was immediately set upon by enraged youths, who beat his head with clubs.

In the crescendoing chaos, there was a sudden fusillade of automatic-weapons fire, and, as if choreographed, the banner wavers crumpled to the ground, one after another, their white shirts slowly staining with a crimson as deep as the scarlet of their fallen banners. While most terrified onlookers threw themselves to the ground, several ran across the litter of stones, bricks, twisted bicycles, and bodies to try to drag the wounded banner wavers to safety. Uncertain what possessed him, Little Li, too, dashed onto the debris-strewn battleground toward one of them. He was just trying to lift him when Little Wang appeared at his side.

"You take his arms, brother, and I'll take his legs!" he shouted.

"Quickly! He's bleeding!" Staggering under the limp, dead weight of their load, they did not stop running until they reached the refuge of a side street.

"You know foreign languages," barked Little Wang breathlessly, gesturing at a parked car with a sticker on its rear window saying FRANCE. Since it had its interior lights on, he began banging on its roof.

"Can you help us?" begged Little Li in English. "Please, help us!"

The front window rolled down and the face of a foreign man smeared with blood looked out.

"Do you need a doctor?" he asked in heavily accented Chinese.

"Yes!" pleaded Little Li, pointing at the youth sprawled on the sidewalk. "He's wounded."

"Where?"

"Stomach."

"We're going to the hospital," said the foreigner, grimacing. "I'm wounded in the leg. Put your guy in the back and we'll take him, too!"

"It's not safe!" interjected his Chinese driver.

"I don't care. Open the fucking door!" insisted the foreigner.

"Who are you?" asked Little Li, wanting to know into whose hands they were consigning this unknown wounded boy.

"A French journalist. Don't worry!" The back door opened, and they loaded the limp body into the back seat.

By the time the Two Virtuous Ones got back to the barricade, several more of the vehicles were ablaze and soldiers were firing indiscriminately into the smoky chaos. Aghast, Little Li watched as one soldier dropped to his knee to steady his weapon, and meticulously squeezed off several rounds at individual targets, like a sniper. Everywhere, people were running, screaming, and dropping.

"Fascists! Animals! Bandits! Turtle eggs!" the terrified crowd screamed hysterically.

Each time there was a lull in the firing, small teams of bystanders sprinted onto the battlefield to try and rescue more wounded. Little Li could no longer locate Little Wang and was about to flee when a young woman with long hair just like Little Hong charged into the mayhem toward a fallen comrade. But she'd hardly taken ten steps when she spun around, clawed at her chest, and dropped to the littered pavement. Without thinking, he ran to her. As a crimson stain spread across her pink blouse, like ink spilled on a blotter, she stared up wide-eyed at him.

"What's happening?" she asked, her brow furrowing.

"I'll help you," he tried to soothe.

"You will?" She closed her young eyes.

Picking up her limp body, he held her against his chest the way a parent might hold a sleeping child. He could feel her small breasts against his shoulder and the warmth of her sticky blood drenching his shirt and smearing his face. He licked his lips. Their saltiness tasted like Yang Ming's tears. Then, as if she'd grown suddenly weary, her head slumped over his shoulder, and her arms began flopping against his back like those of a rag doll. He felt like kissing her, but he knew he should keep running, because from everywhere came the crackling sound of gunfire.

"So—is this the way it ends?" he wondered. Was this young girl ready for the slumber in the hereafter that Bach had so wistfully described in his cantata? Had she lived enough life to be ready for death?

Suddenly everything started to spin. Little Li tried to steady himself by recollecting his father listening to *"Ich habe genug"* with eyes closed and a half-smile on his masklike face:

> *Slumber now, you eyes so weary,*
> *Close into soft and sweet repose!*
> *World, I will not remain here any longer,*
> *I own no part of you*
> *That could matter to my soul.*
> *Here, I must with sorrow reckon,*
> *But there, yes, there, shall I witness*
> *Sweet repose and quiet rest.*
> *My God! When will the lovely "now" come?*
> *When will I journey into peace*
> *And into the cool soil of earth . . .*

Was this the inevitable end of the political dreams Little Hong and his father had both cautioned against? He'd chosen God and music and she'd chosen their daughter and being a mother over politics and struggle. But he'd been a poor listener, and here he was with a dying girl in his arms, running he knew not where. How had he ended up in such an ecstatic heart of darkness?

Little Hong was suddenly gazing down at him, a melancholy look of resignation etched on her lovely face. She seemed to be saying goodbye. He wanted to swim back against the churning current of violence around him to the safety of her embrace, but could not figure out how. And was that not Lisa shrouded in the clouds? Not knowing what else to do, he just kept running.

Suddenly there was another staccato slapping sound, and the already blurry world began spinning even faster. He tried to steady himself by fixing his gaze on the crowd like a distant shoreline. But, a scrim of the same crimson so beloved by Chairman Mao was now slowly falling over everything. He tried crying out to Little Wang, but was unable to make a sound. As he began falling, falling, falling he was no longer frightened. Then his father appeared at the piano, and the heartbreaking beauty of the *Goldberg Variations* filled him with an unexpected sense of calm. How comforting it was to have such heavenly music for this mysterious passage.

But where was he going? To "the lovely 'now'" that Bach had embraced as he pleadingly cried out, "My God! When will the lovely 'now' come?" And why, at such a momentous time, was his old friend, Little Wang, not at his side? Weren't the Two Virtuous Ones forever indivisible? Wherever he was headed, did he have to go there alone?

Then such concerns no longer mattered. The girl in his arms felt no more substantial than a piece of down, and instead of falling, he began floating, up, up, up, on Bach's clear, cold, crisp music. Perhaps it was time, after all, to bid this world goodbye and make his "journey into peace" and "the cool soil of earth"?

As he allowed himself to surrender, he kept floating higher and higher until the only thing that mattered any more was his own liberating sense of weightlessness.

ACKNOWLEDGMENTS

I started this novel decades ago, after repeatedly running into topics crucial to explaining the divide separating the United States and China that remained frustratingly elusive in writing nonfiction. On this long journey I've benefited from much editorial help. Mike Levine helped me see beyond an early draft. Sarah Crichton ably assisted me in honing the narrative. But it is my posse of friends who, by reading endless early drafts and offering much good counsel and encouragement, deserve my deepest thanks. Larry Friedlander; Adam and Arlie Hochschild; Deirdre English; Zha Jianying; Elaine Pagels; Andrew Nathan; Lynn Glaser; Irena Grudszinka Gross; Eric Karpeles; Michael Tilson Thomas; Judith Belzer; Michael Pollan; Sonia Song; Burr Heneman; Ye Wa; Elizabeth Economy; Xi Lian; Winston Lord; Zhu Yuchao; Ezra Vogel; Tom Engelhardt; my wife, Baifang Schell, to whom this book is dedicated; and my son Sasha who helped edit the final proofs. Your collective support bore me up like the wings of angels during some difficult times.

A special thanks to my longtime agent, Amanda Urban; to novelist Michael Ondaatje, who introduced me to Sonny Mehta and Knopf/Pantheon; and to my wonderful, understated new editor, Dan Frank, who has not only given this book a safe harbor, but been its editor.

Finally, I write this in loving remembrance of my brother, Jonathan Schell, whose elegant voice as a writer and decency as a person has always been a true north.

Orville Schell

A NOTE ABOUT THE AUTHOR

Orville Schell is the Arthur Ross Director of the Center on U.S.–China Relations at the Asia Society. From 1996 to 2007, he was dean of the UC Berkeley Graduate School of Journalism. He has written twelve non-fiction books, ten on China, and contributed to numerous publications, including *The New Yorker, The Atlantic, The Nation, Foreign Affairs, Newsweek,* and *The New York Review of Books.* He divides his time between New York and Berkeley, California.

A NOTE ON THE TYPE

The text of this book was set in Sabon, a typeface designed by Jan Tschichold (1902–1974), the well-known German typographer. Designed in 1966 and based on the original designs by Claude Garamond (ca. 1480–1561), Sabon was named for the punch cutter Jacques Sabon, who brought Garamond's matrices to Frankfurt.

Composed by North Market Street Graphics, Lancaster, Pennsylvania
Printed and bound by Berryville Graphics, Berryville, Virginia
Designed by Maria Carella